Ambika Shanmugam's

Fundamentals of Biochemistry for Medical Students

8th Edition

Ambika Shanmugam's

Fundamentals of Biochemistry for Medical Students

8th Edition

Editor

K. Ramadevi MD, PhD
Professor and Head
Department of Biochemistry
Madras Medical College
The Tamil Nadu Dr. M.G.R. Medical University
Chennai

Wolters Kluwer

Sr Publisher: Dr. Binny Mathur
Manager Commissioning: P. Sangeetha
Sr Production Editor: Tamali Deb
Manager Manufacturing: Sumit Johry

3th Floor, Tower B, Building No. 10, Phase – II, DLF Cyber City
Gurgaon, Haryana - 122002

Eight Edition, 2016
Ninth Impression, 2025

ISBN: 978-93-5129-682-9

Published by Wolters Kluwer (India) Pvt. Ltd., New Delhi
Compositor: Design Modus
Printed and bound at One Stop Solutions 99

For product enquiry, please contact – Marketing Department (marketing@wolterskluwerindia.co.in) or log on to our website www.wolterskluwerindia.co.in.

Foreword

Biochemistry has in recent years, become a most vital subject for study in the understanding of the physiology and pathology of human beings and animals. It was in the early years of this century that the first seeds were sown by the discovery of the vitamins which play an important role in the metabolism of the body. Subsequently, rapid developments have taken place and biochemistry has become one of the essential subjects of study for all members of the medical, veterinary and agricultural professions.

This book, which has been written by Dr. Ambika Shanmugam, Professor of Biochemistry, Madras Medical College, deals with the subject in an exhaustive manner and covers many aspects relating to protein metabolism, haematological changes, hormones and acid-base balance which are so essential for a thorough grasp by the physicians and surgeons in treating their patients. We look forward to the day when biochemical investigations will make a breakthrough in the diagnosis of some of the conditions which have so far defied scrutiny, such as cancer and other forms of new growths. It is no longer possible to deal effectively with many disease conditions without thorough biochemical research being conducted, whatever may be the branch of speciality, whether it be neurology, urology, gastroenterology, etc. This book by Dr. Ambika Shanmugam is a welcome addition to the subject and deserves to be in the hands of all practitioners of medicine.

Sir AL Mudaliar
MD, LLD, DSc, DCL

Kensington,
Kilpauk,
Madras-10

Preface to the Eighth Edition

Dr. Ambika Shanmugam's 'Fundamentals of Biochemistry for Medical Students' has been one of the earliest books on biochemistry for medical students. The book is prescribed by many universities and followed by medical, dental, nursing and science students all over India. Though many books are available for learners by different authors, this particular text is designed to meet both the needs of the students—that of easy understanding of the subject and passing the exam with good scores.

I feel privileged to present the revised edition of this prestigious publication. In the revised edition, updates have been included, wherever required. For quick learning, flowcharts have been added at certain places to supplement lengthy descriptions, and a few have been modified. Also, some complex biochemical structures as well as some theoretical details that are not needed by the undergraduate students have been omitted, thus making the text crisp and to the point. Simplicity and clarity of content have been maintained to meet the students' need of an easy-to-understand book.

I sincerely hope that this edition will serve the needs of the students of biochemistry in a still better way. I would very much appreciate and welcome suggestions from students and faculty members for further improvement of the book.

K. Ramadevi

Table of Contents at a Glance

Detailed Table of Contents

1 CHAPTER

Carbohydrates

Chapter Outline

- Chemical Characteristics of Carbohydrates
- Classification of Carbohydrates
- Monosaccharides
- Disaccharides
- Polysaccharides

Carbohydrates include a large group of compounds commonly known as starches or sugars, widely distributed in plants and animals. Chemically, they are described as polyhydric alcohols, having potentially active aldehyde and ketone groups.

In general, carbohydrates are white solids, freely soluble in water with the exception of certain polysaccharides. Carbohydrates of lower molecular weight have a sweet taste.

Biological significance:

1. The chief function of carbohydrates in the body is that of a fuel. When carbohydrates are oxidised in the body, they liberate carbon dioxide, water and energy. They supply the major portion of energy required by living cells.
2. Certain products of carbohydrate metabolism, as will be seen later, act as catalysts to promote oxidation of foodstuffs.
3. Certain carbohydrates can be used as the starting material for the biological synthesis of compounds, such as fatty acids and amino acids.

Occurrence: Carbohydrates are widely distributed in nature in plants and animals. The most important carbohydrate found in plants is starch. It occurs abundantly in the roots, tubers, leaves, vegetables and grains. The carbohydrate found in animals is glycogen. It forms the storage form of carbohydrate in animals and is found abundantly in the liver and muscles. Both starch and glycogen are polysaccharides having high molecular weight; carbohydrates having lower molecular weight are also found in nature. They come under the groups of monosaccharides and oligosaccharides which are white crystalline substances, sweet to taste. They are generally known as **sugars** and are consumed with food.

Sucrose, which is largely taken in food, is obtained from sugarcane. It is also present in the nectar of flowers and in fruits. Glucosides, which are derivatives of carbohydrates, are found in certain plants. Certain glucosides are used in the treatment of heart diseases.

Glucose and fructose which are simple sugars are widely distributed in plants. Glucose is the sugar present in blood and other body fluids. Lactose is present in milk.

CHEMICAL CHARACTERISTICS OF CARBOHYDRATES

Chemically, carbohydrates contain carbon, hydrogen and oxygen. Generally, the composition of carbohydrates is in the proportion of two of hydrogen and one of oxygen atoms as in water (H_2O). Glucose, which is a simple carbohydrate, has a molecular formula of $C_6H_{12}O_6$.

All simple sugars contain a potential aldehyde or ketone group. All the compound sugars which are made up of simple sugar molecules also contain the potential aldehyde group, either in the free form or in the combined form. The importance of a potential aldehyde or ketone group is that it is associated with a reducing property.

CLASSIFICATION OF CARBOHYDRATES

Carbohydrates are classified into four major groups:

1. Monosaccharides
2. Disaccharides
3. Oligosaccharides
4. Polysaccharides

Monosaccharides: They contain only one molecule of sugar and cannot be broken into simpler substances by hydrolysis. Monosaccharides are further subdivided according to the number of carbon atoms contained in their structure, as indicated below:

1. *Diose* has two carbon atoms. Molecular formula, $C_2H_4O_2$.
   For example, glycolaldehyde.
2. *Triose* has three carbon atoms. Molecular formula, $C_3H_6O_3$.
   For example,
   - Glyceraldehyde
   - Dihydroxyacetone

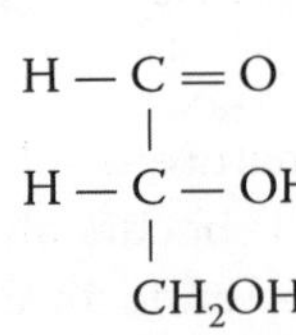

Glyceraldehyde

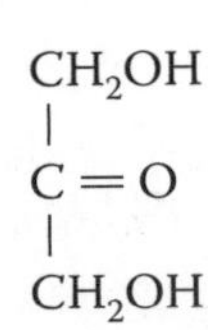

Dihydroxyacetone

3. *Tetrose* has four carbon atoms. Molecular formula, $C_4H_8O_4$.
   For example,
   - Erythrose
   - Threose
   - Erythrulose

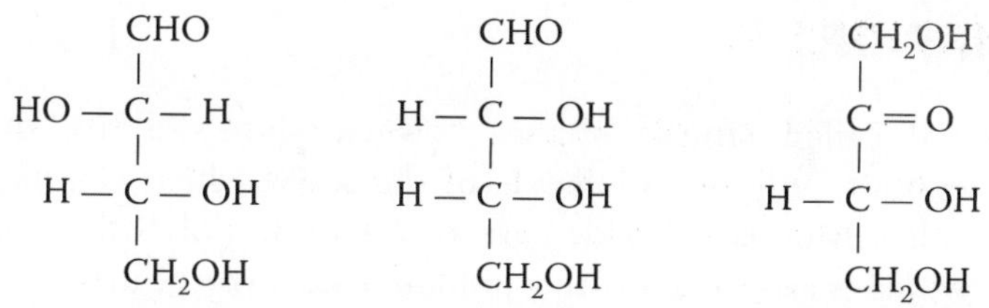

D-Threose D-Erythrose D-Erythrulose

4. *Pentose* has five carbon atoms. Molecular formula, $C_5H_{10}O_5$.
   For example,
   - Ribose
   - Deoxyribose
   - Xylose
5. *Hexose* has six carbon atoms. Molecular formula, $C_6H_{12}O_6$.
   For example,
   - Glucose
   - Fructose
   - Galactose
   - Mannose
6. *Heptose* has seven carbon atoms. Molecular formula, $C_7H_{14}O_7$.
   For example,
   - Sedoheptulose
   - Glucoheptose

Disaccharides: They yield two molecules of monosaccharides on hydrolysis. Disaccharides have a molecular formula of $C_{12}H_{22}O_{11}$.

For example,

1. Sucrose
2. Lactose
3. Maltose

Oligosaccharides: They yield 2–10 monosaccharide units on hydrolysis. Strictly speaking, disaccharides also come under this group.

Examples of oligosaccharides other than disaccharides are as follows:

1. Raffinose—trisaccharide
2. Stachyose—tetrasaccharide
3. Verbascose—pentasaccharide

Polysaccharides: They yield more than 10 molecules of monosaccharides on hydrolysis. Polysaccharides have a molecular formula of $(C_6H_{10}O_5)_x$.

For example,

1. Starch
2. Glycogen
3. Dextrins
4. Cellulose
5. Dextran
6. Inulin

MONOSACCHARIDES

Monosaccharides are called **simple sugars** because they are the simplest units of carbohydrate and contain only one molecule of the sugar which cannot be split further into simpler molecules. Monosaccharides are regarded as polyhydric alcohols having a reducing property which is associated with a potential aldehyde or ketone group, contained in the structure.

Monosaccharides are further classified according to the number of carbon atoms:

1. Diose
2. Triose
3. Tetrose
4. Pentose
5. Hexose
6. Heptose

Diose

The simplest compound to be classed as a carbohydrate is the diose, glycolaldehyde ($CH_2OH{\cdot}CHO$). It is classified as a 'diose', because it contains two carbon atoms. It contains an aldehyde group and therefore it is referred to as aldose. Thus, glycolaldehyde is an aldodiose. It differs from the higher aldoses in that it is not polyhydroxylic and for this reason, some authors do not include this compound among the true carbohydrates.

Triose

The next higher group *trioses* contain three carbon atoms ($C_3H_6O_3$). They are considered true carbohydrates because they contain polyhydroxylic groups. Examples are as follows:

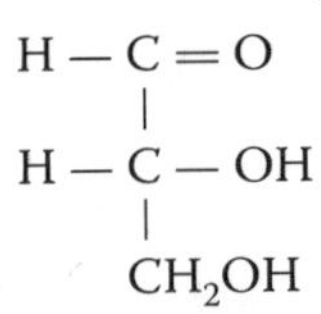

Glyceraldehyde

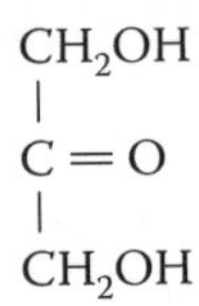

Dihydroxyacetone

Glyceraldehyde, which can be considered as the simplest monosaccharide, is an aldotriose because it is a triose and contains an aldehyde group. Dihydroxyacetone is a ketotriose because it is a triose and contains a ketone group. The phosphate esters of glyceraldehyde and dihydroxyacetone occur as intermediates in the glycolysis of carbohydrates.

Tetroses

Tetroses contain four carbon atoms ($C_4H_8O_4$).

For example,

1. Erythrose
2. Threose
3. Erythrulose

Erythrose and threose are aldotetroses while erythrulose is a ketotetrose.

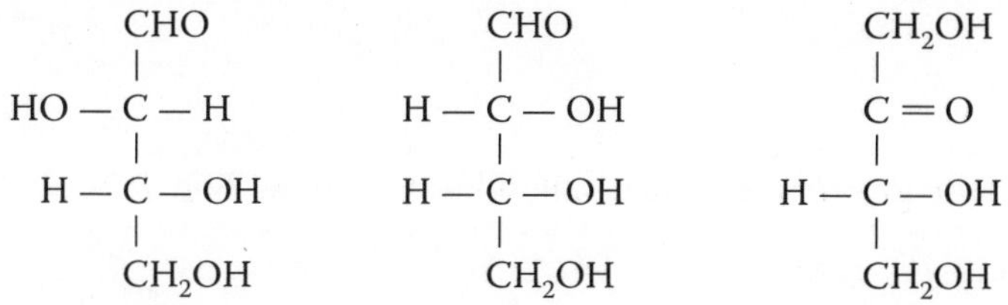

D-Threose D-Erythrose D-Erythrulose

Pentoses

Pentoses contain five carbon atoms ($C_5H_{10}O_5$).

For example,

1. Ribose
2. Deoxyribose
3. Xylulose
4. Arabinose

Ribose and Deoxyribose

Out of the four pentoses, **ribose** and **deoxyribose** (**Fig. 1.1**) are physiologically important, as they are constituents of the nucleic acids. Ribose is also part of riboflavin which belongs to the B complex group of vitamins and certain coenzymes. It has a reducing property because of the free aldehyde group. The structures of ribose and deoxyribose are given below:

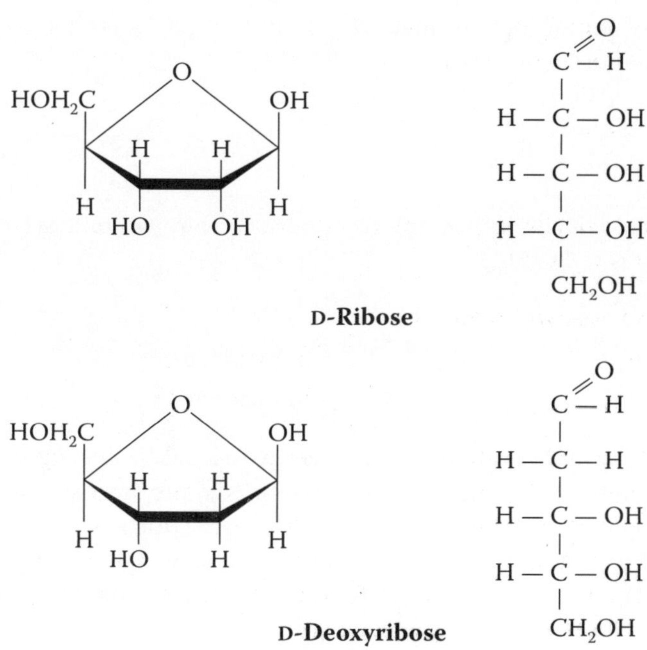

Figure 1.1 Closed and open structures of ribose and deoxyribose.

Note that deoxyribose contains one oxygen atom less than ribose.

Xylulose

Xylulose has a ketone group and is also called ketoxylulose (**Fig. 1.2**).

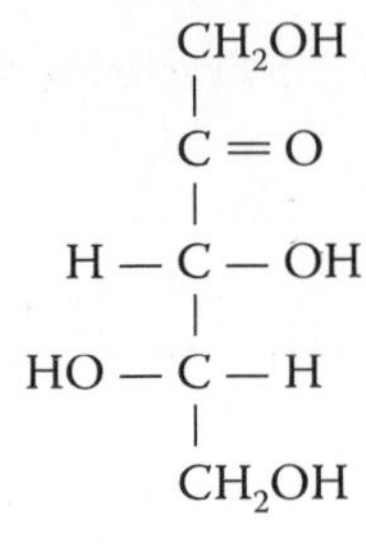

Figure 1.2 Ketoxylulose.

Xylulose is a metabolite of glucuronic acid. It is excreted in the urine of persons suffering from **pentosuria**, which is an inborn error of pentose metabolism.

Arabinose

Arabinose is not of importance in man. It is found in plants with gum arabic and cherry gum and is obtained on hydrolysis.

Hexoses

Hexoses are physiologically important compounds. They contain six carbon atoms. The molecular formula is $C_6H_{12}O_6$.

The common hexoses are as follows:

1. Glucose
2. Fructose
3. Galactose
4. Mannose

Glucose, galactose and mannose are aldohexoses, each having an aldehyde group. Fructose is a ketohexose having a ketone group. Of the hexoses, glucose is the most important, because it is the sugar contained in blood. Glucose and fructose occur freely in plants and fruits. Galactose is a component of lactose which is the disaccharide of milk. Polysaccharides containing mannose are found in ivory nuts, orchid tubers and yeast.

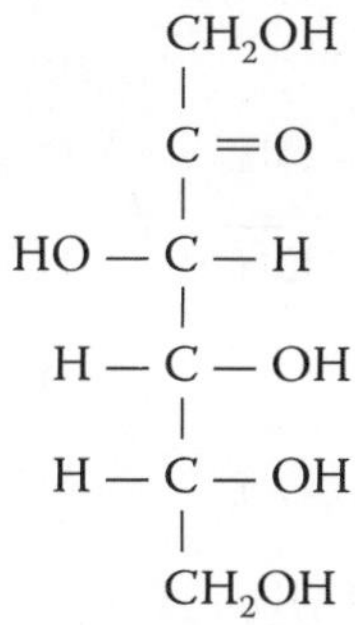

D-Fructose

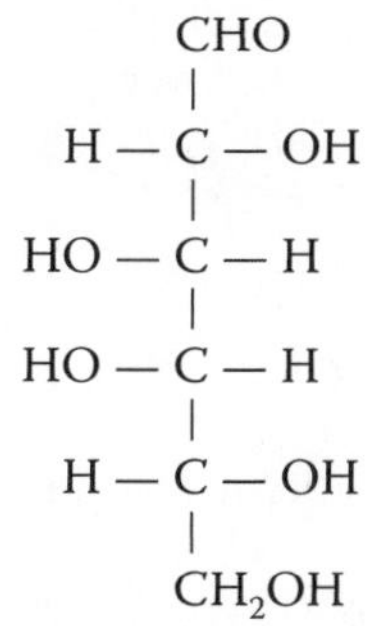

D-Galactose

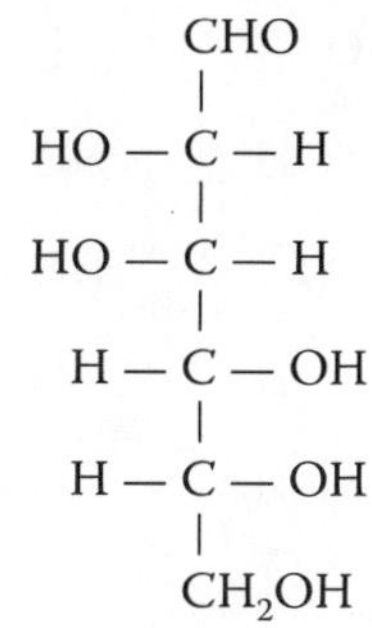

D-Mannose

Hexoses are as a class optically active. It will be seen that the various aldohexoses differ in their structures mainly in the spatial arrangement of hydrogen and hydroxyl groups, around each carbon atom of the molecule. But this little difference is enough to produce marked variation in the physical properties of the different hexoses.

Spatial Configuration of Sugars – Stereoisomerism

Many of the monosaccharides contain the same number of atoms and the same types of groups in their structures. But they are entirely different substances. For example, $C_6H_{12}O_6$ is the molecular formula of hexose. But there are 16 different hexoses possessing structure similar to that of glucose like

$$CHO - CHOH - CHOH - CHOH - CHOH - CH_2OH$$

The spatial arrangement of certain constituent groups such as hydrogen and hydroxyl in each of these varies. This phenomenon is called **stereoisomerism** or **space isomerism** and the sugars are called **stereoisomers**.

A few examples of stereoisomers having the same molecular formula but different space formula are given in **Figure 1.3**.

Asymmetry of carbon atoms and optical activity: Carbohydrates exhibit an important property called the **optical activity** which is closely related to the asymmetry of the carbon atoms contained in them. A carbon atom is said to be asymmetric when it bears four different atoms or groups of atoms at the four valency bonds. This is illustrated in the structure of glyceraldehyde. The second carbon atom is asymmetric because four different groups are attached to the second carbon atom, and these are as follows:

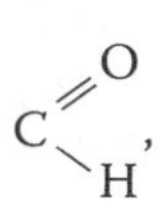 , H, OH and CH_2OH

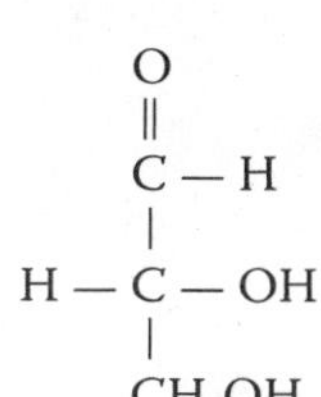

D-Glyceraldehyde

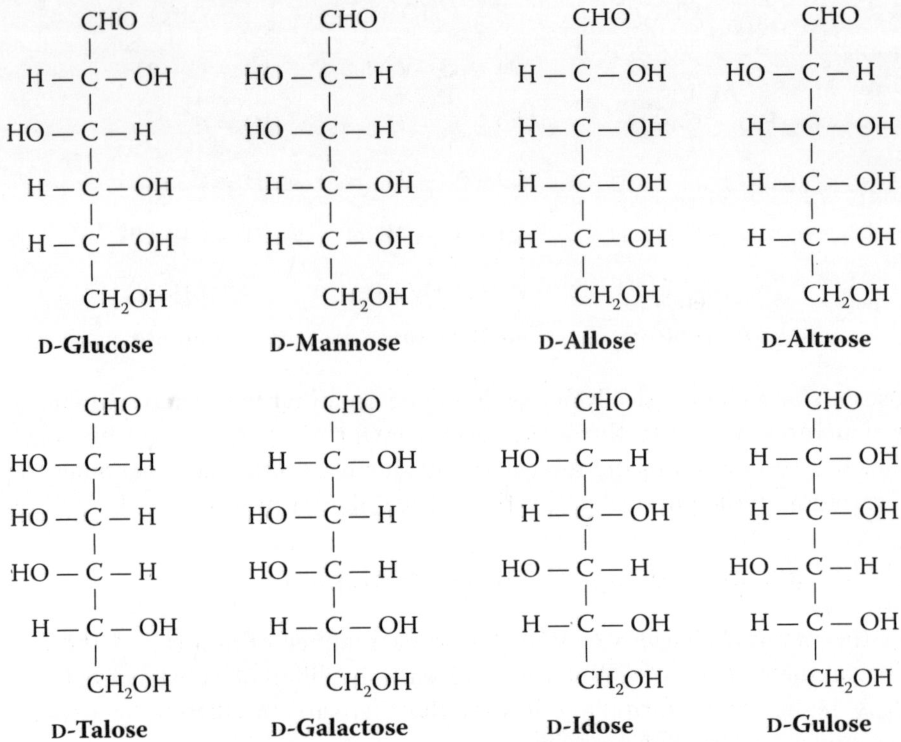

Figure 1.3 Examples of stereoisomers.

It is found that any compound having asymmetric carbon atoms is optically active and exists in more than one form of isomers. The isomers are identical in configuration but differ only in spatial configuration. **Figure 1.4** represents two isomers identical in configuration but differing in spatial arrangements. The central carbon atom marked C is asymmetric because it has four different groups attached, one at each valency.

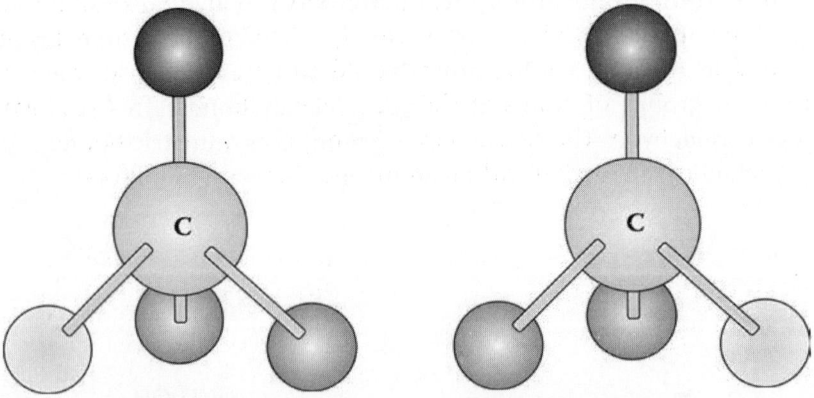

Figure 1.4 Two isomers having asymmetric carbon atoms.

These two isomers are not superimposable as they are mirror images of each other. All such isomers are said to exhibit optical isomerism, which involves optical rotation. This is true of any molecule having an asymmetric carbon atom. Thus, it is assumed that all sugars having asymmetric carbon atoms exist in optically active forms.

The number of possible isomers of any given compound depends upon the number of asymmetric carbon atoms in the molecule. According to Vant Hoff, the number of possible isomers for a given substance is given by the formula $I = 2^n$, where I represents the number of isomers and n represents the number of asymmetric carbon atoms. Thus for glucose which has four asymmetric carbon atoms, the number of isomers would be $(2^4) = 16$. Eight of these would represent the 'D' series and the other eight, which are mirror images of the former, would represent the 'L' series.

Monosaccharides containing asymmetric carbon atoms are glucose, fructose, mannose, galactose and glyceraldehyde.

Optical Isomerism Optical isomerism specifies the peculiar effect undergone by solutions of isomers by plane-polarized light.

Plane-polarized light: A beam of ordinary light may be regarded as a bundle of electromagnetic waves vibrating in all directions perpendicular to the axis of the beam. When such a beam of light is made to pass through a specially cut crystal of certain minerals or a sheet of special plastic known as Polaroid or a crystal of Iceland spar (transparent calcite), all vibrations except those in one plane are eliminated. This is plane-polarized light (**Fig. 1.5**). When such a beam of plane-polarized light is passed through a solution of an optical isomer, and if the plane-polarized light is found to rotate to the left, it is described as **levorotation**. If the plane-polarized light rotates to an equal number of degrees to the right, it is described as **dextrorotation**. This phenomenon exhibited by asymmetric compounds is called **optical isomerism**.

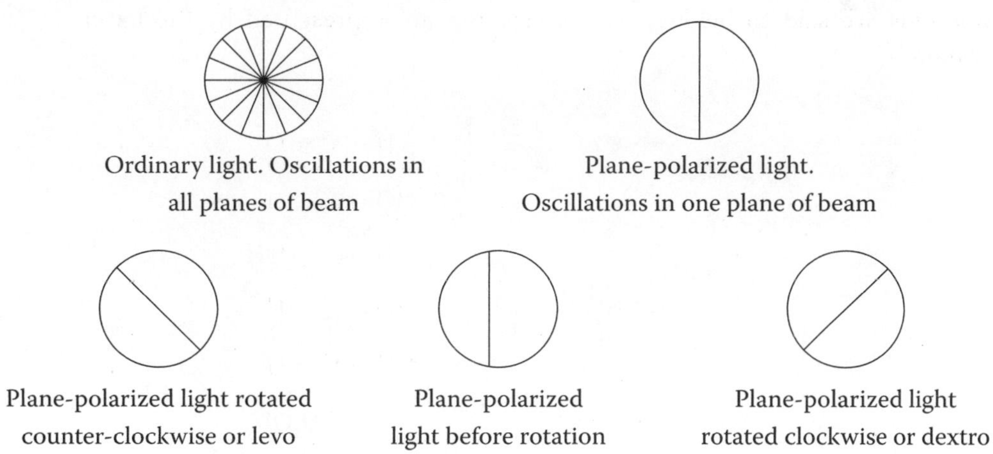

Figure 1.5 Plane-polarized light and optical rotation.

Expression of optical activity: Optical rotation to the left, i.e. laevorotation, is expressed as a minus (–) sign and rotation to the right, i.e. dextrorotation, is expressed as a plus (+) sign.

Expression of spatial isomerism: While the dextrorotation and levorotation of an optical isomer are designated by a plus (+) sign or a minus (–) sign, respectively, they are represented spatially or geometrically in a different way. The geometric representation of the dextrorotatory form is customarily written with the secondary alcoholic hydroxyl group of the carbon atom just adjacent to the terminal primary alcoholic hydroxyl group, extending to the right (**Fig. 1.6**). Such compounds are said to belong to 'D' series and are represented by letter 'D' before their names.

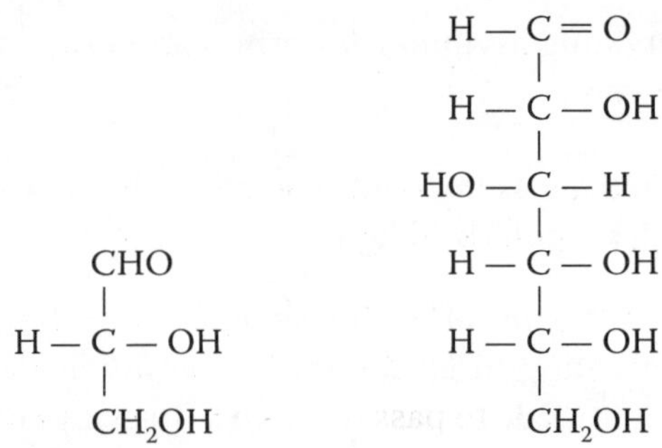

D-Glyceraldehyde **D-Glucose**

Figure 1.6 Dextrorotation.

On the other hand, the geometrical representation of the laevorotatory form is customarily written with the secondary alcoholic hydroxyl group of the carbon atom just adjacent to the terminal primary alcoholic group extending to the left (**Fig. 1.7**). Such compounds are said to belong to 'L' series and are represented by the letter 'L' before their names.

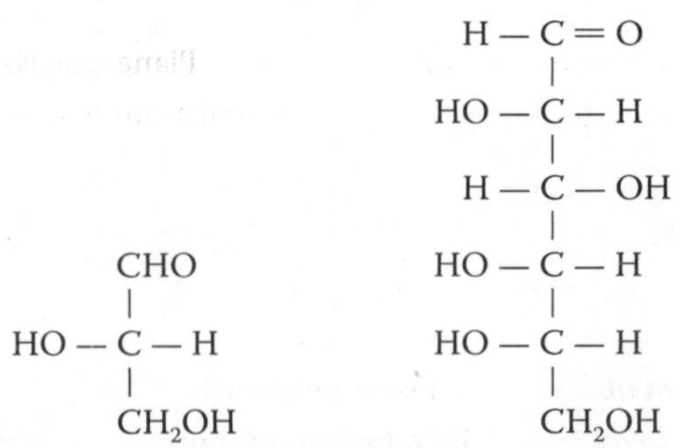

L-Glyceraldehyde **L-Glucose**

Figure 1.7 Laevorotation.

It should be noted that the prefixes 'D' and 'L' have no significance to the direction of optical rotation. They simply designate spatial relationship of the secondary alcoholic group to the right or to the left, respectively, whereas the sign plus (+) or minus (–) represent optical rotation.

Note that the configuration of H and OH groups on the asymmetric carbon atom (C-2) of 'D' and 'L' glyceraldehyde is identical to the configuration of these groups on the asymmetric carbon atom C-5 of 'D' and 'L' glucose, respectively (*see* **Figs 1.6** and **1.7**). Note that the OH of the secondary alcoholic hydroxyl group in the case of 'D' glucose extends to the right, whereas in the case of 'L' glucose, it extends to the left.

Another point to be noted is that the optical rotation of many members of the 'D' series may be levorotatory and that of the 'L' series dextrorotatory. When it is necessary to represent both the spatial configuration and the optical activity of a particular isomer simultaneously, they are expressed as D(–) or D(+) and L(–) or L(+).

Thus, glyceraldehyde can be represented as D(+) or D(–) as indicated alongside. Here, 'D' represents the spatial configuration of the secondary alcoholic hydroxyl group and the plus (+) and minus (–) signs represent the optical rotation

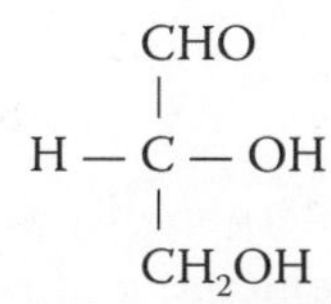

D(+) Glyceraldehyde

D(–) Glyceraldehyde

Glucose

Glucose, a hexose, is present in blood in significant concentration and is physiologically the most important carbohydrate. Glucose is a monosaccharide and has six carbon atoms. It contains an aldehyde group and therefore it is an aldose. Its molecular formula is $C_6H_{12}O_6$. It has five hydroxyl groups. The structural formula of glucose is shown in **Figure 1.8**.

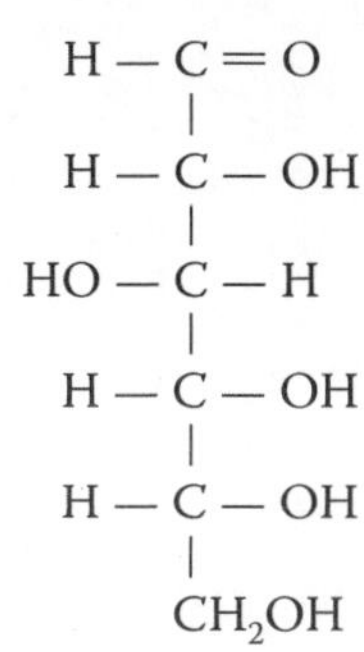

Figure 1.8 Structural formula of glucose.

'D' series and 'L' series—structure differences of α and β glucose:

1. In 'D' series the hydroxyl group of C-5 is on the right, whereas the hydroxyl group of C-5 in the 'L' series is on the left.
2. The ring formation is written on the right side for 'D' series and on the left side for 'L' series.
3. This should not be confused with α and β forms, which distinguish the position of hydroxyl group at C-l. In α form, the hydroxyl group at C-l is on the same side as the ring formation, usually on the right. In β form, the hydroxyl group at C-1 is on the opposite side of the ring formation.

Mutarotation: This means changing of optical rotation. Tanret explained that when a solution of freshly prepared crystalline glucose of α-D form is observed in a polariscope, its initial specific rotation which is +112° gradually decreases and finally becomes steady at +52.5°. If, however, a solution of pure crystals of β-D-glucose is observed in a polariscope, the initial specific rotation of +19° for β-D-glucose gradually increases and finally becomes steady at +52.5°.

The change in rotation is illustrated as

$$\underset{\text{α-D-Glucose}}{+112^\circ \rightarrow} \qquad +52.5^\circ \qquad \underset{\text{β-D-Glucose}}{\leftarrow +19^\circ}$$

This change in optical rotation undergone by solutions of freshly prepared glucose is called **mutarotation**. Thus, both α-D-glucose and β-D-glucose in solution attain a stage of equilibrium, when the optical rotation reaches a steady and stationary value of +52.5°. It is generally accepted that the mechanism of mutarotation involves opening and closing of the hemiacetal ring structure of monosaccharides, to form traces of aldehyde and α and β ring forms. It has also been established that all monosaccharides exist in three forms in nature: (i) aldehyde, (ii) α ring and (iii) β ring forms. Of the three forms, the aldehyde form is said to be extremely unstable and exists only as a transient intermediate. In glucose solutions, it is assumed that approximately two-third of the sugar exists as the β form at equilibrium. Addition of hydroxyl or hydrogen ions catalyses mutarotation.

Pyranoses and Furanoses (Figs 1.9 and 1.10)

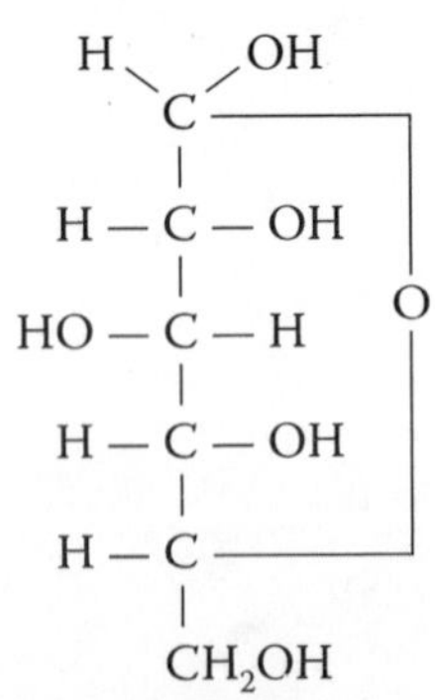

α-D-Glucose

Figure 1.9 Pyranose.

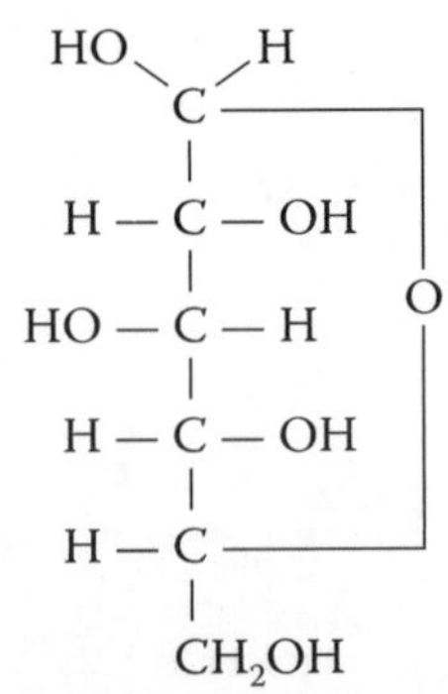

β-D-Glucose

Figure 1.10 Furanose.

Haworth proposed a scheme by which all sugars forming six-membered rings are to be called **pyranoses** as pyran possesses the same ring composed of six members of which five are carbon and one is oxygen (**Fig. 1.11**). Sugars in the pyranose form are most stable.

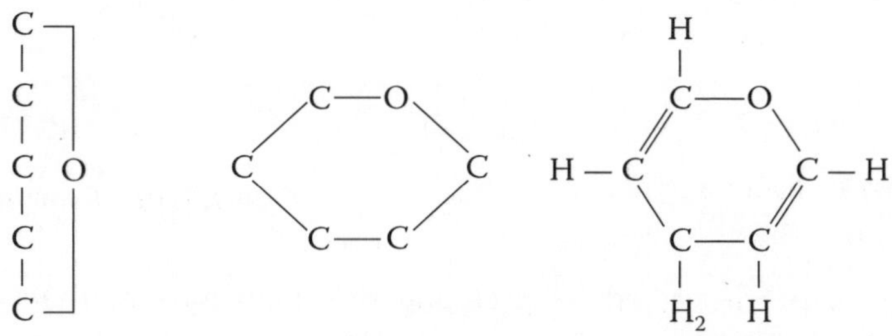

Pyran

Figure 1.11 Structure of pyranose.

In some sugars, condensation takes place between the aldehyde at C-1 and hydroxyl at C-4, when a ring of five members is formed. The five-membered ring structures for fructose of 'D' series are shown in **Figures 1.12** and **1.13**.

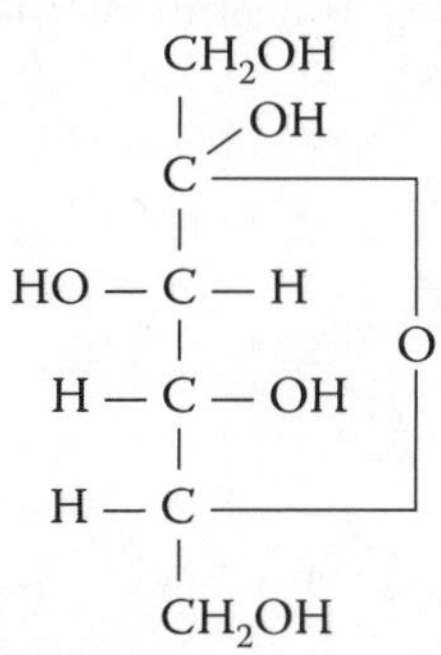

Figure 1.12 α-D-Fructose.

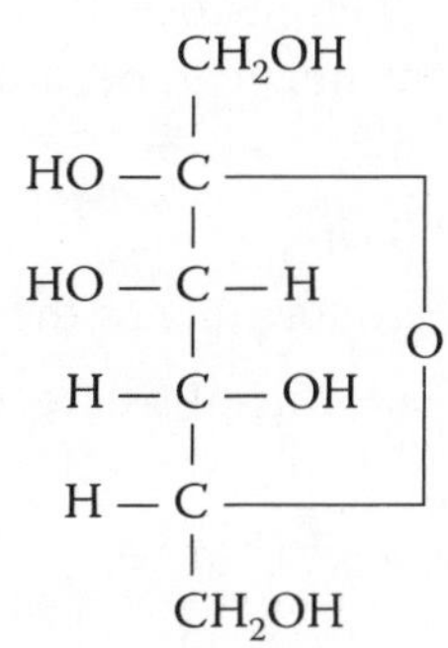

Figure 1.13 β-D-Fructose.

Haworth designated that sugars having a five-membered ring are to be called ***furanoses***, because furan possesses the same ring composed of four carbons and one oxygen (**Fig. 1.14**). Formation of furanoses for monosaccharides is a transitory process and is unstable.

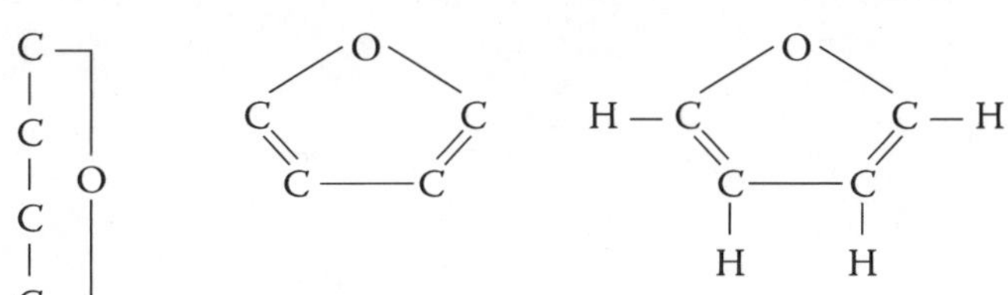

Furan

Figure 1.14 Structure of furanose.

It is customary to write pyranose and furanose ring structures by leaving out the carbon atoms and retaining the oxygen as in **Figures 1.15** and **1.16**.

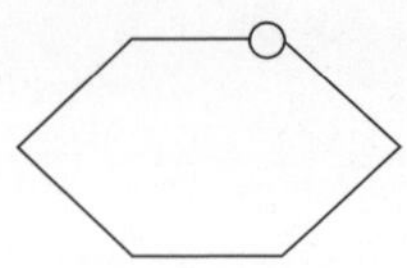

Figure 1.15 Pyranose ring.

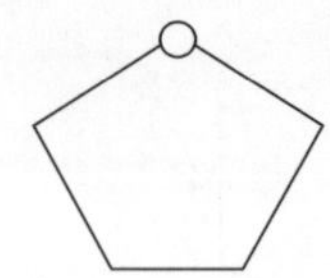

Figure 1.16 Furanose ring.

Individual sugars are described by prefixing the main part of their common name (glucose or fructose) to pyranose or furanose. Thus, glucose which is a six-membered ring is called **glucopyranose** and fructose in the furanose form is called **fructofuranose**.

Fructose

Fructose is called **levulose** or **fruit sugar**. It is called so because it is levorotatory and is found abundantly in sweet fruits. It is also present in honey and is sweeter than sucrose. Fructose can be obtained by hydrolysis of cane sugar and inulin, a polysaccharide. D-Fructose is a ketohexose. Its molecular formula is $C_6H_{12}O_6$, the same as that of glucose. Its structural formula can be shown in three forms:

1. The keto form
2. The α and β ring forms
3. The Haworth formula as furanose and pyranose forms

All the three forms of fructose are shown in **Figure 1.17**.

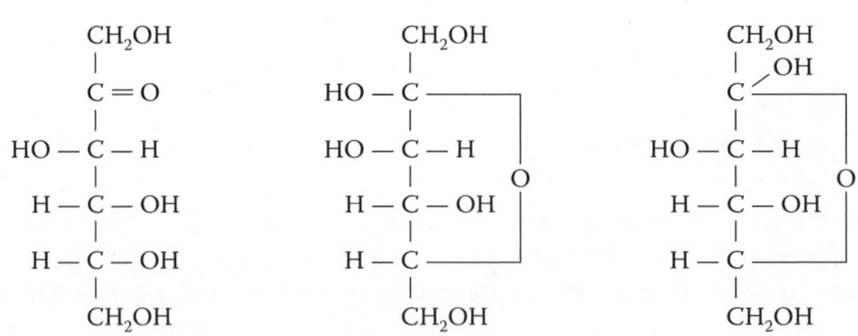

Keto form of D-fructose (1) | **β-D-Fructose** (2) | **α-D-Fructose** (3)

Figure 1.17 Forms of fructose.

Galactose

Galactose is seldom found free in nature. It is obtained when lactose is hydrolysed. Lactose is milk sugar and is a disaccharide consisting of galactose and glucose. Galactose is also a constituent of the glycolipids which are abundantly present in nervous tissues. Galactose is strongly dextrorotatory. The structure of galactose is shown in **Figure 1.18**.

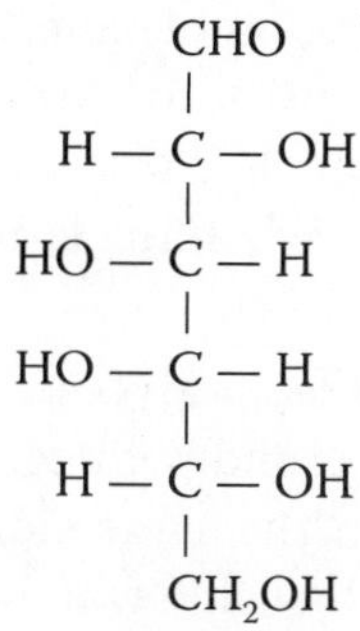

D-Galactose

Figure 1.18 Structure of galactose.

Galactose on oxidation by hot nitric acid yields mucic acid, which is insoluble in water, and also saccharic acid. Galactose forms osazones. It is not fermented by yeast.

Mannose

Mannose does not occur free in nature. But it is widely distributed in combination as the polysaccharide mannan, as in ivory nut. It is a constituent of the prosthetic polysaccharide of albumins, globulins and mucoids. Mannose reduces Benedict's reagent.

Heptoses

Heptoses contain seven carbon atoms. The structure of sedoheptulose, which is a heptose, is shown in **Figure 1.19**. It occurs as an intermediate in the oxidative shunt pathway of carbohydrate metabolism.

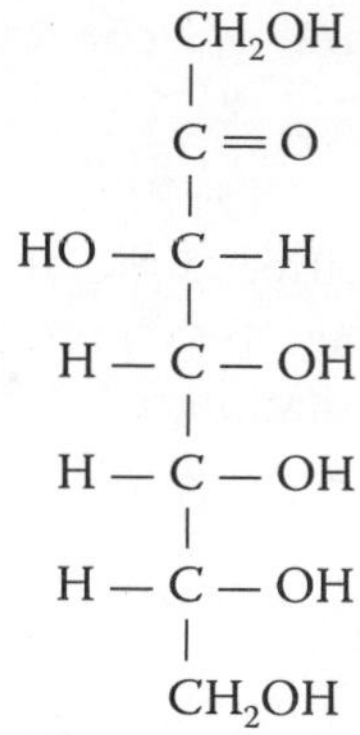

Figure 1.19 Sedoheptulose.

Glycosides

Glycosides or **glucosides** are compounds containing a monosaccharide and a non-carbohydrate group in the same molecule. Glucosides are formed when the monosaccharides react with alcohols in the presence of HCl as a catalyst. The reaction takes place between the OH of C-1 (which is also called glucosidic hydroxyl group) of the sugar and the non-carbohydrate group, when the latter gets attached at C-1 of the sugar in acetal linkage.

The non-carbohydrate group is called **aglycon**. The resulting compound is called a glucoside when the sugar is a glucose; α and β glucosides are present, depending upon the presence of the glucosidic hydroxyl on the same side or on the opposite side of the ring. The simplest glucoside is the methyl glucoside which is formed when a solution of glucose in boiling methyl alcohol is treated with 0.5% HCl as a catalyst (**Fig. 1.20**).

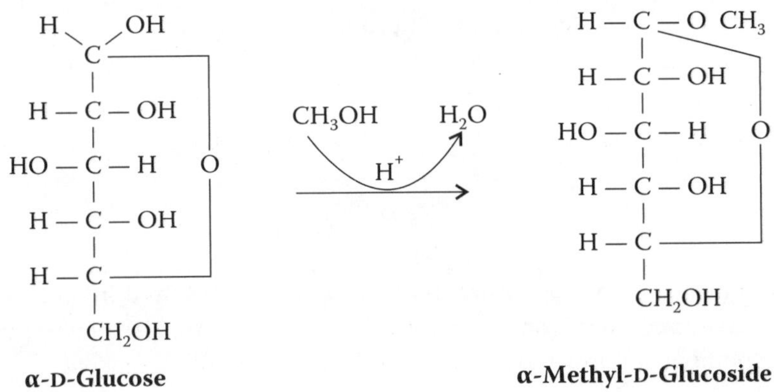

Figure 1.20 Formation of methyl glucoside.

Other glucosides are complex. They are widely distributed in plants. The aglycon may be a sterol or phenol. They are mostly plant pigments, spices and drugs. Some glucosides are of clinical importance. These are cardiac glucosides. They are found in the leaves and seeds of digitalis, the seeds of strophanthus and the bulbs of squill. The cardiac glucoside digitonin contains galactose, xylose and aglycon digitogenin which is a steroid. Other examples of glucosides are as follows:

1. Phlorizin which is found in rose bark is a combination of glucose and phloretin.
2. Amygdalin which is found in bitter almonds is a combination of glucose and mandelonitrile. The union between two monosaccharides to form a molecule of disaccharide is also a glucoside formation.

DISACCHARIDES

Disaccharides are sugars containing two molecules of monosaccharides. When condensation occurs between two monosaccharides, union takes place between C-l of the second monosaccharide and C-4 of the first monosaccharide. Therefore, the C-l of the second monosaccharide is not free in the sense that it has lost its potential aldehyde group whereas the C-l of the first monosaccharide is free and has its potential aldehyde intact. Examples of disaccharides are as follows:

1. Maltose (**Fig. 1.21**)
2. Lactose (**Fig. 1.22**)
3. Sucrose (**Fig. 1.23**)

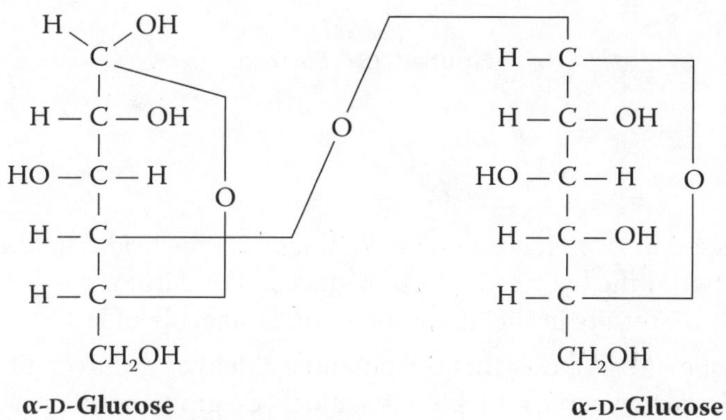

Figure 1.21 Maltose.

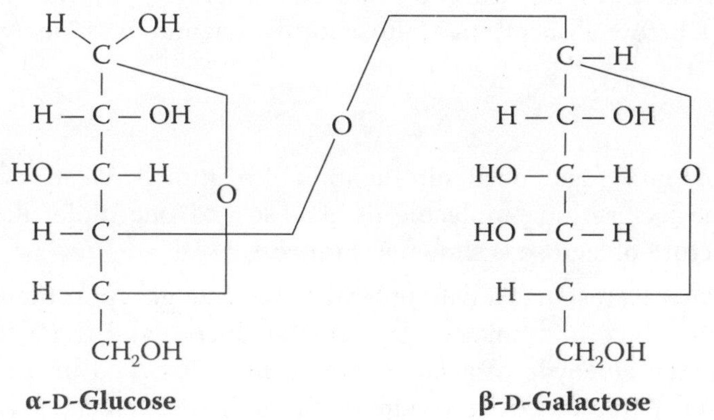

Figure 1.22 Lactose.

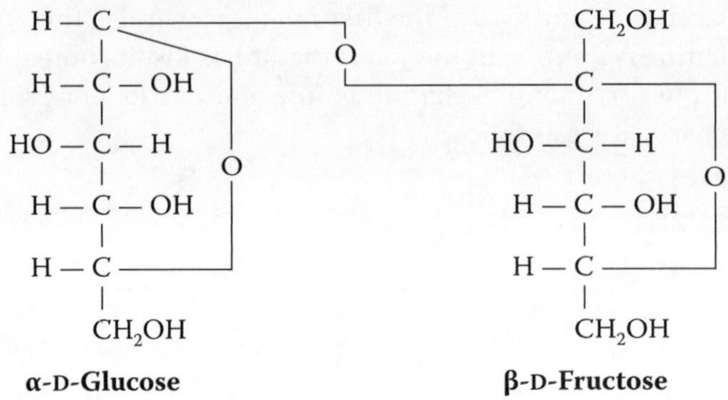

Figure 1.23 Sucrose.

Maltose

Maltose is composed of two glucose units, combined in glucosidic linkage (*see* **Fig. 1.21**). Condensation between the hydroxyl group of glucose 1 at carbon-4 and hydroxyl group of glucose 2 at carbon-1 results in the liberation of one molecule of H_2O.

The structure of maltose shows that the potential aldehyde group of glucose-2 is blocked in the glucoside linkage whereas the potential aldehyde group of glucose-1 is free and can reduce alkaline copper solutions. It is because of this free aldehyde in the first glucose molecule that maltose has the property of reducing sugar.

Maltose is the end product of digestion of starch by the action of salivary amylase ptyalin, in the mouth, and pancreatic amylase, in the intestines. Maltose is formed as an intermediate product in the intestines. It is formed as an intermediate product in the acid hydrolysis of starch. It is split into two molecules of glucose by the enzyme maltase of the intestinal juice before absorption. Maltose forms osazones with phenylhydrazine.

Lactose

Lactose, also called milk sugar, occurs in the milk of mammals. When hydrolysed by acids or by the enzyme lactase, one molecule of glucose and one molecule of galactose are formed. The structure of lactose is shown in **Figure 1.24**.

Just as in maltose, lactose has a true potential aldehyde group in the glucose molecule, not involved in the glucosidic linkage between the glucose and the galactose molecules, whereas the potential aldehyde of galactose molecule is blocked in the linkage. Because of the presence of a free aldehyde group in the glucose molecule, lactose can reduce alkaline copper solutions and is therefore a reducing sugar. Lactose may occur in the urine of pregnant and lactating women, and this is physiological. It exhibits all the reactions of reducing sugars. It is not fermented by yeast.

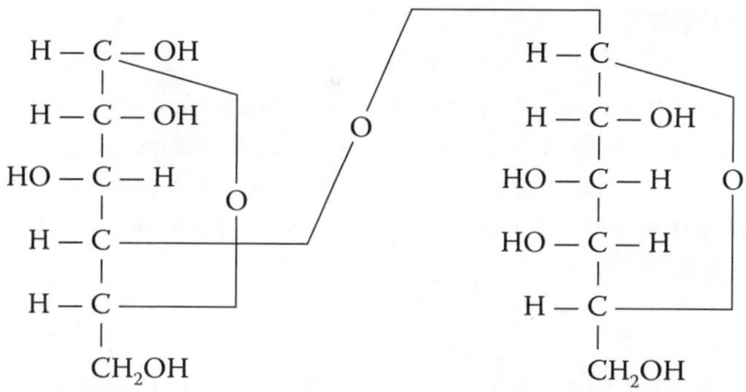

Figure 1.24 Lactose.

Sucrose

Sucrose is cane sugar. It is the most commonly and extensively used sugar in the food. It is widely distributed in plants and is obtained from sugarcane, beetroot, pineapple, honey, fruits and certain palms.

An important property of sucrose is that it is a **non-reducing sugar**, and this is due to its structural peculiarity which is rather unusual. Sucrose is a disaccharide, consisting of one molecule of glucose and one molecule of fructose. The linkage between these molecules is formed between the carbon of the aldehyde group of glucose and the carbon of the ketone group of fructose (*see* **Figs 1.17** and **1.23**). Thus, both the potential aldehyde group of glucose and the ketone group of fructose are blocked in the linkage and the molecule of sucrose has no free reducing group. On account of this structural peculiarity, sucrose is a non-reducing sugar. It does not reduce Benedict's qualitative reagent. It does not undergo mutarotation and does not form osazones like other reducing sugars.

Sucrose before hydrolysis is dextrorotatory. On hydrolysis, it yields glucose and fructose. The product of hydrolysis which consists of glucose and fructose is called **invert sugar** and this is levorotatory. The levorotation is due to the presence of fructose which is by itself more levorotatory than glucose is dextrorotatory. This phenomenon is called **inversion**. Invert sugar is sweeter than sucrose and for this reason, it is used commercially in the manufacture of sweets.

Honey contains plenty of invert sugar and is therefore very sweet. Inversion may be effected by the enzyme sucrase or invertase and by weak acids.

POLYSACCHARIDES

Polysaccharides are composed of a number of molecules of monosaccharides. They represent condensation products of several molecules of simple sugars. They possess high molecular weight and form colloidal solution. The important polysaccharides are (i) starch, (ii) glycogen, (iii) dextrins and (iv) cellulose. Other examples are dextrin and inulin.

Starch

Starch is the storage form of carbohydrate present in plants, being abundantly found in roots, tubers, stem, vegetables, fruits and cereals. The bulk of our diet which consists mainly of rice, wheat and vegetables is a good source of starch. Starch occurs in the form of grains which may be spherical or oval in shape. Microscopically, the starch grains are found to differ in size and shape, according to their sources. Generally, they appear to consist of concentric rings with a hilum in the centre.

Starch which is composed of several glucose molecules is a mixture of two types of molecules, namely amylose, in which glucose molecules are arranged in a linear form, and amylopectin, in which the glucose molecules are arranged in a highly branched form. Amylose forms the inner portion of the starch grain and is soluble in water. Amylopectin forms the outer covering of the starch grain and is insoluble in water. Starch as a whole is insoluble in cold water. When it is heated with water the amylopectin absorbs water, swells up and bursts to form a paste, with amylose diffusing into the water, at a temperature between 60°C and 80°C. The amylopectin, being insoluble, settles down. The mixture of amylose and amylopectin in water is called **starch paste**. The amylopectin can be separated by centrifugation.

Structure of amylose: Amylose is a linear, non-branched polymer of glucose. The glucose units of amylose are linked at the 1–4 carbon atoms of the successive glucopyranose units, as in maltose, and are not branched. In other words, the amylose structure may be considered as an expanded maltose structure, with a free sugar group at one end. Amylose is soluble in water and is less viscous. The molecular weight of amylose is 60,000 corresponding to a chain of 300–400 glucose units (**Fig. 1.25**).

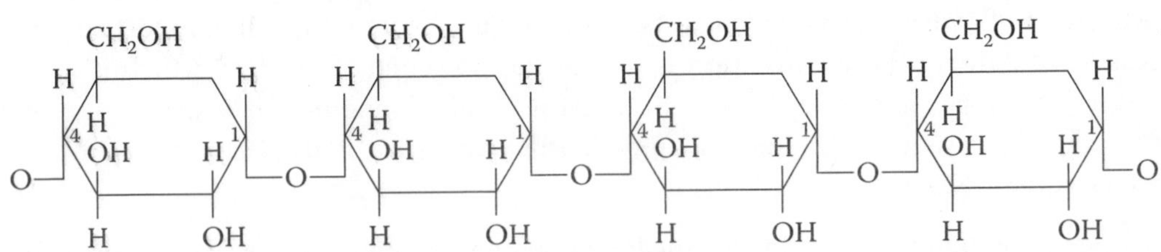

Figure 1.25 Structure of amylose showing 1–4 linkage.

Structure of amylopectin: Amylopectins differ from amylose in that they are larger molecules. They have molecular weight as high as 200,000 or more, corresponding to 1,000–1,500 glucose units. Their molecules are highly branched. They have both

1:4 and 1:6 glucosidic linkages (**Fig. 1.26**). In the figure, the horizontal arrangement of 'G' represents glucose molecules in 1–4 linkage. The branching from the horizontal 'G's represents glucose molecules in 1–6 linkage.

```
      G           G
      G           G
      G           G
      G           G
   GGGGGGGGGGGGGGGGG
         G           G
         G           G
         G           G
         GGGGG       G
         G
```

Figure 1.26 Structure of amylopectin, showing 1–4 and 1–6 linkages.

Hydrolysis of Starch

Starch, which is composed of several glucose units, is hydrolysed to form first maltose and finally glucose molecules. Hydrolysis of starch may be brought about by both enzymes and acids.

Enzymes which hydrolyse starch are amylases, and these are present in saliva as ptyalin and in pancreatic juice as pancreatic amylase. Amylase acts on starch, hydrolysing them into fragments of dextrins and ultimately to maltose molecules. They act at the 1–4 glucoside linkages. The products of hydrolysis are given below starting from starch.

Starch

↓

Soluble starch

↓

Amylodextrin + maltose (+)

↓

Erythrodextrin + maltose (+ +)

↓

Achrodextrin + maltose (+ + +)

↓

Maltose + maltose (+ + + +)

The various products can be demonstrated by their colours obtained with iodine. Thus, the first product soluble starch gives a blue colour (less opaque than the colour obtained with unhydrolysed starch). The next product amylodextrin gives a violet colour and the third product erythrodextrin gives a red colour. Achrodextrin, which is the final product among dextrins, does not give any colour with iodine.

It may be seen that at every stage starting from amylodextrin, maltose is also formed in increasing concentration, as the hydrolysis progresses. The end product obtained by the hydrolysis of starch by the enzyme is maltose. It may be noted that the hydrolysis of starch by acid goes a step further, and the end product is glucose.

For the hydrolysis of starch, certain anions such as Cl^- and Br^- are required to act as activators. The optimum pH for amylase to hydrolyse starch in NaCl solution is 6.9. Complete hydrolysis of starch requires the presence of an intestinal enzyme called oligo-1, 6-glucosidase, which acts at the 1–6 branching point and disintegrates starch completely.

Glycogen

Glycogen or animal starch is the storage form of carbohydrate in animals. It is found in a large amount in liver and muscles and in a smaller amount in other tissues such as kidneys and heart.

Glycogen plays an important role in the metabolism of carbohydrate. Liver glycogen is broken down to glucose which passes into the bloodstream to form blood glucose, if necessary. Muscle glycogen breaks down during muscle contraction to supply energy for contraction. It does not form blood glucose.

Structure of glycogen: Glycogen is a polysaccharide, composed of a number of glucose molecules arranged in the form of glucopyranose units with linkage between 1 and 4 carbon atoms of successive glucose units and branching involving 1–6 linkages of different glucose units. It differs from amylopectin by being shorter, but having more number of branches. The molecular weight of glycogen is high and is about 5,000,000.

Dextrins

Dextrins are formed as intermediate products, during hydrolysis of starch to maltose or glucose, by enzymes or acids. They occur in plants and are present in honey. Dextrins are soluble in water. In cold water, they form an opalescent solution which clears on heating.

All dextrins have free sugar groups and therefore have the property of reducing alkaline copper solution.

Cellulose

Cellulose forms the chief constituent of the structure of the cell wall of plants. It is present in the fibrous part of plants. Structurally, it is composed of long, unbranched chains of β-D-glucopyranose units, joined to one another by 1–4 glucosidic linkages.

It is highly insoluble and resistant to hydrolysis. It therefore passes through the human digestive tract without being attacked by the enzymes, though some bacterial decomposition takes place. On hydrolysis, it yields D-glucose units.

Dextran

Dextran is a polysaccharide, closely related to starch and glycogen. It has a molecular weight of approximately 50,000. It is a polymer of D-glucopyranose units. It is synthesised from sucrose by certain bacteria as occurring in starch and glycogen, where we have 1–4 linkage and branching points between 1 and 6. Structurally, it shows chains of α-glucose units linked at 1–6 carbon atoms and branching points between 1 and 4 carbon atoms. It is just the other way.

Inulin

Inulin is a polysaccharide, each molecule being composed of about 30 D-fructose units. Its molecular weight is about 5000. It occurs as the reserve carbohydrate in the tubers and roots of chickory, dhalia and dandelions and in the bulb of onions and garlic.

Properties: Inulin is a white, more or less crystalline powder. It is sweet to taste. It is readily soluble in hot water, but only slightly soluble in cold water. It does not give any colour with iodine. It has no reducing property.

Inulin is not hydrolysed by any kind of enzymes of the gastrointestinal tract and does not undergo any metabolic change in the body. When injected intravenously, it is excreted quantitatively by glomerular filtration within a short time. It does not undergo any reabsorption in the tubules. This property of inulin clearance is made use of in the determination of the rate of glomerular filtration or inulin clearance in an individual.

2 CHAPTER

Lipids

Chapter Outline

- Classification of Lipids
- Simple Lipids
- Compound Lipids
- Derived Lipids
- Substances Associated With Lipids

Lipids or fats are greasy materials occurring widely in nature. They are generally insoluble in water but soluble in fat solvents. They include substances such as

1. Naturally occurring fats, for example butter and oils.
2. Substances which are chemically related to fats but differ in certain common properties, such as lecithin, a waxy substance, soluble in fat solvents, and also mixing well with water, to form a colloidal solution.
3. Substances which are related to fats, because of certain common properties such as solubility and biological origin, but differ from fat in appearance and chemical nature, for example cholesterol.
4. Oils which are liquid at room temperature.

Occurrence: Fats are widely distributed in plants and animal tissues, from which they can be extracted by fat solvents such as alcohol and ether. In plants, they are particularly present in nuts, seeds and certain leaves. In animals, the nervous system is rich in lipids such as cholesterol, phospholipids and glycolipids. Blood contains lipoproteins. The fat depots such as subcutaneous tissues, mesenteric tissues, fatty tissue around the kidney and yellow bone marrow contain large amounts of fat. Food sources rich in fat are as follows:

1. *Animal sources:* Milk, egg, meat, liver and fish oils
2. *Plant sources:* Nuts, seeds and oils

Biological significance of fats:

1. Lipid forms one of the three main types of food stuffs. As an essential dietary constituent, it performs the important function of supplying fuel to the body yielding more heat and energy than carbohydrates.

2. Certain normal breakdown products of fatty acids in the body, such as acetic acid and bile acids, form important building blocks of biologically active and complex materials such as cholesterol, sex hormones and steroids.
3. Another function of dietary lipid is to supply the essential dietary constituent, known as the *essential fatty acids* (EFA). They cannot be synthesised by the body and therefore should be supplied in the diet in small quantities for optimal growth. Lack of these constituents in adequate amounts produces deficiency symptoms. Examples of EFA are linoleic acid, linolenic acid and arachidonic acid.
4. Deposits of fat underneath the skin exert an insulating effect to the body. They protect the body from excessive heat or cold and act as shock absorbers, for example the mesenteric pad of fat protects the internal organs.
5. Vitamins A, D, E and K which are fat-soluble vitamins are dietary essentials.

CLASSIFICATION OF LIPIDS

The following classification proposed by Bloor is the most accepted classification for lipids:

1. Simple lipids
2. Compound lipids
3. Derived lipids
4. Substances associated with lipids

Simple lipids: Simple lipids are those which contain esters of fatty acids and alcohol. They are further classified into (i) fats and (ii) waxes.

The alcohol in fats is glycerol and the alcohol in waxes is anything other than glycerol. This alcohol has a higher molecular weight.

Compound lipids: Compound lipids contain some other chemical groups in addition to alcohol and fatty acids. There are four subdivisions under this group:

- *Phospholipids:* They contain fatty acid, glycerol, phosphoric acid and a nitrogenous compound. Phospholipids include
  - Lecithin
  - Cephalin
  - Sphingomyelin
- *Glycolipids:* They are lipids containing carbohydrate and nitrogen but no phosphoric acid and glycerol.
- *Sulpholipids:* They are lipids containing sulphate groups.
- *Lipoproteins:* They are lipids attached to proteins. They are present in plasma and tissues.

Derived lipids: Derived lipids are substances derived from groups mentioned above by hydrolysis. They are as follows:

- Fatty acids
- Alcohols other than glycerol
- Glycerides
- Bases

Bases include the following:

- Choline
- Ethanolamine
- Sphingosine
- Serine

Substances associated with lipids:

- Carotenoids
- Vitamins A, D, E and K
- Tocopherols
- Steroids

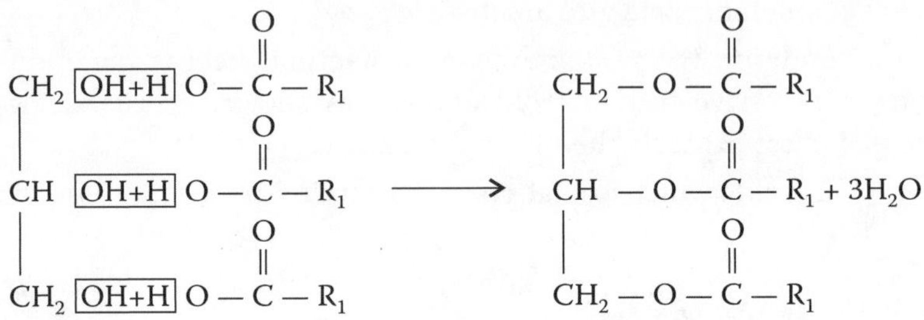

Glycerol **Fatty acid** **Simple glyceride**

SIMPLE LIPIDS

Fats

The common fatty acids present in natural fats are as follows:

Palmitic acid — $CH_3(CH_2)_{14}COOH$

Stearic acid — $CH_3(CH_2)_{16}COOH$

Oleic acid — $CH_3(CH_2)_7CH = CH(CH_2)_7COOH$

Properties of Fats

The following properties apply to lipids in general.

Physical properties:

1. Fats are greasy to touch and leave an oily impression on paper.
2. They are insoluble in water, but are readily soluble in fat solvents such as alcohol, ether and chloroform.
3. Pure glycerides are tasteless, odourless, colourless and neutral in reaction. But after exposure to air for sometime, they become acidic and develop a yellow colour due to partial hydrolysis and oxidation of unsaturated fatty acids contained in them.
4. Fats used in food have specific flavour and colour. The flavour is attributed to the presence of certain substances, absorbed by the fat either from its natural environment or acquired during the processing of the fat; for example, the flavour of butter is due to the presence of bacterial flora, which is carefully controlled to impart a special flavour to butter. The colours of butter, human fat and egg yolk are due to the presence of carotene and xanthophyll contained in them.

5. The hardness or consistency of the fat depends upon the relative amount of saturated and unsaturated fatty acids present in the fat. Fats containing saturated fatty acids are solids at room temperature. Fats containing unsaturated fatty acids are liquid at room temperature and these are oils.
6. Fats have definite melting points. They are usually low and vary in each case. The melting point of a fat is always higher than the temperature at which it solidifies. The melting points of natural fats are not sharp because they are mixtures of several fats. The presence of saturated fatty acids in fats increases the melting point, but the presence of unsaturated fatty acids lowers the melting point. This property causes the fat to be liquid or oil at room temperature.
7. Fats have lesser specific gravity than water and therefore float in water. The specific gravity of solid fat is less than liquid fat.

   One consequence of the low specific gravity of fat is that fat people float in water more readily than thin people.
8. Spreading of fat: When a liquid fat is placed on water, it spreads uniformly over the surface of water and if the quantity is sufficiently small, it will form a layer which is one molecule thick. The purpose of this property is to lower the surface tension and help the transport of fat.
9. Emulsification: Though fats are insoluble in water, they can be broken down into minute droplets and dispersed in water. This is emulsification. A satisfactory emulsion is one which is stable and contains very minute fat droplets with diameter less than 0.5 μm. Examples of naturally occurring emulsions are milk and yolk of egg. But they are not mere fat droplets in water. They contain hydrophilic colloidal particles such as proteins, carbohydrates and phospholipids which act as stabilising agents. Emulsification greatly increases the surface area of the fats, and this is an essential requisite for digestion of fats in the intestines. Emulsification is brought about by
   - Mechanical action; this can be facilitated by mixing mechanically or passing superheated steam
   - Chemical action; this is accomplished by the action of bile salts, which lower the surface tension

Chemical properties:

1. **Hydrolysis:** Fats being esters of glycerol and fatty acids are readily hydrolysed to glycerol and fatty acids, by acids, alkalies, superheated steam and enzymes known as lipases which act on the ester linkages. Two kinds of hydrolysis are known.
   - Enzyme hydrolysis
   - Alkali hydrolysis

   Enzyme hydrolysis is effected by lipase of pancreatic juice. This is important in the digestion of fats.

   Alkali hydrolysis refers to hydrolysis of fats by boiling with alkalies. This is important in industry. The process of alkali hydrolysis is called *saponification* which means 'soap-making'. The alkali salt resulting from saponification is soap. Alkali hydrolysis takes place as shown below:

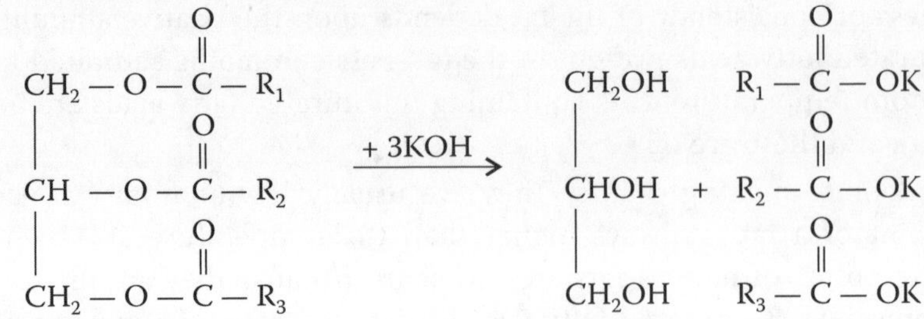

Triglyceride　　Glycerol　　Soap

Soaps: Since the common fats used for making soaps contain predominantly palmitic, stearic and oleic acids, the soaps we use for washing consist largely of the sodium or potassium salts of these fatty acids. The potassium soaps are soft and soluble and the sodium soaps are hard and less soluble in water. When soluble soap is used in hard water which contains calcium and magnesium ions, the efficiency of producing lather is diminished. This is because the fatty acids in the soap are precipitated by the calcium and magnesium salts of the hard water. The precipitation continues until all the calcium and magnesium ions combine with the fatty acids of the soap. Now, additional soap will form lather. But this means that more soap is required for cleaning. Another disadvantage of using hard water is that the precipitated calcium and magnesium salts will cling to the washed clothes and make them harsh and thick. The presence of excess Na^+ and K^+ ions (as in seawater) diminishes the solubility of sodium and potassium soaps. A sodium soap is practically insoluble in a saturated NaCl solution. This is why washing with ordinary soap in seawater is difficult.

Soaps are good cleansing agents because they are effective emulsifying agents. Dirt is held to the surface by greasy substances. Soaps being good emulsifying agents lower the surface tension also. The greasy materials are emulsified by the soaps and the dirt is carried away with them in washing.

Saponification number: This is a constant which is of special value in the identification and characterisation of neutral fat. It is defined as the number of milligrams of KOH required to saponify 1 gram of fat. Roughly speaking, this number varies inversely with the molecular weight of the fat. A high saponification number indicates the presence of a good proportion of fatty acids of low molecular weight. This is because simpler fatty acids take up more KOH than higher fatty acids.

2. **Autoxidation:** Unsaturated fatty acids in fats react with ozone and oxygen to undergo a reaction called autoxidation, in the presence of an appropriate amount of moisture, light, warmth and catalytic substances. Ozonides, peroxides, aldehydes and ketones are formed. Some of the natural oils containing a large proportion of highly unsaturated fatty acids such as linseed oil, when exposed to air and light in a thin layer, absorb oxygen and undergo autoxidation. The fatty acids are oxidised to aldehydes and ketones, which further condense to form tough, elastic, waterproof films. Such oils are called 'drying oils' and are used in the manufacture of paints, varnishes and linoleum.

Rancidity: Autoxidation occurring in natural edible fats is called rancidification. The fat which has become rancid has a disagreeable odour and taste and is unfit for consumption. Rancidification occurs more frequently in summer. The chemical changes which occur during rancidification are known as rancidity.

Rancidity can be considerably prevented by the addition of traces of organic compounds such as phenols, gallic acid and vitamins C and E. Such substances are called *antioxidants*, and these are present in many vegetable oils. This is why certain oils tend to keep better than others, even though unsaturation is the same in both.

Prevention of rancidity: Rancidification of fat may be prevented by

- Proper storage of the fats in air-tight, non-metallic receptacles kept in a cool place, away from light, moisture and warmth. Storing in non-metallic vessels is necessary, because metals such as copper and lead catalyse rancidity.
- Addition of antioxidants such as vitamins C and E.

3. **Addition reaction:** Fats containing unsaturated fatty acids readily add on elements such as halogens and hydrogen at their double bonds.

Iodine value: The number of grams of iodine taken up by 100 grams of a given fat is called its iodine value or iodine number. Iodine number is a measure of the degree of unsaturation of the fatty acid. Since the quantity of iodine absorbed by the fat can be measured accurately, it is possible to calculate the relative unsaturation of fats.

Fats containing a high proportion of unsaturated fatty acids have a characteristically high iodine value. The iodine values and saponification values of some common fats are given in **Table 2.1**.

Table 2.1 Iodine Values and Saponification Values of Fats

Fat	Iodine Value	Saponification Value
Coconut oil	6–10	246–260
Butter	25–50	220–233
Beef fat	36–48	192–200
Pork fat (Lard)	50–70	195–197
Human fat	57–66	193–199
Olive oil	78–90	185–195
Cottonseed oil	106–112	192–196
Cod liver oil	144–168	175–193
Linseed oil	192–195	190–195

Hydrogenation: Unsaturated fats can combine with hydrogen under the influence of a suitable catalyst, such as finely divided nickel, platinum and copper, at high temperature and become more saturated. For example, oleic acid which is an unsaturated fatty acid can be saturated by the addition of 2H atoms (hydrogenation) to give stearic acid.

$$\underset{\text{Oleic acid}}{CH_3(CH_2)_{14}CH = CH\ COOH} \xrightarrow{+2H} \underset{\text{Stearic acid}}{CH_3(CH_2)_{16}COOH}$$

In this way, solid edible fats which are saturated can be made from cheap and comparatively inedible oils such as cottonseed oils and fish oils. Examples of such fats are margarine and *vanaspati*.

Waxes

Waxes are esters of fatty acids with alcohols other than glycerol. One such alcohol is cholesterol. Waxes are insoluble in water, but soluble in fat solvents. They are not easily hydrolysed like fats or digested by lipases. Therefore, they are of no value nutritionally. Examples of waxes are as follows:

1. **Bees wax:** This is secreted by the honey bee to form the honeycomb. The chief ingredient is myricyl palmitate.
2. **Chinese wax:** This is the secretion of an insect.
3. **Carnauba wax:** This is found on the leaves of Carnauba palm of Brazil.
   This is of value in the manufacture of shoe polish, floor waxes, varnishes and candles.
4. **Lanoline:** This is known as 'wool wax'. It is obtained from wool and is used in making ointments. The common wax in the human body is found in the blood plasma, suprarenals and sebaceous glands. They are all esters of cholesterol, i.e. cholesterol palmitate.

The importance of waxes in plants and animals is that they serve as protective agents. The waxy coating on the surface of plants prevents excessive loss of moisture. The waxy coating over fruits such as apples and citrus fruits prevents them from drying and from being infected with fungi and bacteria. In birds, the presence of wax on the surface of feathers and hair helps to keep them soft and pliable. The waxes prevent the aquatic animals from becoming wet.

COMPOUND LIPIDS

Compound lipids are lipids which contain certain chemical groups other than alcohol and fatty acid. They include the following:

1. Phospholipids
2. Glycolipids
3. Sulpholipids
4. Lipoproteins

Phospholipids

Phospholipids are also known as phosphatides. They are important compounds present in all vegetable and animal cells. They are abundantly present in heart, brain, kidneys, egg yolk and soya bean. They are all composed of fatty acid, glycerol, phosphoric acid and nitrogenous base. Phospholipids play an important role in the prevention of fatty liver and in the process of blood coagulation. Thromboplastin, a factor in blood clotting, is a phospholipid. The three important phospholipids are as follows:

1. Lecithin

2. Cephalin
3. Sphingomyelin

Lecithin: A typical lecithin consists of one glycerol molecule esterified to two molecules of fatty acids. One of these fatty acids may be unsaturated and the other saturated. It contains a phosphoric acid molecule and a nitrogenous base, choline (**Fig. 2.1**).

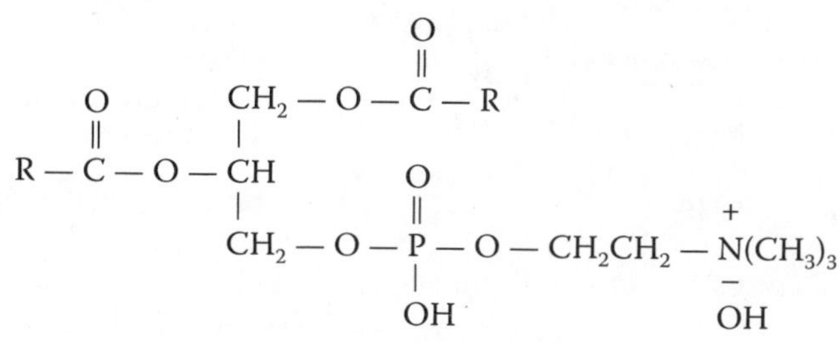

Figure 2.1 α-Lecithin.

Two forms of lecithin, α-lecithin and β-lecithin, are described. α-Lecithin has the phosphoric acid and choline attached to the third carbon atom (α-carbon atom) of glycerol. β-Lecithin has the phosphoric acid and choline attached to the second carbon atom (β-carbon atom) of glycerol. Lecithins are important in the metabolism of fat and in the prevention of fatty livers.

Lecithins are hydrolysed by enzymes called lecithinases to various components. There are four types of lecithinases occurring in nature. Each acts on lecithin at different points. These are as follows:

(i) Lecithinase A
(ii) Lecithinase B
(iii) Lecithinase C
(iv) Lecithinase D

Lecithinase A is found in cobra venom. It is also present in spider venom and poisonous stings. It partially hydrolyses lecithin, splitting off the unsaturated fatty acid component, leaving behind lysolecithin. This action of lecithinase A is specific as it acts only on the unsaturated fatty acid. Lysolecithin is a powerful haemolytic poison, which causes haemolysis of the erythrocytes (**Fig. 2.2**).

Lecithinase B is present especially in pancreas. It hydrolyses both the saturated and the unsaturated fatty acids from the lecithin molecule, leaving behind glyceryl phosphorylcholine (**Fig. 2.2**).

Lecithinase C hydrolyses lecithin at the point between glycerol and phosphoric acid with the liberation of a diglyceride and phosphorylcholine. Lecithinase C is found in plants.

Lecithinase D hydrolyses lecithin by splitting only choline and leaving behind phosphatidic acid (triglyceride phosphoric acid). It is found in leafy vegetables such as cabbage. The action of the different lecithinases on lecithin is shown in **Figure 2.2**.

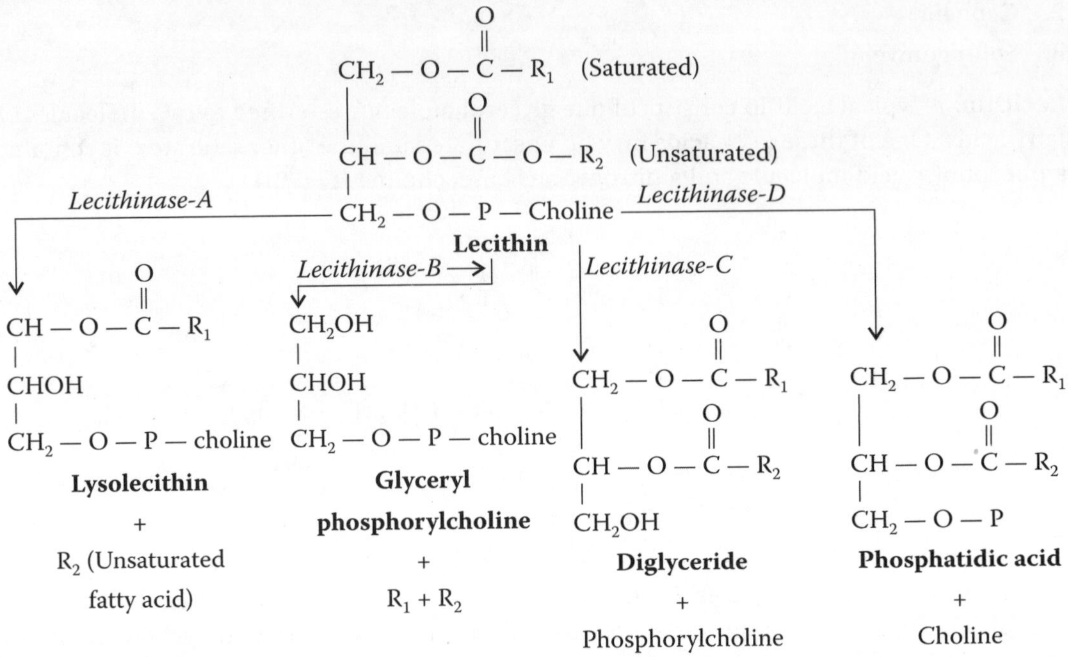

Figure 2.2 Action of lecithinases.

Lecithins form stable compounds with proteins, carbohydrates and various heavy metals. During absorption of fat, the lecithin content of blood increases as the blood lipids increase.

Choline: Choline is trimethyl hydroxyethyl ammonium hydroxide (**Fig. 2.3**). It is a strong quaternary base, as strong as NaOH. It is synthesised from ethanolamine by transmethylation with methionine. Choline is a component of lecithin and sphingomyelin and hence an important constituent of phospholipid.

Functions

- Choline is an important factor in the prevention of fatty liver. Absence of choline in the diet leads to accumulation of fat in the liver of rats, leading to fatty liver. Choline is therefore a lipotropic factor.
- Choline acts as a methyl donor along with methionine and betaine, in transmethylation reactions.
- Acetylcholine, the acetylated derivative of choline, plays an important role in the transmission of nerve impulses.
- When putrefying bacteria act on tissue choline, water is split from choline to produce a poisonous base called neurine.

Source: Choline is present in egg yolk, liver, heart, kidney and milk.

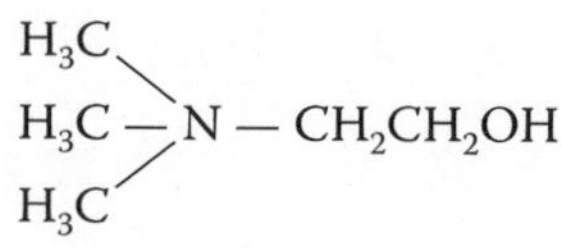

Figure 2.3 Choline.

Cephalins: They occur along with lecithin in all animal and plant cells. They are of similar structure to that of lecithin, but differ from lecithin in that the base attached to phosphoric acid is not choline. It may be one of the three bases, namely ethanolamine, serine or inositol. Therefore, three cephalins are known. They are (i) ethanolamine cephalin, (ii) serine cephalin and (iii) inositol cephalin. Both α- and β-cephalins are known.

Ethanolamine cephalin (phosphatidylethanolamine): The saturated fatty acid component is stearic acid and the unsaturated fatty acid is oleic acid (**Fig. 2.4**).

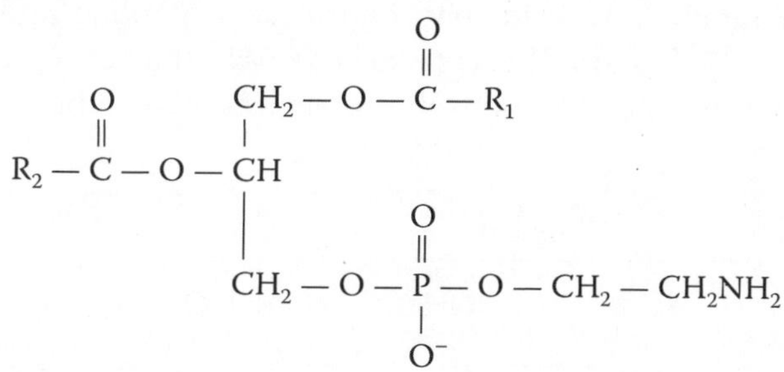

Figure 2.4 Phosphatidylethanolamine.

Serine cephalin (phosphatidylserine): This compound contains amino acid serine instead of ethanolamine. It is found in brain tissues. Traces are detected in blood also (**Fig. 2.5**).

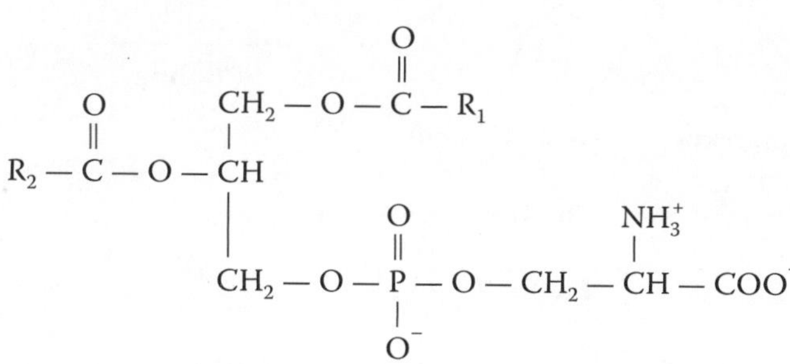

Figure 2.5 Phosphatidylserine.

Phosphatidylinositol (lipositol): This cephalin contains inositol instead of serine. Inositol was first discovered in acid-fast bacteria. It was later found to occur in phospholipids of brain tissues, soya bean and wheat germ (**Fig. 2.6**).

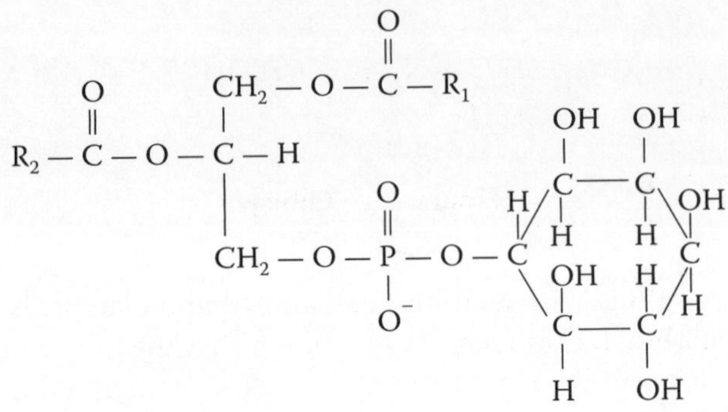

Figure 2.6 Phosphatidylinositol.

Sphingomyelins: They differ radically from cephalin in composition. They are found in brain and nerve tissues (**Fig. 2.7**).

Sphingomyelins contain fatty acid, phosphoric acid, choline and a complex amino alcohol sphingosine or sphingol. The fatty acid (R) is attached to the amino group of sphingosine by amide linkage. The phosphoric acid is attached to one of the hydroxyl groups of sphingosine.

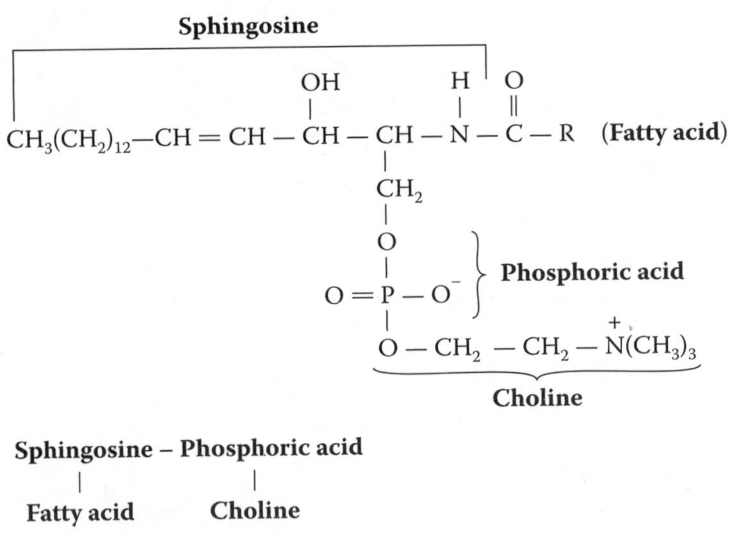

Figure 2.7 Sphingomyelin.

Accumulation of sphingomyelin in liver, spleen and other tissues causes the Niemann–Pick disease.

Glycolipids

Glycolipids may be further subdivided into

1. Cerebrosides
2. Gangliosides

They are known as glycolipids because they contain a sugar in addition to fatty acid and sphingosine. They do not contain phosphoric acid. They are optically active, owing to the presence of asymmetric carbon atoms in the molecules of sphingosine and galactose. They are found in large amounts in the white matter of the brain and myelin sheaths of nerves.

Cerebrosides: They are also known as galactolipids because of their galactose content. They are called cerebrosides as they are found in brain in large amounts. They have no phosphoric acid group. They are composed of

- Fatty acid of high molecular weight
- Sphingosine
- Galactose

Four cerebrosides have been identified according to their fatty acid component. They are as follows:

(i) Cerebroside containing lignoceric acid
(ii) Cerebroside containing cerebronic acid
(iii) Cerebroside containing nervonic acid
(iv) Cerebroside containing oxynervonic acid

Abnormally high concentration of cerebroside (kerasin) is found in the spleen, in Gaucher's disease.

Gangliosides: They are glycolipids containing glucose, galactose and a substance called neuraminic acid, in addition to fatty acid and sphingosine. Gangliosides occur in brain.

Sulpholipids

Sulpholipids are lipids containing sulphur. The chemical nature of sulpholipids is not known well. It is probable that it is a sulphuric acid ester of a glycolipid. Sulpholipids are abundantly present in the white matter of the brain.

Lipoproteins

Lipoproteins are formed by combination of proteins with lipids which include phospholipids, lecithin and cephalin, fatty acid, cholesterol, glycerides and fat-soluble vitamins.

The lipoprotein molecule has lower density than the ordinary protein molecule, due to its combination with lipids. Because of this property, the different fractions of serum lipoproteins can be identified by ultracentrifugation when they float at different rates, due to different densities of each fraction.

Lipoproteins are widely distributed in the body tissues. The various sites of distribution are as follows:

- Cell membrane
- Certain internal structures of cells, such as nucleus, mitochondria and microsomes
- Thromboplastin which converts prothrombin to thrombin
- Egg yolk contains two lipoproteins, known as lipovitellin α and lipovitellin β
- The film that stabilises the fat droplets in milk contains lipoprotein
- Rhodopsin or visual purple is a combination of a protein opsin and retinene aldehyde of vitamin A (fat-soluble vitamin)

- Blood lipoproteins are present in plasma. The lipid fraction consists mainly of cholesterol, phospholipids, triglycerides, traces of fat-soluble vitamins and steroid hormone.

These water-insoluble lipids are combined with the α and β globulin fractions of plasma protein to form water-soluble complexes and are transported in a soluble form. The molecular weight of α-lipoprotein is 200,000. The molecular weight of β-lipoprotein is in the range of 1,300,000. (For more details, refer to blood lipids.)

DERIVED LIPIDS

Fatty Acids

Fatty acid is an important constituent of fat. They are monocarboxylic acids with a hydrocarbon chain. The length of the chain may vary from 2 to 34 carbon atoms. It is obtained by the hydrolysis of fats by acids, alkalies or enzymes. Almost all the fatty acids found in nature have a straight chain and an even number of carbon atoms. The chain may be saturated or unsaturated. The commonest fatty acids that occur in nature are palmitic, stearic and oleic acids. Among these fatty acids, oleic acid is unsaturated.

Classification of Fatty Acids

Fatty acids may be divided into three classes, as follows:

1. Saturated fatty acids
2. Unsaturated fatty acids
3. Cyclic fatty acids

Saturated Fatty Acids

These are fatty acids which do not contain double bonds. They do not exhibit addition reactions and their iodine values are nil. Generally, the presence of saturated fatty acid makes the fat solid, but there are exceptions to this rule. For example, butter which is a solid fat has a higher iodine value (35–50) than coconut oil which is a liquid fat (iodine value 6–10).

Saturated fatty acids are built up on acetic acid which is the first member of the series. The general formula for saturated fatty acids is ($C_nH_{2n+1}COOH$). They contain an even number of carbon atoms. A list of saturated fatty acids occurring in nature is given in **Table 2.2**.

Unsaturated Fatty Acids

These are fatty acids which contain double bonds. Iodine values vary according to the degree of unsaturation. They are generally liquid at room temperature. But there are exceptions to this rule. For example, lard contains unsaturated fatty acids, but it is solid. Unsaturated fatty acids are further divided according to the degree of unsaturation. They

Table 2.2 Saturated Fatty Acids

Names	Formula	Occurrence
Acetic	CH_3COOH	Vinegar
Butyric	$CH_3(CH_2)_2COOH$	Butter
Caproic	$CH_3(CH_2)_4COOH$	Butter
Caprylic	$CH_3(CH_2)_6COOH$	Butter
Capric	$CH_3(CH_2)_8COOH$	Coconut oil
Laurie	$CH_3(CH_2)_{10}COOH$	Coconut oil
Myristic	$CH_3(CH_2)_{12}COOH$	Coconut oil
Palmitic	$CH_3(CH_2)_{14}COOH$	Animal and vegetable fats
Stearic	$CH_3(CH_2)_{16}COOH$	Animal and vegetable fats
Arachidic	$CH_3(CH_2)_{18}COOH$	Peanut oil
Lignoceric	$CH_3(CH_2)_{22}COOH$	Arachis oil

have a general formula of $C_nH_{2n-1}COOH$ with a double bond. They are subdivided into fatty acids containing

- One double bond—Oleic acid—$C_{17}H_{33}COOH$
  $CH_3(CH_2)_7CH = CH(CH_2)_7COOH$
- Two double bonds—Linoleic acid—$C_{17}H_{31}COOH$
  $CH_3\ (CH_2)_4CH = CHCH_2CH = CH\ (CH_2)_7COOH$
- Three double bonds—Linolenic acid—$C_{17}H_{29}COOHCH_3CH_2CH = CHCH_2CH = CHCH_2CH = CH(CH_2)_7COOH$
- Four double bonds—Arachidonic acid—$C_{19}H_{31}COOHCH_3(CH_2)_4\ (CH = CHCH_2)_3CH = CH(CH_2)_3COOH$

There are two hydroxy acids which are unsaturated. They are (i) ricinoleic acid and (ii) dihydroxystearic acid. Both are present in castor oil.

Cyclic Acids

These are fatty acids having a cyclic ring structure containing five carbon atoms. They are unsaturated. Two cyclic acids, hydnocarpic acid (**Fig. 2.8**) and chaulmoogric acid (**Fig. 2.9**), are of interest, because of their presence in chaulmoogra oil which is used in the treatment of leprosy.

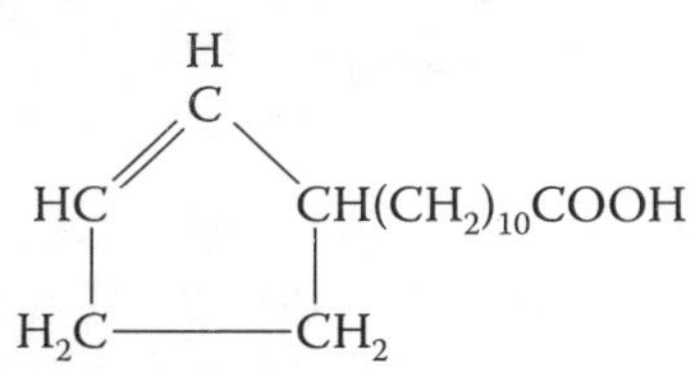

Figure 2.8 Hydnocarpic acid.

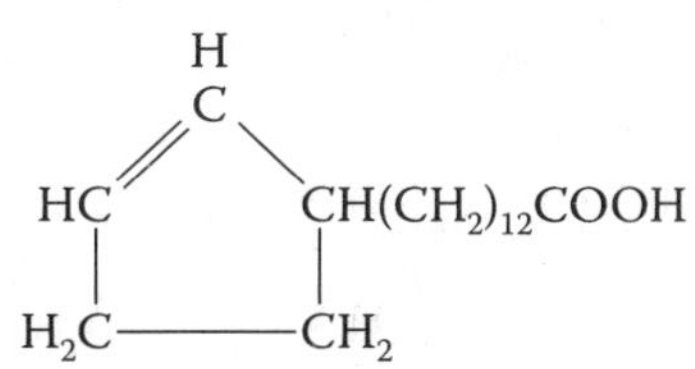

Figure 2.9 Chaulmoogric acid.

Essential Fatty Acids

Certain fatty acids which have specific nutritional importance are called essential fatty acids (EFA). They are long-chain, polyunsaturated fatty acids that cannot be synthesised by the body. They resemble vitamins in that they are required in a small quantity, but are essential constituents of diet.

A few common essential fatty acids are as follows:

- *Linoleic acid*: $CH_3(CH_2)_4CH{=}CHCH_2CH{=}CH(CH_2)_7COOH$
- *Linolenic acid*: $CH_3CH_2CH{=}CHCH_2CH{=}CHCH_2CH{=}CH(CH_2)_7COOH$
- *Arachidonic acid*: $CH_3(CH_2)_4(CH{=}CHCH_2)_3CH{=}{=}CH(CH_2)_3COOH$

Essential fatty acids are nutritionally essential for humans and their deficiency is known to produce eczema-like skin lesions.

Atherosclerosis: Experiments on EFA in the diet of humans have indicated that a diet containing animal fat tends to increase the serum cholesterol whereas a diet containing vegetable fats and EFA in an adequate quantity tend to lower the serum cholesterol. This indicates that unsaturated fatty acids and EFA tend to lower the serum cholesterol. This property of EFA is important in the management of hypercholesterolaemia, which is associated with atherosclerosis or thickening of the arteries.

Other functions of EFA are as follows:

- They are important for the growth of cells.
- They are important for reproductive function.
- They prolong clotting time and increase the fibrinolytic activity.

Diets rich in EFA are as follows:

- Vegetable oils are rich in EFA. Safflower oil contains 75% EFA, corn oil contains 50% EFA, cottonseed oil contains 45% EFA and peanut oil contains 25% EFA.
- Animal fats are poor sources of EFA. Egg contains 9% EFA and lard contains 9% EFA.

Glycerol

Since glycerol is a component of fat, its properties and reactions are described here. Glycerol, commonly called glycerine, is the alcoholic component of triglycerides. It is closely allied to carbohydrates in its chemical structure and properties. But it is closely associated with fats in its occurrence and functions. It is obtained in an enormous quantity as a by-product in the manufacture of soap, by the process of saponification.

Fate of glycerol: Glycerol is utilised in the body as follows:

Glycerol is phosphorylated to form glycerophosphate by the action of ATP and specific phosphokinase.

Glycerophosphate is oxidised to glyceraldehyde-3-phosphate by the enzyme glyceraldehyde-3-phosphate dehydrogenase. Glyceraldehyde-3-phosphate is an intermediate in glycolysis. It may be further oxidised via the Krebs cycle to yield energy.

SUBSTANCES ASSOCIATED WITH LIPIDS

Steroids

Steroids represent a large group of compounds which exist in nature, having a common and characteristic structure based on the cyclopentanoperhydrophenanthrene ring (**Fig. 2.10**).

These compounds vary widely in their occurrence and physiological properties despite their common basic structure.

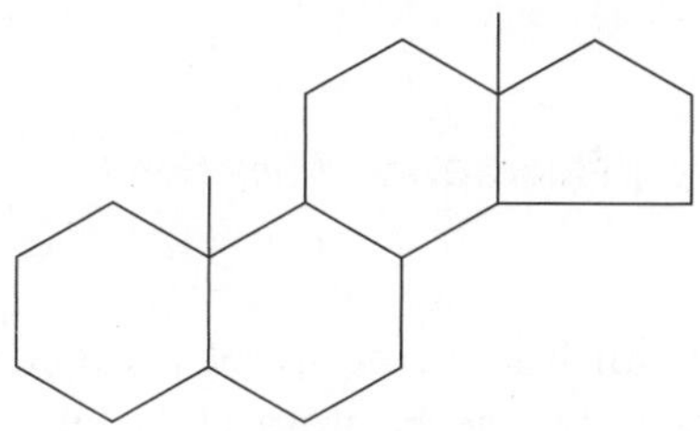

Figure 2.10 Cyclopentanoperhydrophenanthrene ring.

The various substances of physiological interest, having the same steroid structure, are as follows:

1. Sterols
2. Bile acids
3. Steroid hormones
    - Male sex hormones
    - Female sex hormones
    - Adrenocortical hormones
    - Calcitriol

Sterol: Sterol means solid alcohol. They are widely present in animal and plant tissues. They include cholesterol, 7-dehydrocholesterol, coprosterol, ergosterol and calciferol. Among the sterols, cholesterol forms an important physiological compound.

Cholesterol: Cholesterol means solid bile alcohol. It derives its name from the Greek word 'cholesterine' which means 'bile solid' (chole=bile, sterine=solid), as it was first isolated from human gall stones (**Fig. 2.11**).

Source: Cholesterol is widely distributed in all cells of the body. It occurs in large quantities in brain and nerve tissues. It is found in adrenal glands, glandular tissues, plasma and egg yolk. It may be noted that cholesterol occurs in animal fats and not in plant fats.

The concentration of cholesterol in human plasma is 150–220 mg/100 ml of blood.

Structure: Cholesterol is composed of the characteristic cyclopentanoperhydrophenanthrene ring system.

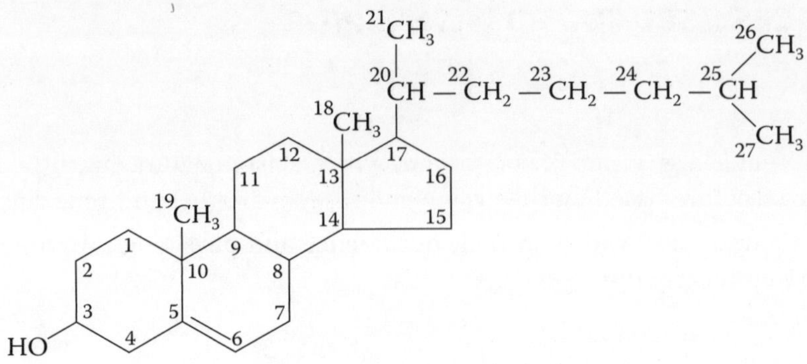

Figure 2.11 Cholesterol.

7-Dehydrocholesterol: This is an important sterol present in the skin. It has one more double bond at C_7–C_8. It has only one H atom at C_7 and none at C_8 (**Fig. 2.12**). It is converted to vitamin D when irradiated with ultraviolet light.

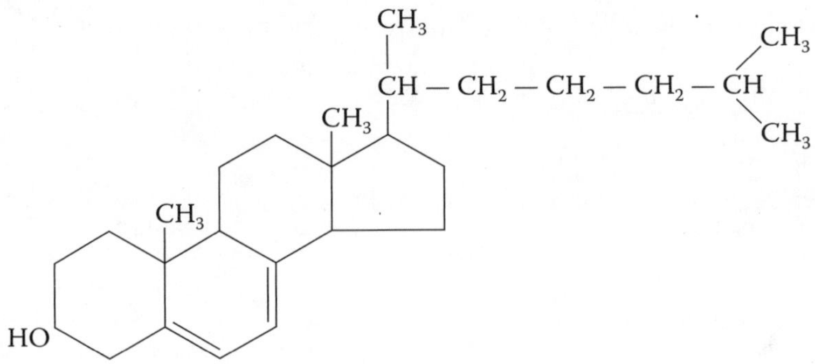

Figure 2.12 7-Dehydrocholesterol.

Ergosterol: It is present in ergot and yeast. It is an important compound, because it is the precursor of vitamin D to which it can be converted by irradiation with ultraviolet light. Its structure is similar to that of 7-dehydrocholesterol but differs in the following aspects (**Fig. 2.13**):

1. It has a double bond in the side chain.
2. It has an additional CH_3 group in the side chain.

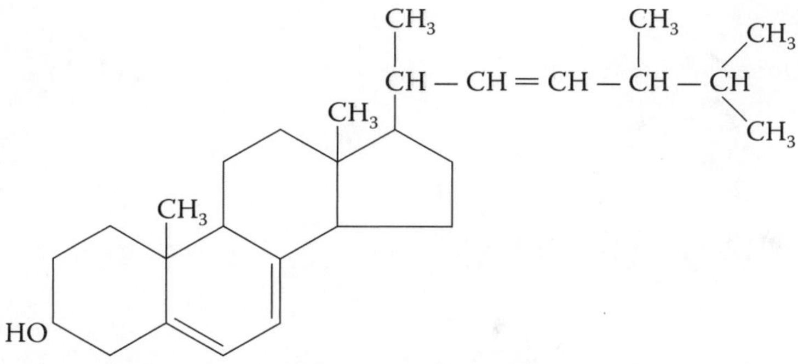

Figure 2.13 Ergosterol.

Coprosterol: Coprosterol is present in faeces. It is the reduced form of cholesterol, formed as a result of reduction by intestinal bacteria. It does not have the double bond between C_5 and C_6.

Bile acids: Bile acids are synthesised from cholesterol. They are important factors in the digestion and absorption of lipids in the intestines. Bile acids contain additional hydroxyl groups (1–3) attached to the steroid nucleus. The side chain has a carboxyl group. Bile acids are conjugated to an amino acid glycine or to a compound called **taurine**, through their carboxyl groups, to form glycocholic acid and taurocholic acid respectively. Four bile acids have been isolated from human bile. These are as follows:

1. Cholic acid (**Fig. 2.14**)
2. Chenodeoxycholic acid
3. Deoxycholic acid (**Fig. 2.14**)
4. Lithocholic acid

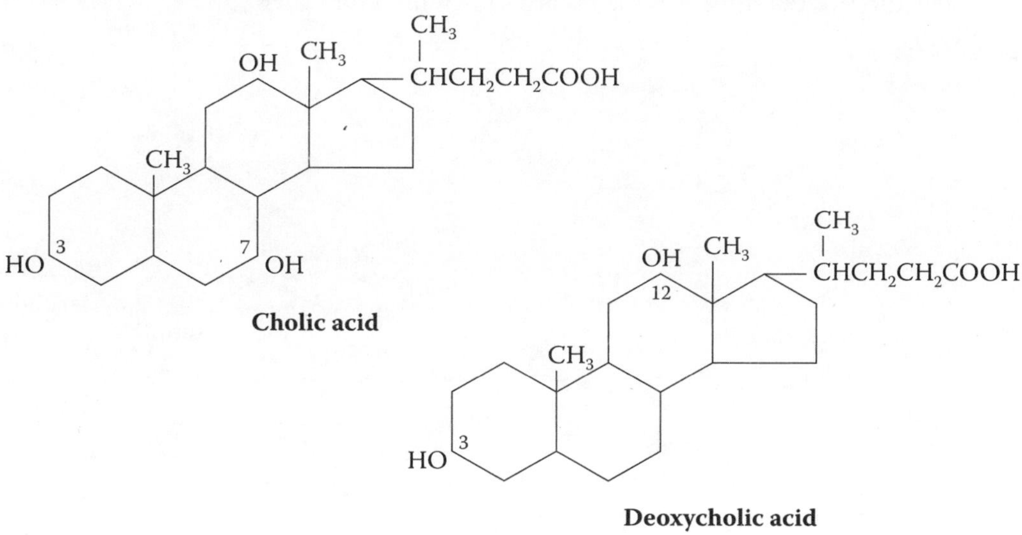

Figure 2.14 Cholic acid and deoxycholic acid.

Sex hormones

Male sex hormones or androgens: These include

- Testosterone (**Fig. 2.15**)
- Androsterone (**Fig. 2.15**)

These do not have the side chain in position 17. They possess either a keto or a hydroxyl group in positions 3 and 17 (**Fig. 2.15**).

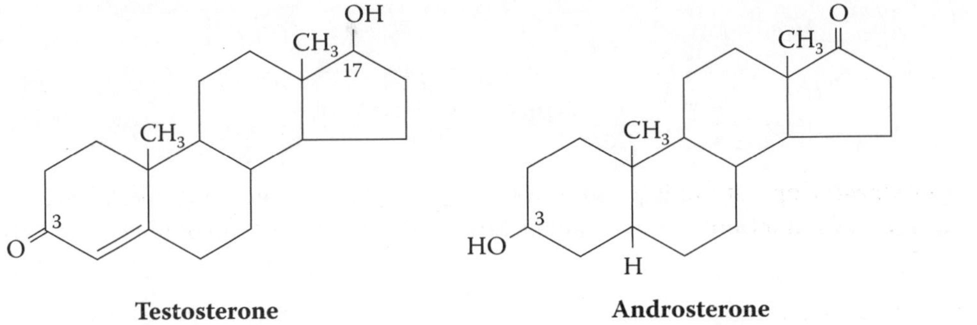

Figure 2.15 Male sex hormones.

Female sex hormones: These include two groups of hormones:

- Oestrogens produced from ovary
- Progesterone produced from corpus luteum

Oestrogens include (i) oestrone, (ii) oestradiol and (iii) oestriol.

The structures of the three oestrogens are shown in **Figure 2.16**.

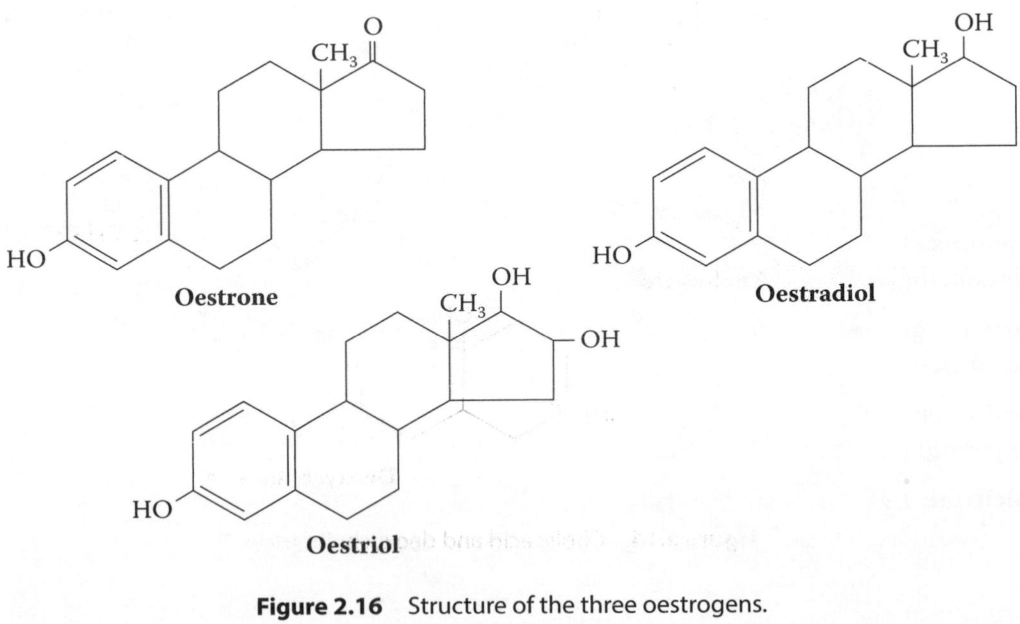

Figure 2.16 Structure of the three oestrogens.

Note that they do not have the side chain in position 17. All three possess a hydroxyl group in position 3. *Oestrone* has a ketone group in position 17. *Oestradiol* has a hydroxyl group in position 17. *Oestriol* has hydroxyl groups in positions 16 and 17.

Progesterone is the hormone of the corpus luteum. It does not have the side chain. It has ketone groups at C_3 and C_{17} (**Fig. 2.17**).

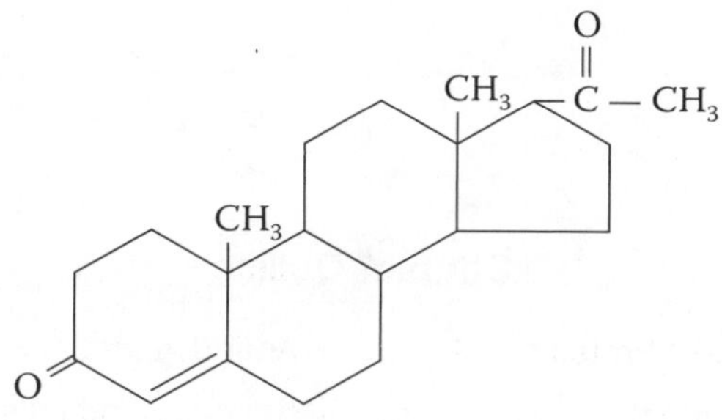

Figure 2.17 Progesterone.

Adrenocortical hormones: Corticosterone contains a ketone group in positions C_3 and C_{17} and has an OH group at C_{11} (**Fig. 2.18**).

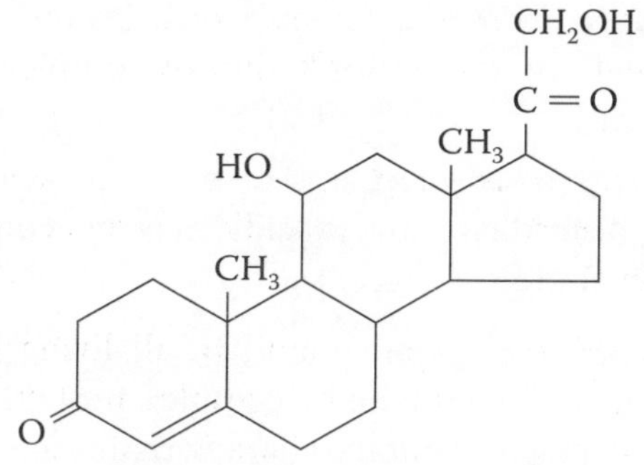

Figure 2.18 Corticosterone.

Saponins: They are haemolytic poisons widely distributed in plants. They are steroids. In solution, they are effective surface active agents.

Cardiac glucosides: They are present in digitalis and squill. They have the cyclopentanoperhydrophenanthrene ring structure.

Toad poisons: They have the structure of steroids. They are cardiac toxins secreted by the parotid glands of toads.

Calcitriol: This is a metabolically active form of vitamin D and is derived from cholesterol.

CHAPTER 3

Proteins

Chapter Outline

- General Properties of Proteins
- Classification of Proteins
- Types of Proteins
- Characteristic Reactions of Proteins
- Amino Acids
- Special Reactions of Protein
- Protein Structure
- Structural Organisation of Proteins

The term 'protein' is derived from the Greek word 'Protos' which means 'OF FIRST IMPORTANCE'. It represents an enormous group of complex nitrogenous compounds, having high molecular weight.

Protein molecules are composed of chains of α-amino acids, united to one another by peptide linkages. The individual amino acids may be considered analogous to the monosaccharides of carbohydrate.

Occurrence and functions: Proteins are found in all living cells. They form essential constituents of protoplasm, cell membrane or complex protein combined with lipids and nucleic acids. Genes which carry hereditary characteristics are nucleoproteins. Wherever they occur, they play a vital role in the biological functions and serve as building blocks for cellular and organic structures. Proteins form components of catalysts called enzymes which are essential for the metabolic reactions.

Proteins are also constituents of most of the hormones which are regulators of the metabolism of important physiological compounds. They form about 15% of the total body weight of an average adult. The proteins in different tissues such as connective tissue, bones, muscles, brain, blood and other biological fluids differ in composition and properties. The protein content of plants is relatively less than that of an animal. In the plants, seeds and cereals contain the highest protein content while the leaves, stem and tubers contain much less protein. All proteins contain carbon, hydrogen, oxygen and nitrogen. Some contain sulphur and some phosphorus. An approximate composition of these elements would be carbon—51%, hydrogen—7%, oxygen—20%, nitrogen—16%, sulphur—1% and phosphorus—2%. It is assumed that all proteins contain about 16% nitrogen.

The physiological significance and functions of proteins are varied but vital. They regulate and integrate the numerous physiological and metabolic processes in the body through hormones, enzymes and nucleoproteins. The plasma proteins help in the maintenance of acid–base balance and osmotic pressure of the body fluids.

GENERAL PROPERTIES OF PROTEINS

1. Proteins are complex substances of high molecular weight, consisting largely of chains of α-amino acids, united in peptide linkage. The constituent amino acids may be obtained by hydrolysis of the proteins.
2. They contain C, H, O, N and sometimes P and S. Elements such as Fe, Cu, I and Zn are occasionally present.
3. The molecular weight of the proteins varies from 6,000 to many millions. Because of the high molecular weight, most proteins are not diffusible through membranes.
4. Proteins are generally soluble in water, weak salt solution, dilute acids and alkalies. Owing to their large size, they form colloidal solution and exhibit the properties associated with the colloidal state of the matter; the number of the molecules occupying a given volume of the solution is lesser. Consequently, properties such as osmotic pressure, surface tension, viscosity, lowering of the freezing point and rising of the boiling point become less.
5. Proteins possess free ionic or electrically charged groups so that they can migrate in an electrical field. Owing to their charges, they combine with ionic reagents giving rise to insoluble compounds.
6. Proteins are precipitated by salts of heavy metals such as silver, mercury and lead in an alkaline medium. Here, the metals combine with the carboxyl groups to form metal proteinate. One important application of this property is the use of proteins as an antidote in metallic poisoning. Egg white and milk are commonly used, when the metal is precipitated along with the proteins of egg and milk.
7. Proteins are precipitated by certain alkaloidal reagents. These are picric acid, trichloracetic acid, phosphotungstic acid, phosphomolybdic acid and sulphosalicylic acid. Here, the proteins react with the NH_2 groups.
8. Proteins are amphoteric substances because they contain both NH_2 and COOH groups. They can react with acids and bases.
9. Some proteins in solution coagulate on heating. They are called heat-coagulable proteins; examples are albumin and globulin.
10. *Colour reaction:* All proteins give colour reaction, when treated with certain reagents. Certain reactive chemical groups situated in the amino acids and the peptide linkages possessed by all proteins are responsible for the production of the colours.
11. Proteins are hydrolysed to their constituent amino acids by boiling with acids and alkali and by the action of appropriate proteolytic enzymes.

CLASSIFICATION OF PROTEINS

Proteins are most conveniently classified on the basis of their physical properties such as solubility and composition. Accordingly, they are classified into three main groups:

I. Simple proteins
II. Conjugated proteins
III. Derived proteins

Each of these main groups is subdivided into a number of subgroups:

I. **Simple proteins**
   1. Albumin
   2. Globulin
   3. Glutelin
   4. Prolamines or gliadins
   5. Scleroprotein or albuminoids
   6. Histones
   7. Protamines

II. **Conjugated proteins**
   1. Nucleoproteins
   2. Phosphoprotein
   3. Mucoprotein and glycoprotein
   4. Chromoprotein
   5. Lipoprotein
   6. Metalloprotein

III. **Derived proteins**
   1. *Primary derivatives*: Denatured protein (metaprotein)
   2. *Secondary derivatives*
      - Proteoses
      - Peptones
      - Peptides
      - Diketopiperazines

TYPES OF PROTEINS

Simple Proteins

These proteins yield only α-amino acids on hydrolysis. The subgroups of simple proteins are described below.

1. **Albumin and globulin:** These are typical examples of simple protein. They contain most of the amino acids. Their characteristic property is coagulation on heating. They differ from one another in their solubility. Albumin is soluble in water whereas globulin is insoluble in water. Another difference is that albumins are precipitated from solution by full saturation with ammonium sulphate, whereas globulins are precipitated by half-saturation with ammonium sulphate.

   Source: Animal sources for albumin are egg albumin, myoalbumin of muscles, serum albumin and lactalbumin of milk. Animal sources for globulin are the same as for albumin, namely globulin of egg, myoglobulin of muscles, serum globulin and lactoglobulin of milk. Plant sources for both albumin and globulin are the same. They are present in the legumen of the peas and beans and in cereals.

2. **Glutelin and gliadin (prolamines):** Both glutelin and gliadin are present in cereals, especially wheat. They form the proteins of wheat. The dough made out of wheat flour contains starch, glutelin and gliadin. It is the gliadin in the wheat flour that forms the sticky mass and binds together the particles of glutelin, starch, etc., to give the dough.

   Both glutelin and gliadin contain large amounts of glutamic acid. Glutelins are insoluble in water and absolute alcohol but soluble in dilute alkalies and acids.

   Gliadin contains a high concentration of amino acid proline and therefore it is also known as prolamine. It contains a large amount of amide nitrogen and is found also in zein of corn. Gliadins are insoluble in water and absolute alcohol but soluble in dilute alcohols (70–80%), dilute acids and alkalies.
3. **Scleroproteins or albuminoids:** These are characterised by great stability and insolubility in water and salt solutions. They are called albuminoids because they are essentially similar to albumin and globulins.

   They form most of the supporting structures of animals, for example collagen in cartilage and white fibrous connective tissues, ossein in bones and dentine in teeth and keratin in hair, nails, hoofs and horns. Keratins have a high sulphur content, mainly in the form of amino acid cystine. Keratins are readily soluble in alkaline sulphides and such solutions are used in the manufacture of hair-removing preparations. Partial hydrolysis of collagen by steam gives a soluble product called **gelatin**.
4. **Histones:** Histones are more complex than protamines. They are basic proteins and contain a fairly large amount of amino acid histidine. They are soluble in water and are not readily coagulated by heat. They occur in the globin of haemoglobin, nucleoproteins and in spermatozoa of fish.
5. **Protamines:** These are simplest of the proteins and contain about eight amino acids. They are soluble in water and are not coagulated by heat. They are basic in nature and this is due to the preponderance of amino acid arginine. Protamines are found in association with nucleic acid in the sperm cells of certain fish.

Conjugated Proteins

Conjugated proteins are composed of simple proteins combined with some non-protein substances known as prosthetic groups. They are classified according to the nature of the non-protein groups or the prosthetic groups to which the proteins are attached:

1. **Nucleoproteins:** These are compounds of protein with nucleic acid. The protein moiety is usually a simple protein like protamines and histones. Nucleoproteins are important compounds found in the protoplasm and nuclei. They are also constituents of chromatin.
2. **Phosphoprotein:** These are proteins containing phosphoric acid, in organic combination, i.e. phosphoric acid is linked to the hydroxyl group of certain amino acids such as serine in the protein. Examples of phosphoproteins are as follows:
   - Casein of milk
   - Vitellin of egg

Phosphoproteins contain about 1% of phosphorus. They are sparingly soluble in water and dilute acids, but readily soluble even in dilute alkalies.

3. **Glycoproteins and mucoproteins:** These proteins are composed of simple proteins and are combined with carbohydrates such as mucopolysaccharides which include hyaluronic acid and chondroitin sulphates. On hydrolysis, mucopolysaccharides yield amino sugars, hexosamine and uronic acid. The distinction between glycoproteins and mucoproteins is based on the amount of carbohydrate. Mucoproteins contain more than 4% hexosamine. Glycoproteins contain less than 4% hexosamine. They are important constituents of the ground substance of the connective tissues and are present in tendons, bones, cartilage, synovial fluid and mucous membrane. They are found in mucin, mucoids and certain proteins in the plasma, which migrate electrophoretically with α_1 and α_2 globulins. They are also found in gonadotropic hormone.
4. **Chromoproteins:** These proteins contain certain heterocyclic compounds such as porphyrins as the prosthetic group. The porphyrins combine with metals giving rise to coloured proteins or chromoproteins. Examples of chromoproteins are haemoglobin, melanoprotein, flavoprotein, cytochrome and chlorophyll.
5. **Lipoproteins:** These are proteins conjugated with lipids such as neutral fat, phospholipids and cholesterol.
6. **Metalloproteins:** These proteins contain metals as their prosthetic group, for example ferritin contains iron, ceruloplasmin contains copper and carbonic anhydrase, an enzyme protein, contains zinc.

Derived Proteins

These are proteins derived from the simple proteins or conjugated proteins by the action of acids, alkalies or enzymes. They are products resulting from partial to complete hydrolysis of the proteins. They include two types of derivatives:

1. **Primary derivatives** like metaproteins, which are denaturation products of proteins resulting from the action of heat, acids and alkalies on proteins. They are heat coagulable.
2. **Secondary derivatives** are obtained at a later stage of hydrolysis. Examples are as follows:
   - *Proteoses:* These are not coagulated by heat but precipitated by saturated salt solutions. Proteoses are further subdivided into *primary proteoses* which are precipitated by half saturation with ammonium sulphate and *secondary proteoses* which are precipitated by full saturation with ammonium sulphate.
   - *Peptones:* These are products of further hydrolytic decomposition. They are soluble in saturated salt solutions and are therefore not precipitated even by full saturation with ammonium sulphate. They are not coagulated by heat.
   - *Peptides:* These are products derived at a still later stage of hydrolysis. They are made up of two or more amino acids and are not coagulable by heat. They are

soluble in saturated salt solution and are not precipitated by saturated ammonium sulphate solution.

CHARACTERISTIC REACTIONS OF PROTEINS

Certain terms which refer to reactions characteristic of proteins require mention and clarification. These are as follows:

1. Hydrolysis
2. Denaturation
3. Precipitation
4. Coagulation

Hydrolysis

Proteins are complex molecules composed of a number of amino acid units, joined to one another by peptide linkages. Hydrolysis of protein involves breaking of the complex protein molecule at the peptide linkages. The mechanism of hydrolysis involves addition of a molecule of water across the peptide bond, resulting in the formation of an amino and a carboxyl group for each peptide bond split, as illustrated in **Figure 3.1**. The figure represents a polypeptide chain formed by three amino acids R_1CHNH_2COOH, R_2CHNH_2COOH and R_3CHNH_2COOH. The proteolytic enzyme has split the polypeptide chain into its constituent amino acids.

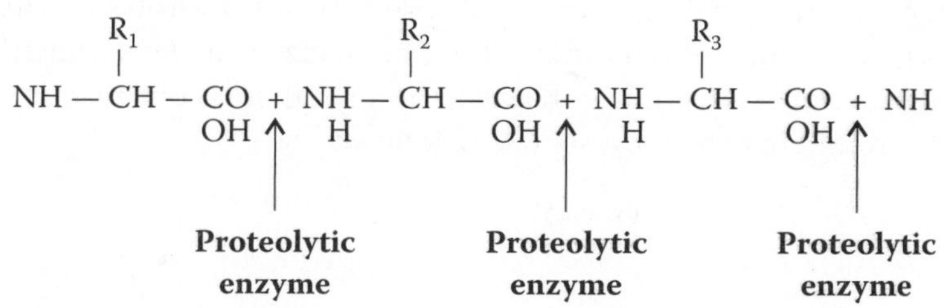

Figure 3.1 Hydrolysis of a polypeptide by the proteolytic enzyme.

Thus, the ultimate end products of hydrolysis of protein are amino acids. Hydrolysis proceeds completely only under adequate physiological conditions and biosynthesis of peptide bonds does not occur by simple reversal of the hydrolytic reaction. There are several ways by which hydrolysis is accomplished in vivo and in vitro. In the body, hydrolysis is effected by proteolytic enzymes. Hydrolysis by enzymes in the body is rapid and complete. Hydrolysis may also be brought about by the following methods:

1. Boiling the proteins in the presence of acids or alkalies
2. Action of the proteolytic enzymes
3. Action of superheated steam

The sequence of events and the various products obtained during hydrolysis are illustrated in **Figure 3.2**.

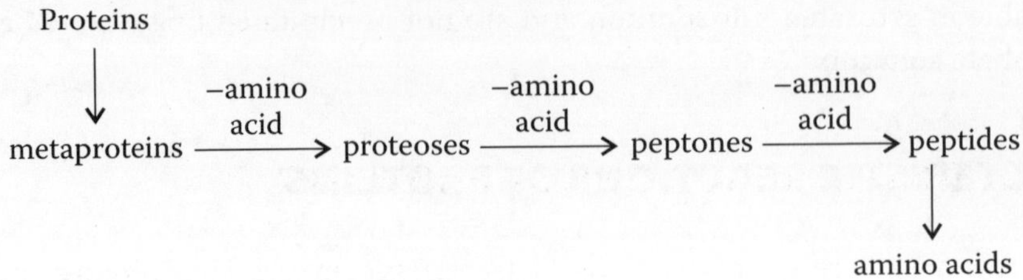

Figure 3.2 Sequence of events during hydrolysis of proteins.

Proteins are first changed to metaproteins, which split liberating amino acids and form proteoses. The latter are formed by the rupture of the protein molecule into several large complexes. Proteoses retain many of the properties of the original protein, but are more soluble. They have peptide linkages and therefore give biuret reaction. They can be precipitated by strong salt solution (ammonium sulphate), because they are relatively large molecules.

Proteoses may be further subdivided into primary proteoses and secondary proteoses depending upon the size of the molecules. The next product of hydrolysis is peptones, which are formed by further loss of amino acids. They have lesser molecular weight and therefore differ from the proteoses in not being precipitated by saturated salt solution. However, they answer biuret reaction, but give a pink colour instead of the usual violet colour. Even the other colour reactions of proteins are obtained with some difficulty. Polypeptides and amino acids are the next products of hydrolysis. They are simpler compounds formed by further liberation of amino acids. They have much less molecular weight, and they do not answer biuret reaction or any other colour reaction. The products of hydrolysis of protein may be represented as follows:

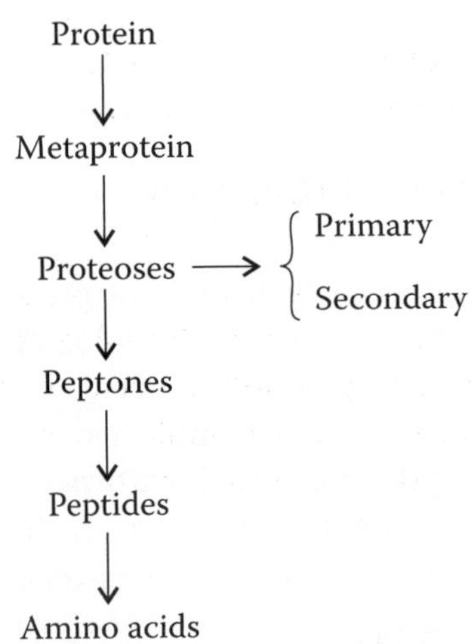

Denaturation

Denaturation means disorganisation of the native (naturally occurring) protein molecule, by which the specific configuration or regular arrangement of the protein molecule is altered to an irregular diffuse arrangement; this leads to changes in the physical and chemical properties of the affected protein.

Denaturation may involve a mere unfolding of the peptide chain (**Fig. 3.3**) or splitting of the protein into smaller units.

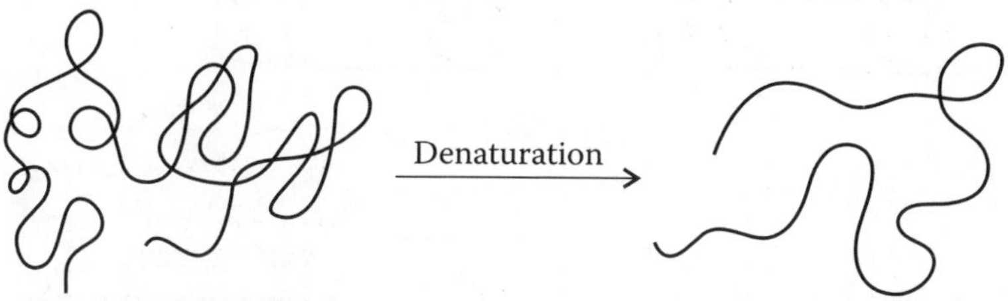

Figure 3.3 Unfolding of the peptide chain.

The agents which bring about denaturation may be discussed under two headings:

1. Physical agents
2. Chemical agents

Physical agents are heat, ultraviolet light, X-rays, high pressure and violent shaking of the protein solution.

Chemical agents are acids, alkalies, enzymes, organic solvents, strong urea solution and high concentration of salt or heavy metals.

The following changes take place in denaturation:

1. **Physical changes:**
   - Solubility decreases.
   - Surface tension is altered.
   - Viscosity increases; therefore, the rate of diffusion decreases.
   - Denaturated protein cannot be crystallised, since crystallisation depends upon a high degree of organisation of the molecule.
2. **Chemical changes:** The structure of the peptide chains of some proteins is held in a coiled form by three types of cross-linkages, namely hydrogen bonds, disulphide and salt linkages. Denaturation causes splitting of one or more of these linkages resulting in unfolding and uncoiling of peptide chains which in turn produce certain chemical changes. As a result of the unfolding process, chemical groups which are essential for the activity of the protein molecules lose their activity. Examples of such chemical groups are as follows:
   - The sulphydryl (SH) group of cysteine
   - The disulphide groups of cystine and insulin
   - The phenolic group of tyrosine
3. **Biological changes:** The denatured proteins are digested more easily and quickly by proteolytic enzymes. The hormonal and enzymatic activities of hormones and enzymes are destroyed when denatured. The antibody function of denatured proteins is altered.

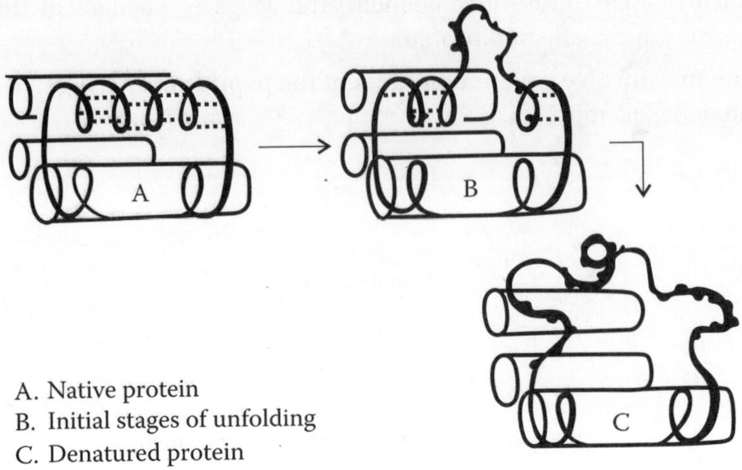

A. Native protein
B. Initial stages of unfolding
C. Denatured protein

Figure 3.4 Stages in denaturation.

Denaturation is the preliminary stage for precipitation and coagulation and may be compared to the formation of meta-protein (**Fig. 3.4**). Denaturation is generally a reversible change, but in some proteins it may bring about an irreversible change. For example, ovalbumin undergoes an irreversible change when denatured by urea, because the two cystine bridges which hold the structure of this protein molecule are broken and it is difficult to restore the structure on account of few linkages, whereas serum albumin undergoes a reversible change when denatured by urea, because there are 18 cystine bridges in the serum albumin molecule, holding the structure of the molecule.

Precipitation

Precipitation is brought about by neutralising the charges of the metaprotein and bringing it to the isoelectric point. This may be brought about by the action of heat, acid, alkali or enzymes. This is also called **flocculation**. In other words, precipitation is clumping together of the denatured metaprotein by neutralisation of the charges. Precipitation is a reversible change, because alteration of the pH to values above or below the isoelectric point, by adding acid or alkali, will result in dissolving the precipitate.

Coagulation

Applying heat to the precipitate of metaprotein is coagulation. Therefore, coagulation requires two preliminary steps.

1. Formation of metaprotein which may be brought about by denaturation
2. Precipitation of metaprotein, brought about by bringing the reaction to the isoelectric point by the addition of acid or alkali or neutral salt solution

When heat is applied to the precipitate of metaprotein, the precipitate is matted together to form an insoluble mass which cannot be brought to solution by altering the pH. Therefore, coagulation is an irreversible reaction.

AMINO ACIDS

Amino acids are the simplest units of a protein molecule and they form the building blocks of protein structure. The general formula of an amino acid can be written as

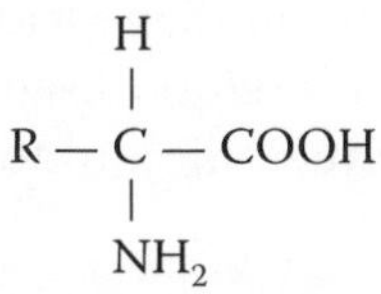

Amino acid structure

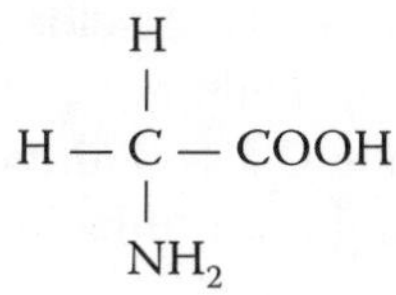

Glycine—an α-amino acid

An amino acid consists of a free NH_2 (amino) and a free COOH (carboxyl) group. Both are attached to the same carbon atom. In the structure of the amino acid shown above, 'R' represents the groups other than the NH_2 and COOH groups. This may be aliphatic or heterocyclic group. In glycine which is the simplest of the amino acids, 'R' represents 'H' atom.

All amino acids are α-amino acids because the NH_2 group is attached to the α-carbon atom which is next to the COOH group. Examination of the structure of an amino acid except glycine reveals that the α-carbon atom has four different groups attached to it, thus making it asymmetric. Because of the presence of asymmetric carbon atoms, amino acids exist in optically active forms. Therefore, it is possible to have a dextrorotatory and levorotatory form in such amino acids. The distinction between dextrorotation and levorotation in amino acids is represented by symbols + (for dextro) and – (for levo). In view of the presence of asymmetric carbon atoms, the configuration of an amino acid may be represented to belong to 'D' or 'L' series. For this purpose, the stearic formula of the amino acid serine, which is α-amino-β-hydroxypropionic acid, is taken as the reference compound. It may be remembered that the reference compound for carbohydrates is glyceraldehyde.

In the stearic configuration for serine (**Fig. 3.5**), the COOH is written on the top, while the amino group is written to the left in the case of L-serine and to the right in the case of D-serine.

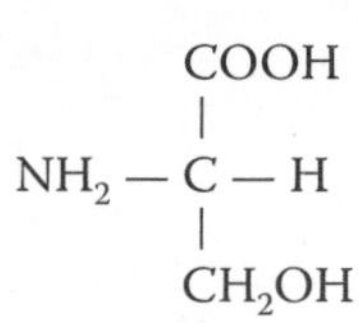

L-serine

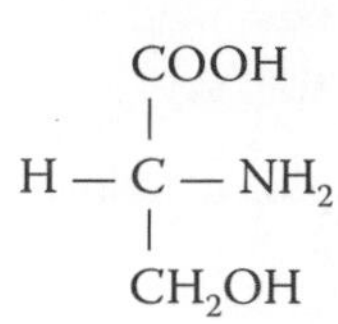

D-serine

Figure 3.5 Stearic configuration of serine.

This distinction will hold good for all amino acids having asymmetric carbon atoms. It may be noted that 'D' and 'L' do not refer to optical rotation but to the stearic configuration of the NH_2 group to the right and left sides of the COOH group, as referred in the stearic formula of serine (*see* **Fig. 3.5**). The direction of optical rotation of an amino acid is indicated by the symbol + or – which follows the designation 'D' or 'L'. The steric configuration and optical rotation of an amino acid may be simultaneously expressed as D(+) or D(–) and L(+) or L(–).

It has been found that L-amino acids are more common than D-forms and most of the naturally occurring amino acids are L-amino acids. Therefore, L-amino acids are called natural amino acids. Since the L-amino acids are more common, the letter 'L' is usually omitted while representing L-amino acids.

Amino acids are widely distributed in plants and animals. Several amino acids have been isolated, many differing from the others in their structures and properties. The amino acids are best studied after grouping them under a classification.

Classification of Amino Acids

Amino acids are classified in different ways. Among these, the classification referring to the numbers of carboxyl groups present in the amino acids and the nature of structure (whether aliphatic, aromatic and heterocyclic) appears simple and convenient. Accordingly, the various amino acids may be classified into six main groups. Another group of amino acids, which are formed as intermediaries during metabolic reactions, forms the seventh group.

1. Monoamino monocarboxylic acids
2. Monoamino dicarboxylic acids
3. Diamino monocarboxylic acids
4. Sulphur-containing amino acids
5. Aromatic amino acids
6. Heterocyclic amino acids
7. Amino acids formed as metabolic intermediaries

Monoamino monocarboxylic acids: These amino acids have one amino group and one carboxylic group in the structure. They are neutral amino acids. Examples are

- Glycine (α-Aminoacetic acid)

$$CH_2NH_2COOH$$

- Alanine (α-Aminopropionic acid)

$$\begin{array}{c} \quad NH_2 \\ \quad | \\ CH_3 - CH - COOH \end{array}$$

- Serine (α-Amino-β-hydroxypropionic acid)

$$\begin{array}{c} \quad\quad NH_2 \\ \quad\quad | \\ CH_2OH\ CH - COOH \end{array}$$

- Threonine (α-Amino-β-hydroxy-*n*-butyric acid)

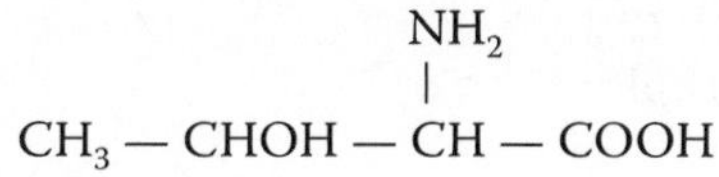

- Valine (α-Amino-isovaleric acid)

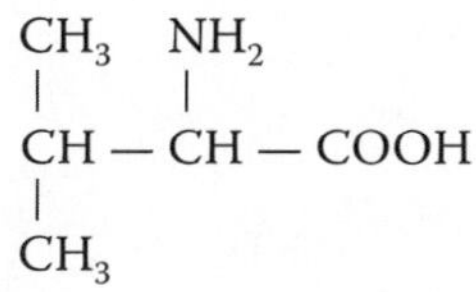

- Leucine (α-Amino-isocaproic acid)

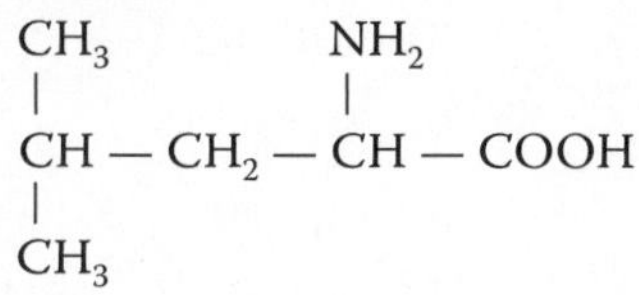

- Isoleucine (α-Amino-β-methyl-*n*-valeric acid)

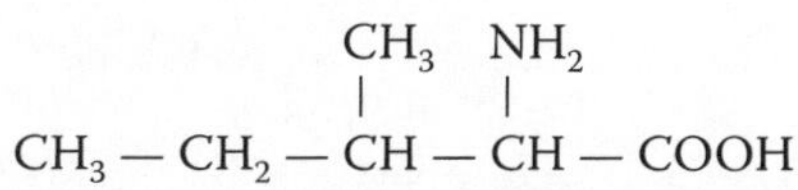

Monoamino dicarboxylic acids: These amino acids contain one amino group and two carboxyl groups. They are acidic amino acids. Examples are

- Aspartic acid (α-Amino-succinic acid)

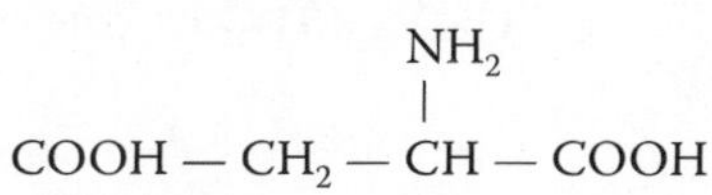

- Glutamic acid (α-Amino-glutaric acid)

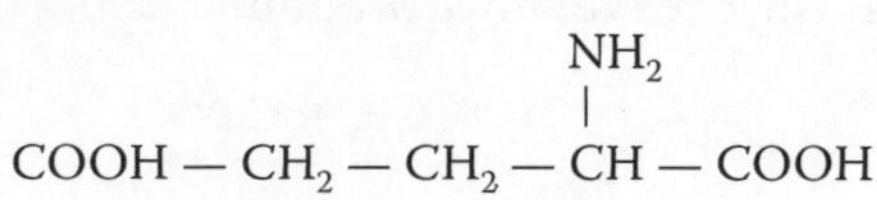

Diamino monocarboxylic acids: These amino acids are α-amino acids containing two amino groups and one carboxyl group. They are also called basic amino acids.

- Arginine (α-Amino-δ-guanidino-*n*-valeric acid)

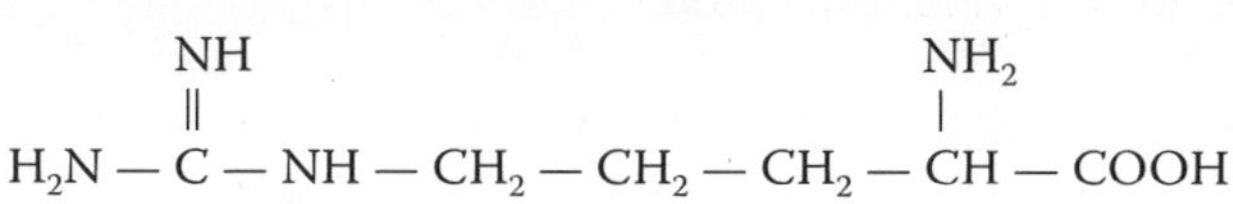

- Lysine (α-ε-Diamino-*n*-caproic acid)

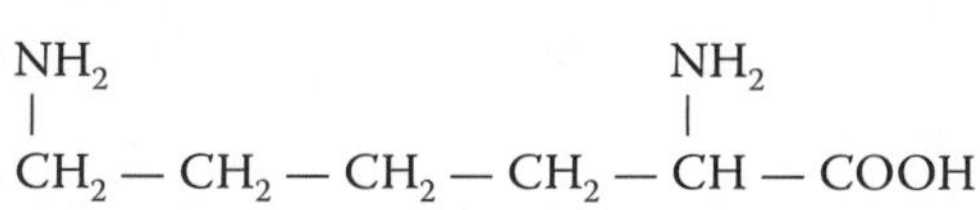

Sulphur-containing amino acids: These amino acids are α-amino acids containing an aliphatic side chain with sulphur atoms.

- Cysteine (α-Amino-β-thiopropionic acid)

$$HS-CH_2-\underset{\displaystyle |}{\overset{\displaystyle NH_2}{\overset{|}{C}}}H-COOH$$

- Cystine (Dicysteine)

$$\begin{array}{l} \quad\;\; NH_2 \\ \quad\;\;\; | \\ SCH_2CHCOOH \\ | \\ SCH_2CHCOOH \\ \quad\;\;\; | \\ \quad\;\; NH_2 \end{array}$$

Cystine consists of two cysteine residues linked by a disulphide linkage.

- Methionine (α-Amino-γ-methylthio-*n*-butyric acid)

$$CH_3-S-CH_2-CH_2-\overset{\displaystyle NH_2}{\overset{|}{C}}H-COOH$$

Aromatic amino acids: They contain aromatic rings. Examples are as follows:

- Phenylalanine (α-Amino-β-phenylpropionic acid)

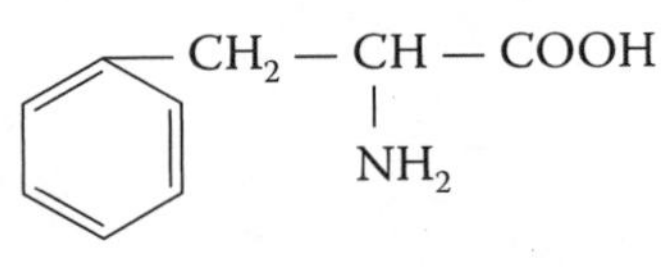

- Tyrosine (α-Amino-β-para-hydroxyphenyl-propionic acid)

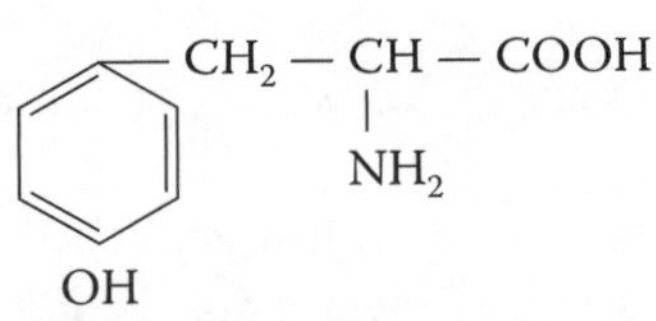

- Tryptophan (α-Amino-β-indole-propionic acid).

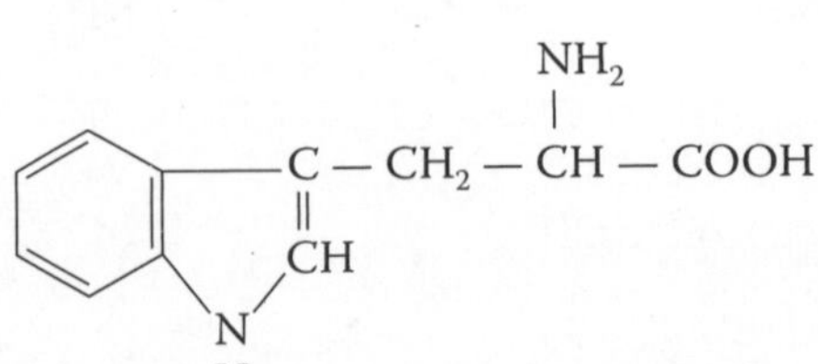

Heterocyclic amino acids: These amino acids contain either an imidazole or an indole ring. Examples are as follows:

- Proline (Pyrrolidine-2-carboxylic acid)

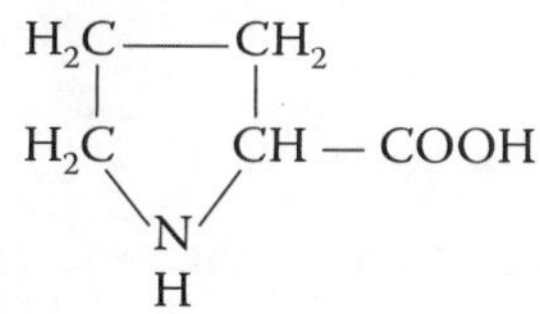

- Hydroxyproline (4-Hydroxyproline)

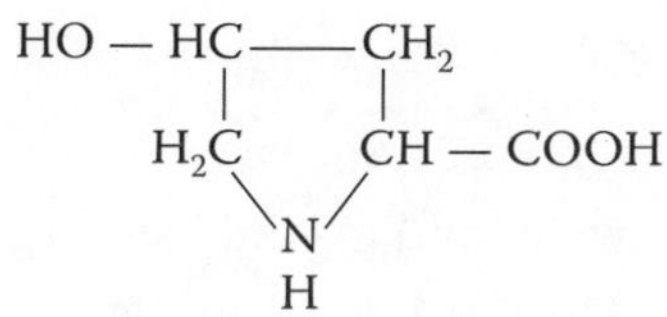

Proline and hydroxyproline are called imino acids.

- Histidine (α-Amino-β-imidazole propionic acid)

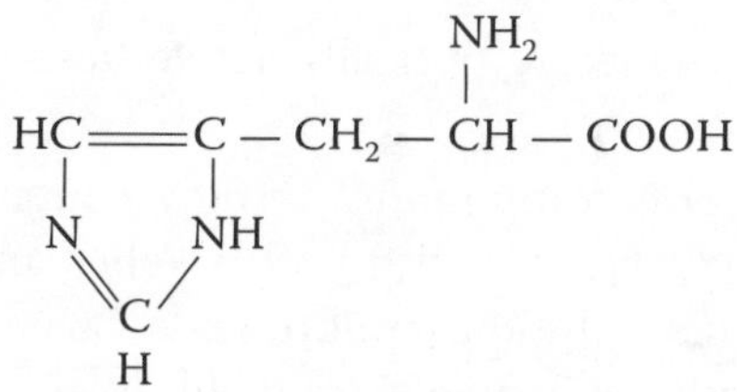

Amino acids formed as metabolic intermediaries: The following amino acids are formed during metabolic reactions. They are physiologically important.

- Di-iodotyrosine

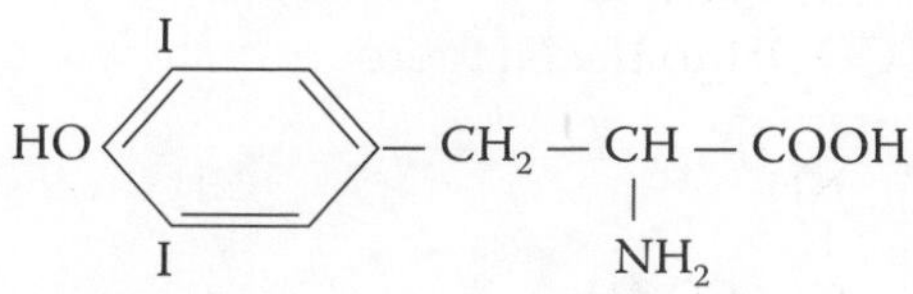

- Thyroxine

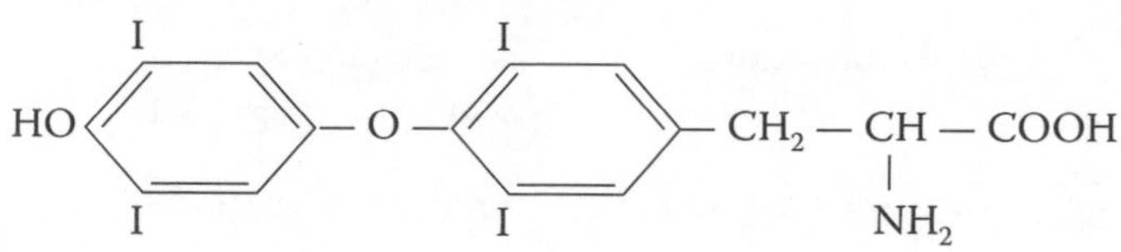

These two amino acids are derivatives of tyrosine and contain iodine atoms. Thyroxine is the active hormone of thyroid.

- Ornithine

Ornithine is an intermediary, derived in the process of synthesis of urea in the body.

- Citrulline

$$\underset{\displaystyle O=C-NH-CH_2CH_2CH_2-CH-COOH}{\overset{NH_2 \qquad\qquad\qquad\qquad\qquad NH_2}{|\qquad\qquad\qquad\qquad\qquad\quad |}}$$

Citrulline is derived from ornithine in the process of formation of urea in the body.

Properties of Amino Acids

Physical properties:

1. Amino acids are white crystalline substances.
2. They are generally soluble in water and insoluble in organic solvents.
3. They have characteristically high melting points, varying from 200°C to 300°C, or even more.
4. Amino acids may be tasteless, sweet or bitter. Sodium glutamate is a valuable flavouring agent and is used in the preparation of certain dishes and sauces.
5. All amino acids except glycine are optically active because they contain asymmetric carbon atoms.
6. Amino acids are amphoteric compounds, as they contain both acidic (COOH) and basic (NH_2) groups. They can react with both alkalies and acids to form salts. It has been found that in an acid solution, amino acids carry positive charges and hence they move towards the cathode in an electric field. In an alkaline solution on the other hand, the amino acids carry negative charges and therefore move towards the anode. But at a certain reaction around neutrality, they are found electrically neutral. This is because the amino acids at this reaction exist as inner salts, carrying an equal number of positive and negative charges. This occurs as a result of dissociation of the H^+ ion, which passes from the COOH to the NH_2 group as shown in **Figure 3.6**.

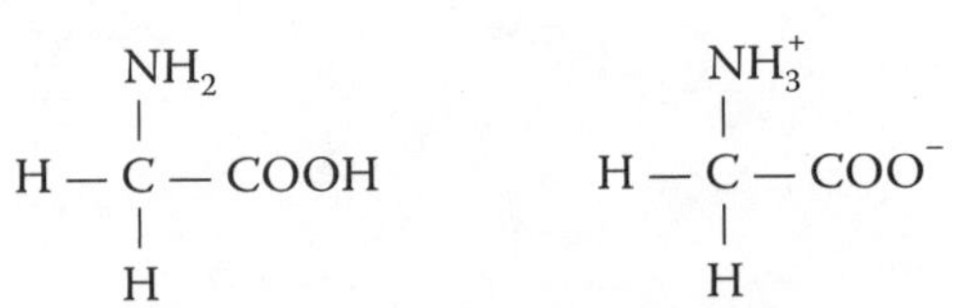

Glycine at pH 7 | **Glycine as a zwitterion at pH 6.1**

Figure 3.6 Amphoteric property of glycine.

The amino acid is said to exist as a zwitterion under such conditions. This theory is called **zwitterion theory**. According to this theory, amino acids possessing double charges (positive and negative) are called zwitterions. They exist as doubly charged molecules and hence are electrically neutral. When an amino acid is in the zwitterion state, it will not migrate to either electrode in an electrical field (**Fig. 3.7**). However, when an acid is added to the amino acid, it assumes a positive charge and moves towards the cathode. Similarly,

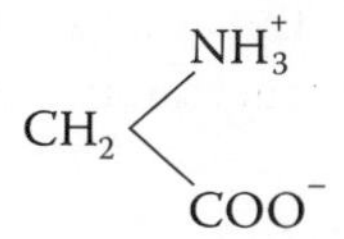

Figure 3.7 Zwitterion.

when an alkali is added, it assumes a negative charge and moves towards the anode. This may be explained with an illustration. A zwitterion reacts with a base; thus

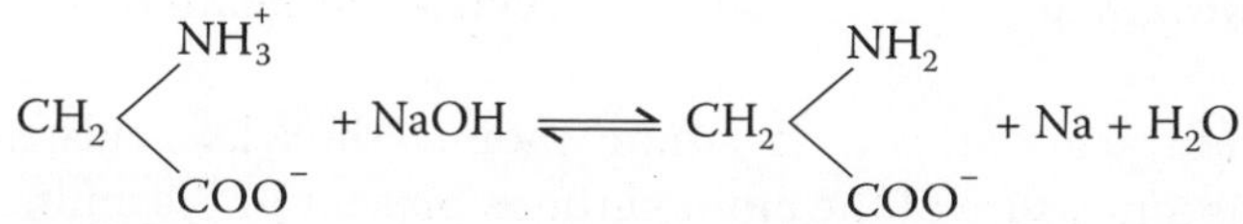

The zwitterion reacts as an acid with a base, by liberating a proton (H^+) from the NH_3 group, resulting in the formation of an organic molecule bearing a net negative charge.

On the other hand, zwitterion reacts with acid as a base, combining with the proton (H^+) of the acid (HCl) and resulting in the formation of an organic compound bearing a net positive charge. These reactions are reversible.

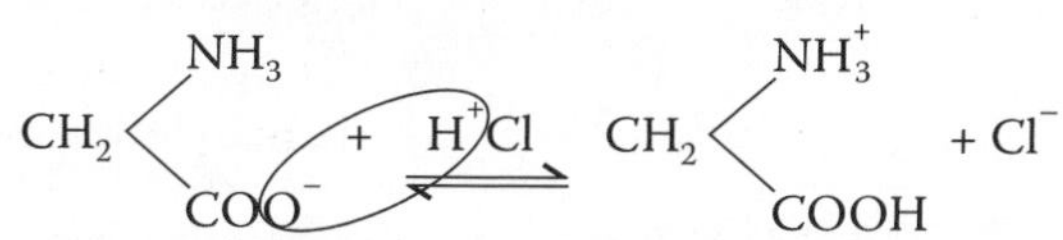

The pH at which the amino acid has no tendency to move either to the positive or to the negative electrode is called its **isoelectric point**. At this pH, the amino acid molecule bears a net charge of zero. The isoelectric point is symbolised by pI. Individual proteins have their own isoelectric points.

Chemical properties: The chemical properties of amino acids are due to their amino groups and carboxyl groups. It may be noted that amino acids that contain more than one NH_2 group are referred to as basic amino acids; when amino acids contain more than one COOH group, they are referred to as acidic amino acids.

1. **Reactions of amino acids due to amino groups**
   - ***Reaction with formaldehyde:*** This reaction is called Sørensen's formol titration. Amino acids dissolve in water to form a neutral solution. The carboxyl groups react with the basic amino groups to form zwitterions. Because of this, the carboxyl groups of α-amino acids in an aqueous solution cannot be accurately titrated with alkalies. Sørensen noted that if amino acid solutions are treated with a large excess of neutralised formaldehyde solution, the mixture becomes acidic and can be titrated sharply with standard alkali, using phenolphthalein as an indicator. The reaction is explained as follows:

     The amino group combines with formaldehyde to form dimethylol amino acid which is an amino acid formaldehyde complex. In this way, the existence of all the amino groups is eliminated, resulting in an acidic solution, due to the presence of only the carboxyl groups. This solution can be titrated against standard alkali, using phenolphthalein as an indicator. The amount of alkali required indicates the amount of carboxyl groups present. The reaction proceeds as follows:

$$\begin{array}{c} NH_3^+ \\ | \\ R-C-COO^- \\ | \\ H \end{array} + OH^- + 2CH_2O \rightleftharpoons \begin{array}{c} HOH_2C-N-CH_2OH \\ | \\ R-C-COO^- \\ | \\ H \end{array} + H_2O$$

Zwitterion **Dimethylol amino acid**

As α-amino acids are mono amino monocarboxylic acids, the acidity of the amino acid is a measure of the amino groups present in the amino acid.

- ***Reaction of glycine with benzoic acid:*** Amino acids act as bases towards acids and form salts. This may be shown by the reaction of glycine with benzoic acid to form benzoyl glycine. The amino groups condense with benzoic acid to form hippuric acid. This phenomenon occurs in man as a process for detoxication of benzoic acid. The reaction proceeds as follows:

$$C_6H_5COOH + HNHCH_2COOH \rightarrow C_6H_5CONHCH_2COOH + H_2O$$

Hippuric acid (benzoylglycine)

- ***Reaction with nitrous acid:*** Nitrous acid reacts with the amino group of amino acids to form the corresponding hydroxy acids and liberate nitrogen gas. The reaction proceeds as follows:

$$\begin{array}{c} NH_2 \\ | \\ R-C-COOH \\ | \\ H \end{array} + HONO \longrightarrow \begin{array}{c} OH \\ | \\ R-C-COOH \\ | \\ H \end{array} + N_2 + H_2O$$

The nitrogen evolved can be volumetrically measured in a manometer. It may be seen that one amino group gives one molecule of nitrogen. The reaction is the basis of Van Slyke's method of estimation of free amino groups in amino acids and protein. The Van Slyke amino nitrogen method is used to follow the rate of hydrolysis of proteins, since for each peptide linkage hydrolysed, an α-amino group is liberated. The amount of amino nitrogen thus increases progressively and comes to a standstill when the hydrolysis of the protein is complete.

- ***Reaction with ninhydrin:*** When a solution of α-amino acid is boiled with ninhydrin (triketohydrindene hydrate), the amino acid is quantitatively deaminated to NH_3 and keto acid by oxidative deamination. The carboxyl group of the keto acid is converted to CO_2 which is evolved in quantitative amounts and therefore can be measured. In this way, this reaction is also specific for the release of CO_2. The ninhydrin is specifically reduced to a compound which condenses with ammonia and more ninhydrin to form a beautiful blue-coloured compound. This reaction is of value in the quantitative estimation of amino acids, proteins and peptides in solution. The reactions may be explained to proceed as follows: oxidative deamination of the amino acid occurs in two stages:

(i) Formation of imino acid:

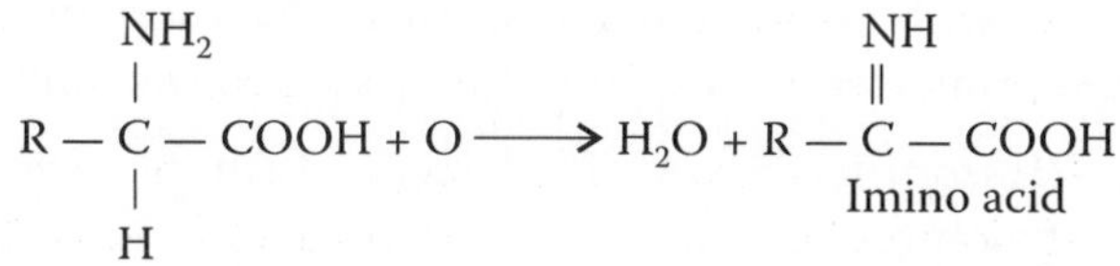

(ii) Formation of NH_3 and keto acid:

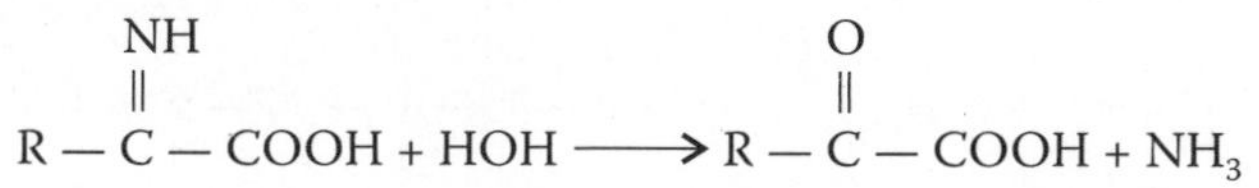

The blue-coloured compound known as 'Ruhemann's purple' is formed by the reaction of some of the ninhydrin with its reduction products hydrindantin and ammonia as follows:

(iii) Ninhydrin + Amino acid → Reduced ninhydrin (hydrindantin) + Ammonia + CO_2 + Aldehyde

(iv) Reduced ninhydrin + Ninhydrin + NH_3 → Blue compound

- ***Reaction with 1-fluoro-2,4-dinitrobenzene (FDNB):*** The reaction of the amino groups of amino acids with 1-fluoro-2, 4-dinitrobenzene (FDNB), also called 'Sanger's reagent', is an important reaction. The reagent (FDNB) condenses with free amino groups in cold mild alkaline solution (bicarbonate) to give dinitrophenyl amino acid.

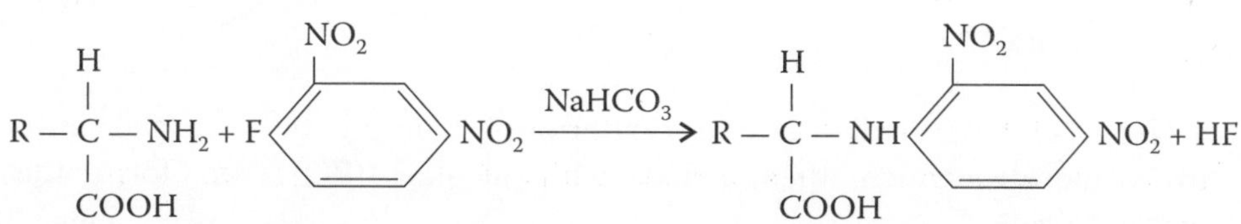

1-Fluoro-2,4-dinitrobenzene **Dinitrophenyl amino acid** or **DNP-amino acid**

The DNP-amino acids are bright yellow in colour and are soluble in ether. The amino acids can be separated from the DNP bond by acid hydrolysis and identified by chromatography. This reaction is of importance because Sanger used this reagent originally to identify and separate the terminal amino acid from the free amino group of the peptide chains of the insulin molecule. By using this technique, Sanger succeeded in determining the sequence of the amino acids in the molecule of insulin which contains 51 amino acids.

- ***Reaction with carbon dioxide-Siegfried's carbamino reaction:*** The free amino groups of amino acids can condense with carbon dioxide to form carbamino compounds. This reaction is called *Siegfried's* carbamino reaction.

$$R-NH_2 + CO_2 \longrightarrow R-NH-COO^- + H^+$$

Carbamino compounds are formed in the blood, when the amino groups in haemoglobin react with carbon dioxide. Carbamino compounds of haemoglobin are important in the transport of CO_2 from the tissues to the lungs.

- ***Formation of diketopiperazines:*** The esters of amino acids condense to form anhydride ring structures containing two amino acid groups. These compounds are called diketopiperazines.

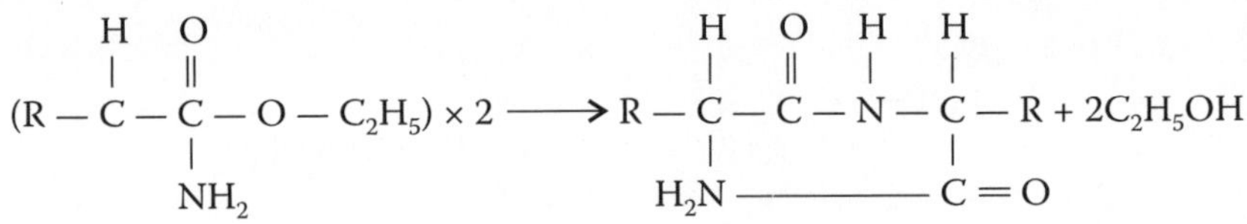

Ester **Diketopiperazine**

- ***Chelation with metal ions:*** Heavy metals such as Cu^{++}, Hg^{++}, Mn^{++} and Fe^{++} form chelated complexes with amino acids in which both carboxyl and amino groups are involved.

2. **Reactions due to carboxyl groups:**
   - ***Formation of esters:*** Amino acids react with alcohols in the presence of HCl to form ester.

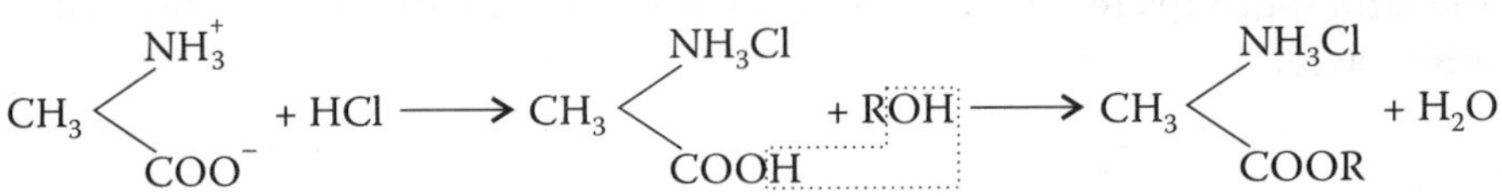

The HCl first breaks up the zwitterions' structure to form the amino acid hydrochloride, which then reacts with alcohol (ROH) to form the ester hydrochloride.

- ***Decarboxylation—formation of amine:*** When amino acids are treated preferably in the presence of barium hydroxide, CO_2 is lost and the corresponding amine is formed. Decarboxylation of histidine to histamine which takes place in the large intestine by the bacterial enzymatic action is an example of this reaction.

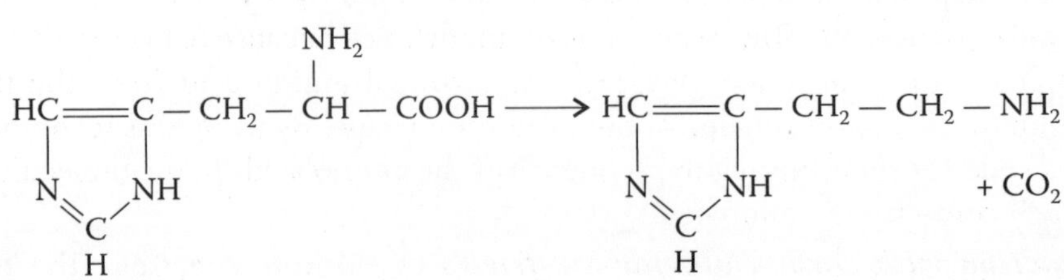

Histidine **Histamine**

- ***Amide formation:*** Amino acid esters form amides when treated with anhydrous or alcoholic ammonia.

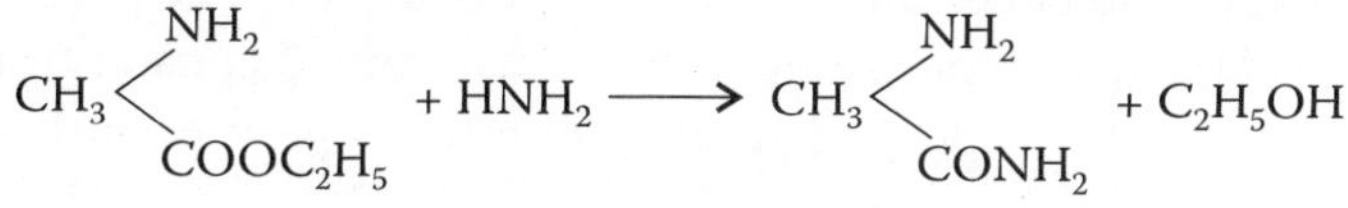

Ester **Amide**

Chromatography

Methods of separating amino acids: The separation and identification of individual amino acids from a mixture of protein involve laborious and difficult procedures. A simple and convenient method for the separation and identification of amino acids in a protein solution comprises a technique called **chromatography**. Strictly speaking, chromatography applies to the separation of a variety of compounds of biochemical interest, including fatty acids, carbohydrates and amino acids. In clinical chemistry, chromatography is applied to separate and identify amino acids, sugars, lipids and various other compounds of clinical interest, present in urine and other biological fluids.

Chromatography may be defined as a technique in which the components of mixture containing amino acids and many other physiologically important substances are made to migrate at different rates in an apparatus. This involves equilibration of the solutes (amino acids) between a stationary and a moving phase. The stationary phase is the supporting medium such as filter paper or silica gel on which the mixture of amino acids (or other substances to be separated) is made to migrate. The moving phase consists of a mixture of two immiscible solvent systems, of which one is usually water which has a stronger affinity for the supporting medium. The other solvent has lesser affinity for the stationary phase and carries the solutes across the stationary phase.

Paper Chromatography

This is the most widely used procedure for the separation and identification of amino acids. It is referred to as paper chromatography because filter paper is used as the supporting medium.

The procedure is simple and inexpensive and is carried out as follows.

A strip of filter paper is suspended vertically with the lower end dipping into a mixture of water and an organic solvent of amino acids such as *n*-butyl alcohol, *n*-propyl alcohol, phenol, isobutyic acid or collidine, contained in a shallow trough.

The mixture of water and organic solvent moves up the filter paper in ascending chromatography, whereas in the case of descending chromatography, the solvent placed in a trough at the top, from which the paper hangs, moves down the filter paper. The water represents a stationary solvent phase because water is strongly held by the paper, while the organic solvent moves up the filter paper, since paper has lesser attraction for the organic solvent than water. At the onset of the procedure, a small quantity of the amino acid mixture is spotted on the paper, about 5 cm from the end of the paper, which dips into the solvent contained in a wide and shallow vessel. The other end of the paper is supported at a convenient height. The paper and the solvent mixture are enclosed in a covered glass cylinder or in a big bell jar, and the temperature is maintained constant, so that the solvent moves up the paper in an atmosphere saturated with the vapour of both water and organic solvent at the temperature (**Fig. 3.8**).

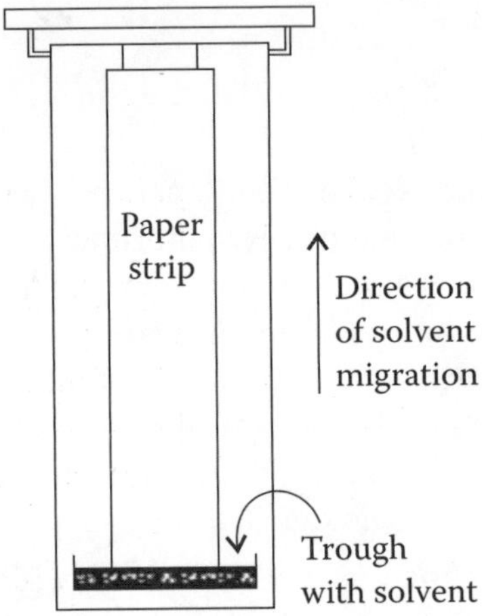

Figure 3.8 Cross-section of apparatus for ascending paper chromatography.

Now the solvent moves up the strip gradually and goes over the solute spot carrying the solute along with it, thus partitioning the solute from the stationary water phase on the paper. Depending upon the solubility of the solutes contained in the mixture of amino acids, the solutes migrate up to certain distances on the filter paper, at different rates, and afterwards stop migrating. But the moving organic solvents still rise up the paper, leaving behind the solute on the stationary phase, i.e. paper. Thus, another partition has taken place now. The run is stopped after several hours, say 8–10 hours, by which time the solvent would have run up a convenient distance. The solute appears as a characteristically localised spot at the point where it stopped migrating.

The strip of paper is now removed and the position of the solvent front is marked with a pencil. The strip is dried and sprayed with a solution of ninhydrin in acetone which stains the amino acid spots purple, thus enabling to visualise the position of the different amino acids migrated on the paper strip. This migration rate is expressed as the R*f* value, which is defined as the ratio of the distance of the spot from the spotted line to the distance of the solvent front from the spotted line:

$$Rf \text{ value} = \frac{\text{Distance of the spot from the spotted line}}{\text{Distance of the solvent from the spotted line}}$$

R*f* values are characteristic for different amino acids when chromatographed under the same experimental conditions. When a mixture of amino acids is chromatographed, a vertical series of spots representing the different amino acids is obtained (**Fig. 3.9**). This is known as **single-dimension chromatography**. However, there will be an overlapping of the spots if the *Rf* values are too close as in the case of some amino acids. Each spot which represents an amino acid can be identified by comparing its *Rf* value with that obtained by running chromatography of a solution of known amino acid composition on the adjoining side of the same paper simultaneously. The *Rf* value of the known amino acid which corresponds with that of the unknown amino acid is taken to represent the unknown amino acid; quantitative estimation of the amino acids under investigation may be done by

1. **Elution:** This consists in cutting out the stained amino acid spot and eluting the colour of the stain with a suitable solvent and comparing in a photoelectric colorimeter with that of a standard.
2. **Scanning:** This is measurement of the density of the stained spot, in a densitometer.

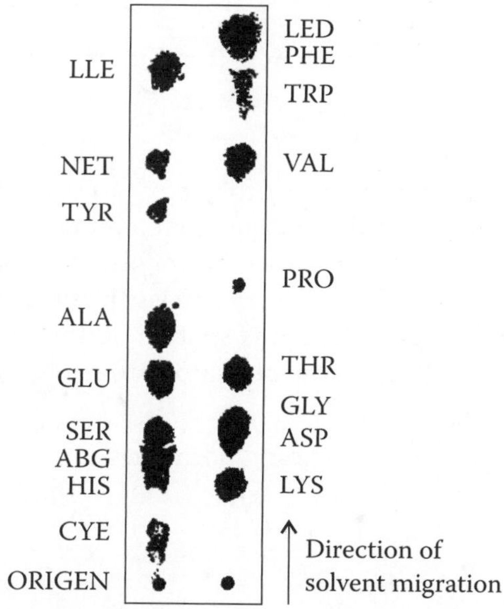

Figure 3.9 Paper chromatography—single-dimension chromatogram of amino acids.

Two-dimensional paper chromatography is an improvement on the single-dimension chromatography. In this technique, two spots of the amino acid mixture are spotted at the right and left corners of a square sheet of filter paper. It is first chromoatographed with one solvent mixture (e.g. phenol-ammonia-water). The paper is dried and turned through 90° and chromatographed for another period of run with another solvent mixture, say collidine-water. As it is chromatographed twice in two different directions, it is called two-dimensional chromatography. By using this technique, it is possible to obtain a better separation of the amino acids especially when there is overlapping of spots in the single-dimension technique (**Fig. 3.10**).

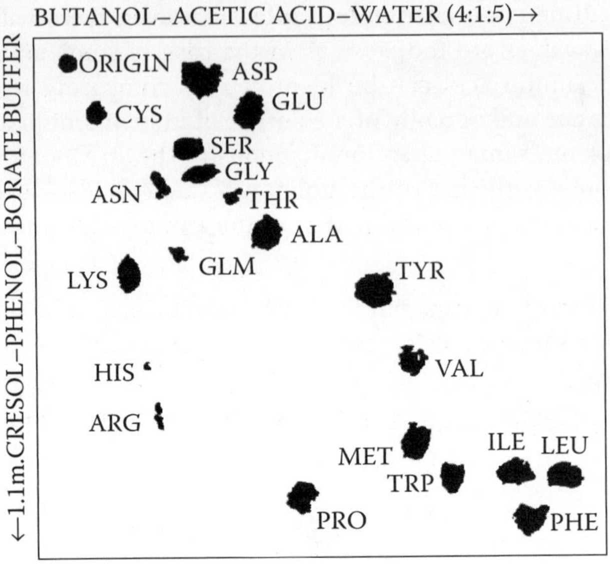

Figure 3.10 Paper chromatography—double-dimensional chromatogram of amino acids.

A further modification on paper chromatography has replaced both the single- and double-dimensional techniques and this is called thin layer chromatography (TLC). In this technique, the filter paper is replaced by a thin uniform layer of an adsorbent-like fine silica gel or alumina, which is spread as a slurry on glass plates of different sizes. The plates are dried and then the amino acid solution is spotted on the adsorbent layer as done on filter paper. The advantages of TLC over paper chromatography are as follows:

1. Better separation of spots
2. Many more compounds such as lipids and hormones can be separated very well
3. The separation in TLC takes place three or four times quicker than in paper chromatography

Gas Chromatography

Gas chromatography is a technique used to separate complex mixtures of chemical compounds which are volatile either in their natural state or after the formation of their derivatives, by selective partition between a stationary solid or liquid and a mobile gas phase. In clinical chemistry, this technique is employed to separate and determine the concentration of plasma lipids, blood alcohol and urinary steroids, using microquantities of the test material.

In gas chromatography, the moving phase is one of the inert gases such as hydrogen, helium, argon or nitrogen, called as the carrier gas. The stationary phase may be a solid like alumina or Kiselghur or may be a liquid like silicone oil or polyethylene glycol supported by inert solids such as glass beads or ground fire bricks. The stationary phase is packed in long or coiled metal or glass tubes called columns. The carrier gas is passed into the columns through a regulator from a storage cylinder. In practice, the test sample, for example a mixture of fatty acids (which has to be first converted into their methyl esters), is injected, at one end of the column where it is instantaneously volatalized by elevated temperature (175–200°C) and is swept through the inert solids in the columns by the constantly flowing stream of inert gas. As with other types of chromatography, the individual components are adsorbed and retained by the stationary phase at different rates depending upon their affinity for the stationary phase. Consequently, the gases which have lesser affinity for the stationary phase move through the column at a quicker rate and emerge out of the column earlier than those which have a stronger affinity. As the individual fatty acid esters emerge out of the column one by one at different intervals, they pass to a highly sensitive detector which transmits the output to a recorder. This records the data automatically on a chart as a series of peaks. The area under each peak is proportionate to the concentration of the particular component in the mixture. Each component is identified by comparison with the gas chromatographic pattern of a standard mixture of known composition.

SPECIAL REACTIONS OF PROTEIN

Certain special reactions of proteins and their application in clinical biochemistry are dealt with briefly in this section.

Colloidal nature: Aqueous solutions of protein are colloidal and are opalescent in appearance. Colloids are of bigger dimensions measuring from 1 to 200 mμ in diameter.

(1 micron [μ] = 0.001 mm) 1 mμ = 0.001 μ.

The stability of a protein molecule in a solution is due to two factors: (i) electrical charge it carries and (ii) the hydration or the covering of water around the protein molecule.

A protein molecule which contains both these factors is called an emulsoid. When these two factors are removed, the protein molecules lose their stability and clump together to form a precipitate.

Molecular weight: The colloidal nature of a protein solution is due to the high molecular weight of the protein molecules. Proteins form giant molecules due to their high molecular weight, which ranges from 5,000 to many millions. The large size of the protein molecule has special significance in the metabolic processes. A large size makes the molecule difficult to move about and limits diffusibility. This keeps the protein at its work spot, preventing it from wandering. This is seen best in enzymes and hormones which are macromolecular proteins, having specific action. Further, being macromolecular they have the advantage of acting on substrates which are smaller molecules, by adsorbing them on their surface. The molecular weights of some proteins of physiological importance are given below:

Egg albumin	=	44,000
Insulin	=	12,000
Serum albumin	=	69,000
Serum γ-globulin	=	180,000
Fibrinogen	=	450,000
Thyroglobulin	=	630,000

Electrophoresis of Proteins

Migration of particles in a solution between electrodes is called electrophoresis. Since proteins have their own isoelectric points at any given pH (**Table 3.1**), they will bear net charges of different magnitudes. As a result, when a mixture of protein is placed in an electrical field, the individual components of the mixture migrate at different velocities. This phenomenon is utilised in the procedure of electrophoretic analysis, which has a wide application in clinical medicine. If the pH of the plasma is adjusted by the addition of a proper buffer to a value alkaline to the isoelectric points of all the fractions of plasma protein, then the plasma proteins will all carry negative charges but of different magnitudes. When an electric current is passed through the plasma protein, the different fractions of plasma migrate towards the anode, at characteristically different rates. By electrophoretic analysis of plasma protein, the various fractions of plasma protein could be separated, and a study of the electrophoretic pattern gives valuable information about the distribution of plasma protein fractions in health and disease. The technique and apparatus for electrophoresis were first developed by Tiselius and Longsworth. Tiselius used a U-tube, which he filled with a protein solution, overlaid by a buffer solution of the same ionic strength, pH and conductivity, and applied current to the two ends of the U-tube. Separation of the various proteins present occurred at the junction between the buffer and the protein solution, as they migrated towards the opposite electrode, giving rise to new moving boundaries which were photographed through a special optical system. Electrophoretic separation of plasma protein is most conveniently carried out on strips of special filter paper.

Table 3.1 Isoelectric Points of Proteins

Proteins	pH
Serum albumin (human)	4.7
γ-Globulin (human)	6.4
Lactalbumin	5.12
Haemoglobin (man)	6.7
Carbonic anhydrase	5.3
Pepsin	1

Paper Electrophoresis

The technique of paper electrophoresis is simple and inexpensive and requires only microquantities of plasma for separation. The electrophoresis apparatus in its simplest form consists of two troughs to contain buffer solution, through which electric current is passed (**Fig. 3.11**).

The plasma under investigation is mixed with bromophenol blue, a blue-coloured stain, and spotted at the centre of a strip of special filter paper, saturated with an alkaline buffer solution. Barbitone buffer of pH 8.6 is used. The centre of the filter paper is supported vertically over a glass rod. The ends of the paper dip in buffer solution contained in two troughs placed on either side of the glass rod. The entire system is covered with an airtight transparent lid.

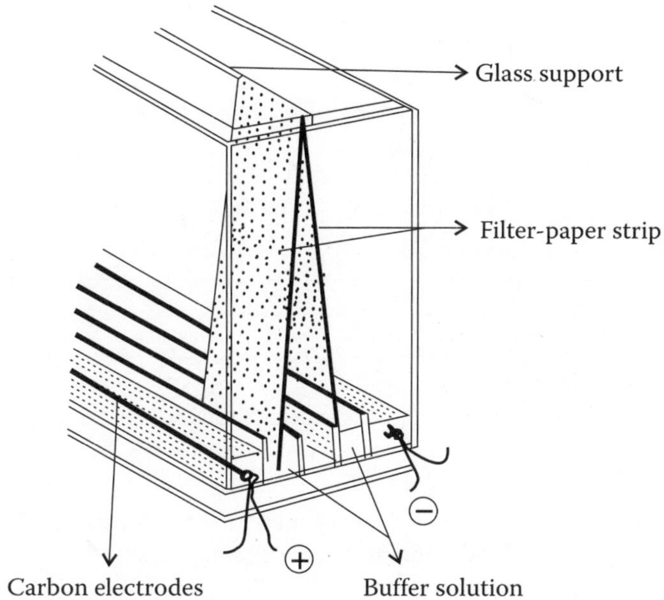

Figure 3.11 Diagram of an electrophoresis apparatus.

An electric current of proper amperage and voltage is passed across the paper, when the charged protein fractions bearing different charges migrate at different rates. The moving boundary of the migrating proteins, stained blue, can be seen moving towards the anode. After a run of about 5–6 hours, the current is stopped and the separated fractions of plasma protein, which lie in succession behind the moving boundary, are fixed in their places by heating the paper in an oven at 110°C for half an hour. The paper is then stained with a solution containing bromophenol blue. The different fractions appear as blue-coloured bands across the filter paper starting from the moving boundary backwards. If a quantitative estimation is required for each fraction, the bands may be carefully cut and eluted or the bands may be scanned optically in a densitometer. In human plasma, five different bands can be identified on paper electrophoresis. These are designated in the order of decreasing mobility, as albumin, α_1-globulin, α_2-globulin, β-globulin, fibrinogen and γ-globulin (**Fig. 3.12**).

Albumin, being the fastest moving fraction of the proteins of plasma, forms the farthest band on the paper while γ-globulin, which is the lowest moving protein, forms a band at the other end of the pattern. The rest of the fractions take their positions in between these two bands.

Media such as starch, agar, polyacrylamide gel and cellulose acetate strips are also used instead of the special filter papers for electrophoresis. These media give better separation of the protein fractions than filter papers.

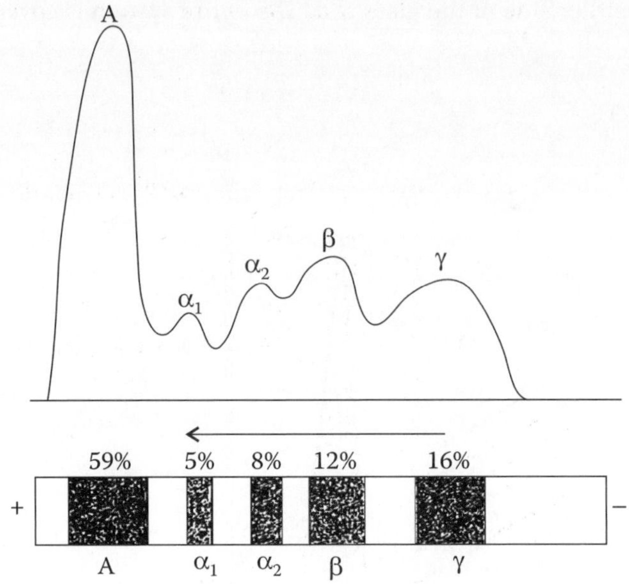

Figure 3.12 Graphical representation of the concentration of serum protein fractions as obtained by scanning in a densitometer.

The concentration of the different protein fractions in normal human plasma as obtained by scanning in a densitometer is expressed in percentage, as follows:

Albumin—55.2%
Globulin (total)—44.8%
Albumin/Globulin ratio—1.23
α_1-globulin—5.3%
α_2-globulin—8.7%
β-globulin—13.4%
γ-globulin—11.0%
Fibrinogen—6.5%

It has been found that the lipoproteins of plasma circulate along with the α- and β-globulins and the γ-globulins contain the circulating antibodies.

Paper electrophoresis is widely used in the diagnosis of certain diseases. The characteristic changes observed in the electrophoretogram of some diseases are shown in **Figure 3.13**.

The albumin component is lowered in conditions which present albuminuria as in nephritic syndrome. Another characteristic finding in nephritic syndrome is the well-marked band of α_2-globulin.

The albumin content is lowered in chronic liver diseases associated with cirrhosis. In addition, the γ-globulin band has an increased concentration and is intensely marked.

The albumin content is decreased in extensive 'burns', due to extravasation of fluid, and in malnutrition, due to hypoproteinaemia. A well-marked band is seen in the region of γ-globulin in a malignant bone disease called multiple myeloma.

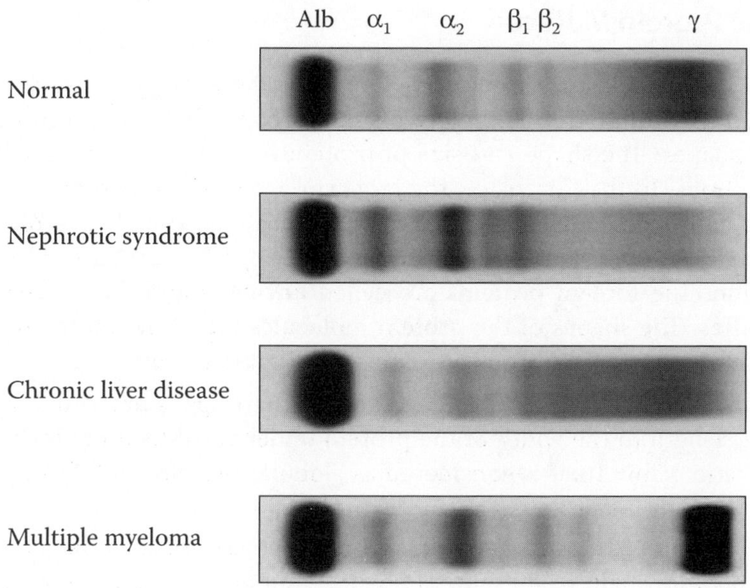

Figure 3.13 Electrophoretic pattern of serum protein in health and disease.

Protein Allergy

When certain foreign proteins are introduced into the body either by injection, ingestion or absorption through the respiratory tract, untoward reactions referred to as *allergic reactions* may occur. An initial administration of a small dose of a foreign protein to a person by injection may not reveal any visible effects. But if the same is repeated, say after a week, the subject may develop a severe reaction, sometimes resulting in death. The reaction is known as *anaphylactic shock.* It is apparent that the initial dose of the foreign protein has sensitized the individual to subsequent doses of the same protein. Anaphylactic shock can be prevented by injecting frequent but small doses of the foreign protein, as this will build a tolerance to the protein. This is known as *desensitisation.* Protein allergy may manifest in milder ways also. For example, some persons who are sensitive to specific proteins may develop symptoms such as headache, urticarial rash, eczema and asthma, when they come in contact with those proteins. Such individuals are said to be allergic to the proteins. The proteins of milk, eggs, fish and meat are the common food allergens. Plant pollens are the commonest respiratory allergens.

PROTEIN STRUCTURE

The architecture of a protein molecule is complex but well organised. To understand this, a clear idea of certain basic details regarding the mode of arrangement of the structural units inside the molecule is necessary. These may be discussed under two headings, namely

1. Shape of the protein molecule
2. Internal structure of the protein

Shape of the Protein Molecule

It has been determined by application of special techniques, such as streaming birefringence, X-ray diffraction and electron microscopy, that protein molecules possess characteristic shapes. The shape and size of protein molecules serve a special purpose in biological functions. In the first place, the large surface of enzyme proteins is most suited to attract the substrates during enzyme action. Secondly, the shapes of γ-globulin are modified in such a way that they can combine with foreign proteins and remove them from circulation. The foreign proteins are called **antigens** and the altered globulins are called **antibodies**. The shapes of the protein molecules found in nature are classified into two major groups, namely (i) fibrous proteins and (ii) globular proteins.

The arbitrary dividing line to differentiate the two groups is determined by calculating the ratio of the length to the width of the protein under consideration. If the protein has a length/width ratio below 10, it is considered as globular protein, and if the ratio is over 10, it is considered as fibrous protein.

1. **Globular protein:** A typical globular protein consists of a rather compactly folded or coiled peptide chain or a group of chains. Globular proteins have a high degree of regularity in their structure. Most of the easily crystallisable proteins fall under this group (**Fig. 3.14**).

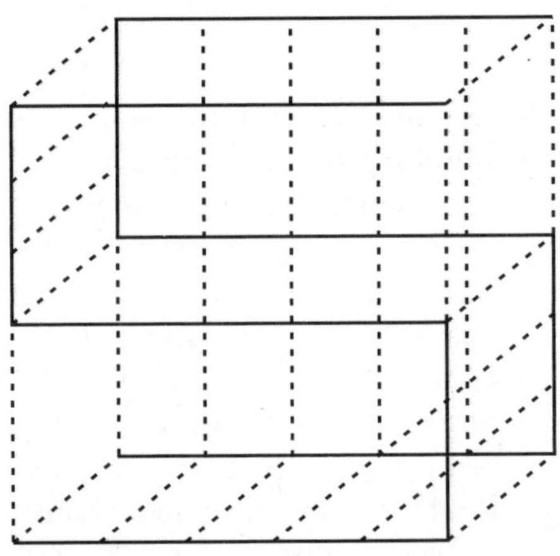

Figure 3.14 Globular protein.

Examples of globular proteins are insulin, albumin and globulin of plasma.

2. **Fibrous protein:** They are insoluble in water and form extracellular components. A fibrous protein consists of an elongated peptide chain or a group of such chains. Each chain may be extended or helically coiled along its length. The peptide chains may be united by cross-linkages like disulphide (**Fig. 3.15**). Examples of fibrous proteins are as follows:
   - Keratin found in hair, skin, etc.
   - Fibrinogen
   - Muscle proteins, namely actin, myosin and actomyosin

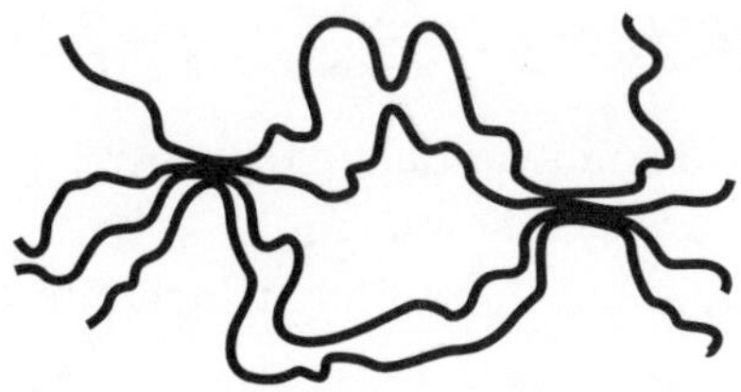

Figure 3.15 Fibrous protein.

Internal Structure of the Protein

The study of the internal structure of protein deals with the following details:

1. The overall quantitative amino acid composition
2. The number of peptide chains in the molecule
3. The number of amino acids in the peptide chains
4. The forces involved in holding the chain, in specific folded configuration

All these aspects are discussed briefly in this chapter.

A protein molecule is composed of several amino acids linked with one another in peptide linkage. The amino acid composition can be determined by special analytical procedures.

Peptide Linkage

A complex protein molecule can be considered to be a large polypeptide containing several peptides, which in turn are composed of amino acids linked to one another by peptide linkages. The simplest peptide consists of two amino acids joined by a peptide linkage. This is called a **dipeptide**. Formation of a peptide linkage may be represented as follows:

$$\underbrace{NH_2\text{—}\underset{\underset{CH_3}{|}}{CH}\text{—}\overset{\overset{O}{\|}}{C}\text{—}}_{\textbf{Alanine}}\boxed{OH+H}\underbrace{\text{—}\overset{\overset{H}{|}}{N}\text{—}\underset{\underset{CH_2OH}{|}}{CH}\text{—}COOH}_{\textbf{Serine}} \longrightarrow \underbrace{H_2N\text{—}\underset{\underset{CH_3}{|}}{CH}\text{—}CONH\text{—}\underset{\underset{CH_2OH}{|}}{CH}COOH}_{\textbf{Alanyl serine}} + H_2O$$

A protein molecule containing three amino acids, linked to one another by peptide linkages, is a tripeptide. For example, glycylalanylglycine is a tripeptide. Similarly, further lengthening of the amino acids will form a polypeptide chain. Each peptide chain contains a free terminal carboxyl group (COOH) at the terminal end and a free NH_2 group at the other end.

Biologically important peptides: There are peptides which occur naturally. Important among them are (i) glutathione, (ii) bradykinin and (iii) kallidin. Glutathione is γ-glutamyl-cysteinyl-glycine. Bradykinin and kallidin are potent smooth muscle hypotensive agents liberated from specific plasma proteins by treatment with the proteolytic enzyme trypsin or snake venom.

Linkage Other Than Peptide Bonds

The polypeptide chains are held and maintained in position within the protein molecule by various kinds of bonds. These are as follows:

1. **Disulphide bond:** This is an important bond which interconnects two parallel peptide chains and is formed between two cysteine residues of the adjacent chains. Sometimes, it is formed between two cysteine residues within the same chain. A good example is insulin. $-CH_2$-S-S-CH_2- represents a disulphide bond.
2. **Hydrogen bond:** Another major force which holds and maintains the structure of protein is the hydrogen bond. The peptide chains are held together in a coiled shape by these hydrogen bonds. They are formed between the hydrogen atom of the NH and the O of C=O of a CONH (peptide) linkage, as shown in **Figure 3.16**:

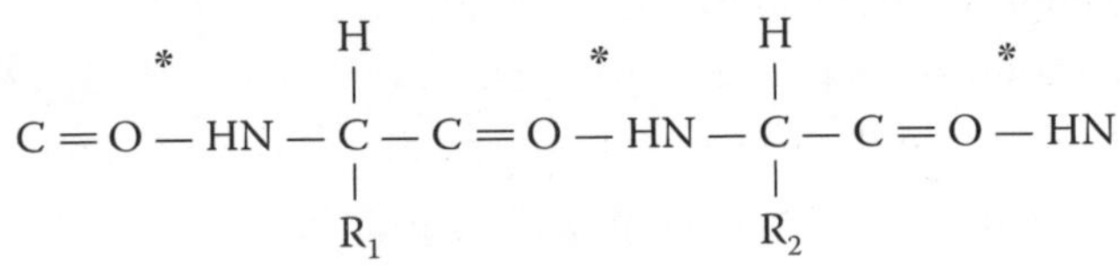

Figure 3.16 Hydrogen bond.

The asterisk marks represent the hydrogen bond.

3. **Salt linkages:** They may be formed between the carboxyl group of one chain and the amino group of the adjacent chain. Salt bridges are formed by the action of an acid group and a basic group as in the case of lysine which possesses an additional NH_2 group and in glutamic acid which possesses an additional COOH group. The salt linkage unites two adjacent peptide chains (**Fig. 3.17**).

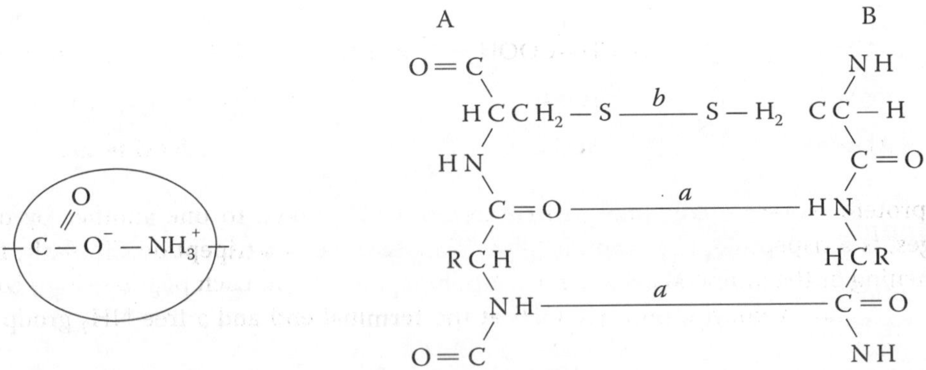

Salt linkage

Two peptide chains A and B are linked by *a*—hydrogen bonds, *b*—disulphide bonds

Figure 3.17 Salt linkage between peptide chains.

One striking feature about proteins is their high degree of specificity in the structure and function. Proteins are composed of several molecules of amino acids joined to one another by peptide bonds. The peptide chains and the sequence of amino acids are organised in a characteristically regular fashion. In 1949, Pauling and Corey have indicated by application of X-ray diffraction techniques and quantitative amino acid analysis that some protein molecules have a definite helical structure and a spatial or three-dimensional configuration. Subsequent studies have shown that the structure of proteins can be considered at four different levels of organisation, namely 'primary', 'secondary', 'tertiary' and 'quaternary' structures. The four levels of the structural organisation of proteins are discussed in this section.

STRUCTURAL ORGANISATION OF PROTEINS

Protein structure can be classified into four levels of organisation, which are as follows:

1. Primary structure
2. Secondary structure
3. Tertiary structure
4. Quaternary structure

Primary Structure

The primary structure of a protein molecule refers to the sequence of amino acids in the polypeptide chain. The amino acids are linked by covalent peptide bonds. The amino acid sequence which is coded by DNA determine the final three-dimensional form adopted by the protein in its native state. It includes the location of the disulphide (cystine) bonds (**Fig. 3.18**).

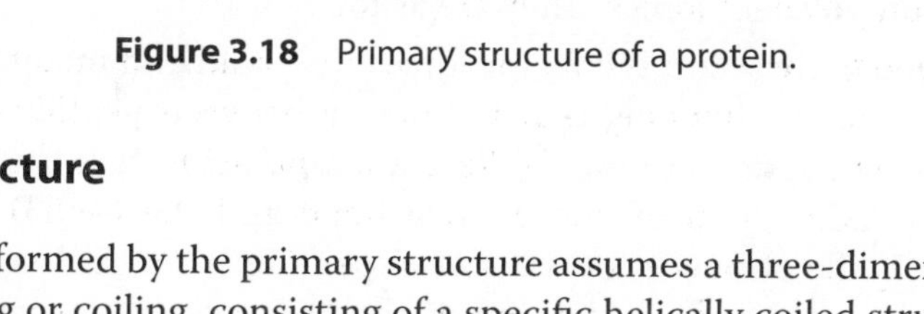

Figure 3.18 Primary structure of a protein.

Secondary Structure

The peptide chain formed by the primary structure assumes a three-dimensional secondary structure by folding or coiling, consisting of a specific helically coiled structure in a regular manner. The coiling is the result of linking of the carboxyl group and the amino group of the neighbouring amino acid residue of the peptide chain, by hydrogen bonds and disulphide bonds.

The hydrogen bonds are formed when a hydrogen atom (H) is shared between the oxygen (O) of the CO and nitrogen (N) of NH of different peptide bonds (**Fig. 3.19**). Refer to **Figure 3.16** also.

The **secondary structure** is formed by the ordering of the polypeptide chain as dictated by the DNA-encoded primary sequence. The secondary structure is particularly present in fibrous proteins where the polypeptide chains have an extended or longitudinally coiled confirmation. It also occurs in segments of polypeptide chains in globular proteins.

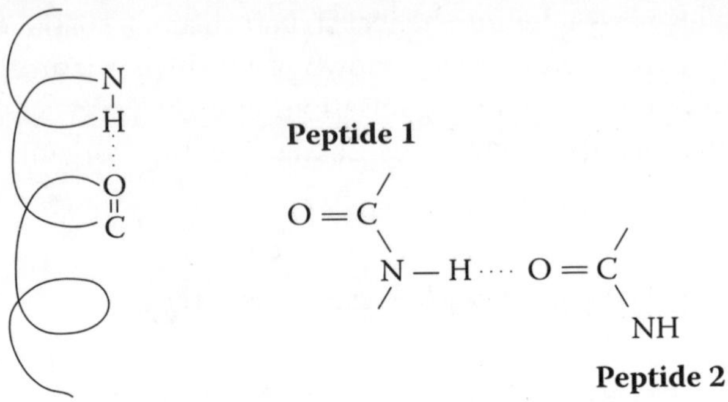

Hydrogen bonds in a peptide bond

Figure 3.19 Secondary structure of a protein.

Tertiary Structure

The polypeptide chain with the secondary structure may be further folded and twisted producing structural coils of different sizes and shapes to form a compact three-dimensional globular molecule called the tertiary structure. The hydrophobic side chains are generally in the interior of the structure away from water and the hydrophilic side chains are found on the outside of the protein structure, in contact with water. The tertiary structure which is the total three-dimensional structure of the protein includes grouping and arrangement of helical chains into specific layers and refers to the geometric relationship of various segments and domains in the protein with individual amino acid residues. It considers the steric relationship of the amino acid residues that are generally far apart in primary structure, but brought closer by folding (**Fig. 3.20**). The structure is stabilised in position by covalent and non-covalent forces. They are as follows:

1. **Hydrogen bonds:** These are the major forces that hold and maintain the structure of protein. Hydrogen (H) bonding may be formed between peptide bonds in the same chain or between peptide bonds of different amino acids. It is the formation of bond between the (–CO) group of one peptide bond and the (–NH) of another nearby peptide bond. If the H bonds form between peptide bonds in the same chain, helical structures such as the α-helix develop. If the H bonds are formed between peptide bonds in different chains, extended structures such as the β-configuration or β-pleated sheet form. These are pleated and the chains are not in straight lines.
2. **Salt bonds** can interact electrostatically to stabilise proteins. Salt bonds or ionic bonds link oppositely charged side chain groups such as the negatively charged carboxyl group ($-COO^-$) of aspartate or glutamate and the positively charged N terminal residue ($-NH_3^+$) of lysine.

3. **Hydrophobic interactions:** Amino acids with non-polar side chains tend to fold into the interior of the protein molecule, where they are shielded from exposure to water. In contrast, amino acids with polar or charged side chains tend to be located on the surface of the molecule in contact with the water molecule of the solvent.
4. **Covalent cross-linkage:** A disulphide bond (SH) is a covalent bond which interconnects two parallel cysteine chains between SH groups resulting in the formation of cystine. The disulphide (S–S) linkage contributes to the stability of the three-dimensional shape of the protein molecules and prevents them from becoming denatured in the various extracellular environment.
5. **Flexibility** of the peptide chain in points of instability and allowing water to entrap to the maximum stabilise the structure to some extent.

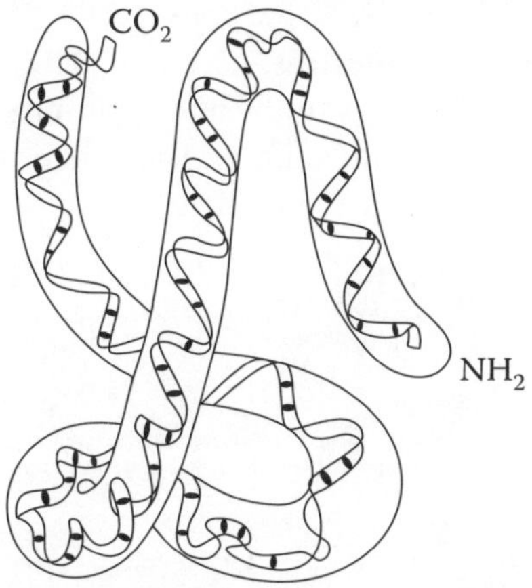

Figure 3.20 Representation of primary, secondary and tertiary structure of a protein. The dots represent α-carbon atoms of amino acids. The sequence of the dots represents the primary structure of the protein. (Note that it has a free NH_2 group at the lower end.) The spiral arrangement of the polypeptide chain represents the helical coiling of the secondary structure. The folding of the entire structure represents the tertiary structure.

Quaternary Structure

Some proteins may exhibit a fourth level of organisation in addition to the first, second and third. It refers to the combination of two or more monomers or subunits of polypeptide chains, each organised with primary, secondary and tertiary structures. The polypeptide chains are held together by non-covalent forces such as hydrogen bonds, salt bonds and interchain hydrophobic interaction between non-polar side chains. Such proteins are said to exhibit quaternary structure. This level of organisation is essential for the activity of proteins such as haemoglobin, ferritin and some enzymes. A well-known example of quaternary protein is haemoglobin which consists of four polypeptide chains, two α- and two β-globin chains, fitting together tightly to form a compact globular structure of the globin molecule (**Fig. 3.21**). The enzyme aspartate transcarbamoylase has a quaternary structure comprised of 12 polypeptide units. The quaternary structure of haemoglobin and

Figure 3.21 Representation of quaternary structure—the ping-pong ball model of apoferritin molecule. The balls represent subunits arranged to form a hollow sphere. The space in between are packed with iron salts to form a molecule of ferritin.

ferritin molecules is represented in **Figures 3.21** and **3.22**, respectively. The ping-pong model arrangement in **Figure 3.22** refers to the apoferritin molecules. Each ball represents a monomer arranged to form a hollow sphere. The space in between the monomers is packed with iron salts to form the ferritin molecule.

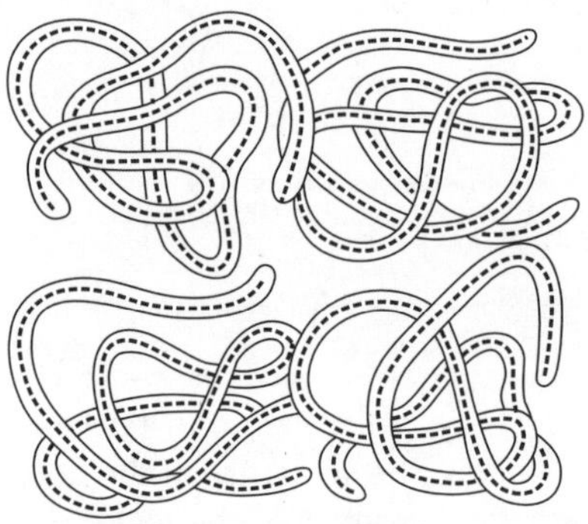

Figure 3.22 Quaternary structure of a haemoglobin molecule. The four polypeptide chains form a compact globular structure of the globin.

4

CHAPTER

Enzymes

Chapter Outline

- Properties of Enzymes
- Classification of Enzymes
- Mechanism of Enzyme Action
- Enzymes of Clinical Interest

Enzymes may be described as complex catalysts produced by living cells, having a high degree of specificity and efficiency, which permit biological reactions to occur rapidly through well-defined pathways. They accelerate the rate of reactions, without being lost in the process. Minute quantities can promote chemical reactions involving numerous metabolic compounds. Enzymes are located in the cells, cytoplasm, mitochondria, tissues and body fluids. The enzymes of glycolytic pathway are located in the non-particulate portion of the cytoplasm, whereas the enzymes of the citric acid cycle are present in the mitochondrion.

Enzymes occurring in biological tissues and fluids are generally mixed with proteins, cells, tissue materials and other enzymes. Some enzymes occur inside the cells and some others outside the cells. Some are soluble and some insoluble.

Separation and isolation of enzymes can be carried out by chromatography.

PROPERTIES OF ENZYMES

1. **Enzymes are catalysts:** In the presence of enzymes, certain chemical reactions proceed faster than in their absence. For example, a solution of lactose does not hydrolyse appreciably at body temperature. But on addition of a minute quantity of the enzyme lactase, hydrolysis takes place rapidly to form glucose and galactose.
2. **Enzymes are proteins:** Most enzymes are simple or conjugated proteins and exhibit all the properties of proteins. Some of them are listed below:
    - They are colloidal in nature and hence are non-dialysable. But there are a few enzymes such as urease, pepsin and trypsin which have been crystallised, and these are dialysable.
    - Being proteins, they have their respective isoelectric points, at which pH they are least soluble.

- Like proteins, they are subject to denaturation by changes in pH or by an increase in the temperature of their solution.
- They are precipitated from solution by protein-precipitating agents such as alcohol, ammonium sulphate and alkaloidal reagents.
- Chemical analysis of purified crystalline enzymes yields composition typical of proteins. They contain C, H, N and S.

3. **Specificity:** One characteristic feature which distinguishes enzymes from a catalyst is its specificity. This means that a given enzyme can catalyse only a comparatively small range of reactions or only one reaction. Since all the biochemical reactions are catalysed by enzymes, there must be a large number of enzymes, which are specific in their own way.

   Three kinds of specificity are described. They are as follows:

   - *Absolute specificity*: When enzymes catalyse only one particular reaction, they are said to exhibit absolute specificity. For example, (i) urease acts only on urea and (ii) esterases act on ester linkage only.
   - *Group specificity*: Enzymes acting on a group of substances possessing a particular type of linkage common to that group of substances are said to exhibit group specificity. For example, amylase hydrolyses the group of substances such as starch, dextrins and glycogen, which have the same type of glucosidic linkages.
   - *Optical specificity*: Almost all enzymes show a high degree of optical specificity. Thus, there are certain enzymes which catalyse the hydrolysis of the same group of substances possessing the same optical activity, i.e. optical isomers. For example,
     - D-amino acid oxidase oxidises D-amino acids.
     - L-amino acid oxidase oxidises L-amino acids.

     D- and L-amino acids refer to the position of the NH_2 groups to the right or the left of the carboxyl group, respectively.

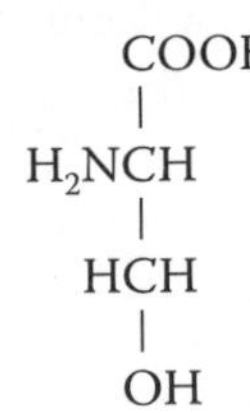

L-Amino acid

CLASSIFICATION OF ENZYMES

Enzymes may be classified into six major groups. Each has many subgroups. They are briefly dealt with in this section.

I. Oxidoreductases
II. Transferases
III. Hydrolases
IV. Lyases
V. Isomerases
VI. Ligases

Oxidoreductases: They catalyse oxidoreduction reactions between two substances. These enzymes are concerned with reactions of biological oxidation and involve transfer of hydrogen atoms or electrons from one substrate to another.

Examples are oxidases, dehydrogenases, peroxidase and catalase.

Transferases: They bring about transfer of certain groups from one organic compound to another. Examples are as follows:

1. *Transaminases:* They effect the transfer of amino groups of certain amino acids to certain keto acids.
2. *Transacylases:* They effect the transfer of acyl and acetyl groups.
3. *Transpeptidases:* They effect the transfer of amino acids or peptides from one peptide to another.

Hydrolases: These enzymes catalyse hydrolysis of substrates having large molecular weight. They bring about hydrolysis, i.e. they add water to the substrates and simultaneously break them.

For example:

1. Carbohydrases split carbohydrates.
2. Esterases split ester linkages.
3. Proteases split peptide linkages.

Lyases: These enzymes catalyse the addition or removal of some chemical group of a substrate by mechanisms other than hydrolysis, oxidation or reduction. They differ from transferases in that the chemical group liberated is not merely transferred from one substrate to another but is liberated in the free state. Depending on the nature of the chemical groups added or removed, lyases are further classified as follows:

1. *Dehydratases:* These enzymes catalyse the reversible removal and addition of a molecule of H_2O from or to their respective substrates. For example:
   - Enolase catalyses

$$\text{2-phosphoglycerate} \underset{+H_2O}{\overset{-H_2O}{\rightleftharpoons}} \text{phosphoenolpyruvate}$$

   - Fumarase catalyses

$$\text{fumarate} \underset{-H_2O}{\overset{+H_2O}{\rightleftharpoons}} \text{malate}$$

2. *Desulphydrases:* These enzymes catalyse the removal of H_2S with pyridoxal phosphate as the coenzyme. For example:
   - Cysteine desulphydrase catalyses

$$\text{cysteine} \xrightarrow{-H_2S} \text{pyruvic acid} + NH_3$$

   - Homocysteine desulphydrase catalyses

$$\text{homocysteine} \xrightarrow{-H_2S} \alpha - \text{ketobutyrate} + NH_3$$

3. *Decarboxylase:* This enzyme catalyses the removal of CO_2 from amino acids to form the corresponding amines and from keto acids to form aldehydes. For example:
   - Dopa decarboxylase catalyses

$$\text{dopa} \longrightarrow \text{dopamine} + CO_2$$

   - Pyruvate decarboxylase catalyses

$$\text{pyruvate} \longrightarrow \text{acetaldehyde} + CO_2$$

Isomerases: These are enzymes which catalyse the interconversion of isomers. For example:

1. Epimerase catalyses

$$\text{L-alanine} \rightleftharpoons \text{D-alanine}$$

2. Maleylacetoacetate isomerase catalyses

$$\text{maleylacetoacetate} \rightleftharpoons \text{fumaryl acetoacetate}$$

3. Triose phosphate isomerase catalyses

$$\text{D-glyceraldehyde-3-phosphate} \rightleftharpoons \text{dihydroxyacetone phosphate.}$$

Ligases: These are enzymes which catalyse the linking together of two compounds, coupled with activation with ATP or GTP. Examples are as follows:

1. Acyl-CoA ligase:

$$\text{Fatty acid} + \text{ATP} + \text{CoA} \rightleftharpoons \text{acyl-CoA} + \text{AMP} + \text{PP}$$

2. Succinyl-CoA ligase:

$$\text{Succinate} + \text{GTP} + \text{CoA} \rightleftharpoons \text{succinyl-CoA} + \text{GDP} + \text{Pi}$$

MECHANISM OF ENZYME ACTION

Enzyme Substrate Combination

The compound on which the enzyme acts is called the substrate. Enzymes, being proteins, have on their surface reactive sites into which the substrates can fit. All enzymatic reactions involve a temporary union of the substrate with the enzymes. The substrate just fits on the reactive site, to form the 'enzyme substrate complex', which is also referred to as the 'Michaelis' complex. After this, some sort of activation of the substrate takes place while it is still situated on the enzyme surface. This combination is called the 'activated complex' (**Fig. 4.1**). The combination weakens the structure of the substrate and the bond in the substrate is strained to the point of rupture. When the bond ruptures, the reaction products are liberated into the solution and the original enzyme molecule is

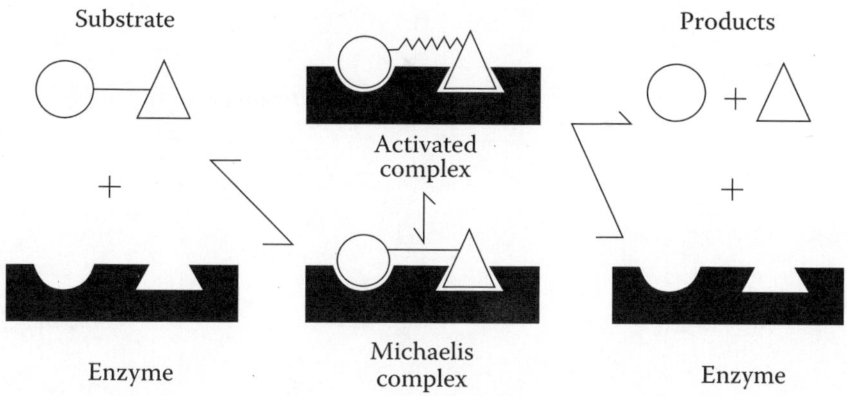

Figure 4.1 Mechanism of enzyme action.

regenerated. The enzyme molecule can now catalyse fresh substrate molecules and repeat the process. The reaction can be written as follows:

$$\text{Enzyme + substrate complex} \rightleftharpoons \text{Enzyme substrate complex. (`Michaelis' complex)}$$

$$\text{Enzyme substrate complex} \longrightarrow \text{Activated complex.}$$

$$\text{Activated complex} \rightleftharpoons \text{Enzyme + products of enzyme action.}$$

Coenzymes

Many enzymes require for their action the presence of certain non-protein compounds which help in accelerating the enzyme action. In contrast to enzymes, these are heat stable and are of smaller molecular weight and are therefore dialysable. These are called **coenzymes** or **prosthetic groups**, depending upon the proximity of their attachment to the enzyme protein. If the activator is firmly attached to the enzyme protein, it is called a prosthetic group. Conjugated proteins are examples of this kind. On the other hand, if the non-protein compounds are not firmly attached to the enzyme protein but exist in a free state in the solution contacting the enzyme protein only at the instant of enzyme action, they are called **coenzymes.** The nature of attachment in the case of prosthetic group and coenzyme is illustrated in **Figure 4.2**.

The entire enzyme system consisting of the enzyme protein and the coenzyme or prosthetic group is called the 'holoenzyme' and the protein portion is sometimes called 'apoenzyme'.

Coenzymes are necessary for enzyme action because they accelerate enzyme action. They are heat-stable, dialysable, non-protein compounds. Most of them are derivatives of vitamin B complex. Coenzymes are usually not firmly attached to the enzyme protein, but exist in the free state in the solution, contacting the enzyme protein only at the instant of enzyme action. Many of the coenzymes act as intermediate carriers of hydrogen atoms in the biological oxidation reduction reactions.

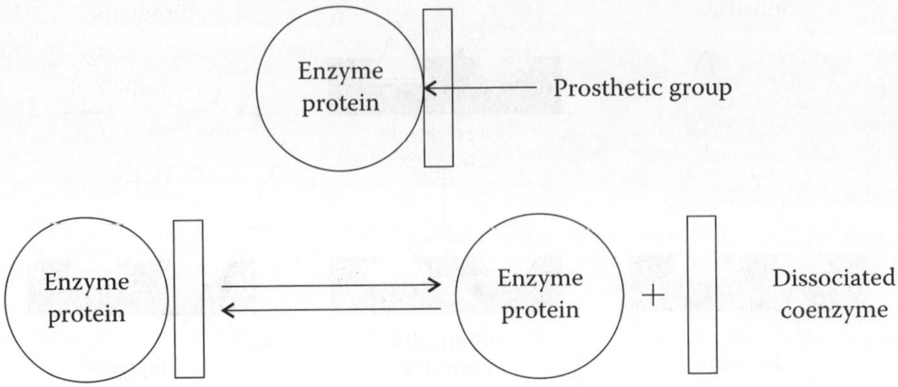

Figure 4.2 Prosthetic group and coenzyme.

Examples of coenzymes are as follows:

1. (a) Thiamine pyrophosphate (TPP)

   (b) Lipothiamide pyrophosphate (LTPP)

   Both are derivatives of thiamine. They act as cocarboxylase or codecarboxylase in the metabolic reactions, particularly of carbohydrates.
2. (a) Diphosphopyridine nucleotide (DPN), now known as nicotinamide adenine dinucleotide (NAD)

   (b) Triphosphopyridine nucleotide (TPN), now known as nicotinamide adenine dinucleotide phosphate (NADP)

   These are derivatives of nicotinic acid. They act as coenzymes of dehydrogenases and function as hydrogen acceptors and donors in biological oxidation–reduction reactions.
3. (a) Flavin mononucleotide (FMN)

   (b) Flavin adenine dinucleotide (FAD)

   These are derivatives of riboflavin. They act as coenzymes to dehydrogenases and function as carriers of hydrogen atoms from one substrate to another in biological oxidation reactions.
4. *Pyridoxal phosphate:* This is the derivative of pyridoxine. It is the coenzyme of decarboxylases and transaminases.
5. Biotin acts as a coenzyme for carboxylase, in carboxylation reactions, i.e. CO_2 fixation. For example, carboxylation of acetyl-CoA to malonyl-CoA is the initial reaction involving synthesis of fatty acids.
6. Coenzyme A, also known as co-acetylase, is the derivative of pantothenic acid. It is the coenzyme for condensing enzymes and functions in the transfer of acyl groups in the fatty acid oxidation reactions.
7. Tetrahydrofolic acid (FH_4) is the derivative of folic acid. It acts as a coenzyme in reactions involving the transfer and utilisation of the formyl groups (one carbon unit).
8. Vitamin B_{12} (cobamide) is the cofactor in transmethylation reactions.

9. Haem (iron protoporphyrin) is the prosthetic group of catalases, peroxidases and cytochrome oxidase.
10. *Uridine derivatives:* Uridine disphosphate glucose (UDPG) and uridine diphosphate galactose (UDP Gal) act as coenzymes in reactions involving epimerisation of galactose and glucose.

    Uridine diphosphate glucuronic acid (UDP gluc) serves as a source of active glucuronide in the formation of bilirubin glucuronide.
11. *ATP and related compounds:* These compounds act as coenzymes in transphosphorylation reactions.
12. *Specific ion activators:* It is found that specific inorganic ions are necessary for certain reactions. Cobalt, Mn, Mg and Zn ions are necessary for the action of various peptide-splitting enzymes.

Proenzymes (enzyme precursors): Certain enzymes are synthesised in an inactive state, in which condition they are known as zymogens. Proenzymes are active agents, which convert certain enzymes secreted in the inactive form to the active form. If the active agent is inorganic, it is called activator, and if it is organic it is called kinase. For example:

$$\text{Pepsinogen} \xrightarrow[\text{Activator}]{\text{HCl}} \text{Pepsin (active)}$$

$$\text{Trypsinogen} \xrightarrow[\text{Kinase}]{\text{Enterokinase}} \text{Trypsin (active)}$$

Lysosomal enzymes: Lysosomes are minute structures, approximately of the size of mitochondria, located within the cytoplasm of all cells. Some have described that they resemble small bags filled with a mixture of powerful digestive enzymes which hydrolyse fats, proteins and nucleic acids. As long as the lipoprotein membrane of the lysosomes remains intact, the enzymes inside the lysosomes confine to the digestion of substances that enter the lysosome. But once the membrane ruptures, the enzymes escape into the cytoplasm which gets rapidly digested leading to dissolution of the cell.

Coenzyme Q (Ubiquinone): This represents an important coenzyme located in mitochondria, where it functions as an electron transport agent. It has quinone in its structure, with a number of isoprene side chains. It is the coenzyme derivative of vitamin K.

Factors Influencing Enzyme Action

The velocity of enzyme-catalysed reactions is influenced by certain factors, which are as follows:

1. Temperature
2. Hydrogen ion concentration
3. Concentration of enzyme
4. Concentration of substrate
5. State of oxidation of enzyme
6. Effect of light and radiation
7. Inhibitors and inactivators

Temperature: The rate of enzyme action increases with an increase of temperature only up to 40°C. The temperature at which the enzyme action is maximum is called the **optimum temperature**. After this point, the enzymes being protein in nature get denatured and the rate of enzyme action comes down (**Fig. 4.3**).

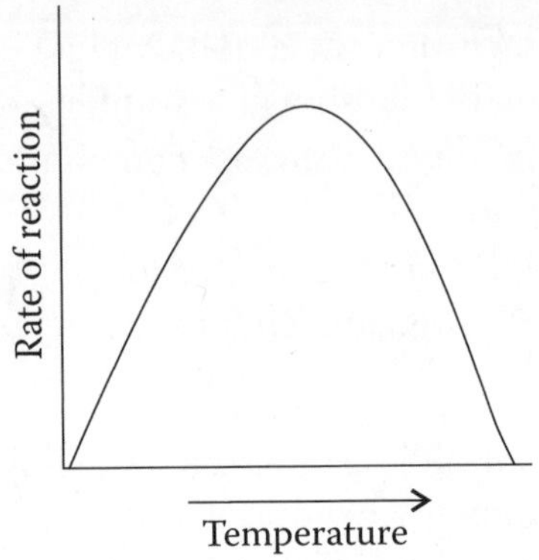

Figure 4.3 Effect of temperature.

Hydrogen ion concentration: The rate of enzyme action increases steadily with an increase in the H^+ ion concentration up to a certain pH where the enzyme action is maximum. This pH is called the **optimum pH**. An increase in H^+ ion concentration beyond this peak point will destroy the enzymes because of their protein nature and bring down the enzyme action (**Fig. 4.4**).

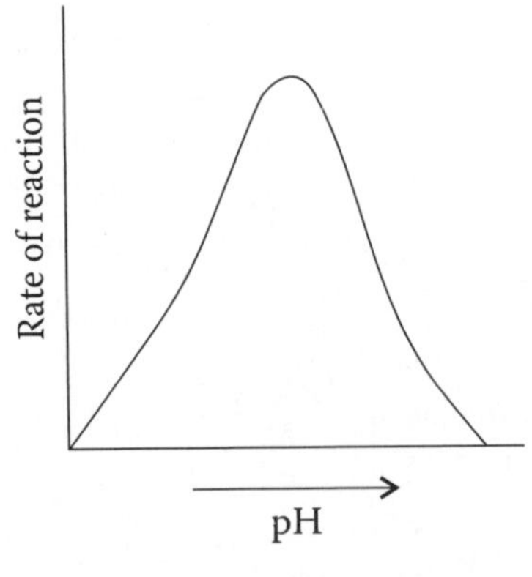

Figure 4.4 Effect of pH.

Concentration of enzyme: When other factors influencing the enzyme reaction remain constant, the velocity of enzyme action increases proportionately to the concentration of enzyme. This being the general rule, it is also possible that the rate of certain enzymatic reactions may be limited at a point where the substrate particles are saturated with enzymes, and a further increase in the concentration of enzyme will have no effect on the rate of enzyme action (**Fig. 4.5**).

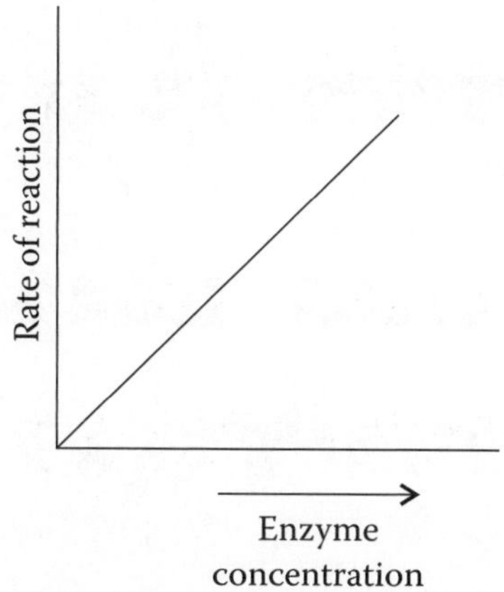

Figure 4.5 Effect of enzyme concentration.

Concentration of substrate: Keeping the concentration of enzyme fixed, the rate of reaction increases proportionately to the concentration of the substrate up to a point beyond which an increase in substrate concentration will not cause a further increase in the rate of the reaction. This is again due to the increasing saturation of the active sites of the enzymes with the substrate molecules, which block further action. The curve is first linear and later assumes a hyperbolic pattern (**Fig. 4.6**).

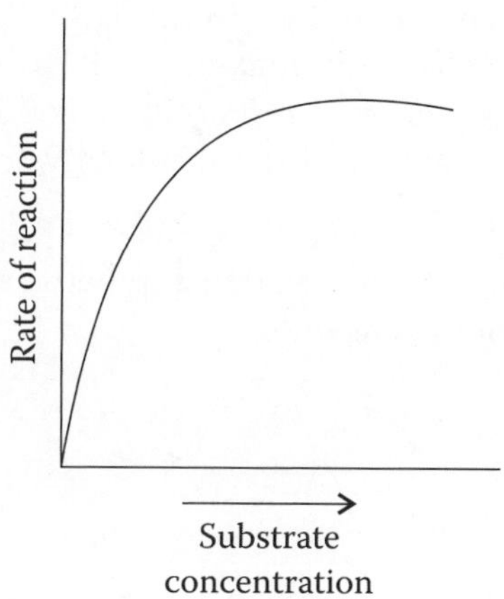

Figure 4.6 Effect of substrate concentration.

Michaelis–Menten's hypothesis: This situation correlating the effect of substrate concentration [S] on the initial velocity υ (velocity of enzyme action when the concentration of the substrate is very low) and maximum velocity V may be explained as follows:

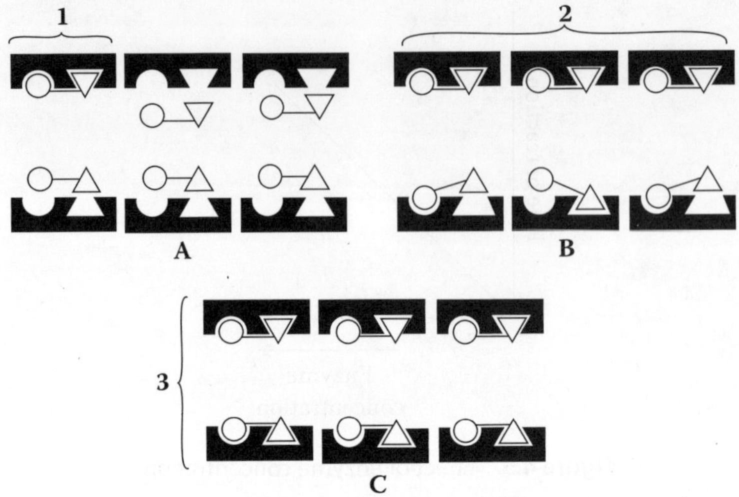

Figure 4.7 Effect of substrate concentration on the velocity of enzyme action.

In **Figure 4.7**, **A** represents six enzyme molecules with active sites, ready to combine with substrate molecules to form enzyme substrate complex. The enzyme action has just started, and one enzyme molecule has combined with a substrate molecule. This initial event is represented by 1 in **Figure 4.7A**.

In **Figure 4.7B**, the enzyme action is in progress. Three out of six enzyme molecules hold substrate molecules on their active sites. In this case, the velocity of enzyme reaction υ corresponds to exactly one-half of the maximal velocity V and the enzyme substrate saturation is exactly half. This situation is represented as 2 in **Figure 4.7B**. The substrate concentration which produces one-half of the maximal velocity is known as K_m value or **Michaelis constant** (**Fig. 4.7B**).

Figure 4.8 graphically represents the relationship between the substrate concentration and the half maximal velocity of the enzyme.

V = Maximal velocity

S = Substrate concentration

K_m = Michaelis constant

$\frac{V}{2} = \frac{1}{2}$ = Maximal velocity

If during enzyme reaction the substrate concentration [S] is increased, the reaction of formation of the maximum amount of enzyme substrate complex will be pushed to the right (**Fig. 4.8A** and **B**).

$$E + S \rightleftharpoons ES$$

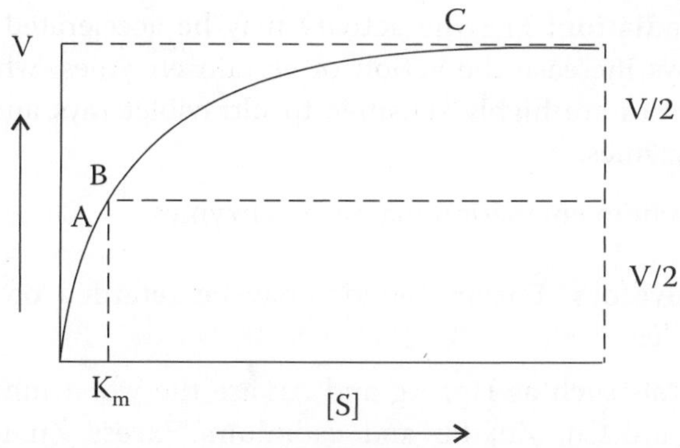

Figure 4.8 Graphic representation of the relationship between substrate concentration and velocity of enzyme action.

In **Figure 4.7C**, all the six enzyme molecules have combined with substrate molecules so that a further increase in substrate concentration will not increase the velocity of reaction beyond the maximal velocity V. This is represented by 3 in **Figure 4.7**.

A hypothesis is derived from these findings, which explains a general relationship between the concentration of substrate and the rate of enzyme action. This hypothesis is known as Michaelis–Menten's hypothesis; it is expressed as

$$\upsilon = \frac{V[S]}{K_m + [S]}$$

Here, υ represents the velocity of enzyme action, V represents the maximum velocity, S is the substrate concentration and K_m is the Michaelis constant which represents the substrate concentration, at half maximal velocity.

Three important derivations follow the hypothesis:

1. When the substrate concentration is so low as to produce half maximal velocity, i.e. K_m value, the velocity υ depends upon the substrate concentration [S] and increases as [S] increases. This may be represented as $\upsilon \approx K[S]$. ≈ means approximately equal to.
2. When the substrate concentration [S] is much greater than K_m, the velocity υ also increases till it reaches the maximal velocity V. This may be represented as $\upsilon = V$.
3. When the substrate concentration [S] is equal to the K_m value, the observed velocity is equal to half the maximal velocity (K_m). This may be represented as $\upsilon = \frac{V}{2}$.

Since the K_m value represents the substrate concentration when the velocity is half maximal, it gives an indication as to how much substrate should be used.

State of oxidation of enzyme: Many enzymes, for example dehydrogenases, contain sulphydryl groups (SH) which are essential for enzyme activity. When such enzymes come into contact with mild oxidising agents, oxygen or air, the SH groups are oxidised to disulphide groups (S-S) resulting in loss of enzyme activity. Full activity may be restored by adding reduced glutathione and cysteine because they contain SH groups.

Effect of light and radiation: Enzyme activity may be accelerated or retarded by light rays. Red and blue rays increase the action of certain enzymes, while radiation has the opposite action. Enzymes are highly sensitive to ultraviolet rays and X-rays. They effect denaturation of the enzymes.

β- and γ-rays and radium emanation inactivate enzymes.

Inhibitors and inactivators: Enzyme action may be retarded or inhibited by certain substances. For example:

1. Salts of heavy metals such as Hg, Ag and Au are the worst inhibitors. Less effective inhibiting metals are Cu, Zn, Pb and cadmium. Excess Zn ions inhibit carbonic anhydrase. Mg^{++} and Ag^{++} ions inhibit myosin.
2. Oxidising agents such as iodine, HNO_3 and H_2O_2 inactivate enzymes.
3. Iodoacetic acid and sodium arsenite inhibit enzyme action by reacting with the active sulphydryl groups (SH) of certain enzymes.
4. Cyanides and carbon monoxide react with the metal in iron porphyrin of the respiratory enzymes and block the enzyme action.

Enzyme Inhibition

Valuable information regarding the mechanism and pathway of enzyme catalysis has been obtained from the study of enzyme inhibition.

Reversible Enzyme Inhibition

There are three types of reversible enzyme inhibition. They are as follows:

1. Competitive
2. Non-competitive
3. Uncompetitive

In reversible inhibition, the inhibitor participates in a rapidly established and easily reversible combination with the enzyme or enzyme substrate complex.

Competitive inhibition: Most drugs act by inhibiting the enzymes responsible for the growth and multiplication of micro-organisms. The drugs have chemical structure closely resembling that of the substrate or the product of reaction and therefore compete with the substrate, to bind with the enzyme reversibly, at its active site forming enzyme inhibitor complex (EI) instead of enzyme substrate complex (ES).

$$E + S \rightleftharpoons ES \rightleftharpoons E + P$$

$$E + I \rightleftharpoons EI$$

EI cannot yield product and the enzyme reaction results in the formation of a non-productive complex. The overall rate of the enzyme reaction is retarded. However, EI dissociates and releases the enzyme. It can then bind to a substrate if it is present or if excess substrate is added. Thus, inhibition is reversed by the addition of substrate and the inhibitor is dislodged from the enzyme. This is *competitive inhibition.*

Two well-known examples of competitive inhibitors are considered here.

- *Succinate dehydrogenase*: Succinate dehydrogenase catalyses the formation of fumaric acid from succinic acid by removal of one hydrogen atom from each α-carbon atom of succinic acid. Malonate (I), an inhibitor having structure similar to succinate, competes with succinate to bind with succinic dehydrogenase and forms EI. This cannot be dehydrogenated as there is no way to remove even one H atom from the single α-carbon of malonate. Oxalic acid and glutaric acid can also inhibit succinic dehydrogenase as they have structure similar to succinic acid.

CH_2COOH	HCCOOH	COOH	COOH	CH_2COOH
|	‖	|	|	|
CH_2COOH	HCCOOH	CH_2	COOH	CH_2
		|		|
		COOH		CH_2COOH
Succinic acid	**Fumaric acid**	**Malonic acid**	**Oxalic acid**	**Glutaric acid**

- *Allopurinol*: Another example of a competitive inhibitor is allopurinol. Allopurinol is used therapeutically in the treatment of gout to control the high uric acid level in serum and tissues.

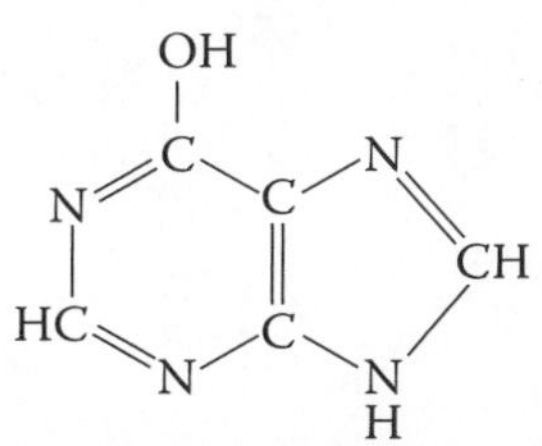

Hypoxanthine

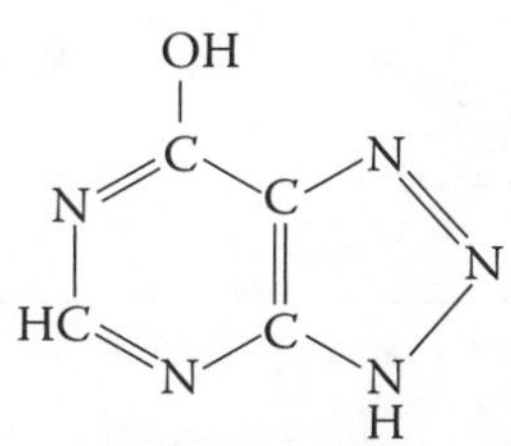

Allopurinol

Allopurinol which resembles hypoxanthine in structure competes with hypoxanthine and inhibits enzyme xanthine oxidase in the conversion of hypoxanthine to uric acid and thus reduces the formation of uric acid.

Non-competitive inhibition: This is another kind of reversible inhibition. In non-competitive inhibition, the inhibitors do not bind at the same site on the enzyme as the substrate. They bind at different sites on the enzyme molecule and often deform the enzyme. The non-competitive inhibitor can react with either free enzyme or the enzyme substrate complex interfering with the action of both.

$$E + I \rightleftharpoons EI$$

$$ES + I \rightleftharpoons ESI$$

The reaction with the enzyme and ES yields two inactive forms—EI and ESI. Increasing the substrate concentration cannot reverse the inhibition.

Uncompetitive inhibition: This is also a form of reversible inhibition. It is neither competitive nor non-competitive but the inhibitor binds only to ES complex instead of enzyme to give an inactive enzyme substrate inhibition complex and thus causes inhibition. The inhibition is not reversed by increasing substrate concentration.

$$ES + I \rightleftharpoons ESI$$

Allosteric Inhibition

An enzyme may have one or more binding sites other than the catalytically active site. The catalytically active site is for the substrate. The other site referred to as the 'allosteric site' is for the modifier substance, also referred to as the 'effector'. The catalytic site and the allosteric site are distinct and are separated spatially on the enzyme molecule. When the effector is bound to the allosteric site, it can cause conformational changes at the binding site of the substrate and prevent the normal binding of the substrate to the enzyme (**Fig. 4.9**). The effect is similar to competitive inhibition, as the binding of the substrate is prevented by the inhibitor. In some cases, there may not be any conformational changes and then the substrate binding proceeds in the usual way. Here, it behaves like a non-competitive inhibitor.

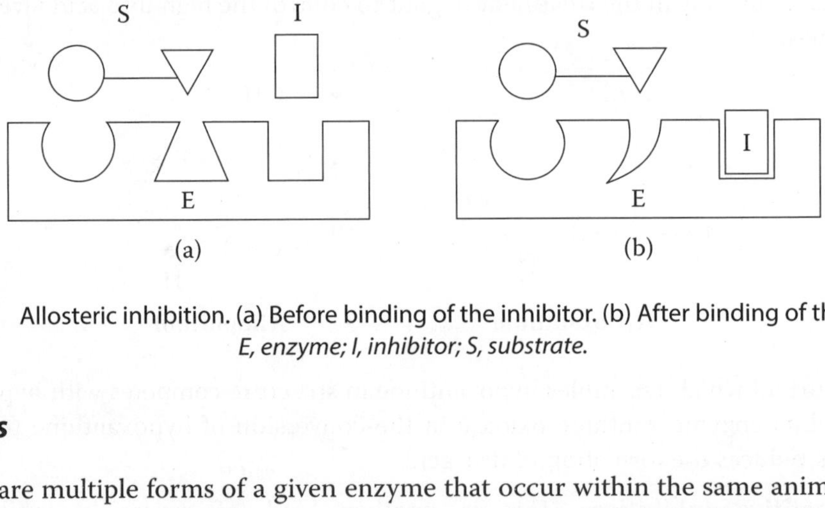

Figure 4.9 Allosteric inhibition. (a) Before binding of the inhibitor. (b) After binding of the inhibitor. *E, enzyme; I, inhibitor; S, substrate.*

Isozymes

Isozymes are multiple forms of a given enzyme that occur within the same animal species. They have different physical properties and chemical characteristics but perform similar catalytic activity. Such multiple forms exhibit variation in charges and can be separated and detected by electrophoresis of cell extracts. They are coded by different genes and therefore differ in amino acid composition and in their isoelectric pH values. They have different inmunological behaviour.

Lactic dehydrogenase (LDH), one of the earliest enzymes studied, occurs as five different isozymes in tissues. They catalyse the same reaction.

$$\text{Lactate} + \text{NAD} \rightleftharpoons \text{Pyruvate} + \text{NADH} + H^{+}$$

All five isozymes have the same molecular weight and all contain four polypeptide chains, each of the same molecular weight. The five isozymes consist of five different combinations of two different kinds of polypeptide chains, designated M and H. One kind of polypeptide chain is found predominantly in heart muscle and this is named H subunit. It has four identical H chains and is designated H_4. The other kind of polypeptide chain predominates in skeletal muscle and is named M subunit. It has four identical M chains and is designated M_4. The other three isozymes have the composition of M_3H, M_2H2 and MH_3.

ENZYMES OF CLINICAL INTEREST

Blood contains several enzymes of which some are of clinical significance. With the exception of few enzymes which are directly concerned with the mechanism of coagulation, others have no direct metabolic function in blood but find their place in blood due to overflow from their sites of origin from where they are released after damage to the cells. Under normal conditions, the concentration of the enzymes present in blood is very low. But the concentration of these enzymes is increased in certain diseases involving damage to the cells of vital organs from where they originate, and therefore quantitative estimation of these enzymes in plasma would serve as an important index in the diagnosis of the clinical conditions. Such enzymes of plasma which are of clinical interest are discussed in this section. They are as follows:

1. Amylase
2. Lipase
3. Trypsin
4. Cholinesterase
5. Phosphatases
    - Alkaline
    - Acid
6. Transaminases
7. Lactate dehydrogenase
8. Creatine kinase
9. Glucose-6-phosphate dehydrogenase
10. Isocitrate dehydrogenase
11. Lysozyme

Amylase: This enzyme originates mostly from the pancreas, and a small amount is secreted by parotid glands. In normal plasma, it is present only in a small amount. Its concentration in plasma is markedly increased in the early stages of acute pancreatitis which is associated with acute destruction of pancreatic tissues. This permits escape of pancreatic amylase in the bloodstream. Acute pancreatitis is a rare condition, which sets in suddenly with severe abdominal pain and high fever. It may prove fatal if not attended to promptly, and this is mostly due to the peritonitis caused by pancreatic juice escaping into the peritoneum. Obstruction of the pancreatic duct will also produce a similar situation resulting in an increased level of amylase in plasma. Serum amylase may be increased in parotitis too.

Lipase: This enzyme originates from pancreas and its level in plasma is increased along with amylase in acute pancreatitis and pancreatic duct obstruction. The lipase of pancreatic juice has a deleterious effect on the fat of the omentum, resulting in fat necrosis and abscess formation.

Trypsin: An increased level of trypsin in plasma occurs during acute stages of pancreatitis along with amylase and lipase. It has been found that the level of plasma trypsin is a more sensitive and reliable index of pancreatic disease than either plasma amylase or lipase.

Cholinesterase: The plasma cholinesterase originates mainly in the liver. Its level in plasma is decreased in liver diseases and malnutrition. It has been found that certain drugs, particularly the alkyl fluorophosphates used in the treatment of myasthenia gravis, depress the activity of cholinesterase to a considerable extent. The cholinesterase level is increased in renal diseases.

Phosphatases: These enzymes comprise a large group of hydrolysing enzymes involved in the process of digestion and intermediary metabolism. They are present in blood as alkaline phosphatase and acid phosphatase.

1. ***Alkaline phosphatase*** has an optimum pH of about 9 and is therefore known as alkaline phosphatase. It is formed mainly in the bones, especially by the osteoblasts, but some are formed in the liver also. Because of its osteoblastic origin, the enzyme content in the plasma is increased in skeletal diseases which show a high osteoblastic activity and this is accompanied by improper mineralisation as in the case of osteomalacia, rickets, hyperparathyroidism and Paget's disease. The concentration of plasma alkaline phosphatase is also increased in biliary obstruction as in obstructive jaundice. This occurs most probably due to impairment of biliary excretion, when the enzyme escapes into the lymphatics and then into the bloodstream. The enzyme level is decreased in a hereditary condition called hypophosphatasia, which is characterised by defective skeletal mineralisation.

   Alkaline phosphatase favours mineralisation of bones by mobilising PO_4^- ions and Ca^{++} ions from the blood and depositing them on the surface of the bones.

2. ***Acid phosphatase*** has an optimum pH of 4.9. Normal plasma contains a very small amount of acid phosphatase. It is present in the liver, red cells and spleen in small amounts. It is interesting to note that this enzyme is formed mainly by mature prostatic epithelial cells from where it passes into the prostatic secretion. For this reason, it has been found that the activity of acid phosphatase in adult prostate is 100 times more than in other tissues. But the activity in pre-adolescent boys is negligible as it is not formed by immature prostatic cells. The clinical significance of serum acid phosphatase lies in the diagnosis of cancer of prostate, especially metastatic stage, when the enzyme escapes into the bloodstream and shows increased activity.

Transaminases: These enzymes belong to the group of transferases. Two transaminases present in serum are of clinical interest. They are as follows:

1. ***Aspartate amino transferase (AST)/Serum glutamic oxaloacetic transaminase (SGOT):*** Normal serum contains only a small amount of GOT. It is present in abundance in cardiac muscles. It is also found in skeletal muscles. The SGOT level increases markedly in conditions of extensive damage to muscles, especially cardiac muscles, when the GOT released from the damaged muscle escapes into the bloodstream. Since cardiac muscle is rich in GOT, myocardial infarction is followed by a rapid increase in the SGOT level. Estimation of SGOT is widely sought for to confirm the diagnosis of myocardial infarction. GOT acts by catalysing the transfer of

amino group of the aspartic acid to α-ketoglutaric acid, to form oxaloacetic acid and glutamic acid.

$$\text{Aspartic acid} + \alpha\text{-Ketoglutaric acid} \rightleftharpoons \text{Oxaloacetic acid} + \text{Glutamic acid.}$$

2. ***Alanine amino transferase (ALT)/Serum glutamic pyruvate transaminase (SGPT):*** Normal serum contains only a small amount of GPT. Liver tissue is rich in GPT. On account of this, the SGPT level increases markedly in patients with acute hepatic disease, where liver cells are damaged. SGPT is considered a more specific index of hepatocellular damage. GPT acts by catalysing the transfer of the amino group from alanine to α-ketoglutaric acid to form pyruvic acid and glutamic acid:

$$\text{Alanine} + \alpha\text{-Ketoglutaric acid} \rightleftharpoons \text{Pyruvic acid} + \text{Glutamic acid.}$$

Lactate dehydrogenase (LDH): This enzyme has gained much clinical interest recently, and measurement of its activity in blood is considered useful in the diagnosis of certain pathological conditions. It is present in high concentration in the heart, liver, kidneys, skeletal muscles and erythrocytes. The serum LDH level increases in patients with leukaemia, generalised cancer and acute hepatitis. LDH acts by catalysing the reversible conversion of pyruvic acid to lactic acid. An interesting point about this enzyme is that it exists in five distinct forms, and these are called isoenzymes or isozymes. It has been found that cardiac muscle is rich in one form of LDH, i.e. isozyme LDH_1. The concentration of this isoenzyme has been found to increase rapidly within 24 hours following the onset of myocardial infarction and reach a normal value after a week. Therefore, measurement of the serum isozyme pattern of LDH during the course of myocardial infarction is useful in the diagnosis and prognosis of the disease. Similarly, concentration of isozyme 5 of LDH is found high in liver diseases. The five isoenzymes of serum LDH can be recognised by subjecting the serum to electrophoresis. LDH_1, being the fastest moving fraction, can be recognised as the farthest band while LDH_5, the slowest moving fraction, can be seen nearer the point of application of the serum. (Refer to page 92.)

Creatine kinase (CK): This enzyme is present in myocardium and skeletal muscles. The serum CK level is raised in early myocardial infarction and in progressive muscular dystrophy.

Glucose-6-phosphate dehydrogenase (G-6-P-D): This enzyme is present in erythrocytes. An adequate concentration is essential to initiate a complex metabolism which yields reduced glutathione, which, in turn, is necessary for the maintenance of the integrity of the erythrocytes. It has been observed that low levels of glutathione are associated with hereditary deficiency of G-6-P-D in erythrocytes. Low concentration of G-6-P-D in erythrocytes is found to lead to an increased susceptibility of the erythrocytes to haemolysis after the ingestion of drugs such as sulphonamides, acetanilide, naphthalein and antimalarial drugs.

Isocitrate dehydrogenase (IDH): This enzyme is distributed in all tissues. It is an enzyme of the Krebs cycle. Its level in serum is raised in hepatic diseases showing liver cell damage, as in infective hepatitis and malignancy in liver. Its level is normal in myocardial infarction.

Lysozyme: This enzyme is present in plants and animals. In humans it is widely distributed, being present in tears, nasal secretion, saliva, synovial fluid, plasma and gastric juice. A fairly high amount of the enzyme is produced by the intestinal mucosa and excreted in the faeces.

The physiological function of lysozyme is not clear. It has been observed that the enzyme acts on the cell wall of many bacteria and hydrolyses the acetyl aminopolysaccharides contained in the cell wall. It is assumed that the bacteriolytic action of the enzyme which is present in high concentration in tears, mucous membrane, etc., helps in protecting the body against bacteria that are inhaled or ingested with food.

Antienzyme: Extracts of intestinal parasites such as *Ascaris* contain substances called antienzymes, which inhibit the action of digestive enzymes—pepsin and trypsin. This is probably the reason why the worm escapes digestion in the intestines. The antienzymes which are protein in nature are also found in pancreas and raw egg white.

5

CHAPTER

Vitamins

Chapter Outline

- Fat-Soluble Vitamins
- Water-Soluble Vitamins
- Antivitamins

Lind in 1753 proved that **scurvy**, a dreadful disease among sailors, could be cured by giving them oranges and lemons to eat. Eijkman in 1867 found that a disabling disease named **beriberi** could be cured by administration of rice polishings. Hopkins in a series of experiments carried out during the period 1907–1912 found that animals maintained on purified carbohydrate, protein, fat and minerals failed to grow, became ill in a short time and died. But when the purified diet was supplemented by small quantities of milk, the animals maintained growth. He observed that certain accessory factors found in natural products were required in small amounts to keep the animals from running into states of deficiency. In 1911, Funk led the hypothesis that these accessory food factors are necessary for the health and growth of the experimental animals, and in their absence they developed deficiency diseases such as Beriberi and Scurvy. He named them vitamins. In 1915, McCollum and Davis showed that some vitamins were fat soluble and some were water soluble but both were required as accessory food factors.

Vitamins are not related chemically, but are considered as a group because of the similarity in their functions. Vitamins, besides being accessory food factors, are essential for metabolic reactions and form coenzymes to many enzyme systems. Most of the vitamins, especially the members of the B complex group, are synthesised in considerable amounts by the bacterial flora in man.

The vitamins were named one after another as they were discovered as A B C D and so on, and each had a different chemical nature. The nature of solubility was made use of in classifying them into two groups, namely (i) fat-soluble vitamins, closely associated with the lipids of naturally occurring food, which include vitamins A, D, E and K, and (ii) water-soluble vitamins, which include vitamins of B complex group and vitamin C.

FAT-SOLUBLE VITAMINS

Vitamin A (Retinol)

Vitamin A is derived from certain pigments called **carotenoids** which are widely distributed in nature. They are known as provitamins A.

Provitamins A include four compounds, which are as follows:

1. α-Carotene
2. β-Carotene
3. γ-Carotene
4. Cryptoxanthin

The first three are hydrocarbons ($C_{40}H_{56}$) and the fourth is an alcohol derivative of β-carotene (monohydroxy-β-carotene).

Chemistry—structure of Vitamin A (Fig. 5.1): Vitamin A is closely related to β-carotene, from which it is derived. The structures of β-carotene and Vitamin A are given below for comparison:

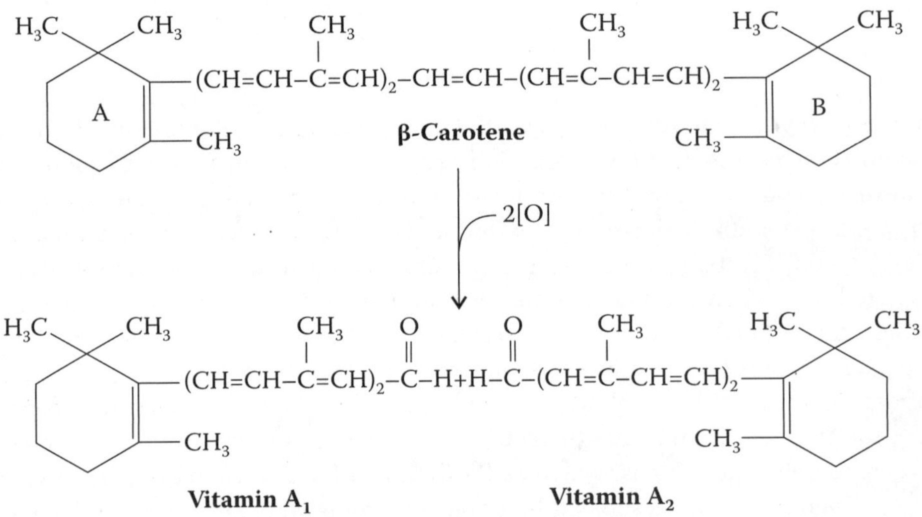

Figure 5.1 Structure of Vitamin A.

Note that β-carotene is a symmetrical molecule containing two terminal β-ionone rings (A and B) at either ends, connected by a long hydrocarbon chain, containing 18 carbon atoms. The hydrocarbon chain has nine conjugated double bonds. The entire structure of β-carotene ($C_{40}H_{56}$) contains 40 carbon atoms. The structure of vitamin A ($C_{20}H_{29}OH$) differs from β-carotene in that it forms half of the structure of a β-carotene molecule. It contains 20 carbon atoms and only one β-ionone ring. It has five conjugated double bonds. Vitamin A molecule has a terminal primary alcohol group whereas β-carotene does not possess an alcohol group. Thus, two molecules of vitamin A are obtained from one molecule of β-carotene, and this takes place by oxidative scission of a molecule of β-carotene, exactly in the middle of the molecule. The central double bond where the splitting takes place is oxidised to form an aldehyde which is further reduced to form alcohol. Thus, each molecule of vitamin A has a terminal primary alcohol group. Two forms of vitamin A occur in nature. They are vitamin A_1 and vitamin A_2. There is another form known as neovitamin A which is a stereoisomer of vitamin A_1. Vitamin A_2 differs from vitamin A_1 in certain aspects.

1. **Structural form:** Vitamin A_2 has an additional unsaturated linkage in the β-ionone ring, between carbon atoms 3 and 4.
2. **Biological activity:** Vitamin A_2 has only 40% of biological activity as that of vitamin A_1, whereas neovitamin A which is the stereoisomer of vitamin A_1 has about 70–80% of biological activity of vitamin A.

Properties:

1. Vitamin A and the provitamins are insoluble in water and are soluble in most fat solvents.
2. Both provitamins and vitamin A are destroyed by exposure to light and oxidation. They are however protected from being destroyed by the presence of antioxidants, for example vitamin E.
3. Though vitamin A and provitamins are not thermolabile, heat accelerates their destruction in the presence of oxygen.
4. Vitamin A content of food is considerably lowered by dehydration, but is not affected by canning or freezing.
5. Vitamin A, being an alcohol, forms esters. It can be oxidised to form an aldehyde. 'Retinene', which is an intermediate in the rhodopsin cycle, is vitamin A aldehyde.
6. *Spectral absorption (Carr-Price test):* When vitamin A in anhydrous solvents (like chloroform) is treated with antimony trichloride, a blue colour develops. This test is known as Carr-Price test and is made use of in the quantitative estimation of vitamin A. When this coloured solution is observed spectroscopically, characteristic absorption bands at different wavelengths are observed as indicated below. β-carotene gives a green colour instead of blue.

   Vitamin A_1: 620 mμ

   Vitamin A_2: 693 mμ

   β-carotene: 590 mμ

Absorption and metabolism: Vitamin A exists as long-chain, fatty acid esters of retinol in the diet of animal products. It is present in the form of β-carotene in vegetables. The retinol esters are hydrolysed in the intestinal lumen and absorbed as retinol. The β-carotene is split oxidatively in the middle of its long hydrocarbon chain by the enzyme β-carotene dioxygenase to form two molecules of **retinal** (retinaldehyde). In the intestinal mucosa, the retinal is reduced by a specific reductase to form retinol. Some retinal is oxidised to **retinoic acid** in the intestines. The retinoic acid formed is absorbed through the portal system and metabolised to oxidation products and excreted in urine and bile. The absorbed retinol is re-esterified as retinyl palmitate in the cells of intestinal mucosa and is absorbed via the lymphatics into the blood. Being fat soluble, absorption of retinol and carotene is favoured by conditions that facilitate absorption of lipids. The presence of tocopherols and other oxidants in the intestines helps to protect the vitamin from destruction in the intestines. Absorption is seriously interfered by the presence of unassimilable oils such as liquid paraffin, and the vitamin is carried out in the faeces. The retinyl esters from the circulation are taken up by the liver (where they are hydrolysed to retinol and subsequently re-esterified) and stored in the liver. In subjects with liver damage, including that due to alcohol, the capacity for storage of vitamin A is impaired and the concentration of retinol in blood is decreased. As needed, retinyl palmitate that is stored in the liver is hydrolysed to retinol and is transported in the blood, bound to a special transport protein known as retinol-binding protein. The retinol-bound protein complex, known as holoretinol-binding protein, delivers retinol to the target tissues. This action of retinol is similar to that of hormone.

Normal plasma contains 18–60 μg of vitamin A and 100–300 μg of carotene in 100 ml. Under normal conditions, the levels of both these substances in blood are maintained by the conversion of carotene to vitamin A and by mobilisation of vitamin A from the liver.

Excretion: Very small quantities of vitamin A are excreted under normal conditions. Administration of mineral oils (liquid paraffin), especially in children and old people, causes excessive loss of the vitamin in the faeces. Normally, vitamin A or carotene is not present in urine.

Food sources: Vitamin A occurs mainly in animal sources. Important among them are liver oils of fish such as halibut, cod and shark, and egg yolk, butter and milk. Carotenes are found mainly in green vegetables, apricots, sweet potatoes, corn and in yellow-coloured vegetables such as carrots.

Requirements: The recommended daily requirement of vitamin A for adults is 750 μg. The requirement for infants and young children is 300 μg. Women during pregnancy and lactation require 1200 μg per day.

Functions and deficiency manifestations: The functions of vitamin A are related to the three major retinoids, namely retinol, retinal and retinoic acid. Retinol is necessary for growth and reproduction. The action of retinol as a hormone has been mentioned. Retinal plays an important role in the physiological mechanism of vision. Retinoic acid is necessary for the synthesis of glycoproteins.

The functions of vitamin A are best studied along with deficiency manifestations, as both are closely interrelated.

1. Vitamin A is essential for growth. It plays an important role in the construction of normal bone. Deficiency causes defective endochondral bone formation and decreased osteoblastic activity. The bones become cancellous and lose their structural details.
2. Vitamin A is necessary for the functional integrity of the epithelial cells of the skin and mucous membranes. Deficiency results in keratinisation of the cells.

   The ***skin*** becomes dry, scaly and rough, resulting in the formation of follicular hyperkeratosis. It occurs commonly on the extensor surfaces of the arms, thighs, shoulders and back. Acne vulgaris, which occurs on the face, and 'corns', which occur on feet, are considered variations of keratinisation of the epithelial cells.

   Mucous membrane: Vitamin A deficiency may cause a widespread atrophy of the mucous membrane of living cells, leading to keratinisation resembling epidermis. This can occur in the mucous membrane of the eyes, lacrimal glands, respiratory tract, gastrointestinal tract and genitourinary tract.

Eyes: The conjunctiva is most commonly affected. Keratinisation of the conjunctiva and lacrimal glands leads to dryness of the eyes, photophobia and follicular conjunctivitis. This condition is called **xerophthalmia**. Bitot's spots, which are small triangular silvery foam-like patches, appear on the conjunctiva due to keratinisation of the conjunctival epithelium. When keratinisation involves corneal epithelium, vision is impaired. In severe cases, the corneal epithelium becomes inflammed resulting in keratomalacia, which may ultimately lead to blindness due to secondary infection and perforation of the cornea.

Respiratory tract: The mucous membrane of the nose, nasal sinuses, pharynx and tracheobronchial tract may get keratinised, resulting in impairment of the local resistance to infection. For this reason, vitamin A is referred to as 'anti-infective vitamin'.

Genitourinary tract: When the mucous membrane of the urinary tract gets keratinised, calculi formation occurs. The desquamated cells form the nidus on which salts of calcium and phosphorus from urine precipitate and form calculi.

3. ***Vision:*** Vitamin A has a specific role to play in the physiological mechanism involved in vision. An early sign of vitamin A deficiency in man is inability to see objects in dim light, especially after exposure to bright light. This condition is called 'night blindness' or nyctalopia. The mechanism which concerns the active participation of vitamin A to maintain normal vision is described by Wald as a cyclic phenomenon, which involves constant splitting and resynthesis of a light-sensitive vitamin A containing pigment present in the retina. This cyclic mechanism is known as **Wald's visual cycle** (**Fig. 5.2**).

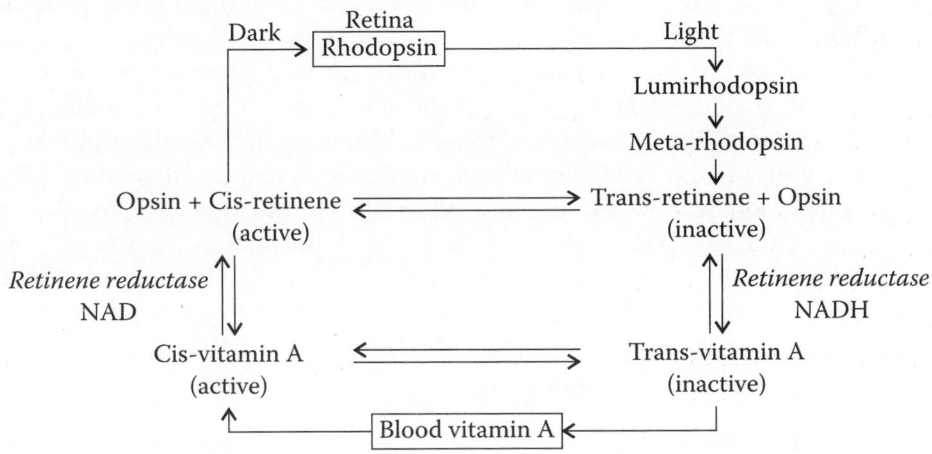

Figure 5.2 Rhodopsin–Vitamin A cycle (Wald's visual cycle).

There are two types of receptor cells in the retina. These are cones and rods. Cones are specialised for colour and detailed vision in bright light and rods are specialised for visual acuity in dim light (night vision).

When light waves fall on these receptors, chemical changes are produced, which, in turn, liberate nerve impulses. They in turn pass to the brain and produce a photochemical process. Vitamin A plays an important role in the photochemical process. The rod cells contain a photosensitive pigment called *rhodopsin* which is also called *visual purple.* It is a conjugated protein containing *opsin* which is the protein and retinene (retinal: vitamin A aldehyde), the prosthetic group. Similarly, the cones contain a photosensitive pigment *iodopsin,* which is also called *visual violet.* This is also a conjugated protein containing protein photopsin and retinene. When light strikes the retina, rhodopsin is converted to unstable orange-coloured products lumirhodopsin and meta-rhodopsin. Finally, it is split to form a yellow-coloured mixture of opsin and trans-retinene termed 'retinal', which is inactive vitamin aldehyde. Trans-retinene (visual yellow) is reduced to trans-vitamin A by retinene reductase and NADH. Trans-vitamin A, which is inactive, passes into the blood. (All trans-isomers are inactive and cis forms are active.) Resynthesis of rhodopsin occurs in dim light or darkness, when cis-vitamin A (active form) is formed, and enters the retina from the blood. Cis-vitamin A is oxidised to cis-retinene by the reverse action of retinene reductase (oxidation) and NAD. Cis-retinene couples with opsin to form the active visual purple rhodopsin in the retina.

The reactions explained above may be summarised as follows:

Bright light converts rhodopsin to inactive compounds, depleting it from the retina. This is associated with difficulty in seeing after entering a dark room from a well-lighted place. This is a physiological phenomenon and in a few seconds, rhodopsin is synthesised and vision improves. It should be noted that rhodopsin is synthesised in the dark. Under normal conditions, this is a routine and rapid process, because an equilibrium is maintained in the retina such that the rate of breakdown of rhodopsin is equal to the rate of its synthesis. But if there is a deficiency of vitamin A, the rate of resynthesis is delayed and the individual continues to have difficulty in seeing objects in darkness. This is the defect in night blindness (nyctalopia) and is the result of deficiency of vitamin A. The condition may be assessed by subjecting the person to 'dark adaptation' test, which measures the ability of the individual to adapt to dim illumination after seeing a bright light. If the dark adaptation time is prolonged, it is a sign of vitamin A deficiency because deficiency causes inability to resynthesise rhodopsin.

4. ***Growth and reproduction:*** Deficiency of vitamin A has been known to cause impairment in growth and reproduction.

Effects of vitamin A excess: Hypervitaminosis A occurs as a consequence of administration of large doses of concentrated forms of vitamin A, especially to infants and children. This includes symptoms such as drowsiness, painful joints, periosteal thickening of long bones and loss of hair. Peeling of skin is seen in Eskimos who eat the liver of polar bears rich in vitamin A.

Vitamin D

Vitamin D includes a number of compounds that are chemically related to sterols and exhibit the property of preventing and curing rickets. The precursors of vitamin D are known as provitamins D. They occur as inactive compounds in nature. Two provitamins considered important are as follows:

1. Ergosterol—Provitamin D_2
2. 7-Dehydrocholesterol—Provitamin D_3

Ergosterol occurs in plants and is found in ergot fungi and yeast whereas 7-dehydrocholesterol occurs in animal sources. It is present in the oily secretions in mammalian skin. Both are inactive. The D vitamins are formed from these two provitamins.

Chemistry: Ergosterol and 7-dehydrocholesterol are sterols possessing similar structural characteristics. They have the same empirical formula and are isomers. They differ only in the structure of the side chain. The structures of ergosterol and 7-dehydrocholesterol are shown in **Figures 5.3** and **5.4**, respectively.

Properties: Vitamins D are soluble in fat solvents. They all have identical absorption spectra and absorb various wavelengths in the ultraviolet spectrum. They do not absorb visible light. Vitamins D are quite stable if kept in dark. They are resistant to oxidation and heat.

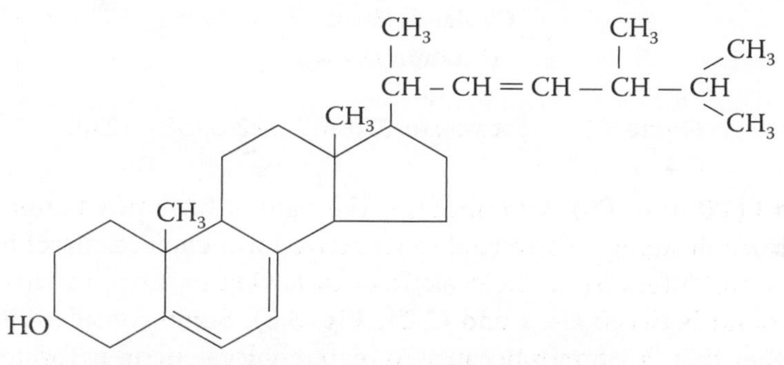

Figure 5.3 Ergosterol (provitamin D_2).

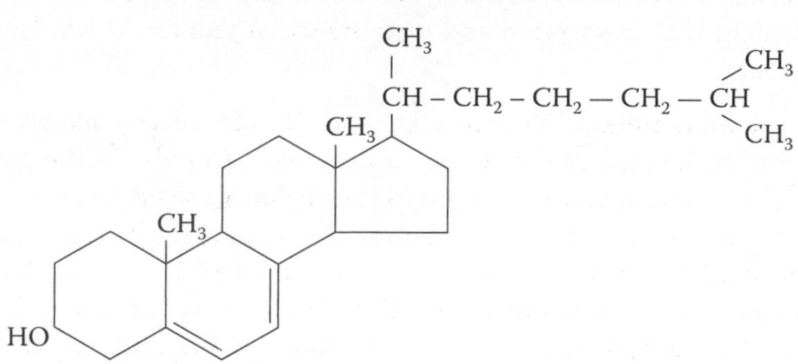

Figure 5.4 7-Dehydrocholesterol (provitamin D_3).

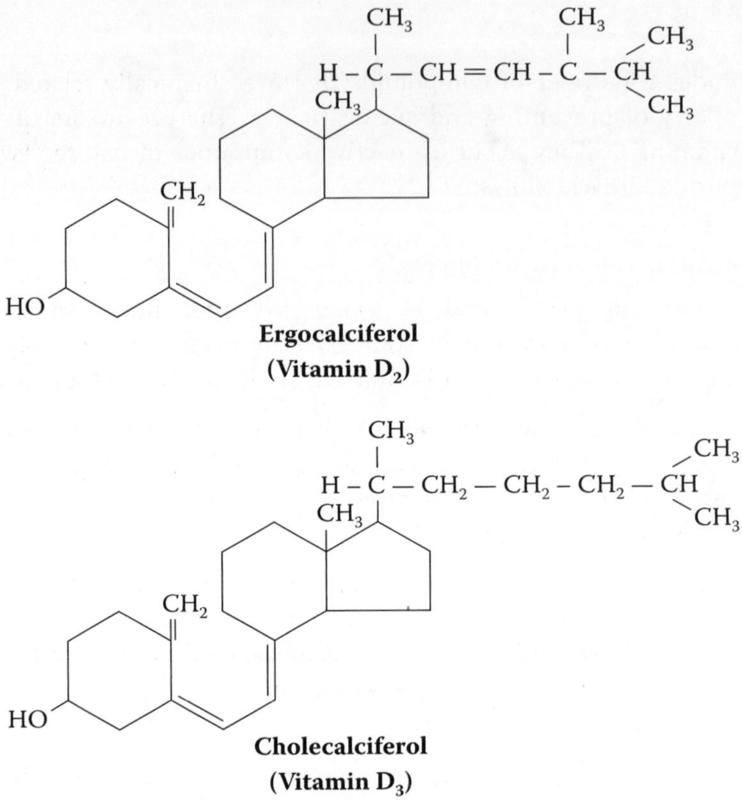

Figure 5.5 Ergocalciferol (D_2) and cholecalciferol (D_3).

Cholecalciferol (Vitamin D_3): Vitamin D_3 is the natural form of vitamin D occurring in man. 7-Dehydrocholesterol is converted to its active form cholecalciferol by irradiation of skin. Ergocalciferol differs from cholecalciferol in having an extra methyl group at C-24 and a double bond between C-22 and C-23 (**Fig. 5.5**). Some consider cholecalciferol as a hormone rather than a vitamin because in man, cholecalciferol is formed in one organ of the body, the skin, and it acts on distant target organs, namely the intestines and the bones. Ergocalciferol and cholecalciferol are important in nutrition and therapeutics. This section dealing with absorption and metabolism of vitamin D will have reference to cholecalciferol only.

Absorption and metabolism: Vitamins D_2 and D_3 are readily absorbed from small intestines, facilitated by factors that favour absorption of lipids. In the plasma, they are bound to a specific globulin and are carried in the chylomicrons to the liver, where vitamin D_3 undergoes hydroxylation on the 25 position, by a specific vitamin D_3 25-hydroxylase (**Fig. 5.6**) to form 25-hydroxycholecalciferol, also known as 25-hydroxy-D_3 or calcifediol. This hydroxylation occurs in microsomes. 25-hydroxy-D_3 is the major circulating form of vitamin D and is carried by a special α-2 globulin. 25-hydroxy-D_3 is also the major storage form present in the liver. A considerable fraction of 25-hydroxy-D_3 undergoes enterohepatic circulation.

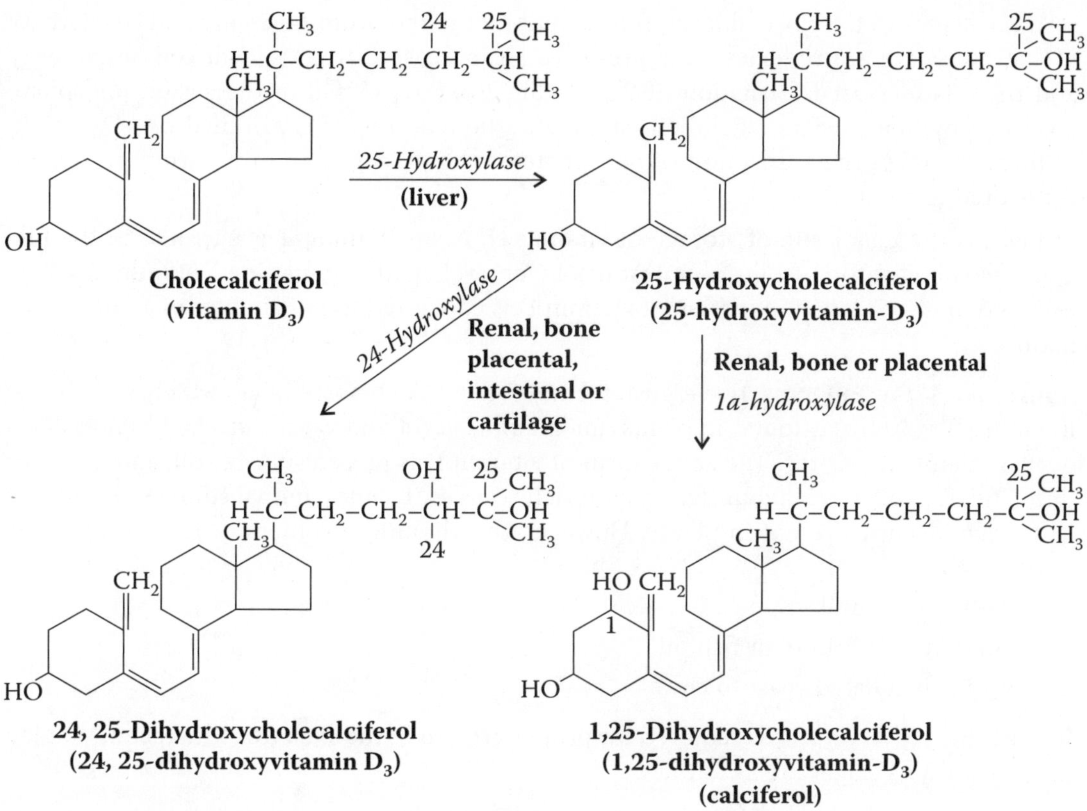

Figure 5.6 Hydroxylation of cholecalciferol (D_3) and formation of 25-hydroxy-D_3, 1,25-dihydroxy-D_3 and 24, 25-dihydroxy-D_3.

Further hydroxylation of 25-hydroxy-D_3 can occur on position 1 to form 1, 25-dihydroxy-D_3 by a specific mitochondrial enzyme known as 25-hydroxy-D_3 1-hydroxylase which is present in the renal tubules. This product is the most potent metabolite of vitamin D and it functions as a hormone. It regulates calcium and phosphate metabolism along with parathyroid hormone by increasing intestinal absorption of calcium and by mobilising calcium from bones into blood circulation. It also enhances calcium reabsorption from kidney. Yet another hydroxylation can occur at the 24 position of 25-hydroxy-D_3 to form 24, 25-dihydroxy-D_3 by a mitochondrial enzyme present in the renal tubules.

It has been observed that in serum, the level of 1, 25-dihydroxy-D_3 is reciprocally related to that of 24, 25-dihydroxy-D_3 and this is regulated by parathyroid hormone. A fall in serum calcium as in hypocalcaemia induces parathyroid glands to secrete more parathyroid hormone, which, in turn, stimulates the renal 1-hydroxylase to generate 1, 25-dihydroxy-D_3. Simultaneously, parathyroid hormone reduces the 24-hydroxylase pathway and reduces the level of 24, 25-dihydroxy-D_3. 1, 25-dihydroxy-D_3 increases intestinal absorption of calcium and also increases reabsorption of calcium from kidney and bone, and thus the serum calcium is restored to a normal level. With the restoration of serum calcium to the normal level, the secretion of parathyroid hormone and the activity of 1-hydroxylase are reduced. This produces an increase in the 24-hydroxylase pathway and there is increased formation of 24, 25-dihydroxy-D_3. A fall in the serum phosphate level as in hypophosphatemia directly stimulates the synthesis of 1, 25-dihydroxy-D_3 which, in turn, enhances the absorption of phosphate by the intestine, and the serum phosphate is restored to a normal level.

Liver is the major site of storage of vitamin D. A small amount is excreted in the bile and this is reabsorbed from the intestines by enterohepatic circulation. Vitamin D is not excreted in urine. A major portion of vitamin D is converted to metabolites of an unknown nature.

Sources of Vitamin D: Inactive ergosterol and 7-dehydrocholesterol are widely distributed in nature. Ergosterol is found in plants, for example ergot and yeast. 7-Dehydrocholesterol occurs in animal sources. The active form of vitamin D is present in egg yolk and fish liver oils. Cod liver oil and Halibut liver oil are rich sources. Besides animal sources, vitamin D is not significantly present in plants. However, the vitamin D content of the food may be increased by

1. Irradiation of milk
2. Addition of calciferol or fish oil
3. Feeding irradiated yeast to cows

Requirement: Vitamin D is required for proper growth of the skeleton. The recommended doses at various stages are as follows:

1. *Infants:* 400–800 I.U. daily
2. *Children and adolescents:* 400 I.U. daily
3. *During pregnancy and lactation:* 400–800 I.U. daily

Exposure to sunlight produces an adequate amount of vitamin D in the skin.

Functions: The overall function of vitamin D is to increase the absorption, retention and utilisation of calcium and phosphorus for proper mineralisation of the bones. The details are as follows:

1. Vitamin D facilitates absorption of calcium and phosphorus from the distal ileum where absorption is otherwise poor.
2. Vitamin D is necessary for promoting proper growth of bone in man. This is accomplished by
   - Promoting endochondral growth of long bones and mineralisation of the zone of provisional calcification. This is described as the antirachitic action of vitamin D.
   - Supplying proper proportion of calcium and phosphorus to the skeleton, thus promoting mineralisation of the skeleton.
   - Hydrolysing phytate, thus suppressing the rachitogenic effects of phytate.

Deficiency manifestations: Deficiency of vitamin D in children produces rickets. This is characterised by (i) a defect in the endochondral bone growth and (ii) a defect in the mineralisation of the zone of provisional calcification of long bones and the corresponding areas of flat bones and cartilage cells continue to grow, but the ossification is retarded.

X-ray photography of bones in rickets is characteristic, showing wide transparent gaps at the growing ends which denote the proliferation of cartilage cells.

Children with rickets manifest characteristic symptoms. (i) The cranial sutures are widened and the fontanelles remain open during infancy. (ii) Formation of rickety rosary may be evident, due to enlargement of the costochondral junction. (iii) Other deformities such as kyphosis, pelvic deformities, pot belly and bow legs are seen in severe deficiency. These deformities are the result of bending of the ends of the long bones due to the force of muscle pull. (iv) A delay in dentition is common.

Deficiency of Vitamin D in adults causes **osteomalacia** which means softening of bones. The bones are inadequately calcified leading to osteoporosis. Osteomalacia can occur during pregnancy and lactation where there is an increased demand for the vitamin and in women who observe purdah and are thus not exposed to sunlight. The pelvic bones are particularly affected and get deformed. This leads to complications during childbirth.

Hypervitaminosis D: Absorption of calcium and phosphorus from intestines is increased in vitamin D toxicity, leading to increased levels of these minerals in blood. Calcification of tissues has been reported in animals.

Vitamin E (Tocopherols)

Vitamin E comprises a number of compounds, which are chemically known as tocopherols.

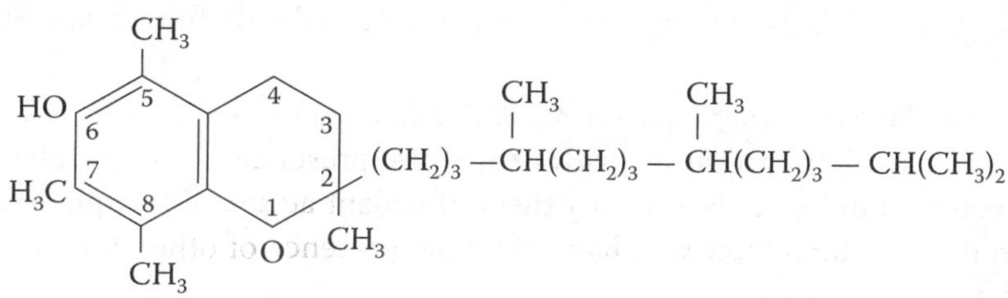

Chemistry: Structure of vitamin E

Four naturally occurring tocopherols have been identified. They are α-, β-, γ- and δ-tocopherols. They differ from one another in the number and position of methyl groups on the chroman ring. Out of the four tocopherols, α-tocopherol is the most active.

Properties:

1. Tocopherols form esters because of the presence of the phenolic hydroxyl group.
2. Both free and ester tocopherols are soluble in fat solvents.
3. Tocopherols are very susceptible to oxidation, and this leads to loss of vitamin activity. This property which is characteristic of tocopherols is known as the antioxidant property of tocopherols and is due to the phenolic hydroxyl group. As they are extremely susceptible to oxidation, they protect less susceptible compounds by breaking up the chain of oxidation reactions. This property is made use of in the commercial use of tocopherols as antioxidants, to prevent oxidation of fats. The stabilising effect of vitamin E in fats is greatly facilitated by the presence of other substances such as

ascorbic acid, pyruvic acid and phosphoric acid which act as synergists. Most of these substances are antioxidants themselves.

Esterification removes the antioxidant property of vitamin E but the vitamin activity is not affected.

4. Vitamin E compounds are very stable to heat in the absence of oxygen. But ultraviolet light and oxidation destroy the vitamin activity.

Absorption, metabolism and excretion: Tocopherols, both free and ester forms, are readily absorbed from the small intestines. Being fat soluble, they require bile acids for absorption.

The average concentration of vitamin E in adults is 1 mg/100 ml of serum. Vitamin E is transported chiefly in the serum α-lipoprotein fraction. It is present in small amounts in all tissues. Liver is probably a temporary site of storage of tocopherols.

Under normal conditions, very little of the vitamin is excreted in the urine or faeces.

Food sources: Tocopherols occur abundantly in plants. All green plants, especially lettuce and alfalfa, are rich sources of the vitamin. Vegetable oils such as wheat germ oil and seed germ oils are particularly rich sources. Milk, eggs and meat are also good sources.

Requirement: A daily allowance of 20–25 mg of vitamin E has been recommended for man.

Functions: Though there is no conclusive evidence that vitamin E has any specific function to perform in man, it is believed that it is closely connected with four important metabolic reactions.

1. It has a specific function based on its antioxidant activity. Vitamin A and carotene, which are particularly prone to oxidation in the presence of unsaturated fatty acids, are protected from being oxidised by the antioxidant action of tocopherols. Vitamin E action in the intestinal tract is enhanced by the presence of other antioxidants such as ascorbic acid.
2. Vitamin E has a specific effect on selenium metabolism. Selenium facilitates digestion and absorption of lipids including Vitamin E.
3. Vitamin E along with glutathione peroxidase, which has selenium as an integral part, provides the first line of defence against the formation of peroxides that cause damage to the cell membrane. Thus, vitamin E protects cell membranes, particularly their unsaturated fatty acid constituents, from oxidative damage against peroxidation.
4. Tocopherol acetone, a metabolite of tocopherol, is necessary for the biosynthesis of coenzyme Q which is a component in the electron transport chain.

Deficiency manifestations in certain species of animals: Two characteristic deficiency manifestations occur in certain rodent species. They are as follows:

1. Sterility
2. Muscle dystrophy

The antioxidant and protective action of vitamin E on cell membrane is utilised in preventing a large number of degenerative diseases. Vitamin E is now considered effective in the treatment of circulatory disturbances, particularly intermittent claudication.

Vitamin K

Substances which have vitamin K activity are naphthoquinones. There are three important forms of vitamin K. These are Vitamin K_1 (**Fig. 5.7**), Vitamin K_2 (**Fig. 5.8**) and Vitamin K_3 (**Fig. 5.9**).

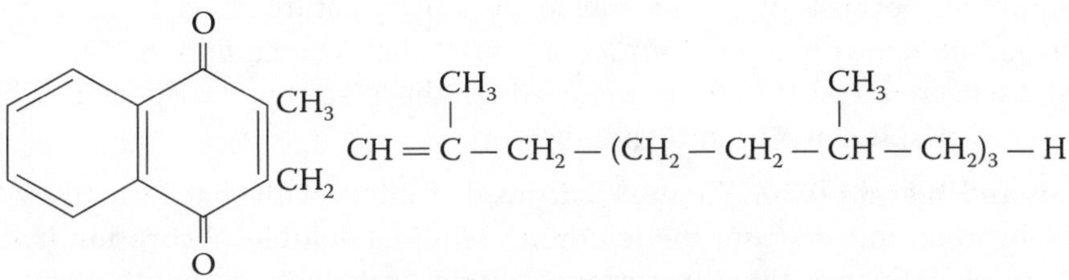

Figure 5.7 Vitamin K_1.

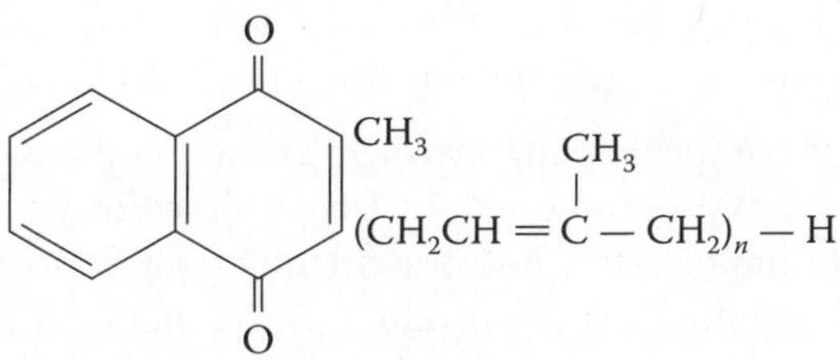

Figure 5.8 Vitamin K_2 (menaquinone) ($n = 6, 7$ or 9).

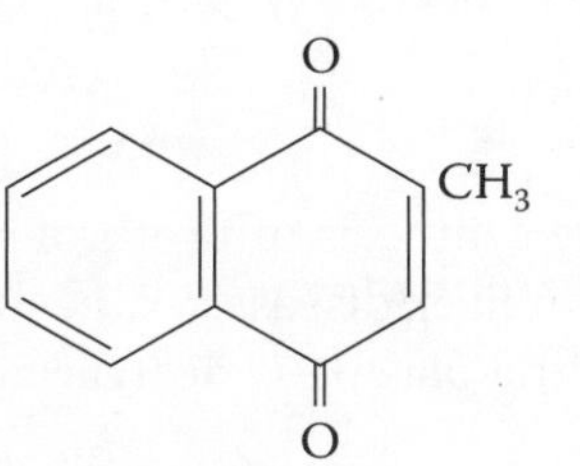

Figure 5.9 Vitamin K_3 (menadione).

Chemistry: All vitamin K are derivatives of 2-methyl-1, 4-naphthoquinone ('menadione' nucleus).

Vitamin K_1 (phylloquinone) is 2-methyl-3-phytyl-1, 4-naphthoquinone. It was originally isolated from alfalfa leaves. It has a phytyl chain attached in position 3 of the menadione nucleus.

Vitamin K_2 (farnoquinone or menaquinone) is 2-methyl-3-difarnesyl-1, 4-naphthoquinone. It has a long difarnesyl chain attached at position 3. It was originally isolated from putrified fish meal.

Vitamin K_3 (menadione), vitamin K synthetic, is 2-methyl-1, 4-naphthoquinone. This is the simplest and most potent synthetic vitamin K.

K-vitamins are fairly stable to heat, but are readily destroyed by light. They are destroyed by alkali and alcohol.

Coenzyme Q (ubiquinone): This is the coenzyme derivative of vitamin K. It is called ubiquinone because of its wide distribution in nature. It is a 2,3-dimethoxy-5-methylbenzoquinone, with a polyisoprenoid side chain at carbon 6. Coenzyme Q is a recently discovered cofactor. It is involved in the electron transport mechanism of respiratory enzymes. It exists in mitochondria.

Absorption and metabolism: Vitamin K from diet along with that formed by intestinal bacteria is absorbed mostly from the jejunum. Being fat soluble, absorption is influenced by factors which influence the absorption of lipids. Adequate amounts of bile salts are necessary for optimal absorption. In blood, vitamin K is not present in significant amounts, though it passes readily from the mother to the foetus during pregnancy. Nothing is known about the storage of vitamin K in man. It is utilised or metabolised rapidly.

Excretion: Vitamin K is not excreted in urine or bile. But large quantities are present in faeces, and this is mostly derived from the intestinal bacterial flora.

Sources: Food sources are principally derived from plants. Green leafy vegetables, alfalfa, cabbage, tomatoes and oat shoots are rich sources of vitamin K. Dietary supply of vitamin K_2 is of little importance, because adequate amounts are synthesised by the normal bacterial flora. Vitamin K_2 is the product of the metabolism of most bacteria and is present in large amounts in putrid fish.

Requirement: Since a sufficient quantity of the vitamin is synthesised by intestinal bacteria under normal conditions, there is no necessity for dietary requirement of vitamin K. However, exogenous supply is necessary only in conditions of potential vitamin K deficiency.

Functions:

1. Vitamin K is essential for the synthesis of prothrombin by the hepatic cells. Synthesis of prothrombin is impaired in liver diseases. When there is a deficiency of vitamin K, the prothrombin content of the plasma is decreased and the clotting time of blood is prolonged.
2. Vitamin K_3 (menadione) has been postulated to play an important role in oxidative phosphorylation in the mitochondria. Coenzyme Q functions as an electron carrier in the terminal electron transport system.
3. Vitamin K is used therapeutically as an antidote for anticoagulant drugs which are used in the treatment of thrombosis.

Deficiency: Vitamin K deficiency rarely results from dietary inadequacy, because the vitamin is synthesised by intestinal bacteria. Deficiency may arise in the following conditions:

1. In newborn babies, the plasma prothrombin level is low during the first few days due to deficient synthesis of vitamin K, because of (i) insufficient intestinal bacterial flora, (ii) inadequate bile flow and (iii) intestinal hypermotility.

In severe cases of vitamin K deficiency in newborn babies, uncontrollable haemorrhage may occur with bleeding in the brain, gastrointestinal tract and the umbilical cord.

2. Antibiotics, when administered orally, inhibit the intestinal bacterial flora and produce a deficiency in the synthesis of the vitamin.
3. Biliary obstruction as in obstructive jaundice may cause absence of an adequate amount of bile salts in the intestine and thus impair the absorption of vitamin K.
4. Chronic diarrhoea and sprue also produce the same problem of inadequate absorption of vitamin K.
5. In hepatocellular damage, liver cells are unable to synthesise prothrombin, in spite of adequate supply of vitamin K.

Prothrombin time: In vitamin K deficiency, coagulation of blood is delayed. This is because of deficient formation of prothrombin and certain factors concerned with coagulation, namely factors VII, IX and X. Prothrombin time is a useful clinical index in assessing the extent of deficiency of prothrombin. The normal prothrombin time is 16–18 seconds; when there is a deficiency, it may increase beyond 30 seconds.

WATER-SOLUBLE VITAMINS

Vitamin B Complex

B Complex group of vitamins comprises a large number of water-soluble vitamins which are nutritional essentials for all forms of life, from the lowest form of yeast and bacteria to the highest form, the man. Apart from being important nutritionally, they form essential components as coenzymes to certain important intracellular enzyme systems. Originally, the name B complex was applied to a factor present in rice polishings, yeast and liver, which if deficient in the diet was found to cause beriberi. But later, a number of components were differentiated and isolated from the B complex group and were named according to their chemical composition and properties. Accordingly, at least 11 individual components were discovered and they are enumerated in this section. Most of them are synthesised by the microorganisms which flourish in the intestinal flora.

The components of vitamin B complex are as follows:

1. Thiamine—Vitamin B_1, aneurine, anti-beriberi factor
2. Riboflavin—Vitamin B_2, lactoflavin
3. Niacin—Nicotinic acid, P-P factor of Goldberger
4. Pyridoxine—Vitamin B_6, rat antidermatitis factor
5. Pantothenic acid—Filtrate factor
6. Biotin—Vitamin H, anti-egg white injury factor
7. Folic acid group—Vitamin M – pteroyl glutamic acid
8. Lipoic acid—Thioctic acid
9. Inositol—Mouse antialopecia factor
10. Para-aminobenzoic acid (PABA)

11. Vitamin B_{12}—Cyanocobalamin, cobamide, antipernicious anaemia factor, extrinsic factor of Castle

Thiamine (Aneurine)

Chemistry: Free thiamine is basic and is less heat stable. Structurally, it contains a pyrimidine ring and a thiazole ring. It is a 2, 5-dimethyl-6-aminopyrimidine combined with 4-methyl-5-hydroxyethyl thiazole (**Fig. 5.10**).

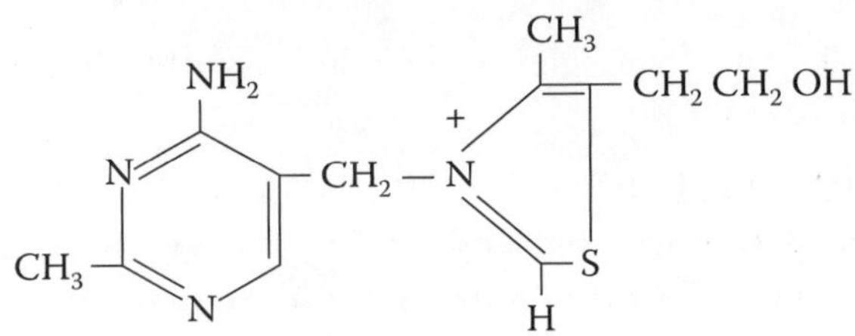

Figure 5.10 Thiamine.

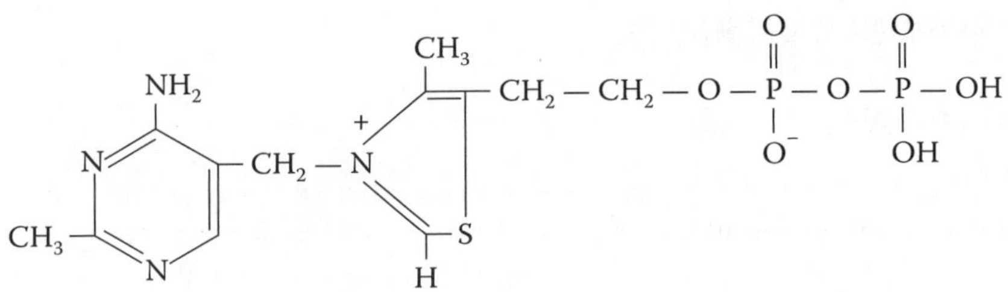

Figure 5.11 Thiamine pyrophosphate.

Metabolic role: The most important ester of thiamine is thiamine pyrophosphate (TPP) (**Fig. 5.11**). It is also known as cocarboxylase. It functions as a coenzyme in metabolic reactions involving decarboxylation of certain α-keto acids such as pyruvic acid and α-ketoglutaric acid. TPP also serves as a coenzyme in the transketolation reaction which occurs in the direct oxidative pathway of carbohydrate metabolism. TPP is an essential coenzyme of the enzyme system which helps in synthesis of fats from carbohydrates and proteins.

Lipothiamide: This is a thiamine-containing coenzyme. It is formed by the combination of lipoic acid with thiamine. Lipothiamide forms lipothiamide pyrophosphate (LTPP) by phosphorylation. LTPP also acts as a coenzyme in the oxidative decarboxylation reaction of α-keto acids along with TPP and coenzyme A. Oxidative decarboxylation of α-keto acids, such as pyruvic acid, and α-ketoglutaric acid are important metabolic reactions in the aerobic phase of carbohydrate metabolism.

Biosynthesis and metabolism: Synthesis of thiamine in man is limited. The main source of the vitamin is from the diet. Free thiamine which is the form present in food is readily absorbed from the small intestine. It is phosphorylated to TPP in the liver and exists in the blood cells largely as TPP combined with protein in the concentration of 6–12 μg/100 ml of blood.

Food sources: Plants, vegetables and seeds are rich sources of thiamine. The outer coverings of cereal grains (rice polishings) are particularly concentrated with thiamine. Other sources of thiamine are peas, nuts and yeast. Ham and pork are particularly rich in thiamine. Being water soluble and heat labile, thiamine is destroyed and lost in cooking water.

Excretion: About 10% of the ingested thiamine is excreted in the urine.

Daily requirement: The amount required is assessed in terms of calories intake. Thus for each 1000 calories, 0.5 mg is recommended and for an average man who takes 3000 calories, 1.5 mg of thiamine is the recommended daily requirement.

Deficiency manifestations: Deficiency of thiamine causes a disease known as **beriberi**. It occurs in an endemic form among rice eaters in certain places. The disease is characterised by three varieties of manifestations, namely cardiovascular, neurological and gastrointestinal, with oedema in some cases.

Cardiovascular manifestations include palpitation, dyspnoea, cardiac hypertrophy and dilatation of the heart leading to congestive heart failure.

Neurological manifestations include peripheral polyneuritis, giving rise to symptoms such as tingling sensation on the skin, numbness and weakness of the limbs and paraplegia. Haemorrhagic polioencephalitis, also known as Wernicke's encephalopathy, is characterised by haemorrhage in the brain.

Gastrointestinal symptoms include anorexia and diarrhoea.

Oedema may occur in beriberi, due to congestive heart failure or protein under nutrition. In such cases, it is referred to as **wet beriberi**. In beriberi, the levels of thiamine and thiamine pyrophosphate are decreased in blood and urine, whereas the levels of pyruvic acid and lactic acid in blood are increased.

Riboflavin

Chemistry: Riboflavin is an orange-yellow compound containing the pentose sugar ribose (ribitol) and a heterocyclic substance called isoalloxazine.

The first carbon of the ribityl group is attached to the ninth position of isoalloxazine which has three rings in its structure, namely benzene, azine and pyrimidine (**Fig. 5.12**).

Riboflavin is slightly soluble in water and alcohol, but insoluble in fat solvents. It forms a yellow solution having a yellowish-green fluorescence. Riboflavin is heat stable but sensitive to light. On irradiation with ultraviolet rays or even ordinary light, it undergoes irreversible decomposition.

Riboflavin is reversibly reduced by reducing agents such as thiosulphate, hydrogen sulphide and hydrogen to form a colourless compound called leuco-riboflavin. In the living cell, it forms two phosphorylated derivatives. These are as follows:

1. Riboflavin phosphate or flavin mononucleotide (FMN)
2. Flavin adenine dinucleotide (FAD)

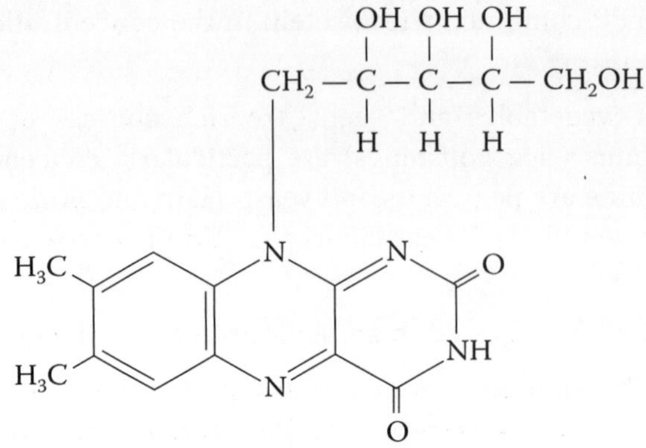

Figure 5.12 Riboflavin.

FMN contains one nucleotide group. It forms the prosthetic group for cytochrome C reductase and amino acid dehydrogenase for L-amino acids (refer to **Chapter 16, Biological Oxidation.**)

FAD contains two nucleotide groups. It is the prosthetic group of diaphorase, D-amino acid dehydrogenase, glycine oxidase and xanthine oxidase.

Functions of riboflavin: This vitamin is a constituent of several enzyme systems involved in intermediary metabolism.

These enzymes are called flavoproteins. The phosphorylated derivatives FMN and FAD serve as coenzymes for the enzymes involved in biological oxidation–reduction reactions. They also serve as bridges over which hydrogen atoms pass between two substrate molecules. (For details of its role in biological oxidation, refer to **Chapter 16, Biological Oxidation.**) FMN and FAD function as coenzymes for amino acid oxidases, glycine oxidase and xanthine oxidase. Riboflavin is necessary for the normal metabolism of tryptophan and for oxidation of fatty acids.

Biosynthesis: Riboflavin is synthesised by all higher plants. Tender parts of the plants like the tender leaves and buds contain more riboflavin than the older ones. In man, it is synthesised by the intestinal bacteria but as the quantity is not sufficient, it has to be supplied in the diet.

Metabolism: Riboflavin is readily absorbed in the intestines after phosphorylation to riboflavin phosphate. It is present in blood and all tissue cells mostly as FMN and FAD. It is secreted in the milk and excreted in urine and faeces. A major portion of riboflavin is metabolised in the body to unknown compounds.

Food sources: Yeast, milk, eggs, liver, leafy vegetables, whole grains and nuts are rich sources of riboflavin.

Daily requirement: The recommended daily requirement for adults is 1.5–1.8 mg. Pregnant and lactating women and growing children require 2.0–2.5 mg daily.

Deficiency manifestations: Characteristic lesions appear in the mouth region, and the face is affected in severe cases. Lips appear red and shiny, with characteristic painful fissures at the angles of the mouth called **cheilosis**. Painful glossitis with a swollen and abnormally red (magenta coloured) tongue having large flattened papillae occur in severe cases. Localised seborrheic dermatitis occurs on the nose, nasolabial folds and ears giving the appearance of shark skin. Eyes are affected in severe cases of deficiency, leading to photophobia, opacity and ulceration of cornea and sometimes cataract formation.

Niacin

(Nicotinic acid: Pellagra-preventing factor of Goldberger).

Chemistry: Niacin is pyridine-3-carboxylic acid. Niacinamide or nicotinamide is the acid amide of nicotinic acid.

Nicotinic acid **Nicotinamide**

Figure 5.13 Niacin.

Niacin derives its name from nicotine, from which it can be prepared by oxidation. In tissues, it is present as nicotinamide which is the physiologically active form (**Fig. 5.13**).

They are white, needle-shaped crystals, soluble in alkali but slightly soluble in water. It forms two phosphorylated compounds, which act as coenzymes to dehydrogenases in metabolic reactions. These are as follows:

1. Nicotinamide adenine dinucleotide (NAD), previously known as diphosphopyridine nucleotide (DPN) and coenzyme I. It contains one niacinamide + 2 D-ribose + 2 phosphoric acid + one adenine molecules.
2. Nicotinamide adenine dinucleotide phosphate (NADP), previously known as triphosphopyridine nucleotide (TPN) and coenzyme II. It contains one niacinamide + 2 D-ribose + 3 phosphoric acid + one adenine molecules.

The two coenzymes are interconvertible.

Physiological functions: Niacin in the form of NAD and NADP play an important role in metabolic reactions.

1. NAD and NADP are coenzymes to dehydrogenases. They serve as agents transferring hydrogen atoms from one substrate to another in biological oxidation. (For details, refer to **Chapter 16, Biological Oxidation.**)
2. Nicotinamide has an important relationship with protein, because it is the end product of the metabolic pathway of tryptophan which is an essential amino acid.
3. Pharmacologically, it has a stimulating effect on the central nervous system. Nicotinic acid produces vasodilatation, causing flushing of the face, neck and arms due to increased peripheral blood flow.

Biosynthesis: Niacin is synthesised in the body from tryptophan, an essential amino acid. Administration of tryptophan or proteins rich in tryptophan is followed by increased excretion of niacin metabolites. Diets deficient in tryptophan produce a deficiency of niacin in the body. Niacin is also synthesised to some extent by intestinal bacteria.

Metabolism: Nicotinic acid and nicotinamide are readily absorbed from the intestines; they are present in blood, mostly in the erythrocytes. Niacin is excreted in urine either as niacinamide or as nicotinuric acid which is the glycine conjugate of nicotinic acid. The largest portion is excreted as methyl derivative, namely *N*-methyl-nicotinamide. The methylation is done in the liver by the labile methyl groups supplied by methionine.

Food sources: Yeast, liver, milk, tomatoes and green leafy vegetables are good sources.

Daily requirement: The recommended daily requirement for adults is 17–21 mg. An increased amount is required during adolescence, pregnancy and lactation. These requirements are influenced by the protein content of the food, because of the ability of tryptophan to supply much of the niacin required by the body. 60 mg of tryptophan yield 1 mg of niacin.

Deficiency manifestations: Deficiency of niacin causes **pellagra**. Administration of niacin cures the condition. Hence, niacin was named as pellagra-preventing factor (P-P factor) of Goldberger, who originally discovered the vitamin. The three characteristic symptoms of this condition, namely dermatitis, diarrhoea and dementia, are referred to as three 'D's and these are exhibited as skin, gastrointestinal and cerebral manifestations.

Dermatitis refers to skin lesions. The skin appears red, thickened and scaly. The lesions are found characteristically distributed on areas exposed to sunlight and subjected to pressure, like face, neck, dorsal aspects of forearms, elbows, wrists, knees and legs.

Gastrointestinal manifestations include abdominal pain with alternating constipation and diarrhoea, the latter becoming a permanent feature later. Stomatitis, gingivitis and glossitis are also common.

Cerebral manifestations include depression and neurological symptoms.

Pyridoxine (Vitamin B_6)

Pyridoxine refers to a group of naturally occurring pyridine derivatives, possessing vitamin B_6 activity. When it was first discovered, it was considered essential for rats and was named rat antidermatitis factor (**Fig. 5.14**).

Chemistry: Pyridoxine is a derivative of pyridine. The naturally occurring pyridoxines include pyridoxol, pyridoxal and pyridoxamine. All three forms exhibit vitamin B_6 activity.

Pyridoxol (or pyridoxine) has a CH_2OH in the fourth position. It is 2-methyl-3-hydroxy-4, 5-dihydroxymethyl-pyridine. Pyridoxal has a CHO in position 4 whereas pyridoxamine has CH_2NH_2 in the same position. The phosphorylated derivative of pyridoxal, pyridoxal phosphate, is an important coenzyme which participates in several metabolic reactions. Pyridoxine is highly soluble in water. It is readily destroyed by exposure to light, but is stable to heat (**Fig. 5.15**).

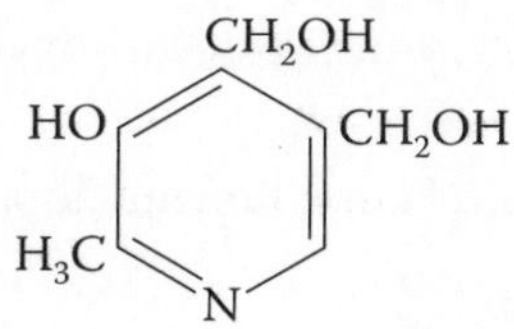

Pyridoxol (pyridoxine)

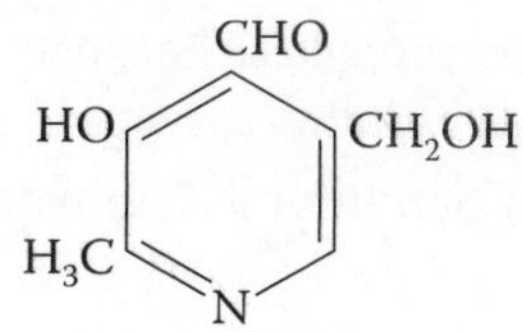

Pyridoxal

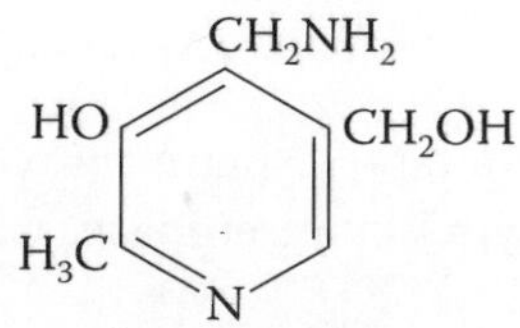

Pyridoxamine

Figure 5.14 Pyridoxine and derivatives.

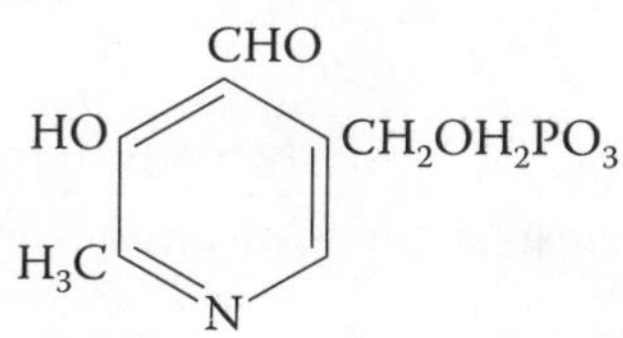

Figure 5.15 Pyridoxal phosphate.

Physiological role: Vitamin B_6 is principally concerned with the metabolism of amino acids. Pyridoxal phosphate acts as an active coenzyme and takes part in many metabolic reactions.

1. It acts as a cotransaminase in transamination reactions, involving the reversible transfer of an α-amino group between an amino acid and α-keto acid. Two examples are given below:

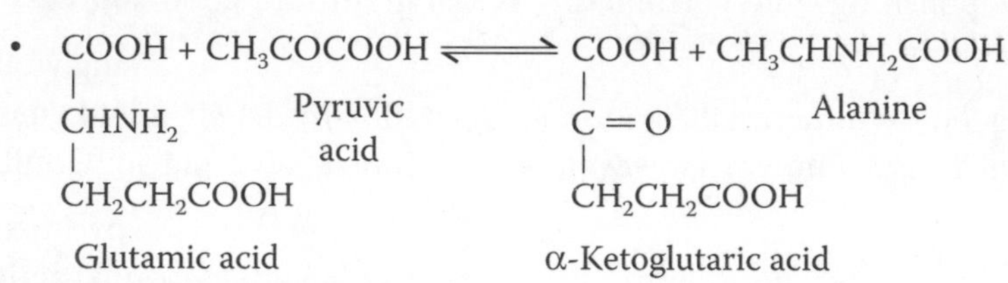

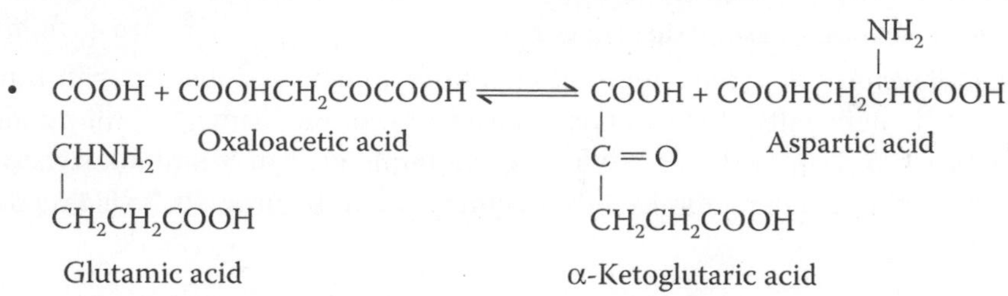

2. It is a codecarboxylase because it acts as a coenzyme in decarboxylation reactions. Examples are as follows:
   - Decarboxylation of 3, 4-dihydroxyphenylalanine ('dopa') forms dopamine.

$$\text{Dopa} \xrightarrow{-\,CO_2} \text{Dopamine.}$$

   - Decarboxylation of glutamic acid forms γ-aminobutyrate.

$$\text{Glutamic acid} \xrightarrow{-\,CO_2} \gamma\text{-aminobutyrate.}$$

3. It is essential for the normal metabolic pathway of tryptophan. Pyridoxal phosphate acts as a coenzyme to the enzyme kynureninase, which is involved in the conversion of tryptophan to nicotinic acid.
4. It acts as a coenzyme to deaminases which are involved in the deamination of amino acids, for example serine and threonine.
5. It acts as a coenzyme in transsulphuration reactions. *Example:* In the metabolism of cysteine, sulphur from methionine is transferred to serine to form cysteine.
6. It acts as a coenzyme in desulphuration reaction. *Example:* Cysteine is converted to pyruvate by removal of sulphur.
7. Pyridoxal phosphate acts as a cofactor in the conversion of linoleic to arachidonic acid.
8. Pyridoxine helps in the active transport of amino acids and certain metabolic ions across cell membranes.
9. It has been recently discovered that pyridoxine plays an important role in the metabolism of brain.

Biosynthesis and metabolism: Synthesis of vitamin B_6 by intestinal bacteria in man is limited. Therefore, it is necessary that the vitamin be adequately supplied in the diet. Pyridoxol, pyridoxal and pyridoxamine are nutritionally interconvertible in man. Among these, the phosphorylated derivatives of pyridoxal and pyridoxamine are functionally active. The major metabolic product of pyridoxine is 4-pyridoxic acid, which is excreted in urine.

Food sources: Yeast, rice polishings and germinating cereal grains are good sources. The highest concentration occurs in royal jelly (bee).

Requirement: As there is no definite manifestation associated with deficiency of vitamin B_6, the exact requirement is not known. However, a daily intake of 2 mg for adults is recommended.

Deficiency manifestations: Though no definite manifestations have been established in vitamin B_6 deficiency, several possible disorders have been observed. These are as follows:

1. *Epileptiform convulsions:* It is reported that epileptiform convulsions occur in infants when vitamin B_6 is deficient. This has been traced to the impairment of the function of B_6 as a codecarboxylase in the conversion of glutamic acid to γ-aminobutyric acid (GABA), which further gets metabolised to succinic acid in the brain. It is also reported

that GABA, which functions as a regulator of neuronal activity in normal individuals, is deficient in brain when there is a deficiency of B_6.

$$\text{Glutamic acid} \xrightarrow[\textit{Decarboxylase}]{\text{Pyridoxal phosphate}} \gamma\text{-Aminobutyric acid} + CO_2$$

$$\downarrow$$

$$\text{Succinic acid}$$

2. Nausea and vomiting in pregnancy have been reported to occur due to deficiency of B_6. It is suggested that B_6 deficiency is created in pregnancy because of the diversion of the vitamin to the increasing demands of the foetus.
3. In humans, a reversible type of hypochromic microcytic anaemia develops, when there is a deficiency of B_6. The anaemia improves after administration of vitamin B_6.
4. Clinical reports have shown that an apparent pyridoxine deficiency occurs in patients receiving high doses of tuberculostatic drugs (isonicotinic acid hydrazide [INH]). They develop neuritis and neuropathy. This condition is cured by the administration of pyridoxine. It is believed that INH forms a hydrazone complex with pyridoxal, resulting in inactivation of the vitamin.

Pantothenic Acid

Pantothenic acid is essential for nutrition. It is also known as a 'filtrate factor' because it was found difficult to separate it from pyridoxine contained in the filtrate, when it was first discovered.

Chemistry: The structure of pantothenic acid consists of an alanine chain in peptide linkage with a dihydroxy-dimethyl-butyric acid.

$$CH_2OH - \underset{\underset{CH_3}{|}}{\overset{\overset{CH_3}{|}}{C}} - CHOH - CO - NH - CH_2 - CH_2COOH$$

Pantothenic acid

Pantothenic acid is viscous and soluble in water. It is heat labile. The free acid is destroyed by acid or alkali. The calcium and sodium salts of pantothenic acid are more stable. In tissues, it is present in the form of coenzyme A (CoA), mostly bound to the protein apoenzyme. It is the coenzyme for acetylation reactions.

Pantothenate is joined on one side with adenosine-3-phosphate by a pyrophosphate bridge and on the other side with β-mercaptoethylamine by a peptide linkage (**Fig. 5.16**). The terminal thiol (SH) group of β-mercaptoethylamine is the reactive site of CoA.

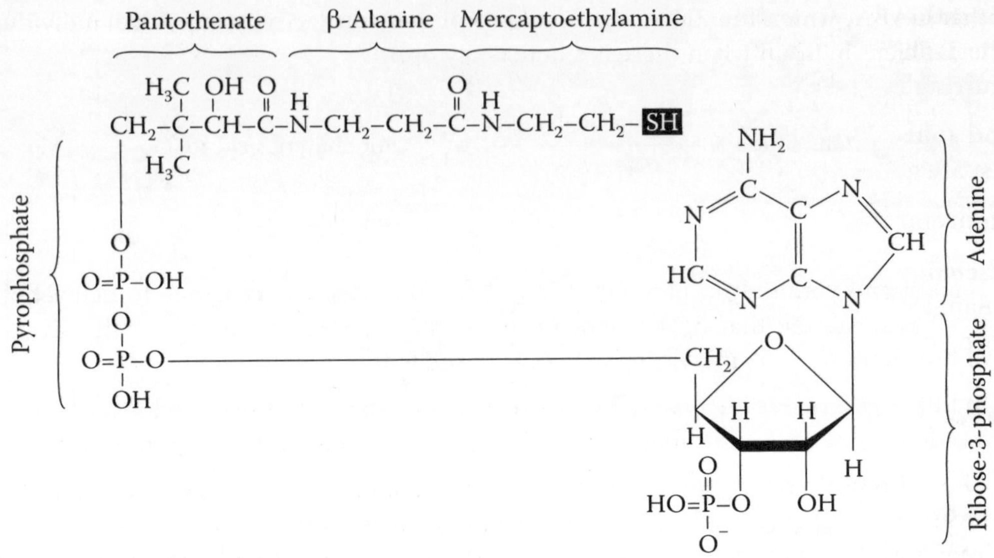

Figure 5.16 Structure of coenzyme A.

CoA reacts with acetate to form acetyl-CoA, a high-energy compound. It is also known as 'active acetate'.

Metabolic role: The metabolic functions of pantothenic acid are due to its coenzyme derivative CoA, which participates in several metabolic reactions. CoA gains further importance after its conversion to form acetyl-CoA. In this form, a number of important metabolic reactions are initiated. These are enlisted below.

1. Acetyl-CoA participates in the initial reaction of the citric acid cycle, by combining with oxaloacetic acid to form citric acid. It is also formed during the intermediary stages of fat and protein metabolism, thus occupying a key position in the common metabolic pathway of carbohydrate, fat and protein.
2. Acetyl-CoA combines with choline to form acetylcholine.
3. Acetyl-CoA forms ketone bodies during oxidation of fatty acids.
4. Acetyl-CoA is the precursor of cholesterol. It is the main source for the synthesis of cholesterol, as well as steroid hormones, which possess a similar structure to that of cholesterol.
5. Sulphonamide drugs are detoxified by acetylation with acetyl-CoA.
6. In the citric acid cycle, coenzyme A is required for the conversion of α-ketoglutarate to succinyl-CoA. The latter is necessary for the synthesis of haem.
7. CoA plays an important role in lipid metabolism. The first step in the oxidation of fatty acids is initiated by CoA.
8. Acyl carrier protein (ACP) contains protein-bound pantothenic acid and is involved in the biosynthesis of fatty acids.
9. Certain amino acids require CoA for their activation.

Biosynthesis and metabolism: Pantothenic acid is synthesised mostly by the intestinal bacteria. It is present in blood and all tissues in small amounts, the highest concentration occurring in liver. It is catabolised to certain unknown products and excreted in urine.

Food sources: Royal jelly is a rich source of pantothenic acid. Egg yolk, kidney, liver and yeast are good sources.

Requirement: The recommended daily requirement is 5–12 mg for adults.

Deficiency manifestations: No definite deficiency manifestations have been recognised in man. However in animals, changes in skin leading to dermatitis and in hair resulting in greying of the hair and alopecia have been reported.

Biotin

Biotin is also called 'anti-egg white injury' factor because egg white contains a protein called avidin, which combines with biotin in the intestinal tract and prevents absorption of biotin from intestines.

Chemistry: Biotin is a heterocyclic sulphur-containing monocarboxylic acid (**Fig. 5.17**). Biotin crystals are soluble in water and are heat stable. Avidin, a protein present in egg white, forms a stable and inactive complex with biotin. The coenzyme of biotin is biocytin. It is a combination of biotin and lysine. It occurs in nature, firmly bound to the enzyme protein.

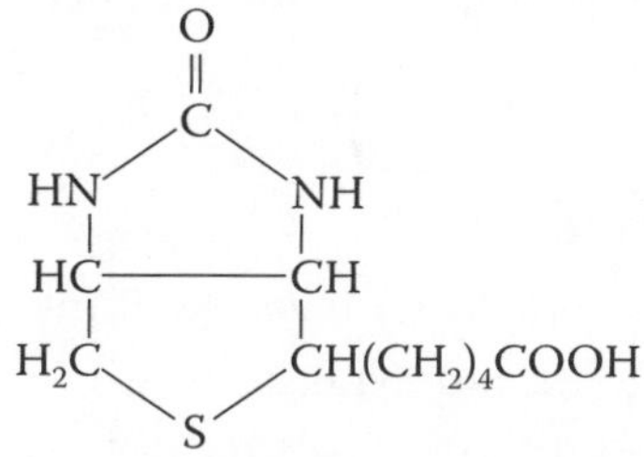

Figure 5.17 Biotin.

Metabolic functions:

1. The most important function of biotin is its role as a coenzyme for carboxylases, which catalyse 'carbon dioxide fixation' or carboxylation. Examples are as follows:
    - In the first step of the non-mitochondrial pathway of fatty acid synthesis, acetyl-CoA is converted to malonyl-CoA by acetyl-CoA carboxylase and biotin coenzyme.

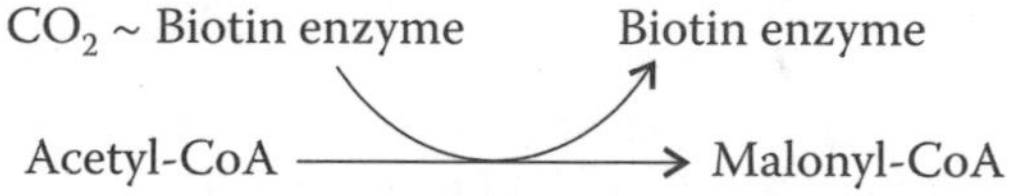

- Biotin coenzyme acts as a coenzyme to pyruvic carboxylase in the carboxylation of pyruvate to form oxaloacetate.

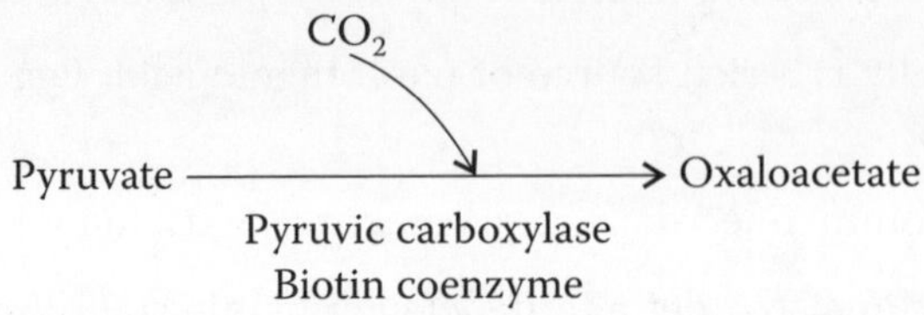

2. It assists in the deamination of amino acids such as aspartic acid, serine and threonine.
3. It helps in the synthesis of purine structure.
4. Biotin is required for the conversion of ornithine to citrulline in synthesis of urea.

Biosynthesis and metabolism: Biotin is synthesised mainly by intestinal bacteria. It is excreted in urine and faeces.

Food sources: Royal jelly, egg yolk, liver and kidney are good sources of the vitamin.

Requirement: Man does not depend upon the dietary supply of the vitamin, because it is abundantly produced by intestinal bacteria.

Deficiency manifestations: Manifestations due to deficiency of biotin are rare in man. However, biotin deficiency induced experimentally by giving a low biotin diet containing one dozen raw eggs manifested symptoms such as dermatitis of the extremities, depression, lassitude, muscle pain, anorexia and vomiting. All these symptoms were relieved by administration of biotin.

Folic Acid Group

This group of vitamins has a characteristic structure. It includes three chemical groups:

1. A pteridine nucleus (pyrimidine and pyrazine rings)
2. A para-amino benzoic acid (PABA)
3. Glutamic acid

A pteridine nucleus together with PABA is known as pteroic or pteroyl moiety (**Figs 5.18** and **5.19**).

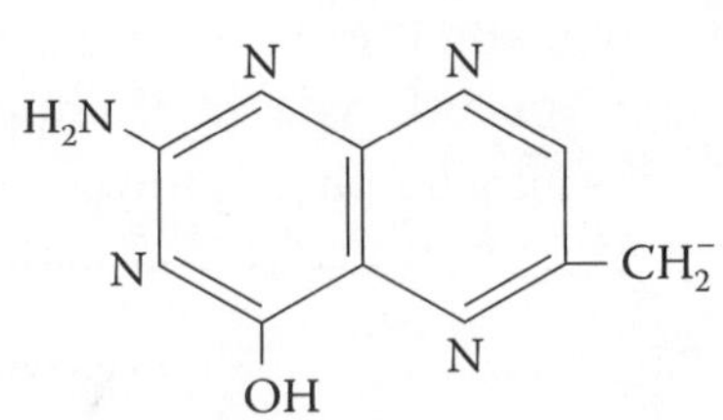

Figure 5.18 Pteridine group.

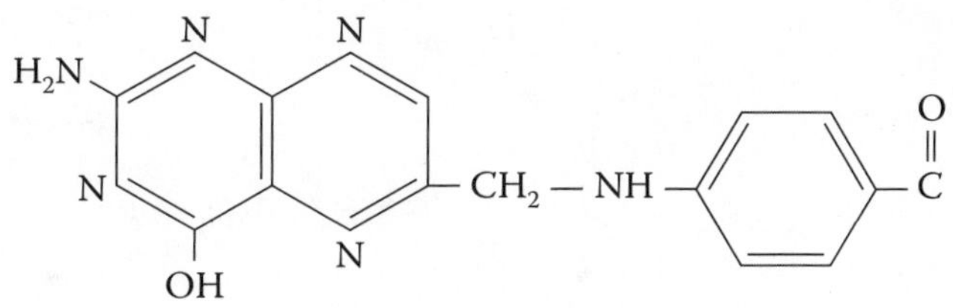

Figure 5.19 Pteroyl moiety.

There are at least three forms of folic acid which occur naturally and are important nutritionally. They differ from one another in the number of glutamic acid residues attached to the pteroyl moiety. All are pteroyl glutamates.

The folic acid which occurs in the liver contains one glutamic acid and is called pteroylmonoglutamic acid (PGA; **Fig. 5.20**). The second form of folic acid is known to contain three glutamic acid residues and is called pteroyltriglutamic acid.

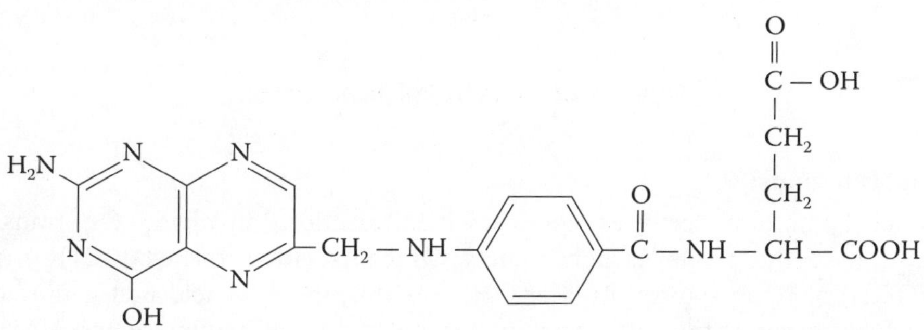

Pteridyl **PABA** **Glutamic acid**

Figure 5.20 Pteroylmonoglutamic acid—folic acid.

The third form of folic acid contains seven glutamic acid residues and is called pteroyl heptaglutamic acid.

Structure of folic acid (PGA): In pteroyl monoglutamic acid, the pteridine nucleus is joined through a methylene linkage to the amino group of PABA. The amino group of PABA is in peptide linkage with glutamic acid (*see* **Fig. 5.20**).

Folinic acid: This is the reduced formylated derivative of folic acid. It is also known as *citrovorum factor* (CF) because it is found necessary for the optimal growth of a lactobacillus, known as *Leuconostoc Citrovorum*. Structurally, it differs from PGA in having a CHO group in addition (**Fig. 5.21**).

Folinic acid is more powerful than folic acid in action. Ascorbic acid and vitamin B_{12} are required for the conversion of folic acid to folinic acid. The active coenzyme of folic acid is the tetrahydro derivative known as tetrahydrofolic acid (FH_4) (**Fig. 5.22**).

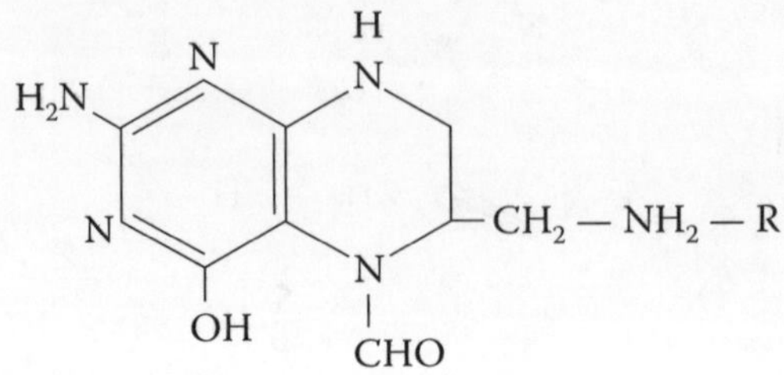

Figure 5.21 Folinic acid (citrovorum factor).

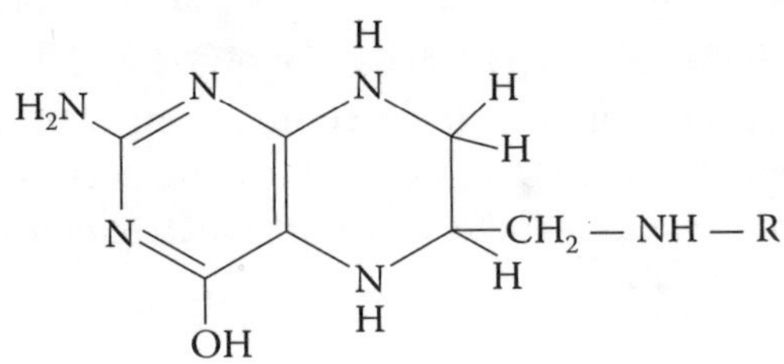

Figure 5.22 Tetrahydrofolic acid (FH_4).

Metabolic functions:

1. Folic acid vitamins serve as coenzymes in reactions involving the transfer and utilisation of the single carbon moiety, which is either formyl (–CHO), formate (HCOOH) or hydroxymethyl (–CH_2OH). For this, the folic acid first gets reduced to FH_4 which serves as the coenzyme, by enzymes folic acid reductase and NADPH, the latter serving as a hydrogen donor for the reduction.
2. Folic acid participates in the reactions concerned with the synthesis of purine, pyrimidine and nucleic acids. The latter are required for normal growth and reproduction of cells.
3. Along with vitamin B_{12}, folic acid helps in the transmethylation of homocysteine to methionine, ethanolamine to choline and uracil to thymine.
4. Folic acid in conjunction with vitamin B_{12} functions as an important factor in reactions concerned with the normal growth and maturation of red blood cells. Both vitamins help in the development of red cells beyond the megaloblastic stage. Thus, deficiency of these two vitamins exhibits evidences of arrested development of blood elements in bone marrow and accumulation of megaloblasts and myeloblasts. The peripheral blood shows a picture of the macrocytic type of anaemia.
5. Folic acid is required for the normal metabolic pathway of histidine, particularly in the conversion of formimino-glutamic acid to glutamic acid.

Biosynthesis and metabolism: Folic acid is synthesised by the intestinal microorganisms. Folinic acid is formed by reduction and formylation of folic acid, for which ascorbic acid and vitamin B_{12} are required. Thus, administration of folic acid results in the urinary excretion of FH_4 in a normal person, but in subjects with scurvy (deficiency of ascorbic acid), only small amounts of FH_4 are excreted due to impairment in the formation of folinic acid. It has been reported that scorbutic monkeys develop a megaloblastic anaemia which could be corrected by administration of tetrahydrofolic acid.

Food sources: Folic acid vitamins are particularly present in green leafy vegetables, cauliflower and yeast. Liver and kidney are good animal sources.

Requirement: There is no definite requirement for a normal human. However, an increased amount is required during pregnancy and lactation.

Deficiency manifestations:

1. Megaloblastic anaemia occurs when folic acid is deficient in nutrition. Rapid recovery occurs after treatment with folic acid.
2. Sprue and symptoms such as glossitis, diarrhoea and anaemia are cured by the administration of folic acid.
3. Macrocytic anaemia of pregnancy responds to treatment with folic acid.

Folic acid antagonists: Just as folic acid is concerned with the growth and development of cells, antagonists to folic acid are found to be clinically useful in the treatment of malignant diseases. It has been found that 4-amino folic acid or aminopterin functions as an antagonist to folic acid, as it inhibits growth and multiplication of cells. Aminopterin is used in the treatment of leukaemia, which is characterised by a malignant multiplication of leucocytes. The mechanism of inhibition is attributed to the failure in the formation of FH_4 and folinic acid which are required for the synthesis of nucleoprotein and cell growth.

α-Lipoic Acid

Lipoic acid is not a vitamin, but is closely associated with vitamin coenzymes such as thiamine pyrophosphate and coenzyme A. Lipoic acid is a growth-promoting factor for certain strains of bacteria. It was originally named pyruvate oxidation factor (POF), as it was found necessary for the oxidative decarboxylation of pyruvate to form acetate by *Streptococcus faecalis*.

Chemistry: Lipoic acid is a sulphur-containing fatty acid and is 6, 8-dithio-octanoic acid containing two sulphur atoms and eight carbon atoms (**Fig. 5.23**). It is abbreviated as $\begin{matrix}S\\S\end{matrix}\!>$ Lip.

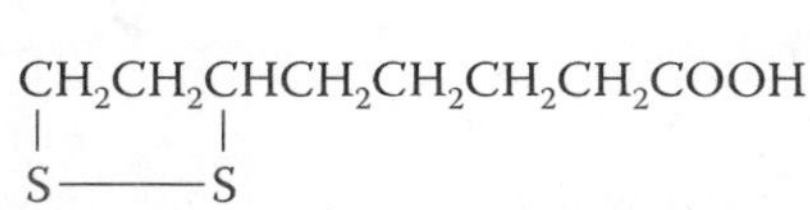

Figure 5.23 α-Lipoic acid.

Functions: Lipoic acid functions as a cofactor in conjunction with thiamine pyrophosphate in the initial oxidative decarboxylation of α-ketoacids. For example, (i) pyruvate → acetyl-CoA and (ii) α-ketoglutarate → succinyl-CoA. It is present in liver, kidney, yeast, bacteria and green plants.

Inositol

Strictly speaking, inositol is not classified as vitamin because it occurs in plants and animals in much larger quantities than vitamins and has no catalytic action.

Chemistry: It is a cyclic compound with structure similar to that of glucose. Its empirical formula is $C_6H_{12}O_6$ and chemically it is hexahydroxycyclohexane; it is sweet in taste and is also known as muscle glucose. Glucose is its precursor. There are nine isomers of inositol, and out of these only one, meso-inositol which is also called myo-inositol, is important (**Fig. 5.24**).

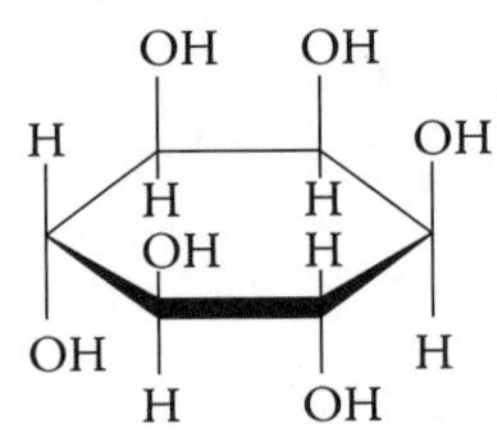

Figure 5.24 Meso-inositol.

Functions:

1. Because of its alcoholic nature, inositol forms esters with acids. The most important of these is phytic acid, the hexaphosphate ester, formed with phosphoric acid. The importance of phytic acid is that it forms phytins, which are highly insoluble salts, with calcium and magnesium in the intestines, preventing absorption of these minerals.
2. Inositol along with choline is considered to have lipotropic action in experimental animals.

Biosynthesis and metabolism: Glucose is probably the precursor of inositol. It is also synthesised by intestinal bacteria. Inositol is readily absorbed from the intestines.

Occurrence and food sources: Inositol is present in plants and animal tissues. In the form of phytic acid, it occurs in seeds and cereal grains. Fruits, vegetables and grains are good sources. It is also present in milk.

No deficiency manifestations have been reported in man.

Para-Aminobenzoic Acid

Para-aminobenzoic acid (PABA), which was originally regarded as B vitamin, is now considered to function solely as a component of folic acid (**Fig. 5.25**). It forms one of the three components of the folic acid group of vitamins. PABA is required for the growth of certain micro-organisms and functions by counteracting the bacteriostatic action of sulphonamide drugs. This is because of the structural similarity of both the compounds. The result is that the microorganisms multiply in the presence of sulphonamide drugs if PABA is not excluded.

Figure 5.25 Para-aminobenzoic acid.

Vitamin B_{12}

Vitamin B_{12} was isolated in 1948 from liver, as a red crystalline compound, containing cobalt. It has derived the names of cobalamin and cyanocobalamin because of the presence of cobalt and cyanide (CN) groups, respectively, in its structure. Other names of vitamin B_{12} are *antipernicious anaemia factor* and *extrinsic factor of Castle.*

Structure: Vitamin B_{12} has a complex structure. The molecule is large, containing 63 carbon atoms. Its molecular weight is 1350. The structure of vitamin B_{12} is shown in **Figure 5.26**. The important features of the structure of vitamin B_{12} are as follows:

1. A macrocytic porphyrin-like ring structure in which two pyrrole rings, A and D joined directly without a methene bridge, form the major part of the structure.
2. In the centre of the ring structure, there is a trivalent cobalt atom, which is attached by co-ordinate linkages to the N atoms of the pyrrole nuclei. The central structure is referred to as 'corrin' ring system.
3. To the cobalt is attached a cyanide (CN) group.
4. Below the corrin ring system, there is a nucleotide ring which is connected at one end to the central cobalt atom and at the other end through the phosphate of the nucleotide to an amino-propanol chain, which, in turn, is attached to the propionic acid side chain of ring C of the porphyrin-like structure.

Properties:

1. Vitamin B_{12} crystals are red in colour and the colour is attributed to the activity of the vitamin. They are stable to heat.
2. The presence of the CN ion in the molecule gives the designation of cyanocobalamin to the vitamin. Removal of the CN ion from the molecule makes it cobalamin. Substitution of the cyanide group with a hydroxyl group forms hydroxocobalamin (B_{12a}). Substitution of the cyanide group with a nitro group forms nitrocobalamin (B_{12c}). All these derivatives have similar biological action and among these, hydroxocobalamin is considered more active than the others.
3. An important property of vitamin B_{12} is its capacity of binding with protein. For example, the intrinsic factor is a protein with which vitamin B_{12} combines readily in the stomach, before absorption of the vitamin from the intestines.

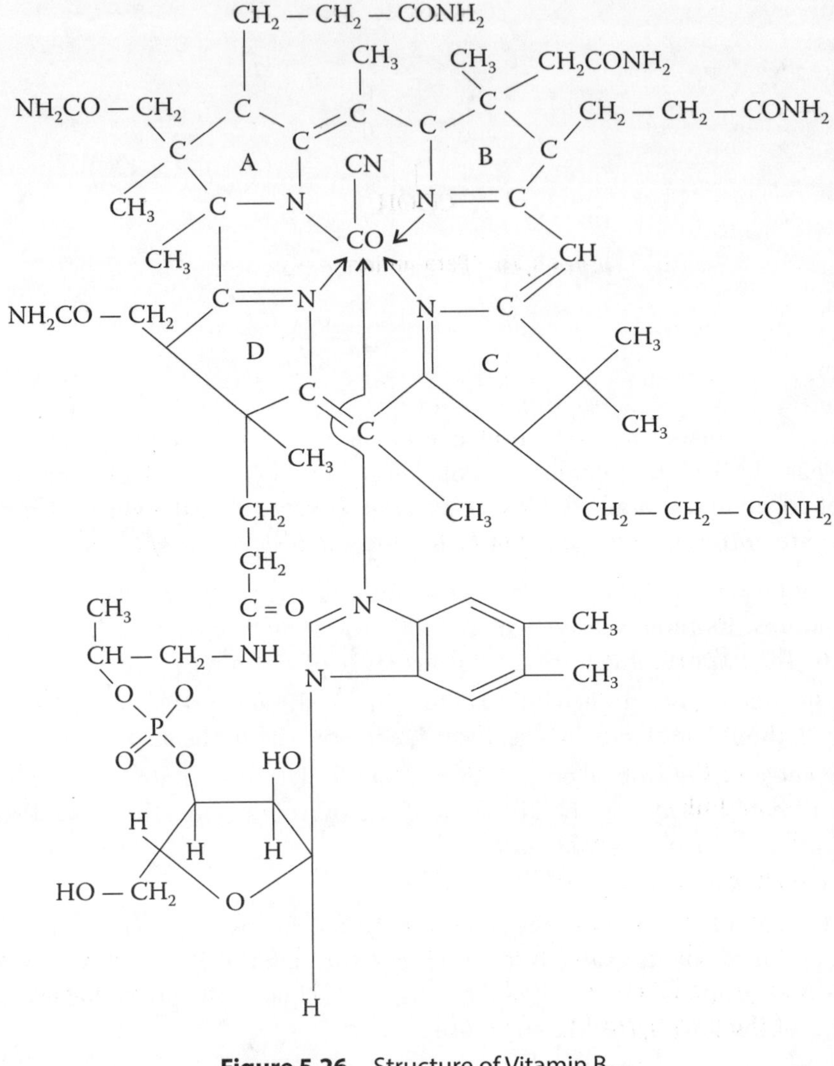

Figure 5.26 Structure of Vitamin B_{12}.

4. The coenzyme forms of vitamin B_{12} are called cobamides and they have been isolated from microorganisms and liver tissues. Structurally, they differ from vitamin B_{12} in that they have an adenine deoxy nucleoside group in place of the CN ion. There are three forms of cobamides.

Metabolic functions:

1. Vitamin B_{12} helps in the formation of labile methyl groups.
2. Methyl groups are required for the synthesis of thymine and therefore for the synthesis of nucleic acids.
3. Vitamin B_{12} functions as a cofactor in transmethylation reactions which are involved in the biosynthesis of methionine.
4. Vitamin B_{12} is involved in the biosynthesis of protein in the microsomal system.

5. Cobamide coenzyme is required for proper utilisation of propionic acid, i.e. in the conversion of propionate to succinate, when methyl malonyl-CoA is converted to succinyl-CoA by the enzyme methyl malonyl isomerase.
6. Cobamide takes part in the interconversion of glutamate and β-methylaspartate, which takes place in the bacterial system.
7. Vitamin B_{12} is concerned with the maintenance of sulphydryl group (SH). In vitamin B_{12} deficiency, marked deficiency of glutathione and CoA occurs.
8. Vitamin B_{12} along with folic acid are important factors for the maintenance of normal haemopoiesis. Both vitamins function to promote the development of red cells beyond the megaloblastic stage. Deficiency of vitamin B_{12} and folic acid results in the accumulation of megaloblasts in the bone marrow, leading to the development of a macrocytic type of anaemia and this is the picture observed in pernicious anaemia. These abnormalities are corrected by administration of vitamin B_{12} and folic acid, as they stimulate the maturation of the megaloblasts, to form mature red blood cells. For this reason, vitamin B_{12} is given the name of 'erythrocyte maturation factor'.

Biosynthesis and metabolism: Vitamin B_{12} (cobalamin) is synthesised by intestinal microorganisms. It is present in normal animal liver where it exists mostly as adenosylcobalamin. Lesser amounts of methyl cobalamin and hydroxocobalamin are also present in the liver.

Absorption, storage and circulation: Absorption of vitamin B_{12} occurs in the intestines, particularly from ileum. It requires the presence of an intrinsic factor which is a highly specific non-dialysable and thermolabile glycoprotein secreted by the parietal cells of the gastric mucosa. It also requires free HCl for its absorption. Absorption of vitamin B_{12} is impaired in the absence of intrinsic factor and free HCl, and such a condition can arise after surgical removal of the stomach. This will lead to development of vitamin B_{12} deficiency and anaemia.

As the cobalamin-intrinsic factor complex which is formed during absorption crosses the ileal mucosa, the intrinsic factor is released and cobalamin is transferred to a plasma transport protein known as transcobalamin II. Transcobalamins I and III are also cobalamin-binding proteins and are present in the plasma and liver, the latter providing an effective storage form for cobalamin. They bind the vitamin more permanently whereas transcobalamin II gives up its vitamin B_{12} to the tissues and is the functionally important carrier. Some cobalamin is excreted in the bile, but this is partly reabsorbed in normal people with a fresh intrinsic factor in an enterohepatic circulation. The major circulating cobalamin is methylcobalamin. Liver is the major storage organ and 70% of the total cobalamins is stored in the liver as 5-deoxyadenosylcobalamin. The normal concentration of plasma vitamin B_{12} is 0.008–0.042 μg/100 ml.

Requirement: The daily requirement of vitamin B_{12} is 2–4 μg. Much more is required in case of pernicious anaemia.

Food sources: Vitamin B_{12} content of food is very low. Only foods of animal origin contain an appreciable amount of the vitamin. For example, liver, kidney, eggs, meat and milk are good sources of vitamin B_{12}.

Deficiency manifestations: A tendency for the development of vitamin B_{12} deficiency has been reported in pure vegetarians, as this vitamin is present predominantly in foods of animal origin, with very little present in vegetables. These persons have subnormal serum concentration of vitamin B_{12} and they develop symptoms such as glossitis and peripheral sensory disturbances. Gross deficiency of vitamin B_{12} causes pernicious anaemia which manifests the same abnormalities of blood formation as encountered in folic acid deficiency, namely evidences of arrested development of blood elements in bone marrow, with accumulation of megaloblasts and myeloblasts. A peripheral blood picture shows a macrocytic type of anaemia. Other characteristic manifestations of pernicious anaemia are as follows:

1. Atrophy of the mucous membrane of the mouth and tongue with inflammation, resulting in glossitis, stomatitis and pharyngitis
2. Degenerative lesions of the posterior and lateral columns of the spinal cord, resulting in peripheral sensory disturbances, hyperactive reflexes and paralysis

Pernicious anaemia arises due to failure of the secretion of the intrinsic factor by the gastric fundus in an adequate quantity to facilitate absorption of vitamin B_{12} from the intestines. Pernicious anaemia may occur in patients, following surgical removal of the stomach (total gastrectomy) and extensive resection of small intestines, the latter creating the problem of a reduced surface area for absorption of the vitamin.

Vitamin C (Ascorbic Acid)

Vitamin C is known as the antiscorbutic vitamin, because it was found to cure a deficiency disease called *scurvy* which was prevalent among sailors who could not get fresh fruits and vegetables for a long period when they were in a ship. It was recognised as early as the sixteenth century that oranges and lemons had a curative value for scurvy. The vitamin was isolated in 1928 and synthesised in 1933.

Chemistry: Ascorbic acid has a structure similar to that of L-glucose and it is a derivative of glucose.

Ascorbic acid may be described as an enediol lactone of gulonic acid, which has a configuration similar to that of L-glucose (**Fig. 5.27**). It contains two enolic hydroxyl groups attached to the second and third double-bonded carbon atoms. The acidity of ascorbic acid is due to the dissociation of the enolic hydrogen atoms of these carbon atoms. It contains a lactone ring which ties up the carboxyl group with the fourth carbon atom. There are two asymmetric carbon atoms, C-4 and C-5, which make the vitamin optically active. Two optical isomers, dextro and levo forms, exist in nature. The levo form is active and dextro form inactive.

Properties:

1. Pure ascorbic acid appears as white crystals.
2. Ascorbic acid is readily soluble in water but insoluble in most solvents.
3. It has a sour acid taste.
4. Ascorbic acid is extremely unstable and gets easily oxidised to dehydroascorbic acid, in the presence of air, light, hydrogen peroxide, ferric chloride, iodine and methylene blue.

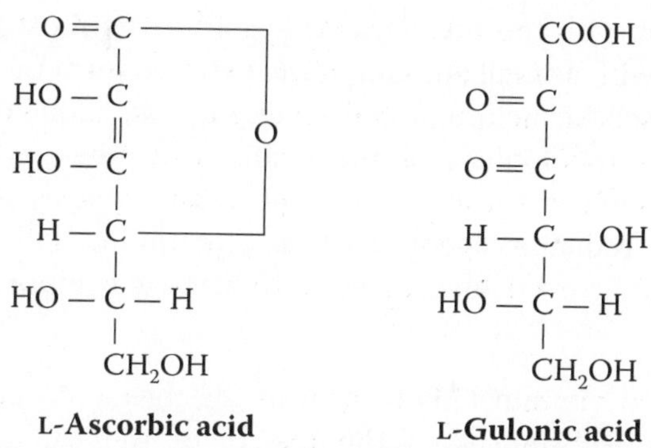

Figure 5.27 Structure of L-ascorbic acid and L-gulonic acid.

5. Ascorbic acid has a strong reducing property. When oxidised, it reduces the substance used for oxidation. The reaction can be readily reversed by the action of reducing agents, both in vitro and in vivo (**Fig. 5.28**).
6. Because of its solubility in water and its susceptibility to undergo irreversible oxidative degradation to inactive compounds, much vitamin C is lost during cooking, processing and storage procedures.
7. Ascorbic acid oxidase, an enzyme present in vegetables and fruits, accelerates the oxidation of vitamin C in the presence of oxygen. The oxidation occurs more rapidly if the vegetables are bruised and stored, as the enzyme readily escapes from the damaged cells.

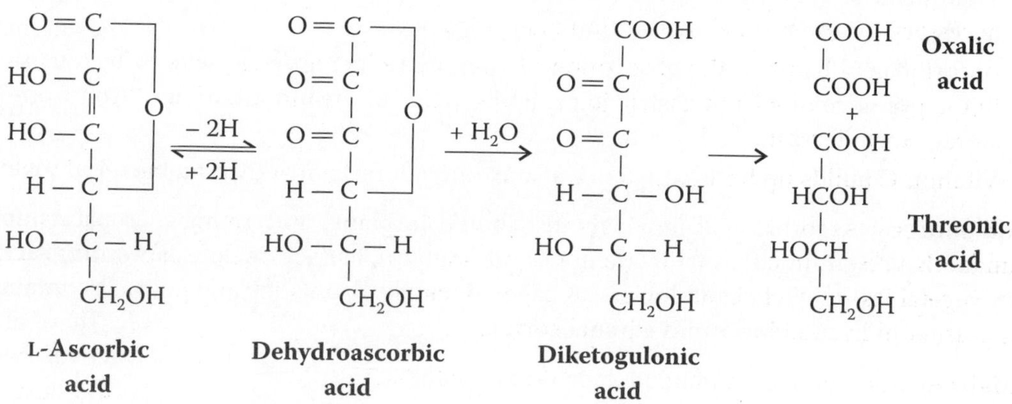

Figure 5.28 Metabolism of ascorbic acid.

Absorption and metabolism: Man cannot synthesise ascorbic acid. Therefore, the entire human requirement has to be supplied by the diet.

Ascorbic acid is readily absorbed from the small intestines and subcutaneous tissues. There is no particular organ for storage of the vitamin, though liver and adrenal cortex contain high concentration of vitamin C. Normal plasma contains 0.6–1.5 mg of ascorbic acid per 100 ml of blood. White blood cells and platelets contain 20–40 times more of ascorbic acid than plasma. In the body, ascorbic acid exists mostly in the reduced form which is in equilibrium with a small amount of the oxidised form under normal conditions. About 50–75% of the ascorbic acid ingested undergoes metabolic degradation to inactive compounds such as diketogulonic acid and oxalic acid. The remaining portion of the vitamin is excreted as such in the urine. It is necessary that ascorbic acid is preserved in its reduced form by reducing agents such as glutathione and cysteine, as otherwise the oxidised form will get irreversibly converted to inactive compounds.

Metabolic functions:

1. The chief function of vitamin C is to help in the formation and maintenance of the intercellular ground substances of the matrix of the capillary walls, collagen of connective tissues, osteoid tissues of bone and dentine of teeth. The clinical signs observed in scurvy are mainly due to the defective development of these structures. Vitamin C is particularly required for the repair and healing of wounds.
2. Because of its existence in two reversible forms, vitamin C is involved in cellular oxidation-reduction reactions, where it functions as a hydrogen transport agent.
3. Ascorbic acid acts as a coenzyme in one of the steps of tyrosine metabolism, i.e. in the conversion of p-hydroxyphenyl pyruvate to homogentisic acid.
4. Ascorbic acid is also required for the normal metabolism of tryptophan, when it gets converted to 5-hydroxytryptophan (serotonin pathway).
5. Vitamin C is necessary for the normal growth, maturation and reproduction of cells, in the sense that in its presence, folic acid is reduced and formylated to folinic acid which is required for the synthesis of nucleic acid.
6. Vitamin C is required for the conversion of folic acid to folinic acid, both being necessary for the normal maturation of erythrocytes.
7. Ascorbic acid helps in the absorption of iron, by reducing ferric salts to ferrous salts in the presence of HCl of gastric juice. It also helps in the mobilisation of iron from its storage form ferritin.
8. Vitamin C builds up body resistance against infections by inactivating bacterial toxins.

Food sources: Ascorbic acid is widely distributed in plants and animals. In plants, it is abundantly present in citrus fruits (lemons and oranges), berries, melons, sprouting seeds, leafy vegetables, spinach, cauliflower, cabbage, tomatoes, drumstick and guava. In animals, it is present in liver, kidneys and adrenal cortex.

Requirements: The recommended daily requirement is 75–100 mg.

Deficiency manifestations: Deficiency of ascorbic acid produces a disease called *scurvy*, which exhibits characteristic features. These are associated with failure in the development of specialised cells that promote normal deposition of collagen, osteoid and dentin, and formation of the intercellular cement substance of the capillaries. These defects are exhibited by the following symptoms which are characteristic of scurvy:

1. Widespread haemorrhage due to fragility of capillaries is seen as petechial, subcutaneous, subperiosteal and internal bleeding.

2. Painful, tender and swollen joints, restricting movements, is a common feature. This again is due to haemorrhage inside the joints and inflammation of the ends of bones.
3. Defective teeth formation with swollen spongy, tender and bleeding gums which retract causing loosening of teeth are characteristic features of scurvy.
4. Defective skeletal growth due to defective bone formation may be seen by X-ray examination.

ANTIVITAMINS

Antivitamins are chemical substances that possess structures similar to those of certain vitamins and on introduction into the body, they behave antagonistically towards these vitamins preventing their normal activities. The antivitamins compete with their structurally similar vitamins for the same specific reaction sites on enzyme surfaces. A few examples of vitamins with their respective antivitamins are given below:

1. Thiamine—pyrithiamine
2. Riboflavin—dichlororiboflavin, isoriboflavin
3. Nicotinic acid—3-pyridine sulphonic acid
4. Pyridoxine—isonicotinic acid hydrazide
5. Folic acid—aminopterin
6. Vitamin K—dicoumarol

6 CHAPTER Nucleoproteins and Nucleic Acids

Chapter Outline

- Nucleotides and Their Importance
- Nucleosides and Their Biological Importance
- Nucleic Acids: Composition and Structure
- Metabolism of Nucleic Acid

Nucleoproteins are conjugated proteins. They contain nucleic acids which are non-protein prosthetic groups attached to simple proteins such as protamines or histones. Nucleoprotein is an essential constituent of the nuclei of animal and plant cells and has derived its name because of its existence in nuclear material. It is also found in the cytoplasm, particularly associated with the ribosomes which are specially concerned with the biosynthesis of proteins. They are present in all living cells, namely bacteria, virus and chromosomes. Nucleoprotein, being a primary constituent of chromatin, plays an important role in the process of cell division and transmission of hereditary factors. Abnormality in the process of normal cell growth and reproduction results, when there is an alteration in the formation of nucleoproteins.

When nucleoproteins are hydrolysed by either acids or enzymes, they are broken down to their components, nucleic acids and simple protein. The simple proteins follow the usual reactions common to proteins (**Fig. 6.1**).

Nucleic acids were first reported by Miescher in 1871. They have high molecular weight. They contain phosphoric acid, pentose sugar and purine and pyrimidine bases.

Nucleic acids are of two types:

1. Ribose nucleic acid (RNA)
2. Deoxyribose nucleic acid (DNA)

The main feature which distinguishes the two nucleic acids is the pentose contained in each. In RNA, the pentose is ribose and in DNA, it is deoxyribose.

RNA is present largely in the cytoplasm of actively growing cells which are engaged in the production and secretion of protein. The concentration of RNA increases with an increase in protein synthesis.

DNA is always present in the nuclei of cells and is confined to the chromosomes. A very small amount is present in mitochondria, which are outside the nuclei.

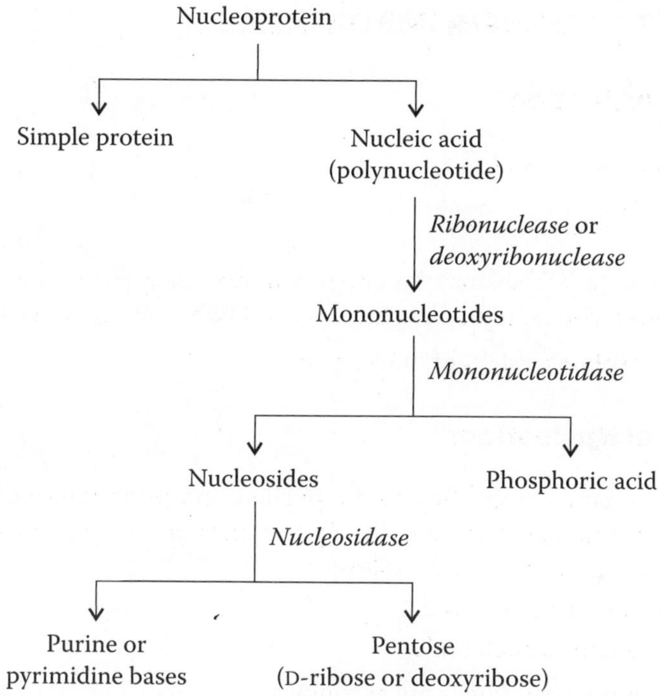

Figure 6.1 Hydrolysis of nucleoproteins.

Biological functions of nucleic acids: Nucleic acids play a vital role in the biosynthesis of cellular proteins.

1. Ribonucleic acids are involved in the actual process of synthesis of protein molecules.
2. The concentration of RNA is increased in organs which show high energy intake due to treatment with thyroxine, insulin and cortisone.

   The concentration of RNA is diminished in high fat diets and in states of deficiency of thiamine and vitamin B_{12}.
3. According to the current concept, RNA is speculated to be associated with memory storage function in the brain.
4. Viruses which invade plant and animal cells contain RNA, whereas bacteriophage which are viruses infecting bacterial cells contain DNA. Viruses after invading living cells multiply the synthesis of the nucleic acid and the protein of which they are composed, thus altering the metabolism of the host cell.
5. DNA participates in two important roles in the life of the cells:
   - During cell division, it undergoes replication and transmits an exact copy to each of the daughter cells.
   - It provides genetic information and directs synthesis of a specific protein.
6. Nucleic acids are concerned with mutation and carcinogenesis of living cells. Agents such as X-rays, ultraviolet light and nitrogen mustard, which are considered mutagenic and carcinogenic, produce abnormal types of nucleic acids in the cells.

NUCLEOTIDES AND THEIR IMPORTANCE

Structure of a Nucleotide

Each nucleotide unit consists of

1. A phosphoric acid
2. A pentose
3. A nitrogenous base, which may be either a purine or a pyrimidine. Out of the four mononucleotides, two contain a purine base and two a pyrimidine base.

Nucleotides are phosphoric esters of nucleosides.

Nomenclature of Nucleotides

The nucleotides are named according to the purines and pyrimidines contained in them. The purines are adenine and guanine. The pyrimidines are uracil, cytosine and thymine. Nucleotides containing purines are as follows:

1. Adenylic acid (adenine nucleotide)
2. Guanylic acid (guanine nucleotide)

Nucleotides containing pyrimidines are as follows:

1. Uridylic acid (uracil nucleotide)
2. Cytidylic acid (cytosine nucleotide)
3. Thymidylic acid (thymine nucleotide)

The structures of adenylic acid and cytidylic acid are shown in **Figures 6.13** and **6.14** later in the text.

The structures of uridylic and guanylic acid are shown in **Figure 6.2**.

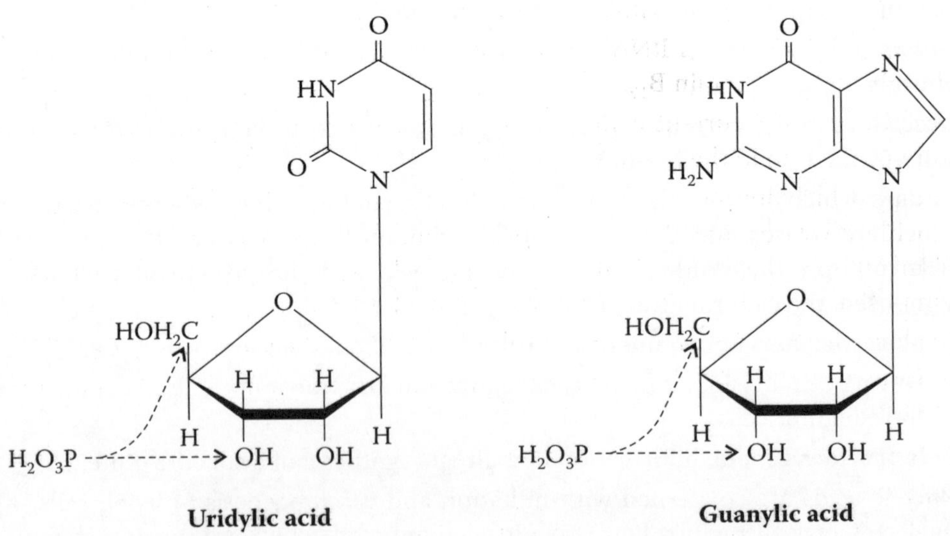

Figure 6.2 Structures of uridylic and guanylic acid.

Free Nucleotides and Their Biological Importance

Besides the nucleotides which form integral components of the nucleic acids, the following nucleotides exist in a free state in the tissues:

1. Adenlylic acid (AA) is also known as adenosine monophosphate (adenosine-3, monophosphate) or AMP. It is important because of its metabolic role in the activation of phosphorylase (**Fig. 6.3**).

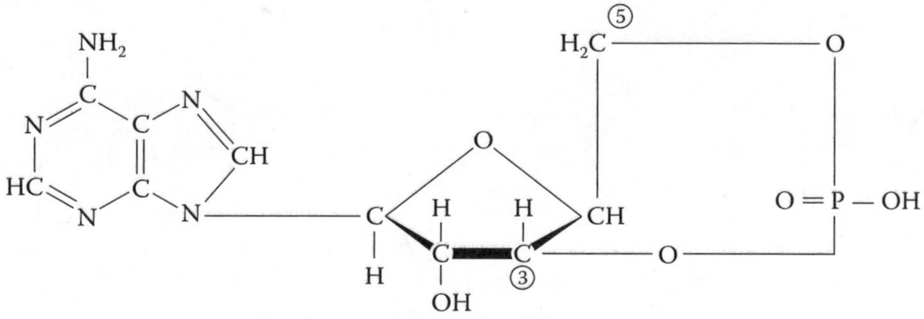

Figure 6.3 3′-5′-Adenylic acid (cyclic AMP).

2. Adenosine diphosphate (ADP)
3. Adenosine triphosphate (ATP). Both ADP and ATP act as transfer agents for phosphate groups and are involved in oxidative phosphorylation. They serve as sources of high-energy phosphate (**Fig. 6.4**).
4. *Adenosine-3′-5′-cyclophosphate (cyclic AMP)*: This is an unusual cyclic derivative of adenosine-5-monophosphate. It is involved in the activation of phosphorylase.
5. *Guanosine diphosphate (GDP)*: This is a guanine nucleotide derivative. It is involved in phosphorylation concerned with the oxidation of α-ketoglutaric acid to succinyl-CoA.
6. *Guanosine triphosphate (GTP)*: This compound serves as a source of high-energy phosphate.
7. *Uracil nucleotides*:
   - Uridine derivatives, namely uridine diphosphate glucose (UDPG) and uridine diphosphate galactose (UDP Gal), function as coenzymes in reaction concerned with epimerization of galactose and glucose. UDPG is a precursor in reactions involving glycogen synthesis.
   - Uridine diphosphate glucuronic acid (UDP Gluc): This serves as a source of active glucuronide for conjugation reactions requiring glucuronic acid, for example in the formation of bilirubin glucuronide.
   - Uridine triphosphate (UTP) is a high-energy phosphate compound.
8. *Cytosine derivatives*: Cytidine triphosphate (CTP) is a high-energy phosphate compound. It reacts with phosphoryl choline to form cytidine diphosphate choline (CDP-choline), which combines with the diglyceride to form phospholipid.

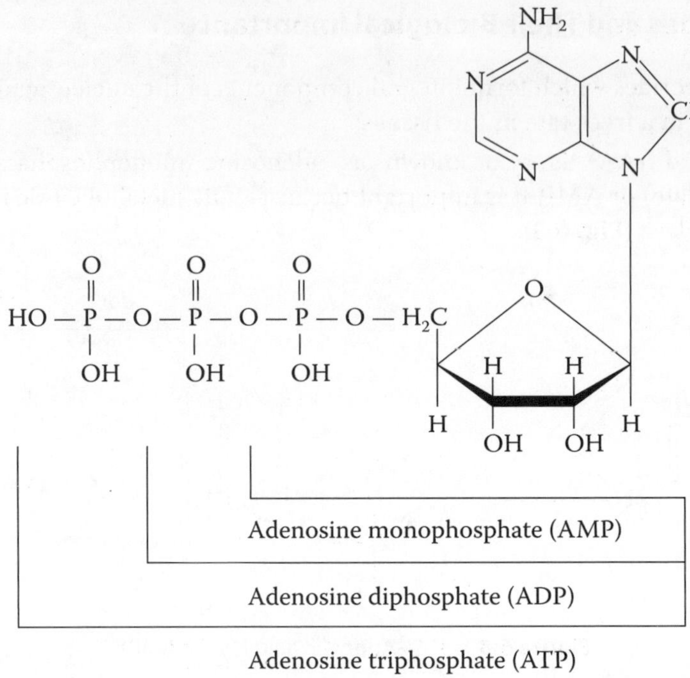

Figure 6.4 Adenylic system.

9. *B vitamins and nucleotides*: Coenzyme derivatives of riboflavin and niacin are nucleotides.
    - Riboflavin coenzymes are as follows:
        - Flavin mononucleotide (FMN; **Fig. 6.5**)
        - Flavin adenine dinucleotide (FAD; **Fig. 6.6**)

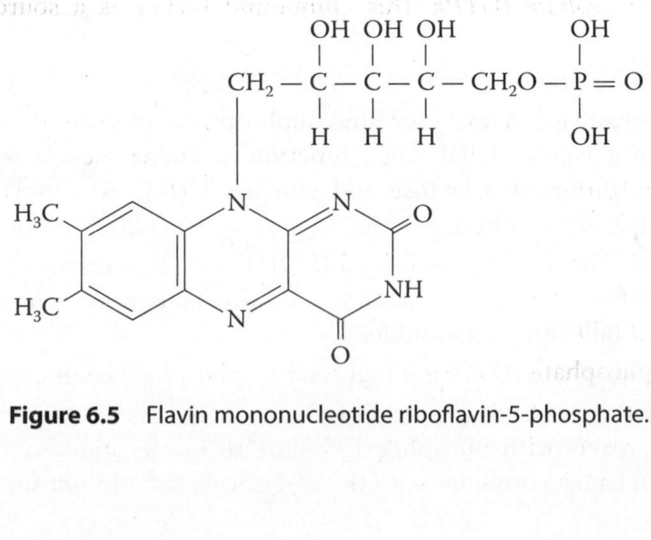

Figure 6.5 Flavin mononucleotide riboflavin-5-phosphate.

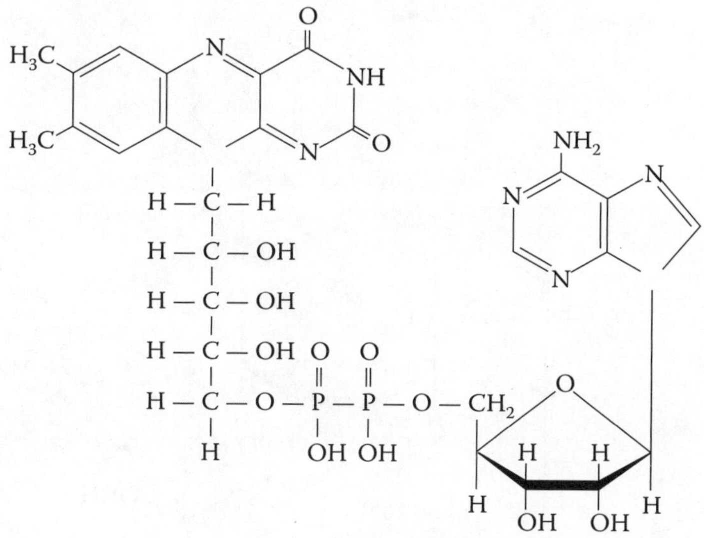

Figure 6.6 Flavin adenine dinucleotide.

- Niacin coenzymes are as follows:
  - Nicotinamide adenine dinucleotide (NAD; **Fig. 6.7**)
  - Nicotinamide adenine dinucleotide phosphate (NADP; **Fig. 6.8**)

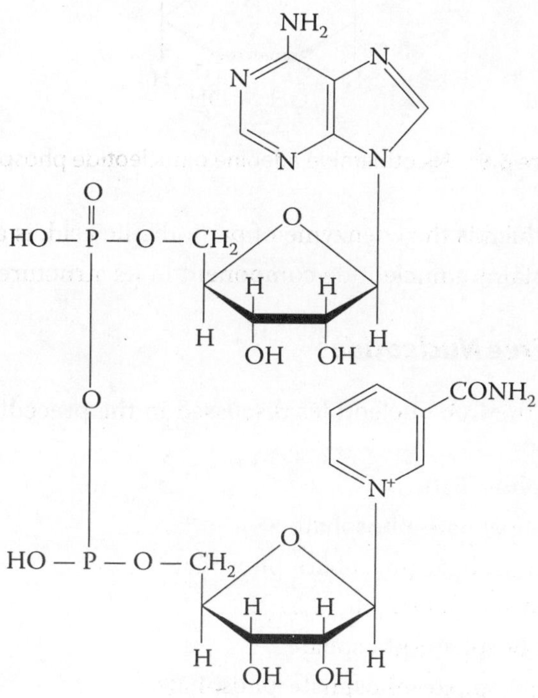

Figure 6.7 Nicotinamide adenine dinucleotide.

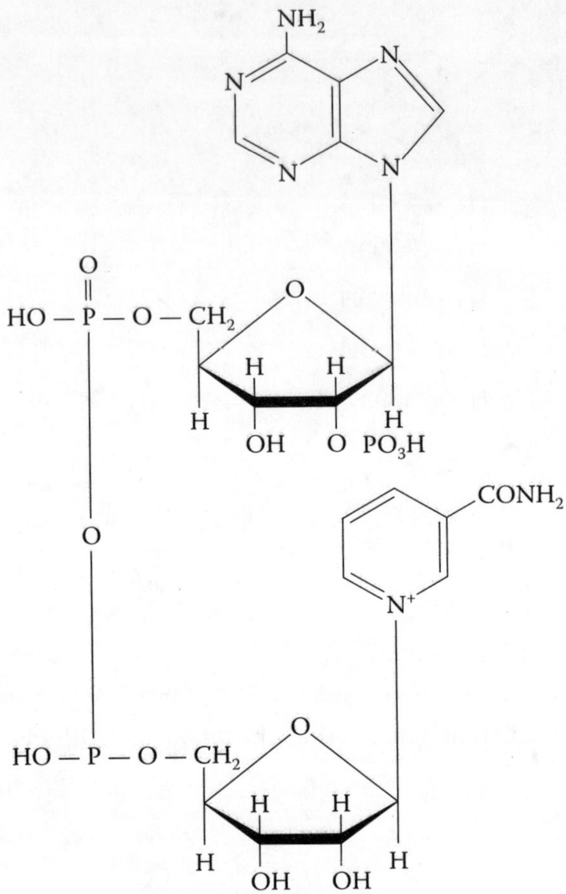

Figure 6.8 Nicotinamide adenine dinucleotide phosphate.

- Coenzyme A, which is the coenzyme of pantothenic acid, is a nucleotide.
- Vitamin B_{12} contains a nucleotide component in its structure.

Word Formulae of Free Nucleotides

The word formulae of the free nucleotides discussed in the preceding text may be written as follows:

1. AMP: Adenosine-phosphate
2. ADP: Adenosine-phosphate-phosphate
3. ATP: Adenosine-phosphate-phosphate-phosphate
4. AMP: Cyclic-adenosine-phosphate (3,5)
5. GDP: Guanosine-phosphate-phosphate
6. GTP: Guanosine-phosphate-phosphate-phosphate
7. UDPG: Uridine-phosphate-phosphate-glucose
8. UDP: Gal-Uridine-phosphate-phosphate-galactose

9. UDP: Gluc-Uridine-phosphate-glucuronate
10. UTP: Uridine-phosphate-phosphate-phosphate
11. CTP: Cytidine-phosphate-phosphate-phosphate
12. FMN: Riboflavin-phosphate
13. FAD–Flavin-ribose-phosphate-phosphate-ribose
    |
    adenine
14. NAD–Adenine-ribose-phosphate-phosphate-ribose
    |
    nicotinamide
15. NADP–Adenine-ribose-phosphate-phosphate-ribose
    | |
    phosphate nicotinamide
16. CoA: Pantothenate + ATP + mercaptoethylamine
17. Vitamin B_{12}

NUCLEOSIDES AND THEIR BIOLOGICAL IMPORTANCE

Nucleosides are structural subunits of nucleic acids and are products of enzymatic or chemical hydrolysis of nucleic acids. The knowledge about the structural composition of nucleosides has allowed chemical synthesis of nucleosides that are being used as antibotics and anticancer agents, for example Puromycin and Zidovudine.

Structure of a Nucleoside

A nucleoside is composed of a purine or pyrimidine base linked to a pentose sugar, either ribose or deoxyribose, through a glucoside linkage.

Examples of nucleosides: The nucleosides are named according to the purines and pyrimidines contained in them. Nucleosides containing purines are as follows:

1. Adenosine (adenine + ribose): AR
2. Guanosine (guanine + ribose): GR

Nucleosides containing pyrimidines are as follows:

1. Uridine (uracil + ribose): UR
2. Cytidine (cytosine + ribose): CR
3. Thymidine (thymine + ribose): TR

S-Adenosyl methionine, which is also known as active methionine, is a biologically important nucleoside containing adenine (adenine nucleoside). It is an important prerequisite for the transmethylation reaction of methionine.

$$\text{Adenine} - \text{ribose} - \underset{}{\overset{\overset{CH_3}{|}}{S}} - CH_2CH_2CHNH_2COOH$$

S-Adenosylmethionine

In addition to the purines and pyrimidines mentioned already, there are some nitrogenous bases, which are formed as products of metabolism. These are hypoxanthine, xanthine, allantoin, orotic acid and uric acid (**Figs 6.9** and **6.10**).

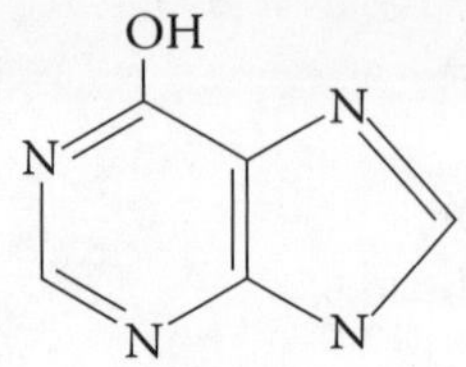

Hypoxanthine

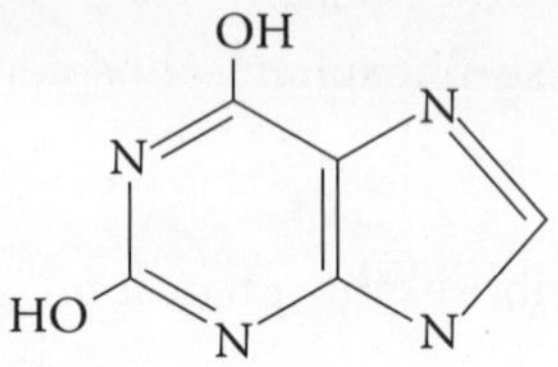

Xanthine

Figure 6.9 Products of purine degradation.

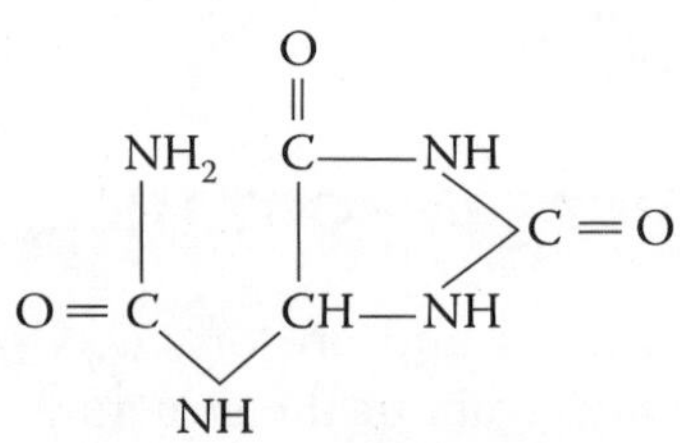

Allantoin

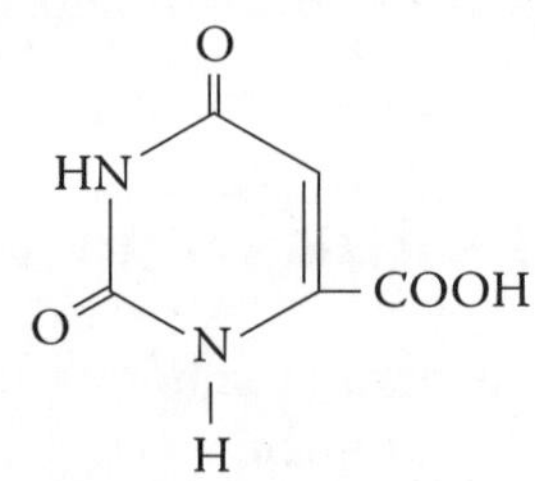

Orotic acid

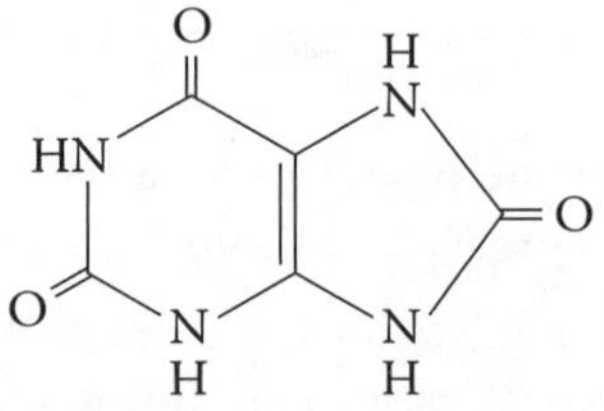

Uric acid (keto form)

Figure 6.10 Nitrogenous bases formed as products of metabolism.

NUCLEIC ACIDS: COMPOSITION AND STRUCTURE

The constituents of RNA and DNA are given in **Table 6.1**.

Both the nucleic acids contain phosphoric acid. Both have purines, adenine and guanine. Both have one pyrimidine in common, i.e. cytosine.

The two nucleic acids differ in the following aspects:

1. The sugar component of RNA is ribose. The sugar component of DNA is deoxyribose. It is this factor which decides whether a nucleic acid is RNA or DNA.

2. The second pyrimidine component of RNA is uracil. The second pyrimidine component of DNA is thymine. Traces of another pyrimidine, methylcytosine, occur in some DNA of animal origin and in larger amounts in wheat germ DNA.

Table 6.1 Constituents of RNA and DNA

Ribonucleic Acid	Deoxyribonucleic Acid
Phosphoric acid	Phosphoric acid
Ribose	Deoxyribose
Adenine	Adenine
Guanine	Guanine
Cytosine	Cytosine
Uracil	Thymine
Cytosine	Methylcytosine

Ribonucleic Acid

Four types of RNA have been distinguished, based on their functions. They are all involved in protein synthesis. These are as follows:

1. Messenger RNA (mRNA)
2. Ribosomal RNA (rRNA)
3. Soluble RNA (sRNA)
4. Viral RNA

Messenger RNA (mRNA): These are RNAs which carry the genetic information stored in the DNA of the nucleus to the site of protein synthesis. mRNA has a high molecular weight.

Ribosomal RNA: These are associated with the ribosomes of the endoplasmic reticulum in the cytoplasm. They have comparatively low molecular weight. There are four types of rRNA.

Soluble RNA (sRNA): These are also known as transfer RNA (tRNA). They are a soluble form of RNA. They are extremely soluble in aqueous solvents, in contrast to the ribosomal and viral forms of RNA. They have low molecular weight. There are different types of sRNA, about 20 in number. Each type combines with a specific amino acid and carries it to the ribosome and deposits it on the RNA template which is the site of protein synthesis. It finds out the definite code word on the mRNA.

Viral RNA: These are present in virus, for example the RNA present in tobacco mosaic virus. They have very high molecular weight. They have a protective coating of protein mixed with the RNA which helps to form the highly organised rod shape for the viral particle. The viral RNA also function as DNA.

Products of Hydrolysis of Nucleic Acids

These are the nitrogenous bases, pentose sugars and phosphoric acid. The nitrogenous bases are pyrimidines and purines.

Nitrogenous bases

- Pyrimidines
- Purines

Pyrimidine Bases

These are (i) uracil, (ii) thymine, (iii) cytosine, (iv) methylcytosine and (v) hydroxymethylcytosine. The numbering which is done according to the original Fischer system and the structural formulae of the pyrimidines are shown in **Figure 6.11**. Pyrimidines are capable of undergoing keto-enol tautomerism. The structures shown below are the keto forms. Pyrimidine bases are derived from the parent compound, the pyrimidine.

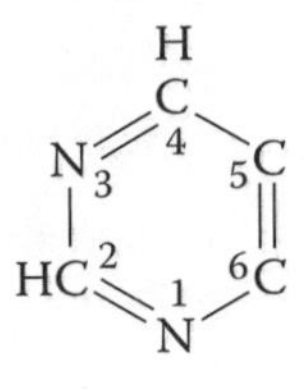

Pyrimidine

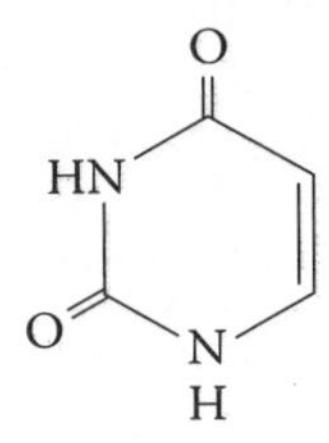

Uracil (2,6-dioxypyrimidine)

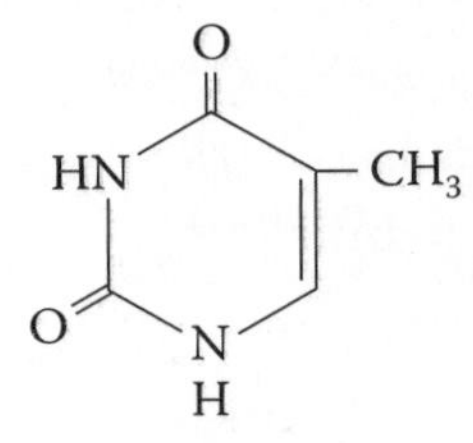

Thymine (5-methyluracil)

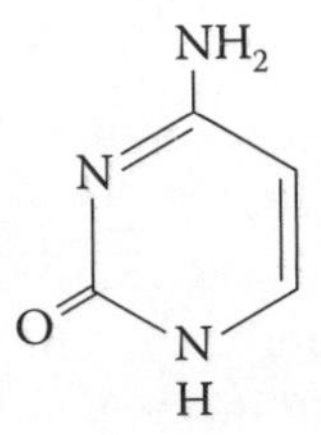

Cytosine (2-oxy-6-amino-pyrimidine)

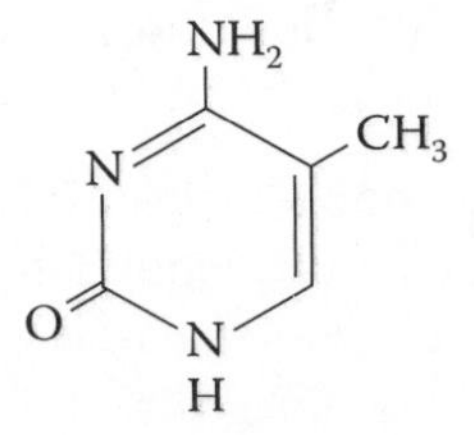

5-Methylcytosine

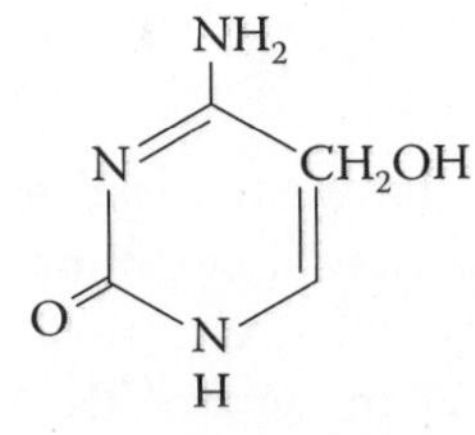

5-Hydroxymethyl-cytosine

Figure 6.11 Pyrimidine bases.

Purine Bases

The two major purine bases are adenine and guanine. The numbering system and the structural formulae of the purines are shown in **Figure 6.12**. Like pyrimidine, purines are capable of undergoing keto-enol tautomerism. The structures shown in the following text are of the enol form. Purine bases are derived from the parent compound purine. The structure of purine contains a pyrimidine ring and an imidazole ring.

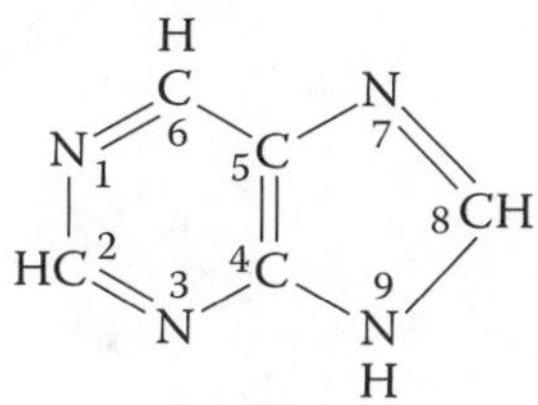

Purine

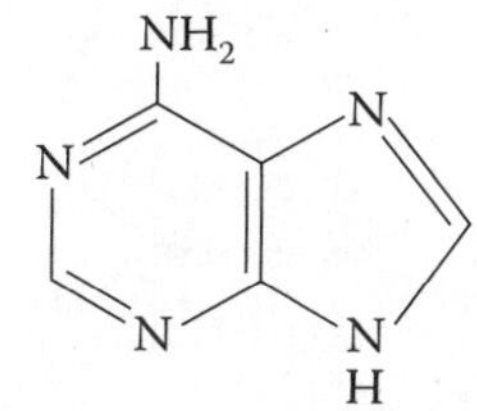

Adenine (6-aminopurine)

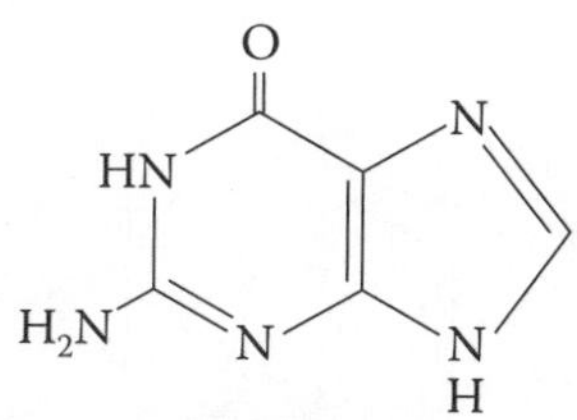

Guanine (2-amino-6-hydroxypurine)

Figure 6.12 Purines.

Pentose Sugars

The two pentose sugars contained in nucleic acids are (i) ribose in RNA and (ii) deoxyribose in DNA. The structural formulae of the two sugars have been shown in **Figure 1.1**. They exist in their furanose forms.

The general mode of linkage of the three components in the nucleotides and the nature of the internucleotide linkage are described below.

1. The ribose which exists in the furanose form is attached to the N atom in the ninth position of the purine in the case of purine nucleotide (**Figs 6.13** and **6.15**).
2. The ribose is attached to the N atom in the third position of the pyrimidine in the case of pyrimidine nucleotide (**Figs 6.14** and **6.16**).

In a nucleic acid, the nucleotides are interlinked through a phosphoric acid between the third position of the ribose of the first nucleotide and the fifth position of the ribose of the second nucleotide (**Figs 6.15** and **6.16**).

The mode of internucleotide linkage may be illustrated as in **Figure 6.17**. The diagonal lines indicate the linkage between the pentose of one nucleotide and the phosphoric acid of the next nucleotide.

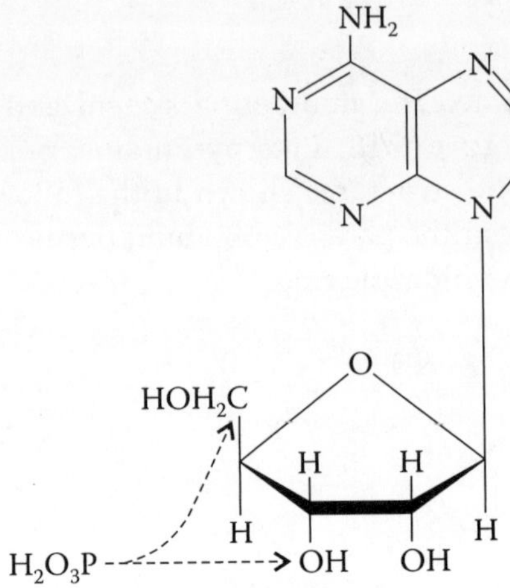

Figure 6.13 Adenylic acid (purine nucleotide).

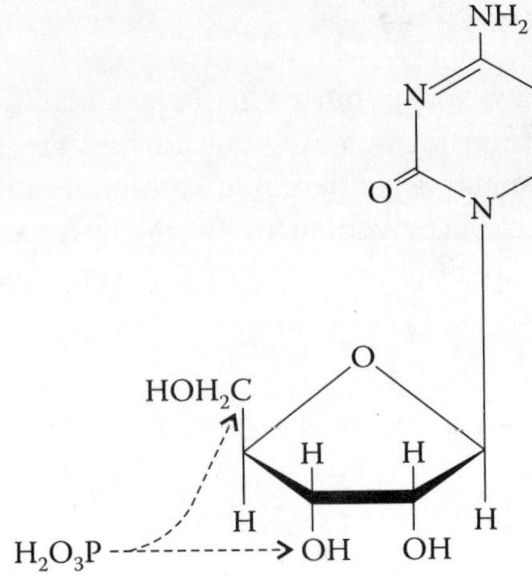

Figure 6.14 Cytydilic acid (pyrimidine nucelotide).

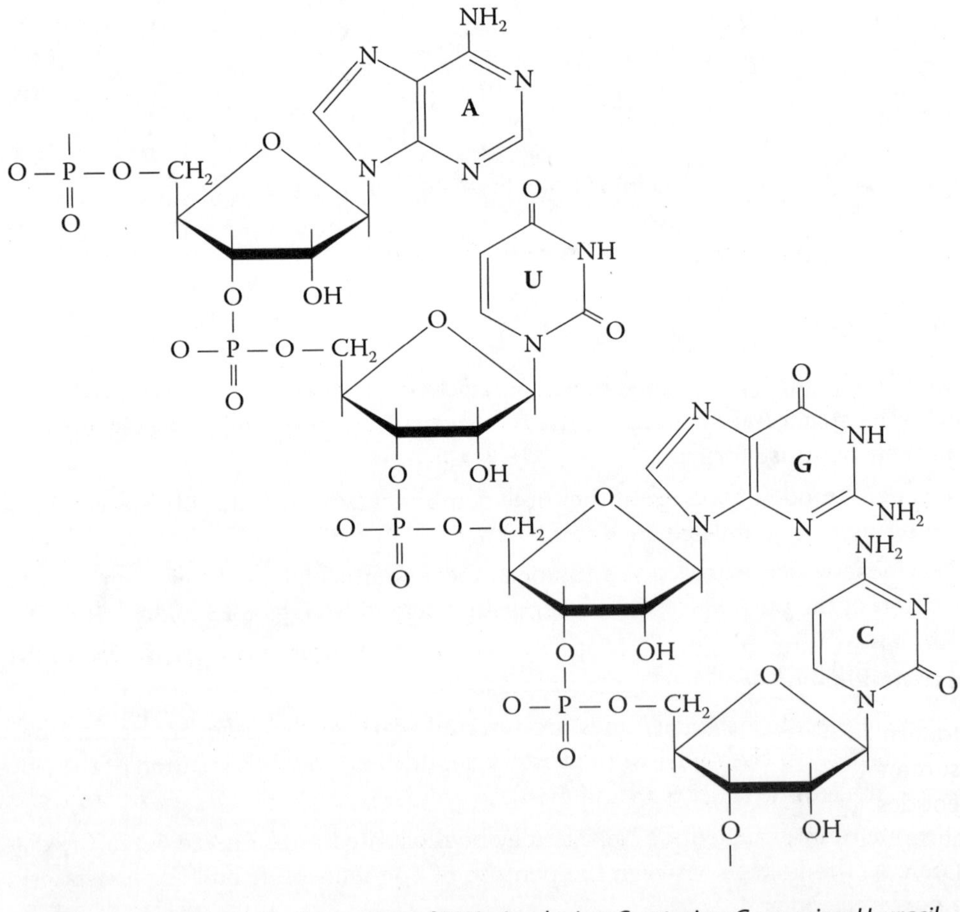

Figure 6.15 Structure of a section of RNA. *A, adenine; C, cytosine; G, guanine; U, uracil.*

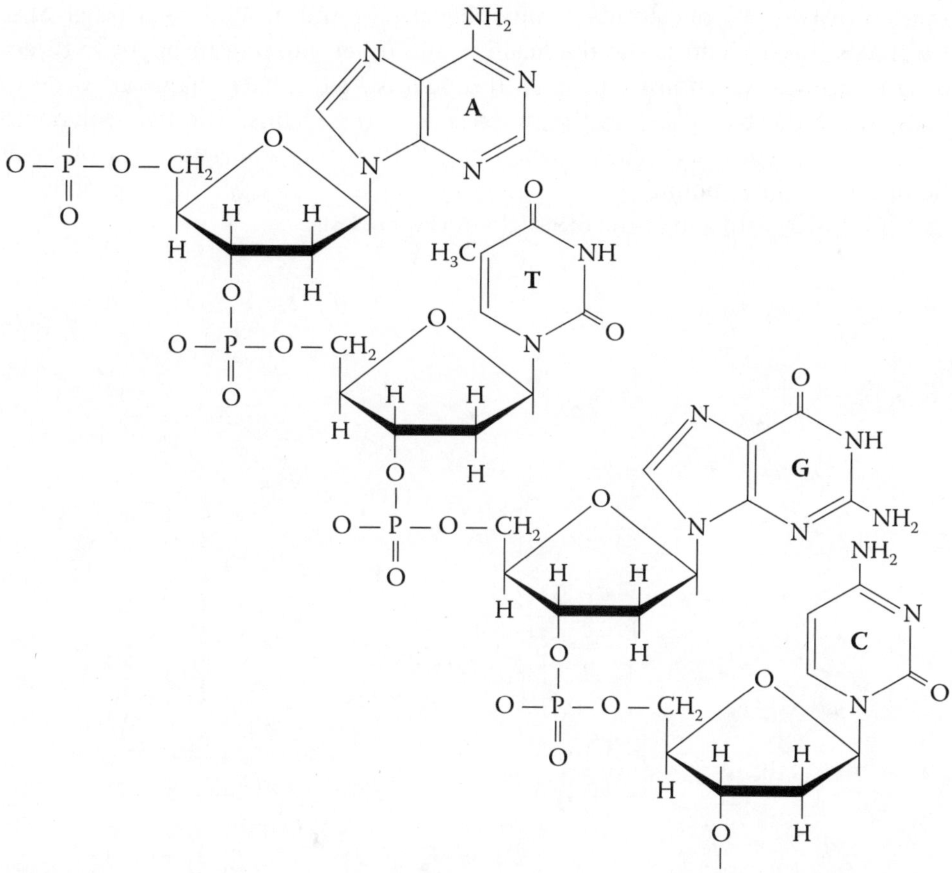

Figure 6.16 Structure of a section of DNA. *A, adenine; C, cytosine; G, guanine; T, thymine.*

Base—Pentose—PO_4

Base—Pentose—PO_4

Base—Pentose—PO_4

Base—Pentose—PO_4

Figure 6.17 Mode of internucleotide linkage.

Modern studies by applying techniques such as ultra-centrifugation, viscosity measurements and X-ray diffraction reveal that nucleic acids are highly polymerised nucleotides. The molecular weight of a typical tetranucleotide is 1286. It may increase to values twice or thrice 1286, up to 3,000,000 or more. The currently accepted structure for DNA is that proposed by Watson and Crick. Accordingly, the structure of DNA is composed of two polynucleotide chains helically wound around each other against a cylindrical axis. Each chain is the duplicate of the other running in opposite directions, consisting of groups which are repeated. The pentose-phosphate chains are seen on the outer side, while the bases are on the inner side of the chains. The two polynucleotide chains are held together by hydrogen bonding between appropriate pairs of bases, i.e. adenine of one chain is bound with thymine of another chain. Similarly, guanine of one chain is bound with cytosine of the other chain (**Fig. 6.18**).

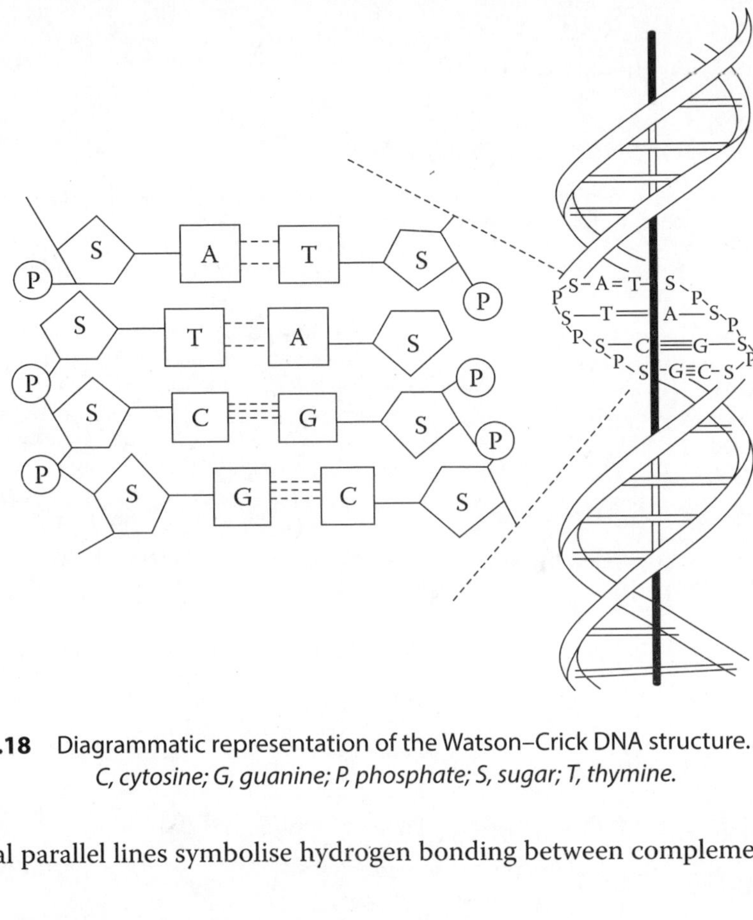

Figure 6.18 Diagrammatic representation of the Watson–Crick DNA structure. *A, adenine; C, cytosine; G, guanine; P, phosphate; S, sugar; T, thymine.*

Horizontal parallel lines symbolise hydrogen bonding between complementary bases.

METABOLISM OF NUCLEIC ACID

The major components of a molecule of nucleic acid are purine bases, pyrimidine bases, phosphate and pentose sugars, namely ribose and deoxyribose. Ribose and deoxyribose are derived from the hexose monophosphate pathway. Phosphate is available from the phosphate metabolic pool of the body.

The important aspects of nucleic acid metabolism are biosynthesis of purine and pyrimidine nucleotides, degradation (catabolism) of purines and pyrimidines, and salvage pathway for purines and pyrimidines.

Biosynthesis of Purine and Pyrimidine Nucleotides

Most of the purines and pyrimidines are synthesised within the body utilising amphibolic intermediates that furnish small molecules as precursors for biosynthetic reactions. This is known as 'de novo synthesis'.

Synthesis of Purine

The major site of synthesis of purine nucleotides is liver, though intestinal mucosa and thymus are also capable of synthesising purines.

By using the isotopic labelling technique, the sources of the nitrogen and carbon atoms of the purine ring have been traced to small fragments derived from glycine, aspartate, glutamate, CO_2 and formate. **Figure 6.19** illustrates the sources of C and N atoms of the purine ring. It may be seen that the major part of the purine ring is derived from glycine. The sequence C-4, C-5 and N-7 is derived from glycine. C-6 is furnished by CO_2. C-2 and C-8 arise from formate and are carried via tetrahydrofolate derivatives. N-l is derived from the amino group of aspartate. N-3 and N-9 arise from the amide N of glutamine.

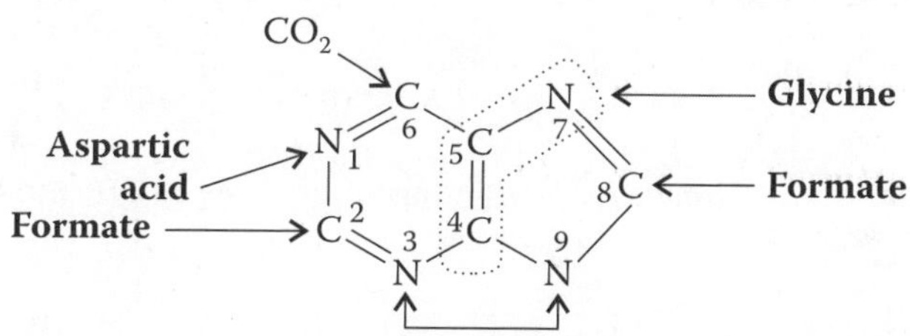

Figure 6.19 Sources of carbon and nitrogen atoms of a purine ring.

Synthesis of Pyrimidine

Most of the pyrimidines are synthesised de novo in the body like purines. The major site of synthesis is liver. By using isotopically labelled precursors, the sources of the carbon and nitrogen atoms of the pyrimidine ring have been traced to small fragments derived from CO_2, amide N of glutamine and aspartate. **Figure 6.20** illustrates the sources of C and N atoms of the pyrimidine ring. N-1, C-4, C-5 and C-6 are derived from aspartate. C-2 is derived from CO_2. N-3 is derived from the amide nitrogen of glutamine.

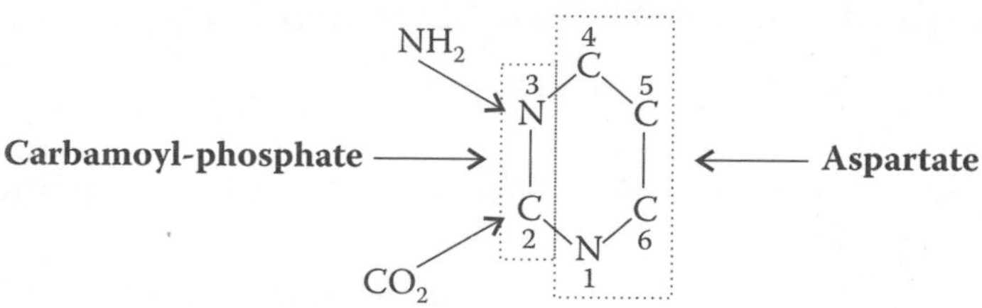

Figure 6.20 Source of carbon and nitrogen atoms in synthesis of pyrimidine.

Salvage Pathways for Purines and Pyrimidines

It is necessary to recycle free purine and pyrimidine bases for reuse in biosynthesis of nucleotides and nucleic acids, because the de novo synthesis of nucleotides is expensive in terms of utilisation of high-energy phosphate bonds, particularly for purine biosynthesis. The recycling reactions involve the so-called **salvage pathways**. They require expenditure of much less energy than the de novo synthesis. Liver provides purines and their nucleosides for salvage and utilisation by tissues that are incapable of synthesising them such as human brain, red blood cells and polymorphonuclear leucocytes (**Fig. 6.21**). It is known that up to 90% of the purines formed in man are salvaged and recycled.

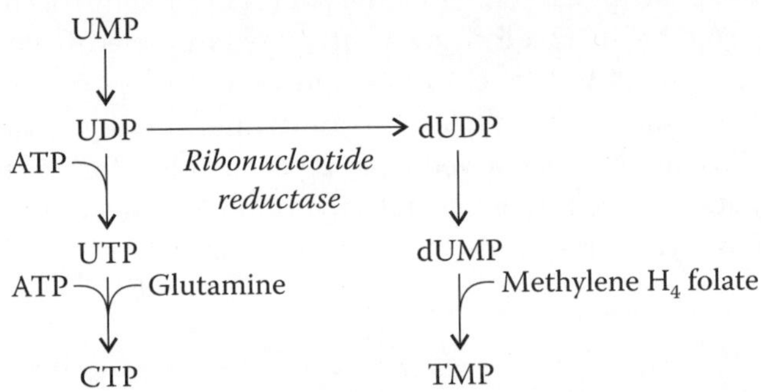

Figure 6.21 Pathway of biosynthesis from UMP to CTP and TMP.

Purine Salvage Pathways

Purine salvage pathways have two mechanisms:

1. The major salvage mechanism involves phosphoribosylation of free purines by using PRPP to form the corresponding purine nucleotide: Two enzymes, namely hypoxanthine guanine phosphoribosyl transferase (HGPRT) and adenine phosphoribosyl transferase (APRT), catalyse the reactions.
   - HGPRT catalyses the formation of GMP from guanine and IMP from hypoxanthine.

$$\text{Guanine} + \text{PRPP} \xrightarrow{\textit{HGPRT}} \text{GMP}$$

$$\text{Hypoxanthine} + \text{PRPP} \xrightarrow{\textit{HGPRT}} \text{IMP}$$

   - APRT catalyses the formation of AMP from adenine.

$$\text{Adenine} + \text{PRPP} \xrightarrow{\textit{HGPRT}} \text{AMP}$$

2. A second salvage mechanism involves direct phosphorylation of a purine ribonucleoside by ATP to form the nucleotide.

   In a reaction catalysed by adenosine kinase, adenosine is converted to AMP.

$$\text{Adenosine} + \text{ATP} \longrightarrow \text{AMP}$$

Pyrimidine Salvage Pathway

Mammalian cells salvage pyrimidine nucleosides to their respective nucleotides by phosphorylation. Uridine and cytidine are converted to uridine mono PO_4 (UMP) and cytidine mono PO_4 (CMP), respectively. These reactions are catalysed by uridine and cytidine kinase, respectively.

$$\text{Uridine} + \text{ATP} \longrightarrow \text{UMP}$$

$$\text{Cytidine} + \text{ATP} \longrightarrow \text{CMP}$$

Fate of Absorbed Nucleoprotein

In the intestine, nucleoprotein of food is split into protein and nucleic acids by the proteases. The protein follows the metabolic pathway of other proteins. The nucleic acids, RNA and DNA, are specifically split by ribonuclease and deoxyribonuclease of pancreatic juice to their constituent mononucleotides. The nucleotides are acted upon by nucleotidases of succus entericus, to form nucleoside and phosphoric acid. The nucleosides are split further by nucleosidases to their constituent purine and pyrimidine bases and sugars. The purines (adenine and guanine) are absorbed, and part of them is utilised for synthesis of tissue nucleic acids. Some adenine may be converted to guanine. The major part of adenine and guanine is catabolised.

Catabolism of Purines and Pyrimidines

Catabolism of Purines

Adenosine and guanosine are purine nucleosides. The catabolic pathways of purines are shown in **Figure 6.22**. The end product of purine degradation is uric acid.

Adenosine is first deaminated to form inosine by the action of adenosine deaminase. Inosine is phosphorolysed by purine nucleoside phosphorylase which splits inosine into the free base hypoxanthine and ribose-1-phosphate. Hypoxanthine is oxidised to xanthine by xanthine oxidase. Traces of iron and molybdenum are required for the enzyme action.

Guanosine is phosphorolysed to guanine by the action of purine nucleoside phosphorylase. In the next step, guanine is deaminated by guanine deaminase to xanthine which represents an intermediate, common to the catabolic pathway of adenine and guanine. Xanthine is further oxidised by the same xanthine oxidase to form uric acid which is excreted in urine. Uric acid is the major end product of purine catabolism in man and higher apes. Allopurinol, an inhibitor of xanthine oxidase, inhibits the formation of uric acid. For this reason, allopurinol is used in the treatment of a clinical disorder called **gout** in which the serum uric acid level is markedly increased (hyperuricaemia). Hypoxanthine and xanthine which are more soluble than uric acid are excreted in urine during treatment with allopurinol.

In other mammals and in birds, uric acid is further degraded to allantoin by uricase. Allantoin is highly water soluble. Uricase is absent in man.

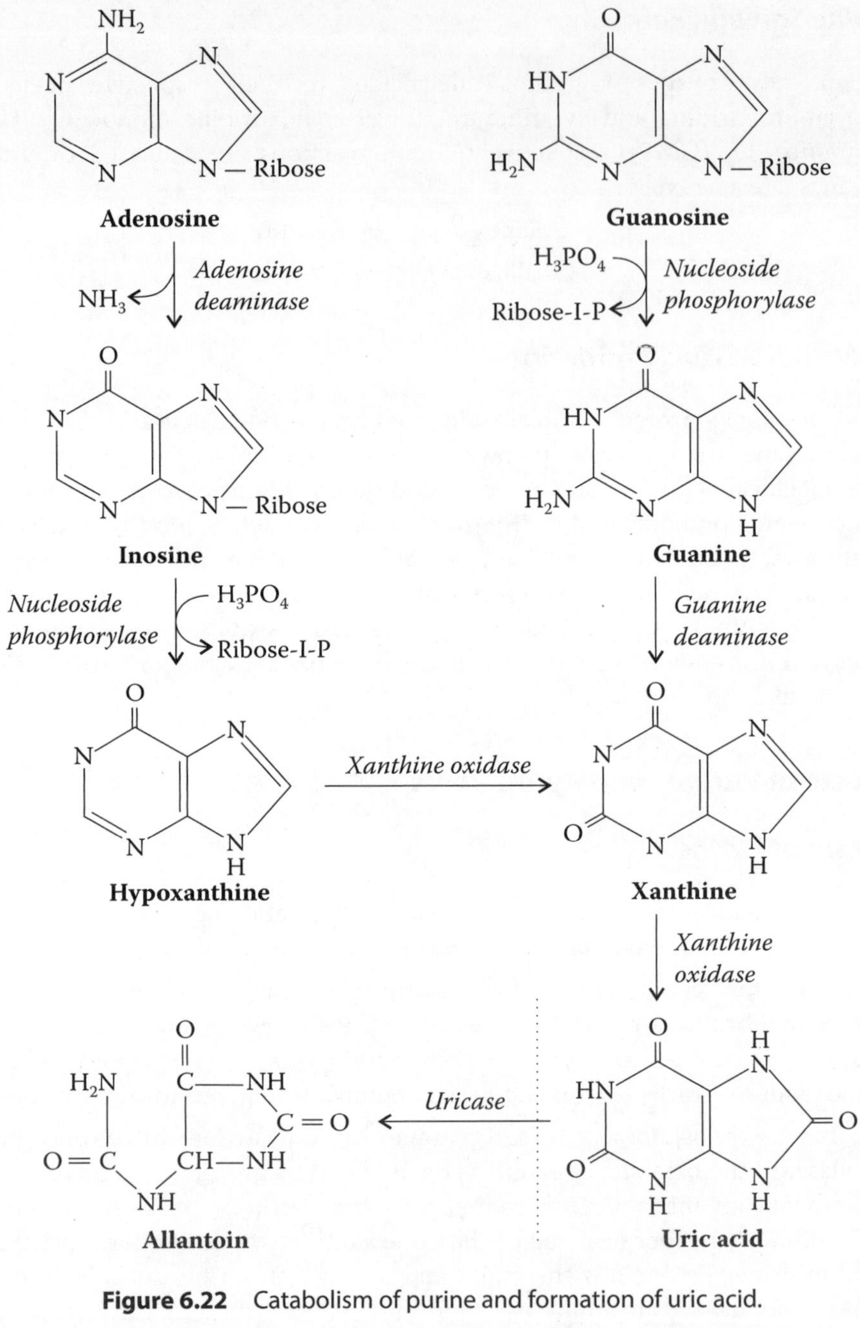

Figure 6.22 Catabolism of purine and formation of uric acid.

Food rich in nucleoprotein such as sweet bread, kidney, liver, glandular meat, high protein diet, mushroom and spinach produces increased excretion of uric acid in urine.

Hypouricaemia: A low level of serum uric acid and increased excretion of hypoxanthine and xanthine in urine is observed in persons who have xanthine oxidase deficiency due to a genetic disorder. In such conditions, xanthine gets rapidly filtered in the glomerular filtrate and fails to get reabsorbed by the renal tubules. In severe xanthine oxidase deficiency, patients may exhibit lithiasis (formation of xanthine calculi) with xanthinuria.

Uric Acid Metabolism

Purine nucleosides, namely adenosine and guanosine, are degraded and converted to uric acid which is the end product of purine catabolism in man. It is formed by the conversion of xanthine, catalysed by xanthine oxidase which is present in liver and intestinal mucosa. From the liver, uric acid is transported in the bloodstream to the kidneys and is excreted in urine. The serum uric acid level in a normal adult is 2–6 mg per 100 ml. A normal adult excretes 400–600 mg uric acid in 24 hours.

Miscible uric acid pool: The body synthesises about 150 mg more of uric acid than the amount excreted in urine per day. The excess uric acid formed is evidently destroyed in the body. The quantity of the total miscible uric acid pool amounts to about 1200 mg under normal conditions.

Hyperuricaemia: It is a condition in which the serum urate level exceeds the solubility limit of 7.0 mg/100 ml. The serum becomes supersaturated and crystals of sodium urate may precipitate out from serum and deposit on tissues around. Hyperuricaemia carries an increased risk of developing a disease called **gout** and formation of renal calculi due to massive deposits of sodium urate crystals in the kidneys.

Gout is a genetic disorder of purine catabolism. It is caused by excessive formation of uric acid due to increased purine biosynthesis by the de novo pathway. Two characteristic features in gout are hyperuricaemia and uricosuria.

With the overproduction of uric acid, the serum uric acid level is elevated and exceeds the solubility limit of 7.0 mg%. Crystals of monosodium urate precipitate out from serum and are deposited in the articular cartilages and synovial membranes of joints, mainly those of lower limbs. The abnormal deposits of urate form the characteristic nodules known as **tophi** or **gouty nodules**. Deposits of gouty nodules in joint spaces produce an inflammatory reaction resulting in acute gouty arthritis, which can develop to chronic gouty arthritis.

Uricosuria: With elevation of serum uric acid, there is increased urinary excretion of uric acid, especially in acid urine with pH less than 5.75. This leads to the deposition of sodium urate crystals in the kidneys resulting in the formation of renal calculi. The cause for the hyperuricaemia in gout has been identified to two factors:

1. Overactivity of PRPP synthetase
2. Partial deficiency of HGPRT

Both factors accelerate the rate of purine biosynthesis.

Clinically, gout manifests symptoms of acute and painful arthritis, the most frequently affected joints being the metatarsophalangeal joints. The arthritis usually appears abruptly and later at regular intervals. The affected individuals show hyperuricaemia with serum uric acid levels ranging from 6 to 20 mg%, while the normal serum uric acid concentration is 2–6 mg%. Patients with prolonged hyperuricaemia and gout often develop progressive impairment of renal function due to deposit of sodium urate crystals and calculi formation in the kidney. Microscopic examination of urine deposit reveals the presence of uric acid crystals.

Lesch–Nyhan syndrome: Lesch–Nyhan syndrome is an X-linked disorder of purine biosynthesis, occurring only in males at a very early age. The biochemical abnormalities in this rare genetic disorder are excessive purine synthesis, overproduction of uric acid and hyperuricaemia. The defect is due to a complete deficiency of hypoxanthine guanine phosphoribosyl transferase (HGPRT), an enzyme of the purine salvage pathway catalysing the formation of GMP and IMP from either guanine or hypoxanthine, using PRPP as the donor of ribosyl moiety. When there is lack of HGPRT, guanine and hypoxanthine are not salvaged and are degraded further to uric acid. The accompanying rise in the intracellular level of PRPP enhances the synthesis of purine. Consequently, there is an increase in synthesis of purine, while the levels of GMP and IMP decrease. The reactions are as follows:

$$\text{Guanine} + \text{PRPP} \xrightarrow{HGPRT} \text{GMP}$$

$$\text{Hypoxanthine} + \text{PRPP} \xrightarrow{HGPRT} \text{IMP}$$

Clinically, children affected with this disease begin to bite their fingers and lips and develop a bizzare tendency of self-mutilation. Mental deficiency and spasticity are other characteristics of the Lesch–Nyhan syndrome.

Hyperuricaemia leads to massive deposits of uric acid in the kidneys and formation of calculi early in life. This is followed by gout and renal impairment.

Von Gierke's disease: Von Gierke's disease is primarily a glycogen storage disease. It is a genetic disorder caused due to an inherited deficiency of glucose-6-phosphatase, an enzyme required for the conversion of glucose-6-phosphate to glucose. It is characterised by hypoglycaemia and a high level of serum uric acid. Glucose-6-phosphate accumulates because of the failure of the liver to convert it to glucose. This enhances the hexose monophosphate shunt pathway and increases the intracellular level of ribose-5-phosphate. This in turn increases the cellular PRPP levels which drive purine biosynthesis to abnormally high rates, resulting in excessive uric acid production, leading to hyperuricaemia.

Immunodeficiency diseases: Two immunodeficiency diseases are associated with purine metabolism. Both are autosomal recessive disorders.

1. Adenosine deaminase deficiency
2. Purine nucleoside phosphorylase deficiency

Adenosine deaminase catalyses conversion of adenosine to inosine and deoxyadenosine to deoxyinosine. Purine nucleoside phosphorylase catalyses cleavage of inosine to yield hypoxanthine and ribose 1-P or deoxyribose-1-P (**Fig. 6.23**).

Adenosine deaminase deficiency (Add) is associated with a severe combined immunodeficiency disease (SCID) in which both thymus-derived lymphocytes (T cells) and bone marrow-derived lymphocytes (B cells) are sparse and dysfunctional. There is gross immunodysfunction with susceptibility to fungal, bacterial and viral infections. In adenosine deaminase deficiency, there is accumulation of adenosine and deoxyadenosine.

Excess deoxyadenosine is either excreted or converted to dATP (deoxyadenosine triphosphate). The cellular concentration of dATP is markedly increased. High concentration of dATP interferes with DNA synthesis. dATP is a toxic substance.

Adenosine (deoxyadenosine)

NH_3 ← ↓ *Adenosine deaminase*

Inosine (deoxyinosine)

↓ *Purine nucleoside phosphorylase*

Hypoxanthine + Ribose-1-P (deoxyribose-1-P)

Figure 6.23 Degradation by adenosine deaminase and purine nucleoside phosphorylase.

Purine nucleoside phosphorylase deficiency is associated with a severe thymus-derived lymphocyte deficiency (T cells). It manifests a milder form of immunodeficiency. It shows increased intracellular accumulation of dGTP (deoxyguanosine triphosphate) and dATP (deoxy adenosine triphosphate) and increased urinary excretion of hypoxanthine. There is a marked increase in the uric acid production and reduced excretion of uric acid. dGTP is a toxic substance.

Orotic aciduria: In this genetic disorder, there is deficiency or absence of orotate phosphoribosyl transferase and orotidylate decarboxylase. This causes excessive production of orotic acid (OA). The characteristic features in orotic aciduria are high levels of blood OA and excretion of a high amount of OA in urine. Urine deposits show crystals of OA. Clinically, the affected children develop a severe megaloblastic anaemia and retarded growth.

Catabolism of Pyrimidine

Catabolism occurs mainly in the liver. The two pyrimidine bases—uracil and thymine—derived by hydrolysis of the respective nucleotides are degraded by similar pathways. Uracil is degraded to β-alanine. Thymine is degraded to β-aminoisobutyric acid. The major end products of pyrimidine catabolism are β-alanine and β-aminoisobutyric acid. They are highly water soluble and are excreted in urine. The following is the scheme of the catabolic pathway of pyrimidines:

Uracil and thymine are reduced to their dihydro derivatives dihydrouracil and dihydrothymine, respectively, by NADPH. They are further hydrolysed when their rings open to form β-ureidopropionic acid from dihydrouracil and β-ureidoisobutyric acid from dihydrothymine. β-ureidopropionic acid is hydrolysed further to form β-alanine, CO_2 and NH_3. β-Ureidoisobutyric acid is hydrolysed simultaneously to form β-aminoisobutyric acid, CO_2 and NH_3. β-alanine and β-aminoisobutyric acid are further cleaved to form NH_3 which goes to form urea, acetic acid and propionic acid (**Fig. 6.24**).

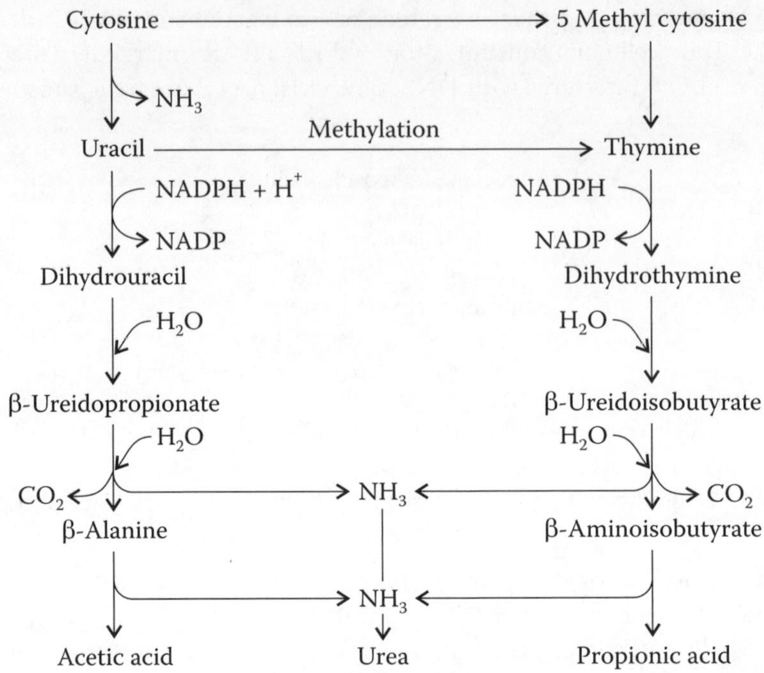

Figure 6.24 Pathway of pyrimidine catabolism.

β-aminoisobutyric acid is excreted in urine and is derived from degradation of thymine. Increased amounts of β-aminoisobutyric acid are excreted in leukaemia patients and cancer patients undergoing chemotherapy or radiation therapy, where a large number of cells are destroyed and DNA is degraded.

Inhibitors of Purine and Pyrimidine Metabolism

Inhibiting the synthetic pathways of purines and pyrimidines will reduce the turnover of nucleic acids.

This has importance in the treatment of cancer, because the production of nucleic acids in malignant tissues is very high. Many compounds have been found as inhibitors and they can be considered under the following four groups:

1. Antifolate drugs
2. Glutamine analogues
3. Purine and pyrimidine analogues
4. Antibiotic, antitumour substances

Antifolate drugs: Folate derivatives play an important role in the synthesis of purines. Antifolate drugs are structural analogues of folic acid and can act by competing with folate derivatives in the various enzymatic reactions and block synthesis of purines. For this reason, antifolate drugs are used in the treatment of different forms of cancer.

Examples of antifolate drugs are as follows:

- Methotrexate
- Aminopterin

Methotrexate is used in the treatment of leukaemia.

Glutamine analogues: They inhibit all reactions involving the transfer of the amide group of glutamine, including the entry of N-3 and N-9 into the purine ring. They inhibit the synthesis of GMP and conversion of UTP to CTP. These reactions are very critical for the synthesis of the purine ring. Compounds that inhibit these reactions are called glutamine antagonists.

Examples of glutamine antagonists are as follows:

- Azaserine
- Diazonorleucine

Purine and pyrimidine analogues: Many compounds have been screened as structural analogues of purines and pyrimidines. They interfere with the synthesis of nucleic acids.

Examples of purine analogues are as follows:

- 6-Mercaptopurine
- 6-Thioguanine

  These two drugs are used in the treatment of acute leukaemia.
- Allopurinol is 4-hydroxy-pyrazolopyrimidine, a purine analogue. It inhibits xanthine oxidase activity and prevents breakdown of purine at the level of either xanthine or hypoxanthine that is more soluble in urine than uric acid.

  It is used in the treatment of hyperuricaemia and gout.

Examples of pyrimidine analogues are as follows:

- 5-Fluorouracil
- 5-Iodouracil

Both these drugs are structurally similar to uracil. They block the formation of thymidine.

5-Fluorouracil is used in the treatment of solid tumours. 5-Iodouracil is used in the treatment of herpes infection.

Antibiotic, antitumour substances: There are several antibiotic compounds that inhibit the synthesis of nucleic acids by combining with them and making them inactive. Some among them are actinomycin, mitomycins and phleomycin.

- Actinomysin is an antitumour compound. It probably forms complexes with DNA and arrests its activity. It also inhibits the synthesis of RNA.
- Mitomycins are a group of bactericidal and cytotoxic antibiotics, prepared from streptomycetes. They inhibit DNA synthesis.
- Phleomycin is an antibiotic, antitumour agent. It inhibits DNA synthesis.

7 CHAPTER

Oxygen Transport Proteins

Chapter Outline

- Myoglobin
- Haemoglobin

Transport of oxygen is mediated by two proteins in the body, which are as follows:

1. Myoglobin
2. Haemoglobin

MYOGLOBIN

Myoglobin is a haemoprotein present in the muscle cells of red skeletal muscle fibres and cardiac muscle. It is a small globular protein with a molecular weight of 17,000.

Structure of Myoglobin

Structurally, myoglobin consists of a single polypeptide chain which has 153 amino acid residues, with L-valine at the NH_2 terminal. It is bent and folded into eight helical segments to give a compact globular structure.

Starting at the N terminus, each of the segments is given an alphabet letter designation A to H. The eight helical segments are designated as A B C D E F G H. Each segment carries about 7–20 amino acid residues in length. The polypeptide has a molecule of haem which is an iron-containing porphyrin identical with the haem of haemoglobin. The iron which is in the ferrous state (Fe^{++}) is coordinately linked to the nitrogen atom of a histidine residue of the polypeptide chain (**Fig. 7.1**). The haem fits into a tiny crevice situated between helix E and helix F. The outer surface of the myoglobin is charged (polar) and the interior of the structure is non-polar except two histidine residues which are polar. The three-dimensional globular structure of a myoglobin molecule is represented in **Figure 7.1**.

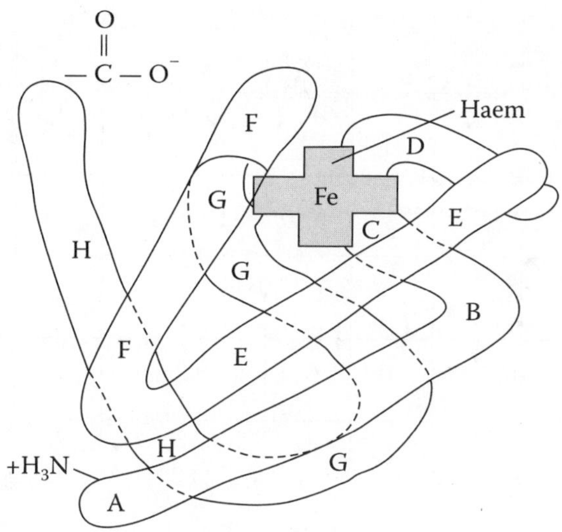

Figure 7.1 Structure of myoglobin. The eight helical segments are given alphabet letter designation.

Properties of Myoglobin

Myoglobin has high affinity for oxygen (O_2). It is capable of reversible oxygenation and deoxygenation. It combines with O_2 to form oxymyoglobin:

$$Mb + O_2 \rightleftharpoons MbO_2$$

The O_2-binding site in myoglobin is on the haem molecule. The Fe^{++} iron (ferrous) in the haem opens one of its coordinate bonds attached to the histidine residue of the polypeptide chain and binds with a molecule of O_2 (*see* **Fig. 7.3b** later in the text). This process is known as **oxygenation**.

The affinity of myoglobin to O_2 is much higher than haemoglobin to O_2 (**Fig. 7.2**). Myoglobin is saturated about 95% with O_2 at PO_2 of 100 mmHg as is present in lungs. At PO_2 40 mmHg as is present in venous blood, myoglobin is 90% saturated with O_2. At PO_2 20 mmHg as in capillaries, myoglobin continues to retain O_2 and is 80–85% saturated with O_2. Thus over a range of PO_2 values between 100 and 20 mmHg, oxymyoglobin releases very little O_2 unlike oxyhaemoglobin. The O_2 saturation drops sharply to about 20% only at PO_2 5 mmHg or even lower PO_2 as is present in active red cells and as required for cytochrome enzymes.

The affinity of myoglobin for O_2 at varying partial pressure of O_2 and the dissociation of oxymyoglobin at different ranges of PO_2 are illustrated in **Figure 7.2**. The O_2 saturation curve for myoglobin is a rectangular hyperbola whereas the curve obtained for haemoglobin is sigmoid in shape (S shaped) (**Fig. 7.2**).

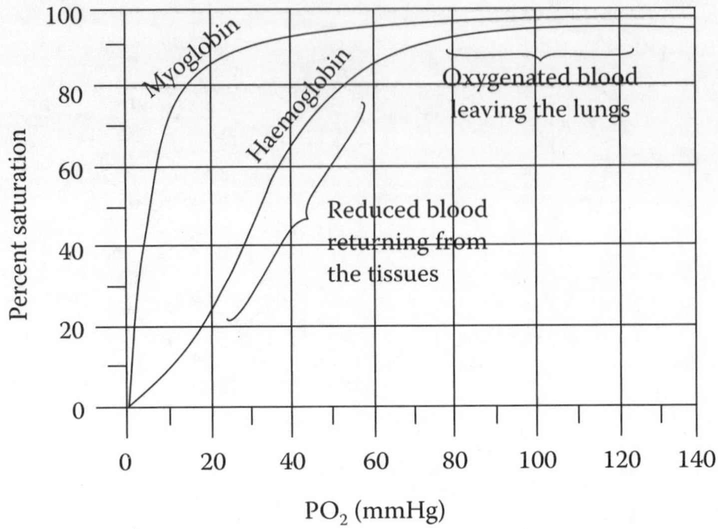

Figure 7.2 Oxygen dissociation curves of myoglobin and haemoglobin.

Function of Myoglobin

The main function of myoglobin is that it stores O_2. It is found in skeletal muscle cells, where it stores oxygen in the red muscle fibres. Oxymyoglobin releases the bound O_2 to the peripheral tissues at very low O_2 tension, for example as in severe muscular exercise, for use by muscle mitochondria.

Similar release of O_2 takes place in cardiac muscle during periods of oxygen debt.

HAEMOGLOBIN

Haemoglobin is the red-colouring matter of blood and is present inside the erythrocytes. The normal concentration of haemoglobin is 14–16 grams per 100 ml of blood. It has a molecular weight of 67,000.

Internal Structure of Haemoglobin

A molecule of haemoglobin (Hb) consists of

1. Globin moiety
2. Haem moiety

Globin moiety: Globin moiety forms the protein part of haemoglobin. It is composed of four parallel layers of closely packed polypeptide chains arranged in the configuration of a tetrahedron. The four polypeptide chains form two pairs of chains and each pair has identical amino acid composition arranged in an identical sequence (two α-chains and β-chains). Each α-chain has 141 amino acid residues and each β-chain has 146 amino acid residues. The total number of amino acid residues in a molecule of haemoglobin is 574.

Each polypeptide chain is linked covalently to the Fe^{++} ions of a haem molecule through the N atoms of two of their histidine residues (**Fig. 7.3**). The four polypeptide subunits with their identical haem molecules are packed into a globular tetramer. The peptide chains are held together and the structure stabilised by hydrophobic bonds, hydrogen bonds and salt bridges. The normal adult haemoglobin is composed of one pair of α-chains and one pair of β-chains and is designated as Haemoglobin A (HbA).

HbA comprises about 97% of the total haemoglobin in normal adult blood. It is synthesised in bone marrow.

In the course of a lifetime, five different globin chains are synthesised in humans. They vary in their primary structure, i.e. in the amino acid composition. They are named as α, β, γ, δ and ∈ chains. All normal haemoglobins contain 2α chains and these are paired mostly with a pair of β-chains. A few variants of haemoglobin are paired either with γ, δ or ∈ (embryonic) chains.

Three different types of haemoglobin are normally present in the post-natal life. They are HbA_1, HbA_2 and HbF, the foetal form.

HbA_1 or **HbA** is the major form of haemoglobin in normal adult blood. It is represented as $\alpha_2\beta_2$.

HbA_2 is composed of one pair of α-chains like those in HbA and one pair of δ (delta) chains. Its globin structure is represented as $\alpha_2\delta_2$. The δ-chain differs from β-chain in that the glycine in the 16th position of β-chain is replaced by arginine. About 2–3% of HbA_2 is present in normal adult blood.

Foetal haemoglobin F (HbF) is the main haemoglobin present in foetal blood. It is composed of one pair of α chains similar to those of HbA and one pair of γ-chains instead of the β chains of HbA.

HbF is represented as $\alpha_2\gamma_2$. The γ-chains have the same number of amino acids as in β-chains. But the terminal amino acid sequence in the γ-chain is glycine. The γ-chains have a higher amount of serine and leucine and less of valine than in β-chains. As the foetus grows, HbF is replaced by HbA and at birth the haemoglobin of the newborn contains 85% of HbA and 15% of HbF. A characteristic property of HbF is that it is resistant to denaturation by alkali whereas HbA is readily denatured.

Embryonic haemoglobin (Hb∈) is present in the erythrocytes in the embryonic life. It is composed of one pair of α chains and one pair of ∈ chains and is represented as $\alpha_2\epsilon_2$. As the embryo grows to the foetal stage, Hb∈ is replaced by HbF.

Haem moiety: Haem is a compound of protoporphyrin IX containing iron as ferrous (Fe^{++}) iron in the centre. Each of the peptide chains of the globin subunit is linked covalently to the Fe^{++} iron of the respective haem molecule through N atoms of two of their histidine residues (**Fig. 7.3**). The four haem molecules of the two pairs of polypeptide chains lie in four pockets formed by the folding of the corresponding polypeptide chain, on the surface of the haemoglobin molecule.

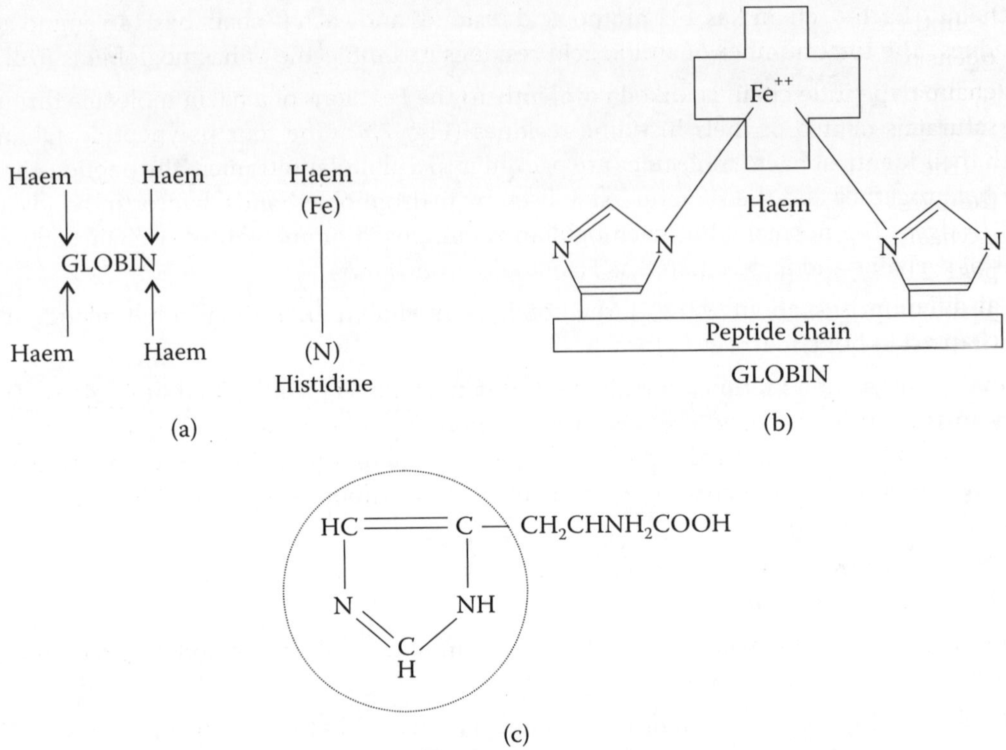

Figure 7.3 (a) and (b) Representation of the mode of attachment of haem with globin through the N atom of histidine. (c) Structure of histidine.

Properties and Reactions of Haemoglobin

1. **Buffering capacity:** Haemoglobin is an effective buffer. Its isoelectric point is 6.8. The buffering capacity of haemoglobin is due to the presence of a large number of histidine residues in the globin fraction. It is estimated that a molecule of haemoglobin has 35 histidine residues. Histidine exerts its buffering action through its ionisable group imidazole (**Fig. 7.3c**).

   The encircled portion is the imidazole moiety of histidine.

2. **Transport of oxygen:** Haemoglobin has a high affinity for oxygen (O_2) at high oxygen tension and readily forms a loose complex known as oxyhaemoglobin (HbO_2). This process is known as **oxygenation**. It also releases O_2 readily when exposed to low O_2 tension.

$$Hb + O_2 \rightleftharpoons HbO_2$$

   The physiological importance of this reaction is that haemoglobin has the capacity to combine reversibly with O_2 to form oxyhaemoglobin (HbO_2) in lungs, where high oxygen tension exists and releases O_2 in tissues where low oxygen tension prevails. This property of haemoglobin provides an excellent system for transport of O_2 from lungs to the tissue cells.

In the process of oxygenation, each of the four Fe^{++} ions of the four haem molecules opens one of its two covalent bonds attached to the histidine residue of the polypeptide chain of globin and binds with a molecule of O_2. Oxyhaemoglobin which is fully saturated contains four oxygen molecules.

The affinity of haemoglobin for oxygen at varying partial pressures of oxygen, the kinetics of saturation of haemoglobin with oxygen and the dissociation of oxyhaemoglobin are explained under the heading 'oxygen dissociation curve' on page 216. The affinity of myoglobin for O_2 and the dissociation of oxyhaemoglobin at different gaseous pressures of O_2 have been illustrated in **Figure 7.2** earlier in the chapter. **Figure 7.4** illustrates the oxygen dissociation curve of haemoglobin.

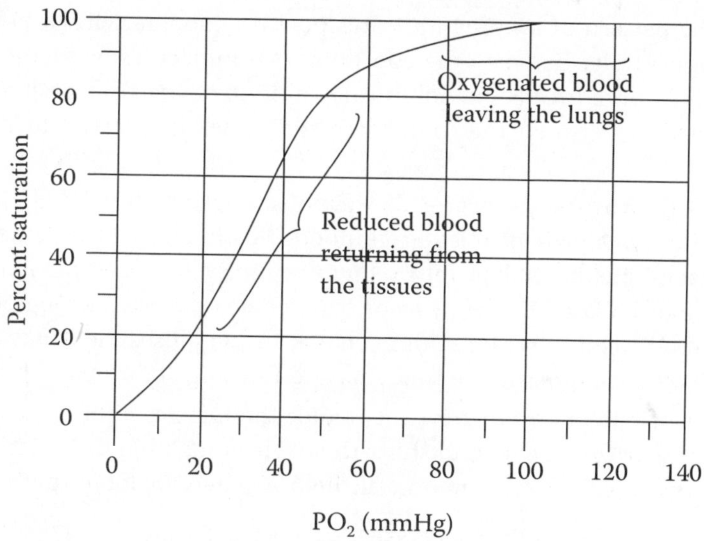

Figure 7.4 Oxygen dissociation curve of haemoglobin.

It may be seen that normally about 97–98% of the oxygen transported from the lungs to the tissues is carried in the haemoglobin molecule in reversible combination. The degree of combination of oxygen with haemoglobin or the dissociation of oxyhaemoglobin to release oxygen is determined by the tension of the oxygen (PO_2) in the medium surrounding the haemoglobin. At the tension of oxygen in the blood as it is leaving the pulmonary capillaries (104 mmHg), haemoglobin is saturated approximately 97% with oxygen (**Fig. 7.4**). When the blood that has circulated in the peripheral tissues returns to the lungs and enters the pulmonary capillaries, it has a PO_2 of 40 mmHg. At this tension, haemoglobin is about 70% saturated with oxygen (**Fig. 7.4**). At PO_2 of 20 mmHg, as prevailing in capillaries of active muscles, haemoglobin is only about 20% saturated with oxygen. This means that oxyhaemoglobin releases rapidly its bound oxygen over a range of PO_2 values between 100 and 20 mmHg. The relationship between the percentage saturation of the haemoglobin in blood and the oxygen tension of the blood is shown in **Figure 7.4**. It depicts the oxygen dissociation curve of haemoglobin. The shape of the oxygen haemoglobin dissociation curve is sigmoid.

The high affinity of haemoglobin for oxygen at high oxygen tension and its capacity to deliver a greater amount of oxygen at relatively high oxygen tension are possible because of the interaction between the four haem molecules, each carrying a binding site for oxygen.

3. **Cooperative binding of oxygen (haem–haem interaction):** There are four haem molecules, one for each subunit of a haemoglobin molecule, and there are four binding sites for O_2. Each haem molecule binds with one molecule of O_2 in a step-wise manner. The binding of the first O_2 molecule to one haem molecule increases its affinity for O_2 and this facilitates binding of the second, third and fourth O_2 molecules to the other three haem molecules. The last O_2 molecule is bound more tightly than the first. This indicates that as O_2 is bound to one site, the affinity to bind more O_2 to other sites is increased. The pattern of binding indicates positive cooperativity. It is because of this **positive cooperativity** between the coordinate O_2 molecules of haemoglobin that the oxygen-binding curve for haemoglobin is sigmoid in shape. The positive cooperativity due to interaction between the four haem molecules is referred to as **haem–haem interaction**.
4. **Role of 2,3-diphosphoglycerate:** 2,3-Diphosphoglycerate (DPG), a product of glycolytic pathway, is present inside red blood cells in almost the same concentration as that of haemoglobin. It has much higher affinity for haemoglobin than oxygen. One molecule of DPG binds firmly to one molecule of deoxyhaemoglobin in a central cavity formed between the two β-globin chains and stabilises the deoxygenated form of haemoglobin by cross-linking the β-chains and forming additional salt bridges.

   High levels of DPG in erythrocytes enhance the formation of deoxyhaemoglobin at low partial pressure of oxygen and shifts the oxyhaemoglobin dissociation curve to the right. Thus, its presence in red blood cells helps oxyhaemoglobin to unload oxygen.

   $$HbO_2 + DPG \rightleftharpoons Hb\ DPG + O_2$$

   In the lungs where the PO_2 is high, haemoglobin is almost completely oxygenated despite the presence of DPG.

   In the capillary beds of peripheral tissue where PO_2 is much lower, erythrocyte concentration of DPG increases and promotes release of more oxygen from haemoglobin, thus ensuring adequate oxygen supply to tissues.

   Elevated levels of DPG in cells have been noted in tissue hypoxia as in anaemia, cardiopulmonary insufficiency and high altitudes.
5. **Combination with carbon monoxide:** Carbon monoxide binds competitively with haemoglobin to form carboxyhaemoglobin at the same site on haemoglobin as oxygen, with an affinity 200 times more than oxygen. Carboxyhaemoglobin is a stable compound. Unlike oxyhaemoglobin, dissociation of carboxyhaemoglobin to carbon monoxide and haemoglobin can occur only at high partial pressure of oxygen. Since carbon monoxide prevents formation of oxyhaemoglobin, transport of oxygen by haemoglobin to tissues is reduced. Tissues suffer lack of oxygen supply and this results in tissue and cellular anoxia. Inhalation of carbon monoxide in large amounts is common in persons who are exposed to leaky gas burners and incomplete combustion of wood.

6. **Formation of carbamino haemoglobin:** A small amount of carbon dioxide, about 10–15%, is transported in the red blood cells as carbamino haemoglobin. In this reaction, some of the free amino groups of the terminal valine residues of the β-globin subunits readily combine with CO_2 in a reversible reaction to form carbamino haemoglobin.

$$CO_2 + HbNH_2 \rightleftharpoons HbNHCOO^- + H^+$$

7. **Glycosylation of haemoglobin:** A small amount of glycosylated haemoglobin named haemoglobin A_{1c} (HbA_{1c}) is present in red blood cells. HbA_{1c} is formed by glycosylation, a reaction which involves non-enzymatic condensation between the aldehyde group of D-glucose and the amino terminal valine of the β-chains. The reaction is favoured by a high glucose level and HbA_{1c} has clinical significance. Normally, the HbA_{1c} level in blood is low, about 3–5% of the total haemoglobin, but in prolonged hyperglycaemia as in uncontrolled diabetes mellitus, the HbA_{1c} level increases and may reach 12–15% of the total haemoglobin. The blood level of HbA_{1c} in diabetes serves as a valuable index to assess the control of hyperglycaemic status in diabetes mellitus over the previous period of 120 days, the lifespan of RBC.
8. **Effect of carbon dioxide:** Haemoglobin facilitates transport of carbon dioxide produced in peripheral tissue to lungs for exhalation.

   Bohr effect: An increase in the CO_2 tension causes dissociation of the haemoglobin–oxygen dissociation curve and shift of the curve to the right, promoting release of oxygen from oxyhaemoglobin. The shift of haemoglobin oxygen curve to the right by increasing CO_2 tension is termed **Bohr effect**. It is mainly due to the increased hydrogen ion concentration resulting from increased carbonic acid generation from CO_2.

   The Bohr effect has important physiological significance. Cells metabolising at high rates produce CO_2 and lactic acid which act to increase the H^+ ion concentration in the cells' environment. As the H^+ ion concentration increases, the acidity of blood increases. The excess H^+ ions are buffered by haemoglobin (Hb). Hb binds with H^+ ions and carries them to the lungs. In the lungs O_2 binds to the deoxygenated haemoglobin, forces the H^+ ions from the deoxyhaemoglobin and releases them. The released H^+ ions combine with bicarbonate ion (HCO_3^-) and form carbonic acid (H_2CO_3). This dissociates to CO_2 and H_2O with the aid of carbonic anhydrase. CO_2 is exhaled in the lungs.

Abnormal Haemoglobin Derivatives

Certain derivatives of haemoglobin are of clinical importance because of their presence in blood in certain abnormal conditions. These are carboxyhaemoglobin, sulphaemoglobin and methaemoglobin. Clinical manifestations associated with these derivatives are described in the following text.

1. **Carboxyhaemoglobinaemia** is a condition in which blood contains carboxyhaemoglobin (HbCO). This can occur after exposure to a large amount of carbon monoxide as in those who are exposed to coal gas, leaky gas burners and incomplete combustion of wood. Carbon monoxide produced in a large amount is rapidly absorbed through

lungs and binds with haemoglobin forming carboxyhaemoglobin with an affinity 200 times more than that of oxygen. Formation of oxyhaemoglobin is considerably reduced and release of oxygen to tissues is decreased. The combined effects produce significant tissue and cellular anoxia. Clinically, symptoms such as headache, confusion and fainting occur at 30–50% carbon monoxide saturation. 60% saturation and above are often fatal.

Blood which contains carboxyhaemoglobin shows a characteristic cherry-red colour. On spectroscopic examination, the blood shows two absorption bands in the green region of the spectrum, similar to those of oxyhaemoglobin. But the bands are not altered by addition of reducing agents.

2. **Sulphaemoglobinaemia** is a condition in which Hb contains sulphur. It cannot bind O_2. The affected persons suffer from marked cyanosis and dyspnoea. Sulphaemoglobinaemia can occur due to habitual use of drugs containing inorganic sulphides which combine with oxyhaemoglobin, to form sulphaemoglobin. It is also found in cases of prolonged sulphaemoglobin therapy and in cases of chronic and severe constipation, when more than the normal amount of H_2S is formed in the intestines. Spectroscopically, the blood shows three absorption bands, more or less similar to those of methaemoglobin.
3. **Methaemoglobinaemia** is a condition in which the level of methaemoglobin in blood is high and exceeds 10% of the total haemoglobin. In haemoglobin, the iron in haem is in a ferrous (Fe^{++}) state and this is necessary for transport of oxygen. In methaemoglobin, the iron in haem is in the ferric (Fe^{+++}) state and this cannot transport oxygen. The affected individual suffers from oxygen deprivation. Under a normal condition, methaemoglobin is steadily formed in erythrocytes, but is rapidly reduced to haemoglobin by an enzyme system known as the **NADH cytochrome b_5 methaemoglobin reductase system**, leaving behind a small amount of 0.4–1% of methaemoglobin in blood. This enzyme system present in the erythrocytes consists of NADH, which is generated from glycolysis, a flavoprotein named cytochrome b reductase and cytochrome b_5. The Fe^{+++} iron of the methaemoglobin is reduced to the Fe^{++} state by the action of this enzyme system. There are two types of methaemoglobinaemia:
   - Inherited
   - Acquired

   Inherited methaemoglobinaemia: This is due to one of the following two causes:

   (i) Presence of haemoglobin M

   (ii) Deficiency of cytochrome b_5 reductase enzyme

   — Methaemoglobinaemia due to the presence of HbM is explained in page 171.

   — Methaemoglobinaemia due to deficiency of the cytochrome b_5 reductase enzyme has the following clinical features:

   - Individuals affected by the deficiency of cytochrome b_5 reductase have a lifelong cyanosis, depending on the level of methaemoglobin in blood. Some may have compensatory polycythaemia. Severe cases may be associated with mental retardation and dwarfing.

***Acquired methaemoglobinaemia*:** This is more common than the inherited type. It results from ingestion and exposure to a wide variety of drugs and chemicals that oxidise Fe^{++} (ferrous) iron to Fe^{+++} (ferric) iron.

Analgesics and antipyretic drugs such as acetanilide and phenacetin, nitrites such as amyl nitrite and nitroglycerine, and sulphonamides are known to cause acquired methaemoglobinaemia in some individuals.

Exposure to several industrial chemicals such as aniline, nitrobenzene and phenol causes acquired methaemoglobinaemia by absorption through skin and lungs. Use of well water contaminated with a high amount of nitrites, particularly in the preparation of artificial infant food, is one of the known causes leading to methaemoglobinaemia in infants.

Haemoglobinopathies

Haemoglobinopathies refer to inherited abnormalities in synthesis of the globin structure of haemoglobin. These are manifested by an abnormality in the structural sequence of the amino acids in the polypeptide chains. Such abnormal variants are known as **abnormal haemoglobins**. They are genetically determined and are of clinical importance.

Abnormal haemoglobins are formed by random mutations and may persist with impairment of functions. A mutation is a change or a defect in the nucleotide sequence of a gene. Abnormal mutations in the genes for haemoglobin may result in substitution of a single amino acid residue in one of the globin chains. The mutation may be either harmless or fatal, and this depends on the nature of the amino acid substituted and the point at which substitution occurs in the polypeptide chain. Itano and Pauling were the earliest to discover the abnormal haemoglobin in sickle cell anaemia in 1949. Since then, more than 400 abnormal haemoglobins with variation in structure have been discovered, and they are widely scattered in different parts of the world. The abnormal haemoglobins have been named in an alphabetical order as C D E F G H K L M N O P Q S, etc. But due to the discovery of increasing numbers of the variants subsequently, they are identified by the nature of their peptide chains and also by the places where they were detected, such as Hopkins, Milwaukie, Boston and Hyde Park.

All the variants of haemoglobin (Hb), including A and F, are inherited through genes, on a simple Mendelian principle, i.e. one gene coming from each parent. Under normal conditions, HbA is inherited through the genes from each parent and this results in the formation of haemoglobin A in the offspring. On the other hand, when HbA is inherited from one parent and an abnormal Hb is inherited from the other parent, a **heterozygote** is formed. This will result in the individual being a carrier of the abnormal haemoglobin trait, but at the same time, the presence of the normal 'A' gene will prevent development of serious complications such as anaemia. In this case, the affected individual may appear to be free from having abnormal clinical findings. If both the 'A' genes are replaced by abnormal variants, a **homozygote** results. The offspring suffers from severe complications.

The abnormal variants of haemoglobin are of clinical importance, because they are responsible at the molecular level in producing severe types of haemolytic anaemias. The more common of such variants are haemoglobins S, F, M, C, D and E. They show altered biological function and manifest characteristic clinical findings:

1. **Haemoglobin S** is also known as **sickle haemoglobin**: **HbS** is the most prevalent and important type of haemoglobin. The gene frequency for HbS is highest among the Blacks in the United States. The basic defect in HbS is due to inheritance of a mutant autosomal gene which replaces the glutamic acid residue on the sixth position of the β-chain with valine. The α-chains are normal.
   - *Sickle cell anaemia:* If a homozygous individual inherits the mutant gene from each parent, his haemoglobin gets totally replaced by HbS. When HbS passes through tissues where oxygen tension is low, it gets deoxygenated and forms reduced HbS. On deoxygenation, HbS polymerises within the erythrocytes forming insoluble fibres that distort the erythrocytes. This leads to the formation of the characteristic sickle-shaped red cells that appear as thin, long, boat-shaped particles under a microscope. They are highly fragile and get hemolysed resulting in a severe type of haemolytic anaemia known as **sickle cell anaemia**. The sickle-shaped cells impair circulation when blood flows through capillaries to certain organs, resulting in localised ischaemia and thrombosis, causing acute pain. The painful crisis due to blocking of small vessels by sickle cells is known as a **vaso-occlusive phenomenon**. The characteristic chronic ulcers that occur on the legs in sickle anaemia are due to poor blood circulation caused by sickling of red cells.
   - *Sickle trait:* If a heterozygous individual inherits the mutant gene from one parent only, the individual gets both HbS and HbA in an equal amount in the blood. He is usually free of clinical symptoms and is said to have sickle trait. Individuals heterozygous for HbS are said to have a resistance to malarial parasites.
2. **Haemoglobin F** is foetal haemoglobin and is present in foetal blood. The concentration of HbF in foetal blood at birth is 70–80% of the total haemoglobin. It decreases rapidly and is reduced to a minimum in about 4–6 months. If HbF persists in adult life, it becomes an abnormal haemoglobin which produces a severe type of haemolytic anaemia known as **thalassaemia major**. In this condition, more than 50% of the haemoglobin is replaced by HbF. The abnormality in HbF lies in the pair of β-chains. These are replaced by a pair of γ-chains. The α-chains are similar to those of HbA. HbF is represented as $\alpha_2A\gamma_2F$.
3. **Thalassaemias** is a group of inherited disorders in which there is a defect in the coordinated synthesis of α- and β-globin chains. This leads to decreased production of haemoglobin and severe haemolytic anaemia. Thalassaemias are classified broadly as α-thalassaemia and β-thalassaemia.
   - In **α-thalassaemia,** the rate of synthesis of α-globin chains is reduced due to genetic deletion of α-genes. When one α-gene is defective, the result is not serious.

     Deletion of two α-genes results in the affected individual to have **α-thalassaemia trait**.

     Deletion of three α-genes produces a chronic haemolytic anaemia. The characteristic feature in this condition is that the erythrocytes contain an increased amount of an abnormal haemoglobin known as **HbH**. This is a tetramer composed of four β-chains (β_4). There are no α-globin chains. This disease is known as **haemoglobin H** or **HbH disease.**

Deletion of all four α-genes is the most severe form of α-thalassaemia. The major haemoglobin found in the erythrocytes of foetus is **Hb Bart's** (γ_4) which is a tetramer composed of 4γ-chains and **HbH** (β_4). There are no α-chains. This condition is found in a congenital abnormality known as **'hydrops fetalis'** which is incompatible with life. Death occurs in utero.

- **β-Thalassaemias** are known to occur in the Mediterranean border, middle-east regions, central Africa and certain parts of India. The defect in β-thalassaemias is due to a mutation which affects the biosynthesis of β-globin mRNA. There is insufficient production of β-globulin. There are two types of β-thalassaemias:

  (i) β-Thalassaemia major

  (ii) β-Thalassaemia minor

  β-Thalassaemia major: This was first described by Cooley and Lee in 1925 and was subsequently known as Cooley's anaemia. Other names by which this condition is known are Mediterranean anaemia and target cell anaemia.

  β-Thalassaemia major is the homozygous type. The genes of the β-globin chains inherited from each parent are defective and carry the abnormal F trait. More than 50% of the haemoglobin is replaced by HbF. There is no detectable β-globin chain. Instead, there is increased synthesis of δ- and γ-globin chains to compensate for the lack of β-chains. An abnormally high amount of α-globin chains is also produced. Free α-chains, being insoluble, precipitate out and cause haemolysis of the red cells. Severe haemolytic anaemia appears in infancy.

  Clinically, a marked pallor sets in as a result of severe anaemia. The blood picture shows microcytic and hypochromic RBCs. The disease is accompanied by enlarged spleen and liver. There is thinning of the cortical bones and deformity of the skull bones. This contributes to the characteristic Mongoloid facies that is seen in patients of thalassaemia major. Hemosiderosis and deposit of a large amount of iron in myocardium occur as a result of repeated blood transfusion given to maintain life. The life expectancy of the affected child is short. Most of them die before they reach adulthood. Hb electrophoresis shows the presence of HbF in an increased amount. It is useful for establishing diagnosis.

  β-Thalassaemia minor: This is the heterozygous type, where one gene from one of the HbF parents carries HbA and the other gene from the other parent carries the HbF trait. As a result, the rate of β-globin synthesis is affected. There is a compensatory increase in the production of HbA_2. It is a milder variety. There are no significant clinical manifestations. The patient may have microcytosis with mild anaemia. It is generally detected in routine blood tests.

4. **Haemoglobin C** is a rare variant. It was detected in the Blacks in Africa. The genetic defect in HbC is due to substitution of glutamic acid in the sixth position of the β-chain with lysine; α-chains are normal.

   Haemoglobin C disease is the homozygous type, in which the abnormal gene for HbC is derived from each parent. Clinically, the patients have mild haemolytic anaemia accompanied by splenomegaly and intermittent jaundice. The disease is detected accidentally. HbC has a tendency to form intracellular crystals.

The terminal portions of the β-chains in haemoglobins A, S and C are indicated below:

HbA - Val - His - Leu - thr - Pro - Glu - Gly - Lys

HbS - Val - His - Leu - thr - Pro - Val - Glu - Lys

HbC - Val - His - Leu - thr - Pro - Lys - Glu - Lys

5. **Haemoglobin D** is detected in Punjab and Gujarat. It is seen combined with HbS. The genetic defect in HbD is that glutamic acid in the 121st position of the β-chain is replaced by glutamine.

   Clinically, homozygotes have mild haemolytic anaemia.

   No symptoms are seen in heterozygotes.

   Electrophoretic mobility is the same as HbS. HbD is distinguished from HbS by the absence of sickling.

6. **Haemoglobin E:** This variant detected in Myanmar and Sri Lanka is rarely seen. The genetic defect in HbE is that glutamic acid in the 26th position of the β-chain is replaced by lysine. Clinical symptoms are the same as in haemoglobin D. Electrophoretic mobility is the same as HbA_2.

7. **Haemoglobin M (HbM):** This is a rare abnormal haemoglobin variant in which a mutation modifies the O_2-binding capability. The defect is due to substitution of an amino acid residue, in either the α- or the β-subunits of the globin moiety. This leads to oxidation of the ferrous (Fe^{++}) iron of the haem to the ferric (Fe^{+++}) form. The oxidised Hb is known as methaemoglobin. Haemoglobin with iron in the ferric (Fe^{+++}) form will not bind O_2 and the ability to transport oxygen is impaired.

   There are five types of HbM variants. Of these, two are α-chain variants affecting α-globin chains and three are β-chain variants that affect β-globin chains.

   The two α-**chain variants** are named as **haemoglobin M (Boston)** and **haemoglobin M (Iwate)**.

   - *Haemoglobin M (Boston):* In the HbM (**Boston**), the histidine which occurs in the 58th position of α-chain is substituted by tyrosine. The β-chains are normal. In HbM (**Iwate**), the histidine which occurs in the 87th position of α-chain is substituted by tyrosine. The β-chains are normal.

     The three β-**chain** variants are named as **haemoglobin M (Hyde Park)**, **haemoglobin M (Saskatoon)** and **haemoglobin M (Milwaukee)**.

     In **HbM (Hyde Park)**, histidine which occurs in the 92nd position of β-chain is substituted by tyrosine.

     In **HbM (Saskatoon)**, histidine which occurs in the 63rd position of β-chain is replaced by tyrosine.

     In **HbM (Milwaukee)**, valine which occurs in the 67th position of β-chain is replaced by glutamic acid. The α-chains are normal.

Methaemoglobinaemia

A rare cause for hereditary methaemoglobinaemia is the presence of HbM in which a mutation changes the amino acid residue to which haem is attached. This alters its affinity for oxygen and favours oxidation of the ferrous form in haem to feme form which is incapable of binding oxygen. The level of methaemoglobin in blood is elevated.

Clinically, the affected individuals manifest a rare form of congenital and familial type of cyanosis. Those affected with HbM Boston and HbM Iwate (α-chain variants) are cyanotic from birth, whereas in those affected with HbM Saskatoon, HbM Hyde Park and HbM Milwaukee (β-chain variants), cyanosis appears 4–6 months after birth, i.e. when HbF disappears from blood and is replaced by HbA.

Tests to Detect Methaemoglobin

1. Blood with elevated levels of methaemoglobin is brownish red when viewed in a glass test tube. The colour does not change upon mixing with air.
2. Spectroscopic examination of blood containing methaemoglobin exhibits three characteristic absorption bands, one in the red region at 630 nm and two in the green region of the spectrum.
3. Haemoglobin M variants have specific electrophoretic mobility and can be detected by electrophoresis.

The electrophoretic migration rate of each haemoglobin variant differs depending on whether the amino acid side chain of the Hb has an anionic amino acid which means that it is charged. They can be identified by comparing with the known standards of different haemoglobin variants (**Fig. 7.5**).

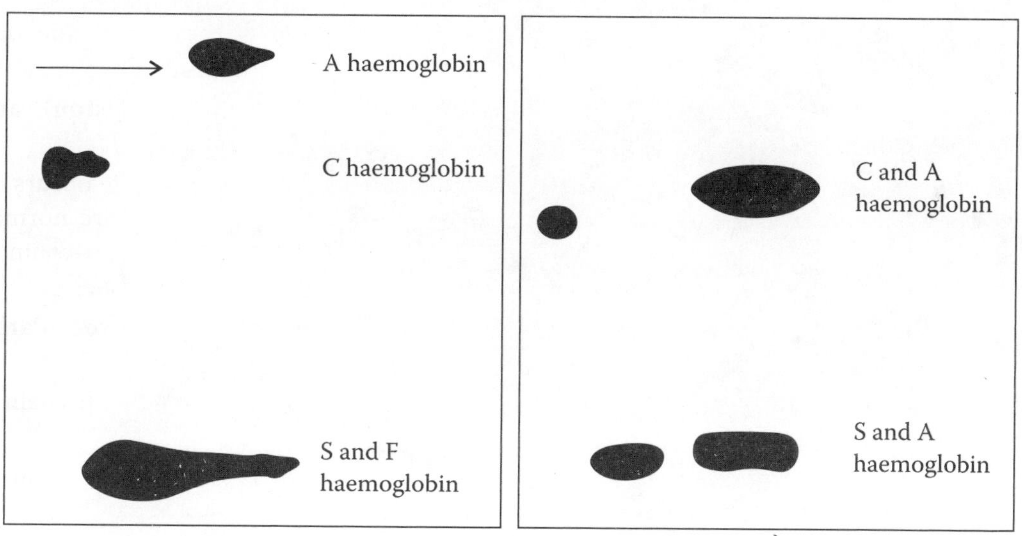

Figure 7.5 Electrophoresis of some haemoglobin variants.

Finger print technique: Ingram developed a technique by which the peptide chains of haemoglobin could be degraded into several peptide fragments by tryptic digestion. This facilitated identification of the composition and sequence of the various amino acids more accurately. For this, the haemoglobin is first denatured by heat and then subjected to tryptic digestion. Trypsin splits the peptide chains only at points where lysine and arginine occur. Since there are approximately 30 molecules of lysine and arginine in each half of haemoglobin molecule, the resultant mixture of peptides contains about 28 peptide fragments, of which 26 are soluble and are rich in lysine and arginine. Ingram subjected the mixture of peptides to electrophoresis on paper in one dimension, followed by chromatography in the other dimension. On staining, the peptides appear as spots taking different positions on the paper. This combined process of separation of peptides by electrophoresis and chromatography is called **finger print technique**. In this manner, **finger prints** or **peptide maps** are prepared for different types of haemoglobin. The separated peptides are further analysed for their amino acid sequence.

8 CHAPTER

Porphyrins and Porphyrias

Chapter Outline

- Chemistry of Porphyrins
- Properties of Porphyrins
- Metabolism of Porphyrins
- Abnormalities in Synthesis of Porphyrins—Porphyrias

CHEMISTRY OF PORPHYRINS

The compounds described in this chapter differ from carbohydrates and fats in that they do not serve the purpose of fuel for supply of energy to the body. They have a unique biochemical importance in the body. Haemoglobin which is the main compound under this group performs the vital function of carrying atmospheric oxygen from the lungs to the various parts of the body. The members of this group are conjugated proteins containing iron porphyrin as their prosthetic groups. The porphyrins which form the outline of the structure of these compounds are cyclic compounds made of pyrrole nuclei. They have the characteristic property of forming complexes with metal ions. The well-known example of iron porphyrin is haem of haemoglobin. Equally important are the cytochromes, which form the intracellular haemoprotein enzyme system. They are concerned directly or indirectly with the ultimate metabolic process common to all substances known as the biological oxidation, which involves combination of oxygen from the lungs with the hydrogen of metabolic substances to form water. Chlorophyll, the photosynthetic pigment of plant, contains magnesium and porphyrin.

To understand the chemistry of porphyrin, comprehensive knowledge of the basic units which form the structure of porphyrin is necessary.

Structure of Porphyrins

Porphyrins are cyclic compounds consisting of four pyrrole units which are linked by methene bridges (–CH =). Each monopyrrole unit contains an acetic acid and a propionic acid side chain (**Fig. 8.1**).

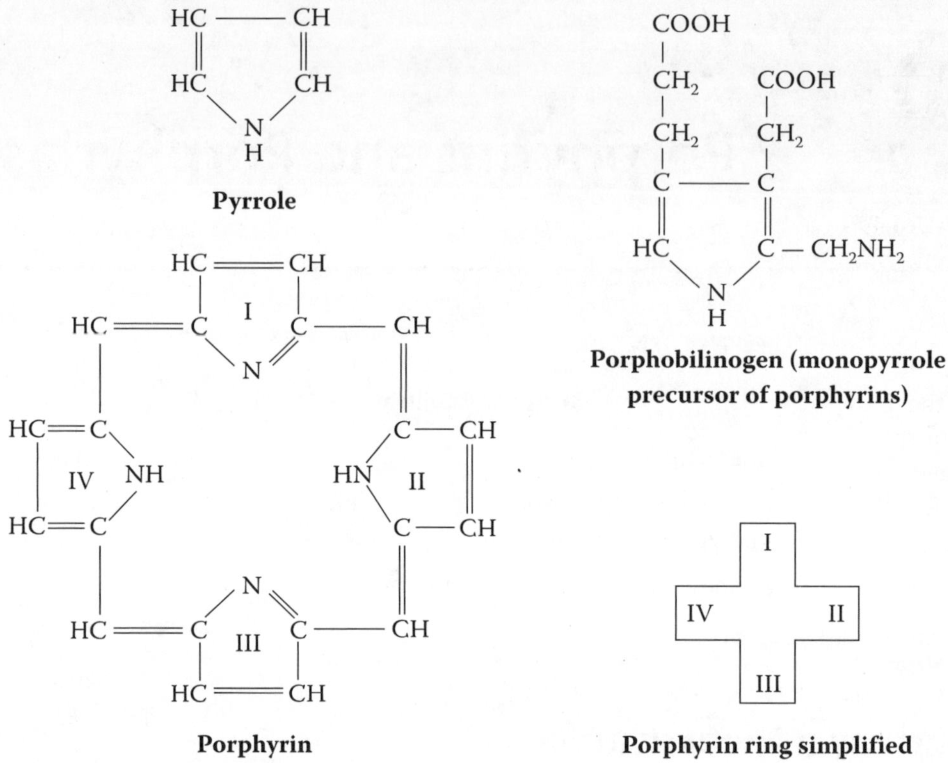

Figure 8.1 Basic pyrrole and porphyrin structures.

There are two types of naturally occurring porphyrins:

1. Uroporphyrins
2. Coproporphyrins

Uroporphyrins: These are called uroporphyrins because they were originally discovered in urine. They are tetra-acetic, tetrapropionic porphyrins, because they contain an acetic acid and a propionic acid side chain in each pyrrole nucleus. The side chains pertaining to acetic acid and propionic acid are represented by letters A and P, respectively, in **Figure 8.2**. There are two isomers of uroporphyrin. These are called uroporphyrin type I and uroporphyrin type III isomers (*see* **Fig. 8.2**).

Type I uroporphyrins are characterised by having their side chain substituents, i.e. acetic acid and propionic acid, in an alternating sequence in all the four pyrrole units whereas this order is reversed in the fourth pyrrole unit of uroporphyrin type **III** (*see* **Fig. 8.2**).

Coproporphyrins: These are called coproporphyrins because they were originally isolated from the faeces. They have tetramethyl, tetrapropionic acid side chains. The methyl groups are formed by decarboxylation of the acetic acid side chains. There are two types of coproporphyrins, namely coproporphyrin I and coproporphyrin III. They are represented in **Figure 8.2**.

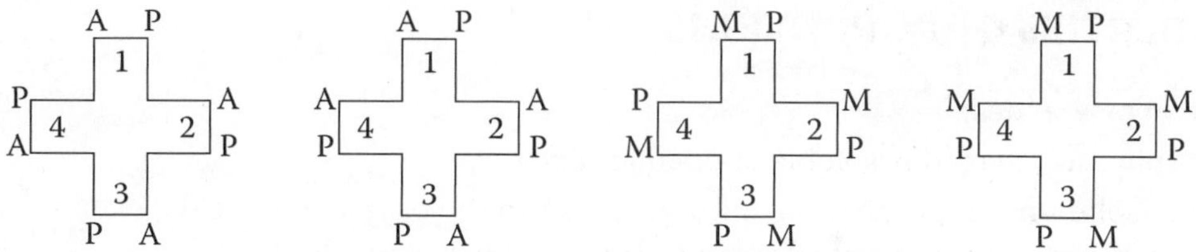

Uroporphyrin I **Uroporphyrin III** **Coproporphyrin I** **Coproporphyrin III**

Figure 8.2 Naturally occurring porphyrins.

In the figure, M represents methyl group and P represents propionic acid. Type I coproporphyrins have their substituents, i.e. methyl and propionic acid side chains arranged in an alternating sequence in all the pyrrole units, whereas this order is reversed in the fourth pyrrole unit in type **III** coproporphyrin.

There are three porphyrin derivatives which are physiologically important. These are mesoporphyrin 9, hematoporphyrin 9 and protoporphyrin 9. They are all derived from type III coproporphyrin.

Mesoporphyrin 9 is tetramethyl, diethyl, dipropionic porphyrin and is derived from type **III** coproporphyrin by decarboxylation of two propionic acid side chains which are converted to ethyl groups (**Fig. 8.3**).

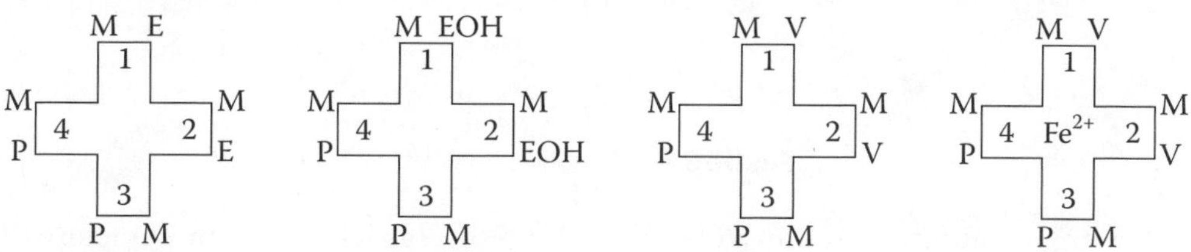

Meso-porphyrin 9 **Hemato-porphyrin 9** **Proto-porphyrin 9** **Haem**

Figure 8.3 Naturally occurring porphyrins derived from coproporphyrin.

Hematoporphyrin 9 is tetramethyl, dihydroxyethyl, dipropionic porphyrin. It is obtained by conversion of the two ethyl groups to hydroxyethyl groups. In **Figure 8.3**, EOH represents hydroxyethyl groups.

Protoporphyrin 9 is tetramethyl, divinyl, dipropionic porphyrin. The vinyl groups are obtained by dehydration of the hydroxyethyl groups (vinyl group is $-CH = CH_2$). This is represented as V in the figure. Haem is formed when iron is added to protoporphyrin 9.

PROPERTIES OF PORPHYRINS

Physical properties:

1. Porphyrins are readily soluble in organic solvents.
2. The solution of porphyrins in organic solvents or mineral acids exhibits a red fluorescence under ultraviolet light. This property is made use of in the qualitative detection and quantitative determination of porphyrins.
3. Characteristic absorption spectra are exhibited by porphyrins in both the visible and the ultraviolet regions. The formation of absorption spectra and the display of red fluorescence are due to the presence of the conjugated double bonds in the porphyrins. When the double bonds of the methene bridges are reduced by the addition of hydrogen atoms to form methylene linkages, the porphyrins are converted to colourless porphyrinogens in which pyrrole units are linked by methylene ($-CH_2-$) bridges.

Chemical properties:

1. The porphyrins behave as weak bases, because of the presence of the tertiary nitrogen atoms in the two pyrroline nuclei of the porphyrin molecule (**Fig. 8.4**). Porphyrins are also acids because of the presence of the carboxyl groups in the side chains. The carboxyl group of porphyrins is readily esterified. Thus, the natural porphyrins are amphoteric compounds. The isoelectric points of porphyrins range from pH 3.0 to 4.5 and within this pH range, porphyrins can be precipitated from an aqueous solution.

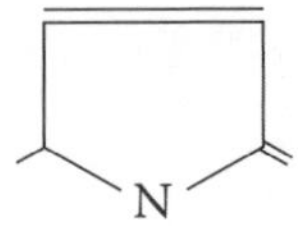

Figure 8.4 Pyrroline nucleus.

2. The nitrogen atoms of the pyrrole nuclei have the capacity to form complexes with certain metals such as copper, zinc, iron and magnesium, the metal occupying a central position in the porphyrin ring. These metal complexes are called **metalloporphyrins**. Of all the metalloporphyins, those in combination with iron are of greatest physiological importance. The iron porphyrins are called **haem**. The iron in haem is in the ferrous form. Haem combines with proteins to form haemoproteins.

   Haem + Globin = Haemoglobin.

   Other examples of metalloporphyrins containing iron are myoglobin which occurs in muscle cells, cytochromes and catalases.

METABOLISM OF PORPHYRINS

Porphyrin metabolism includes the following:

1. Biosynthesis of porphyrin
2. Formation of haem and haemoproteins
3. Excretion of porphyrins

Abnormalities in the synthesis of porphyrins—porphyrias

The overall metabolism of porphyrin is shown in **Figure 8.5**.

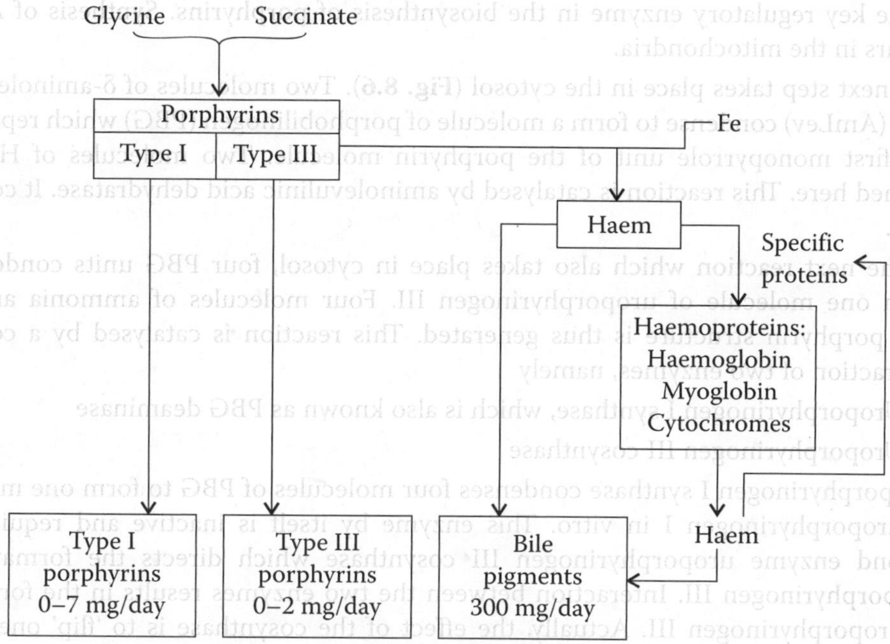

Figure 8.5 Outline of the overall metabolism of porphyrins.

The complex heterocyclic porphyrin ring is synthesised from small units of glycine and succinic acid. Two isomeric types of porphyrins are produced. These are type I and type III porphyrins. Type I porphyrins follow a minor metabolic path and are mostly excreted without being utilised. A small proportion of type III porphyrins is also excreted, but most of them take the major metabolic path which leads to the formation of protoporphyrin. Inclusion of iron to protoporphyrin results in the formation of haem. Haem combines with specific proteins to yield conjugated proteins called haemoprotein such as haemoglobin, myoglobin, cytochromes and catalases (**Fig. 8.5**). Small amounts of bile pigments are derived from the breakdown of haem.

Biosynthesis of Porphyrins

Porphyrins are synthesised largely in the erythroid cells of bone marrow and in hepatic cells. Synthesis of the complex porphyrin ring comprises the following series of reactions. Two materials in small units, namely succinyl-CoA derived from the citric acid cycle and amino acid glycine, are required to start the synthesis (**Fig. 8.6**).

1. The first step involves condensation of one molecule of active succinyl-CoA with one molecule of glycine to form α-amino-β-ketoadipic acid. CoA is released. This reaction takes place in the mitochondria and is catalysed by the enzyme δ-aminolevulinate synthase (ALA synthase). ALA synthase is an inducible enzyme and requires pyridoxal

phosphate to activate glycine. α-Amino-β-ketoadipic acid is rapidly decarboxylated to form 8-aminolevulinic acid (AmLev). The reaction is catalysed by the same enzyme ALA synthase. This step is a rate-limiting step in porphyrin biosynthesis. ALA synthase is the key regulatory enzyme in the biosynthesis of porphyrins. Synthesis of AmLev occurs in the mitochondria.

2. The next step takes place in the cytosol (**Fig. 8.6**). Two molecules of δ-aminolevulinic acid (AmLev) condense to form a molecule of porphobilinogen (PBG) which represents the first monopyrrole unit of the porphyrin molecule. Two molecules of H_2O are formed here. This reaction is catalysed by aminolevulinic acid dehydratase. It contains zinc.
3. In the next reaction which also takes place in cytosol, four PBG units condense to form one molecule of uroporphyrinogen III. Four molecules of ammonia are lost. The porphyrin structure is thus generated. This reaction is catalysed by a complex interaction of two enzymes, namely
   - Uroporphyrinogen I synthase, which is also known as PBG deaminase
   - Uroporphyrinogen III cosynthase

   Uroporphyrinogen I synthase condenses four molecules of PBG to form one molecule of uroporphyrinogen I in vitro. This enzyme by itself is inactive and requires the second enzyme uroporphyrinogen III cosynthase which directs the formation of uroporphyrinogen III. Interaction between the two enzymes results in the formation of uroporphyrinogen III. Actually, the effect of the cosynthase is to 'flip' one of the pyrrole rings to produce type III isomer (uroporphyrinogen III). In the absence of cosynthase, this flipping does not occur and the condensation would take place spontaneously resulting in the formation of type I porphyrins. Under normal conditions, the uroporphyrinogen formed is almost exclusively type III isomer. These form the major metabolic series. Uroporphyrin I derivatives form a minor metabolic series and are excreted without utilisation. But when type I porphyrins are produced in excess, they are toxic and cause photosensitivity and destruction of skin and damage to the central nervous system. It should be remembered that in uroporphyrin I series, the acetic acid and propionic acid side chains are arranged in an alternating sequence in all the four pyrrole units whereas this arrangement is reversed in the fourth pyrrole unit in uroporphyrin III derivatives.
4. The next series of reactions is concerned with the formation of coproporphyrin and derivatives. Coproporphyrins are tetramethyl, tetrapropionic porphyrins. Two series of coproporphyrins occur in nature. These are coproporphyrin I and coproporphyrin III derivatives. The methyl groups and propionic acid side chains are arranged in an alternating sequence in all the four pyrrole units in the I series whereas this arrangement is reversed in the fourth pyrrole unit in coproporphyrin III derivatives.
5. Uroporphyrinogen III is converted to coproporphyrinogen III by decarboxylation of all the four acetic acid side chains to methyl groups. The reaction is catalysed by uroporphyrinogen decarboxylase in the cytosol. This enzyme is also capable of converting uroporphyrinogen I to coproporphyrinogen I. Coproporphyrin I derivatives

form a minor metabolic series and are excreted without utilisation in the body (**Fig. 8.6**).

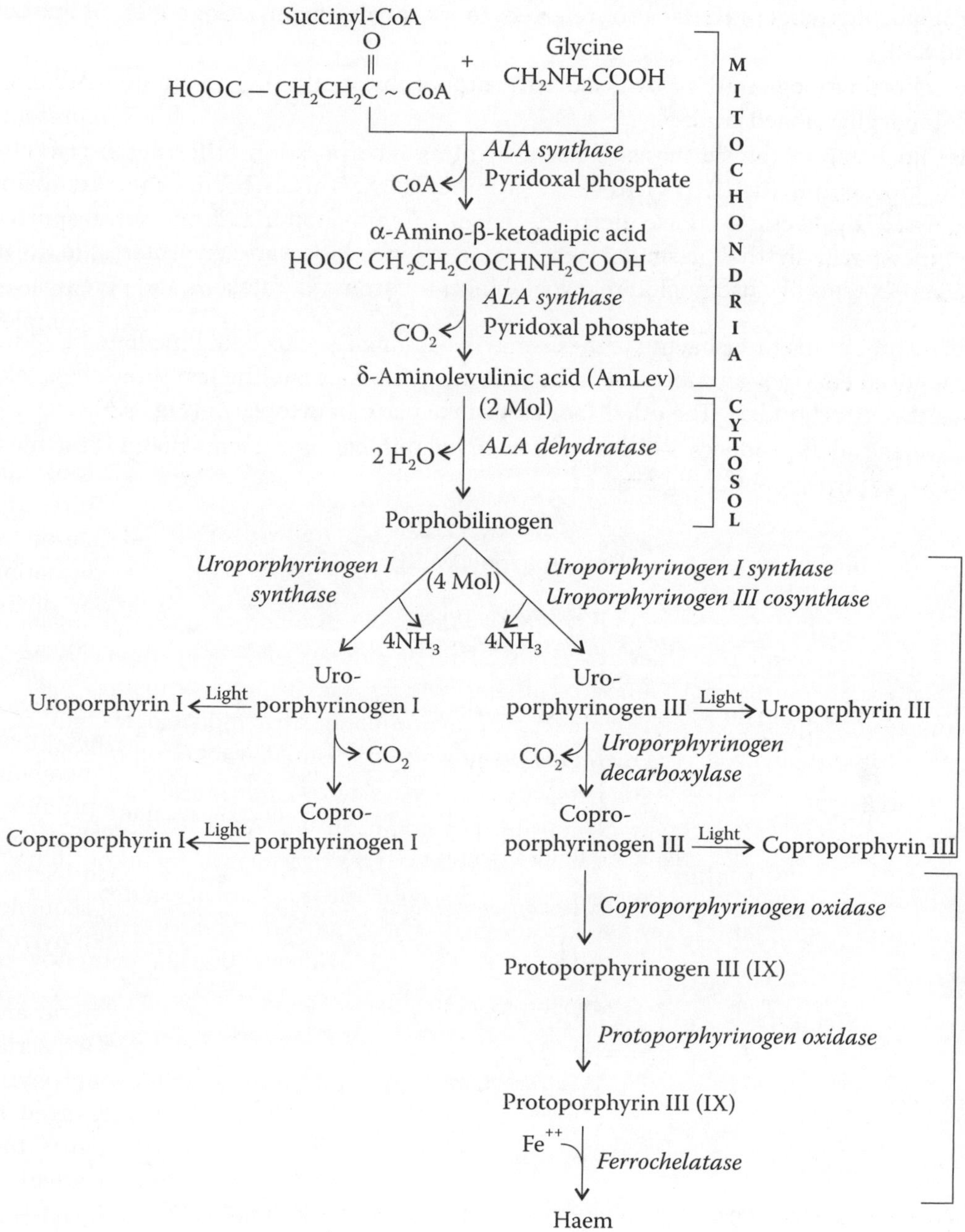

Figure 8.6 Biosynthesis of porphyrin and formation of haem.

6. Next, coproporphyrinogen III enters the mitochondria where it is converted to protoporphyrinogen III. The reaction is catalysed by coproporphyrinogen oxidase. Several oxidations and decarboxylations are involved in this conversion. Protoporphyrinogen III is also referred to as **protoporphyrinogen IX** (**Figs 8.6** and **8.7**).
7. Protoporphyrinogen III is oxidised to protoporphyrin III (IX) in mitochondria by protoporphyrinogen oxidase.
8. The final step in the synthesis of haem involves incorporation of ferrous iron (Fe^{++}) into protoporphyrin III (IX) to form protohaem IX. This is haem. The reaction is catalysed by haem synthase (ferrochelatase) in mitochondria. Iron is transported by transferrin in the plasma. Haem can combine with various proteins to form haemoproteins like haemoglobin, myoglobin, cytochrome C, catalases and peroxidases.

The formation of haem or haem synthesis may be summarised as being mediated by four mitochondrial enzymes and four cytosolic enzymes. The first and the last three steps take place in the mitochondria. The other four steps take place in cytoplasm (**Fig. 8.6**).

An average adult produces 5–6 grams of haemoglobin per day. Haemoglobin is the most abundant porphyrin containing protein.

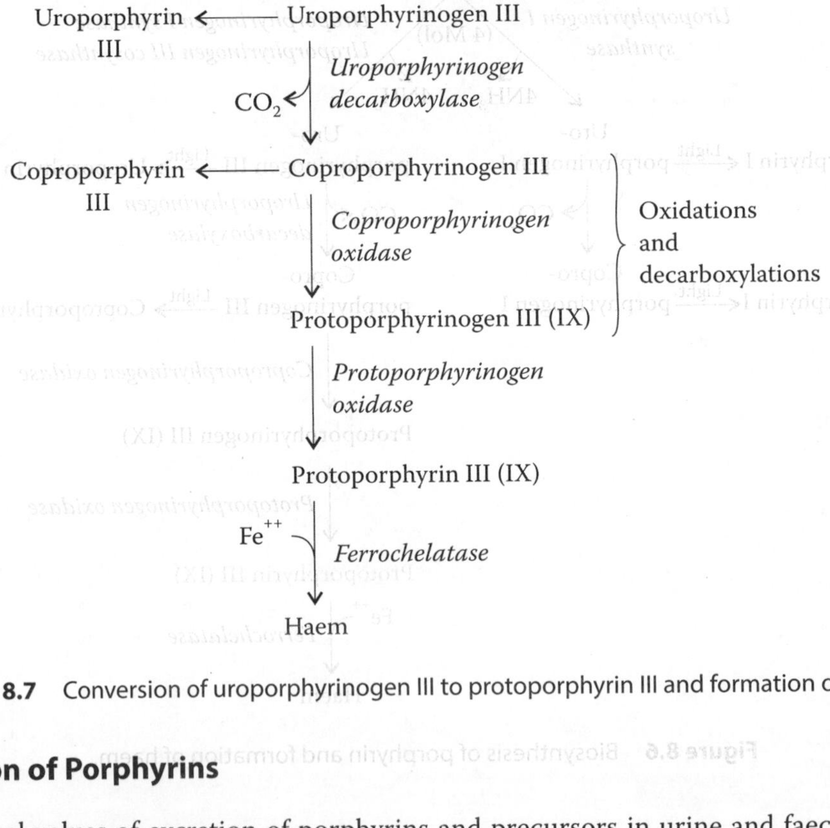

Figure 8.7 Conversion of uroporphyrinogen III to protoporphyrin III and formation of haem.

Excretion of Porphyrins

The normal values of excretion of porphyrins and precursors in urine and faeces and the normal concentration of porphyrins in erythrocytes are given in **Table 8.1**.

Table 8.1 Normal Values of Excretion of Porphyrins

Porphyrins	Urine (μg/24 hr)	Faces (μg/g dry wt)	Erythrocytes (μg/dl cells)
AmLev	4000	–	–
Porphobilinogen	1500	–	–
Uroporphyrin	50	5	Trace
Coproporphyrin	300	50	3
Protoporphyrin	–	120	80

Porphyrinuria: Excretion of an excess amount of porphyrins in urine is porphyrinuria. There need not be any disturbance in porphyrin synthesis. Excretion of coproporphyrins in excess amount may occur as a result of the accelerated rate of synthesis of haem as in haemolytic anaemias or as a result of interference with synthesis of haem, as in the case of lead poisoning, liver diseases and malignant conditions.

ABNORMALITIES IN SYNTHESIS OF PORPHYRINS—PORPHYRIAS

Inherited disorders caused by abnormalities in the pathway of biosynthesis of porphyrins are designated as **porphyrias**. Each of the porphyrias exhibits a characteristic pattern of increased production, accumulation and excretion of high amounts of uroporphyrins, coproporphyrins and intermediates of porphyrin biosynthesis (**Table 8.2**). They represent deviation in the metabolic pathway due to genetic defects of specific enzymes.

Classification of Porphyrias

Porphyrias are classified as follows:

1. Erythropoietic porphyria
2. Hepatic porphyrias
3. Protoporphyria

Erythropoietic porphyria: This is also known as **congenital erythropoietic porphyria** (CEP) which is a rare disease transmitted as a recessive trait. It is more common in males than in females. The characteristic clinical manifestation of CEP is severe photosensitivity which appears in an early age and persists throughout life. Exposure to sunlight leads to erythema, bullae formation and ulceration of the skin which may later become necrotic followed by pigmented scars. Death may occur in childhood. When they survive longer, mutilation affecting nose, ears and fingers is observed. The teeth and bones may be stained red due to deposit of porphyrin and exhibit fluorescence in ultraviolet light.

The site of metabolic error is the bone marrow (erythroid tissue) and the defect lies in the enzymatic conversion of porphobilinogen type I and III porphyrins. Normally, the conversion is towards a preponderance of type III isomers which are the actual precursors of haem, whereas type I isomers are formed in a lesser amount and are excreted without utilisation. In congenital erythropoietic porphyria, there is an imbalance between the relative activities of uroporphyrinogen I synthase and uroporphyrinogen III cosynthase due to genetic deficiency of uroporphyrinogen III cosynthase. This results in increased formation of uroporphyrinogen I which exceeds the formation of uroporphyrinogen III, the normal isomer on the pathway to haem synthesis. Patients with congenital erythropoietic porphyria excrete increased quantities of type I uroporphyrinogen and type I coproporphyrinogen which in the urine are spontaneously oxidised to uroporphyrin I and coproporphyrin I. The urine is coloured red due to the presence of an increased amount of type I uroporphyrinogen and coproporphyrins. Circulating erythrocytes contain a high concentration of uroporphyrin I. Decreased formation of uroporphyrinogen III, which is the precursor of haem, leads to a relative deficiency of haem. This induces ALA synthase in erythropoietic tissues, as a compensatory mechanism, which in turn promotes massive production of type I porphyrinogen.

Hepatic porphyrias: These are rare conditions transmitted as autosomal dominants. The site of metabolic error is liver. There are four types of hepatic porphyrias. All have many features in common such as increased excretion of ALA and PBG in urine during acute attacks; however, excretion of porphyrins in urine and faeces differ in some types. The four types of hepatic porphyrias are as follows:

1. Acute intermittent porphyria
2. Porphyria variegata
3. Hereditary coproporphyria
4. Porphyria cutanea tarda

Acute intermittent porphyria (AIP) is the most common type of hepatic porphyria. It has an autosomal dominant mode of inheritance. Acute intermittent porphyria is characterised by (i) intermittent attacks of acute abdominal pain, (ii) neurological symptoms and (iii) psychiatric symptoms. The symptoms appear as late as the third decade of life. The abdominal symptoms may consist of severe colicky pain with vomiting and fever. The neurological symptoms may vary from peripheral neuritis to complete paralysis of limbs. The psychiatric symptoms may manifest mental disturbance. Barbiturates are noted for precipitating attacks of AIP. Patients with AIP excrete massive quantities of porphobilinogen and aminolevulinate in urine during acute attacks. Both these compounds are colourless. Urine is not coloured.

The metabolic error in AIP is due to an inherited partial deficiency of uroporphyrinogen I synthase which is required for the conversion of porphobilinogen to uroporphyrinogen III, the precursor of haem. This induces a compensatory increase in aminolevulinate synthase activity. This combined with the partial deficiency of uroporphyrinogen I synthase results in a massive accumulation of aminolevulinate and porphobilinogen. The patients do not exhibit photosensitivity as in CEP, because there is no accumulation of porphyrins. Under normal conditions, aminolevulinate synthase is the rate-limiting enzyme. It regulates haem synthesis which is under complete repression. In AIP, the repressor mechanism which controls aminolevulinate synthase is affected by a genetic mutation, resulting in overactivity of aminolevulinate synthase and therefore increased production of aminolevulinate. Drugs such as barbiturate and steroid hormones are known to induce increased formation of aminolevulinate synthase, resulting in the manifestation of AIP.

Porphyria variegate is common in South Africa. It is an autosomal dominant disorder. Clinically it exhibits mainly cutaneous manifestations such as photosensitivity, blister formation and hyperpigmentation of skin exposed to sun or subjected to trauma. In some cases, acute attacks of gastrointestinal symptoms and neurological symptoms similar to those in AIP may occur. During an acute attack, there is increased excretion of aminolevulinate (ALA), porphobilinogen (PBG), uroporphyrin and coproporphyrin in urine. But the outstanding feature is that throughout the course, there is increased excretion of coproporphyrin and protoporphyrin in faeces. The defect is due to a partial deficiency of protoporphyrinogen oxidase which is responsible for the conversion of protoporphyrinogen to haem. This leads to overproduction of all intermediates in the haem synthetic pathway proximal to the block. Accordingly, patients with porphyria variegata excrete excessive quantities of ALA, PBG, uroporphyrin and coproporphyrin in urine and coproporphyrin and protoporphyrin in faeces.

Hereditary coproporphyria is an autosomal dominant disorder. It exhibits symptoms similar to porphyria variegata and acute intermittent porphyria. The unique feature of this disease is excessive excretion of coproporphyrin III in faeces. In the latent phase, the patients may remain asymptomatic. The defect is due to partial deficiency of coproporphyrinogen oxidase which is responsible for the conversion of coproporphyrinogen HI to protoporphyrinogen IX. Further metabolism of coproporphyrinogen HI is blocked. This causes increased excretion in faeces of coproporphyrinogen III which is rapidly oxidised to coproporphyrin III. Formation of protoporphyrinogen which is the precursor of haem is decreased and there is deficiency in the synthesis of haem. This in turn produces depression of AmLev synthase, which results in overproduction and excretion of an increased amount of aminolevulinate and porphobilinogen in urine, particularly during attacks.

Porphyria cutanea tarda is an autosomal dominant disorder. It resembles porphyria variegata in that it manifests mainly cutaneous lesions, varying from photosensitivity to blister formation in areas exposed to sun. Gastrointestinal and neurological manifestations are absent. Urine may be coloured pink or brownish due to increased excretion of a large amount of uroporphyrin III. The defect in porphyria cutanea tarda is due to a partial deficiency of uroporphyrinogen decarboxylase. As a result, further metabolism of uroporphyrinogen III to coproporphyrinogen III is defective. This results in increased excretion of uroporphyrin III in urine.

Protoporphyria: This is also known as erythropoietic protoporphyria. It is an autosomal dominant disorder. Clinical manifestations are similar to those in congenital erythropoietic porphyria. It exhibits photosensitivity followed by erythema and urticaria on exposure to sunlight. The metabolic defect is due to a partial deficiency of ferrochelatase, the enzyme that catalyses the incorporation of ferrous iron to protoporphyrin IX. There is increased excretion of protoporphyrin IX in faeces. Erythrocytes contain an increased quantity of protoporphyrin IX.

Tests for Porphyrin

The following tests are commonly employed to detect the presence of porphyrins in urine:

1. **Colour:** Urine in most types of porphyrias may show varied intensity of red colour due to excretion of increased amounts of uroporphyrins and coproporphyrins.

Table 8.2 Summary of Major Features in Different Types of Porphyrias

Porphyria: Type	Enzyme (±) Activity	Major Symptoms	Products in Urine/Red Cell	Products in Faeces
Congenital erythropoietic porphyria	Uroporphyrinogen III cosynthase (–)	Photosensitivity Cutaneous lesions	Uroporphyrin 1 (+++) Coproporphyrin 1 (+++) Red cell - uroporphyrin 1 (+++)	
Acute intermittent porphyria	ALA synthase (+) Uroporphyrinogen I synthase (–)	Abdominal pain Neuropsychiatric No photosensitivity	ALA (+++) PBG (+++)	
Porphyria variegata	Protoporphyrinogen oxidase (–)	Photosensitivity Abdominal pain Neuropsychiatric	ALA (+++) PBG (+++)	Coproporphyrin (++) Protoporphyrin (++)
Hereditary coproporphyria	Coproporphyrinogen oxidase (–)	Photosensitivity Abdominal pain Neuropsychiatric	ALA (+++) PBG (+++)	Coproporphyrin III (+)
Porphyria cutanea tarda	Uroporphyrinogen decarboxylase (–)	Photosensitivity	Uroporphyrin (+)	Protoporphyrin (+)
Protoporphyria	Ferrochelatase (–)	Photosensitivity	Red cell - protoporphyrin (+)	Protoporphyrin IX (++)

ALA, aminolevulinate; PBG, porphobilinogen.
(+) increased, (–) decreased
Protoporphyrin is present in red cells only in protoporphyria.

2. **Fluorescence in ultraviolet light:** Urine containing porphyrin, acidified with strong mineral acids, emits a characteristic red fluorescence when illuminated by ultraviolet light.
3. **Spectroscopic examination:** Three absorption bands of which two similar to those of oxyhaemoglobin and one nearer to the 'D' line are seen in the case of urine containing porphyrins acidified with 5% hydrochloric acid and viewed against light through a spectroscope. The band nearer the 'D' line (400 nm) is sharp and is characteristic to all porphyrins and it is due to the presence of a porphyrin ring. This band is known as **Soret band.**
4. **Test to differentiate coproporphyrin from uroporphyrin:** Urine containing coproporphyrins I and III is soluble in a mixture of glacial acetic acid and ether, whereas uroprophyrins are not soluble in acetic acid–ether mixture.
5. **Test for porphobilinogen:** Urine containing PBG reacts with Ehrlich's reagent to form a red colour, just as urobilinogen, but the red substance is not extractable with chloroform.

9 CHAPTER

Catabolism of Haem

Chapter Outline

- Degradation of Haem
- Formation of Bile Pigments
- Properties of Bile Pigments
- Metabolism of Bilirubin
- Jaundice
- Unconjugated Hyperbilirubinaemia
- Conjugated Hyperbilirubinaemia

Circulating erythrocytes are destroyed at the end of their lifespan of about 120 days, releasing haemoglobin. Approximately, 6 grams of haemoglobin are formed per day in a human adult under normal conditions. This on degradation produces about 250–300 mg of bilirubin per day. Globin dissociates first from haemoglobin. It may be utilised as such or may be split further into amino acids.

DEGRADATION OF HAEM

The catabolism of haem derived from all haem proteins takes place mainly in the microsomal fraction of the reticuloendothelial cells of spleen, liver and bone marrow by a complex enzyme system known as **haem oxygenase**. It is located in close proximity to the microsomal electron transport system. This enzyme system requires oxygen and reduced NADP (NADPH) as cofactors.

First, haem oxygenase oxidises the ferrous (Fe^{++}) iron of haem to the ferric (Fe^{+++}) form, converting haem to hemin. In the next step, haem oxygenase, with the aid of NADPH and molecular oxygen (O_2), cleaves hemin at the point between I and II pyrrole rings. The ring structure of hemin is opened to form biliverdin IXa, a green pigment. The carbon of the methynyl bridge between I and II pyrrole rings is eliminated as carbon monoxide (**Fig. 9.1**).

Next, the iron from hemin dissociates and enters the iron pool for reutilisation. Biliverdin IXa is then reduced to bilirubin IXa which is orange in colour, by enzyme biliverdin reductase and NADPH. Bilirubin is released in blood.

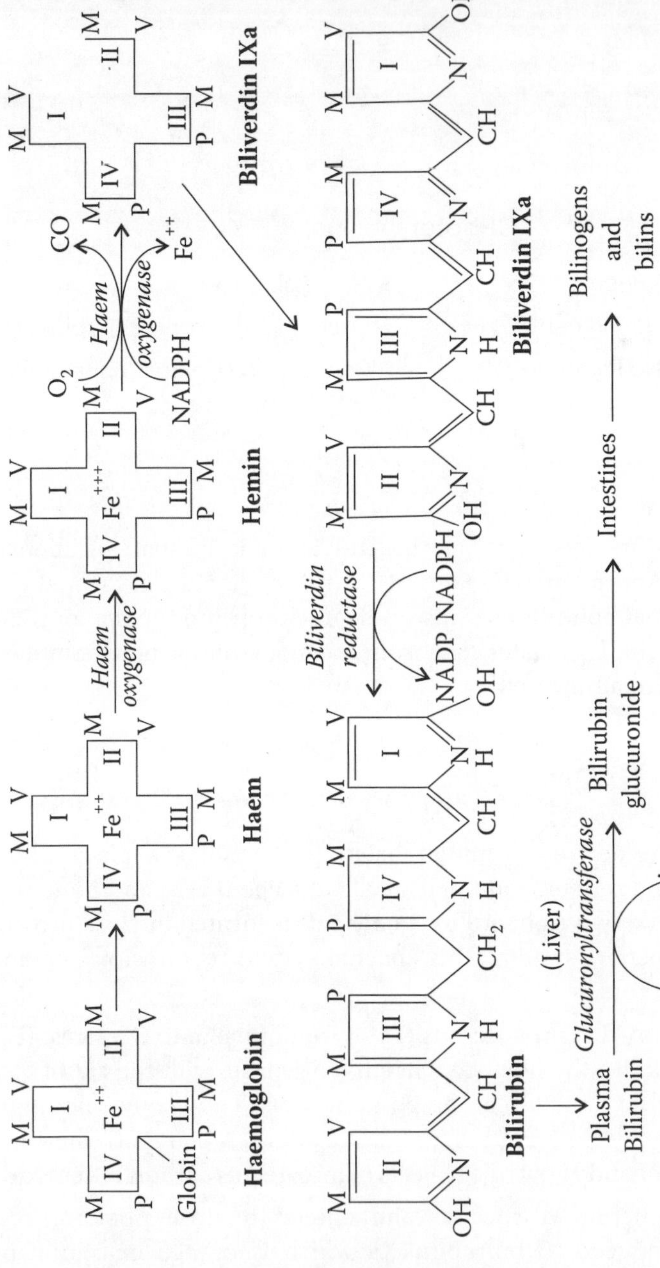

Figure 9.1 Catabolism of haem—formation of bile pigments.

FORMATION OF BILE PIGMENTS

Conversion of hemin to bile pigments and derivatives broadly involves seven steps. The cyclic structure of the protoporphyrin is cleaved between the I and II pyrrole units with opening of the ring and formation of open chain tetrapyrroles (**Fig. 9.2**). These are known as bile pigments. During the process, the following changes take place:

1. The methene carbon bridge between I and II pyrrole rings is oxidised and eliminated as carbon monoxide. At the same time, two hydroxyl groups are introduced at both ends.

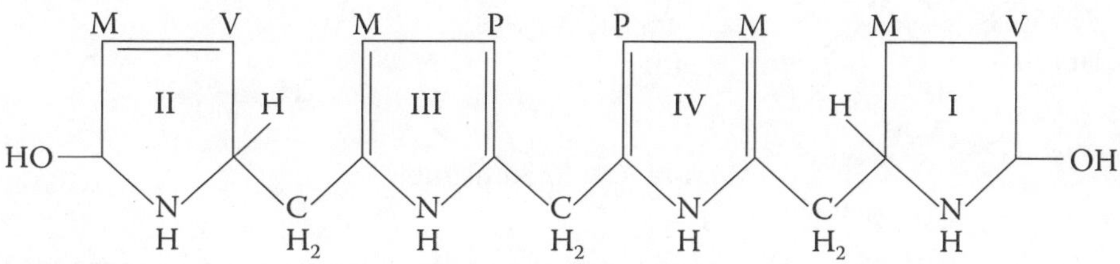

Figure 9.2 Bilane.

2. All the remaining methene linkages are reduced to methylene linkages (CH_2) resulting in the formation of the hypothetical parent compound **bilane**. But the initial bile pigment formed from degradation of haemoglobin is biliverdin which has all three methylene linkages in the oxidised form (methene) as indicated in **Figure 9.3**.

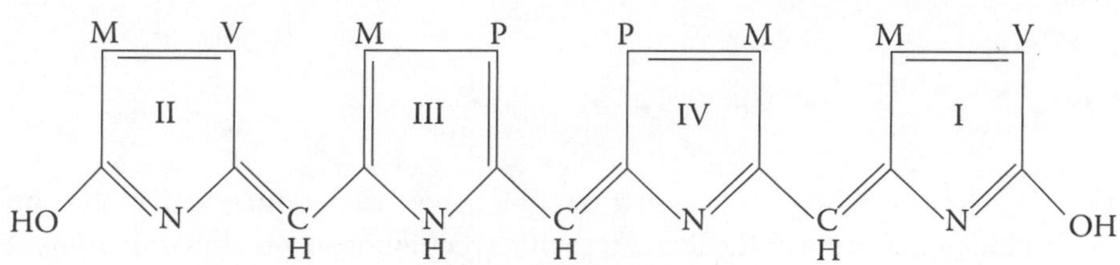

Figure 9.3 Biliverdin.

3. Biliverdin is reduced by the action of biliverdin reductase to form bilirubin which is the major bile pigment present in human bile. In the formation of bilirubin, the methenyl bridge between III and IV pyrrole rings of biliverdin is reduced to the methylene group (**Fig. 9.4**). The bilirubin secreted in bile is conjugated bilirubin and it enters the small intestine.

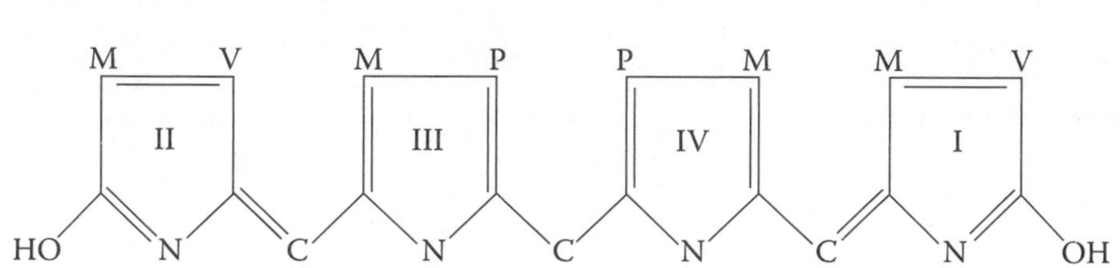

Figure 9.4 Bilirubin.

4. When it reaches the terminal part of ileum and the large intestines, the glucuronides are removed from bilirubin by specific bacterial enzymes and bilirubin is reduced to form mesobilirubin. Two vinyl groups of bilirubin are reduced to ethyl groups in the formation of mesobilirubin (**Fig. 9.5**).

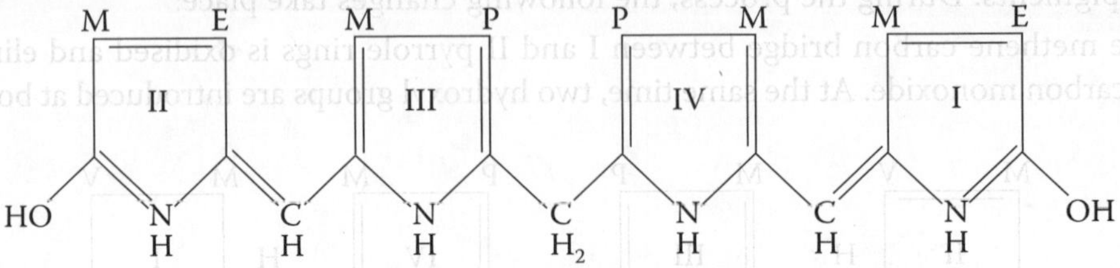

Figure 9.5 Mesobilirubin.

5. Further reduction of mesobilirubin takes place when two methyne linkages are reduced to methylene groups, resulting in the formation of mesobilirubinogen (**Fig. 9.6**).

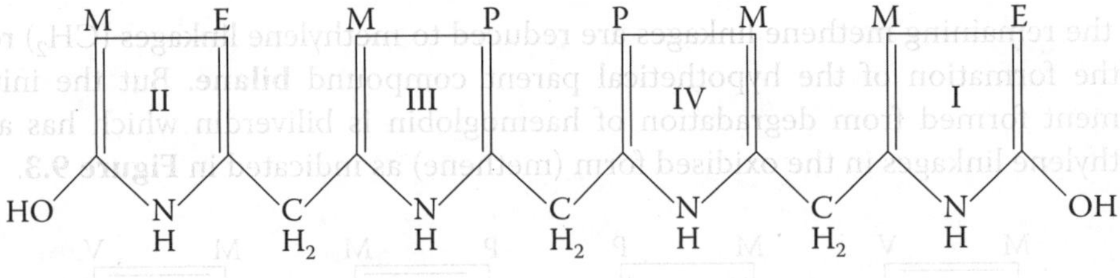

Figure 9.6 Mesobilirubinogen.

6. Further reduction by hydrogenation of the two outer pyrrole nuclei of mesobilirubinogen results in the formation of stercobilinogen which is colourless (**Fig. 9.7**).

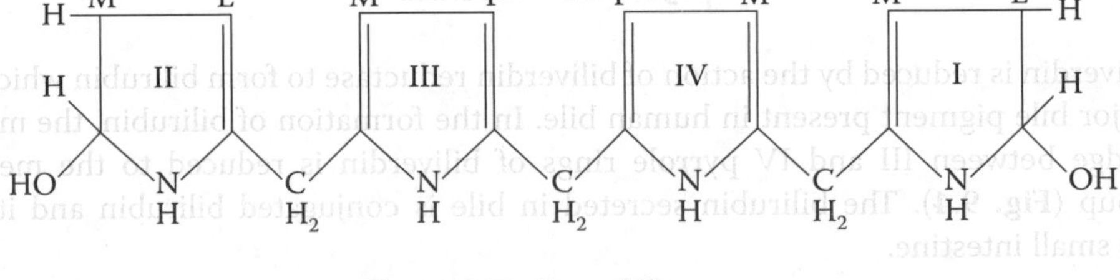

Figure 9.7 Stercobilinogen.

7. Autooxidation in the presence of air converts stercobilinogen to stercobilin, which gives the brown colour to the faeces. Here, the central methylene linkage of stercobilinogen is oxidised (**Fig. 9.8**).

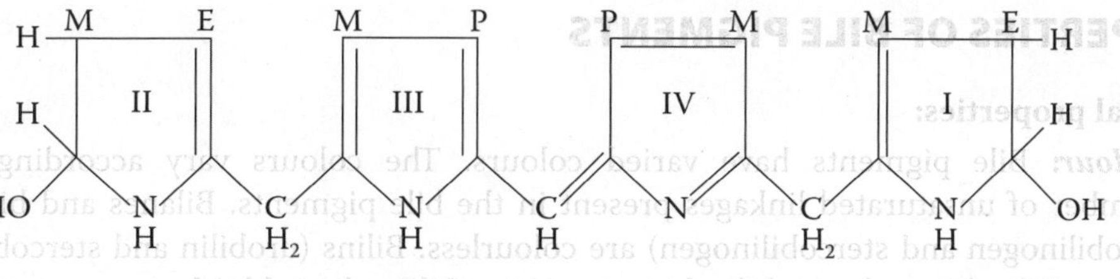

Figure 9.8 Stercobilin.

It may be noted that stercobilin in faeces has the same structure as urobilin in urine. Urobilin is formed when mesobilirubinogen gets oxidised at the central methylene linkage.

The formation of bile pigments and their metabolic pathway may be represented schematically as shown in **Figure 9.9**.

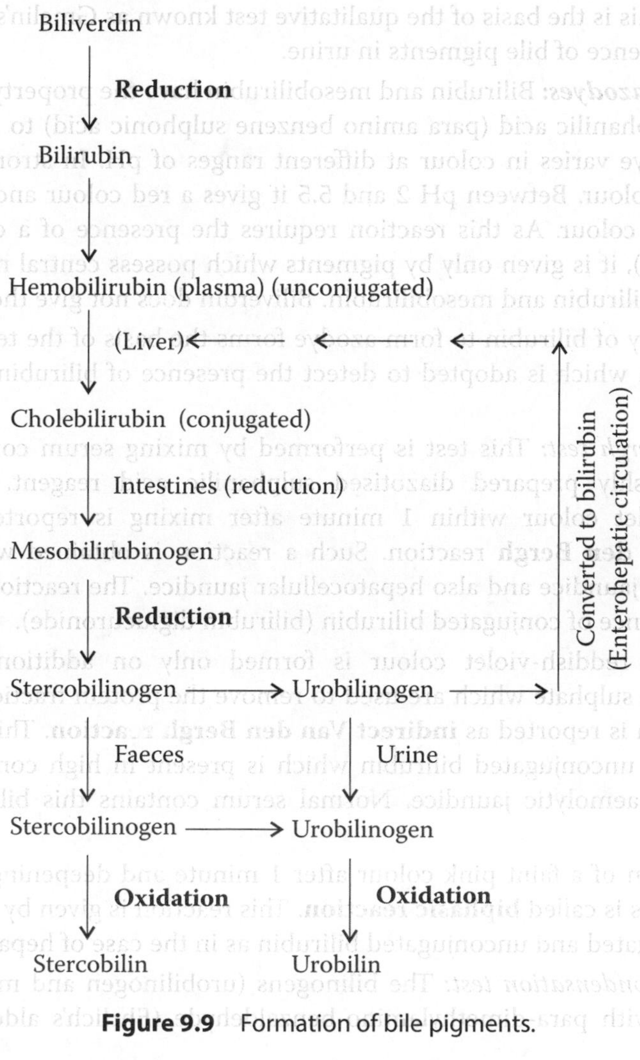

Figure 9.9 Formation of bile pigments.

PROPERTIES OF BILE PIGMENTS

Physical properties:

1. ***Colour***: Bile pigments have varied colours. The colours vary according to the number of unsaturated linkages present in the bile pigments. Bilanes and bilinogens (urobilinogen and stercobilinogen) are colourless. Bilins (urobilin and stercobilin) are yellow. Bilirubin and mesobilirubin are orange. Biliverdin is bluish green.
2. ***Solubility***: The free acid forms of bilirubin and biliverdin and their calcium and barium salts are insoluble in water. The sodium and potassium salts are soluble in water. The conjugated derivatives, both glucuronides and sulphates, are also soluble in water.

Chemical properties:

1. ***Oxidation***: Certain bile pigments on oxidation yield characteristic colours. When bile pigments are treated with oxidising agents such as nitric acid, a play of colours consisting of green, blue and orange, indicating the presence of biliverdin and bilirubin, is observed. This is the basis of the qualitative test known as Gmelin's test employed to detect the presence of bile pigments in urine.
2. ***Formation of azodyes***: Bilirubin and mesobilirubin have the property of coupling with diazotized sulphanilic acid (para amino benzene sulphonic acid) to form azodye. The resulting azodye varies in colour at different ranges of pH. In strong acid, it gives a bluish-violet colour. Between pH 2 and 5.5 it gives a red colour and above pH 5.5, it yields a green colour. As this reaction requires the presence of a central methylene group ($-CH_2-$), it is given only by pigments which possess central methylene groups; examples are bilirubin and mesobilirubin. Biliverdin does not give the reaction.

   The property of bilirubin to form azodye forms the basis of the test called Van den Bergh reaction which is adopted to detect the presence of bilirubin in the jaundiced serum:

   - *Van den Bergh test:* This test is performed by mixing serum containing bilirubin with a freshly prepared diazotised sulphanilic acid reagent. Formation of a reddish-violet colour within 1 minute after mixing is reported as prompt or **direct Van den Bergh** reaction. Such a reaction is obtained with the serum of obstructive jaundice and also hepatocellular jaundice. The reaction is characteristic of the presence of conjugated bilirubin (bilirubin diglucuronide).

     When a reddish-violet colour is formed only on addition of alcohol and ammonium sulphate which are used to remove the protein fraction from bilirubin, the reaction is reported as **indirect Van den Bergh reaction**. This type of reaction is given by unconjugated bilirubin which is present in high concentration in the serum of haemolytic jaundice. Normal serum contains this bilirubin in a small amount.

     Formation of a faint pink colour after 1 minute and deepening of the colour in 2–3 minutes is called **biphasic reaction**. This reaction is given by serum containing both conjugated and unconjugated bilirubin as in the case of hepatic jaundice.
   - *Aldehyde condensation test:* The bilinogens (urobilinogen and mesobilirubinogen) condense with para-dimethylamino-benzaldehyde (Ehrlich's aldehyde reagent) in

acid solution, to give a red colour. The coloured product formed dissolves in organic solvents, and this is in contrast to the formation of red colour by porphobilinogen which does not dissolve in organic solvents.

- *Fluorescence of Zn complexes:* The bilins (urobilin and stercobilin) exhibit a characteristic brilliant green fluorescence when treated with alcoholic zinc acetate solution. This test is called **Schlesinger's test**. The fluorescence disappears on acidification. This test is characteristically positive when performed with the urine of haemolytic jaundice, due to the presence of urobilinogen in high concentration.

METABOLISM OF BILIRUBIN

Liver occupies the central role in the metabolism of bile pigments. Bilirubin metabolism consists of three phases:

1. Uptake and circulation of bilirubin
2. Conjugation of bilirubin
3. Excretion of bilirubin into bile

Uptake and circulation of bilirubin: Following release in plasma, bilirubin which is sparingly soluble in aqueous media circulates in plasma by binding to serum albumin. Each molecule of albumin has two sites of affinity for bilirubin. One is a high affinity site and the other is a low affinity site. In 100 ml plasma, about 25 mg of bilirubin can be tightly bound to albumin at the high affinity site. Excess bilirubin binds only loosely. It can be easily detached and diffused into tissues. The normal concentration of plasma bilirubin is 0.3–1.0 mg/100 ml. Almost all of this is unconjugated bilirubin. It is known as **indirect bilirubin**. It is colloidal in nature because of its attachment to albumin. It is insoluble in water and cannot pass through the glomerular membrane. It reaches liver where the albumin fraction is removed by Kupffer cells and bilirubin is transported to the endoplasmic reticulum through the cytoplasm of hepatocytes, bound to a protein called ligandin.

Conjugation of bilirubin: In the endoplasmic reticulum, bilirubin combines with glucuronic acid to form bilirubin monoglucuronide and bilirubin diglucuronide. This process is known as **conjugation**. This step is necessary to convert unconjugated bilirubin, which is insoluble in water, to a water-soluble derivative so as to be excreted into bile. The reaction is catalysed by uridine diphosphate glucuronyl transferase (UDP-glucuronyl transferase), an enzyme present in the smooth endoplasmic reticulum. The enzyme catalyses the transfer of glucuronide from UDP glucuronic acid to bilirubin, forming bilirubin monoglucuronide (BMG) first and then bilirubin diglucuronide (BDG). Two molecules of BMG may undergo dismutation, catalysed by the enzyme BMG dismutase, to form two molecules of BMG and one molecule of unconjugated bilirubin. UDP glucuronic acid is the donor of glucuronic acid. The reactions take place as follows:

- UDP-glucuronic acid + Bilirubin —*UDP-glucuronyltransferase*→ Bilirubin monoglucuronide + UDP
- UDP-glucuronic acid + Bilirubin monoglucuronide —*UDP-glucuronyltransferase*→ Bilirubin diglucuronide + UDP
- 2 Bilirubin monoglucuronide —*BMG dismutase*→ Bilirubin diglucuronide + Bilirubin

It is found that most of the bilirubin present in bile is bilirubin diglucuronide. A smaller proportion of bilirubin monoglucuronide is also present. Bilirubin diglucuronide and bilirubin monoglucuronide are called **conjugated** bilirubin and **direct** bilirubin, respectively.

The characteristic property of bilirubin glucuronide is that it is soluble in an aqueous medium and is readily excreted into the intestine with bile. Conjugated bilirubin differs from unconjugated bilirubin in the following aspects:

- It is conjugated with glucuronide.
- Conjugated bilirubin does not contain protein.
- It is soluble in an aqueous medium.

Excretion of bilirubin into bile: Bilirubin diglucuronide is excreted into bile canaliculi and from there it enters the hepatic duct. It passes through the common bile duct to empty into the duodenum along with the bile (**Fig. 9.10**). It then enters the intestines where it is reduced by bacterial enzymes to a series of colourless compounds known as bilinogens of which the most important are urobilinogen and stercobilinogen. The latter is excreted in the faeces. On exposure to air, it is oxidised to stercobilin which is the chief pigment of the faeces.

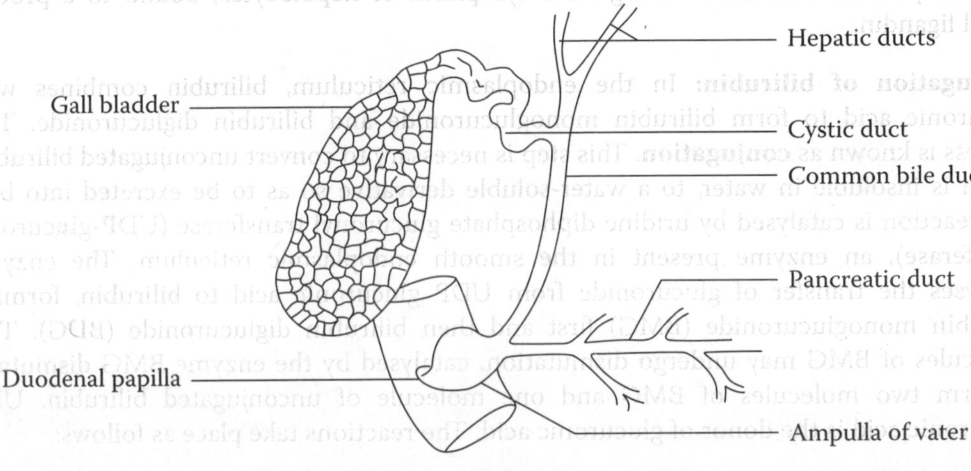

Figure 9.10 Circulation of bile pigments.

A small portion of the urobilinogen (**Fig. 9.10**) from the large intestines is reabsorbed and passes by the portal circulation to the liver, where most of it is reconverted to bilirubin. It is then re-excreted almost entirely as bilirubin into the bile. This is called **enterohepatic circulation of bile pigments**. It is also known as an **intrahepatic urobilinogen cycle**.

A small portion of urobilinogen escapes from the liver to enter the general circulation and then through the kidneys gets excreted as urobilinogen in the urine. When urine is exposed to air, urobilinogen gets oxidised to urobilin. Normally, the amount of urobilinogen excreted in the urine is too small and cannot be detected by the chemical test (Schlesinger's test).

The urobilinogen which escapes reabsorption from the intestines gets converted to stercobilinogen and is excreted in the faeces along with the stercobilinogen derived from enterohepatic circulation. The stercobilinogen excreted in the faeces and the urobilinogen excreted in the urine are chemically identical. The stercobilinogen on exposure to air is oxidised to stercobilin. The formation and circulation of bile pigments are graphically represented in **Figure 9.11**.

JAUNDICE

The normal concentration of bilirubin in blood ranges from 0.3 to 1.0 mg%. When bilirubin in blood exceeds 1 mg%, the condition is known as **hyperbilirubinaemia**. Excess bilirubin (above 2–2.5 mg%) from blood diffuses into the tissues, skin and mucous membrane, colouring them yellow. This condition caused by overflow of bilirubin is called **jaundice**. It can occur due to the following causes:

1. Excessive formation of bilirubin, beyond the capacity of normal liver to excrete
2. Obstruction in the normal excretory passages of the bile in the liver or outside the liver, before reaching the duodenum
3. Dysfunction of the damaged liver cells, resulting in failure to excrete the normal amount of bilirubin produced

Whatever may be the cause of jaundice, bilirubin which accumulates in the blood diffuses into the tissues colouring them yellow. Though jaundice occurs due to well-defined causes as mentioned above, it is common to find overlapping of one or more causes. Jaundice may be classified according to the causes mentioned above as

1. Haemolytic jaundice (pre-hepatic)
2. Obstructive jaundice (post-hepatic)
3. Hepatic jaundice (hepatic)

Haemolytic jaundice: This is known as **pre-hepatic jaundice**. It is caused due to increased destruction of erythrocytes, with release of an increased amount of haemoglobin in the bloodstream. This is followed by excessive haemolysis, resulting in increased production of bilirubin and unconjugated bilirubinaemia. The following are causes known to produce haemolytic jaundice:

- Increased rate of destruction of erythrocytes as seen in haemolytic anaemias, malaria, viral infections and septicaemia
- Incompatible blood transfusion

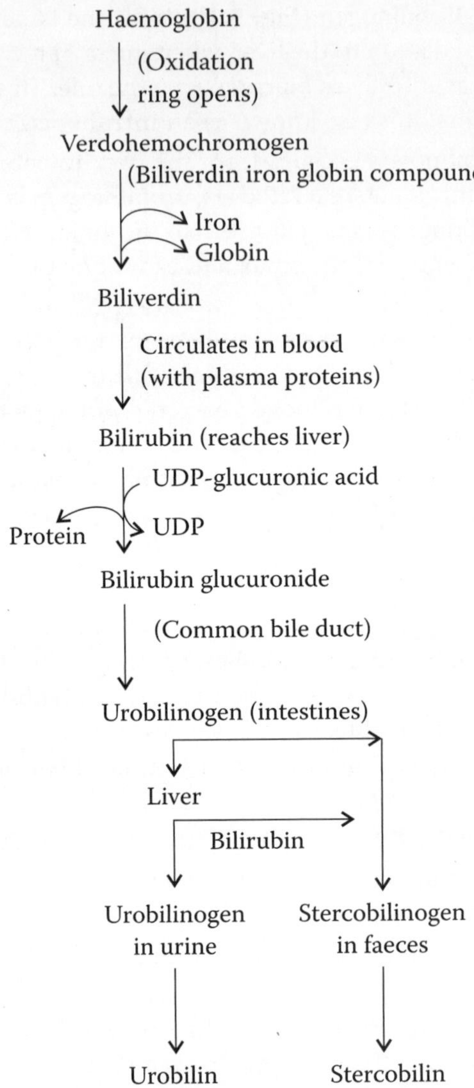

Figure 9.11 Metabolism of bile pigments.

Excessive haemolysis results in the production of excess bilirubin at a rate exceeding the ability of the liver to conjugate and excrete. This leads to hyperbilirubinaemia, mostly unconjugated bilirubin which circulates in blood and enters the liver. There is a small increase in the serum conjugated bilirubin as a result of some conjugation that takes place. Increased production of unconjugated bilirubin leads to the formation of an increased amount of urobilinogen which is reabsorbed from the intestines via portal circulation and reaches liver. Excess urobilinogen escapes from the liver into general circulation, passes through the kidneys and is excreted in urine in a large amount. An increased amount of urobilinogen in urine gives a positive Schlesinger's test. Simultaneously, an increased amount of stercobilinogen is formed which is oxidised to stercobilin in faeces. This contributes to the dark-brown colour of the faeces characteristic of haemolytic jaundice. The biochemical features in haemolytic jaundice may be summarised as follows:

- Increased amount of unconjugated bilirubin in blood, i.e. unconjugated hyperbilirubinaemia. This is indirect bilirubin. In most cases of haemolytic jaundice, the total serum bilirubin level ranges from 3 to 5 mg% only.
- Increased excretion of urobilinogen in urine
- Increased formation of stercobilinogen giving the dark-brown colour to the faeces

Obstructive jaundice, also known as **post-hepatic jaundice**, can occur when there is obstruction in the passage of bile, preventing the flow of bile into the gall bladder and intestines.

The common causes of obstruction are due to

- Blockage of the hepatic duct or common bile duct by gall stones, preventing the flow of bile into the gall bladder and intestines
- Obstruction caused by enlarged glands, tumour of the bile duct and tumour of the head of pancreas
- Stricture or narrowing of the bile duct caused as a result of surgery on the duodenum
- Intrahepatic obstruction as in hepatitis and cirrhosis

The conjugated bilirubin after leaving the liver may get blocked anywhere in its passage to the gall bladder and intestines.

Failing to get excreted in the normal pathway, conjugated bilirubin regurgitates into the bloodstream, after getting absorbed into the hepatic veins and lymphatics. Conjugated bilirubin being free from proteins passes through the glomeruli and gets excreted in the urine in an increased amount, giving the urine a deep yellow or brownish colour. Bile salts circulate in the blood in higher concentration and are excreted along with bilirubin in urine.

Due to the obstruction in the bile passage, conjugated bilirubin fails to enter the intestines. Consequently, urobilinogen is not formed and there is no urobilinogen in urine. Stercobilinogen is not formed and there is no stercobilin in the faeces. This results in excretion of pale or clay-coloured stools, which is a characteristic feature of obstructive jaundice.

The serum alkaline phosphatase level is raised in obstructive jaundice and this is taken as an evidence of biliary obstruction, if bone disease is not present (see page 94).

The characteristic features in obstructive jaundice are as follows:

- Increased level of conjugated bilirubin in blood, i.e. conjugated hyperbilirubinaemia. This is direct-acting bilirubin.
- Highly coloured urine due to excretion of an increased amount of conjugated bilirubin. Only conjugated bilirubin can appear in urine.
- Clay-coloured stool due to absence of stercobilinogen.

Delta bilirubin: A fraction of conjugated bilirubin named delta bilirubin binds covalently to albumin in obstructive jaundice when the level of conjugated bilirubin in plasma is high. It has a longer half-life in plasma than the conventional conjugated bilirubin. This fraction remains elevated during the recovery phase of obstructive jaundice even after the remainder of the conjugated bilirubin has declined to normal levels. This explains why some patients continue to appear jaundiced even after the plasma conjugated bilirubin level has returned to normal.

Hepatic jaundice (toxic and infective): This type of jaundice can result from toxin-induced liver dysfunction such as that caused by chloroform, carbon tetrachloride, acetaminophen, yellow phosphorus and hepatitis virus.

Infective hepatitis is a familiar example of hepatic jaundice caused by hepatitis virus. All these agents produce hepatic parenchymal cell damage and liver dysfunction. This results in producing unconjugated hyperbilirubinaemia because of the impaired conjugating ability and inability to convert urobilinogen to bilirubin. The urobilinogen which is produced in excess finds its way into the general circulation and is excreted in urine. This picture of hyperbilirubinaemia may be aggravated by varying degrees of haemolysis and toxins produced by virus. At a certain stage, the inflammation and damage of the liver cells become severe and this leads to gradual obliteration of the biliary canaliculi, resulting in partial obstruction to the passage of the bile pigments in the liver. The blood and urine at this stage contain high concentration of conjugated bilirubin and the stools may be pale coloured. These findings disappear gradually as the obstruction subsides. But the excretion of urobilinogen would reappear and be present till the disease is active. Thus, hepatic jaundice gives a picture of both haemolytic and obstructive jaundice appearing at different stages of the disease. The acute stage of the disease corresponds with severe hepatitis when evidences of obstruction become pre-dominant. It is at this stage that the urine is highly coloured, and this is due to the excretion of an increased amount of conjugated bilirubin.

The clinical picture of hepatic jaundice varies, depending upon the aetiology. The virus type (infective hepatitis) breaks out in an epidemic form and spreads rapidly, mainly by faecal contamination of the water supply. Loss of appetite, nausea, vomiting and fever are the striking early symptoms. Liver is enlarged in 75% of cases. The serum alkaline phosphatase level is raised in infective hepatitis.

As the causes of jaundice are varied, it is necessary that the type of jaundice be diagnosed and correct treatment instituted promptly. The common laboratory investigations adopted to diagnose the type of jaundice are given in **Table 9.1**.

UNCONJUGATED HYPERBILIRUBINAEMIA

Besides the causes mentioned in the preceding text for the three types of jaundice, hyperbilirubinaemia due to an increase in unconjugated bilirubin can occur in the following conditions:

1. **Neonatal jaundice** is the most common type of unconjugated hyperbilirubinaemia seen in a newborn. It is transient and occurs in normal infants between the second and the fifth days of life and disappears within 2 weeks. It is a normal physiological process and for this reason it is referred to as physiologic jaundice of the newborn. It is more severe in prematures. The serum contains an increased amount of unconjugated bilirubin, usually not exceeding 5 mg%. The jaundice results from an accelerated

Table 9.1 Biochemical Investigations Employed for Diagnosis of Jaundice

Type of Jaundice	Bile Pigment in Serum	Van den Bergh Reaction for Bile Pigment in Serum	Bile Pigment in Urine	Test for Bile Pigment in Urine	Colour of Faeces	Serum Alkaline Phosphatase
Haemolytic	Unconjugated bilirubin	Indirect positive	Urobilinogen	Schlesinger's test—positive	Dark brown	Normal
Obstructive	Conjugated bilirubin	Direct positive	Conjugated bilirubin	Fouchet's test—positive Gmelin's test—positive	Clay colour	Raised markedly
Hepatic	Varies—both conjugated and uncon jugated bili rubin may be present	Biphasic	Varies—both bilirubin and urobilinogen may be present	Varies according to the presence of bile pigment	Varies	Raised slightly

haemolysis and an immature hepatic system for the uptake, conjugation and secretion of bilirubin. In the foetus and at birth, there is a relative deficiency of the hepatic UDP–glucuronyl transferase activity and this accounts for the impaired capacity to conjugate bilirubin with glucuronide. This also explains the reason why jaundice is severe in premature infants. The enzyme activity increases as the infant grows.

In rare circumstances, when the plasma concentration of unconjugated bilirubin exceeds 20–25 mg%, the unconjugated bilirubin penetrates the blood–brain barrier and the infant develops **hyperbilirubinaemic toxic encephalopathy** or **kernicterus**, which can cause mental retardation. Only unconjugated bilirubin can cross the blood–brain barrier and enter the central nervous system, and kernicterus can occur only with unconjugated bilirubin.

Other causes of neonatal jaundice are as follows:

- Congenital obliteration of the bile ducts
- Incompatibility of the Rh blood group factors

2. **Gilbert's disease** is a rare type of jaundice transmitted in an autosomal dominant manner. The affected persons do not suffer from any symptoms, but have mild intermittent jaundice from childhood.

   There is mild unconjugated hyperbilirubinaemia. The jaundice gets exacerbated following prolonged illness, fever and infection. Studies show that there is a defect in the mechanism of bilirubin uptake by the liver parenchymal cells together with a partial deficiency of bilirubin UDP–glucuronyl transferase activity.

3. **Criggler–Najjar syndrome**: This is a rare disorder transmitted in an autosomal recessive manner. It is a congenital non-haemolytic jaundice, characterised by severe

jaundice in which there is marked elevation of unconjugated bilirubin. It is due to a primary metabolic defect in the conjugation of bilirubin. There are two types—I and II.

Type I is the severe form. The defect is due to inherited absence of liver UDP–glucuronyl transferase which catalyses the transfer of glucuronide from UDP–glucuronic acid to bilirubin. Therefore, there is no conjugation. Conjugated bilirubin is not formed in the liver. The serum contains a high concentration of unconjugated bilirubin, sometimes exceeding 20 mg%. The affected infants suffer from severe congenital jaundice and they usually die within the first year of life.

Type II is the milder form and is due to a partial deficiency of UDP–glucuronyl transferase. Serum contains unconjugated bilirubin, but does not exceed 20 mg%. Jaundice is less severe and may not appear until adolescence.

CONJUGATED HYPERBILIRUBINAEMIA

Dubin–Johnson syndrome is an autosomal recessive disorder which consists of hyperbilirubinaemia due to conjugated bilirubin. It is characterised by a chronic intermittent type of jaundice, commonly seen in childhood. The striking feature is the greyish-black colour of the liver and the presence of a brownish-black pigment in the hepatocytes. This disorder is apparently caused by a defect in the biliary secretory mechanism of the liver.

Rotor syndrome is another hereditary disorder associated with elevated levels of plasma conjugated bilirubin. There is no pigment in the liver cells. In this poorly defined disease, an increased excretion of coproporphyrin I and III is found. The relationship of the derangement of coproporphyrin metabolism to bilirubin metabolism is not well understood.

10

CHAPTER

Blood and Cerebrospinal Fluid

Chapter Outline

- Blood
- Immunoglobulins
- Cerebrospinal Fluid

BLOOD

Blood is a body fluid composed of blood cells, nutrients, gases such as oxygen and carbon dioxide and certain other metabolic waste products.

Coagulation of Blood

When blood is shed, it becomes increasingly viscous and within a few minutes it forms a semi-solid gel. This phenomenon is coagulation of blood.

Chemistry of Blood Coagulation

Blood coagulation is a spontaneous but vital phenomenon of defence against prolonged loss of blood which may occur due to various causes, to all living organisms.

According to the original Howell theory of blood coagulation, the essential feature of the process of clotting is the conversion of the soluble fibrinogen, which circulates with plasma protein, to the insoluble fibrin, which is the clot, by the enzyme thrombin. Fibrinogen exists in the circulating blood as such, but thrombin is formed from an inactive circulating precursor prothrombin, only when the blood is shed.

The activation of prothrombin to form thrombin is brought about by Ca^{++} and certain organic activators of obscure composition known as thromboplastins which are derived from damaged tissues, disintegrating platelets and plasma itself.

The formation of prothrombin which takes place in the liver depends upon an adequate absorption of vitamin K.

The various chemical mechanisms involved in the process of coagulation of blood may be described to occur in three stages. They are as follows:

1. **Stage I:** Formation of thromboplastin
2. **Stage II:** Conversion of prothrombin to thrombin
3. **Stage III:** Conversion of fibrinogen to fibrin

These stages of reactions are assisted by certain accelerating factors and limited by certain inhibitory factors. The main events of each of the three stages may be illustrated as follows:

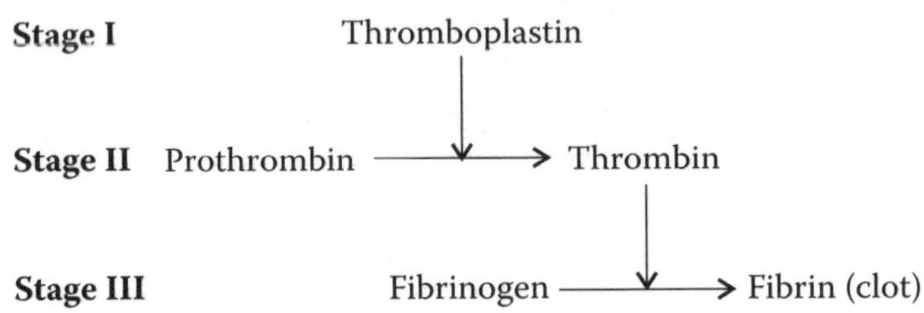

The names of the 12 factors which play an active role in coagulation are listed in **Table 10.1**. Factor VI is deleted since it is believed not to exist.

Table 10.1 Clotting Factors

Factor	Name
I	Fibrinogen
II	Prothrombin
III	Thromboplastin
V	Calcium
V	Labile factor, proaccelerin, accelerator, plasma Ac globulin
VII	Proconvertin, serum prothrombin conversion accelerator (SPCA)
VIII	Antihaemophilic factor (AHF), antihaemophilic globin (AHG)
IX	Christmas factor, plasma thromboplastin component (PTC)
X	Stuart–Prower factor
XI	Plasma thromboplastin antecedent (PTA)
XII	Hageman factor
XIII	Laki–Lorand factor (LLF)

Stage I. Formation of thromboplastin: This stage does not represent the formation of thromboplastin as a single substance but refers to a group of precursors of thromboplastin and reactions thereof for the formation of active thromboplastin. The mechanism of blood clotting is initiated by tissue injury, when thromboplastin precursors from tissues (extrinsic source) are liberated into circulation.

Simultaneously, platelets which contact the rough broken surface of the blood vessels disintegrate, liberating certain activators called platelet factors which are lipid in nature. These platelet factors with the help of two natural components of plasma, namely antihaemophilic factor AHF (VIII) and Christmas factor (Factor IX), form prothromboplastin. These in conjunction with Ca^{++} form active thromboplastin.

Stage II. Conversion of prothrombin to thrombin: In Stage II, thromboplastin converts prothrombin to thrombin in the presence of Ca^{++}

$$\text{Prothrombin} + \text{Thromboplastin} \longrightarrow \text{Thrombin.}$$

Two other substances, namely Factor V and Factor VII, are required to activate this reaction. The reaction is also accelerated by another factor called Factor X, named Stuart–Prower factor. Factor V is called proaccelerin or accelerator (AC) globulin and is inactive by itself. It is converted to active Factor VII which is also called proconvertin or serum prothrombin conversion accelerator (SPCA), by traces of thrombin. According to recent views, it is suggested that an ultimate product of interaction of thromboplastin, Ca^{++}, Factor V, Factor VII and Factor X, designated as 'prothrombinase', is the direct immediate agent which converts prothrombin to thrombin.

Another view suggests that prothrombinase is also formed from 'blood thromboplastin' which in turn is formed by the interaction of certain factors derived from platelets, Factor V (proaccelerin), Factor VIII, AHF (antihaemophilic factor), Factor IX, PTC (plasma thromboplastin component), Factor X (Stuart–Prower factor), Factor XI, PTA (plasma thromboplastin antecedent) and Factor XII. Thromboplastin which is formed thus gets converted to prothrombinase in the presence of Ca^{++}. The mode of formation of prothrombinase from tissue and blood thromboplastin is illustrated in **Figure 10.1**.

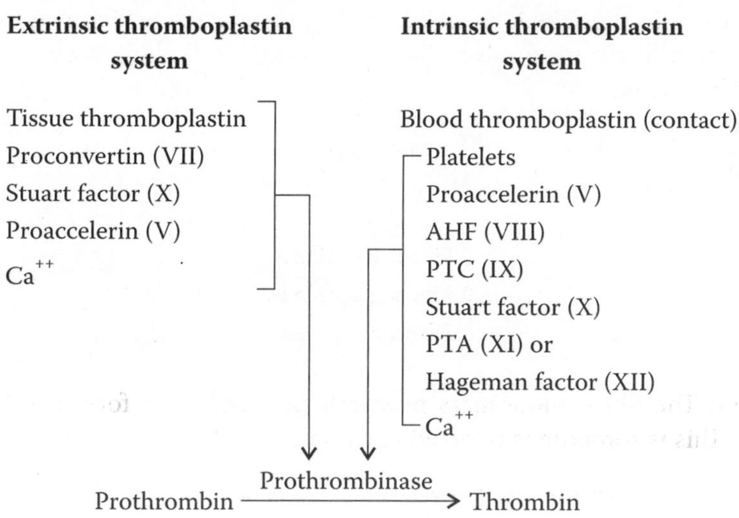

Figure 10.1 Mode of formation of thrombin.

Prothrombin is a glycoprotein present in the α_2-globulin fraction of plasma. It is synthesised in the liver cells in the presence of vitamin K. Prothrombin is considered as a proenzyme because it gets converted to the enzyme thrombin which is the active form.

$$\text{Prothrombin} \longrightarrow \text{Thrombin}$$

Thrombin: This is an enzyme which has a powerful effect on coagulation. It does not exist as such in circulating blood. It is formed when its precursor prothrombin reacts with thromboplastin in the presence of Ca^{++} during clotting.

Calcium ions: Ionic calcium is essential for clotting. It acts by converting prothrombin to thrombin. It is also necessary for the formation of both intrinsic and extrinsic thromboplastin (*see* **Fig. 10.1**). In vitro, clotting of blood is prevented by addition of oxalate, citrate or fluoride. They remove Ca^{++} by forming poorly dissociable calcium compounds.

Stage III. Conversion of fibrinogen to fibrin: In Stage III of clotting, fibrinogen which is a soluble protein circulating in blood is converted to insoluble fibrin (clot), by the action of the enzyme thrombin which acts as a proteolytic enzyme.

The entire reaction may be considered to occur in three stages, namely

1. Proteolysis
2. Polymerisation
3. Clotting

***Proteolysis*:** Thrombin which is a proteolytic enzyme acts specifically on two arginyl-glycine linkages in fibrinogen, splitting it to produce two types of peptides, a pair in each.

The peptides are designated as follows:

- Fibrinopeptide A
- Fibrinopeptide B

The residual portion of the original fibrinogen molecule which has undergone the hydrolysis is termed **fibrin monomer**. Thus, we have the following products derived from proteolysis of fibrinogen:

$$\text{Fibrinogen} \downarrow \begin{array}{c} \text{2 Fibrinopeptide A} \\ \text{2 Fibrinopeptide B} \\ \text{Fibrin monomer} \end{array}$$

***Polymerisation*:** The fibrin monomers promptly polymerise to form a gel meshwork of fibrin polymer. This is sometimes referred to as 'soft clot'.

$$\text{(Fibrin monomers) n} \longrightarrow \text{Fibrin polymer}$$

***Clotting*:** Fibrin polymers, in the presence of Ca^{++} and a serum factor designated as Laki–Lorand factor (LLF) (Factor XIII), and fibrinase, form the more solidified and coarse physiological clot, the fibrin.

$$\text{Fibrin polymers} \xrightarrow{Ca^{++},\ \text{factor XIII}} \text{Fibrin (clot)}$$

Fibrin is laid down as a meshwork of fine threads which entangle the blood cells. These threads are extremely adhesive and make the clot an effective homeostatic agent. Freshly shed blood sets in a soft, jelly-like mass. Gradually, this clot contracts to about 40% of its original volume, when the serum separates out. Therefore, the serum does not contain fibrinogen. The final clot is more solid and tougher. Clots after formation are disposed off, as healing takes place. The process of dissolution of the clot is known as **fibrinolysis**. This is brought about by a proteolytic enzyme called **fibrinolysin** or **plasmin**.

Accelerating mechanism: Thrombin, besides converting fibrinogen to fibrin, also exerts a powerful accelerating action on coagulation. It causes lysis of platelets which in turn activates the thromboplastin-forming mechanism. The latter initiates the mechanism of clotting.

Inhibitors of Coagulation

Once clotting begins, it proceeds at an increasing speed, on account of the presence of clot-accelerating factors. This may result dangerously in intravascular clotting. Such anomalies are prevented by the presence of naturally occurring inhibitors in blood. The best-known inhibitor is heparin. Other substances which reduce coagulation of blood are hirudin (leech extract), cysteine and dicoumarol which is a naphthoquinone derivative.

Heparin is extremely potent. It is water soluble and thermostable. It is an acid mucopolysaccharide, located widely on the walls of fine blood vessels. Heparin is rapidly destroyed in the body by the enzyme heparinase. Therefore, administration of a single dose of heparin will have only a transitory anticoagulant effect for few hours.

Heparin inhibits coagulation in the presence of a cofactor associated with the albumin fraction of serum proteins, by acting at two points in the mechanism of clotting:

1. It acts as antiprothrombin by inhibiting the conversion of prothrombin to thrombin.
2. It acts as an antithrombin by delaying the conversion of fibrinogen to fibrin by thrombin.

In clinical practice, heparin is used in the treatment of intravascular thrombosis to prevent clotting.

Other anticoagulants used in vitro are oxalates (potassium and ammonium), sodium citrate and sodium fluoride. They all form loose complexes with Ca^{++} and prevent clotting by removal of Ca^{++}.

Thrombosis

This phenomenon refers to intravascular clotting due to the formation of thrombus which is a clot formed inside the blood vessels. Thrombus is formed when the circulation is impeded due to the formation of atheromatous patches and damage to the vascular endothelium. Thrombosis occurring in coronary arteries is called **coronary thrombosis** and that occurring in cerebral vessels is called **cerebral thrombosis**.

Coagulation-Related Disease

Haemophilia is a hereditary disease, where clotting occurs at an abnormally slow rate. The sufferers are known as 'haemophilics' or 'bleeders'. It is peculiar in the sense that it affects only males. The defect is due to the deficiency of a component called antihaemophilic globulin in plasma, i.e. Factor VIII which delays the formation of thrombin. The defect is believed to be inherited as a sex-linked recessive trait, transmitted by females to the males who alone exhibit the bleeding tendency. The characteristic findings of this disease are as follows:

1. Bleeding which does not stop. These individuals should be extremely careful not to contact even minor injuries such as trauma or extraction of tooth, since this may result in severe haemorrhage.
2. Marked prolongation of the coagulation time of the blood, while prothrombin time being normal.

Plasma Proteins

Plasma is a solution of complex composition, in which the blood cells are suspended. It is a light straw-coloured fluid, viscous in nature, with a specific gravity ranging from 1.015 to 1.035. Plasma has a fairly high concentration of proteins, varying from 6 to 7.5 grams per 100 ml. The proteins have a complex composition, consisting mostly of simple proteins, mixed with a small amount of conjugated proteins such as lipoproteins and glycoproteins. The main components of plasma proteins are albumin and globulin.

The globulin fraction consists of four distinct subfractions, namely α_1-globulin, α_2-globulin, β-globulin and γ-globulin. A small amount of fibrinogen is present along with the globulins.

The concentration of albumin and globulin estimated separately is of clinical interest and is expressed as the ratio of albumin to globulin (A/G ratio). The normal value for the A/G ratio in a healthy adult ranges from 2 to 1.2:1. In certain pathological conditions, this ratio may be altered slightly or reversed.

Fibrinogen is the precursor of fibrin, which forms the blood clot. It contributes to about 4–6% of the total proteins of plasma. It is removed along with the clot from the serum, during the process of clotting. Fibrinogen is a globulin and has a high molecular weight varying from 350,000 to 450,000. It is precipitated by half-saturation with ammonium sulphate. As fibrinogen is synthesised in liver, any disease affecting an extensive area of the liver will produce a fall in the fibrinogen content of plasma proteins.

Separation of Protein Fractions

The main components of plasma proteins, namely albumin, globulin and fibrinogen, can be separated by simple chemical methods such as salting out process and precipitation; different salts are used for this purpose:

1. **Salting out using ammonium sulphate:** The fractions are salted out by using varying dilutions of ammonium sulphate. Globulin is salted out or precipitated by

half-saturation with ammonium sulphate and albumin is precipitated by full saturation with ammonium sulphate. Fibrinogen can be precipitated by one-fourth saturation with ammonium sulphate. But fractionation using this method is incomplete.

2. **Kjeldahl's method:** Another suitable method for separation of globulin from other proteins is by precipitating it out by the addition of a 22% solution of sodium sulphate. The remaining protein is albumin. This preliminary procedure is carried out in the determination of albumin and globulin fractions in plasma by Kjeldahl's method.
3. **Fractionation by alcohol precipitation:** Fractionation by alcohol precipitation can be adopted for large-scale separation. This involves precipitation of the plasma proteins with various concentrations of alcohol at temperature below 0°. The advantage of this procedure is that denaturation does not occur at such low temperature.
4. **Separation of serum proteins by electrophoresis:** The various fractions of serum proteins can be separated by electrophoresis.

In paper electrophoresis (p. 68), a special filter paper is used for separation. The albumin fraction moves fastest, because of its lowest molecular weight, and occupies the farthest position as a dense band. This is followed by less dense bands of α_1-globulin, α_2-globulin, β-globulin and γ-globulin that occupy positions in this order, because of their decreasing rate of migration. When the paper containing the bands is stained with a special stain, these protein fractions are seen as well-defined bands positioned one behind the other. On this basis, the plasma protein contains six fractions, namely albumin, α_1-globulin, α_2-globulin, β-globulin and γ-globulin and fibrinogen. The bands other than albumin are fractions of globulin. Fibrinogen can be visualised in plasma protein electrophoresis as a thin band between β- and γ-globulin regions. It is not seen in serum protein electrophoresis as it is removed during clotting. The percentage concentration of each protein fraction in normal blood is given on page 70. The serum electrophoretic patterns in some diseases have been shown **Figure 3.13**.

Albumin This is synthesised in the liver and forms about 55–60% of the total plasma protein. The normal concentration of plasma albumin is about 4.5 g/100 ml. Albumin is a globular protein consisting of a single polypeptide chain composed of 610 amino acids. It has a molecular weight of 69,000. Albumin has an isoelectric point of 4.8 and has a negative charge at a physiologic pH of 7.4. This explains the high rate of mobility of the albumin fraction towards the anode in plasma protein electrophoretogram (*see* **Fig. 3.12**).

Albumin performs two important functions:

1. It transports metabolites such as free fatty acids, drugs, bilirubin and several compounds through plasma and extracellular fluid.
2. It plays an important role in maintaining the osmotic pressure of plasma.

The synthesis of albumin is depressed in many diseases, particularly those of liver. The A/G ratio is decreased in the plasma of patients with liver disease. Albuminuria is a common finding in diseases of kidney such as nephritis and nephrotic syndrome. Albumin being of low molecular weight escapes from circulation and passes through diseased kidneys. The loss of albumin in urine is compensated by a relative increase in globulin fraction.

Hypoalbuminaemia: The albumin concentration of plasma protein decreases in the following conditions:

- Albuminuria, when albumin is lost in urine as in nephritis and nephrotic syndrome
- Extravasation of albumin as in burns
- In later months of normal pregnancy, due to haemodilution and hypoproteinaemia
- Due to inadequate intake of dietary protein
- Chronic liver diseases with cirrhosis, due to reduced synthesis of proteins

Fall in plasma albumin concentration leads to retention of water in tissue spaces due to reduction in colloidal osmotic pressure. This is the cause of oedema which is seen in diseases associated with hypoalbuminaemia.

Analbuminaemia: It is a rare disorder characterised by complete absence of serum albumin. It is caused by a mutation that affects splicing in protein synthesis.

Globulin Plasma globulins form about 40–45% of the total protein. The normal concentration of plasma globulin is 2–3.6 g/100 ml. The molecular weight varies from 90,000 to 13,00,000. The globulin consists of a complex mixture of asymmetric protein molecules but exhibits similar electrophoretic mobility. The different fractions of globulin separated electrophoretically are designated as α_1-globulin, α_2-globulin, β-globulin and γ-globulin. Most of the globulins are synthesised in the liver. The γ-globulin is synthesised in the cells of the reticuloendothelial cells of spleen and bone marrow. A brief description of the different fractions of globulin is given below.

α_1- and α_2-globulins contain glycoproteins. High-density lipoprotein (HDL) migrates with α_1-globulin. Ceruloplasmin is present in α_2-globulin.

β-globulin contains lipids such as cholesterol and triglycerides. Low-density lipoprotein (LDL) migrates with β-globulin. The lipoproteins act as carrier molecules for different types of lipids that are not soluble in plasma; β-globulin transports transferrin in plasma.

γ-globulins are made of immunoglobulins. They are circulating antibodies. They confer immunity to the body.

The major functions of globulins are as follows:

1. They serve as easy transport of poorly soluble substances such as cholesterol, triglycerides, fat-soluble vitamins and steroids.
2. Plasma proteins constitute efficient buffers in blood.
3. Immunoglobulins are the circulating antibodies and they confer immunity to the body.

Hyperglobulinaemia: It refers to increased concentration of plasma globulins.

α_1-globulins are increased in acute febrile diseases related to inflammation or destruction of tissues.

α_2-globulin is markedly increased in nephrotic syndrome. The increase in α-globulins is usually compensated by a decrease in albumin.

β-globulin is increased in hyperlipidaemias showing a high level of serum lipids as in atherosclerosis.

γ-globulin is increased in chronic infections in which there is excessive formation of antibodies. It is particularly increased in cirrhosis of liver.

It may be noted that variation in the concentration of the protein fractions can occur without altering the concentration of total proteins. Thus, it is common to find the globulins increased when albumin is decreased and vice versa.

Hypoglobulinaemia and agammaglobulinaemia: These are rare hereditary conditions manifested by partial or complete absence of γ-globulin in serum protein, due to a defect in the production of plasma protein. The affected persons are greatly susceptible to bacterial infections, due to the absence of antibodies.

Fibrinogen It constitutes 4–6% of the total plasma protein. It is a large molecule consisting of two tripeptide units, each unit having two α-, β- and γ-subunits linked by disulphide bonds. It has a molecular weight ranging from 350,000 to 450,000.

Fibrinogen is formed in the liver and is the precursor of fibrin, the clot.

Plasma concentration of fibrinogen is increased in pregnancy and acute infections. It is decreased in liver diseases associated with destruction of liver tissues.

Synthesis of Plasma Proteins

Plasma proteins are synthesised mainly in the liver; γ-globulin is formed in the cells of the reticuloendothelial system, particularly in the plasma cells of spleen, lymphoid tissue and bone marrow. Plasma proteins are formed from amino acids derived from dietary proteins. Among the dietary proteins, lactalbumin, egg white and casein contribute most effectively for the synthesis. It has been estimated that an adult synthesises on an average about 15–20 grams of plasma proteins per day.

Plasma protein, besides being a source of nutrition to tissue proteins, establishes a dynamic equilibrium with the proteins of the tissues.

Functions of Plasma Proteins

1. **Viscosity:** Plasma is viscous because of the high protein content. The viscosity of plasma helps to provide resistance to flow of blood in the blood vessels, thus maintaining blood pressure at a normal level.
2. **Source of nutrition:** Plasma serves as source of nutrition for the tissues. It establishes a dynamic equilibrium with the proteins of tissues. In conditions of protein deficiency, tissue proteins are broken down to maintain the plasma protein level. When serum albumin is administered parenterally, it is utilised effectively for the building up of tissue proteins.
3. **Water exchange:** Albumin plays an important role in the maintenance of plasma osmotic pressure. It exerts a greater osmotic pressure (5.54 mmHg per g%) than globulin, because of its lower molecular weight and higher concentration. Maintenance of osmotic pressure of plasma is important for the proper distribution of water between blood and tissues.
4. **Blood buffers:** Plasma proteins act as efficient buffers for the maintenance of acid–base balance, though the plasma protein buffer pair constitutes only a small fraction of the total blood buffers. Plasma proteins are amphoteric and can combine

with both acids and bases. At normal pH of blood, they act as acids and combine with cations such as sodium in bipod to form sodium proteinate. In acid pH, they combine with the H^+ ion to form acid protein (H^+ protein).

5. **Transport:** Plasma proteins serve as an effective transport medium for several physiologically important compounds which include the following constituents:
   - Lipids form a lipoprotein complex with plasma proteins. They migrate along with α_1-globulin and β-globulin fractions. Lipoproteins also carry phospholipids, cholesterol, neutral fats, fat-soluble vitamins and steroid hormones.
   - Bilirubin combines with albumin and α_1-globulin.
   - Metals such as iron in the form of transferrin and copper in the form of ceruloplasmin are carried in combination with β-globulin.
   - About 40% of serum calcium is bound with plasma protein.
6. **Control of haemorrhage:** Plasma proteins contribute to the mechanism of controlling haemorrhage. Fibrinogen and prothrombin of plasma protein help directly in the process of blood coagulation.
7. **Immunity:** Plasma proteins play an important role in conferring immunity to the body. This is accomplished by the large amount of antibodies present in the γ-globulin. The γ-globulin of a normal healthy person carries antibodies for most of the infectious diseases such as mumps, measles, influenza, poliomyelitis, whooping cough and diphtheria. The antibodies to antigens responsible for various blood groups in man are present in β-globulin.
8. **Enzymes:** Several enzymes which are clinically important and which have varied physiological significance are present in plasma.

IMMUNOGLOBULINS

Immunoglobulins are circulating antibodies synthesised in B lymphocytes and plasma cells in response to the invasion of foreign compounds. They constitute a group of closely related proteins and are associated mostly with γ-globulins of serum proteins. The antibodies react with foreign substances called antigens. They bind to the antigenic sites present on the antigens with remarkable specificity and bring about inactivation and removal of toxins, microbes, parasites or other substances from the body. All immunoglobulins are composed of four polypeptide chains. They comprise two identical heavy chains and two identical light chains, each covalently attached by disulphide bonds. Immunoglobulins are glycoproteins and the heavy chains contain a small amount (2–12%) of carbohydrate.

Classes and Subclasses of Immunoglobulins

There are five major classes of immunoglobulins present in humans. They are IgG, IgA, IgM, IgD and IgE. The differentiation of the classes is based on their molecular weight, structure, electrophoretic mobility, ultracentrifugal properties and immunological properties. IgG and IgA are further subdivided into subclasses such as G1, G2 and G3 for IgG and A1 and A2 for IgA (**Table 10.2**).

IgG comprises approximately 80% of the total serum immunoglobulins and forms the major fraction carrying antibodies. It has a molecular weight of 150,000 and contains about 2–3% of carbohydrate. It has only one basic four-peptide unit in its structure (**Table 10.2**). An important property of IgG is its ability to cross the placenta and thus provide a major line of defence against infection for the first few weeks of a baby's life. IgG diffuses readily into the extravascular spaces where it neutralises bacterial toxins and binds to microorganisms and enhance their phagocytosis.

IgA comprises about 13% of the total serum immunoglobulins. It is primarily found in the mucosal secretions such as saliva, tears and nasal fluids, sweat, colostrum, secretions of lungs and gastrointestinal mucus secretions, where it is the major immunoglobulin concerned in the initial defence against invading viral and bacterial pathogens, prior to their entry into the plasma or other internal space. In plasma, IgA exists mainly as one monomer (basic four-peptide unit) but in the seromucus secretions it is present as a dimer (two peptide units) linked to a polypeptide called J-chain. The molecular weight of the IgA dimer is about 160,000.

IgM is distinguished by its high molecular weight of about 900,000. It is a pentameric molecule made up of five four-peptide units. IgM molecules are confined to the bloodstream and constitute 5–10% of the γ-globulin. It is the initial type of antibody made by newborns and is the first immunoglobulin to appear in the immune response. Because of the high valency, IgM antibodies are extremely efficient agglutinating and cytolytic agents and are a powerful first-line defence against bacteraemia. It has a carbohydrate content of about 10–12% (**Table 10.2**).

Table 10.2 Main Properties of Major Immunoglobulin Classes

Class of Basic Immunoglobulin	Molecular Weight	Number of Basic Four-Peptide Units	Heavy Chain Isotype	Carbohydrate Content (%)	Serum Concentration (mg/100 ml)
IgG	150,000	1	γ	2–3	600–1800
IgA	160,000–720,000	1,2	α	7–12	90–420
IgM	900,000	5	μ	10–12	50–190
IgD	160,000	1	δ	–	0.3–40
IgE	190,000	1	ε	10–12	0.01–0.10

IgD is found in minute quantity in serum and is short lived. It is present together with IgM on the surface of some blood lymphocytes.

IgE is present in serum in very low concentration normally, but it is increased in parasitic infections and allergic conditions. The main physiological role of IgE seems to be protection of the external mucosal surfaces of the body against infections, by local recruitment of antimicrobial agents, through triggering an acute inflammatory reaction. It is brought about by degranulation of the mast cells firmly bound to IgE antibodies when antigens (infectious agents) come in contact with IgE. This is followed by release of inflammatory mediators such as vasoactive amines and a local inflammatory reaction causing an influx of neutrophils and eosinophils that are needed to dispose off the infectious organisms. This process is responsible for the symptoms of hay fever and of extrinsic asthma when patients with allergy come into contact with allergens, for example grass pollen. A similar immune response is produced in persons infested with intestinal worms and in diseases involving protozoal parasites. The IgE production is highly increased in these infections.

The various immunoglobulins in the serum can be separated by a technique called immunoelectrophoresis. The procedure combines electrophoresis of the serum in an agar gel medium with a specific antigen–antibody precipitation reaction. The electrophoretically separated proteins are identified immunologically by applying immune serum to a trough in the agar gel block adjacent to the separated protein fractions, when the specific precipitin antibodies in the immune serum react with the protein fractions, to form visible lines of precipitation within a few hours (**Fig. 10.2**).

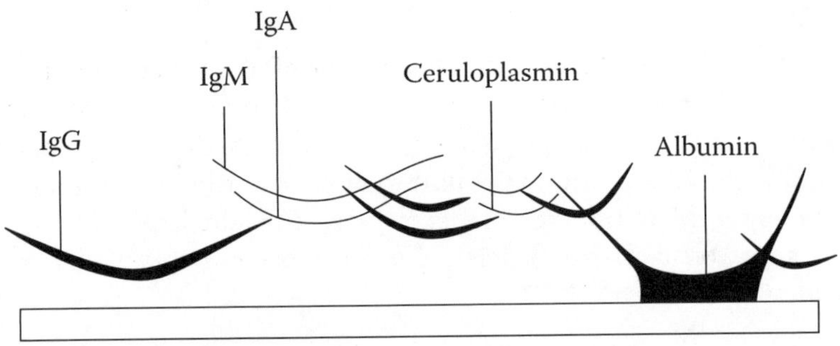

Figure 10.2 Immunoelectrophoresis.

Structure of an Immunoglobulin Molecule

Among the various immunoglobulins, the structure of IgG has been extensively studied. It has been found that IgG molecules can be cleaved by the action of proteolytic enzymes such as papain or trypsin in the presence of a reducing agent such as cystine, into three fragments.

The largest fragment is called Fc fragment. It has no antibody activity. The other two fragments are known as Fab fragments (**Fig. 10.3**). They contain the site for combination of the antibody with the antigens.

Structurally, all immunoglobulin molecules consist of two symmetrical halves, each consisting of two polypeptide chains, of which one is longer and the other shorter. Both halves are joined by disulphide bonds (S-S). Further, the longer and the shorter polypeptide chains in each half are also joined by S-S bonds (**Fig. 10.3**). The longer chain is designated heavy chain (H) and contains 420–440 amino acid residues. The shorter chain is known as light chain (L) and contains 214 amino acid residues (**Fig. 10.3**).

Each chain is divided into specific domains or regions that have structural and functional significance. The half of the light chain (L) which is towards the carboxyl (COO^-) terminus is known as the **constant region (C_L)**. The other half of the light chain which is towards the amino (NH_2) terminal is designated as the **variable (V_L) region**. The heavy chain (H) has the **variable region (V_H)** which is approximately one-fourth of the heavy chain at the NH_2 terminal, and the other three quarters of the heavy chain are referred to as the **constant regions (C_H1, C_H2, C_H3)** of that H chain. V_H and V_L domains are the antigen-binding sites formed at the amino terminal portions of the H and L chains (**Fig. 10.3**).

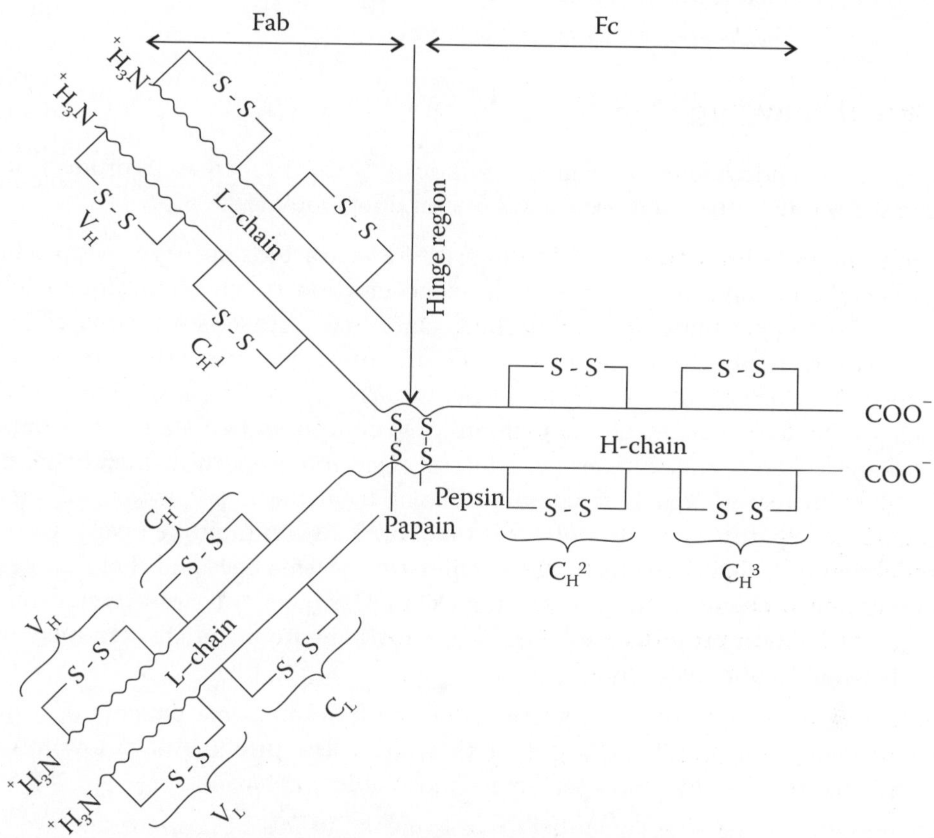

Figure 10.3 Structure of an IgG molecule.

Hinge region is the area between C_Hl and C_H where papain cleaves the immunoglobulin molecule into three fragments. Of these, two are identical. These are the Fab (fragment antigen binding) fragments. They have a molecular weight of 42,000 each. Each has a single combining site for antigen. The third is termed Fc fragment (fragment crystallisable). This is the larger fragment and has a molecular weight of 48,000. It lacks the ability to bind antigen. It has no antibody activity (**Fig. 10.3**).

The light chains are of two major types in man. They are the kappa (κ) and lambda (λ) chains. They can be distinguished by their structural differences in their C_L regions. All immunoglobulins contain either 2κ chains or 2λ chains. The H chain is specific to the class and occurs in five antigenically distinct forms referred to as γ, α, μ, δ and ε chains.

Each immunoglobulin has 2γ, 2α, 2μ, 2δ or 2ε chains and the peptide chains of human immunoglobulins may be represented as follows:

1. IgG contains γ chains and is written as $\gamma_2\kappa_2$ or $\gamma_2\lambda_2$.
2. IgA contains α chains and is written as $\alpha_2\kappa_2$ or $\alpha_2\lambda_2$.
3. IgM contains μ chains and is written as $(\mu_2\kappa_2)_5$ or $(\mu_2\lambda_2)_5$.
4. IgD contains δ chains and is written as $\delta_2\kappa_2$ or $\delta_2\lambda_2$.
5. IgE contains ε chains and is written as $\varepsilon_2\kappa_2$ or $\varepsilon_2\lambda_2$.

Disorders of Immunoglobulins

Disorders of immunoglobulins include conditions with (i) increased production and (ii) decreased production of specific classes of immunoglobulins.

Hyperimmunoglobulinaemia: Certain diseases are characterised by an overproduction of immunoglobulins and an increase in the concentration of specific immunoglobulins in blood. This is hyperimmunoglobulinaemia. One such disease is a plasma cell cancer known as **multiple myeloma**. It is a neoplastic disease characterised by malignant proliferation of a clone of plasma cells in the bone marrow, secreting either IgA or IgG. The abnormal protein known as **myeloma protein** or **M component** appears in serum in high concentration. It is recognised in electrophoresis as an intense well-defined band, mostly in the γ-globulin region, and is strikingly different from the hypergammaglobulinaemia seen in chronic hepatitis and other diseases (*see* **Fig. 3.13**). In multiple myeloma, there is overproduction of L (light) chains by the proliferating plasma cells and these are released in blood as free L chains without combining with H chains and are excreted in urine. These **urinary L chain proteins** are called **Bence Jones protein** and are identified by their specific thermosolubility behaviour.

Bence Jones protein excreted by some of the multiple myeloma patients in urine is a peculiar protein, antigenically related to IgG or IgA. The proteins have low molecular weight and are identified by their specific thermosolubility behaviour.

They are precipitated when acidified urine is heated to 50–60°C and redissolve almost completely at 100°C. The precipitate reappears on cooling. Bence Jones proteins represent the Ig light (L) chains produced in excess in the malignant plasma cells and are excreted rapidly in urine.

Clinically, multiple myeloma exhibits the characteristic punched-out osteolytic lesions in bones. Other features associated with multiple myeloma are hyperproteinaemia, hypercalcemia and impairment of renal function. The disease is rapidly progressive and fatal.

Macroglobulinaemia: Waldenstrom first described a condition known as macroglobulinaemia, which is characterised by a malignant proliferation of lymphoplasmacytoid cells that secrete IgM. It shows a globulin pattern similar to that of multiple myeloma in electrophoresis, i.e. an intense narrow band in the γ-region or in the β–γ-region.

Immunoglobulin deficiency: This may be caused due to absence or reduced production of specific immunoglobulins. They produce increased susceptibility to infections. Examples are as follows:

1. *X-linked agammaglobulinaemia* is an inherited X-linked defect which affects males. It is associated with absence of IgM and IgA. The affected children suffer from repeated respiratory infections.
2. *Common variable immunodeficiency* is the most common form of immunoglobulin deficiency and is characterised by recurrent pyogenic infections of the sinus and respiratory tract.

CEREBROSPINAL FLUID

Cerebrospinal fluid (CSF), which is formed by the choroid plexus of the brain, is an ultrafiltrate of the plasma. It is present in the cerebral ventricles, spinal canal and subarachnoid spaces. The total volume of CSF is about 100–150 ml. It is a clear, colourless and transparent fluid with a specific gravity of 1.003–1.008. It is alkaline and has the same pH as blood (7.35–7.45). Its bicarbonate content is also the same as that of plasma (40–60 vol%). Its composition is more or less similar to that of plasma without the colloids:

Protein: The protein content of normal CSF is very low, ranging from 20 to 45 mg/100 ml. Most of the protein is albumin, the albumin/globulin ratio being 3:1. The CSF protein, particularly globulin, increases to values higher than 100 mg% in inflammatory diseases of brain and meninges, such as encephalitis, neurosyphilis, abscess, tumours and meningitis.

Glucose: The glucose concentration of normal CSF is less than that of blood and ranges from 45 to 80 mg%. It is raised in encephalitis, but reduced in meningitis.

Chloride: The chloride content of CSF is higher than that of plasma and ranges from 700 to 750 mg%. It is decreased in meningitis, especially the tuberculosis type.

Non-protein substances: The concentration of non-protein substances such as urea and uric acid are nearly the same as those in plasma. Its sodium content is 300–350 mg% and potassium 11–15 mg%.

Calcium and phosphorus: The value for calcium is nearly half of that of plasma, i.e. 4–5 mg%, and this corresponds to the diffusible calcium of plasma. The inorganic phosphorus value is also less than that of plasma.

Magnesium: The magnesium content of normal CSF is about 3 mg%.

11 CHAPTER

Chemistry of Respiration

Chapter Outline

- Diffusion of Gases in the Lungs
- Transport of Oxygen in the Blood
- Oxygen Content and Oxygen Tension in Blood
- Dissociation of Oxyhaemoglobin
- Oxygen Dissociation Curve
- Carbon Dioxide Content and Carbon Dioxide Tension in Blood
- Carbon Dioxide Dissociation Curve

DIFFUSION OF GASES IN THE LUNGS

The term **respiration** refers to the exchange of the two gases, oxygen and carbon dioxide, between the body and the atmospheric air. This chapter deals with the chemical changes that occur during respiration.

A continuous supply of an adequate amount of oxygen to the tissues is necessary for the maintenance of life and normal functioning of cells. During metabolic activity, the cells produce large amounts of CO_2 which need prompt removal from the body. During respiration, O_2 is consumed and CO_2 is liberated by the cells. Both these processes are effectively accomplished by the lungs.

When blood passes through the lungs, the gases in blood and those of alveolar air attain an equilibrium, the gases on either side being separated by the very thin alveolar membrane (1–2 μ). The surface area of the membrane is also large (50–100 m^2), besides being very thin. These two factors help diffusion of gases from either side of the membrane, taking place in accordance with the laws of diffusion of gases. Oxygen being lighter diffuses at a greater rate than CO_2 which is heavier.

Under normal conditions of rest, blood passes through the lungs at a slower rate (takes about 0.75 second) than during severe exercise when it passes quickly (takes about 0.3 second).

It has been established that under normal resting conditions, the PO_2 (partial pressure of O_2) and PCO_2 (partial pressure of CO_2) of blood leaving the lungs (arterial blood) are about 100 and 40 mmHg, respectively (**Table 11.1**).

When the blood reaches the tissue cells, it gives away its O_2 for utilisation by the tissues. At the same time, CO_2 produced in the tissue cells is taken up by the blood leaving the tissues. The PO_2 of venous blood is low, i.e. 40 mm, and the PCO_2 is high, i.e. 46 mmHg. This is in accordance with the simple law of gases which states that gases diffuse from a higher to a lower pressure area. Oxygen passes from the arterial blood, where the PO_2 is higher, to the tissue cells, where the PO_2 is lower. CO_2 passes in the opposite direction.

The venous blood carrying more of CO_2 returns to the lungs where it gets oxygenated by drawing oxygen from the alveolar air. At the same time, the venous blood loses its CO_2 to the alveolar air with which it comes into approximate equilibrium.

Table 11.1 Normal Values of PO_2 and PCO_2 of Blood

	Arterial Blood (mmHg)	Venous Blood (mmHg)
PO_2/PCO_2	100/40	46/46

TRANSPORT OF OXYGEN IN THE BLOOD

Blood carries oxygen from the lungs to the tissues. Under normal resting conditions, a man utilises about 250 ml of O_2 per minute and eliminates about 200 ml of CO_2 per minute, whereas during severe exercise he absorbs and eliminates more than 10 times the volume of these gases.

Oxygen is transported in the blood in two forms:

1. In physical solution
2. In chemical combination as oxyhaemoglobin

Physical solution: The blood holds, at a tension of 100 mmHg, a volume of about 0.3 ml% oxygen in a simple physical solution.

Combination as oxyhaemoglobin: The property of blood to transport oxygen from lungs to the tissues is mainly due to the capacity of haemoglobin to form with oxygen the easily dissociable compound, the oxyhaemoglobin.

The average haemoglobin content of arterial blood is 15 grams per 100 ml. It has been calculated that 1 gram of haemoglobin, when fully saturated, carries 1.34 ml of O_2. Thus, 15 grams of haemoglobin in 100 ml of blood when fully saturated can carry about 20 ml of oxygen. But it is found that arterial blood is only about 95% saturated with oxygen, which means that it contains only 95% of HbO_2 and the rest is present as haemoglobin. Consequently, its oxygen content could be only about 19 ml instead of 20 ml.

OXYGEN CONTENT AND OXYGEN TENSION IN BLOOD

The oxygen in blood exerts different tension in arterial and venous blood. The oxygen tension in arterial blood is about the same as that in the alveolar air, and this is 100 mmHg. The oxygen content of arterial blood is 19 ml per 100 ml of blood.

During resting conditions, the oxygen content of the mixed venous blood is about 14 ml per 100 ml of blood and the oxygen tension of mixed venous blood is 40 mmHg (**Table 11.2**).

But in severe exercise, the oxygen content may be reduced to 3–4 ml and the oxygen tension may be reduced to 20–15 mmHg or even less.

Table 11.2 Concentration and Tension of O_2 and CO_2 in Blood

Nature of Blood	Oxygen		Carbon Dioxide	
	Content per 100 ml	Tension mmHg PO_2	Content per 100 ml	Tension mmHg PCO_2
Arterial blood	19 ml	100 mm	48 ml	40 mm
Venous blood	14 ml	40 mm	55 ml	46 mm

DISSOCIATION OF OXYHAEMOGLOBIN

Oxygen combines with haemoglobin readily to form oxyhaemoglobin which in turn also dissociates readily to form oxygen and haemoglobin. $O_2 + Hb \rightleftharpoons HbO_2$. Hb forms HbO_2 when it gets saturated with oxygen. HbO_2 dissociates when the oxygen saturation is less.

The relative amount of Hb and HbO_2 in blood at a given time depends on the amount of available oxygen, which in turn is proportionate to PO_2, i.e. oxygen pressure. Thus, when PO_2 increases, the formation of HbO_2 also increases. But the degree of saturation or dissociation is not proportional to PO_2. This may be indicated by the experiment described below which explains the mechanism of saturation of Hb and dissociation of HbO_2.

OXYGEN DISSOCIATION CURVE

A series of blood samples were exposed to air, containing oxygen at different partial pressures (PO_2), and the oxygen content (or HbO_2) of each sample was determined. When a graph was plotted with percentage saturation of Hb with oxygen in the *Y*-axis, an 'S'-shaped curve was obtained (**Fig. 11.1**). This curve is known as the 'dissociation curve of oxyhaemoglobin'. It indicates the relative amounts of oxyhaemoglobin (HbO_2) present at different levels of oxygen tension.

The same experiment was repeated with purified haemoglobin (HHb), and the percentage saturation of Hb with oxygen was plotted against different levels of PO_2 (**Fig. 11.1**). The curve obtained differs from that of the oxygen dissociation curve of haemoglobin in that it has the shape of a hyperbola. This difference is due to the presence of electrolytes in blood.

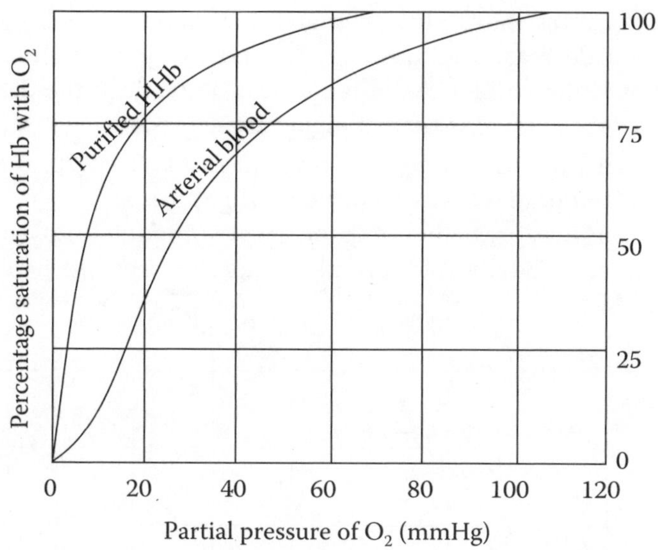

Figure 11.1 Dissociation curve of oxyhaemoglobin. It shows the amount of oxyhaemoglobin and reduced haemoglobin at different levels of oxygen tension.

The oxygen dissociation curve reveals certain factors of great physiological significance. These factors which relate to the peculiar behaviour of Hb towards variations in PO_2 are as follows.

1. **Influence of PO_2 on haemoglobin**
   - At a PO_2 of 100 mmHg, only about 95% of Hb is saturated with oxygen. This means that about 95% is in the form of HbO_2 and about 5% is in the reduced form (Hb).
   - Haemoglobin reached a saturation of 90% at a PO_2 of 70 mmHg. The ability of the blood to carry oxygen beyond PO_2 of 70 mmHg varied only slightly with variation in PO_2. In other words, dissociation of HbO_2 between PO_2 50 and 100 mmHg is comparatively little.
   - The dissociation of oxyhaemoglobin increases greatly, as the PO_2 falls to 40 mmHg, when the blood carries only about 14 ml of oxygen. It gives away 5 ml of oxygen to tissues for utilisation.
   - At oxygen tension below 40 mmHg, the curve descends sharply. This indicates ready dissociation of HbO_2, liberating oxygen which diffuses into tissue fluids. Venous blood which leaves the tissues with an oxygen tension of 40 mmHg has an oxygen content of about 14 ml%.
   - It may be noted that this peculiar behaviour of Hb towards PO_2 is responsible for the uptake of oxygen by the blood in the lungs, where the PO_2 is high (100 mm), and the release of oxygen from the blood to the tissues, where the PO_2 is low (40 mm).
2. **Effect of PCO_2:** The effect of CO_2 tension on the saturation of Hb at different levels of PO_2 is shown in **Figure 11.2**.

   When CO_2 tension is increased in the blood, there is increasing dissociation of HbO_2. The equation $O_2 + Hb \rightleftharpoons HbO_2$ is shifted to the left. With an increase in

CO_2 tension, the curves shift to the right and downwards. This is because the affinity of Hb for oxygen decreases, as the CO_2 tension in blood increases. This effect of CO_2 is known as **Bohr's effect**. As in the case of PO_2 effect, the dissociation is more pronounced at lower PO_2 levels than at higher levels.

As may be seen from the curve, variations in PCO_2 from 20 to 80 mm, at higher PO_2 levels of 90–100 mmHg, bring about only slight dissociation of HbO_2, whereas at PO_2 of 40–20 mmHg, as prevailing in tissues, increasing the PCO_2 from 20–80 mmHg causes the dissociation of HbO_2 to take place more rapidly. The percentage saturation of Hb falls from 40 to 20.

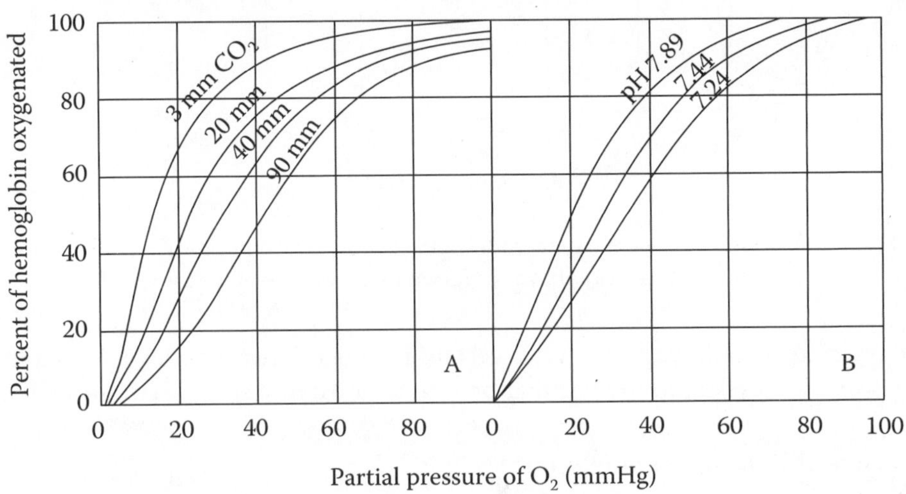

Figure 11.2 Effect of PCO_2 and pH on oxygen dissociation curve.

3. **Effect of pH:** An increase in the acidity (fall in pH) shifts the curve to the right, which means less oxygen is bound by Hb. This effect is well marked at higher levels of PO_2 (**Fig. 11.2**). The same phenomenon takes place in the tissues where the pH is low. In tissues, CO_2 which enters the capillaries increases the H^+ ion concentration and releases oxygen from oxyhaemoglobin, whereas in lungs, which eliminates CO_2 from the alveolar air, the acidity of blood is much less and therefore more oxygen is fixed by haemoglobin. Thus, in tissues, where the CO_2 content is high, the pH is low and the dissociation of HbO_2 to release more oxygen is rapid.
4. **Effect of temperature:** An increase in temperature tends to increase the dissociation of HbO_2, thereby diminishing the capacity of binding oxygen. The result is that the curve is shifted to the right. In muscular activity, the local rise in temperature favours the dissociation of HbO_2, when oxygen is released and delivered to the tissues.
5. **Effect of electrolytes:** Oxyhaemoglobin dissociates, giving up oxygen more readily in the presence of electrolytes than in their absence.
6. **Effect of altitude:** At high altitude, oxygenation of Hb is poor, and therefore the percentage of HbO_2 is low. But adequate amounts of oxygen are taken up from alveolar air in spite of the prevailing CO_2 content.

CARBON DIOXIDE CONTENT AND CARBON DIOXIDE TENSION IN BLOOD

Arterial blood contains 48 ml of CO_2 per 100 ml. Venous blood contains 55 ml of CO_2 per 100 ml.

CO_2 tension in alveolar air is 40 mmHg.

CO_2 tension in venous blood is 46 mm at rest.

About 200 ml of CO_2 are produced per minute during the oxidative process in the tissues at the resting period. A much larger amount of CO_2 is produced during strenuous exercise. The CO_2 produced in the tissues is transported in the blood.

CARBON DIOXIDE DISSOCIATION CURVE

Blood containing reduced haemoglobin and blood containing oxygenated haemoglobin behave differently with regard to uptake of CO_2, under different conditions of CO_2 pressure. This has been established by determining the CO_2 content of a series of blood samples subjected to different CO_2 pressures and plotting the results in a graph. The graph is called the 'carbon dioxide dissociation' curve.

In the graph shown in **Figure 11.3**, CO_2 pressure is plotted on the abscissa and volume of CO_2 in 100 ml of blood on the ordinate. The uptake of CO_2 volume at different PCO_2 for reduced blood and oxygenated blood is noted. The graph reveals certain important findings.

1. The blood with reduced haemoglobin takes up a larger volume of CO_2 than oxygenated blood. Similarly, in the body, there is increased uptake of CO_2 in the tissues which is due to increased reduced haemoglobin content.
2. In the case of oxygenated blood, there is evolution of CO_2 rather than uptake.

   The graph in **Figure 11.4** shows the CO_2 uptake by reduced and oxygenated blood to form carbamino haemoglobin at different pressures of CO_2. It is observed from the graph that formation of carbamino haemoglobin, both by reduced blood and by oxygenated blood, increases with increasing PCO_2 only up to 10 mm of PCO_2. Above this level, both types of blood do not show any increase in the uptake of CO_2, towards the formation of carbamino haemoglobin.
3. Another striking feature of the curves is that at a given PCO_2 level, reduced blood takes up about 5 ml more of CO_2 than oxygenated blood.

   These findings indicate that in tissues, the formation of carbamino haemoglobin (uptake of CO_2) is not increased significantly with an increase in CO_2 pressure but increases with the formation of reduced haemoglobin.

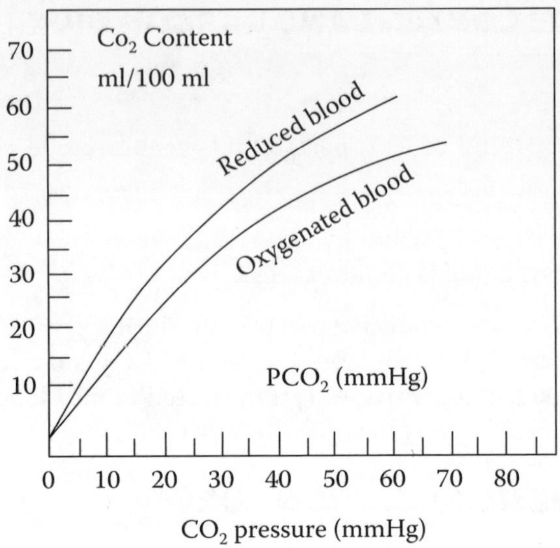

Figure 11.3 Carbon dioxide dissociation curve of reduced and oxygenated blood.

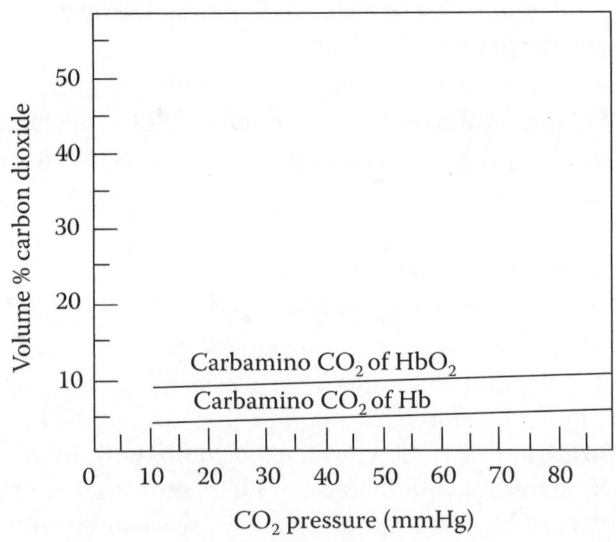

Figure 11.4 Formation of carbamino haemoglobin by reduced and oxygenated haemoglobin at different PCO$_2$.

12 CHAPTER Changes Undergone by Foodstuffs in the Alimentary Tract

Chapter Outline

- Digestive Enzymes and Their Action
- Bile
- Intestinal Fermentation and Putrefaction

DIGESTIVE ENZYMES AND THEIR ACTION

All foodstuffs except water, inorganic salts, vitamins and monosaccharides are hydrolysed into smaller molecules in the digestive tract, prior to absorption from the intestines. The process of hydrolysis is accomplished by the enzymes of the digestive fluids, namely saliva, gastric juice, pancreatic juice and intestinal juices.

Main events of digestion: Foodstuffs entering the mouth are exposed to the digestive action of saliva, which is secreted by the salivary and buccal glands. The food passes through the pharynx and oesophagus and enters the stomach where it is subjected to the digestive action of gastric juice.

The partially digested food mixtures are periodically emptied into the duodenum where they are digested by the enzymes of pancreatic juice. The food mixture passes down the intestines where it is acted upon by the enzymes of the intestinal secretion. The various end products formed by the hydrolytic action of digestion are absorbed mainly in the small intestines. The unabsorbed material passes into the colon where it is concentrated to a large extent by reabsorption of water. From there, it is excreted ultimately along with intestinal bacteria and products of their metabolism, as faeces.

The digestive action of saliva, gastric juice, pancreatic juice and intestinal secretions is mainly due to the enzymes contained in them. These enzymes are hydrolytic in nature. Their actions on the foodstuffs are briefly discussed.

Salivary Digestion

Saliva, which keeps the mouth moistened, is the mixed secretion of salivary, parotid, submaxillary and sublingual glands. About 1000–1500 ml of saliva are secreted daily. It has a slightly acidic pH (6.35–6.85). In addition to inorganic and organic constituents, it contains the enzyme ptyalin which acts on carbohydrates.

Ptyalin, which is also called **salivary amylase**, belongs to the group of hydrolysing enzymes. It hydrolyses starch and glycogen at the 1–4 glucosidic linkages, to a series of products.

The first product of hydrolysis is soluble starch whose formation is indicated by disappearance of the opalescence of the starch solution. It gives a blue colour with iodine, but no free reducing sugar is liberated. Further action of salivary amylase consists in the splitting of the second glucosidic linkage from a free end of the long chain of glucose residues which make up the starch molecule. This action facilitates formation of disaccharide maltose and a series of smaller polysaccharide molecules, the dextrins. The various dextrins differ in molecular size and complexity. The higher members (amylodextrin) resemble starch and give a blue or violet colour with iodine. As the molecules become smaller by formation of more maltose, a red colour is given with iodine, indicating the formation of erythrodextrin which is the next product of hydrolysis. Lower members (achro dextrin) do not give any colour with iodine. Thus, during the action of amylase on starch, free maltose is produced almost immediately and this increases progressively in amount. At the same time, the colour reaction with iodine changes from blue to red and finally becomes colourless. This indicates products of hydrolysis which are formed in stages. Thus, soluble starch gives a blue colour, amylodextrin gives a violet colour, erythrodextrin gives a red colour but achrodextrin does not produce any colour with iodine. Maltose is the end product of enzyme hydrolysis.

Ptyalin requires the presence of certain anions, particularly CF and Br ions, for effective action. The optimum pH for amylase activity in the presence of CF ions is pH 6.7–6.9. Removal of CF ions by dialysis inactivates ptyalin activity.

Ptyalin is destroyed below pH 4–5 and this is the reason why it becomes inactive when it reaches the stomach. But actually, some salivary digestion proceeds for 15–30 minutes in the stomach owing to the slow accumulation of acid. Amylase acts more readily and vigorously on cooked rather than raw starch.

Mucin: Saliva contains mucin which is another organic constituent. It is a glycoprotein containing glucosamine and glucuronic acid. It makes saliva viscous. Mucin is insoluble in water and dilute acids and can be precipitated from saliva by the addition of dilute acid.

Saliva, besides moistening and lubricating the masticated food mass to facilitate smooth swallowing, forms an important channel for excretion of certain harmful substances such as mercury, lead, cyanide and iodide. Potassium thiocyanate, which is present in saliva in traces, is derived from certain fruits and tobacco smoke.

Gastric Digestion

Gastric juice is a composite secretion of three types of cells of gastric mucosa, namely parietal cells, chief cells and columnar cells. It is a colourless liquid and has an acidic pH. The chief inorganic constituents include enzymes and mucin. About 2–3 litres of gastric juice are secreted in 24 hours.

The enzymes of gastric juice are pepsin, rennin (in young) and lipase. Gastric juice contains HCl which is an important adjunct in the process of digestion. Gastric juice does not contain amylase, but the action of ptyalin on carbohydrates continues for a short period till the contents in the stomach become highly acidic. Gastric juice contains mucin.

Pepsin, which is the main digestive component of gastric juice, is a proteolytic enzyme. It is secreted by the gastric mucosa as pepsinogen which is inactive. Pepsinogen is converted to active pepsin by HCl in gastric juice (pH 1–2), and by pepsin itself at pH lower than 5, by its autocatalytic action. The optimum pH of pepsin is 1.5–2.5.

Pepsin is an endopeptidase, because it catalyses the hydrolysis of peptide linkage at all points in the protein molecule, resulting in the formation of smaller peptide units, namely metaproteins, proteoses and peptone, in this order of priority. But pepsin brings about only partial digestion of protein, i.e. up to the stage of peptone in the stomach. It has been observed that pepsin acts with preference on linkages involving amino groups of tyrosine and phenylalanine. It also acts more favourably on denatured proteins possessing SH groups. It does not act on keratins, protamines, histones and mucoproteins. Though pepsin acts best on other proteins at pH around 2, it is capable of converting casein to paracasein even at pH 7, particularly in the presence of Ca^{++} ions, resulting in the formation of insoluble paracaseinate. Thus, pepsin has a milk-clotting action in adults.

Rennin (rennet, chymosin): Rennin is a milk curdling enzyme. It is not present in the gastric juice of human adults, but is present in infants prior to the formation of pepsin. Like pepsin, it is secreted by gastric mucosa as prorennin, which is inactive. It is converted to active rennin by HCl in gastric juice. Its optimum pH is 6–6.5. Its acts only on casein, converting it to paracasein which is soluble. Paracasein later forms, in the presence of Ca^{++} ions, insoluble, calcium paracaseinate.

$$\text{Casein} \xrightarrow{\textit{Rennin}} \text{Paracasein} \xrightarrow{Ca^{++}} \text{Calcium paracaseinate}$$

The milk curdling action of rennin in infants is taken up by pepsin and chymotrypsin in adults. But the digestive action of pepsin and trypsin is too rapid such that paracasein is quickly digested to proteoses without forming a clot.

Gastric lipase: This is a fat splitting enzyme. Very little digestion of fats takes place in the stomach, because the optimum pH of the lipase is 5.5–7, whereas the pH of the gastric juice is about 2, and lipase is destroyed in the stomach at this high acidity. However, the lipase may become active in infants in conditions of low acidity and in cases of achylia gastrica. Hydrolysis of fats takes place favourably in the small intestines, where the pH is on the alkaline side.

Hydrochloric acid: The most important inorganic constituent of gastric juice is HCl. It facilitates enzyme action by maintaining appropriate pH for the action of gastric enzymes. HCl is secreted by the gastric parietal cells. The concentration of HCl in gastric juice when freshly secreted is about 0.5–0.6%, with a pH of about 0.87. The concentration soon gets diluted to about 0.2%, because it is neutralised by (i) the alkaline mucus secreted by the pyloric portion of the stomach and (ii) the regurgitation of alkaline pancreatic juice into the stomach. Further dilution occurs by mixing of HCl with food and water. Thus, the acidity of the gastric juice varies widely from 0.05 to 0.1 N depending upon (i) the actual amount of HCl secreted by parietal cells, (ii) the extent of its dilution with other gastric secretions, foods and water and (iii) the buffering action of mucus.

Functions of Gastric HCl:

1. The main function of gastric HCl is to provide the necessary pH for the digestion of protein in the stomach by pepsin.
2. Its activates pepsinogen to pepsin.
3. It facilitates swelling, denaturation and hydrolysis of proteins, prior to digestion.
4. It facilitates absorption of iron.
5. It stimulates secretion of secretin.
6. It hydrolyses disaccharides.
7. It has a germicidal action by which fermentation by microorganisms in the stomach is restricted.

Mucin: Gastric mucin is a glycoprotein and is slightly alkaline. It forms a coating on the interior of the stomach and serves to protect the mucosa from the acidity of gastric juice.

Pancreatic Digestion

The food from the stomach is emptied into the first part of the duodenum where it is exposed to the action of the pancreatic juice, intestinal secretion and bile. The acidity of the gastric content (chyme) entering the duodenum is neutralised by the alkaline pH prevailing there. Pancreatic juice which is secreted by the acinar cells of the pancreas is alkaline and is the most important of the digestive juices, since it contains powerful enzymes capable of digesting all three classes of food, namely proteins, carbohydrates and fats.

The enzymes of pancreatic juice are as follows:

1. Proteolytic enzymes that split proteins
   - Trypsin
   - Chymotrypsin
   - Carboxypeptidase
2. Pancreatic amylase which hydrolyses starch
3. Pancreatic lipase which hydrolyses fats

These enzymes, responsible for the effective digestion of the food mixture, are briefly dealt in this section.

1. (a) **Trypsin** is secreted by pancreas as inactive trypsinogen. It is converted to active trypsin in the intestines by the enzyme enterokinase which is present in the intestinal juice (succus entericus). Trypsin acts on the products of peptic digestion, splitting them into smaller units. The optimum pH of trypsin is 8–9. Trypsin is an endopeptidase, hydrolysing all types of protein, breaking them down even to the stage of amino acids. It readily acts on denatured proteins, proteoses and peptones, converting them to polypeptides, dipeptides and amino acids. Trypsin does not clot milk. Pancreatic extract contains a trypsin inhibitor which is a polypeptide.

(b) **Chymotrypsin** closely resembles trypsin in its properties. It is secreted as inactive chymotrypsinogen which is activated to chymotrypsin by trypsin. The optimum pH of chymotrypsin is 8–9. It is an endopeptidase. Like trypsin, it acts on denatured proteins, proteoses and peptones, liberating polypeptides, dipeptides and amino acids. It differs from trypsin in that it clots milk like rennin and pepsin.

(c) **Carboxypeptidase** is an exopeptidase, because it acts at the end of the polypeptide chain having a free carboxyl group, splitting off single terminal amino acids. Its optimum pH is around 7.4. It contains zinc. **Peptidases** constitute a mixture of enzymes, namely (i) carboxypeptidase, (ii) aminopeptidase and (iii) dipeptidase, present in intestinal juices. Such a mixture of enzymes in the intestinal juices is also known as **erepsin**.

2. **Pancreatic amylase (diastase, amylopsin):** This is the amylolytic enzyme of pancreatic juice. It acts on polysaccharides in the same manner as that of ptyalin, but more powerfully. It differs from ptyalin in that it has the power of digesting even raw starch. Pancreatic amylase requires Cl^- ions for its action. Its optimum pH is 6.9. The enzyme acts by hydrolysing starch and glycogen in the intestines through stages of dextrins, and the end product formed is maltose. This is further hydrolysed to glucose by the intestinal enzyme maltase.

   The concentration of pancreatic amylase in blood is elevated in acute pancreatitis, which is an inflammatory condition of pancreatic tissues.

3. **Pancreatic lipase (steapsin):** This is the most important enzyme for the digestion of fats. It splits fats into fatty acid and glycerol. Its optimum pH varies from 7 to 8.8.

   The activity of pancreatic lipase in the duodenum is facilitated by the following factors:

   - Presence of bile acids, Ca^{++} ions, certain amino acids and peptides
   - Presence of fatty acids having higher molecular weights
   - Presence of fatty acids with a higher degree of unsaturation

   This indicates that fats containing unsaturated fatty acids such as oleic and linolenic acids are more rapidly hydrolysed than triglycerides.

   Hydrolysis of fats is greatly facilitated by emulsification, whereby a larger surface of the fats is made available for the action of lipase. Emulsification is an important prerequisite for hydrolysis of fats because it is insoluble in aqueous media. Emulsification is potentiated by

   - Mechanical action of the stomach and intestines
   - Presence of bile salts which help in lowering the surface tension
   - Presence of monoglycerides and soaps (formed by hydrolysis) which are also surface active substances

   The products of hydrolysis of fat usually consist of monoglycerides, diglycerides, fatty acids and undigested fats, in varying proportions, because the conditions in the intestines are not optimal for complete hydrolysis of ingested fats to glycerol and fatty acid.

Cholesterol esterase: Pancreatic juice contains cholesterol esterase, which along with bile salts catalyse the esterification of cholesterol with fatty acids. Esterification of cholesterol is necessary for its absorption from the intestines.

Phospholipases: Pancreatic juice contains phospholipases which act on phospholipids. Phospholipase A acts on lecithin and cephalin, splitting off a fatty acid from each. They leave behind compounds called lysolecithin and lysocephalin, respectively. Both have a haemolytic property. Phospholipase B acts on these compounds and removes the second fatty acid in each to yield glyceryl phosphoryl choline in the case of lecithin and glyceryl phosphoryl ethanolamine or glyceryl phosphoryl serine in the case of cephalin. Phosphodiesterase splits off the glycerol and phosphatase removes the bases.

Nucleases: Pancreatic juice contains two more enzymes, namely ribonuclease and deoxyribonuclease, which hydrolyse the nucleic acids into individual mononucleotides.

Intestinal Juice (Succus Entericus)

Intestinal juice is a mixture of different compositions secreted by the cells or the mucosal glands of the small intestines at different levels. It is also known as succus entericus. The pH of the intestinal juice varies at different levels of the intestine, depending upon (i) the concentration of the gastric acidity entering the duodenum, (ii) the quantity of pancreatic juice present, (iii) the composition of the diet and (iv) the degree of bacterial action.

The intestinal juice contains the following enzymes, apart from other inorganic and organic constituents:

1. Disaccharidases
2. Peptidases
3. Polynucleotidases
4. Nucleosidases
5. Enterokinase
6. Phosphatase
7. Lecithinase

Disaccharidases: These are enzymes which hydrolyse disaccharides. They hydrolyse the glucosidic linkage of the disaccharides to form the corresponding monosaccharides.

Examples of specific disaccharidases are as follows:

- Maltase—splits maltose into two molecules of glucose
- Sucrase—splits sucrose into glucose and fructose
- Lactase—splits lactose into glucose and galactose

Hereditary deficiency of intestinal maltase and lactase will result in disaccharide intolerance. In such conditions, ingestion of lactose and sucrose fails to produce a rise in blood glucose. The characteristic feature of this condition is the passage of watery stools, of low pH, and this is due to the presence of acids produced by bacterial fermentation of the unhydrolysed disaccharides.

Peptidases: These enzymes hydrolyse peptide chains. There are two main types of peptidases:

- *Aminopeptidase:* These are exopeptidases acting on the peptide linkage of terminal amino acids, possessing a free amino group.
- *Tripeptidases and dipeptidases:* They split tripeptides and dipeptides into their individual amino acids (**Fig. 12.1**).

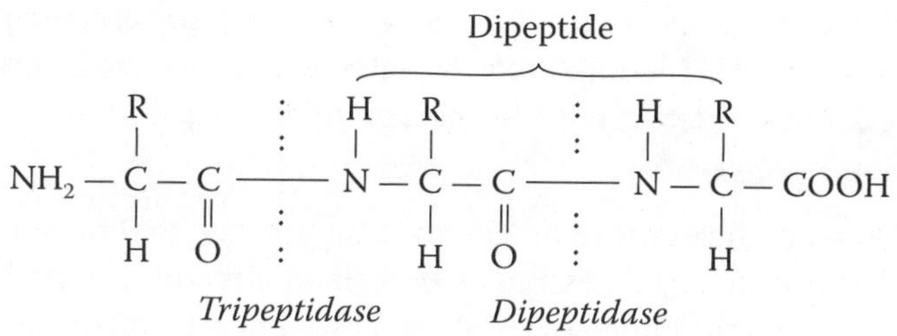

Figure 12.1 Action of tripeptidase and dipeptidase.

Nucleotidase: This enzyme hydrolyses and splits the nucleotide into phosphoric acid and nucleoside.

Nucleosidase: This enzyme splits the nucleosides into their nitrogenous bases and sugars.

Enterokinase: This enzyme is secreted by the duodenal mucosal cells. It converts trypsinogen to trypsin. It does not have any direct digestive action.

Phosphatase: The enzyme phosphatase present in the intestinal juice splits the phosphate from organic phosphate derivatives such as glycerophosphate and hexose phosphate.

Lecithinase: Intestinal juice contains a lecithinase which splits lecithins to yield fatty acids, glycerol, phosphoric acid and choline.

It may be seen that, by the action of various digestive enzymes, the foodstuffs ingested are hydrolysed and split into their simplest constituents. The end products of digestion of carbohydrates and proteins are monosaccharides and amino acids, respectively. The end products of fats are fatty acids, glycerol and monoglycerides and diglycerides.

Summary of digestion of foodstuffs:

Carbohydrates: Digestion of polysaccharides (starch and glycogen) begins in the mouth by ptyalin. The action of ptyalin may continue for a short period in the stomach till the gastric acidity inactivates the enzyme. Polysaccharides are partially hydrolysed to dextrins and maltose by ptyalin. In the intestines, the unhydrolysed polysaccharides and dextrins are further split to maltose by pancreatic amylase. Maltose along with other disaccharides, such as lactose and sucrose, are hydrolysed by maltase, lactase and sucrase of intestinal juice to their constituents, glucose, galactose and fructose.

Proteins: Both native and denatured proteins are hydrolysed step by step by pepsin of gastric juice and by trypsin and chymotrypsin of pancreatic juice to form polypeptides and small amounts of amino acids. Casein forms insoluble paracasein by the action of rennin in infants and by the action of pepsin and chymotrypsin in the case of adults.

Lipids: Very little digestion of fat takes place in the stomach. The main digestion of fat begins in the intestines where they are first emulsified by bile salts. Further emulsification is carried out by products of fat digestion. The emulsified fats are hydrolysed by pancreatic lipase, which is the most important lipolytic enzyme of pancreatic juice, and by the lipase of intestinal secretion incompletely to fatty acids, glycerol, monoglycerides and diglycerides. Some amount of triglycerides escape hydrolysis and are present among the products of digestion.

Nucleoproteins: Dietary nucleoproteins are split by proteolytic enzymes to nucleic acids and proteins. The latter undergo digestion as described already. The nucleic acids are split by ribonuclease and deoxyribonuclease of pancreatic juice to form oligonucleotides and mononucleotides. Phosphodiesterases of intestinal secretion split the oligonucleotides into mononucleotides which are further split into nucleosides and inorganic phosphate by non-specific phosphatases.

BILE

Fresh human bile is a clear, golden, yellow liquid formed and secreted by the liver. It is slightly viscous and tastes bitter. Its pH varies from 7.5 to 8.5.

About 500–700 ml are secreted daily by the liver. A part of it, about 500 ml, is stored in the gall bladder, where it is concentrated and periodically discharged into the small intestines. The bile in gall bladder is more viscous and has a greenish tinge, because of the presence of bile pigments.

During digestion, gall bladder contracts to supply bile to the intestines via the common bile duct. The bile mixes with the pancreatic juice and exerts an important influence on the digestion of fats of food.

Bile contains about 1–4% of solids; of this, about 25% are inorganic constituents. These are mainly bicarbonates and chlorides of sodium and potassium.

The remaining part contains organic materials. The organic constituents of bile include bile salts, bilirubin, cholesterol and smaller amounts of phospholipids, fats, fatty acids, mucin, urea and the enzyme alkaline phosphatase.

The inorganic constituents and bile pigments are products of excretion and are removed from blood by the liver cells, by biliary excretion. The bile salts and bile cholesterol are formed in the polygonal cells of liver. The liver alkaline phosphatase also originates from these cells. Mucin is formed from the epithelium of bile duct and mucosa of gall bladder. The cholesterol of bile is synthesised by the liver.

The composition of hepatic bile differs from the gall bladder bile, as given in **Table 12.1**.

Table 12.1 Composition of Hepatic Bile and Gall Bladder Bile

	Hepatic Bile (pH 7.1–8.5)	Gall Bladder Bile (pH 5.5–7.7)
Constituents	**Percentage of Total Bile**	**Percentage of Total Bile**
Specific gravity	1.009–1.013	1.026–1.032
Water	97.00	85.92
Solids	2.52	14.08
Bile acids	1.93	9.14
Mucin and bile pigments	0.53	2.98
Cholesterol	0.06	0.26
Fats and fatty acids	0.14	0.32
Inorganic salts	0.84	0.65
pH	7.1–8.5	5.5–7.7

Bile Acids and Bile Salts

Bile acids are the end products of cholesterol catabolism in the body. Approximately 0.7 gram bile acids are produced and lost in faeces per day. They are eliminated via bile because tissues cannot break down the steroid nucleus. The bile acids enter the bile as conjugates of glycine and taurine. The primary bile acids—cholic acid and chenodeoxycholic acid—are formed in the liver from cholesterol with various intervening stages as shown in **Figure 12.2**.

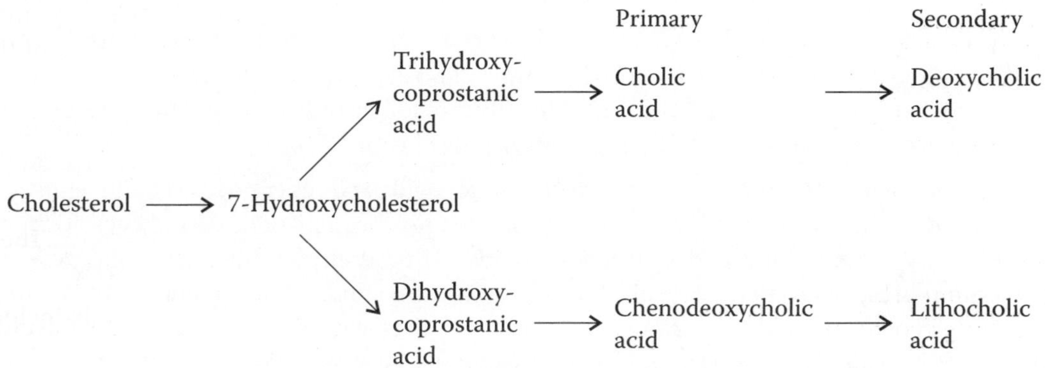

Figure 12.2 Formation of bile acids.

Deoxycholic acid and lithocholic acid are secondary bile acids formed from cholic acid and chenodeoxycholic acid, respectively. Cholic acid forms the largest amount of the bile acid in the bile itself and comprises a maximum of 60% of the total. The formation of primary and secondary bile acids is illustrated in **Figure 12.3**.

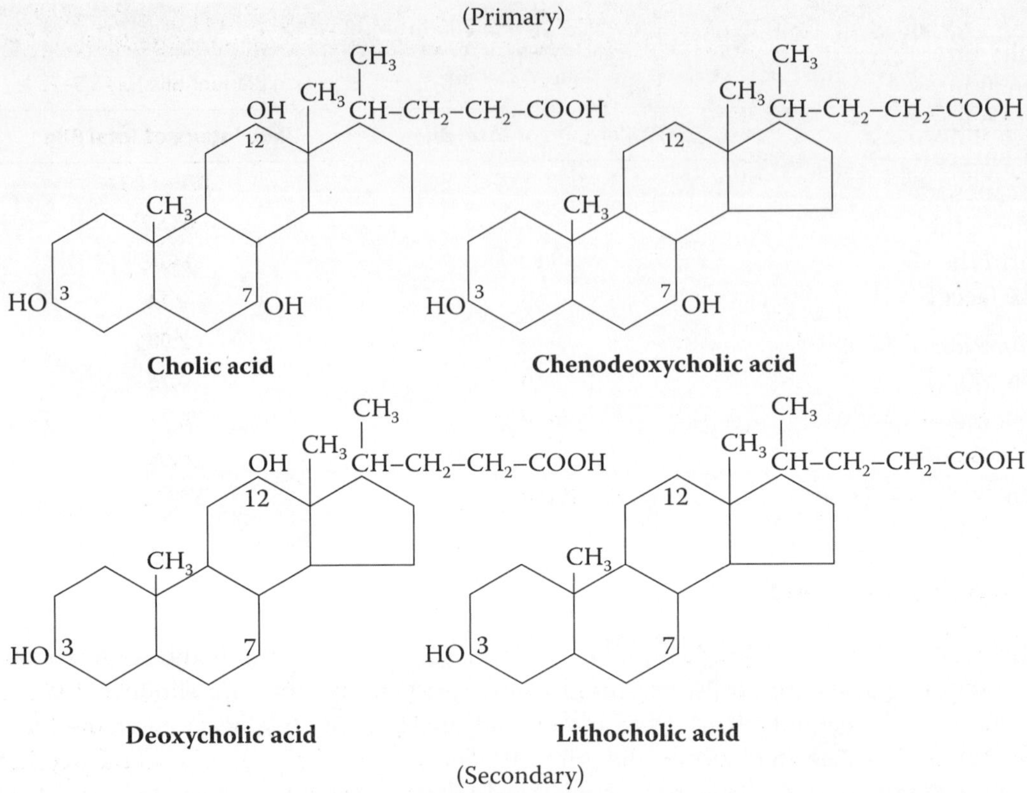

Figure 12.3 Bile acids.

Cholic acid is a saturated sterol having three (OH) groups located in positions 3, 7 and 12. Chenodeoxycholic acid has two (OH) groups in positions 3 and 7. Deoxycholic acid has two (OH) groups in positions 3 and 12. Lithocholic acid has only one OH group located on C-3. The structure of the four bile acids is shown in **Figure 12.3**.

Bile salts: Before excretion in the bile, cholic acid and chenodeoxycholic acid are conjugated in the liver with either glycine or taurine through peptide linkages forming the bile salts, glycocholic and taurocholic acids. They then combine with sodium and potassium present in the bile and form the water-soluble alkaline bile salts, namely sodium glycocholate and sodium taurocholate, and then get excreted in the bile. Glycine and taurine conjugates are stronger acids than the free bile acids and therefore remain completely ionised at the pH in the gall bladder and small intestines. Prior to conjugation, cholic acid is preliminarily activated with coenzyme A by an activating enzyme present in liver microsomes to form cholyl-CoA.

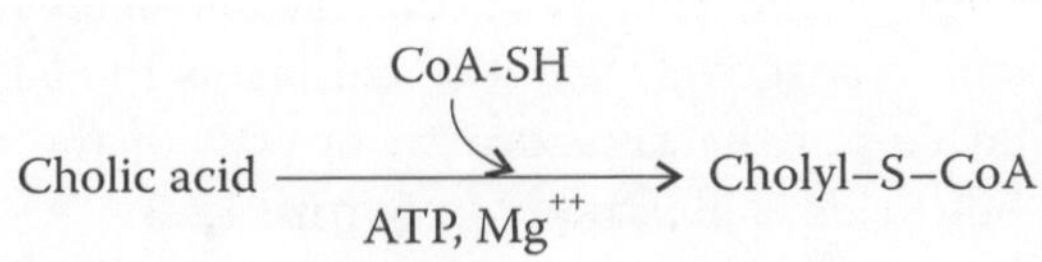

In human bile, glycocholate predominates over taurocholate in a ratio of 3:1. Bile salts after excretion in the intestinal tract are almost completely reabsorbed from the small intestines and are carried by the portal blood, back to the liver for resecretion into the bile. The recycling of bile acids takes place several times after each large meal. This is **enterohepatic circulation** of bile salts. A smaller amount of less than 500 mg a day escapes reabsorption during each enterohepatic cycle. They pass to the large intestines where the bacteria in the colon remove the glycine or taurine and the 7-hydroxyl group to form the secondary bile acids, deoxycholic acid and lithocholic acid. These are excreted in the faeces. Lithocholic acid is mostly excreted in the faeces.

Functions:

1. The bile salts facilitate digestion of fats in the intestine by being emulsifying agents. They lower the surface tension of water and this enables them to emulsify the fats, when a larger surface area of the fats is exposed to the action of pancreatic lipase. Fat-soluble vitamins are also absorbed along with the fats.
2. In the intestines, bile acids combine with monoglycerides and diglycerides to form tiny particles called micelles, which are about 1/100th of the size of the usual emulsified triglyceride particle. This facilitates absorption of fat.
3. Bile salts activate pancreatic lipase and cholesterol esterase at an acid pH, which exists in the upper part of small intestines.
4. They facilitate absorption of cholesterol and fat-soluble vitamins by forming loose, water-soluble complexes with them. The formation of water-soluble complexes with fats which are originally water insoluble is called 'hydrotropic' action.
5. Bile salts, being the natural stimuli to the secretion of hepatic bile, increase the flow of a greater volume of bile.
6. Bile salts help in maintaining cholesterol in solution in the bile. However, when the ratio of bile acid to cholesterol concentration drops to a critical level, cholesterol gets precipitated and this is one of the factors which causes the formation of gall stones.

Bile pigments: Bilirubin glucuronide is the main bile pigment of bile and bile owes its colour to this pigment. A small amount of urobilinogen which escapes metabolism in liver, after absorption from the intestines, may also be present. Both these pigments are formed from degradation of haem which is derived by disintegration of haemoglobin. Bilirubin which is carried in the blood bound with albumin is separated from albumin in the liver where it gets conjugated with glucuronic acid. It is excreted in the bile as bilirubin glucuronide. The circulation of bile pigments is discussed in **Chapter 9, Catabolism of Haem**. Abnormalities in the formation, conjugation, circulation and excretion of bile pigments lead to jaundice.

Cholesterol: Bile contains a fairly large amount of cholesterol. It is presumed that the biliary cholesterol is synthesised in the liver itself and has no relation to the cholesterol of plasma. Liver cells remove cholesterol from the bloodstream and metabolise it to form bile acids which are excreted in the bile.

INTESTINAL FERMENTATION AND PUTREFACTION

After absorption of food from the small intestines, the residue passes into the large intestines. Here, a considerable amount of water is absorbed and the intestinal content gets more solidified.

The microorganisms present in the large intestines act upon these products, causing fermentation, putrefaction and decomposition. The faecal matter, which is the ultimate product formed, contains a considerable amount of these microorganisms and products of their metabolism. Microorganisms which enter the alimentary canal few hours after the infant is born multiply abundantly in the colon. They thrive in the small intestines to some extent, but do not survive in the stomach, because of the acidity of the gastric juice. However, they can flourish in conditions where achlorhydria is present.

In the large intestines, microorganisms act on the products of digestion and produce substances of varied nature. The bacterial action involves oxidation, decarboxylation, deamination and reduction and these reactions are catalysed by bacterial enzymes.

In man, the products formed may be harmful, such as toxic amines and phenols, or beneficial, such as vitamins. Substances which are neither harmful nor beneficial such as urobilinogen are also products of putrefaction.

The most important of the beneficial products formed by the action of intestinal bacteria are vitamins **K** and **B** complex members. Among the B complex vitamins, folic acid, biotin and vitamin B_{12} are synthesised in amounts sufficient to meet the daily requirements. It is for this reason that prolonged treatment with broad-spectrum antibiotics is sustained with adequate doses of vitamin B complex, lest the bacteria which synthesise these important vitamins be destroyed by the antibiotics.

Action of bacteria on carbohydrates: Bacterial action on carbohydrates in the large intestines is referred to as **intestinal fermentation**. The end products are (i) organic acids such as lactic, oxalic, succinic, formic, acetic and propionic acids and (ii) gases such as methane, carbon dioxide and hydrogen.

Though these products do not produce a harmful effect, the gases when formed in excess may lead to distension of the abdomen and cause discomfort. The gases are normally eliminated during the passage of wind.

Action of bacteria on fats: Bacterial enzymes hydrolyse lipids to fatty acids and glycerol which are the normal products of digestion. Toxic amines such as neurine and muscarine may be produced from choline, the component of lecithin.

Action of bacteria on proteins: The action of bacteria on protein is referred to as **putrefaction**. More harmful products are formed by the action of bacteria on proteins. The bacterial enzymes act on amino acids which escape absorption in the small intestines, subjecting them through processes involving decarboxylation, deamination, oxidation and reduction.

Amino acids: Simpler amino acids are decarboxylated to amines or deaminated to short-chain fatty acids, as shown in **Figure 12.4**.

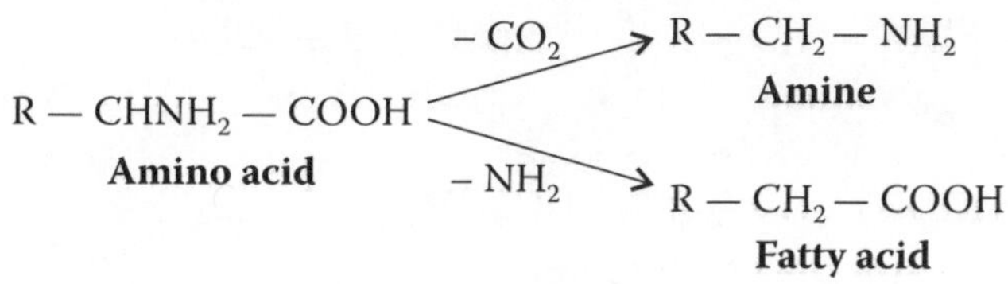

Figure 12.4 Action of bacteria on amino acids.

Among aromatic amino acids, tyrosine is converted to phenol and cresol while tryptophan is converted to skatole and indole.

Tyrosine undergoes the following changes:

1. It may undergo decarboxylation to form tyramine which in turn may be reduced to form cresol and then phenol.

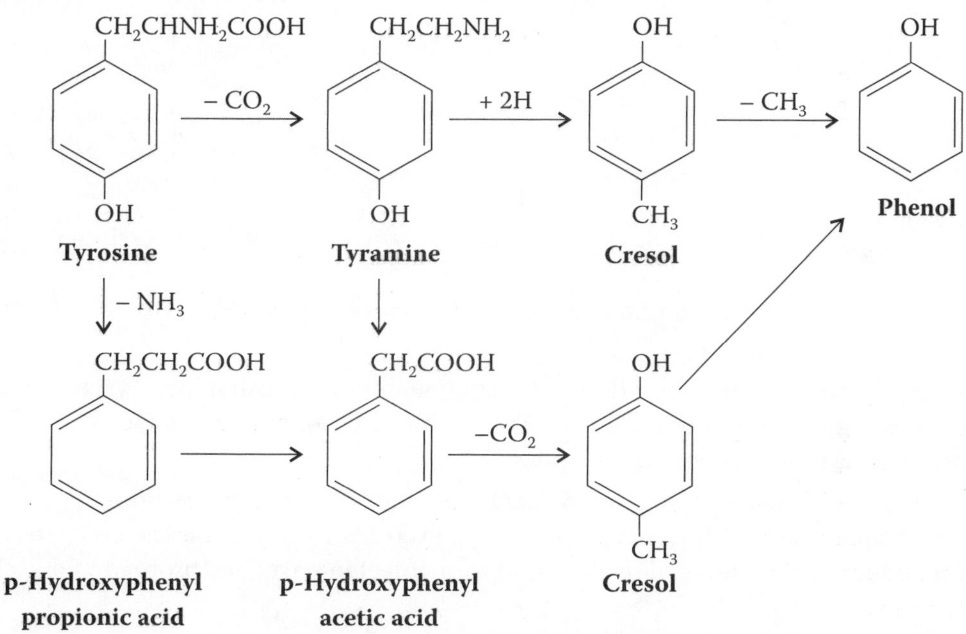

Figure 12.5 Changes undergone by tyrosine.

2. It may undergo deamination to form p-hydroxyphenyl propionic acid, p-hydroxyphenylacetic acid and cresol (**Fig. 12.5**).

Tryptophan undergoes a series of reactions and forms skatole and indole. For this, tryptophan may primarily undergo decarboxylation to form indole ethylamine (tryptamine) or deamination to form indole propionic acid. Both indole ethylamine and indole propionic acid are converted to skatole and indole. The reactions are shown in **Figure 12.6**. Skatole and indole contribute to the characteristic foul odour of the faeces. Normally, they are formed in small amounts but when formed in large amounts they produce toxic effects.

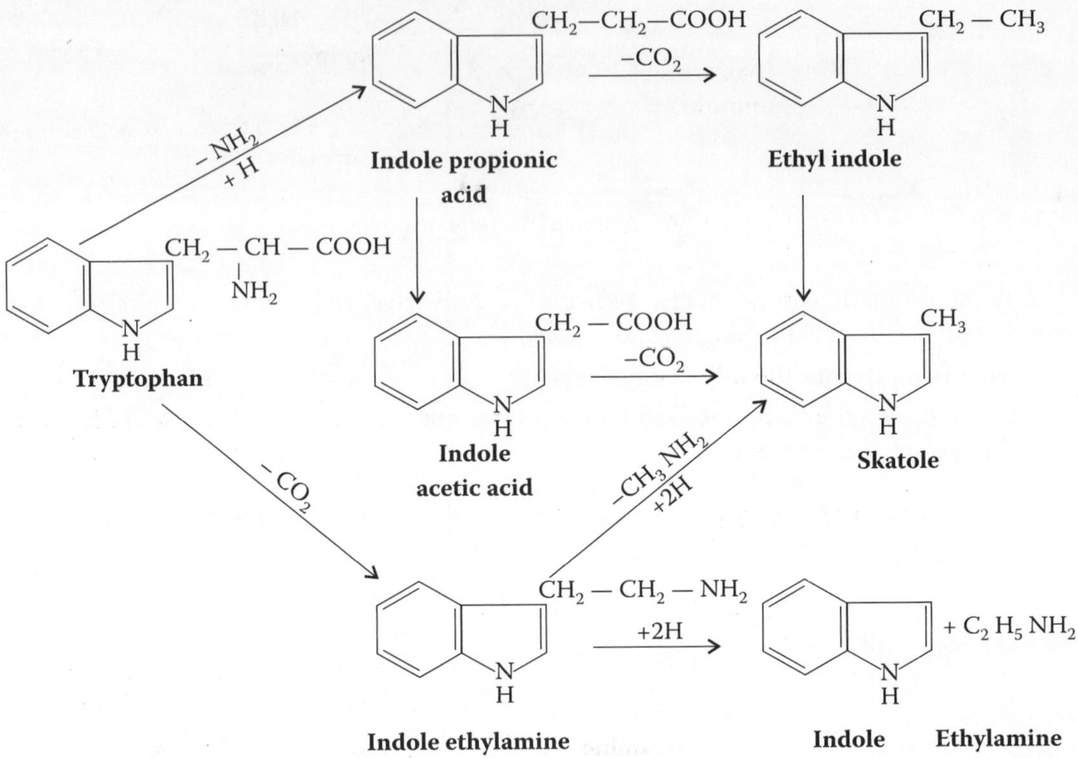

Figure 12.6 Changes undergone by tryptophan.

Similar decarboxylation reactions of histidine produce histamine. Lysine produces cadaverine, arginine produces agmatine and ornithine produces putrescine. Most of these amines are powerful vasopressor compounds.

Cystine, a sulphur containing amino acid, undergoes a series of reactions to eventually form mercaptans and H_2S. These products are excreted largely in faeces, contributing to the foul odour of the faeces. Some amount of mercaptans may be absorbed and excreted in the urine.

Miscellaneous Action

Bilirubin: Bacterial enzymes in the intestines act on bilirubin and reduce it to urobilinogen and stercobilinogen, which subsequently get oxidised to urobilin and stercobilin. The unabsorbed portions of bilins contribute to the normal brown colour of the faeces.

Ammonia: A considerable amount of ammonia is formed as a product of putrefaction on nitrogenous substances. Under normal conditions, this ammonia is absorbed into the portal circulation but is rapidly removed from the blood by the liver. This function of liver may be impaired in liver diseases, when the concentration of ammonia in blood increases to toxic levels resulting in ammonia intoxication. The characteristic manifestations of hepatic coma are due to ammonia intoxication.

CHAPTER 13

Detoxication Mechanisms

Chapter Outline

- Detoxication
- The Mechanism

DETOXICATION

Detoxication refers to the chemical processes that occur in the body, to convert toxic substances to non-toxic substances for excretion.

The toxic substances may include the following:

1. Foreign organic compounds, for example drugs used for therapeutic purposes or chemicals used for diagnostic purposes.
2. Products which are formed in the intestines due to normal metabolic reactions, for example putrefaction products produced in the intestines through bacterial enzymatic reaction or normal digestion products.
3. Sex hormones and bile pigments, which are normal physiological compounds, are eliminated to some extent as sulphate and glucuronide.

The detoxified products are excreted either in the faeces or in urine. Liver is the main site for the detoxication process, though kidneys also participate in the process.

THE MECHANISM

The following chemical mechanisms are involved in detoxication:

1. Oxidation
2. Reduction
3. Hydrolysis
4. Conjugation

Oxidation

Many foreign organic compounds are subjected to oxidation in the body. It may be said that aliphatic compounds are more easily oxidised than aromatic compounds. A classification of the important types of oxidation reactions is as follows:

1. **Oxidation of primary alcohols:** Aliphatic and aromatic alcohols are oxidised to their corresponding acids.

(a) Methyl alcohol ⟶ Formic acid.

$$CH_3OH \xrightarrow{O_2} HCOOH + H_2O.$$

Methyl alcohol is a highly toxic substance. When consumed, it produces blindness.

(b) Benzyl alcohol ⟶ Benzoic acid

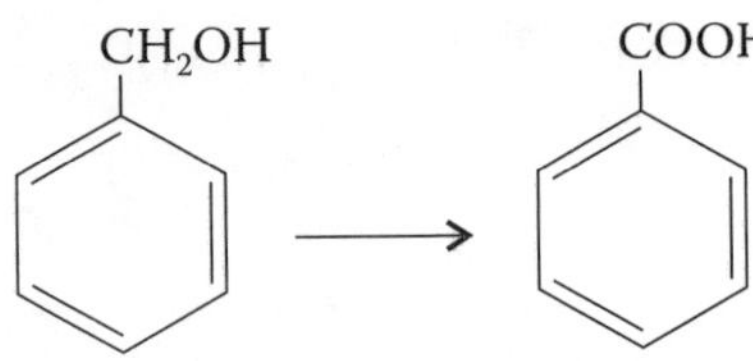

2. **Oxidation of aromatic hydrocarbons:** Aromatic hydrocarbons, such as benzene, are oxidised to phenols.

Benzene ⟶ Phenol

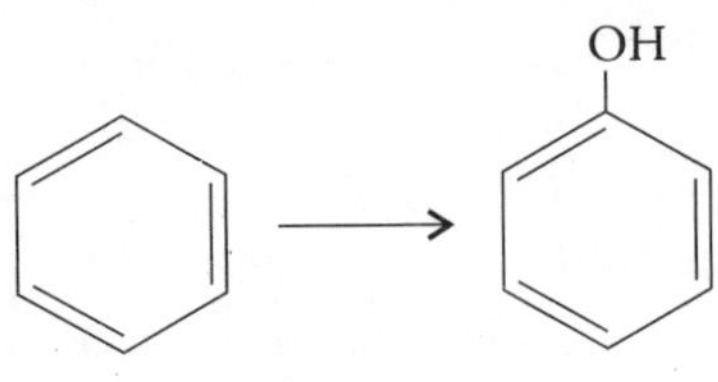

Rarely, the aromatic ring may open to a slight extent, resulting in the formation of compounds such as muconic acid.

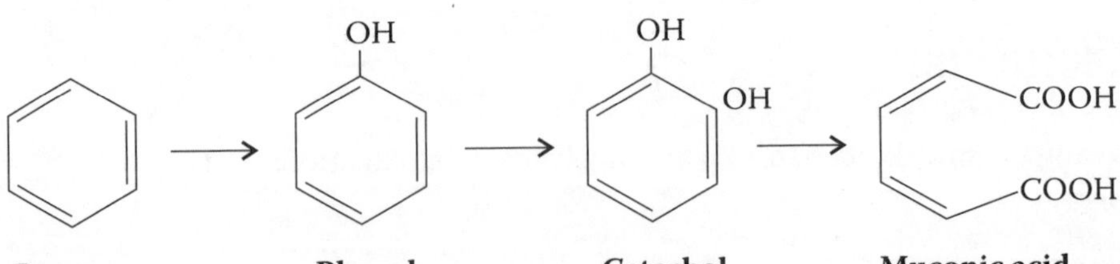

Benzene **Phenol** **Catechol** **Muconic acid**

3. **Oxidation preliminary to conjugation:** Preliminary oxidation, which is a necessary step for conjugation, may occur. For example, benzene may first get oxidised to phenol, which can then combine with sulphuric or glucuronic acid.

Reduction

In man, reduction is less common than oxidation. It has been observed that certain metabolites, which are formed due to reduction, are more toxic than the original compounds.

Examples of reduction as a mechanism of detoxication are as follows:

1. Conversion of picric acid to picramic acid which later gets excreted in urine

Picric acid ⟶ Picramic acid

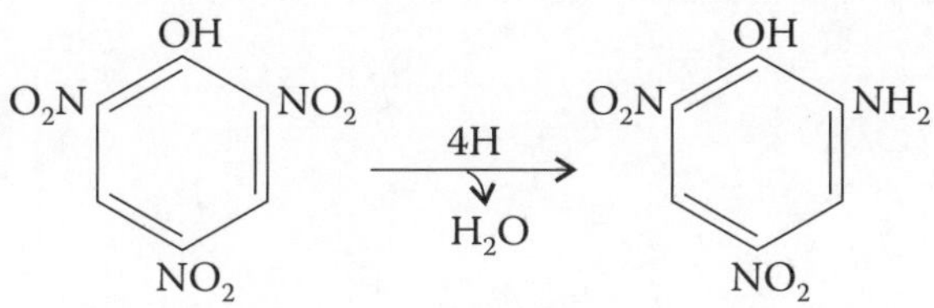

2. Certain aldehydes, for example chloral, may be reduced to the corresponding alcohol which may undergo conjugation later, to form the glucuronide.

$$CCl_3CHO \xrightarrow{2H} CCl_3CH_2OH \xrightarrow[\text{acid}]{\text{Glucuronic}} CCl_3CH_2OC_6H_9O_6$$

Trichloroethyl glucuronide

Simultaneous reduction and oxidation may take place in the same compound.

e.g., ρ-Nitrobenzaldehyde ⟶ ρ-Aminobenzoic acid

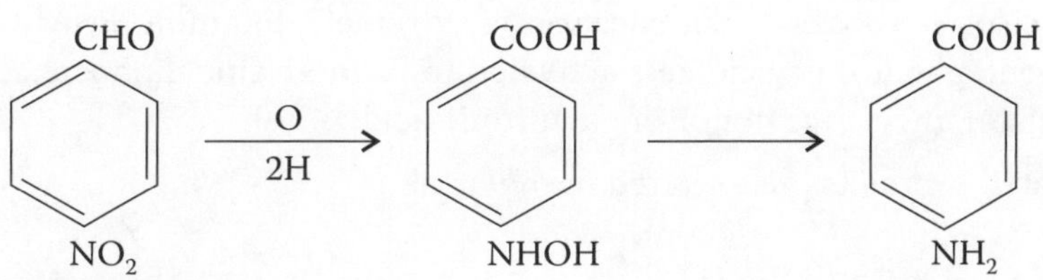

ρ-Nitrobenzaldehyde **ρ-Aminobenzoic acid**

Hydrolysis

Some of the compounds which are ingested for therapeutic purposes undergo hydrolysis in the body. Examples are given below.

1. Acetylsalicylic acid ⟶ Salicyclic acid + Acetic acid.
2. Digitalis ⟶ Sugars + Aglucones.

Conjugation

For the purpose of detoxication, conjugation usually follows oxidation, reduction or hydrolysis of foreign compounds although some compounds are conjugated without previous alteration.

Conjugation is the coupling of a foreign substance or one of its metabolites with a compound occurring normally in the body, to form a detoxified product which is eliminated thereafter. The normally occurring compound of the body is referred to as the conjugating agent. Conjugation in man occurs in the liver. Eight types of conjugation have been recognised and eight conjugating agents are known. These are as follows:

1. Glucuronic acid
2. Sulphuric acid
3. Glycine
4. Cysteine
5. Glutamine
6. Acetic acid
7. Methyl group
8. Thiosulphate

Besides dealing with toxic substances, conjugation occurs also to certain products of metabolism, produced normally in the body. For example, bilirubin, androgen, oestrogen and adrenocortical hormones undergo conjugation with glucuronic acid and sulphate. Here, conjugation helps in maintaining the concentration of the biologically active bilirubin and other hormones in the blood. It also facilitates their excretion from blood in the urine.

Glucuronic acid: This substance is a derivative of glucose, and combination with glucuronic acid for purposes of detoxication is extremely common. Prior to serving as a conjugating agent, glucuronic acid gets activated to form uridine diphosphate glucuronate (UDP glucuronate), the active donor of glucuronic acid.

The conjugated products are excreted in the urine.

Sulphuric acid: Sulphuric acid serves as a conjugating agent for detoxication of compounds with phenolic hydroxyl groups, for example phenol and indole. Phenolic hydroxyl groups combine with sulphuric acid to form esters known as ethereal sulphates and these are excreted in the urine. Prior to conjugation, an enzymatic mechanism is involved by which sulphate is converted in the presence of ATP and Mg^{++} to active sulphate (3′-phosphoadenosine-5′-phosphosulphate), which serves as the donor of sulphuric acid.

$$SO_4^{=} + ATP \longrightarrow \text{Active sulphate}$$

Examples:

1. Phenols with sulphuric acid form phenol sulphate

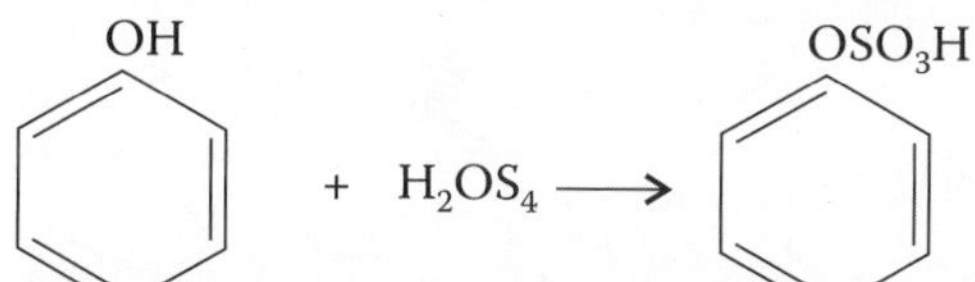

Phenol **Phenol sulphate**

2. Indole (indoxyl) with sulphuric acid forms indoxyl sulphuric acid. Indican is the potassium salt of indole.

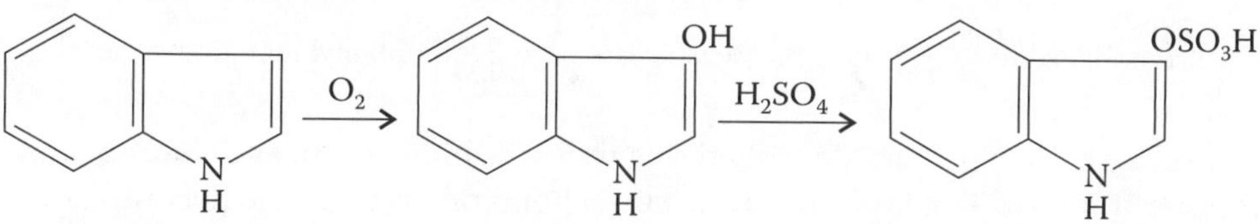

Indole **Indoxyl** **Indoxyl sulphuric acid**

Formation of indican from indole is a well-known reaction of putrefaction of tryptophan in the intestines. Indican is excreted in the urine.

Glycine: This amino acid seems to attach itself particularly to acids. It couples mainly with certain aromatic acids to form aroglycine compounds. Glycine also couples with the carboxyl group of the aliphatic chain of cholic and deoxycholic acids to form glycine conjugates of these bile acids.

A well-known example of conjugation with glycine is the formation of hippuric acid, when an animal is fed with benzoic acid. Hippuric acid is excreted in the urine.

Glycine + Benzoic acid ⟶ Hippuric acid

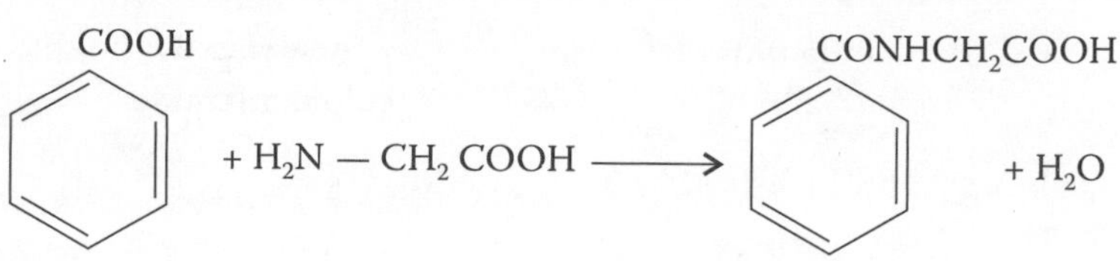

Benzoic acid **Hippuric acid**

Another example is coupling with nicotinic acid to form nicotin uric acid, which is then excreted in the urine.

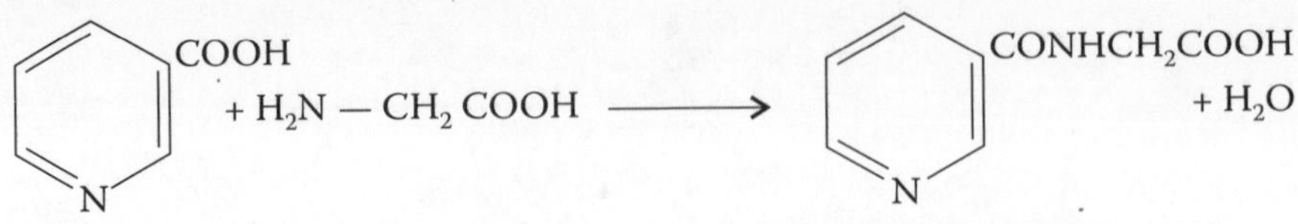

Nicotinic acid **Nicotinuric acid**

Cysteine: Detoxication with cysteine occurs to a limited extent in man. Cysteine couples with certain aromatic compounds such as bromobenzene which then gets acetylated to form the corresponding mercapturic acid derivative.

$$\text{Bromobenzene + Cysteine + Acetic acid} \longrightarrow \text{Bromophenyl mercapturic acid.}$$

Other substances which are detoxified this way are chloro, iodo, and fluorobenzene and naphthalene. They are all converted to the corresponding mercapturic derivatives.

Acetic acid: Acetylation by acetic acid generally involves the amino groups. Sometimes, acetylation of para hydroxyl groups may occur. Formation of acetylcholine is an example of this type.

A well-known example of acetylation of the aromatic amino group is acetylation of para-aminobenzoic acid and sulphanilamide. For this, acetic acid is activated to form activated acetyl-CoA by the action of CoA and ATP. The acetylated derivative is excreted in the urine.

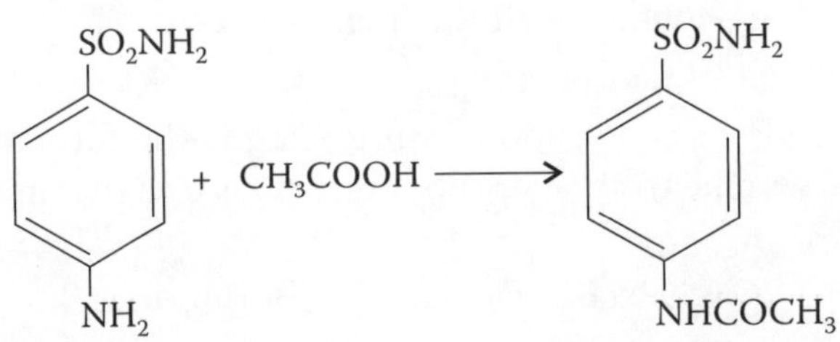

Sulphanilamide **Acetylated sulphanilamide**

Glutamine: Phenylacetic acid is detoxicated by conjugation with glutamine to form phenyl acetylglutamine.

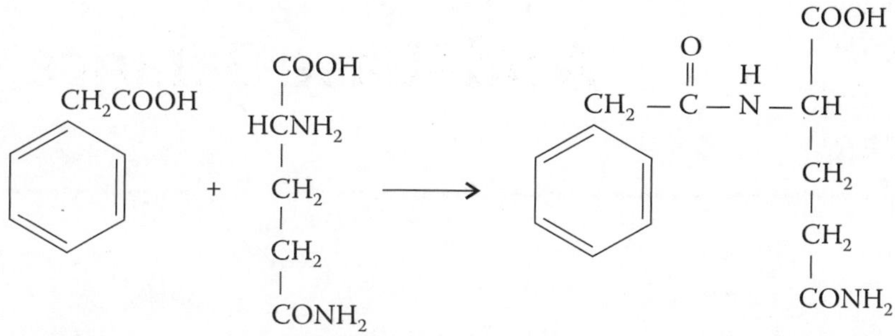

Phenyl accetic acid **Glutamine** **Phenyl acetylglutamine**

Methylation: This mechanism as a detoxication process is rather limited in the body. The methyl donor for such reactions is S-adenosylmethionine. Examples of methylation reactions are as follows:

1. Nicotinamide is conjugated by the methyl group and excreted in urine as methyl nicotinamide.

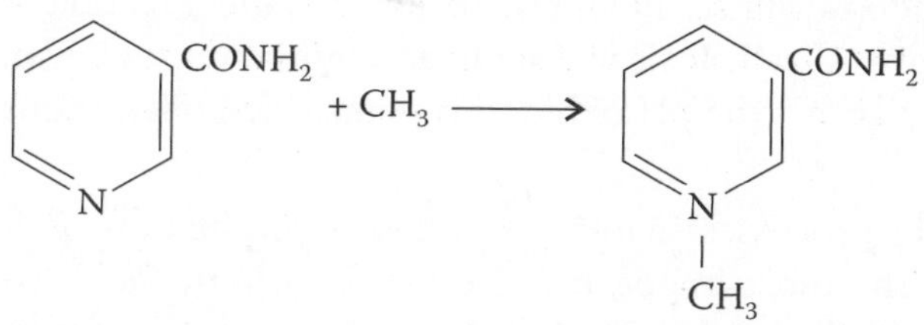

Nicotinamide ***N*-Methylnicotinamide**

2. Norepinephrine is conjugated with the methyl group to form epinephrine.

Thiocyanate formation: Toxic cyanides combine with thiosulphate to form relatively non-toxic thiocyanates. The reaction is catalysed by the enzyme thiosulphate. Cyanide sulphur transferase (rhodonase) found in the saliva is derived from cyanides present in fruits

$$HCN + Na_2S_2O_3 \longrightarrow HCNS + Na_2SO_3.$$

14 CHAPTER

Acid–Base Balance

Chapter Outline

- Buffer Systems of Blood
- Effect of Carbon Dioxide on Blood pH
- Regulation by the Respiratory Mechanism
- Regulation by the Renal Mechanism
- Metabolic and Respiratory Disturbances of Acid–Base Balance

The reaction of blood is faintly alkaline, with a pH range of 7.35–7.45. If the pH falls below 7.3, symptoms of acidosis will set in and pH below 7 is incompatible with life. Similarly, if the pH increases above 7.5, alkalosis will set in and if it increases beyond 7.8, death occurs. Therefore, it is essential that the pH of blood is maintained nearly constant without undue fall or rise.

Normal metabolic processes involve continuous production of fairly large amounts of acid substances. The most important of these is carbonic acid (CO_2); other acids are sulphuric, phosphoric, hydrochloric acids and organic acids such as pyruvic, lactic, uric, acetoacetic and β-hydroxybutyric acids. H_2CO_3 is formed in the process of cellular oxidation. Sulphuric acid is formed by the oxidation of sulphur of ingested protein. Phosphoric acid is formed from the oxidation of phosphorus of ingested proteins, nucleoproteins and phospholipids. The organic acids mentioned above contribute about 80–120 millimoles daily under normal conditions.

Foods also provide a certain amount of basic substances but usually less than acid substances. Both acids and bases are thrown into the bloodstream as they are formed, and the body is faced with the necessity of continuously removing relatively large quantities of them. Further, these substances must be transported to the organs of excretion via the extracellular fluids (ECF) without unduly affecting their H^+ ion concentration which is maintained at pH 7.4 approximately, under normal conditions. The pH of blood remains remarkably constant between pH 7.3 and 7.5, in spite of the constant formation of acid and basic substances. The mechanisms operating in the body to accomplish the maintenance of acid–base balance are outlined as follows:

1. Buffer systems of blood
2. Respiratory mechanisms

3. Renal mechanism
   - Excretion of excess acid or base
   - Formation and excretion of ammonia

At this point, it is necessary to have a clear idea of the two terms 'bases' and 'acids' which are frequently referred to in this chapter.

According to the theory of Brønsted, a base is any substance that combines with the H^+ ion, i.e. protons.

An acid is defined as a substance that yields H^+ ions (protons) in solution. Accordingly, $H_2 + CO_3$ is an acid because, in solution, it dissociates into H^+ and HCO_3^- ions

$$H_2CO_3 \longrightarrow H^+ + HCO_3^-.$$

H^+ is the proton. HCO_3^- is a base because it combines with H^+ ion.

BUFFER SYSTEMS OF BLOOD

Acids and bases after their formation in the cells pass via the extracellular fluids to the site of excretion, i.e. lungs and kidneys, without causing undue change in the pH of the ECF. This is chiefly due to the presence of efficient buffer systems which are present in the fluids and erythrocytes.

Each buffer system consists of a mixture of weak acid (HA) and its salt (BA). The H^+ ion concentration of a buffer system will remain constant if the ratio of the numerator to the denominator remains constant:

$$[H^+] = K\frac{[BA]}{[HA]}.$$

But even slight addition or removal of either acid or base to the buffer system will change the ratio of the H^+ ion concentration of the system.

The important buffers which are present in blood are as follows:

Plasma	Erythrocytes
$\frac{H_2CO_3}{BHCO_3}$	$\frac{H_2CO_3}{BHCO_3}$
$\frac{\text{H. Protein}}{\text{B. Protein}}$	$\frac{HHb}{BHb}$
$\frac{BH_2PO_4}{B_2HPO_4}$	$\frac{HHbO_2}{BHbO_2}$
$\frac{\text{H. Organic acid}}{\text{B. Organic acid}}$	$\frac{BH_2PO_4}{BH_2PO_4}$
	$\frac{\text{H. Organic acid}}{\text{B. Organic acid}}$

The numerators are the acid components and the denominators are their basic salts. Plasma contains H. Protein/B. Protein, but has no Hb system whereas the Hb system of buffers is present in the erythrocytes.

Out of all these buffer systems, only a few are present in fairly high concentration, to be of significance in the regulation of acid–base balance. These are as follows.

In the plasma:

1. The bicarbonate system = $\frac{H_2CO_3}{BHCO_3}$
2. The plasma protein system = $\frac{\text{H. Protein}}{\text{B. Protein}}$

In the erythrocytes:

1. The bicarbonate system = $\frac{H_2CO_3}{BHCO_3}$
2. The HB system = $\frac{HHb}{BHb}, \frac{HHbO_2}{BHbO_2}$

The phosphate pair is less effective, because of its low concentration in plasma. The bicarbonate system which is present in both erythrocyte and plasma is most important, as it acts against fixed, non-volatile acids also. It neutralises more than 50% of all acids stronger than H_2CO_3.

Acids and Alkalies in the Blood

The chief acid present in the blood is CO_2. It is present in solution in the form of H_2CO_3 and is buffered promptly. It yields by dissociation in water, H^+ ions as indicated below:

$$H_2O + CO_2 \rightleftharpoons H_2CO_3 \rightleftharpoons H^+ + HCO_3^-$$

The only alkali present as such in blood is the bicarbonate HCO_3. It dissociates in water as follows:

$$NaHCO_3 + H_2O \longrightarrow H_2CO_3 + Na^+ + OH^-$$

It should be remembered that the presence and the dissociation of bicarbonate will increase the OH^- ion concentration of the solution, thereby increasing its alkalinity. Basic radicals such as Na^+, K^+, Ca^{++} and Mg^{++} ions are consumed in large amounts in an ordinary diet, especially in vegetable food, and they must be promptly disposed off to prevent excessive alkalinity of the blood.

Formation of Carbon Dioxide and Its Distribution in Blood

CO_2 is formed in large amounts in the body as the end product of normal metabolism. In tissues, about 200 ml of CO_2 is formed per minute at rest and 4 litres in maximal exercise. CO_2 enters the bloodstream and from there it reaches the lungs.

In the blood, during rest, 100 ml of arterial blood contains 48 ml of CO_2, of which 35.6 ml (75%) is present in the plasma and 12.6 ml (25%) in the red blood cells (RBC). The distribution of CO_2 in plasma and RBC is graphically illustrated in **Figure 14.1**.

The amount of CO_2 (35.6 ml) in the plasma is present in three forms:

1. About 1.6 ml of CO_2 is present in solution with water to form H_2CO_3.
2. About 34 ml is present as bicarbonate, combined with sodium to form $NaHCO_3$.
3. A very small amount of CO_2 is present as a carbamino compound, which is a combination of the amino groups of plasma proteins.

The amount of CO_2 (12.6 ml) in the RBC is present in the following three forms:

1. About 0.8 ml of CO_2 is present in solution with water to form H_2CO_3.
2. About 9.6 ml is present as bicarbonate, combined with sodium to form $NaHCO_3$.
3. About 2.2 ml of CO_2 is present as carbamino compounds. Haemoglobin contains NH_2 groups which form a carbamino compound with CO_2.

It is the amount of CO_2 which is present in solution with water to form H_2CO_3 that contributes to the acidity of the blood and needs buffering. This corresponds to 1.6 ml of CO_2 in plasma and 0.8 ml of CO_2 in RBC, per 100 ml of blood.

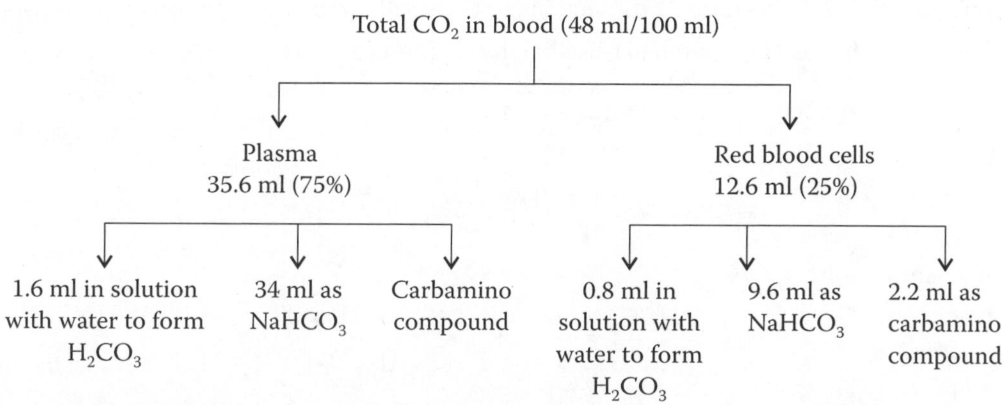

Figure 14.1 Graphic illustration of the distribution of CO_2 in blood.

Carbamino Compound

Some amount of CO_2 forms carbamino compounds with Hb, by combination with the free NH_2 groups in haemoglobin. The compound is called carbamino haemoglobin.

$$Hb{\cdot}NH_2 + CO_2 \rightleftharpoons Hb{\cdot}NHCOOH.$$

The major portion of carbamino compounds is in the red blood cells (2.2 ml/100 ml of blood) because of the presence of a large amount of amino groups in the Hb. The concentration of carbamino haemoglobin is more in the venous blood which also contains more reduced Hb (**HHb**).

EFFECT OF CARBON DIOXIDE ON BLOOD pH

Henderson–Hasselbalch equation: It has been calculated that at the pH of blood (7.4), a ratio of 20:1 must exist between the fractions of bicarbonate and carbonic acid. This ratio is calculated from the Henderson–Hasselbalch equation as follows:

The H^+ ion concentration of a weak acid solution HA and its salt BA is represented as

$$(H^+) = \frac{BA}{HA}; \quad K = [H^+]$$

Here K is the dissociation constant, H^+ is the concentration of hydrogen ions, HA is the concentration of the acid and BA is the concentration of the salt.

It means that the H^+ ion concentration of such a buffer pair will remain constant if the ratio of the numerator to the denominator remains constant.

In a logarithmic form, the relation is written as follows:

$$pH = pK + \log \frac{BA}{HA}$$

$$pK \text{ for } H_2CO_3 \text{ is } 6.1$$

To keep pH at 7.4, the ratio of these acids to their salts must be kept constant.

Substituting in the Henderson–Hasselbalch equation for H_2CO_3,

$$7.4 = 6.1 + \log \frac{BHCO_3}{H_2CO_3}$$

$$1.3 = \log \frac{BHCO_3}{H_2CO_3}$$

Since antilog of 1.3 = 20,

$$\frac{BHCO_3}{H_2CO_3} = \frac{20}{1} \quad \text{or} \quad \frac{20}{1} = \frac{BHCO_3}{H_2CO_3}$$

Any increase or decrease in H^+ ion concentration will be met by an adjustment in this reaction. As long as this ratio is maintained, the pH of the blood will be normal, but when this ratio is altered, the acid–base balance of the blood will be disturbed.

The CO_2 which is present as H_2CO_3, both in the plasma and in RBC, are buffered promptly by two buffer systems. They are as follows:

1. Hb buffer system
2. Plasma proteins buffer system

Haemoglobin Buffer System

Action on H_2CO_3

The buffering capacity of Hb is attributed to the effect of the imidazole groups, which are constituents of the histidine components of the globins of Hb in the erythrocytes. It is assumed that, within the range of pH 7.0–7.45, the buffering capacity of the imidazole groups of the histidine components is dependent on their degree of dissociation, which in turn is dependent on the degree of oxygenation of Hb.

Thus, if the Hb is more oxygenated, the imidazole groups become more acidic and therefore more dissociated and consequently, the buffering capacity is also increased. Oxygenated Hb (HbO_2) is a stronger acid than reduced Hb.

When the Hb is less oxygenated or contains no oxygen as in the case of reduced Hb (Hb), the imidazole groups become less acidic and therefore less dissociated and consequently the buffering capacity is also decreased.

The formation of HbO_2 in the lungs, its dissociation and conversion to HHb in tissues, and disposal of H^+ ions as CO_2 by the lungs are illustrated in **Figure 14.2**.

In the tissues where O_2 tension is reduced, HbO_2 dissociates delivering O_2 to the cells and forms reduced Hb.

$$HbO_2 \rightleftharpoons Hb + O_2$$

At the same time, CO_2 produced in the course of metabolism enters the blood, where it is hydrated to form H_2CO_3 which promptly ionises to form $H^+ + HCO_3^-$.

$$CO_2 + H_2O \rightleftharpoons H_2CO_3 \rightleftharpoons H^+ + HCO_3^-$$

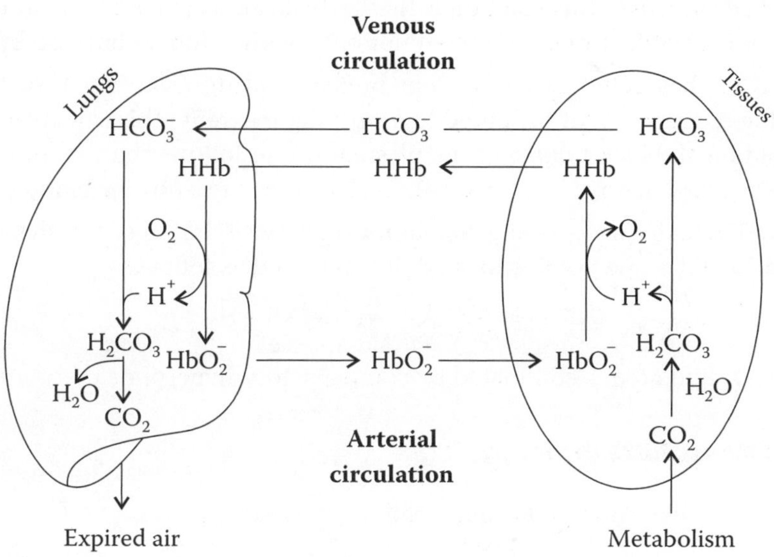

Figure 14.2 Buffering action of haemoglobin.

Reduced Hb acting as an anion accepts the H^+ ions, forming the so-called acid-reduced Hb (HHb); very little change in pH occurs, because the newly arrived H^+ ions are buffered by the formation of a very weak acid, i.e. one in which ionisation is suppressed.

$$Hb + H^+ \longrightarrow HHb$$

When the blood returns to the lungs, HHb combines with O_2 to form HbO_2 and H^+ is liberated.

$$HHb + O_2 \rightleftharpoons HbO_2 + H^+$$

The newly formed H^+ ions react with bicarbonate [HCO_3^-] to form H_2CO_3. Because of the low CO_2 tension in the lungs, the equilibrium shifts towards the production of CO_2 which is continually eliminated in the expired air.

$$HCO_3^- + H^+ \rightleftharpoons H_2CO_3 \rightleftharpoons H_2O + CO_2\uparrow$$

Buffer System for Fixed Acids

When any non-volatile acids such as lactic, phosphoric or sulphuric acid enter the bloodstream, they at once interact with the bicarbonate present in the plasma, i.e. $H_2CO_3/BHCO_3$ buffer system, as shown below:

1. $HCl + NaHCO_3 \longrightarrow H_2CO_3 + NaCl$
2. $HL + NaHCO_3 \longrightarrow NaL + H_2CO_3$

In each case, the salts NaCl and NaL are formed with liberation of carbonic acid. The salts get excreted by the kidneys, and carbonic acid being volatile is eliminated by the lungs. The advantage of this reaction is that lactic acid, which is a comparatively strong acid and also non-volatile, can get excreted not only by the kidneys but also by the lungs.

Thus, $NaHCO_3$ has acted as an efficient buffer, clearing away much of the H^+ ions, thereby altering the reaction of the blood to a very slight extent. This is why the term 'alkali reserve' is used for the bicarbonate of the plasma. It also follows that, as long as $NaHCO_3$ is present in the plasma, no acid stronger than H_2CO_3 can exist in the blood as such.

Buffering of HL takes place during violent muscular exercise. In severe diabetes mellitus and starvation, acid ketone HAK is formed. It is buffered as follows:

$$HAK + NaHCO_3 \rightleftharpoons NaAK + H_2CO_3$$

The extra CO_2 liberated is eliminated by compensatory hyperpnoea.

Protein and Phosphate Buffer System

These may also be involved in buffering action but to a minor extent.

$$\text{Protein} + H^+ \rightleftharpoons H^+ \text{ Protein}$$

$$HPO_4^{=} + H^+ \rightleftharpoons H_2PO_4^-$$

If a fixed base, for example NaOH, enters the extracellular fluid, it reacts with the acid components of these buffer systems, chiefly H_2CO_3, as follows:

$$H_2CO_3 + NaOH \rightleftharpoons NaHCO_3 + H_2O$$

$$H^+ \text{ protein} + NaOH \rightleftharpoons Na\cdot\text{protein} + H_2O$$

$$H_2PO_4^- + NaOH \rightleftharpoons Na\cdot HPO_4^{=} + H_2O$$

Isohydric Transport of CO_2

At a pH of 7.25, 1 mmol of HbO_2 yields 1.88 mEq of H^+ ion whereas 1 mmol of Hb which is less ionised yields only 1.28 mEq of H^+ ion.

This shows that reduced Hb, which is a weaker acid than HbO_2, has a higher H^+ ion-binding capacity than HbO_2. It yields only 1.28 mEq of H^+ ion and binds 0.6 (1.88–1.28) mEq more of H^+ ion.

Similarly, in the tissue capillaries, the elimination of each mmol of O_2 (from HbO_2) permits binding of 0.6 mEq more of H^+ ion, by Hb to form HHb.

This also permits the formation of 0.6 mmol of $BHCO_3^-$ derived from 0.6 mmol of CO_2 without causing any change in the pH. It should be noted that in the tissues, 0.6 mmol of H^+ ion is completely buffered as a result of the reduction of HbO_2 to form HHb. The buffering of H^+ ions by the Hb without causing any change in the pH is called **isohydric action**.

Chloride Shift or Hamberger's Phenomenon

It has been found that 60% of the buffering capacity of blood is due to Hb and another 25% is contributed by the phosphate buffer system in the red blood cells. Thus, 85% of buffering action takes place inside the red blood cells. But most of the buffered CO_2 is carried as bicarbonate in the plasma.

The process by which the buffered CO_2 appears in the plasma and circulates as $NaHCO_3$ is described by the chloride bicarbonate shift phenomenon or **Hamberger's phenomenon** (**Fig. 14.3**).

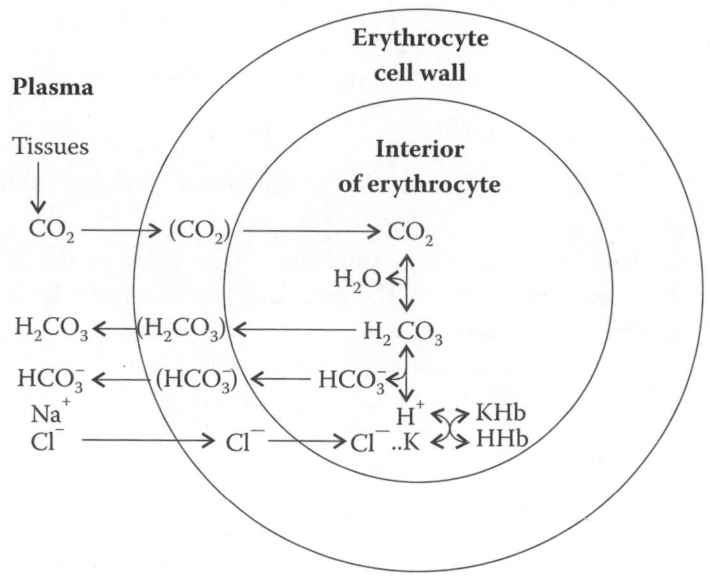

Figure 14.3 Chloride shift mechanism.

When CO_2 liberated from tissue metabolism enters the erythrocytes, it combines with H_2O to form H_2CO_3 readily, because of the catalytic action of carbonic anhydrase, an enzyme present in the erythrocytes. The same enzyme can also dissociate H_2CO_3 to $H_2O + CO_2$ equally rapidly.

$$H_2O + CO_2 \rightleftharpoons H_2CO_3$$

The erythrocyte wall is permeable to CO_2, HCO_3^-, Cl^- and H^+ ions.

Another fact that should be remembered is that most of the sodium ions are in the plasma and most of the potassium ions are inside the cells. In the erythrocytes, a good portion of Hb combines with potassium to form KHb. Sodium is present in the plasma as NaCl.

The concentration of H_2CO_3 which is formed by the action of carbonic anhydrase inside the erythrocytes increases.

H_2CO_3 dissociates to H^+ and HCO_3^- ions.

The H^+ ion is buffered by the intracellular buffer, mainly KHb. The reactions may be summarised as follows:

$$CO_2 + H_2O \xrightleftharpoons{\textit{Carbonic anhydrase}} H_2CO_3$$

$$H_2CO_3 \rightleftharpoons H^+ + HCO_3^- \text{ (diffuses outside the cell)}$$

$$H^+ + KHb \rightleftharpoons K^+ + HHb$$

$$\text{also, } KHCO_3 \rightleftharpoons K^+ + HCO_3^-$$

$$K^+ + Cl^- \text{ (from outside)} \longrightarrow KCl$$

$$NaCl \longrightarrow Na^+ \text{ (outside the cell)} + Cl^- \text{ (diffuses inside the cell)}$$

$$Na + HCO_3^- \longrightarrow NaHCO_3$$

The erythrocyte wall is permeable to HCO_3^- ion which therefore diffuses from the erythrocytes into the plasma.

According to the laws of membrane equilibrium, the ratios of the concentration of individual diffusible monovalent ions in the cells and plasma must be equal, as shown below:

$$\frac{[HCO_3^-]\text{ cells}}{[HCO_3^-]\text{ plasma}} = \frac{[Cl^-]\text{ cells}}{[Cl^-]\text{ plasma}}$$

Therefore, as HCO_3 ion passes from the erythrocytes into the plasma, Cl^- ion which was balanced by Na^+ ion from the plasma passes in the opposite direction into the cells.

As the electrical neutrality of the cell and plasma fluids should be preserved, the numbers of negative ions, i.e. Cl^- and HCO_3 exchanged, must be identical. The Cl^- ion entering inside the erythrocytes is balanced electrically by the K^+ ions which were previously balanced by HCO_3^- ion and Hb while the HCO_3^- ions entering the plasma are balanced by the Na^+ ions previously balanced by the diffused Cl^- ion. As a result of these changes, most of the HCO_3^- ions, although formed originally in the erythrocytes, are actually transported in the plasma. Without this ionic exchange, almost the entire uptake of CO_2 as bicarbonate would occur in the erythrocytes. It has been shown that about 70% of the added CO_2 is transported in the blood as bicarbonate, of which about 60% is carried in the plasma and the rest in the erythrocytes.

It should be noted that all these reactions are reversed in the lungs where the blood becomes arterial and chloride from inside the cells shifts back into the plasma, thus liberating the intracellular potassium to buffer the newly formed oxyhaemoglobin. In the plasma, the diffused Cl^- ion combines with Na^+ ion which is liberated by the removal of CO_2 during respiration.

Carbonic anhydrase: This is an enzyme, present in the erythrocytes, closely associated with haemoglobin. In the purified form, carbonic anhydrase is shown to be a protein, containing one atom of zinc per molecule. It specifically catalyses the splitting of H_2CO_3 to H_2O and CO_2. The reversible reaction ($CO_2 + H_2O \rightleftharpoons H_2CO_3$), which takes place in tissues, is also catalysed by carbonic anhydrase.

Carbonic anhydrase is present in a large amount in the parietal cells of the stomach, where it helps in the formation of HCl. It is also present in the distal tubules of the kidney, where it is involved in the secretion of H^+ ions. Carbonic anhydrase is present in smaller amounts in muscle tissue, pancreas and spermatozoa.

Buffering Action of Plasma Proteins

CO_2 is buffered only to a lesser extent by the plasma protein buffer system $\frac{\text{H. protein}}{\text{B. protein}}$ and this occurs as shown below:

$$CO_2 \text{ from } H_2CO_3$$

$$CO_2 + H_2O \rightleftharpoons H_2CO_3$$

$$H_2CO_3 + \text{B. Protein} \rightleftharpoons BHCO_3 + H^+ \text{ protein}$$

H^+ protein is a weaker acid compared to H_2CO_3.

REGULATION BY THE RESPIRATORY MECHANISM

The respiratory mechanism plays an important role in the regulation of acid–base balance, mainly because

1. The respiratory centre is sensitive to very slight changes in pH and PCO_2
2. CO_2 readily diffuses from the blood into the alveolar air across the pulmonary alveolar membrane

An increase in the blood PCO_2, say by 1.5 mmHg, or a slight increase in the H^+ ion concentration of the blood results in a 100% increase in pulmonary ventilation, due to the stimulation of the respiratory centre.

The increased respiration helps removal of the excess CO_2 from the extracellular fluids into the expired air. Similarly, a fall in blood PCO_2 or H^+ ion concentration produces depression in the activity of the respiratory centre, leading to slow, shallow respiration, hypoventilation and retention of CO_2 in the blood. This continues until the blood regains normal PCO_2 and restoration of pH. Thus, the respiratory mechanism greatly helps to maintain the normal ratio of $H_2CO_3/BHCO_3$ as 1/20, in extracellular fluids, in spite of constant addition of H_2CO_3 formed by metabolic activity.

REGULATION BY THE RENAL MECHANISM

The lungs can deal only with the volatile acid (CO_2) effectively but not with fixed acids or bases. Non-volatile fixed acids, such as lactic, pyruvic, hydrochloric, phosphoric and sulphuric acids which are continuously produced, are effectively buffered by the bicarbonate system, but at the expense of the **alkali reserve** $BHCO_3$, which is the chief component of the buffer system available for this purpose. Consequently, the alkali reserve of the body would eventually be exhausted if $BHCO_3$ is not restored promptly. Lungs can only eliminate the H_2CO_3 but cannot restore the alkali reserve.

This can be done by the kidneys which are the ultimate regulators of the acid–base balance. Kidneys provide the most important final defense mechanism for the regulation of acid–base balance of the fluids. Kidneys work more slowly than the lungs, but when fully in action, they are extremely effective. They contribute in maintaining the alkali reserve by reabsorbing, secreting and excreting acidic or basic substances, as and when necessary.

The reaction of the urine varies with the blood reaction. Under normal conditions, the pH of urine is about 6.0 and that of plasma is 7.4. The increase in the titrable acidity of urine is due to the acid substances removed from the plasma, by renal action.

In **acidaemia**, the urine is highly acidic. The maximal attainable acidity is pH 4.5. Excess acid is eliminated by excretion in urine. In **alkalaemia**, the urine is highly alkaline and the maximal alkalinity may reach pH 8.2. Excess alkali is eliminated by excretion in urine. It is this capacity of the kidney to excrete excess acid or alkali in the urine that contributes to the maintenance of the normal H^+ ion concentration of the body fluids. The H^+ ions secreted by the tubular cells are handled primarily in three ways, namely

1. Reabsorption of bicarbonate
2. Buffering by the phosphate buffer system
3. Formation of ammonia (NH3)

These three processes are considered under the following headings:

1. Bicarbonate mechanism
2. Phosphate mechanism
3. Ammonia mechanism

Bicarbonate mechanism: The kidneys regulate acid–base balance by two mechanisms:

- Bicarbonate reabsorption
- Bicarbonate generation

Bicarbonate reabsorption: At a normal plasma bicarbonate level, 90% of the bicarbonate filtered at the glomeruli is reabsorbed in the proximal tubules and the remainder in the distal tubules. The sequence of reactions is as follows (**Fig. 14.4**):

(i) Bicarbonate (HCO_3^-) is filtered through glomeruli.

(ii) The filtered bicarbonate combines with H^+ secreted by the tubular cells and forms H_2CO_3.

$$HCO_3^- + H^+ \longrightarrow H_2CO_3$$

(iii) H_2CO_3 dissociates to CO_2 and H_2O in the proximal tubule. The reactions are catalysed by carbonic anhydrase present within the tubular lumen.

$$H_2CO_3 \longrightarrow CO_2 + H_2O$$

(iv) This CO_2 diffuses into the tubular cells, along a concentration gradient.

(v) Inside the tubular cells, carbonic anhydrase catalyses the combination of CO_2 with H_2O to form H_2CO_3 and the newly formed H_2CO_3 dissociates into H^+ and HCO_3.

$$H_2O + CO_2 \longrightarrow H_2CO_3 \longrightarrow HCO_3^- + H^+$$

H^+ is secreted into the tubular fluid and is exchanged for Na^+ from the tubular filtrate.

(vi) HCO_3^- formed in the same reaction diffuses into the extracellular fluid accompanied by the reabsorbed Na^+.

This process is **reabsorption of bicarbonate**. The H^+ secreted in the tubular fluid repeats the reactions from (ii) (**Fig. 14.4**).

Bicarbonate generation: In this mechanism, operating in the renal tubular cell, there is net loss of H^+ from the body as well as net gain of HCO_3^-. Whenever a mmol of H^+ is secreted into the urine, a mmol of HCO_3^- passes into the extracellular fluid with sodium. The bicarbonate is formed in the cell and is derived from cellular CO_2 and not from filtered bicarbonate and therefore represents a net gain of bicarbonate (**Fig. 14.5**). Bicarbonate generation coupled with H^+ ion secretion is well suited for correcting acidosis. Continued secretion of H^+ and generation of HCO_3^- depend on the presence of other filtered buffers (B^- in **Fig. 14.5**). In their absence, the acidity in the tubular lumen will increase and further H^+ secretion will be inhibited.

Renal ion exchange mechanism: The bicarbonate mechanism depends on the formation of H^+ and HCO_3^- from CO_2 and H_2O within the tubular cells, by the action of carbonic anhydrase present in the tubular cells. The H^+ formed in this reaction is actively secreted into the tubular fluid in exchange for Na^+. At this point, Na^+ has been reabsorbed in exchange for H^+ ions and sodium bicarbonate has been generated within the tubule cell. The sodium and bicarbonate are then pumped out of the cell into the extracellular fluid. The exchange of Na^+ for H^+ in this reaction is referred to as **ion exchange mechanism**.

Phosphate mechanism: *Buffering by phosphate buffers:* Some H^+ ions secreted by the tubular cells are buffered by the phosphate buffer system $HPO_4^=/H_2PO_4^-$ in the urine (**Fig. 14.6**). Na_2^{++} $HPO_4^=$ and Na^+ $H_2PO_4^-$ that are excreted in varying proportions depending on the pH of the blood constitute the principal buffers in the urine. Under

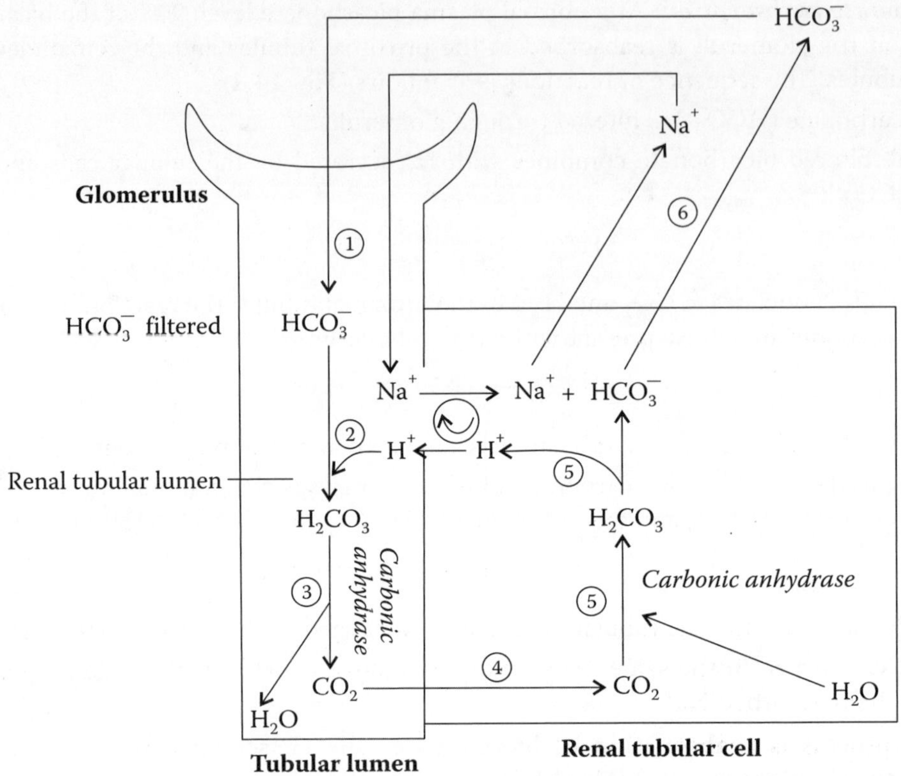

Figure 14.4 Bicarbonate reabsorption by renal tubular cells.

normal conditions, the glomerular filtrate contains Na_2^{++} $HPO_4^=$ and $Na{+}H_2PO_4^-$ in the ratio of 4:1.

$$\frac{Na_2^{++}\ HPO_4^=}{Na^+\ H_2PO_4^-} = \frac{4}{1}$$

But at pH 4.8, i.e. at maximal acidity, the ratio of $Na{+}H_2PCO_4^-$ to $Na_2^{++}HPO_4^=$ in the glomerular filtrate will be 99:1.

$$\frac{Na^+\ H_2PO_4^-}{Na_2^{++}\ HPO_4^=} = \frac{99}{1}$$

In extreme acidaemia, practically all the $BHCO_3^-$ is reabsorbed in the tubules and the phosphates are excreted in the form of Na^+ $H_2PO_4^-$, the acid component of the buffer system. There is no excretion of $BHCO_3^-$. The conversion to acid phosphate and the process of acidification of urine take place in the distal tubular cells, as illustrated in **Figure 14.6.** The metabolic CO_2 formed in the cells is rapidly converted to H_2CO_3 by the action of carbonic anhydrase present in the tubule cells **(Fig. 14.6)**.

Ammonia mechanism: Under ordinary dietary conditions, a normal adult excretes 30–50 mEq of ammonia daily. But the urinary ammonia increases, if the plasma H^+ ion concentration rises. A decrease of urinary ammonia occurs in alkalosis.

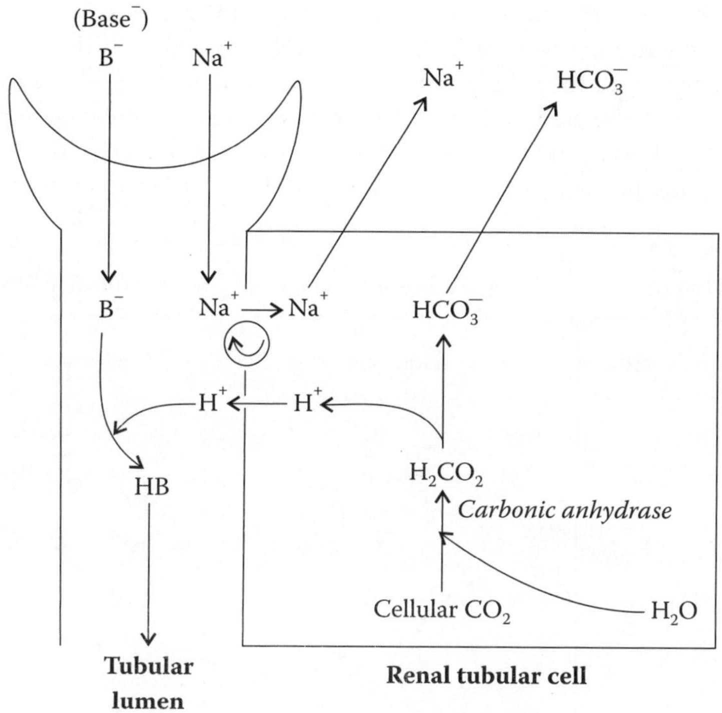

Figure 14.5 Bicarbonate generation of renal tubular cells.

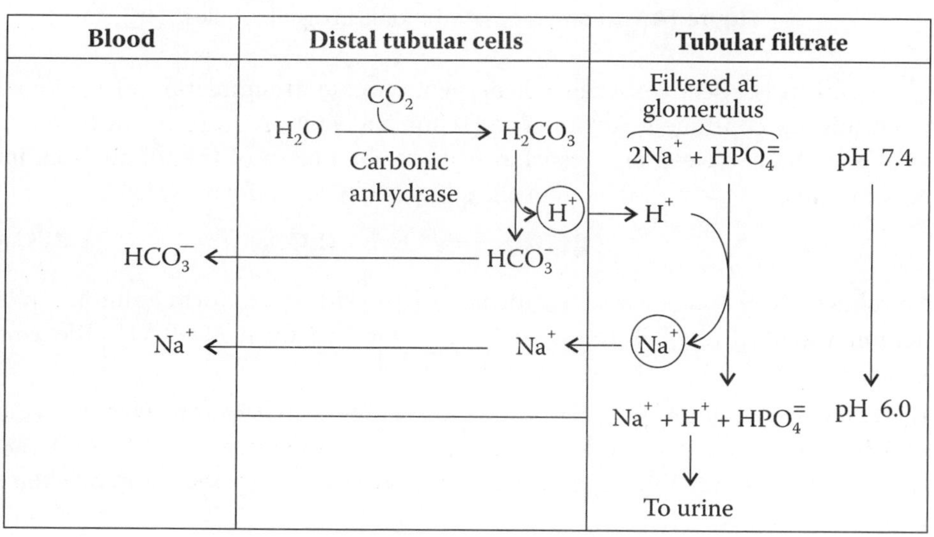

Figure 14.6 Buffering of H^+ ions by phosphate buffer.

It is important to note that the urinary ammonia is formed in the cells of the distal tubules which is also the site of acidification of urine (**Fig. 14.7**). About 60% of ammonia is derived from glutamine. Glutaminase hydrolyses glutamate into glutamine and NH_3 in the renal mitochondria. The remaining 40% is derived from the amino groups of amino acids by oxidative deamination. The gaseous ammonia (NH_3) formed in the distal tubular cells diffuses into the lumen of the tubules and enters the tubular fluid, where it combines with the H^+ ion present in the acidified urine to form NH_4^+ ions. It must be remembered that NH_3 is a gas and NH_4^+ is an alkaline radicle which cannot exist freely. The NH_4^+ radicle acts as a cation and combines with anions such as Cl^- and SO_4^- to form ammonium salts.

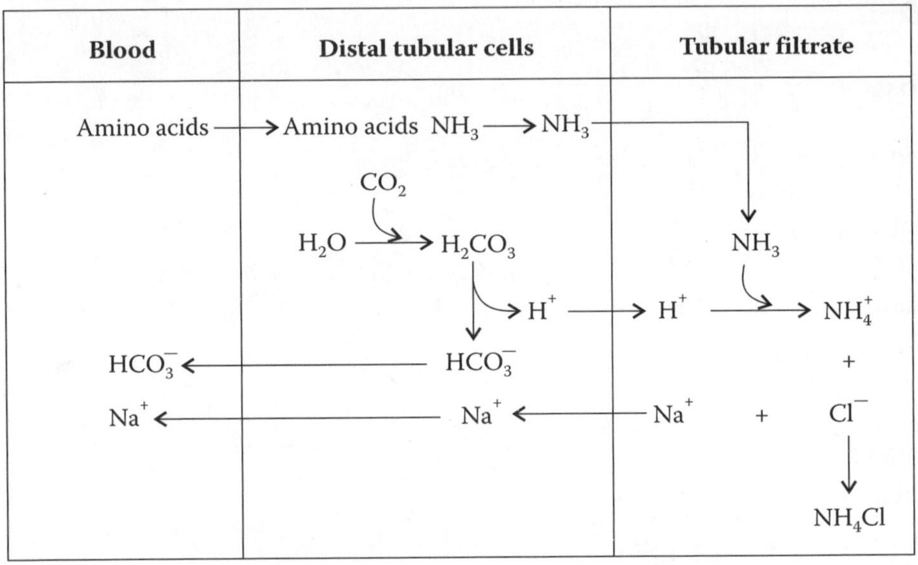

Figure 14.7 Formation of ammonia in distal tubules.

The mechanism is effective because it prevents undue accumulation of H^+ ions in the fluid by permitting continued exchange of H^+ for Na^+ ions. As a result of this, a certain amount of fixed base is freed and transferred from the lumen of the tubule back into the blood. For example, in blood, HL is neutralised by $NaHCO_3$ to form NaL.

$$HL + NaHCO_3 \longrightarrow NaL + H_2CO_3$$

In the tubules, NaL reacts with NH_3 formed by the kidneys to form ammonium lactate. The Na^+ ion which is freed is returned to the blood to form $NaHCO_3$. The ammonia mechanism thus spares the fixed base, i.e. alkali reserve of the plasma.

By the efficiency of ammonia mechanism, the kidneys make more NH_3 in acidaemia, to deal with the excess of acid radicles and less NH_3 or none at all in alkalaemia, because excess base is already available. The urinary ammonia is thus increased in acidaemia and decreased in alkalaemia.

Alkali Reserve

The plasma bicarbonate is known as 'alkali reserve' because, among the plasma electrolytes, bicarbonate plays an important role in the process of neutralisation of the acidic compounds, which enter the blood and tissues. Plasma bicarbonate forms the first line of defense when any acid substance is introduced into the body. Any tendency to tilt the acid–base balance of the body will disturb the normal pattern of bicarbonate and carbonic acid ratio from 20:1. The pH of the blood which ranges from 7.35 to 7.45 either decreases causing acidosis or increases causing alkalosis.

METABOLIC AND RESPIRATORY DISTURBANCES OF ACID–BASE BALANCE

Acidosis and Alkalosis

The normal pH of plasma varies from 7.35 to 7.45. At pH 7.4, the ratio of HCO_3^-/H_2CO_3 (pCO_2) is 20:1 and the total CO_2 is 25–28 mmol/L.

Acidosis is a condition when the pH of the plasma falls below 7.4 and the ratio of HCO_3^-/pCO_2 is less than 20.

Alkalosis is a condition when the pH of blood tends to rise above 7.4. At this pH, the ratio of HCO_3^-/pCO_2 is above 20.

Changes in the values of the ratio and pH may result from pulmonary or metabolic dysfunction. If the imbalance is caused by an alteration of pCO_2, it is respiratory in origin. Conversely, an alteration in HCO_3^- is considered to be of metabolic origin.

Acidosis and alkalosis are classified as follows:

1. (a) Respiratory acidosis
   (b) Respiratory alkalosis
2. (a) Metabolic acidosis
   (b) Metabolic alkalosis

Respiratory Causes

All individuals in health or sickness produce large amounts of acids every day. The major acid is H_2CO_3. This acid is volatile and is normally exhaled by lungs as CO_2. Inability of the lungs to perform this task adequately leads to respiratory acidosis or alkalosis.

Respiratory acidosis: It arises as a result of hypoventilation of the alveoli and CO_2 accumulates in the body. The rate of respiration is diminished. The plasma pCO_2 is elevated.

The common causes of respiratory acidosis are as follows:

1. Chronic obstructive pulmonary diseases (COPD), namely emphysema and heart failure with pulmonary oedema
2. Diseases of the central nervous system and neuromuscular disorders
3. Inadequate artificial respiration

Respiratory alkalosis: It arises as a result of hyperventilation and elimination of an excessive amount of CO_2 from the body. The rate of respiration is increased. The plasma pCO_2 is decreased.

The most common cause of hyperventilation is due to anxiety. Hyperventilation may arise due to hysteria, high altitude, anaemia, central nervous system injury involving respiratory centre, salicylate poisoning and in fever.

Metabolic Causes

Increased production of metabolic acids can produce reduction in the plasma HCO_3^- content. Conversely, retention of abnormal amounts of alkalies can produce an increase in the plasma HCO_3^- content.

Metabolic acidosis: In this condition, there is **reduction of plasma HCO_3^- content**. Metabolic acidosis can be caused due to either accumulation of acids or loss of bicarbonate from the body. Accumulation of acids is observed in the following conditions.

1. *Diabetic ketoacidosis:* Due to excess production of ketone bodies
2. *Acute renal failure:* There is decreased excretion of H^+ due to tubular dysfunction in acute renal failure. In chronic renal failure, there is increased excretion of bicarbonate in urine and this is due to inadequate reabsorption of bicarbonate by the renal tubular cells.
3. *Lactic acidosis:* Overproduction of lactic acid can occur when there is an increase in anaerobic metabolism and tissue oxygen is depleted. A good example is muscular exercise. Other conditions where lactic acidosis occurs are during shock and during convulsion.
4. *Starvation:* Excessive production of ketone bodies leads to ketosis in starvation.
5. Severe diarrhoea causes excessive loss of HCO_3^- from the body due to loss of alkaline pancreatic secretion.
6. *Ingestion of methanol:* Methanol is oxidised to formic acid (HCOOH) in the body, resulting in acidosis.
7. *Salicylate intoxication:* Plasma HCO_3^- is lowered. Severe HCO_3^- depletion leads to metabolic acidosis.

Metabolic alkalosis: The primary defect in metabolic alkalosis is **increase in plasma HCO_3^-**. Metabolic alkalosis can arise from

1. Intake of excess alkali. An alkali commonly taken by many people is sodium bicarbonate.
2. Abnormal loss of acid from the body can occur in protracted vomiting as in pyloric stenosis or gastric lavage when gastric HCl is lost.
3. Rapid loss of body water as in diuresis can temporarily increase the plasma HCO_3^- content and cause metabolic alkalosis.

Compensatory Mechanisms

At normal pH 7.4 of blood, the ratio of HCO_3^-/PCO_2 is 20:1 and the total blood HCO_3^- is 22–26 mEq/L.

Alteration in these values can arise from pulmonary or metabolic dysfunction, producing either acidosis or alkalosis. The four primary types of acid–base imbalance that can produce such alterations are respiratory acidosis, respiratory alkalosis, metabolic acidosis and metabolic alkalosis.

Respiratory acidosis arises from carbonic acid excess and there is an increased plasma pCO_2.

Respiratory alkalosis is caused by carbonic acid deficit and there is a decreased plasma pCO_2.

In **metabolic acidosis,** there is a bicarbonate deficit and there is decreased plasma HCO_3^-.

In **metabolic alkalosis,** there is bicarbonate excess and there is an increase in plasma HCO_3^-.

In any of the above conditions, the pH of plasma will be abnormal and the ratio HCO_3^-/PCO_2 will be less than 20 in acidosis and greater than 20 in alkalosis. These four conditions are **uncompensated acidosis** and **alkalosis.**

Various compensatory mechanisms begin to operate, when the plasma pH deviates from the normal range. The general principle of compensation is that, since an abnormal condition has altered one of the factors of the HCO_3^-/pCO_2 ratio, the pH can be readjusted back towards the normal, by a compensatory alteration of the other factor of the ratio. If HCO_3^- changes, the original HCO_3^-/PCO_2 ratio can be restored by changing pCO_2, in the same direction. If the primary change is in pCO_2, the original ratio can be restored only by altering HCO_3^- in the same direction. The immediate response is hypoventilation followed by increased renal excretion of HCO_3^-. As a result of hypoventilation, the plasma pCO_2 increases.

Normal values of arterial blood gases and pH:

pH = 7.34–7.44

pCO_2 = 35–45 mmHg

pO_2 = 80–100 mmHg

HCO_3^- = 22–26 mEq/L

The changes in the plasma buffer constituents in uncompensated and compensated acidosis and alkalosis are shown in **Table 14.1**.

Table 14.1 Acid–Base Balance Disturbances—Compensatory Mechanisms

Buffer Constituents	Average Normal Value	Acidosis				Alkalosis			
		Metabolic		Respiratory		Metabolic		Respiratory	
	N	U	C	U	C	U	C	U	C
pH	7.4	↓	N	↓	N	↑	N	↑	N
HCO_3^-/PCO_2	20	↓	N	↓	N	↑	N	↑	N
HCO_3 (mmol/L)	22–26	↓	↓	N	↑	↑	↑	N	↓
pCO_2 (mmHg)	35–45	N	↓	↑	↑	N	↑	↓	↓

U, uncompensated; C, compensated
↑ = increase
↓ = decrease
N = Normal

15 CHAPTER
Methods of Investigating Intermediary Metabolism

Chapter Outline

- General Methods
- Isotope Methods

GENERAL METHODS

Intermediary metabolism refers to the sequence of chemical reactions undergone by the foodstuffs, from the time of ingestion to excretion of the metabolic products. This is diagrammatically represented in **Figure 15.1**.

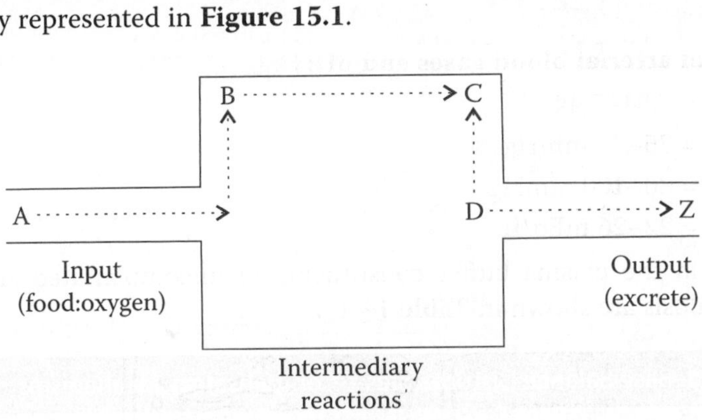

Figure 15.1 Diagrammatic representation of intermediary metabolism.

In **Figure 15.1**, 'A' represents the foodstuffs entering the body. 'Z' represents waste products which are excreted. During the interval between ingestion of 'A' and excretion of 'Z', 'A' undergoes a series of changes by getting converted in stages to intermediary metabolites B, C and D. The identity of the intermediary metabolites is difficult and requires study by applying special methods.

Investigation of the intermediary metabolism may be conducted in vivo and in vitro. 'In vivo' means investigation in the living organism. 'In vitro' means investigation in a glass vessel. We will first deal with 'in vivo' methods and then proceed to 'in vitro' methods.

'In Vivo' Methods

A few important techniques applied in the study of 'in vivo' methods are discussed below.

1. Feeding animals with the chemical under investigation
2. Administration of enzyme inhibitors
3. Surgical removal of organs
4. Inducing genetic variants

Feeding animals with chemicals: The oldest 'in vivo' method consists in feeding or injecting a normal animal with the chemical under investigation. This is followed by demonstration of an increase in one or more metabolites of the chemical compound in the excreta or tissues. This procedure was found to be of limited use, as the data obtained were not reliable. Further, there is no proof that the changes observed have occurred to the chemical compounds which were administered. However, this method is successful if it is desired to demonstrate accumulation of a particular metabolic intermediate due to deficiency of one or more enzymes as occurring in metabolic disorders.

Administration of enzyme inhibitors: Based on the findings mentioned above, certain enzyme inhibitors were administered to experimental animals to create the desired pathological states, and the accumulated compounds were then measured.

Study by surgical removal of organs: Surgical removal of vital organs such as liver or an endocrine gland is sometimes adopted to demonstrate the role of the organ in the concerned metabolic process. For example, pancreatectomy produces marked changes in the metabolism of carbohydrates and fat, resulting in diabetes mellitus.

Inducing genetic variants: Another method is to induce genetic variants by irradiation and administration of chemicals. The mutant strain produced suffers metabolic blockages similar to the type encountered in the inborn errors of metabolism.

But all these techniques are rarely adopted these days, because of the introduction of more modern and reliable procedures.

'In Vitro' Methods

Most often, it is difficult to pursue intermediary metabolism in a living animal. Investigation in a single organ or tissues is adopted in such cases. 'In vitro' techniques which are generally employed are as follows:

1. Perfusion experiments
2. Tissue culture experiments
3. Warburg's technique of manometric measurements

Perfusion experiments: In this technique, the compound under investigation is added to an artificial salt mixture and pumped into organs such as liver and kidney. After a specified period, the perfusion fluid is analysed for products of metabolism. For example, when liver is perfused with alanine, the perfusate contains an increased amount of pyruvic acid, indicating that deamination of alanine to pyruvic acid takes place in the liver cells.

Tissue culture experiments: This technique consists in growing explants of animal tissues in nutrient media, under aseptic conditions. The technique is particularly useful in studying the individual nutritional requirements of the tissue under investigation.

Warburg's technique of manometric measurements: Otto Warburg devised the use of certain types of manometric apparatus to investigate the metabolism of foodstuffs and the intermediary metabolism in tissues. This method is reliable and is widely used. The principle underlying this technique is that tissues after removal from the body environment maintain for more than 1 hour the normal metabolic pattern which could be directly followed and measured.

The technique consists in shaking very thin slices of tissues, in a medium containing the buffer and substrate required for its metabolism. The CO_2 evolved by the metabolic process is absorbed by alkali placed in a centre well of the flask in which the tissues are shaken. The O_2 utilised by the tissues is then measured by the fall in pressure observed in a manometer attached to the flask. After completion of the experiment, the changes in the concentration of substances in the media or in tissue slices are determined and correlated with the uptake of oxygen.

By applying the Warburg technique, much finer materials than tissue slices which would facilitate free entrance of the substrate into the cells during the experiment are used with advantage. These are as follows:

- *Mince or 'Brei' of the tissues:* This is obtained by grinding the tissue in a grinder. The drawback in using mince tissues is that they are crude and heterogeneous.
- *Cell-free homogenate:* This can be prepared by using a mechanical blender. It contains variable amounts of nuclei, mitochondria, microsomal fraction and soluble phase of the cytoplasm.

Cell-free homogenate is well suited for investigation of the metabolic process because of its adequate dilution. The effects of the added substrates and cofactors can be easily demonstrated in such materials. Cell-free homogenate may be further refined by subjecting it to differential centrifugation. This facilitates separation of the individual particulate fraction which can be separately followed in the localisation of the intracellular metabolic processes.

Spectrophotometers are used to follow metabolic reactions involved in biological oxidation, as most of the cofactors of biological oxidation have different absorption spectra in the reduced and oxidised states.

Microorganisms are widely used as experimental materials to follow certain metabolic processes, because of their wide distribution and unity of life. A few metabolic pathways occurring in mammalian tissues were originally discovered in yeast, bacteria and fungi.

ISOTOPE METHODS

Isotopes are extensively used in the investigation of intermediary metabolism. Since radioactive isotopes emit radiation, their concentration in any given sample is expressed in terms of intensities of radiation emitted. The amount of radiation emitted from a given sample containing radioactive isotopes is also proportional to the number of radioactive atoms of the particular isotope present at that time.

Based on these findings, compounds requiring investigation are labelled with radioactive isotopes and administered into the body. The compound can be followed in tissues with particular reference to its uptake in tissues. They can be traced till they are excreted. The conversion of one compound to another can be proved by isotope labelling. Metabolic intermediaries which are labile and cannot be demonstrated by other techniques can also be proved by isotope labelling.

Labelled salts are readily available and can be purchased for the purpose of investigation. They are introduced into the biological system, which may range from an intact animal to a purified enzyme.

The isotope content of the metabolic product is assayed by using various methods, after isolating it in a pure state. The methods usually adopted for assaying isotopes are as follows:

1. Falling drop method
2. Mass spectrometer
3. Geiger–Muller counter
4. Scintillation counters

Falling drop method: Since the atomic weight of the isotope is much greater than the normal element, a method which measures the density in a falling drop apparatus has been developed to assay stable isotopes. For example, the density of D_2O which contains deuterium H^2 is much greater than H_2O. The rate of descent of a drop of sample of heavy water through a column of organic solvents of known density gives an idea of the isotope used.

Mass spectrometer: Assays of stable isotopes are done in the mass spectrometer. This consists in ionisation of the sample in a gaseous state into electrons and heavy positive ions by using an electron beam. Ions of any desired mass can be collected at a collecting plate by regulation of the electrical and magnetic field. The quantity of ions collected is proportional to the ion current resulting from the ions and this can be registered by a device.

Geiger–Muller counter: Radioactive isotopes are best determined by using Geiger–Muller counter. Rays from radioactive isotopes enter an ionisation chamber which contains gas. The rays interact with the gas and produce ions which in turn cause discharge of current. This current is amplified and automatically recorded in a counting device. The number of counts over a specified period is proportional to the current discharged by the rays entering the ionisation chamber. The concentration of isotopes in a given sample is expressed as counts per unit time per unit weight of the sample.

Scintillation counters: Another method used widely for assaying a radioactive isotope is by using scintillation counters. The principle of the working of the counters is as follows. The sample containing radioactive isotopes is mixed with phosphor. The radiation emitted by the sample is converted to flashes of light which are picked up by a photomultiplier tube. This device converts the light flashes to electrical impulses, which in turn are sufficiently amplified and then registered in a counter.

16 CHAPTER Biological Oxidation

Chapter Outline

- Oxidation–Reduction
- The Electron Transport Chain
- Miscellaneous Redox System
- Bioenergetic System
- High-Energy Phosphate Compounds

OXIDATION–REDUCTION

The ultimate aim of any metabolism is its complete oxidation to form CO_2 and H_2O. For example, carbohydrate gets oxidised through the Krebs cycle to form CO_2 and H_2O. Proteins are deaminated and ammonia is excreted. The carbon skeleton which is left behind is finally oxidised to CO_2 and H_2O via the Krebs cycle. Fats are completely oxidised resulting in the formation of acetate, which may condense with another acetate to form acetoacetate or get oxidised completely via the Krebs cycle to form CO_2 and H_2O. This oxidation of foodstuffs in animal tissues, which involves uptake of O_2 and release of CO_2 with the liberation of energy, is called **biological oxidation**. Biological oxidation is also known as **tissue oxidation** or **cellular respiration**.

The process of oxidation which occurs in the cells is accomplished by specific enzymes and coenzymes in a stepwise fashion:

1. Removal of electrons (hydrogen atoms) from the substance being oxidised, which is called the substrate or reductant
2. Union between hydrogen atoms from substrate and oxygen, to form H_2O

Removal of electrons from substrates: In biological oxidation, oxidation is considered as removal of electrons, with an increase in valency and reduction as a gain in electrons with a decrease in valency. For example, oxidation of ferrous to ferric ions means removal of an electron from ferrous.

$$Fe^{++} \underset{\text{Reduction}}{\overset{\text{Oxidation}}{\rightleftharpoons}} Fe^{+++} + e^-$$

An electron as such is not stable in the free state and therefore gets immediately attached to another substance. In other words, every oxidation is accompanied by a reduction. All such reactions are termed oxidation–reduction reactions and abbreviated as redox. The electron donor is called the *reductant* and the electron acceptor the *oxidant*.

Now it is clear that for oxidation, two systems are required—one is the reductant and the other is the oxidant. Streams of electrons pass from the reductant, which has lesser affinity for the electrons, to the oxidant, which has higher affinity for the electrons. This affinity for the electron by the oxidant is called the 'electron affinity' or 'redox potential'.

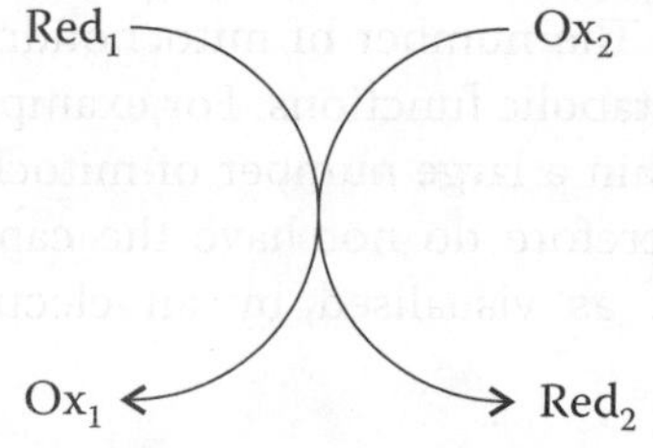

Figure 16.1 Reduction–oxidation system.

In biochemistry, oxygen has the highest redox potential or electron affinity, and therefore electrons pass from systems of hydrogen donor which have lower potential to systems of higher potential which accept hydrogen. In biological oxidation, cellular enzyme systems accomplish oxidation by removing hydrogen from the substrate without inclusion of oxygen. Thus, the system (reductant) which transfers its electrons is changed to its oxidant form while the system (oxidant) which accepts electrons gets converted to the reductant form. This reaction, which couples oxidation and reduction, is illustrated in **Figure 16.1**.

Union between hydrogen and oxygen atoms: The ultimate achievement of biological oxidation is the union between the hydrogen atoms with oxygen atom to form water (H_2O) and liberate energy. These redox reactions which are associated with movements of electrons up the redox potential scale is an energy-yielding process, and there would be a gap between the substrate system and the oxidant system.

This follows that a direct transfer of the electrons from the substrate to the oxidant would cause a sudden liberation and burst of energy, when most of it would be wasted and the direct combination of the electrons of H_2 with oxygen would be an explosive phenomenon. But in biological processes, there is no such explosion and the reactions take place smoothly without causing any rise in temperature. This is because the cells transfer their hydrogen pairs step by step to oxygen. This process also facilitates liberation of energy in correspondingly small amounts.

In order to effect this stepwise process, the cells in biological oxidation make use of systems known as an electron carrier system, whose redox potential is intermediary between substrate and oxygen. This enables the electrons to pass along a gradually increasing potential. These links or carrier systems vary from the simple type of oxidative system to complex forms and they are all enzymes activated by their coenzymes. Most of these coenzymes are derivatives of vitamin B complex and a few are metals such as copper and iron.

Site of cellular oxidation: All the enzymes and coenzymes required for biological oxidation are contained in minute particles called 'electron-transport particles' in the mitochondria. These particles, each having a molecular weight of about 1,560,000, are attached to the inner membrane of the mitochondria, particularly on the cristae.

Mitochondria: These are cytoplasmic subcellular organelles, present in human cells in hundreds. They vary in size and shape. In an electron micrograph, they appear as ellipsoidal, rod shaped or spherical bodies measuring about 0.5–5 μ in length and 0.1–0.6 μ in width. They are described as **powerhouse** of cells because their major function is to convert energy released from oxidation of carbohydrate, fat and protein from food to the chemical energy of cell (**ATP**). The number of mitochondria in tissues depends upon its capacity to perform aerobic metabolic functions. For example, cardiac and liver tissues are highly aerobic tissues and contain a large number of mitochondria, whereas erythrocytes have no mitochondria and therefore do not have the capacity to generate energy. The structure of a mitochondrion as visualised by an electron microscope is shown in **Figure 16.2**.

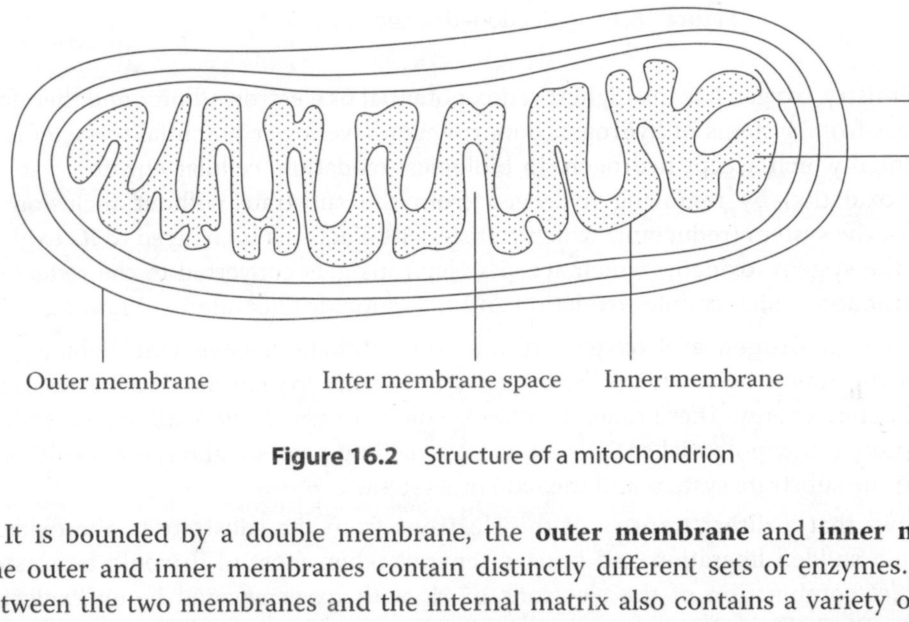

Figure 16.2 Structure of a mitochondrion

It is bounded by a double membrane, the **outer membrane** and **inner membrane**. The outer and inner membranes contain distinctly different sets of enzymes. The space between the two membranes and the internal matrix also contains a variety of enzymes. The outer membrane is simple and is composed of 50% lipid and 50% protein. It is permeable to most small molecules. It has relatively few enzymatic or transport functions. Monoamine oxidase and acetyl-CoA synthetase are among the enzymes that are present in the outer membrane. The inner membrane is folded and highly convoluted so as to produce a number of partitions known as the **cristae** that extend into the matrix. The inner membrane is structurally and functionally more complex than the outer membrane and consists of layers of protein and lipid molecules. It shows highly selective permeability and contains enzymes involved in the electron transport chain and enzymes of oxidative phosphorylation. Various dehydrogenases and several transport systems involved in transferring metabolic intermediates between the cytosol and the matrix are also present in the inner membrane. The inter membrane space is the space between the outer and the inner membranes.

Matrix is the space surrounded by the inner membrane and is filled with fluid. Many enzymes are located in the matrix. Important among them are as follows:

1. Enzymes of the tricarboxylic acid cycle with the exception of succinate dehydrogenase which is located in the inner membrane
2. Enzymes of β oxidation of fatty acids
3. Enzymes of haem synthesis
4. Enzymes of urea synthesis

The location of different enzymes, present in various compartments of mitochondria, are given in **Table 16.1**.

Table 16.1 Location of Enzymes in Mitochondria

Outer Membrane	Inner Membrane	Inter Membrane Space	Matrix
Monoamine oxidase	Succinate dehydrogenase	Adenylate kinase	Most of Krebs cycle enzymes except succinate dehydrogenase
Kynurenine hydroxylase	NADH dehydrogenase	Nucleoside diphosphate kinase	Fatty acid β-oxidation system enzymes
Nucleoside diphosphate kinase	β-hydroxybutyrate dehydrogenase		Glutamate dehydrogenase
Fatty acyl-CoA synthetases	Cytochromes b, c_1, c, a, a_3		Glutamate oxaloacetate transaminase
Phospholipase A	Carnitine acyl-CoA		Carbamoyl phosphate synthetase
NADH: Cytochrome c reductase	Adenine nucleotide translocase		Ornithine transcarbamoylase
Choline phosphotransferase	Glutamate-aspartate translocase		Coproporphyrinogen oxidase
			Protoporphyrinogen oxidase
			Ferrochelatase

THE ELECTRON TRANSPORT CHAIN

The enzymes of the cellular oxidation are arranged in succession as an integrated chain and are bound to the cristae of mitochondria. They function as carriers, transferring electrons from different substrates to oxygen. The substrates and the soluble proteins are contained in the matrix of the mitochondria.

The metabolite which gets activated by its specific dehydrogenase is situated at one end of the chain and the molecular oxygen at the other end. The hydrogen and electron acceptors, which are serially arranged in between, function by transferring the electrons in succession to reach finally the molecular oxygen to form H_2O. This chain of carriers including the terminal oxygen system (½ O_2/H_2O) is known as the electron transport chain or the respiratory chain (**Fig. 16.3**).

Coenzymes and Prosthetic Groups of the Respiratory Chain of Enzymes

The actual carriers of the hydrogen atoms and electrons in the respiratory chain of enzymes are either coenzymes or prosthetic groups.

The phosphorylated derivatives of nicotinic acid, namely nicotinamide adenine dinucleotide (NAD) and nicotinamide adenine dinucleotide phosphate (NADP), are the main carriers of hydrogen atoms for many dehydrogenases.

The phosphorylated derivatives of riboflavin, namely flavin mononucleotide (FMN) and flavin adenine dinucleotide (FAD), also act as main carriers as well as intermediate carriers of hydrogen atoms for some dehydrogenases.

Lipoic acid which contains a disulphide group, though not a component of the chain, participates in the oxidation–reduction reaction while functioning as a cofactor in oxidative decarboxylation reactions.

Iron porphyrin structures present in various cytochromes (Cyt), as Cyt b, Cyt c_1, Cyt a and Cyt a, function as intermediary carriers of electrons while cytochrome oxidase (Cyt a_3), which also contains the iron porphyrin group, acts as the most important terminal link in the electron transport chain (**Fig. 16.3**).

Coenzyme Q, also known as **ubiquinone**, is an additional oxidation cofactor. It has the structure of a quinone with a polyisoprenoid side chain. The location of this enzyme in the electron transport chain is identified to be situated before the cytochromes.

$$SH_2 \longrightarrow NAD/NADH + H^+ \longrightarrow FAD/FADH_2 \longrightarrow CoQ/CoQH_2$$

$$\downarrow$$

$$\tfrac{1}{2}\,O_2 \longleftarrow \text{Cyt } a_3 \longleftarrow \text{Cyt a} \longleftarrow \text{Cyt c} \longleftarrow \text{Cyt } c_1 \longleftarrow \text{Cyt b}$$

Figure 16.3 Schematic representation of an electron transport chain.

The main types of enzymes involved in biological oxidation may be classified as oxidases and dehydrogenases.

1. Oxidases
   - Water forming
   - Hydrogen peroxide forming
   - Other enzymes
     - Oxygenases
     - Hydroxylases

2. Dehydrogenases
   - Flavin-linked dehydrogenase
   - Nicotinamide nucleotide–linked dehydrogenase
   - Lipoate-linked dehydrogenase.

Oxidases

Oxidases comprise the simplest type of enzyme system where only one electron carrier is interposed between the substrate and the oxygen. The carrier couples directly with oxygen to form H_2O or H_2O_2 (**Fig. 16.4**).

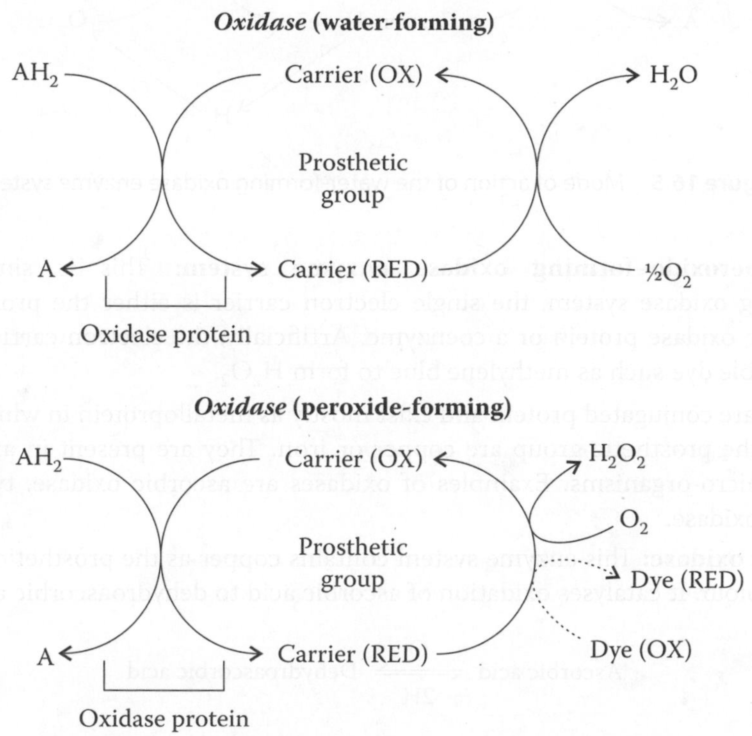

Figure 16.4 Oxidase system with one electron carrier.

There are two types of oxidase enzyme systems. They are as follows:

1. Water-forming oxidases
2. Hydrogen peroxide–forming oxidases

Water-forming oxidase enzyme system: This system catalyses the transfer of a pair of hydrogen atoms which include hydrogen ions plus electrons, from substrate AH_2 to a carrier which in turn passes them on to oxygen; the carrier which is oxidised is restored to its original form. H_2O is formed as the end product. The reduction and oxidation of the electron carrier repeat themselves in a cyclic manner as illustrated in **Figure 16.5**.

The carrier of the electrons in the oxidase system of enzymes is the metal part of the enzyme system. Actually, the hydrogen atoms of the substrate dissociate into hydrogen ions and electrons. The hydrogen ions pass into the solution, and the electrons are transferred by the metal to oxygen. The oxygen which is negatively charged combines with H_2 ions from the solution to form water.

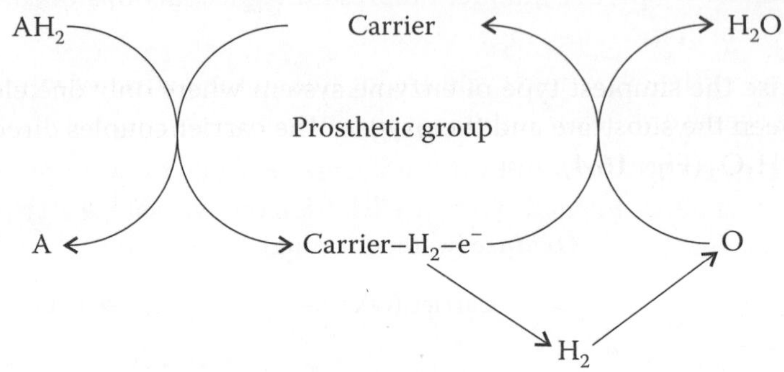

Figure 16.5 Mode of action of the water-forming oxidase enzyme system.

Hydrogen peroxide–forming oxidase enzyme system: This is similar to the water-forming oxidase system; the single electron carrier is either the prosthetic group (metal) of the oxidase protein or a coenzyme. Artificially, the electron carrier can couple with a reducible dye such as methylene blue to form H_2O_2.

Oxidases are conjugated protein and exist mostly as metalloprotein in which the metals which form the prosthetic group are copper or iron. They are present in animal tissues, plants and micro-organisms. Examples of oxidases are ascorbic oxidase, tyrosinase and cytochrome oxidase.

1. **Ascorbic oxidase:** This enzyme system contains copper as the prosthetic group and is blue in colour. It catalyses oxidation of ascorbic acid to dehydroascorbic acid.

$$\text{Ascorbic acid} \underset{2H}{\overset{O}{\rightleftharpoons}} \text{Dehydroascorbic acid}$$

2. **Tyrosinase:** This is also a copper-containing enzyme. It is present in skin and retina where it participates in the formation of melanin. It oxidises tyrosine to dihydroxyphenylalanine (DOPA) and then to a quinone which later gets converted to melanin. Tyrosinase also helps in the formation of adrenaline by forming the common intermediate DOPA.

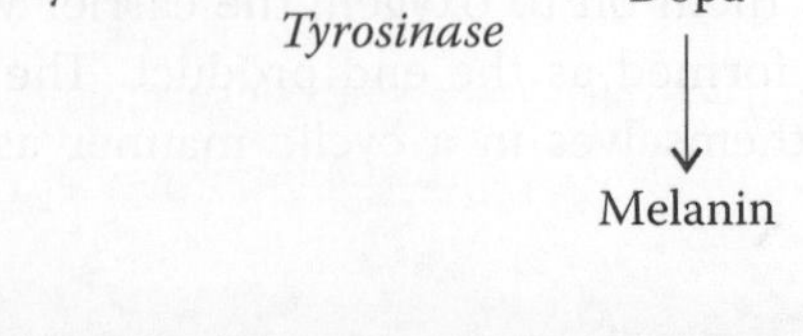

3. **Cytochrome oxidase:** This enzyme contains an iron porphyrin prosthetic group as well as a copper-containing component and is identical with cytochrome a_3 of the cytochrome system of enzymes. It is attached firmly to the granular constituents of the cytoplasm. The iron atom undergoes reversible reduction and oxidation to the ferrous and ferric states. This enzyme is particularly important in cell oxidation because a total failure in cellular oxidation can be brought about by cyanide which inhibits this enzyme. Thus, death caused by cyanides is due to inhibition of cytochrome oxidase.

Oxygenases and Hydroxylases Two more groups of oxidative enzymes require mention here. They are as follows:

1. Oxygenases
2. Hydroxylases

Oxygenases: They catalyse reactions in which oxygen atoms from molecular oxygen are directly incorporated into the substrate molecule. They also act on cyclic substrates resulting in the cleavage of the ring.

Examples are

- Homogentisic oxygenase
- Tryptophan oxygenase

$$\text{Homogentisate} \xrightarrow{\textit{Homogentisic oxygenase}} \text{Maleylacetoacetate.}$$

$$\text{Tryptophan} \xrightarrow{\textit{Tryptophan oxygenase}} \text{Formylkynurenine.}$$

Hydroxylases: They are enzymes which catalyse hydroxylation reactions. Tyrosinase referred under oxidases also acts as a hydroxylase. It participates in the synthesis of melanin. The first product of oxidation of this enzyme is DOPA, which also acts as the reducing agent or cosubstrate. A few hydroxylases which participate in metabolic reactions are given in **Table 16.2**.

Table 16.2 Oxygenases and Hydroxylases

Enzyme	Coenzyme or Prosthetic Group	Cosubstrate	Reactions
Oxygenases			
Homogentisic oxygenase	Fe^{++}	–	Homogentisate → maleylacetoacetate
Tryptophan oxygenase	Haem		Tryptophan → formylkynurenine
Hydroxylases			
Tryptophan-5-hydroxylase	–	–	Tryptophan → 5-hydroxytryptophan
Dopamine hydroxylase	–	Ascorbate	Dopamine → norepinephrine

Dehydrogenases

Dehydrogenases are enzymes which first activate the hydrogen atoms in a metabolite. Unlike oxidase, dehydrogenase does not react directly with oxygen. Instead, a chain of hydrogen or electron carrier is interposed between the metabolite and molecular oxygen.

Structure of the dehydrogenase enzyme system: The dehydrogenase enzyme is made up of two parts:

1. Protein part called the apodehydrogenase
2. Non-protein part which is the coenzyme

The coenzymes are readily auto-oxidisable and are derivatives of vitamin B complex. They are FMN, FAD, NAD and NADP.

Groups of dehydrogenases: Three groups of dehydrogenases have been identified:

1. Flavin-linked dehydrogenase
2. Nicotinamide nucleotide–linked dehydrogenase
3. Lipoate-linked dehydrogenase

Flavin-linked dehydrogenase: The main links of the flavin-linked dehydrogenase enzyme system are flavoproteins, cytochromes and cytochrome oxidase. In tissues, the coenzymes of flavoprotein, namely FMN and FAD, participate in the oxidation–reduction reactions, by functioning as the primary acceptors of hydrogen atoms from the metabolite. A diagram of the components of a flavin-linked dehydrogenase enzyme system is shown in **Figures 16.6** and **16.7**.

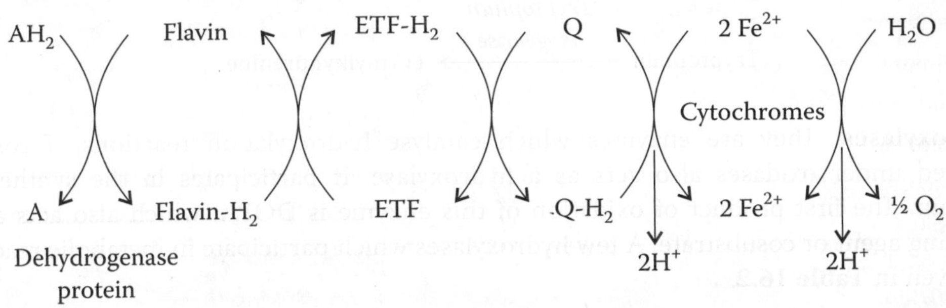

Figure 16.6 Flavin-linked dehydrogenase enzyme system.

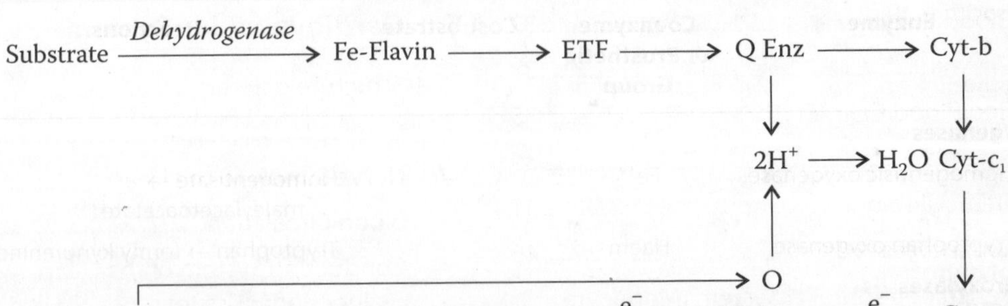

Figure 16.7 Outline of the flavin-linked dehydrogenase enzyme system.

Flavins link with accessory carriers, namely electron transfer ring flavoprotein 'ETF' (sometimes), coenzyme Q system, cytochrome system, cytochrome oxidase, in this order. The dehydrogenase enzyme bound to flavin first catalyses the activation of two hydrogen atoms from the substrate and transfers them in succession to another flavin carrier, an intermediate flavoprotein known as ETF, and then to coenzyme Q. Here the hydrogen atoms which reduce coenzyme Q to hydroquinone dissociate to H^+ ions which go into solution and electrons which pass on to the cytochrome system. The cytochromes b, c and a in this order act as transelectronases; the last of the cytochromes, cytochrome a, transfers the electron to cytochrome oxidase (a_3) which passes it on to oxygen which is now negatively charged. It then combines with H^+ ions released earlier, to form H_2O. At each stage, when hydrogen atoms and electrons pass from one carrier to another in the flavin-linked enzyme system, each carrier gets reduced and oxidised in turn. Examples of reactions catalysed by flavin-linked dehydrogenases are given in **Table 16.3**.

Table 16.3 Dehydrogenases

Dehydrogenase Enzymes	Coenzyme or Prosthetic Group	Reaction
Flavin-linked		
Succinate dehydrogenase	Fe, FAD	Succinate $\rightleftharpoons$ fumarate
Choline dehydrogenase	FAD	Choline $\longrightarrow$ betaine–aldehyde
Dimethylglycine–dehydrogenase	Fe, flavin (+ETF)	Dimethylglycine $\longrightarrow$ sarcosine + HCHO
Sarcosine dehydrogenase	Fe, flavin (+ETF)	Sarcosine $\longrightarrow$ glycine + HCHO
Nicotinamide nucleotide-linked		
Lactate dehydrogenase	NAD, (NADP)	Lactate $\rightleftharpoons$ pyruvate
Malate dehydrogenase	NAD, (NADP)	Malate $\rightleftharpoons$ oxaloacetate
Glucose dehydrogenase	NAD, (NADP)	Glucose $\longrightarrow$ gluconate
L. Glutamate dehydrogenase	NAD, (NADP), Zn	Glutamate $\rightleftharpoons$ α-ketoglutarate + NH_3
Glyceraldehyde-3-phosphate dehydrogenase	NAD, –SH	Glyceraldehyde-3-phosphate + phosphate $\rightleftharpoons$ diphosphoglycerate
Glucose-6-phosphate–dehydrogenase	NADP	Glucose-6-phosphate $\longrightarrow$ gluconate-6-phosphate
Isocitrate dehydrogenase	NADP	Isocitrate $\rightleftharpoons$ oxalosuccinate $\longrightarrow$ α-ketoglutarate + CO_2
Lipoate-linked		
Pyruvate dehydrogenase system	Lipoate, TPP, Mg^{++}	Pyruvate $\longrightarrow$ acetyl-lipoate + CO_2
Ketoglutarate dehydrogenase system	Lipoate, TPP, Mg	Ketoglutarate $\longrightarrow$ succinyl-lipoate + CO_2

Nicotinamide nucleotide–linked dehydrogenase: This system is also known as coenzyme-linked dehydrogenase. It constitutes a larger group of dehydrogenases. Coenzymes NAD or NADP are utilised as the primary carriers of hydrogen atoms. The secondary carrier is a metalloflavoprotein (FAD) which may be specific for the individual coenzyme present (NAD or NADP). These flavoproteins are called cytochrome reductases, because they pass their hydrogen atoms to the cytochrome system. But truly, they are coenzyme Q reductases, because coenzyme Q occupies a position between metalloflavoprotein and cytochromes in the chain. The other accessory carriers of the chain following metalloflavoproteins are coenzyme Q, cytochrome system and cytochrome oxidase. A diagram of the components of a nicotinamide nucleotide–linked dehydrogenase chain is shown in **Figure 16.8**.

The hydrogen atoms released by the action of the dehydrogenase pass on first to the primary carrier, next to NAD or NADP where they may remain temporarily but later they pass through the rest of the carriers in succession in the same order as illustrated in **Figure 16.8**.

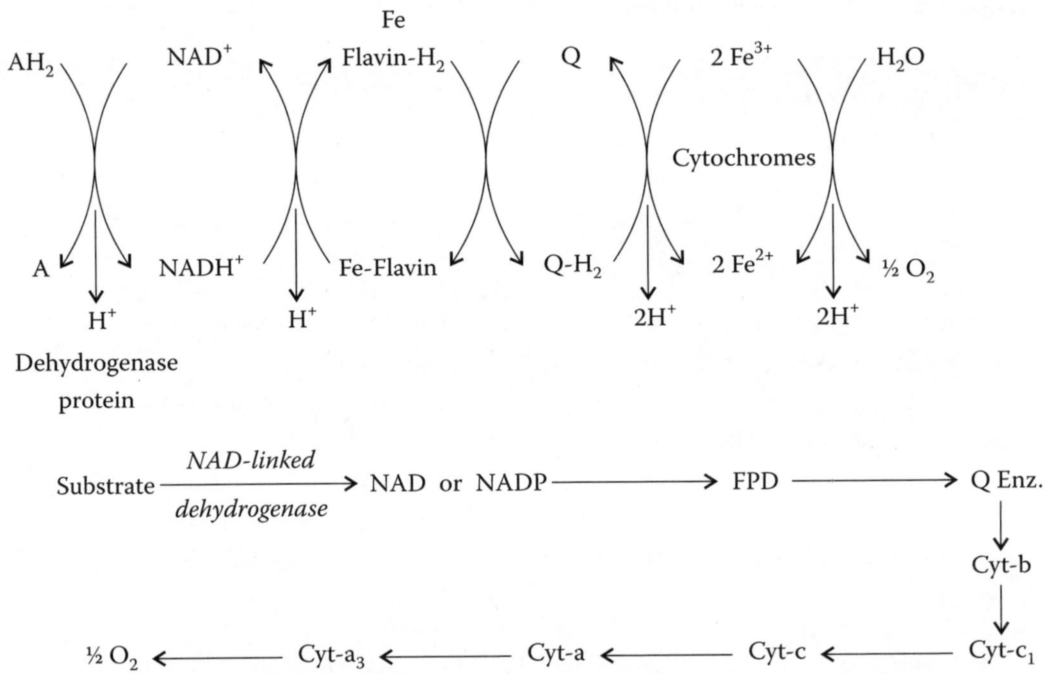

Figure 16.8 Nicotinamide nucleotide-linked dehydrogenase and accessory carriers.

At the point of coenzyme Q, the hydrogen atoms dissociate to H^+ ions which go into the solution and electron, which passes on to the cytochromes. The electron, leaving cytochrome oxidase, is passed on to oxygen. It combines with the H^+ ions released earlier to form H_2O. The carriers in the chain, which carry hydrogen atoms and electrons in succession, get alternatively reduced and reoxidised as they are passed down the chain from one carrier to another. The overall reaction may be illustrated as

$$\text{NAD 2H} + \tfrac{1}{2}\,O_2 \xrightarrow{\text{Via, carriers}} \text{NAD} + H_2O.$$

Metabolic reactions catalysed by nicotinamide nucleotide–linked dehydrogenase are given in **Table 16.3**.

Lipoate-linked dehydrogenase: This comprises a more complex system of enzymes. It is utilised in the initial oxidative decarboxylation reactions of keto acids, whereby CO_2 from metabolites are removed, resulting in the formation of the corresponding acyl-CoA. Such reactions are catalysed by a group of enzymes which include the specific decarboxylase, lipoate reductase-transacetylase and dihydrolipoate dehydrogenase. Lipoate, which functions as the main acceptor of the hydrogen atoms from the keto acids, gets alternately reduced and oxidised at the disulphide group. During the course of the reaction, the keto acid condenses with the disulphide group of lipoic acid which is bound to the enzyme system, to form the acetylated lipoate in the case of pyruvate and succinylated lipoate in the case of α-ketoglutarate. The disulphide groups of lipoate get reduced to disulphydryl groups, when combination with the sulphydryl group of CoA is effected. Lipoate is regenerated to the oxidised form when the hydrogen atoms pass on to the flavin prosthetic group of the specific dehydrogenase which in turn pass the hydrogen atoms to an NAD carrier. From this point, the hydrogen atoms enter the oxidative chain in the same pathway as that utilised by the coenzyme-linked dehydrogenases.

Pyruvate dehydrogenase system and ketoglutarate dehydrogenase systems are examples of this kind (*see* **Table 16.3**).

The lipoate-linked dehydrogenase system is shown in **Figure 16.9**.

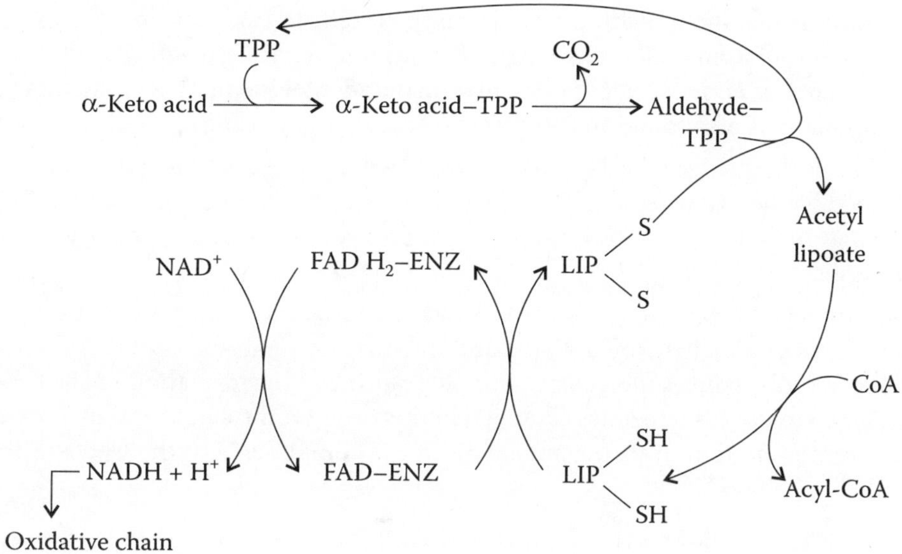

Figure 16.9 Lipoate-linked dehydrogenase system.

Cytochromes

Keilin in 1925 discovered a group of intracellular haemoprotein enzymes, which are widely distributed in animal tissues. He established that they act as catalysts along the major pathway of biological oxidation and named them cytochromes. They are present mostly in the mitochondria of the cells.

Cytochromes, which are combinations of haem and proteins, have characteristic absorption spectra but they differ from those of haemoglobin and its derivatives.

The cytochromes are divided into three major groups, according to the nature of the prosthetic group contained in them. The differences in the prosthetic groups also result in corresponding differences in the absorption spectra.

The main groups of cytochrome with their respective prosthetic haem groups and their corresponding absorption bands are given below:

1. Cytochrome a = Formyl porphyrin—iron prosthetic group (580–590 mμ)
2. Cytochrome b = Protoporhyrin—iron prosthetic group (556–558 mμ)
3. Cytochrome c = Haem-linked to the protein by 2 thioether linkages (441–550 mμ)

The iron component of the cytochromes can exist in either the ferrous or the ferric state depending upon the state of reduction or oxidation.

Cytochrome a: It is assumed that two cytochromes 'a' exist—one is the cytochrome 'a' proper and the other is cytochrome 'a_3,' which is also known as cytochrome oxidase or Warburg's respiratory enzyme. Cytochrome 'a' is an electron-transferring cytochrome, like other cytochromes in the chain.

Cytochrome oxidase (a_3): This is the terminal catalyst in the oxidation system of cellular respiration and is firmly attached to the mitochondria. It effects direct union of hydrogen derived from the metabolite with molecular oxygen to form H_2O. Like other cytochromes, it contains an iron atom which changes to ferrous and ferric states during reduction and oxidation. A copper-containing component which undergoes oxidation–reduction, like the haem component, is also found to be present in cytochrome oxidase.

The other cytochromes b and c are intermediates in the oxidation system and function as transelectronases, transferring electrons from coenzymes such as reduced NAD and flavoproteins. It should be noted that cytochromes do not transfer hydrogen atoms but electrons only.

Among the cytochromes, cytochrome b has the lowest oxidation–reduction potential, which increases gradually through C_1, C and finally to cytochrome oxidase (a_3). The latter in its reduced form reduces molecular oxygen, resulting in the formation of H_2O. Electrons are transferred to the cytochromes arranged in this order in the electron transport chain. A schematic representation of the arrangement of the components of the electron transport chain is shown below:

$$SH_2 \longrightarrow NAD \longrightarrow FAD \longrightarrow Co\,Q \longrightarrow Cyt\ b \longrightarrow Cyt\ c_1 \longrightarrow Cyt\ c$$

$$\downarrow$$

$$\tfrac{1}{2}\,O_2 \longleftarrow Cyt\ a_3 \longleftarrow Cyt\ a$$

Cytochrome b: This group which has a molecular weight of 30,000 is found in the mitochondria, where it forms part of the respiratory chain and is located next to the Q enzyme.

Cytochrome b_5: Cytochrome b_5, which is closely related to cytochrome b, has been identified in the microsome where it probably participates in the electron transport reactions.

Cytochrome c: This catalyst has been studied most thoroughly. It is a haemoprotein with a molecular weight of 11,600. The porphyrin ring is linked by primary valency bonds to the protein through SH groups of two cysteine side chains. The resulting thioether bonds are very stable. In the electron transport chain, it occupies a position just after cytochrome C_1.

Cytochrome C_1 or E is closely related to cytochrome C. It has a molecular weight of 37,000 and forms a component of the respiratory chain. Its location in the electron transport chain is between cytochromes b and c. It has been found in heart and skeletal muscles.

MISCELLANEOUS REDOX SYSTEM

Living tissues contain several enzyme systems that do not come under the classification described so far. They are as follows:

1. Hydroperoxidases which include
   - Peroxidase
   - Catalase
2. Ascorbic acid
3. Glutathione

Hydroperoxidases: Some oxidative chains end up with the formation of H_2O_2 instead of H_2O. This might lead to accumulation of a large amount of peroxide in the tissues, and it is necessary that they are disposed off promptly because they are toxic. This is accomplished by a set of enzymes called hydroperoxidases. They are oxidising enzymes which cannot be classified under the regular enzymes discussed previously, because they differ in their action. The enzyme system consists of a substrate and a hydrogen donor, besides the specific hydroperoxidase enzyme. The enzyme oxidises the hydrogen donor after transferring their H_2 atoms to the substrate, which in turn becomes reduced. Two enzymes, namely **peroxidase** and **catalase**, fall under this category. The substrates are common for both peroxidase and catalase, but the donors are different.

These enzymes are present in all living tissues. Peroxidases are more prevalent in plants and catalases in animals. They are iron-porphyrin proteins like haemoglobin. They differ from haemoglobin in that iron remains in the ferric state during the reaction. They are inhibited by cyanide, azide sulphide and hydroxylamine. The reactions catalysed by both the enzymes may be represented as follows:

Peroxidases: The substrate is H_2O_2. It is reduced by a hydrogen donor (H_2R) to a reduced substrate $2H_2O$. The hydrogen donor is oxidised to oxidised donor (**R**).

$$H_2O_2 + H_2R \xrightarrow{Peroxidase} 2H_2O + R$$

Catalases: In this case, both substrate and donor are H_2O_2. The resulting products are O_2 and reduced substrate, $2H_2O$.

$$H_2O_2 + H_2O_2 \xrightarrow{\textit{Catalase}} 2H_2O + O_2$$

Physiological importance:

Hydroperoxidases are not considered physiologically important. However, a few of their functions in biological oxidation need mention here.

- Peroxidases occur in the thyroid gland, salivary glands, erythrocytes and leucocytes. A peroxidase present in thyroid gland mitochondria oxidises iodide to iodine, which can be used to iodinate tyrosine.
- A protective function for catalase in the cell is suggested, because it disposes the H_2O_2 resulting from the action of certain dehydrogenase.

Ascorbic acid and glutathione: These substances readily undergo reduction and oxidation and form a reversible oxidation–reduction system. For this reason, it was assumed for many years that these compounds participate in biological oxidation–reduction reactions. But at present, this view has been ruled out.

Ascorbic acid can be oxidised and reduced by glutathione easily.

Ascorbic acid on oxidation loses two hydrogen atoms and gets converted to dehydroascorbic acid which in turn can be reduced to the original form of ascorbic acid.

Reduction of ascorbic acid is brought about by the SH group in glutathione, a tripeptide (glutamyl-cysteinyl-glycine) abbreviated as GSH. Two molecules of GSH on oxidation link between the S atom of each, to form a large molecule which is abbreviated as GS-SG.

$$2\,\text{GSH} \underset{+2\text{H}}{\overset{-2\text{H}}{\rightleftharpoons}} \text{G—S—S—G.}$$

$$\text{Ascorbic acid} \underset{2\,\text{GSH}}{\overset{\text{G—S—S—G}}{\rightleftharpoons}} \text{Dehydroascorbic acid}$$

Glutathione is present in the tissues and tissue fluids mostly in the reduced form. This serves to maintain tissue ascorbic acid in its reduced form.

Oxidation of glutathione (SH group) occurs by the action of glutathione peroxidase of erythrocytes and the cytochrome system of enzymes. The disulphide form, in turn, is reduced by NADPH and glutathione reductase.

Physiological importance:

- Glutathione is the coenzyme for the enzyme glyceraldehyde-3-phosphate dehydrogenase, and the enzyme pair is known as glyoxylases I and II.
- It functions as a preserver of sulphydryl groups in compounds.
- It also prevents inactivation of SH groups by heavy metals.
- Glutathione participates in the detoxication process and in the formation of mercapturic derivatives.

- Ascorbic acid is involved in the conversion of proline to hydroxyproline during the synthesis of collagen. It helps in the formation of norepinephrine from dopamine.

BIOENERGETIC SYSTEM

Source and Formation of Energy

The capacity to do work is known as energy. Energy is required for anabolic and catabolic activities of the organism. The store of energy is kept at a constant level by an external source of supply in the form of food.

Directly or indirectly, the green plants form an important source of food to all animals and organisms. The radiant energy of the sun is utilised in the formation of complex compounds from simpler substances (photosynthesis). For example, glucose, a high-potential energy compound, is formed from CO_2 and H_2O which are compounds of low-potential energy. Free energy of 688,500 calories per molecule of glucose is supplied in the form of solar radiation. On oxidation of glucose to CO_2 and H_2O, this stored-up energy is available for other reactions.

$$C_6H_{12}O_6 + 6O_2 \longrightarrow 6CO_2 + 6H_2O + 688{,}500 \text{ Cal.}$$

Energy is generated by the oxidation of different kinds of food.

Stages of Energy Production

Oxidation of foodstuffs occurs in the following three stages:

1. Hydrolysis
2. Intermediate metabolism
3. Oxidation

Hydrolysis: Carbohydrates, fats and proteins are hydrolysed in the gastrointestinal tract to hexoses, glycerol, fatty acids and amino acids. A small amount of free energy that is liberated is lost as heat.

Intermediate metabolism: The hydrolytic products are metabolised further through various pathways, to reach the final stage of oxidation.

Hexoses are phosphorylated and are catabolised to form pyruvic acid. Pyruvic acid on oxidative decarboxylation forms acetyl-CoA. Fatty acids are oxidised to form acetyl-CoA. Glycerol enters the pathway of carbohydrate metabolism via triose-phosphates. Most of the amino acids are deaminated to form keto acids. The nitrogen of the amino groups is converted to urea, but the keto acids of some amino acids (ketogenic) form acetyl-CoA, while others (glucogenic) form pyruvic acid and other intermediates of the tricarboxylic acid cycle. Some useful energy, more than the amount utilised, is obtained during this stage.

Oxidation: In this final stage, acetyl-CoA and all other products of intermediate metabolism are oxidised to CO_2 and H_2O through the tricarboxylic acid cycle. The most useful energy of the cell is liberated during this phase.

Formation of Adenosine Triphosphate

Adenosine triphosphate (ATP) is mainly formed by

1. Substrate level phosphorylation *and*
2. Oxidative phosphorylation.

Substrate-level phosphorylation: ATP is formed by transfer of energy to ADP from a higher energy compound, at the substrate level without the participation of the respiratory chain. Examples are certain reactions of glycolysis and citric acid cycle.

- 1,3-diphosphoglyceric acid + ADP → 3-phosphoglyceric acid + ATP.
- Phosphoenol pyruvate + ADP → ATP + pyruvic acid.
- Succinyl-CoA + GDP + Pi → Succinic acid + GTP + CoA.

  GTP + ADP → GDP + ATP.

It has been found that a maximum of 7,600–7,800 calories of free energy, equivalent to one high-energy bond per molecule of the substrate, are generated and trapped for the transfer of electrons in one step. The disadvantage of substrate phosphorylation is that much energy is liberated and most of it is wasted, because of the one-step transfer.

Oxidative phosphorylation: This process refers to oxidation of a substrate coupled with phosphorylation of ADP to ATP and is accompanied by transport of electrons in the mitochondrial electron chain. The energy liberated at every step of electron transport is stored as energy-rich phosphate, and very little energy is wasted. Examples may be cited from reactions of the tricarboxylic acid cycle.

1. Isocitrate ⟶ oxalosuccinate.
2. Succinate ⟶ fumarate.
3. Malate ⟶ oxaloacetate.

It has been calculated that for each atom of oxygen utilised, three atoms of phosphorus are incorporated into the high-energy bonds, and therefore three molecules of high-energy phosphate are formed. The high-energy phosphates play an important role in energy exchange reactions. The energy yielded by the oxidative breakdown of sugars, lipids and amino acids is captured and stored in the form of high-energy phosphate bonds. They are released by the hydrolysis of the bond, whenever it is necessary.

HIGH-ENERGY PHOSPHATE COMPOUNDS

Among biochemically important compounds, a group of phosphorylated substances exist, which differ from other phosphate-containing compounds in that the phosphorus is bound to the compound by means of a bond in which resides a relatively high amount of energy.

This type of bond is called the high-energy bond, and it is customary to represent such a bond by the symbol ~ph. The compound R containing the bond may be represented as R ~ ph. Removal of the ~ph (phosphate) group by hydrolysis causes release of a large amount of energy equivalent to 10,000–12,000 calories per g mol.

The high-energy phosphate compounds are closely associated with the oxidative breakdown to metabolites, participating in the transfer and capture of chemical energy released during the process.

Following are examples of high-energy phosphate compounds:

1. **Adenosine triphosphate (ATP)**

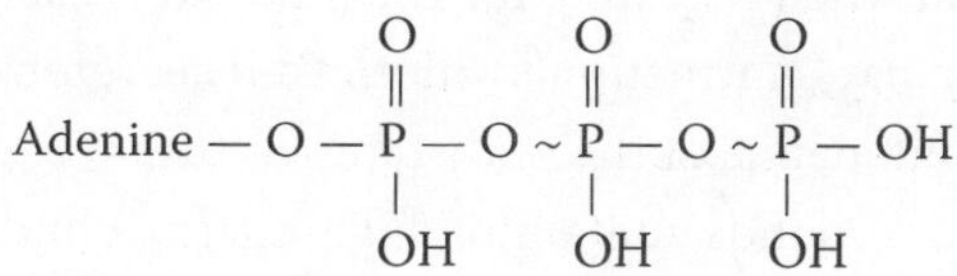

This compound contains two high-energy phosphate bonds. For full structure, see pages 137 and 138.

2. **Adenosine diphosphate (ADP)**

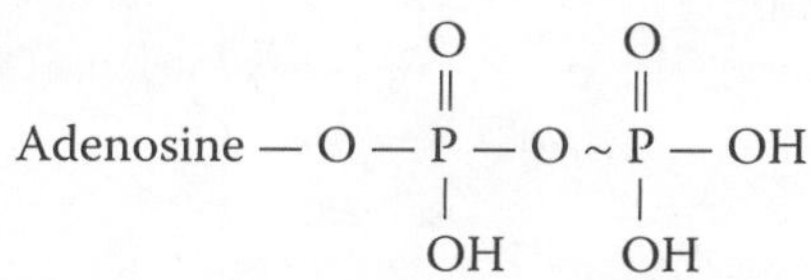

This compound contains one high-energy phosphate bond. For full structure, see pages 137 and 138.

3. **Creatine phosphate**

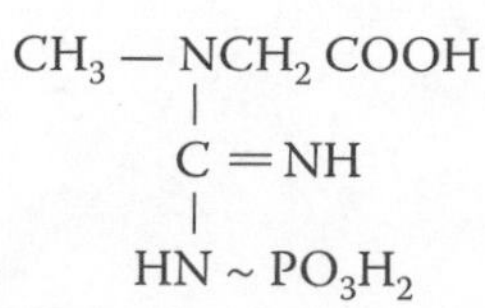

This compound contains one high-energy phosphate bond. It forms the reserve source of energy for muscle contraction and is present in muscles.

4. **1,3-Diphosphoglyceric acid**

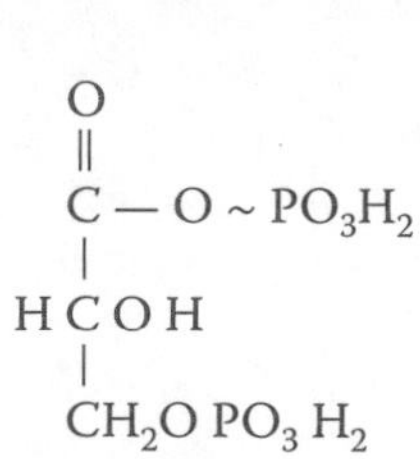

This compound contains one high-energy phosphate bond.

5. **Phosphenolypyruvic acid**

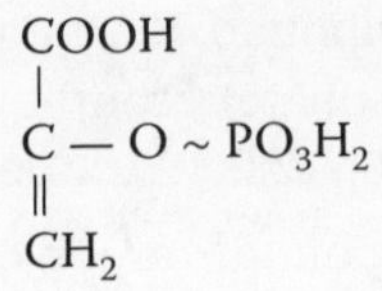

This compound contains one high-energy phosphate bond.

Role of high-energy phosphate groups: These groups serve as a source of energy for utilisation by cells directly. When not in use, they are stored and the energy locked in them. They are used as and when required, for the following reactions:

- To perform work (muscular contraction, osmotic and secretory functions)
- To liberate heat for maintenance of the body temperature
- To effect synthesis of compounds containing high-energy bonds such as ATP

The phosphate groups of the high-energy phosphate compounds may be transferred directly to another organic compound without much loss of the high energy of the bond dissipated as heat. The phosphorylated compound may or may not have a high-energy phosphate bond, but the total energy content of the molecule is much higher than the non-phosphorylated compound.

17 CHAPTER Metabolism of Carbohydrate

Chapter Outline

- Absorption of Carbohydrates
- Carbohydrate as a Source of Energy
- Intermediary Metabolism of Carbohydrate
- Chemistry of Muscle Contraction
- Regulation of Blood Sugar
- Metabolism of Other Hexoses
- Glycogen Storage Diseases

Since glucose is the most important carbohydrate existing in physiological amounts in the body and is easily absorbed from the diet, the metabolism of carbohydrate resolves itself to the study of the metabolism of glucose and its main derivatives. Besides, other monosaccharides such as fructose and galactose are ultimately converted to glucose in the liver.

The ingested carbohydrates, i.e. polysaccharides and disaccharides, are hydrolysed to monosaccharides by the enzymes present in the salivary, pancreatic and intestinal secretions. Glucose is the most important end product and is absorbed much more than other sugars. Fructose and galactose are also formed, but in a lesser amount. However, when there is a large intake of sucrose and lactose, fructose and galactose will be present in significant quantities. Pentoses may be present in small amounts. All the monosaccharides are completely absorbed in the small intestines.

ABSORPTION OF CARBOHYDRATES

The rates of absorption for the different monosaccharides vary. It is found that galactose is absorbed most rapidly, glucose next, fructose more slowly, then mannose and pentose come last.

Absorption of sugars is facilitated by the extensive surface area provided by the projecting villi which line intestinal mucosa. The villi which are richly supplied by a network of blood vessels and lacteals are lined with cells that are metabolically active. According to a recent concept, absorption of sugars involves two processes:

1. Selective permeability
2. Active transport

Selective permeability: This process is assumed to facilitate absorption of smaller molecules and prevent bigger molecules from being absorbed. If this is true, it is not understood why pentoses which are smaller molecules are not absorbed more rapidly than hexoses and why there is a difference in the rate of absorption of individual hexoses.

Active transport: It is also assumed that a kind of membrane transport system involving active absorption against a concentration gradient is involved. This means that the concentration of sugars on the seroside is more than that on the mucosal side. Though the exact nature of the transport is not known, the process requires metabolic energy. The monosaccharides which are actively absorbed pass in their original form into the interstitial fluid and then into the portal capillaries to portal blood, to reach the liver. In the liver, other sugars such as fructose and galactose which are absorbed also get converted to glucose.

Fructose may be converted to glucose by one of two routes (see fructose metabolism). (i) It may be phosphorylated to fructose-6-phosphate by hexokinase and then converted to glucose-6-phosphate which may be dephosphorylated to glucose by a phosphatase. (ii) It may be phosphorylated first to fructose-1-phosphate by fructokinase and later to fructose-1-6-diphospate, which then gets converted to fructose-6-phosphate and ultimately form glucose. In the case of galactose, it is first phosphorylated to galactose-1-phosphate and then converted to glucose-1-phosphate, which forms glucose-6-phosphate and ultimately glucose (*see* **Fig. 17.3**).

When liver functions are impaired as in liver disease, conversion of fructose and galactose to glucose does not occur efficiently; instead, they enter the bloodstream as such and get excreted in urine.

Fate of Glucose After Absorption

In the liver, glucose may undergo a variety of chemical changes depending on the physiological need of the body.

1. When there is a physiological demand for energy, glucose may be oxidised completely to carbon dioxide, water and energy.
2. In the absence of a physiological demand for oxidative energy, excess glucose may be converted to glycogen and deposited in liver, muscles and tissues.
3. When it is necessary to maintain the blood glucose level, liver glycogen is converted to glucose which enters the blood.
4. Excess glucose after conversion to glycogen may be converted to fatty acids and stored as triglycerides in the fat depots.
5. Under special circumstances, as in muscle contraction, only partial degradation (glycolysis) may take place, resulting in the formation of lactic acid, which is largely disposed off by the liver.

6. Small amounts of glucose may be directly or indirectly utilised for the synthesis of other carbohydrates such as ribose and deoxyribose which are required for the synthesis of nucleic acids. Glucose can form glucuronic acid, which is involved in detoxication reactions, and galactose, which is a component of glycolipids and lactose.
7. Glucose may contribute to the synthesis of the carbon skeleton of certain amino acids known as the glucogenic amino acids.

CARBOHYDRATE AS A SOURCE OF ENERGY

The major function of carbohydrate in metabolism is to serve as fuel and get oxidised to provide energy for other metabolic processes. The metabolic intermediates are used for various biosynthetic reactions. For this purpose, carbohydrate is utilised by cells mainly in the form of glucose. A major part of dietary glucose is converted to glycogen for storage. Glucose is degraded in the cell by way of a series of phosphorylated intermediates mainly via two metabolic pathways:

1. Embden–Meyerhof pathway of glycolysis
2. Citric acid cycle (tricarboxylic acid cycle or Krebs cycle)

These pathways include exergonic reactions and yield energy primarily in the form of adenosine triphosphate (ATP). ATP is utilised as a common intermediary for all energy-requiring processes. Besides glucose, dietary fatty acids and amino acids are also utilised as metabolic fuel for living cells and used as sources of energy. All three nutrients are metabolised through the **citric acid cycle**.

INTERMEDIARY METABOLISM OF CARBOHYDRATE

The metabolism of glucose in a mammalian organism may be considered under the following subdivisions:

1. **Glycolysis:** The oxidation of glucose or glycogen to pyruvate and lactate by the Embden Meyerhof pathway
2. **Glycogenesis:** The synthesis of glycogen from glucose
3. **Glycogenolysis:** Breakdown of liver glycogen
4. **Oxidation of pyruvate to acetyl-CoA:** Oxidation of pyruvate, prior to entry into the citric acid cycle
5. **Hexose monophosphate shunt pathway** (also called **pentose phosphate pathway**): This is an alternate aerobic pathway for oxidation of glucose.
6. **Gluconeogenesis:** Formation of glucose or glycogen from non-carbohydrate sources

An overview of the intermediary carbohydrate metabolism is schematically represented in **Figure 17.1**.

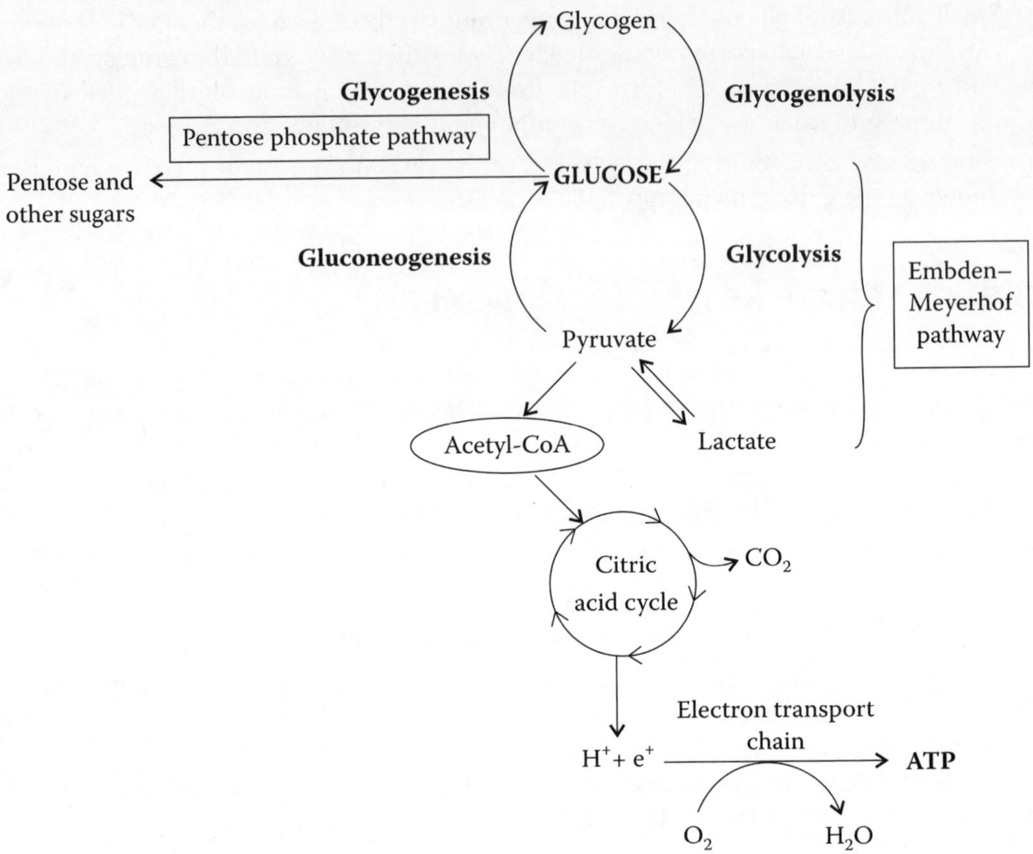

Figure 17.1 Intermediary carbohydrate metabolism.

Glycolysis (Embden–Meyerhof Pathway)

The process whereby glucose or glycogen is oxidised to pyruvic acid and lactic acid (in the absence of oxygen) is known as **glycolysis**. All the enzymes of glycolysis are found in the extra-mitochondrial soluble fraction of the cell, the cytosol. The reactions of glycolysis are schematically represented in **Figures 17.2** and **17.4**. The sequence of reactions occurring in glycolysis may be considered in four stages:

1. Initial phosphorylation
2. Conversion to trioses
3. Oxidative step
4. Formation of pyruvate and lactate

Initial phosphorylation or glucokinase reaction: Glucose enters into the glycolytic pathway by phosphorylation to glucose-6-phosphate. This is an important reaction which takes place in all tissues, but it occurs mainly in liver and muscle. Entry of glucose into cells for utilisation is facilitated by this reaction and is accomplished by the enzyme

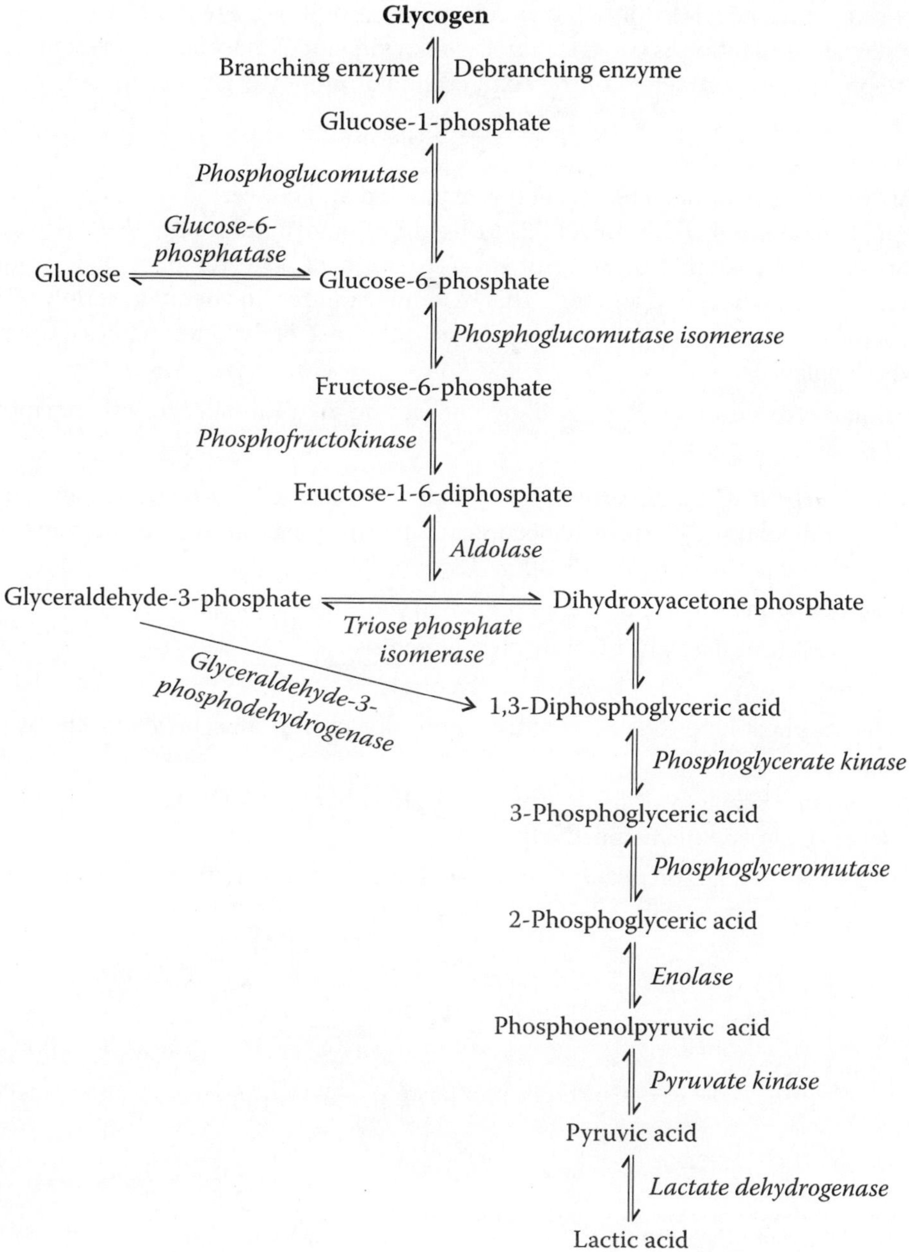

Figure 17.2 Scheme showing the reactions of glycolysis.

glucokinase. **Hexokinase** catalyses the phosphorylation of glucose and other hexoses. **Glucokinase** catalyses the phosphorylation of glucose. The function of glucokinase is to remove glucose from the blood following a meal. The reaction is accompanied by considerable loss of free energy.

Glucose is phosphorylated by ATP which serves as a phosphate donor to form glucose-6-phosphate. The reaction is catalysed by the enzyme glucokinase in the presence of Mg^{++} ions. The phosphate is attached to the sixth carbon atom of the glucose molecule.

$$\text{Glucose} + \text{ATP} \longrightarrow \text{Glucose-6-P} + \text{ADP}$$

In this reaction, one molecule of ATP is expended and converted to ADP and the high-energy phosphate bond (HEB) of ATP is utilised in the formation of glucose-6-phosphate. The reaction is irreversible because of the formation of an ester phosphate (glucose-6-phosphate) at the expense of an HEB. This reaction requires an adequate supply of insulin. When there is decreased secretion of insulin as in the case of diabetes mellitus, the reaction proceeds sluggishly.

Glucokinase reaction is depressed by the action of pituitary growth hormone and adrenocortical hormones.

Metabolic pathways of glucose-6-phosphate: Glucose-6-phosphate is an important compound in glycolysis, because it occupies a central position and forms a junction for several metabolic pathways (**Fig. 17.3**).

1. It is formed from glucose by initial phosphorylation.
2. It is formed from liver glycogen by glycogenolysis.
3. It is formed from muscle glycogen by glycolysis.
4. Glucose-6-phosphate serves to form both liver and muscle glycogen by way of glycogenesis.
5. Fructose and galactose form glucose-6-phosphate via fructose-6-phosphate and galactose-1-phosphate, respectively.
6. The rest of the reactions of the glycolytic pathway up to pyruvic acid proceeds from glucose-6-phosphate (**Fig. 17.4**).

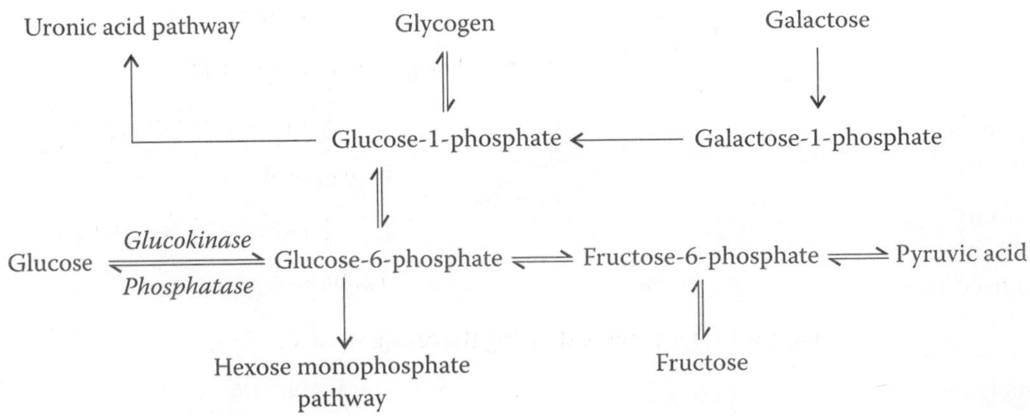

Figure 17.3 Metabolic pathways of glucose-6-phosphate.

7. Another pathway called the hexose monophosphate shunt pathway emerges out from glucose-6-phosphate.
8. Glucose-6-phosphate may be converted to glucuronic acid, via glucose-1-phosphate. This pathway is called **uronic acid pathway**.

Conversion to trioses: First, glucose-6-phosphate is converted to fructose-6-phosphate. The reaction is catalysed by the enzyme phosphohexose isomerase.

Secondly, fructose-6-phosphate is phosphorylated by ATP, to form fructose-1-6-diphosphate. The reaction adds another phosphate linkage at the first carbon atom. ATP which serves as the phosphate donor is converted to ADP.

$$\text{Fructose-6-P} + \text{ATP} \xrightarrow[\text{Mg}^{++}]{\textit{Phosphofructokinase}} \text{Fructose-1-6-di-P} + \text{ADP}$$

The reaction which is catalysed by phosphofructokinase is the same type of reaction as that of initial phosphorylation. Because of the formation of ester phosphate at the expense of a high-energy bond from ATP, it is an irreversible reaction.

In the next reaction, fructose-1-6-disphosphate is split at the midpoint, by the enzyme aldolase, into two molecules of triose phosphates, namely glyceraldehyde-3-phosphate and dihydroxyacetone phosphate.

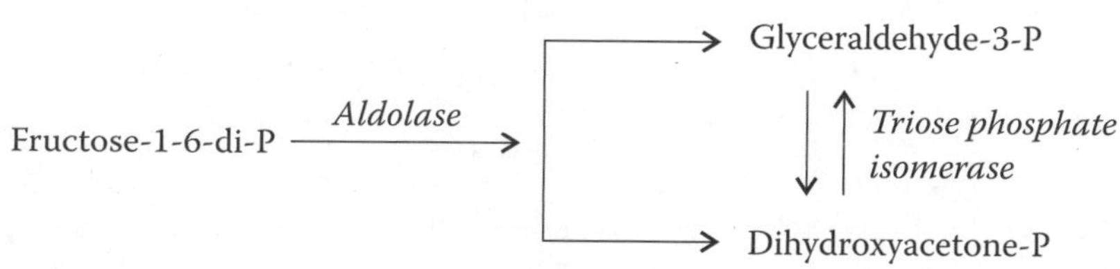

Interconversion of glyceraldehyde-3-phosphate and dihydroxyacetone phosphate to form an equimolecular mixture takes place by the action of triose phosphate isomerase. Since the dihydroxyacetone phosphate is changed to another molecule of glyceraldehyde-3-phosphate, two molecules of glyceraldehyde-3-phosphate are available for oxidation in the next step.

Oxidative step: This is important because this is the first reaction in glycolysis where HEB molecules (ATP) are generated. In this reaction, glyceraldehyde-3-phosphate is oxidised to 1, 3-diphosphoglyceric acid which contains a high-energy bond attached to the first carbon atom. The reaction is catalysed by a double-headed enzyme glyceraldehyde-3-phosphate dehydrogenase which involves the action of coenzymes, namely glutathione, which contains a sulphydryl group (SH) and NAD. It is a complex reaction and may be explained to occur in three steps, namely condensation, dehydrogenation and phosphorolysis.

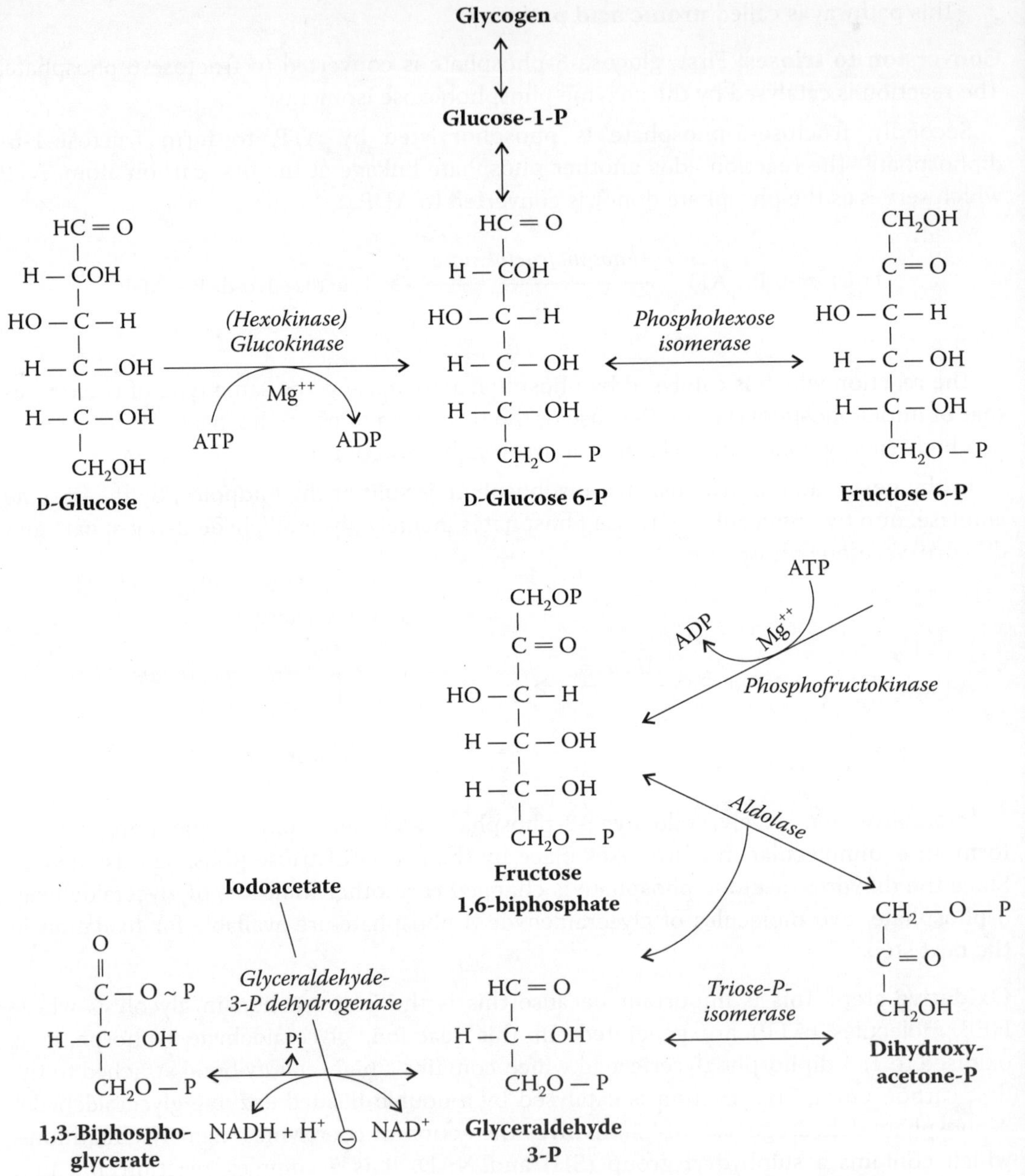

Figure 17.4 Glycolysis: Embden–Meyerhof pathway. (*Contd...*)

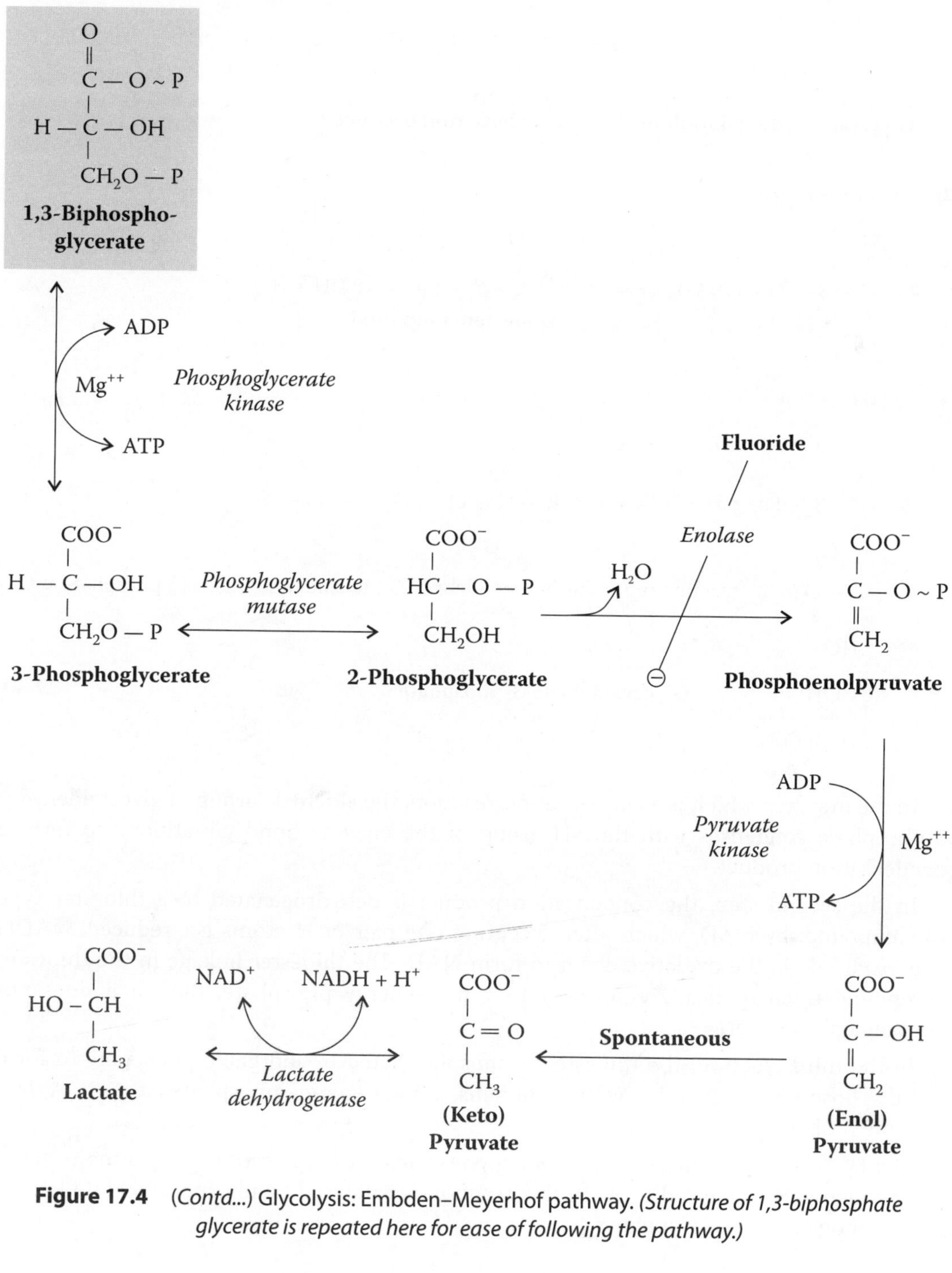

Figure 17.4 (Contd...) Glycolysis: Embden–Meyerhof pathway. *(Structure of 1,3-biphosphate glycerate is repeated here for ease of following the pathway.)*

1. *Condensation*

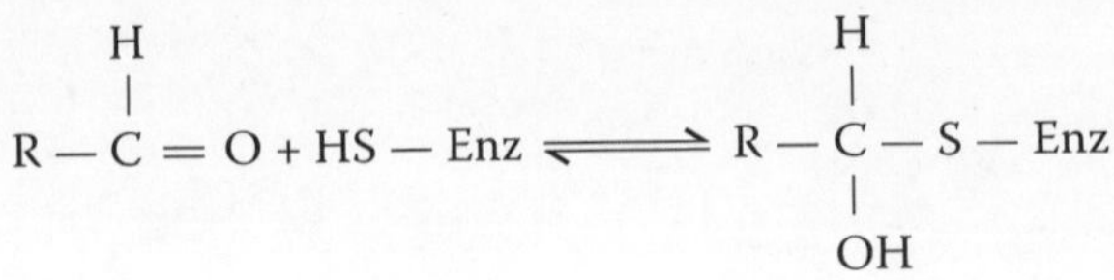

Glyceraldehyde Glutathione Condensation product

2. *Dehydrogenation*

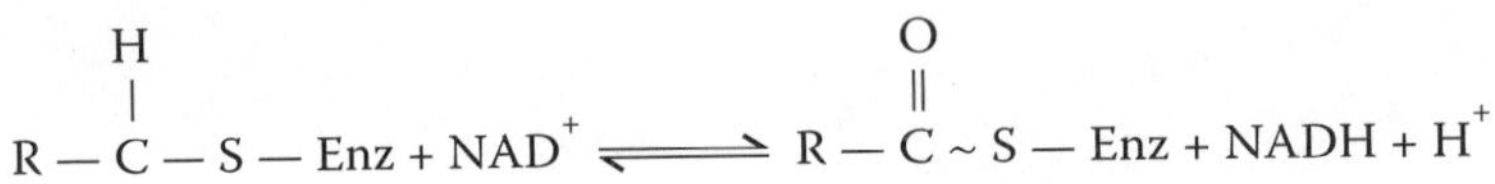

Thioester compound

3. *Phosphorolysis*

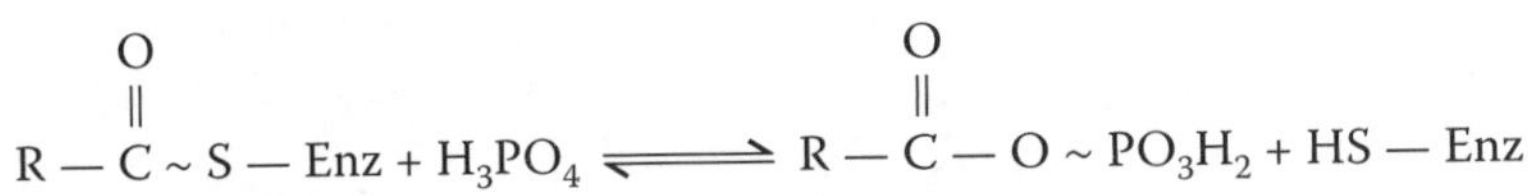

$R-\overset{H}{\overset{|}{C}}=O$ in the reaction represents glyceraldehyde-3-phosphate which has a phosphate at C-3.

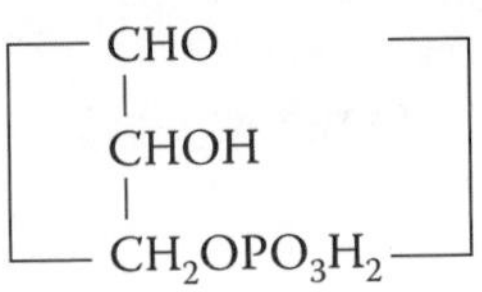

Glyceraldehyde-3-phosphate

In the first step which is a condensation reaction, the aldehyde group of glyceraldehyde-3-phosphate condenses with the SH group of the enzyme bond glutathione to form a condensation product.

In the second step, the condensation product is dehydrogenated to a thioester type of compound, by NAD, which after accepting one pair of H atoms get reduced. NADH gets oxidised via the oxidative chain to form NAD. The thioester linkage in the thioester compound is energetically equivalent to a high-energy phosphate, though it does not contain a phosphate.

In the third reaction, the thioester is phosphorylated by inorganic phosphate to form 1,3-disphosphoglyceric acid, which contains a high-energy phosphate at C-1. A free enzyme is liberated.

The HEB contained in 1,3 disphosphoglyceric acid at C-l is captured by a molecule of ADP which gets converted to ATP. This reaction is catalysed by phosphoglycerate kinase; 3-phosphoglycerate is left behind.

$$\text{Glyceradehyde-3-P} + H_3PO_4 \xrightarrow[\text{Glutathione, NAD}]{\textit{Glyceraldehyde 3-P-dehydrogenase}} \text{1,3-Diphosphoglycerate}$$

$$\text{1,3-Diphosphoglycerate} + \text{ADP} \xrightarrow[Mg^{++}]{\textit{Phosphoglycerate kinase}} \text{3-Phosphoglycerate} + \text{ATP}$$

Since each molecule of glucose metabolised results in the formation of two molecules of glyceraldehyde-3-phosphate, two HEBs (two ATP molecules) are produced for each molecule of glucose. At this stage, 3-phosphoglycerate is converted to 2-phosphoglycerate by phosphoglyceromutase, when the phosphate from the third carbon atom moves to the second carbon atom.

$$\text{3-Phosphoglycerate} \xrightarrow{\textit{Phosphoglyceromutase}} \text{2-Phosphoglycerate}$$

In the next reaction, 2-phosphoglycerate is dehydrated by enolase to form phosphoenolpyruvate which contains an HEB at the second carbon atom.

$$\text{3-Phosphoglycerate} \xrightarrow{\textit{Enolase}} \text{Phosphoenolpyruvate} + H_2O$$

Enolase is inhibited by **fluoride**. This property is made use of to prevent glycolysis, prior to estimation of blood glucose.

Formation of pyruvate: Next, the high-energy phosphate of phosphoenolpyruvate is transferred to ADP when ATP is formed. The reaction is catalysed by pyruvate kinase. Two molecules of ATP are produced for each glucose molecule oxidised. Phosphoenolpyruvate is converted to enolpyruvate which spontaneously gets converted to the keto form of pyruvic acid. This reaction is accompanied by considerable loss of free energy and is irreversible.

$$\text{Phosphoenolpyruvate} + \text{ADP} \xrightarrow{\textit{Pyruvate kinase}} \text{Enolpyruvate} + \text{ATP}$$

$$\text{Enolpyruvate} \xrightarrow{\textbf{Spontaneous}} \text{Ketopyruvate}$$

Keto pyruvic acid may be reduced to lactic acid, if there is lack of oxygen and anaerobiosis prevails. The hydrogen atoms for the formation of lactic acid may be derived from NADH which is produced in the process of oxidation of glyceraldehyde-3-phosphate to 1–3-diphosphoglycerate.

$$\text{Pyruvate} + \text{NADH} + H^+ \xrightarrow{\textit{Lactate dehydrogenase}} \text{Lactate} + NAD^+$$

The enzyme catalysing this reaction is lactate dehydrogenase. Reduced NAD after releasing the hydrogen atoms in this reaction once again gets oxidised to NAD which then participates as a hydrogen acceptor in the oxidative step. But if aerobic conditions are available, lactic acid is not formed and pyruvic acid forms the end product of glycolysis.

Reversibility of the Reactions in Glycolysis

It is important to note that all the reactions in glycolysis from glucose to lactic acid are reversible except three reactions, namely

1. Glucose + ATP $\xrightarrow{\textit{Glucokinase}}$ Glucose-6-P + ADP

2. Fructose-6-P + ATP $\longrightarrow$ Fructose-1-6-di-P + ADP

3. Phosphoenolpyruvate + ADP $\xrightarrow{\textit{Pyruvate kinase}}$ Enolpyruvate + ATP

The first and second reactions are phosphorylations of the irreversible phosphokinase type, forming ester phosphates, at the expense of HEBs of ATP. The third reaction produces ATP.

Summary of Glycolysis

During glycolysis, NAD is reduced to NADH. At the same time, 3-phosphoglyceraldehyde is oxidised to 1–3-diphosphoglycerate. To conserve coenzyme NAD, NADH must be reoxidised. Under anaerobic conditions, this is done when pyruvic acid is converted to lactic acid. In the presence of oxygen, NADH can be oxidised to NAD with the help of the respiratory enzymes.

The H atoms are carried by the flavoprotein enzymes and the cytochrome system of enzymes, until they reach molecular oxygen with which they combine to form H_2O.

Energy Production in Glycolysis

During glycolysis, ATP molecules are used and formed in the reactions given in **Table 17.1**.

Table 17.1 Energetics of Glycolysis

Reactions	ATP Used	ATP Formed
Glucose + ATP $\longrightarrow$ Glucose–6–phosphate	1	
Fructose-6-phosphate + ATP $\longrightarrow$ Fructose-1,6-diphosphate	1	
Reoxidation of 2(NADH + H^+) formed in reaction catalysed by glyceraldehyde-3-phosphate dehydrogenase, in the respiratory chain		6
2(1,3-diphosphoglyceric acid) $\longrightarrow$ 2(3-phosphoglyceric acid)		2
2(phosphoenolpyruvic acid) $\longrightarrow$ 2(enolpyruvic acid)		2
	−2	10

The net gain of ATP molecules during glycolysis is eight as may be seen from the table. It should be noted that oxidation of 2 NADH arising from oxidation of glyceraldehyde-3-phosphate to 1, 3-diphosphoglyceric acid via the oxidative chain will contribute an extra

6 (2 × 3) ATP molecules. 2 × 3 HEBs are produced, as this is oxidative phosphorylation. This accounts for a total of eight molecules of ATP in glycolysis.

Inhibition of Glycolysis

Inhibition can occur during two reactions in glycolysis.

1. Glyceraldehyde-3-P + $H_3PO_4 \longrightarrow$ 1,3-Diphosphoglyceric acid + NADH + H^+

This reaction may be inhibited by iodoacetate. Arsenate can also interfere with this reaction, not by inhibition but by competing with phosphate in the first carbon atom to form 1-areseno-3-phosphoglycerate which hydrolyses spontaneously to give 3-phosphoglyceric acid without generating ATP in the next step. This is an example of uncoupling of oxidation from phosphorylation.

2. 2-Phosphoglyceric acid $\longrightarrow$ Phosphoenolpyruvate + H_2O

Enolase which catalyses this reaction is inhibited by fluoride. Addition of fluoride to blood prior to glucose estimation prevents glycolysis.

Glycogenesis

Glycogenesis is synthesis of glycogen from glucose. Synthesis of glycogen occurs mostly in liver and muscles. Glycogenesis begins with glucose-6-phosphate formed by phosphorylation of glucose. This reaction is common as the first reaction in the pathway of glycolysis from glucose and as the first reaction in glycogenesis. Glucose-6-phosphate is then reversibly converted to glucose-1-phosphate in a reaction catalysed by the enzyme phosphoglucomutase. This process requires Mg^{++} and a small amount of glucose 1-6-diphosphate.

$$\text{Glucose-6-P} \rightleftharpoons \text{Glucose-1-P.}$$

Glucose-1-phosphate undergoes reversible conversion to take part in the synthesis of glycogen. The formation of glycogen occurs as a series of reactions via a uridine pathway (**Fig. 17.5**).

Glucose-1-phosphate reacts with uridine triphosphate (UTP) to form the active nucleotide, uridine diphosphate glucose (UDPG). The reaction is catalysed by the enzyme UDPG pyrophosphorylase. Pyrophosphate (PPi) is liberated.

$$\text{Glucose-1-P + UDP} \xrightarrow{\textit{UDPG-pyrophosphorylase}} \text{UDPG + PPi}$$

UDPG serves as the source of glucose units for the synthesis of glycogen. In the presence of a pre-existing primer of a glycogen chain (R), which acts as a nucleus for the synthesis of fresh glycogen molecules, the activated glucose units separating from UDPG molecules get linked to one another by glucosidic linkages between the first and the fourth carbon atoms (1 → 4) of the adjacent glucose molecules. The reaction is catalysed by glycogen synthetase. The chain of glucose units thus formed gets attached to the outer end of the primer glycogen chain. UDP which is liberated after separation of glucose units gets phosphorylated to form UTP by the action of nucleoside diphosphate kinase. In this manner, the addition of glucose molecules (G) takes place up to eight units. Units of this length are sometimes termed **amylose chains**. Now a second enzyme called the *branching enzyme* acts by establishing connection between the first and the sixth carbon atoms of the adjacent amylose chains. The branches grow by further addition of 1 → 4 glucosyl units, and a glycogen molecule is formed ultimately. Glycogen molecules are large and have high molecular weight (1–4 millions). The structure is characteristic with many branching points looking like branches of a tree. The reactions involved in glycogen synthesis are illustrated in **Figure 17.5**.

UDP-Glucose + R (Glycogen primer) —*Glycogen synthetase*→ RGGGGGGGGG

↓ **Glycogen-amylose from** / Branching enzyme

RGGGGGGGGG
|
GGGGGGGGGG

Glycogen-branched from

Figure 17.5 Representation of reactions involved in glycogen synthesis.

Glycogenesis is stimulated when the level of blood glucose is raised above normal. Besides hexoses, certain amino acids (alanine) and fats (glycerol) contribute to the formation of glucose and glycogen. The formation of glucose from non-carbohydrate sources is known as **gluconeogenesis** or **neoglucogenesis**.

Glycogen Synthetase (Glycogen Synthase) Glycogen synthetase is also known as **glucosyl transferase**. It is present in muscle and liver in two interconvertible forms. Synthase D is the dependent form and is totally dependent for its activity on the presence of glucose-6-phosphate. Synthase I is the independent form. It is not dependent on the presence of glucose-6-phosphate. It implies that synthase I is the active form of the enzyme and synthase D is the inactive form of the enzyme.

Synthase D (inactive) is converted to synthase I (active) by synthase phosphatase. The reaction involves dephosphorylation of a serine residue within the enzyme protein. Synthase I is converted to synthase D by phosphorylation and this leads to inactivation of glycogen synthase. The phosphate donor is ATP. This reaction is catalysed by synthase kinase, a cAMP-dependent protein kinase, active only in the presence of cyclic AMP (cAMP). It implies that glycogen synthesis may be inhibited by the production of cAMP which in turn may be formed by the stimulating action of epinephrine and glucagon. The conversion of synthase D to synthase I is favoured by insulin, thus favouring glycogen synthesis.

Glycogenolysis

Glycogen formed may thus be stored in liver and muscles. The process of breakdown of liver glycogen to glucose is called glycogenolysis (**Fig. 17.6**).

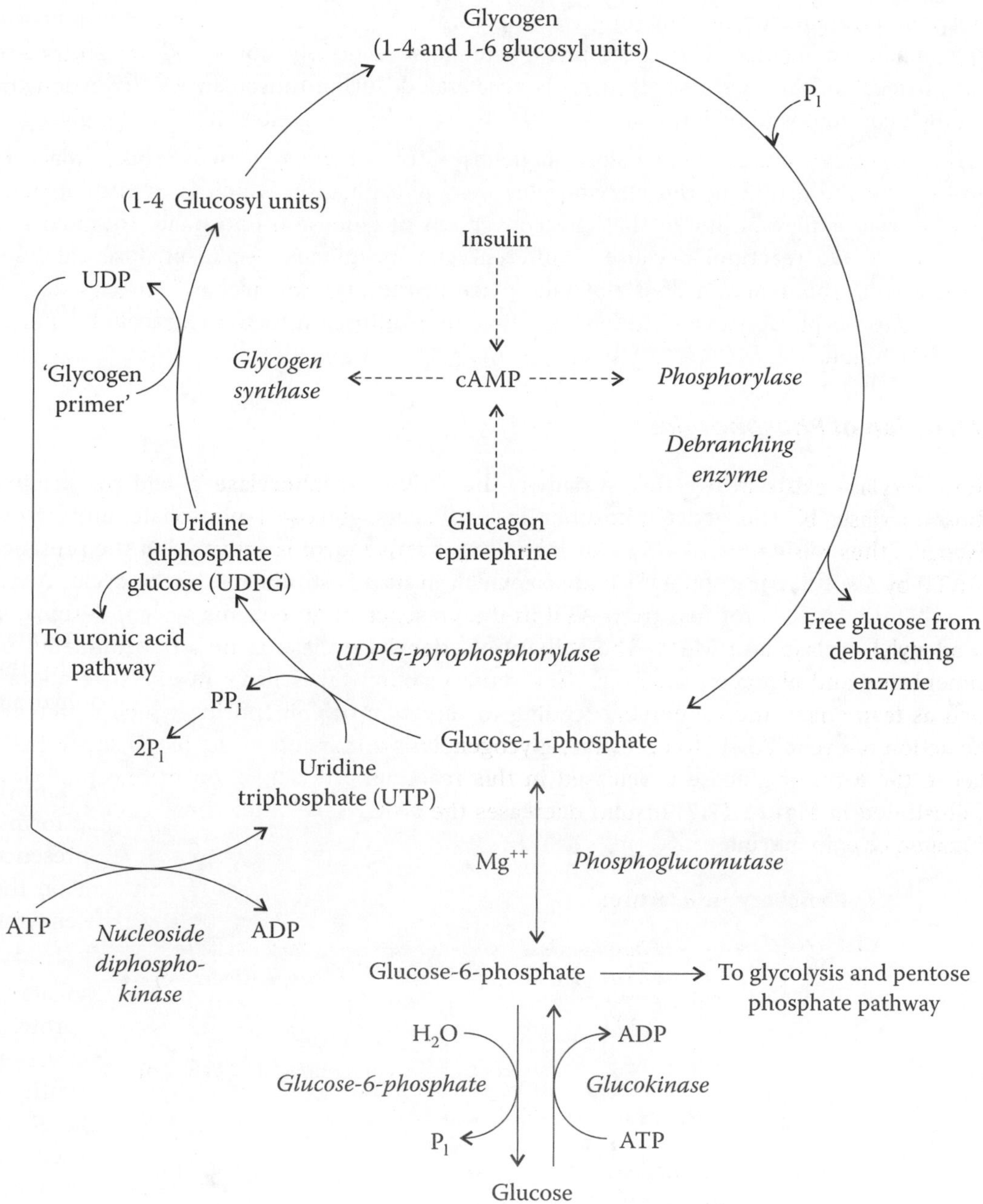

Figure 17.6 Pathway of glycogenesis and glycogenosis in the liver.

First, glycogen is reversibly converted to glucose-1-phosphate. This reaction is catalysed by two enzymes, namely phosphorylase and debranching enzyme. Phosphorylase first acts on the 1–4-glucosidic linkages of the glycogen molecule, breaking it at this point. Glucose-1-phosphate is formed in the presence of inorganic phosphate and simultaneously the 1–6 linkage is split by the action of the debranching enzyme. Thus, the combined action of phosphorylase and the debranching enzyme converts glycogen to a number of glucose-1-phosphate molecules. Glucose-1-phosphate gets reversibly converted to glucose-6-phosphate. Phosphorolysis of glycogen is accelerated during muscular activity, when the blood glucose tends to be low.

The next reaction, i.e. conversion of glucose-6-phosphate to glucose, takes place in the liver by the action of the enzyme glucose-6-phosphatase, which is present in liver and kidneys. It may be noted that the conversion of glucose-6-phosphate to glucose is not a reversible reaction, because a different enzyme glucose-6-phosphatase catalyses the reaction. This reaction does not take place in the muscles because muscles do not have glucose-6-phosphatase. The glucose liberated diffuses into the extracellular fluids, including blood.

Activation of Phosphorylase

Phosphorylase exists in two forms, namely the active phosphorylase 'a' and the inactive phosphorylase 'b'. The active phosphorylase 'a' splits glucose-1-phosphate units from glycogen, thus raising the blood sugar level. The inactive form is activated in the presence of ATP by a specific phosphorylase kinase which in turn is stimulated by the cyclic 'AMP' (cAMP). The latter is formed from ATP in the presence of an enzyme system designated as adenylyl cyclase and Mg^{++}. The activity of adenylyl cyclase is in turn stimulated by epinephrine and glucagon (in liver). The same reaction takes place in violent emotions such as fear, anger and excitement leading to secretion of epinephrine which stimulates the action of cyclic 'AMP' to accelerate glycogenolysis and increase the blood sugar. Extra fuel in the form of glucose is released in this reaction. The activation of phosphorylase is illustrated in **Figure 17.7**. Insulin decreases the cAMP level after it has been raised by glucagon or epinephrine.

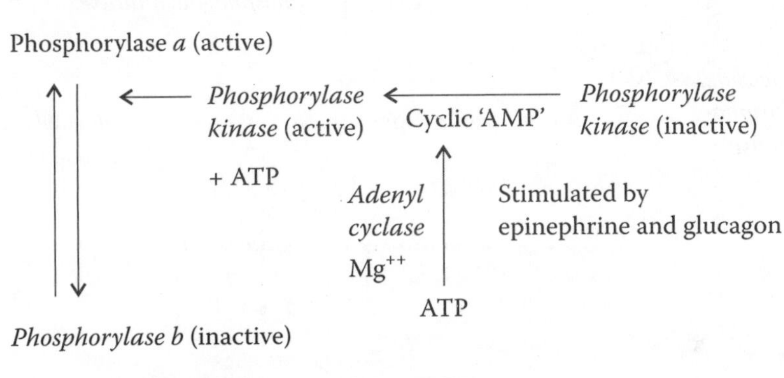

Figure 17.7 Activation of phosphorylase.

Oxidation of Pyruvate to Acetyl-CoA

The conversion of pyruvic acid to acetyl-CoA is the central step linking the glycolytic pathway with the aerobic oxidative pathway or the citric acid cycle. The conversion is accomplished by oxidative decarboxylation catalysed by the complex pyruvate dehydrogenase enzyme system which comprises an aggregate of three specific enzymes, namely

1. Pyruvate decarboxylase
2. Dihydrolipoyl transacetylase
3. Dihydrolipoate dehydrogenase

The reaction is complex involving decarboxylation and dehydrogenation requiring coenzymes TPP, lipoic acid, coenzyme A, NAD, FAD and Mg^{++} ions. The sequence of the reactions may be represented as follows:

1. Formation of 'active pyruvic'

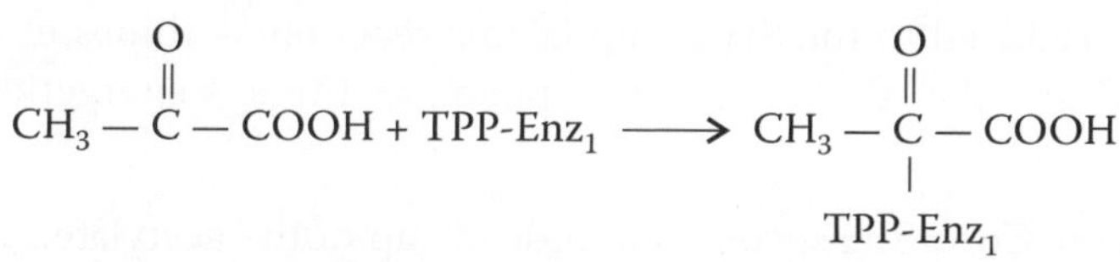

2. Formation of 'active acetaldehyde'

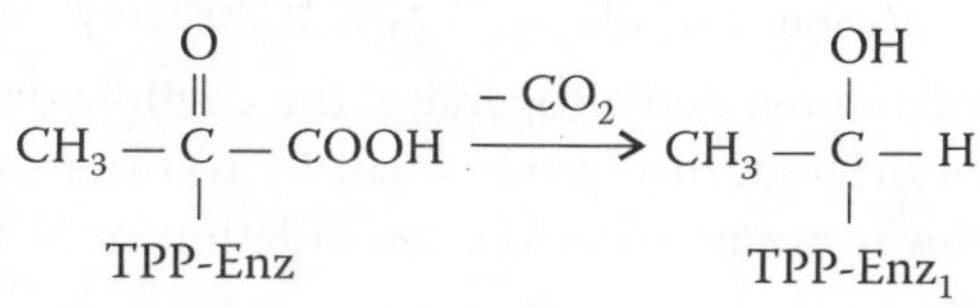

3. Formation of acetylated lipoate

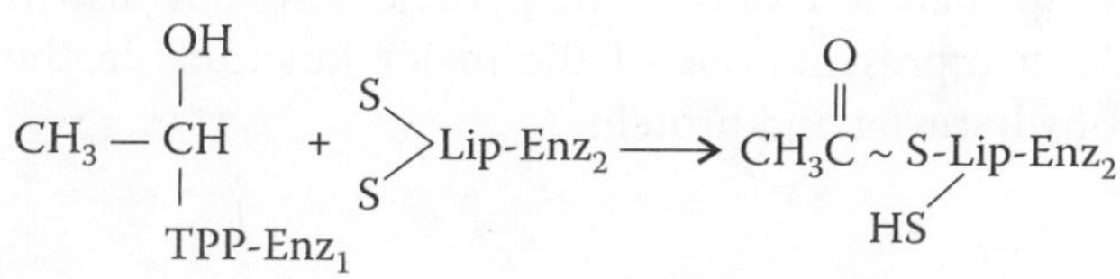

4. Formation of acetyl-CoA

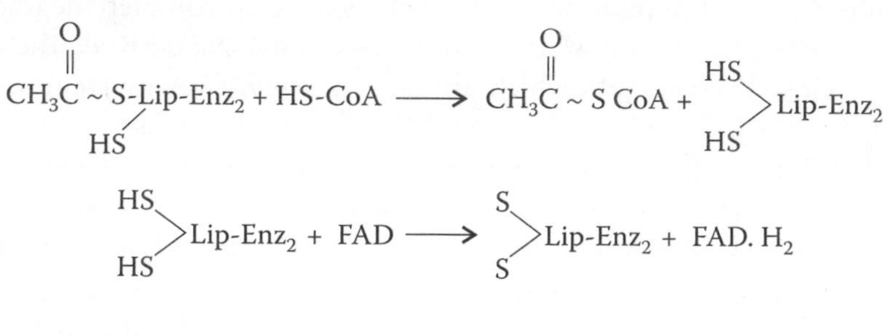

5. $$FAD.H_2 + NAD \longrightarrow FAD + NADH + H^+$$

$$NADH + H^+ + O \longrightarrow NAD + H_2O_2$$

Formation of active pyruvate: The first step is the formation of active pyruvate. This involves condensation of pyruvic acid with the enzyme-bound TPP (TPP-Enz_1), in the presence of Mg^{++} when the α-carbon atom of pyruvic acid gets bound to the C-2 of the thiazole ring of thiamine of TPP, resulting in the formation of an intermediate, 'active pyruvate' or enzyme-bound lactyl-TPP.

Formation of active acetaldehyde: In the second step, 'active pyruvate' loses CO_2 to form 'active acetaldehyde' which is also known as enzyme-bound hydroxyl ethyl-TPP.

Formation of acetylated lipoate: In the third step, 'active acetaldehyde' condenses with the disulphide group of the lipoate bound-enzyme system (Lip-Enz_2) to form the acetylated lipoate, by simultaneously accepting the acetyl group from active acetaldehyde. One of the sulphide groups is reduced to the SH group in this reaction. A thioester linkage is formed between the acetyl and the 'S' of acetylated lipoate, and this is energetically equivalent to an HEB.

Formation of acetyl-CoA: The second sulphide group of the acetylated lipoate undergoes reduction to the sulphydryl form when the acetylated lipoate condenses with the sulphydryl group of coenzyme-A. Thioacyl exchange takes place and acetyl-CoA is liberated. This reaction takes place in the presence of dihydrolipoyl transacetylase.

In the presence of dihydrolipoyl dehydrogenase, the disulphydryl form of lipoate-bound Enz_2 is reconverted to the original disulphide form by transfer of the 2 H atoms to FAD, which in turn transfers the H atoms to NAD. Reoxidation of $NADH_2$ takes place via the aerobic oxidative chain.

Acetyl-CoA is the end product of this reaction. It is an important intermediate metabolite, which is formed not only from pyruvic acid but also from certain amino acids and fatty acids. It represents one of the major junctions in the integration of the metabolism of carbohydrate, fat and protein.

Citric Acid Cycle

Citric acid cycle is the aerobic phase of carbohydrate metabolism and follows the anaerobic pathway from the stage of pyruvic acid. The cycle deals with complete degradation of the acetyl moiety of acetyl-CoA from whatever precursor it may be derived. The cycle may be considered as a closed system into which are fed the acetyl-CoA molecules. To place the system into its proper perspective with regard to glucose metabolism we must remember that for every glucose molecule, two pyruvates are produced at the stage of glycolysis in cytoplasm. These pyruvates are transferred into the mitochondria and are oxidatively decarboxylated to two acetyl-CoA units, and two molecules of CO_2 are released.

As already mentioned, the formation of acetyl-CoA is the link between glycolysis and the citric acid cycle and is at the central point of major metabolic pathways, namely carbohydrate, fat and amino acids. Thus, the cycle gains maximum importance in that all three important foodstuffs take part in the cycle and serve as a common metabolic pathway for the oxidation of foodstuffs. The series of reactions of the citric acid cycle occurs mostly in mitochondria. The reactions are effected in a cyclic manner, and the cyclic mechanism which comprises these reactions is known by various names, namely **'tricarboxylic acid' cycle**, **'citric acid' cycle** and **'Krebs' cycle**. The reactions of the tricarboxylic acid cycle are represented in **Figure 17.8**. The numbers represent eight reactions of the cycle. They are explained one by one in the following section.

All the enzymes of the citric acid cycle are located in the matrix of mitochondria expect succinate dehydrogenase which is located in the inner membrane.

One molecule of acetyl-CoA and one molecule of oxaloacetate are required to start the cycle. Oxaloacetate is formed by carboxylation of pyruvate, catalysed by pyruvate carboxylase.

$$CH_3-\overset{\overset{\large O}{\|}}{C}-COOH + CO_2 \longrightarrow O=\underset{\underset{\large CH_2COOH}{|}}{C}-COOH$$

Pyruvic acid **Oxaloacetic acid**

The cycle starts with the condensation of oxaloacetate with acetyl-CoA to form citrate (1) (*see* **Fig. 17.8**). At the same time, CoA is liberated. One molecule of H_2O is added in this reaction which is catalysed by the condensing enzyme citrate synthetase. It is an irreversible reaction, since it proceeds with the liberation of a large amount of energy amounting to 7720 calories.

$$\text{Oxaloacetate + Acetyl-CoA} \longrightarrow \text{Citrate + CoA}$$

The next reaction is the stepwise production of *cis*-aconitate (2a) and then isocitrate (2b). This involves an equilibration between citrate, *cis*-aconitate and isocitrate.

$$\text{Citrate} \rightleftharpoons \textit{Cis}\text{-aconitate} \rightleftharpoons \text{Isocitrate}$$

The first part of the reaction, i.e. conversion of citrate to *cis*-aconitate, involves dehydration of citrate and therefore removal of one molecule of H_2O, thus creating a double bond for *cis*-aconitate. In the second part of the reaction, *cis*-aconitate is rehydrated to isocitrate with inclusion of one molecule of H_2O. These two reactions (2a) and (2b) are reversible and are catalysed by the enzyme aconitase. The enzyme is inhibited by fluoroacetate which condenses with the oxaloacetate to form fluorocitrate, the actual inhibitor of aconitase. In the next reaction (3), isocitrate is reversibly dehydrogenated to oxalosuccinate, by isocitrate dehydrogenase and coenzyme NAD. This enzyme is located in the mitochondria. NAD which accepts the two H atoms is reduced to $NADH_2$. The two H atoms acquired by NAD are oxidised to H_2O via the respiratory chain of catalysts. NAD is regenerated.

$$\text{Isocitrate} \rightleftharpoons \text{Oxalosuccinate}$$

$$NADH + H^+ + O \longrightarrow NAD + H_2O$$

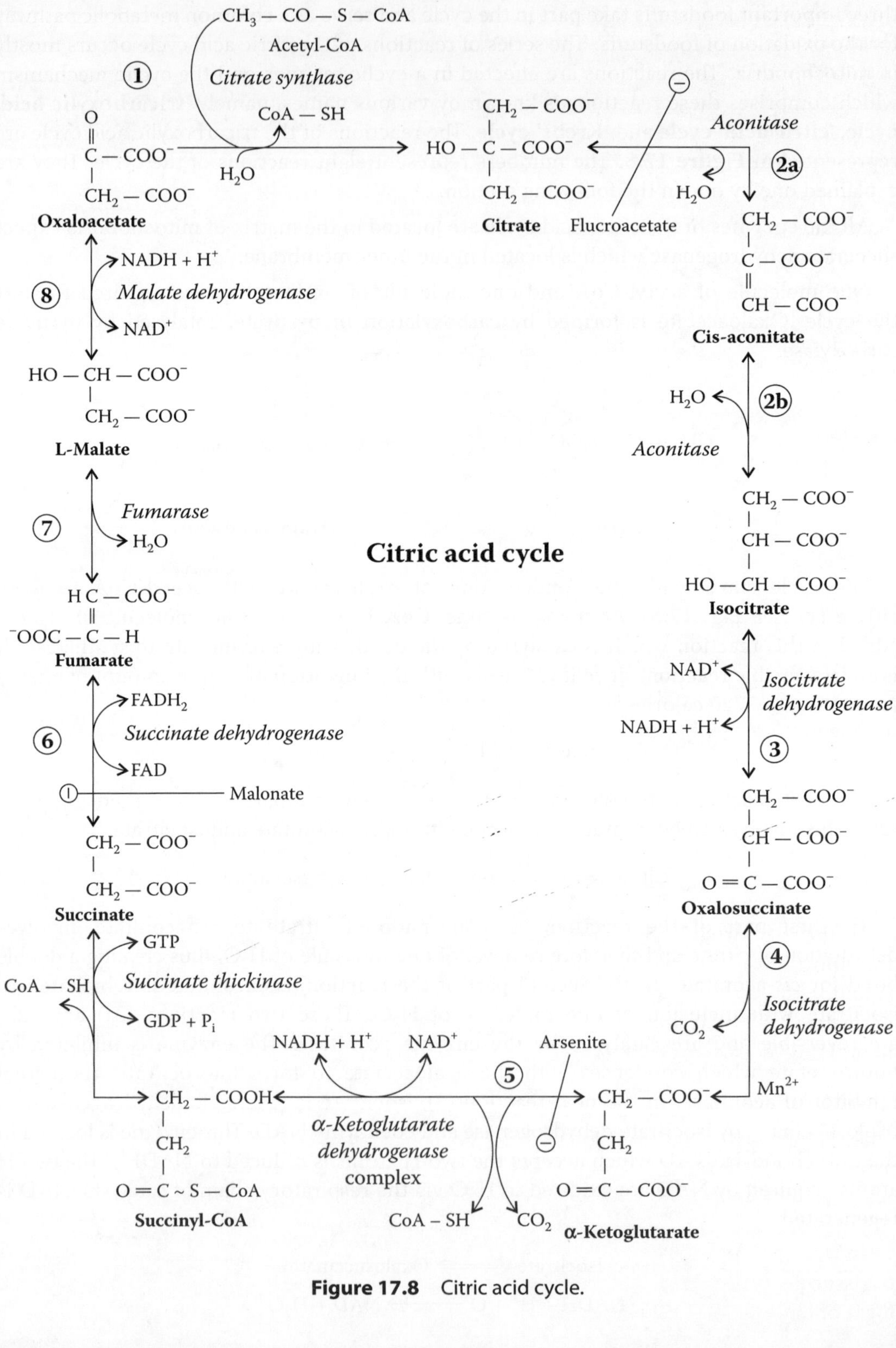

Figure 17.8 Citric acid cycle.

Oxalosuccinate is a keto acid and is not a free intermediate. It gets decarboxylated to form α-ketoglutarate by another isocitrate dehydrogenase which is specific for NAD, in the presence of Mn^{++} (4). This enzyme is also found in the mitochondria.

$$\text{Oxalosuccinate} \xrightarrow{-CO_2} \alpha\text{-Ketoglutarate}$$

In the next reaction (5), α-ketoglutarate undergoes oxidative decarboxylation to form succinate. This involves the series of complex reactions undergone by the initial oxidative decarboxylation of pyruvate. This is an irreversible reaction and is catalysed by the α-ketoglutarate dehydrogenase enzyme system in the presence of cofactors TPP, lipoic acid, NAD, FAD, CoA and Mg^{++} ions. The same aggregate of three specific enzymes, mentioned under oxidative decarboxylation of pyruvic acid, participates in the reaction. They are α-ketoglutarate decarboxylase, dihydrolipoyl trans-succinylase and dihydrolipoate dehydrogenase. Arsenite inhibits the reaction allowing α-ketoglutarate to accumulate. The reactions occur as follows.

In the first step, 'active α-ketoglutaric acid' is formed when α-ketoglutaric acid condenses with the enzyme-bound TPP ($TPP\text{-}Enz_1$), in the presence of Mg^{++} ions.

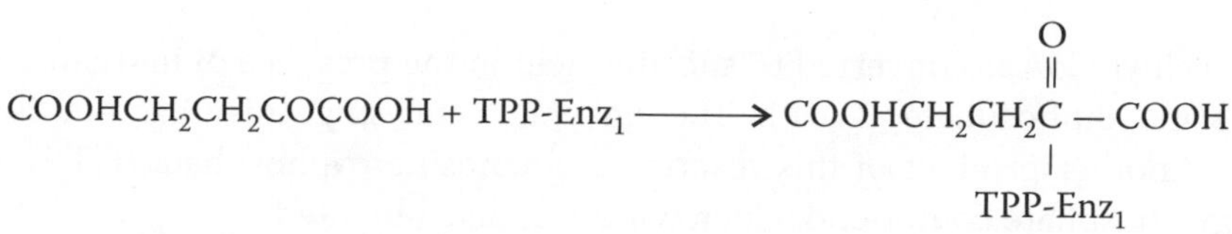

In the second step, TPP-enzyme bound succinyl semialdehyde is formed, after liberation of one molecule of CO_2 from 'active α-ketoglutaric acid'.

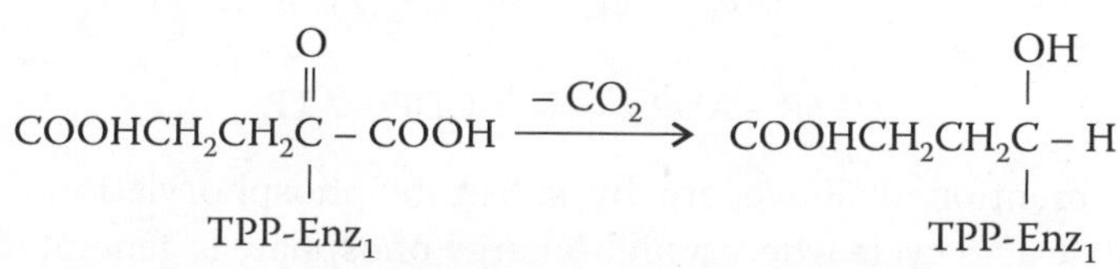

In the third step, TPP-bound succinyl semialdehyde condenses with the disulphide of the lipoate-bound enzyme system ($Lip\text{-}Enz_2$) to form succinylated lipoate in which one sulphide is reduced to the SH group. A thioester linkage is formed, between the succinyl derivative and the 'S' moiety of the succinylated lipoate. The thioester linkage is equivalent to an HEB.

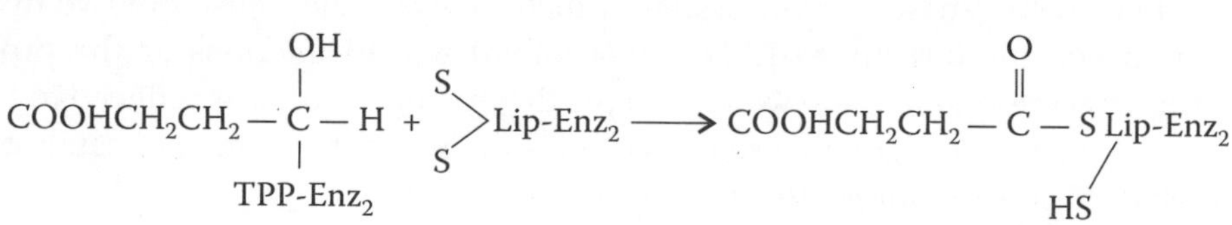

In the next reaction, succinyl-CoA is formed, in the presence of dihydrolipoyl transsuccinylase, when the succinylated lipoate condenses with CoA. The disulphydryl form of lipoic acid is also formed.

$$COOHCH_2CH_2-\overset{\overset{\displaystyle O}{\|}}{C}\sim\begin{matrix}S\\HS\end{matrix}\!>\text{Lip-Enz}_2 + \text{HS-CoA} \longrightarrow COOHCH_2CH_2-\overset{\overset{\displaystyle O}{\|}}{C}\sim S\,CoA + \begin{matrix}HS\\HS\end{matrix}\!>\text{Lip-Enz}_2$$

In the presence of dihydrolipoate dehydrogenase, the disulphydryl form of lipoate-bound Enz_2 is reconverted to the original disulphide form by transfer of the two hydrogen atoms to FAD, which in turn transfers them to NAD.

$$\begin{matrix}HS\\HS\end{matrix}\!>\text{Lip-Enz}_2 + FAD \longrightarrow \begin{matrix}S\\S\end{matrix}\!>\text{Lip-Enz}_2 + FAD.\,H_2$$

$$FADH_2 + NAD \longrightarrow FAD + NADH + H^+$$

Reoxidation of $NADH_2$ takes place via the usual aerobic oxidative chain.

$$NADH + H^+ + O \longrightarrow NAD + H_2O.$$

Next, succinyl-CoA is converted to succinic acid in the presence of inorganic phosphate and guanosine diphosphate (GDP). The enzyme catalysing this reaction is succinate thiokinase. Another product of this reaction is guanosine triphosphate (GTP), which is a high-energy phosphate compound. Coenzyme A is also liberated.

$$HOOC\ CH_2CH_2CO \sim S\ CoA + H_3PO_4 + GDP \rightleftharpoons HOOC\ CH_2CH_2COOH + GTP + CoA{\cdot}SH$$

GTP transfers its HEB to ADP which is converted to ATP. This reaction is catalysed by a phosphokinase.

$$GTP + ADP \rightleftharpoons GDP + ATP.$$

The reactions mentioned above are by substrate phosphorylation. This is the only reaction in the citric acid cycle where a high-energy phosphate is generated at the substrate level. Alternative reactions of succinyl-CoA other than its role in the citric acid cycle are as follows:

1. Succinyl-CoA is utilised in the acetylation of sulphonamide.
2. It is utilised in the synthesis of porphyrin ring.

Succinate is further dehydrogenated to form fumarate (6). This reaction is catalysed by the succinate dehydrogenase enzyme system, which catalyses the transfer of two hydrogen atoms from succinate, directly to FAD (flavoprotein) which functions as the prosthetic group of this enzyme system. FAD which accepts the hydrogen atoms is reduced to $FADH_2$. These two hydrogen atoms are oxidised to H_2O via the respiratory chain of catalysts. FAD is regenerated. Malonate inhibits this reaction.

$$\text{Succinate} \rightleftharpoons \text{Fumarate}$$

$$FADH_2 + O \longrightarrow FAD + H_2O$$

Next, fumarate is reversibly hydrated to malate by fumarase (7). In this reaction, one molecule of H_2O is added to fumaric acid to give malic acid. No coenzyme is required for this reaction.

$$\text{Fumarate} \underset{-\,H_2O}{\overset{+\,H_2O}{\rightleftharpoons}} \text{Malate}$$

Malate is finally dehydrogenated reversibly to oxaloacetate (8) by malate dehydrogenase and coenzyme NAD. NADP can also act as the coenzyme, but it acts at a slower rate. NAD which accepts the hydrogen atoms is reduced to $NADH_2$. These two hydrogen atoms are oxidised to H_2O via the usual aerobic oxidative chain. NAD is regenerated.

$$\text{Malate} \rightleftharpoons \text{Oxaloacetate}$$

$$\text{NADH} + H^+ + O \longrightarrow \text{NAD} + H_2O$$

Oxaloacetate with which the citric acid cycle was started is regenerated. The cycle repeats, starting with the molecule of regenerated oxaloacetate. It is stated that theoretically one molecule of oxaloacetic acid can catalyse oxidation of an infinite number of acetyl groups (acetyl-CoA). The overall oxidation of pyruvic acid may be written as

$$\text{Pyruvate} \longrightarrow (\text{Acetyl-CoA}) \longrightarrow \text{Oxaloacetate}$$

Each time the circuit is completed, 1 molecule of pyruvic acid is dissimilated; 3 molecules of CO_2 are evolved and 10 atoms of H are formed, which combine with 5 atoms of oxygen to form 5 molecules of H_2O by way of the oxidative chain. Three molecules of H_2O are taken up in the hydration reaction so that the final result is

$$CH_3CO\ COOH + 5(O) \longrightarrow 2H_2O + 3CO_2.$$

When oxidation occurs in tissues, the energy formed is captured in HEBs. It has been calculated that at least a total of 38 HEBs are generated for each molecule of glucose undergoing oxidation to CO_2 and H_2O. Assuming each high-energy bond to be equivalent to 7,500 calories, a total energy of 285,000 calories (7,500 × 38) are captured in ATP during oxidation of one molecule of glucose.

Energetics of the Citric Acid Cycle During the aerobic phase, 24 molecules of ATP are formed for 2 acetate units and none utilised. Thus, the total number of ATP molecules produced during glycolysis and citric acid cycle would be (8 + 24) = 32. Formation of ATP occurs, wherever there is uptake of molecular oxygen, as in oxidative reactions concerned with the regeneration of NAD, NADP and FAD, from their reduced forms. There are five reactions where there are uptake of oxygen, and ATP are formed in these five reactions. In these reactions, removal of electrons from the substrate is accompanied by liberation of high energy, which is temporarily stored as ATP.

The number of ATP molecules liberated in each of these five reactions depends upon whether the uptake of oxygen is coupled with oxidative phosphorylation or substrate phosphorylation.

It has been found that three molecules of high-energy phosphate are formed when oxidation is coupled with oxidative phosphorylation, as in the transfer of electrons from the substrate, step by step, via the oxidative system. Examples are conversion of isocitrate to oxalosuccinate, succinate to fumarate and malate to oxaloacetate. Four molecules of HEBs are produced, when oxidation is coupled with substrate phosphorylation, and the electrons couple with oxygen directly, without the participation of the respiratory chain. Examples are conversion of pyruvate and α-ketoglutarate to acetyl-CoA and succinate, respectively.

But exception to these rules arises, because during the oxidation of succinate, it yields only two instead of three molecules of HEB, as it bypasses some of the oxidative chains and couples directly with the cytochromes. Similarly, oxidation of pyruvate yields only three instead of four HEBs, because one HEB is used to 'drive' the synthesis of citrate. The number of ATP molecules formed at the different stages during the aerobic phase is given in **Table 17.2**.

Table 17.2 Production of ATP for Each Turn of Citric Acid Cycle

Reactions Catalysed by	Method of Production of ATP	Number of ATP Produced
Isocitrate dehydrogenase	Oxidation of 2(NADH + H^+) in the respiratory chain	6
α-Ketoglutarate dehydrogenase	Oxidation of 2(NADH + H^+) in the respiratory chain	6
Succinate thiokinase	Oxidation at substrate level	2
Succinate dehydrogenase	Oxidation of $FADH_2$ in the respiratory chain	4
Malate dehydrogenase	Oxidation of 2(NADH + H^+) in the respiratory chain	6
	Total	24

ATP, adenosine triphosphate.

As may be seen from **Table 17.2**, 24 ATP are produced from two acetate molecules for each turn of the citric acid cycle. While calculating energy yield for the complete oxidation of one molecule of glucose, we should include the ATP formed by the oxidation of two pyruvate molecules to two acetyl CoA molecules, catalysed by the pyruvate dehydrogenase enzyme system, as this step links the glycolytic pathway with the citric acid cycle.

Oxidation of two pyruvate to two acetyl CoA yields six ATP molecules. (2 pyruvate ⟶ 2 acetyl CoA) = 6 ATP.

The total number of ATP generated from oxidation of one molecule of glucose would be as follows:

Glycolysis (includes oxidation of $2NADH_2$)	8 ATP
Conversion of pyruvate to acetyl-CoA	6 ATP
Citric acid cycle	24 ATP
Total	38 ATP

Role of Liver in Carbohydrate Metabolism

Liver plays an important role in carbohydrate metabolism by promoting glycolysis, glycogenesis, glycogenolysis, gluconeogenesis and utilisation of carbon dioxide. These processes operate smoothly in accordance with physiological requirements. **Figure 17.9** shows the major metabolic pathways glucose-6 PO_4 can take in the liver.

The presence of the enzyme glucose-6-phosphatase in the liver is responsible for maintaining an equilibrium between blood glucose, glycogen, pyruvate and other glucogenic materials in normal health (**Fig. 17.9**). Owing to the presence of glucose-6-phosphatase in the liver, liver glycogen can directly form blood glucose by way of glucose-1-phosphate and glucose-6-phosphate. In addition, any glucogenic substance in the liver can form blood glucose via glucose-6-phosphate without passing through the stage of liver glycogen. An adequate concentration of glucose-6-phosphate is necessary to maintain a normal blood sugar level. The glycogen content of human liver, at any given time, is the resultant of glycogenolysis and glycogenesis. When there is a deficiency of glucose-6-phosphatase in the liver, glycogenolysis is retarded and blood glucose is reduced, whereas glycogenesis occurs in the usual manner, resulting in an abnormal accumulation of glycogen in the liver. This is the defect in **Von Gierke's disease**, a glycogen storage disease.

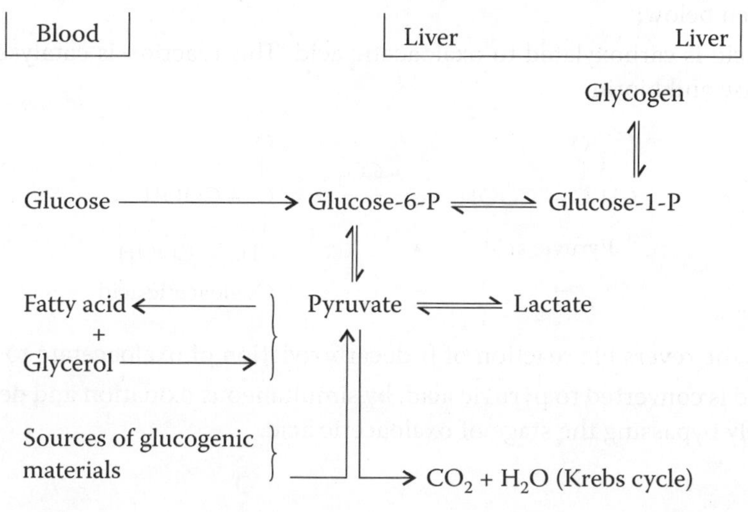

Figure 17.9 Diagrammatic representation of the role of liver in maintaining equilibrium between glucose, glycogen and pyruvate.

The conversion of non-carbohydrate substances to glucose and glycogen is called **gluconeogenesis**. This process takes place mostly in the liver and is essential for the maintenance of normal concentration of glucose in blood and glycogen in liver and muscles. The non-carbohydrate sources for gluconeogenesis include glucogenic amino acids such as aspartic acid, glutamic acid, alanine and certain intermediaries of carbohydrate metabolism, namely lactic acid, pyruvic acid, succinic acid, fatty acid and glycerol. The glucogenic amino acids after undergoing deamination or transamination form α-ketoacids, which enter the carbohydrate metabolism and get converted to glycogen and glucose. Gluconeogenesis occurs especially in the following circumstances:

1. Intake of high protein diet resulting in the absorption of large amounts of amino acids
2. During muscular exercise, when large amounts of lactic acid escape as a result of glycolysis, the liver picks up the lactic acid and converts it to liver glycogen and blood glucose via the Cori cycle
3. During starvation, tissue proteins are broken down in excess, and the amino acids are utilised for gluconeogenesis

The same process takes place in a diabetic state also and this contributes to the emaciation of the body. Gluconeogenesis is enhanced by carbohydrate deprivation and adrenocortical hormones. It is retarded by insulin.

Utilisation of CO_2: Liver, in contrast to other tissues, can readily synthesise its own supply of oxaloacetic and pyruvic acids for the tricarboxylic acid cycle, as long as a source of pyruvic acid and CO_2 are available. Liver utilises CO_2 liberated as a by-product during metabolism, not only in reactions of carbohydrate metabolism but also in metabolism of other substances.

A few examples of utilisation of CO_2 in carbohydrate metabolism (tricarboxylic acid cycle) are given below:

1. Pyruvic acid is carboxylated to oxaloacetic acid. This reaction is catalysed by pyruvate carboxylase and biotin.

$$\underset{\text{Pyruvic acid}}{CH_3C(=O)-COOH} \xrightarrow{+CO_2} \underset{\text{Oxaloacetic acid}}{\begin{matrix} C(=O)-COOH \\ | \\ CH_2-COOH \end{matrix}}$$

This is the reversible reaction of β-decarboxylation of oxaloacetate to pyruvate.

2. Malic acid is converted to pyruvic acid, by simultaneous oxidation and decarboxylation, completely bypassing the stage of oxaloacetic acid.

$$\underset{\text{Malic acid}}{\begin{matrix} HO-CH-COOH \\ | \\ CH_2-COOH \end{matrix}} + NAD \longrightarrow CH_3C(=O)-COOH + NADH_2 + CO_2$$

The enzyme catalysing this reaction is malic enzyme (malic dehydrogenase). Assimilation of CO_2 in liver may be regarded as a necessary preliminary to reactions of the citric acid cycle.

3. In another reaction, not exactly concerned with the citric acid cycle, succinyl-CoA is synthesised from propionate by carboxylation and the reaction is catalysed by a carboxylase and biotin.

Another reaction which is concerned with an early step in the synthesis of fatty acids refers to carboxylation of acetyl-CoA to malonyl-CoA. The reaction is catalysed by acetyl-CoA carboxylase and biotin.

Alternate Aerobic Pathway: Pentose Metabolism (Oxidative Shunt or Hexose Monophosphate Shunt Pathway)

Though it has been established that the main pathway for oxidation of glucose is via glycolysis and Krebs cycle, certain mammalian tissues follow alternate aerobic pathways and bring about direct oxidation without passing through glycolysis, due to the presence of another series of enzymes.

Out of the various alternate pathways, one pathway has been well established and has gained importance. This is called the **oxidative shunt** or **pentose shunt** or **hexose monophosphate** (HMP) **shunt pathway (Fig. 17.10)**. Another name by which it is referred to is **Warburg–Dickens–Lipmann pathway**. It is a cyclic mechanism analogous to the tricarboxylic acid cycle in which molecular oxygen is utilised in the early part of the reactions and is present in the cytosol.

The importance of this pathway is that it generates NADPH which is necessary for the formation of glutathione in a reduced state. It is required to maintain the integrity of the red cell membrane and prevent haemolysis. The pathway is active in brain cells, liver, mammary glands, testes and adrenal cortex. The pathway does not yield ATP.

The sequence of reactions begins with glucose-6-phosphate, which follows an aerobic instead of the usual glycolytic pathway.

For the sake of simplicity, the reactions of the pathway can be divided into two broad phases:

I. Conversion of hexose to pentose
II. Conversion of pentose to hexose

I. Conversion of hexose to pentose:

1. Glucose-6-phosphate is oxidised (dehydrogenated) to 6-phosphogluconic acid by glucose-6-phosphate dehydrogenase ('Zwischenferment') and coenzyme NADP.

$$\text{Glucose-6-P} + \text{NADP} \xrightarrow[\text{}]{\textit{Glucose-6-P dehydrogenase}} \text{6-Phosphogluconic acid} + \text{NADPH} + \text{H}^+$$

2. 6-Phosphogluconic acid is first oxidised (dehydrogenated) by 6-phosphogluconate dehydrogenase and NADP and subsequently decarboxylated to form ribulose-5-phosphate.

$$\text{6-Phosphogluconic acid} + \text{NADP} \xrightarrow{\textit{6-Phosphogluconate dehydrogenase}} \text{Ribulose-5-P} + \text{NADPH} + \text{H}^+$$

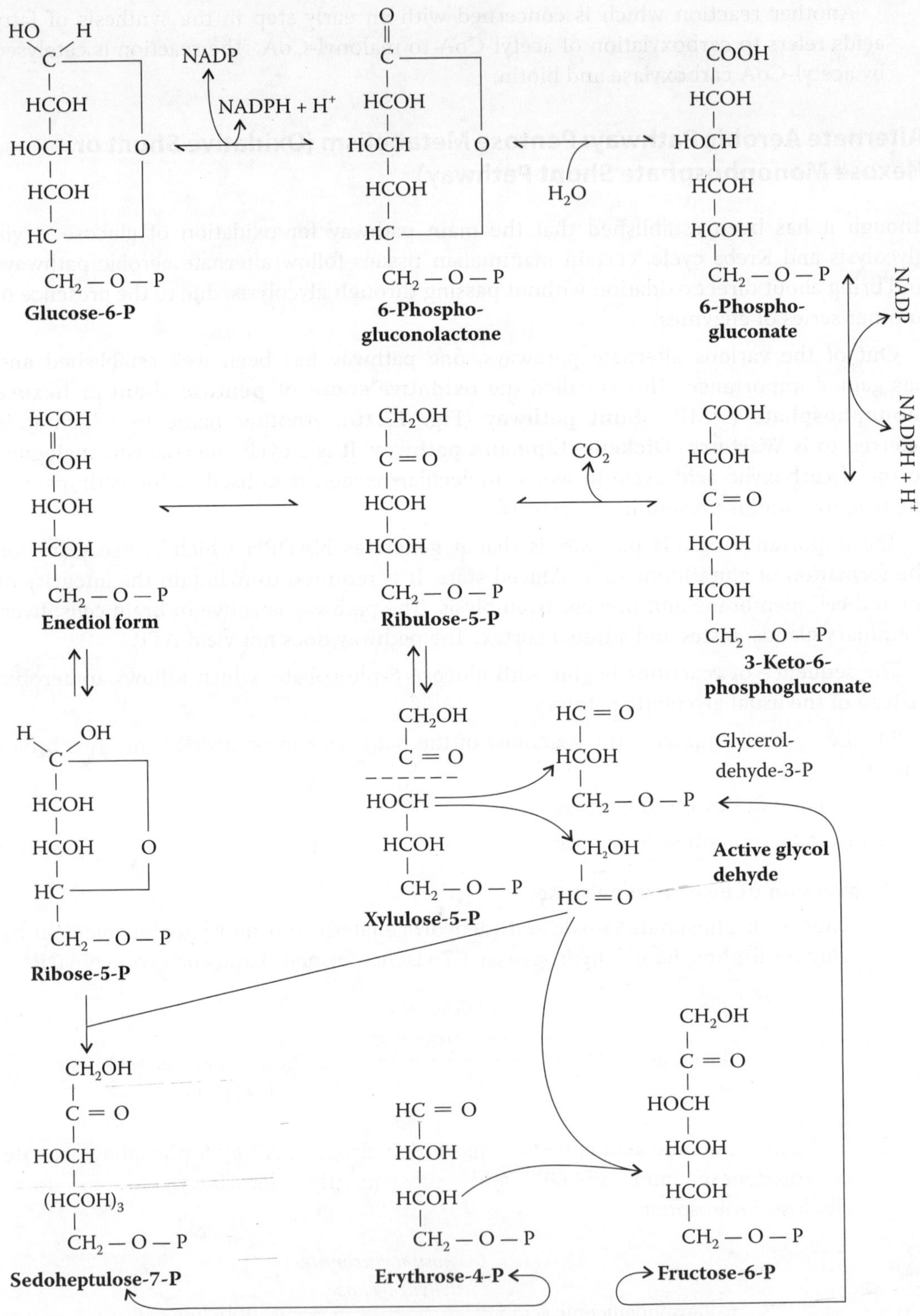

Figure 17.10 Hexose monophosphate shunt pathway.

Ribulose-5-phosphate is in equilibrium with ribose-5-phosphate, through an enediol, catalysed by phosphoriboisomerase.

$$\text{Ribulose-5-P} \xrightleftharpoons{\textit{Phosphoribo-isomerase}} \text{Ribose-5-P}$$

3. Ribulose-5-phosphate is converted to xylulose-5-phosphate by epimerase.

$$\text{Ribulose-5-P} \xrightarrow{\textit{Epimerase}} \text{Xylulose-5-P}$$

II. Conversion of pentose to hexose:

4. Xylulose-5-phosphate undergoes transketolation to form glyceraldehyde-3-phosphate. During this reaction, a ketol group ('active glycolaldehyde') is removed from xylulose-5-phosphate by the enzyme transketolase with TPP and Mg^{++} ions acting as cofactors.

$$\text{Xylulose-5-P} \xrightarrow{\textit{Transketolase}} \text{Glyceraldehyde-3-P + 'Active glycolaldehyde'}$$

5. The ketol fragment removed from xylulose-5-phosphate condenses with ribose-5-phosphate to form an unusual seven carbon sugar sedoheptulose, by the action of a transketolase.

$$\text{Ketol + Ribose-5-P} \xrightarrow{\textit{Transketolase}} \text{Sedoheptulose}$$

6. Finally, a transaldolase transfers the upper dihydroxyacetone moiety of sedoheptulose to glyceraldehyde-3-phosphate to form the hexose, fructose-6-phosphate leaving a tetrose residue, erythrose-4-phosphate. Fructose-6-phosphate can be readily converted to glucose-6-phosphate.
7. Addition of a ketol fragment to erythrose-4-phosphate, by the transketolase reaction, will give fructose-6-phosphate.

$$\text{Ketol + Erythrose-4-P} \longrightarrow \text{Fructose-6-P}$$

The cycle repeats starting with glucose-6-phosphate which is regenerated at the end of each cycle.

The reactions of the pathway may be summarised; thus

1. $$\underset{\text{+ NADP}}{\text{Glucose-6-P}} \xrightarrow{\substack{\textit{G-6-P} \\ \textit{dehydrogenase}}} \text{6-Phosphogluconic acid + NADPH + } H^+$$

2. $$\underset{\text{+ NADP}}{\text{6-Phosphogluconic acid}} \xrightarrow{\substack{\textit{6-P-G} \\ \textit{dehydrogenase}}} \text{Ribulose-5-P + } CO_2 \text{ + NADPH + } H^+$$

$$\text{Ribulose-5-P} \xrightarrow{\textit{Phosphoribo-isomerase}} \text{Ribose-5-P}$$

3. Ribulose-5-P $\xrightarrow{\textit{Epimerase}}$ Xylulose-5-P

4. Xylulose-5-P $\xrightarrow{\textit{Transketolase}}$ Glyceraldehyde-3-P + 'Active glycolaldehyde'

5. Ketol + Ribose-5-P $\xrightarrow{\textit{Transketolase}}$ Sedoheptulose-7-P
fragment

6. Sedoheptulose-7-P + Glyceraldehyde-3-P $\longrightarrow$ Fructose-6-P + Erythrose-4-P

Erythrose-4-P + Ketol fragment $\longrightarrow$ Fructose-6-P

Fructose-6-P $\rightleftharpoons$ Glucose-6-P

Metabolic Significance of the Hexose Monophosphate Pathway

1. The major function of the hexose monophosphate shunt pathway is to furnish and maintain a continuous supply of reduced NAD and NADP which are required for various metabolic reactions.
2. A direct correlation exists between the activity of certain enzymes involved in this pathway, particularly glucose-6-phosphate dehydrogenase and fragility of red blood cells. It has been found that a hereditary defect of this enzyme in erythrocytes is associated with a tendency towards haemolysis, particularly when the cells are subjected to the toxic effects of certain drugs.
3. Reduced NADP is required for the enzyme system concerned with the synthesis of fatty acids. It is found that in active mammary glands where there is increased synthesis of fatty acids, the HMP pathway is particularly active because it supplies enough NADPH, essential for the synthesis of fatty acids. Injection of insulin promotes formation of glucose-6-phosphate and thus indirectly stimulates the HMP pathway which in turn helps in the synthesis of NADPH required for the synthesis of fatty acids.
4. It forms an important pathway by which pentose is synthesised and metabolised in the body. Pentoses are essential for the synthesis of nucleotides and nucleic acids.

Other pathways of glucose metabolism:

Uronic acid (glucuronic acid) pathway: This is a minor pathway by which glucose gets converted to glucuronic acid, ascorbic acid and pentose. The reactions start with glucose-6-phosphate as in the HMP pathway.

1. Glucose-6-phosphate is converted to glucose-1-phosphate by the enzyme phosphoglucomutase.
2. Glucose-1-phosphate reacts with uridine triphosphate (UTP), in the presence of UDPG–pyrophosphorylase, to form the active nucleotide uridine diphosphate–glucose (UDPG). All steps up to this point are similar to those of glycogenesis in the liver.

3. UDP–glucose is oxidised at carbon atom 6, first to uridine–diphosphate–glucuronic acid (UDP–glucuronic acid) by UDPG–dehydrogenase and NAD and then to glucuronic acid.

   UDP–glucuronic acid is the active form of glucuronic acid, which takes part in conjugation reactions and formation of bilirubin glucuronide.

4. Glucuronic acid is then reduced in the presence of NADPH to L-gulonic acid, which is the direct precursor of ascorbic acid in animals which are capable of synthesising this vitamin.

   In man, ascorbic acid cannot be synthesised and L-gulonic acid is oxidised to 3-ketogulonic acid and then to L-xylulose which is converted to its isomer, D-xylulose. This is accomplished by first getting L-xylulose reduced to xylitol in the presence of NADPH.

5. Xylitol is later oxidised in the presence of NAD to D-xylulose which gets converted to xylulose-5-phosphate. It may be remembered that D-xylulose-5-phosphate is a metabolite of the HMP pathway. The reactions may be summarised as follows:

1. $\text{Glucose-6-P} \xleftrightarrow{\textit{Phospho-glucomutase}} \text{Glucose-1-P}$

2. $\text{Glucose-1-P + UTP} \xleftrightarrow{\textit{UDPG-pyrophosphorylase}} \text{UDPG + PPi}$

3. $\text{UDPG + NAD} \xleftrightarrow{\textit{UDPG-dehydrogenase}} \text{UDP-glucuronic acid + NADH + H}^+$

   $\text{UDP-glucuronic acid + H}_2\text{O} \longrightarrow \text{UDP + D-Glucuronic acid}$

4. $\text{D-Glucuronic acid + NADPH + H}^+ \longrightarrow \text{L-Gluconic acid + NADP}$

   $\text{L-Gluconic acid + NAD} \longleftrightarrow \text{3-Keto-gulonic acid + NADH + H}^+$

   $\text{3-Keto-L-gulonic acid} \xrightarrow{-\,CO_2} \text{L-Xylulose}$

   $\text{L-Xylulose + NADPH + H}^+ \longleftrightarrow \text{Xylitol + NADP}$

5. $\text{Xylitol + NAD} \longleftrightarrow \text{D-Xylulose-5-P + NADH + H}^+$

Essential pentosuria: This is a rare hereditary disease, characterised by excretion in the urine of unusually large quantities of L-xylulose. This condition is different from the transient pentosuria which follows ingestion of large amounts of fruits. In essential pentosuria, the person affected appears quite normal and does not suffer from any other ill effects. It is believed that this may be due to a block in the pathway concerned with the conversion of L-xylulose to xylitol, due to the absence of the enzyme necessary for the reduction of L-xylulose to xylitol. As the renal clearance of L-xylulose is very high, and the renal tubular reabsorption very little, L-xylulose cannot be demonstrated in the blood of these patients.

Gluconeogenesis

A continuous supply of glucose is necessary as a source of energy for the metabolism of the nervous system and erythrocytes and for the maintenance of blood glucose within normal limits. It is the major fuel that will supply energy for skeletal muscle contraction under anaerobic condition. Glucose is required in adipose tissue as a source of glycerides and glycerol. Glucose also serves to clear the metabolic products of other tissues from blood, for example lactate produced by muscle and glycerol produced by adipose tissue.

When the supply of glucose from dietary sources is not available in an adequate amount for the varied metabolic reactions, the requirements are met by synthesis of glucose from non-carbohydrate sources. The formation of glucose or glycogen from non-carbohydrate sources is known as **gluconeogenesis**. Several enzymatic pathways have been developed in certain specialised tissues for gluconeogenesis. The principal organs responsible for gluconeogenesis are the liver and kidneys.

Gluconeogenesis and glycolysis are opposing metabolic pathways and share a number of enzymes. The mechanism in gluconeogenesis involves reversal of glycolysis and citric acid cycle. Reactions that are not reversible are substituted by alternate reactions. Thus, glucose or glycogen can be formed from any substance that is a derivative of glycolysis or citric acid cycle.

The main non-carbohydrate sources utilised for gluconeogenesis are amino acids, lactate and glycerol. The amino acids that can synthesise glucose or glycogen are classified as shown in **Figure 17.11**.

Glucogenic Amino Acids

Glucogenic amino acids enter the glycolytic pathway and citric acid cycle through intermediates as indicated in **Table 17.3**.

Table 17.3 Amino Acid Substrates for Gluconeogenesis

Glucogenic Amino Acids Entering Through				
Pyruvate	**α-Ketoglutarate**	**Succinyl-CoA**	**Fumarate**	**Oxaloacetate**
Serine	Arginine	Isoleucine	Phenylalanine	Aspartate
Glycine	Histidine	Methionine	Tyrosine	
Cysteine	Proline	Valine		
Cystine	Glutamate			
Threonine	Glutamine			
Alanine	Ornithine			
	Citrulline			

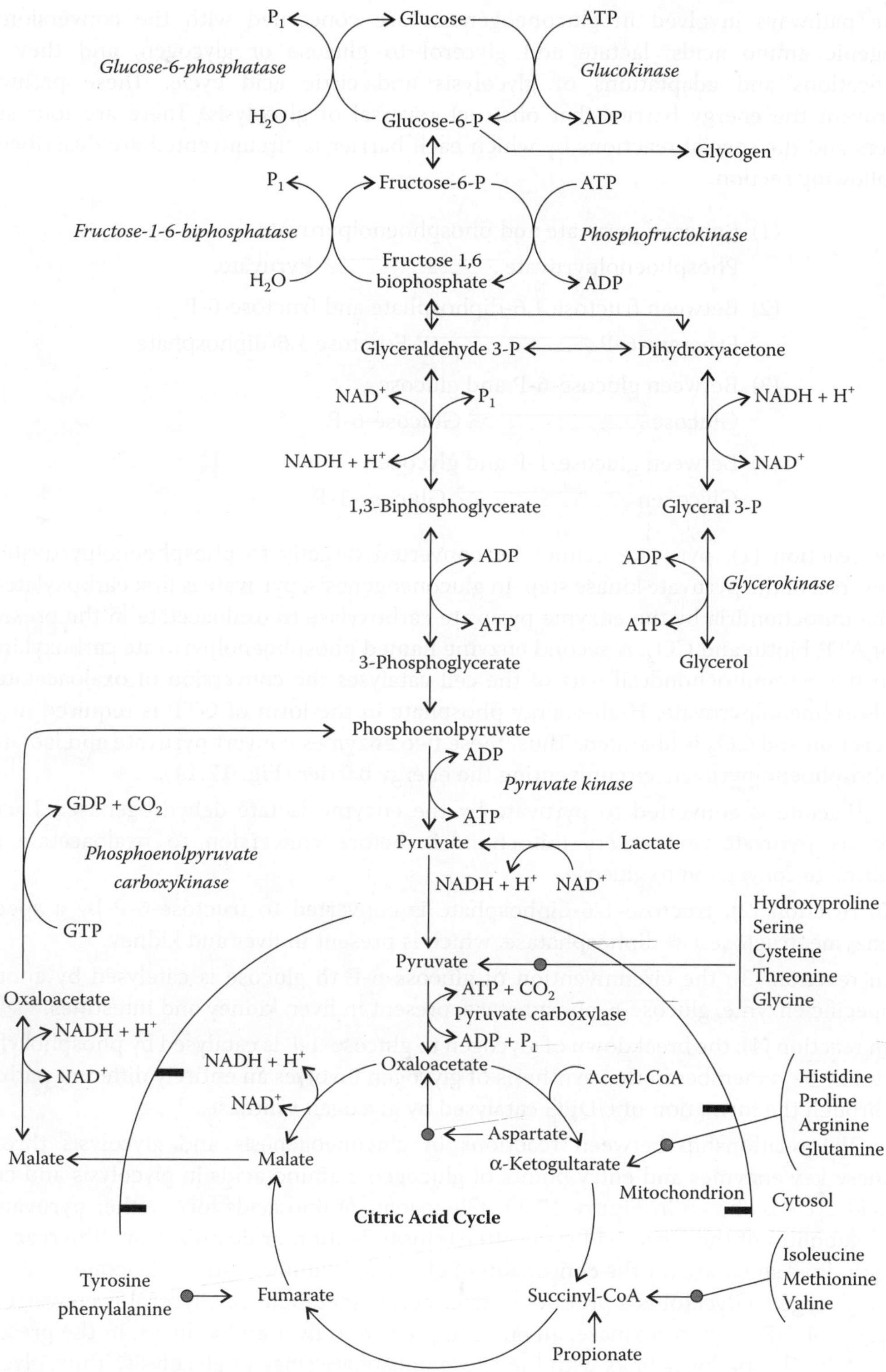

Figure 17.11 Major pathways of gluconeogenesis and glycolysis.

The pathways involved in gluconeogenesis are concerned with the conversion of glucogenic amino acids, lactate and glycerol to glucose or glycogen, and they are modifications and adaptations of glycolysis and citric acid cycle. These pathways circumvent the energy barrier that obstruct reversal of glycolysis. There are four such barriers and the special reactions by which each barrier is circumvented are described in the following section.

(1) Between pyruvate and phosphoenolpyruvate
Phosphoenolpyruvate $\rightleftharpoons$ Pyruvate.

(2) Between fructose 1,6-diphosphate and fructose-6-P
Fructose-6-P $\rightleftharpoons$ Fructose 1,6-diphosphate.

(3) Between glucose-6-P and glucose
Glucose $\rightleftharpoons$ Glucose-6-P.

(4) Between glucose-1-P and glycogen
Glycogen $\rightleftharpoons$ Glucose-1-P.

1. In reaction (1), pyruvate cannot be converted directly to phosphoenolpyruvate by reversal of the pyruvate kinase step. In gluconeogenesis, pyruvate is first carboxylated in the mitochondria by the enzyme pyruvate carboxylase to oxaloacetate in the presence of ATP, biotin and CO_2. A second enzyme named phosphoenolpyruvate carboxykinase in the extramitochondrial part of the cell catalyses the conversion of oxaloacetate to phosphoenolpyruvate. High-energy phosphate in the form of GTP is required in this reaction and CO_2 is liberated. Thus, these two enzymes convert pyruvate and lactate to phosphoenolpyruvate circumventing the energy barrier (**Fig. 17.11**).

   (Lactate is converted to pyruvate by the enzyme lactate dehydrogenase.) Lactate forms pyruvate and enters mitochondria before conversion to oxaloacetate and ultimate conversion to glucose.
2. In reaction (2), fructose-1-6-diphosphate is converted to fructose-6-P by a specific enzyme, fructose 1-6-diphosphatase, which is present in liver and kidney.
3. In reaction (3), the circumvention of glucose-6-P to glucose is catalysed by another specific enzyme, glucose-6-phosphatase, present in liver, kidney and intestines.
4. In reaction (4), the breakdown of glycogen to glucose-1-P is catalysed by phosphorylase. It may be remembered that synthesis of glycogen involves an entirely different pathway through the formation of UDPG catalysed by glycogen synthase.

   The relationship between reactions in gluconeogenesis and glycolysis through these key enzymes and entry points of glucogenic amino acids in glycolysis and citric acid cycle is shown in **Figure 17.11**. Glucogenic amino acids form either pyruvate or metabolites of the citric acid cycle after transamination or deamination. The reactions described so far are for the conversion of glucogenic amino acids and lactate to glucose or glycogen. Glycerol is a product of triglyceride metabolism. Glycerol is converted to glycerol-3-P by glycerokinase, an enzyme present in liver and kidneys, in the presence of ATP. This pathway links with the triose phosphate stage of glycolysis. Thus, glycerol may be converted to blood glucose by making use of the above enzymes.

CHEMISTRY OF MUSCLE CONTRACTION

Chemistry of Muscle

Muscles contain glycogen, proteins and nitrogenous constituents. The proteins of the muscle fibrils are concerned with muscle contraction. Two of the proteins which are directly involved in muscle contraction are (i) actin and (ii) myosin. Szent Gyorgi in 1941 discovered that two types of **actin** exist. These are (i) globular actin or G. actin, which has a low viscosity, and (ii) fibrous actin or F. actin, which has a high viscosity. It is believed that F. actin, which has a strong affinity for myosin, combines with myosin in the ratio of 1:3 to form the contractile unit **actomyosin.**

Myosin is a fibrous protein. The striking property of myosin is its enzymatic activity. As an enzyme, it is known as myosin adenosine triphosphatase or ATP-ase. It helps in the splitting of ATP which is the initial event in the process of muscle contraction. The nitrogenous constituents concerned with muscle contraction are phosphocreatine, creatine, ATP, ADP, carnosine and anserine. Muscles utilise ATP as the direct source of energy for contraction. ATP for this purpose is derived mainly from the oxidation of carbohydrates, fats and amino acids, through the mechanism associated with the Krebs cycle. The breakdown of glycogen through glycolysis supplies sufficient energy to maintain muscle contraction up to a certain extent.

Muscles contain a large amount of creatine phosphate. They serve as an important reserve of high-energy phosphate groups from which energy can be derived whenever required. Immediately after their utilisation, they are resynthesised so that a reserve of high-energy phosphate groups is always maintained.

Contraction of muscle is accompanied by liberation of energy. Some of the energy is used for work and the rest of it is liberated as heat.

The main events occurring in muscle contraction are as follows:

1. Interaction of ATP and actomyosin (contractile unit) to form an activated substance
2. Contraction of the activated substance, thus performing work, with the liberation of inorganic phosphate and ADP
3. Relaxation of the muscle fibre after completion of contraction

Principal Chemical Reactions of Muscle Contractions

The principal chemical reactions involved in muscle contractions are as follows:

1. Breakdown of ATP
2. Breakdown of creatine phosphate
   - Lohmann's reaction
   - Myokinase reaction
3. Restoration of creatine phosphate

Breakdown of ATP: The immediate source of energy for the mechanical contraction of muscle is derived from the breakdown of ATP. As described by Szent Gyorgi, the initial event in muscular contraction is the action of ATP on actomyosin. Simultaneously, ATP is hydrolysed by ATP-ase of myosin to form ADP, inorganic phosphate and energy. The actomyosin dissociates to its constituents, actin and myosin. The reaction may be represented as follows:

$$ATP \longrightarrow ADP + PO_4 + \sim ph.$$

Here ~ ph represents the high energy released during the breakdown of ATP. The formation and dissociation of actomyosin are presumed to occur as follows. According to the 'sliding filaments' concept of Hanson and Huxley, actomyosin, the contractile units, are formed as follows. On the initiation of muscle contraction by an impulse, the sarcoplasmic reticular membrane gets depolarised, liberating Ca^{++} from the storage sites. These ions activate the myosin–actin–ATP system, causing sliding movement of arrays of actin filaments in between myosin filaments which are stationary, resulting in overall contraction of the length of the units (**Fig. 17.12**). Relaxation is the reverse of the process of contraction. A substance called 'relaxing factor' derived from the sarcoplasmic reticulum binds Ca^{++} within fraction of a second, inactivating them. This causes reversal of actomyosin formation and relaxation of muscle.

Breakdown of creatine phosphate: The subsequent step is to regenerate ATP, since the muscles contain only small amounts and these would be soon exhausted. For this, an emergency mechanism which consists of the breakdown of creatine phosphate operates immediately. This results in the release of an HEB (~ph) from creatine phosphate and formation of creatine. The reaction takes place in the presence of the enzyme creatine kinase. The energy-rich phosphate bond (~ph) is immediately transferred to ADP, to resynthesise ATP. The resynthesis of ATP by this mechanism is called **Lohmann's reaction**.

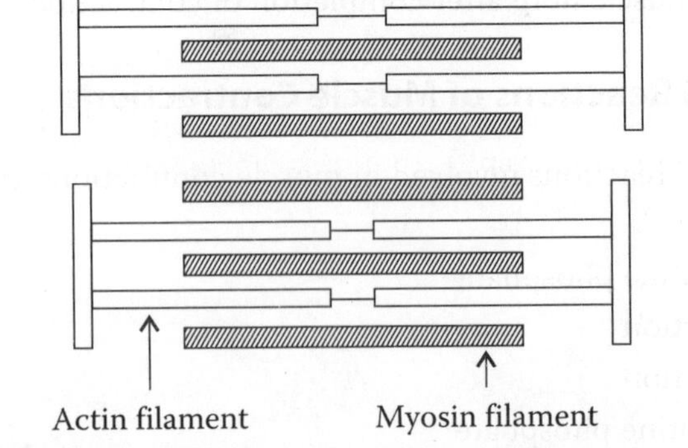

Figure 17.12 Diagram showing behaviour of actin and myosin filaments during muscle contraction. Note the sliding movement of actin filaments and the shortening of their length.

The reactions may be represented as follows:

1. Creatine phosphate $\xrightarrow[\textit{Kinase}]{\textit{Creatine}}$ Creatine + ~ph

2. ~ph + ADP $\rightleftharpoons$ ATP (Lohmann's reaction)

Though the sequence of the reactions is explained in two steps, all these reactions take place concomitantly with the utilisation of ATP during the contractile process.

Creatine phosphate is the most important shortage form of ~ph in muscles. Muscles when relaxed have a high content of creatine phosphate and are good storage materials of potential energy.

Under certain circumstances, when the regeneration of HEBs from other sources is inadequate and the supply of creatine phosphate is low, additional ATP may be provided by a reaction called **myokinase reaction,** which involves combination of 2 moles of ATP in the presence of myokinase, to form 1 mole of ATP and 1 mole of AMP (adenylic acid). However, this is described as a wasteful process, because it requires 2 moles of ADP to produce 1 mole of ATP and the AMP which is formed is rapidly deaminated.

Restoration of creatine phosphate: Recovery takes place either along with Lohmann's reaction or shortly following the reaction. During the recovery phase, creatine phosphate is resynthesised. The HEB required for the conversion of creatine to creatine phosphate is derived from the ATP liberated by glycolysis, which takes place simultaneously. Transfer of phosphate from ATP to creatine to form creatine phosphate is catalysed by the enzyme ATP–creatine transphosphorylase. The relation between ATP and creatine phosphate is represented in **Figure 17.13**. Now, the muscle is in a resting state and has a relatively high concentration of both ATP and creatine phosphate. Such a muscle is in a fit condition for further contraction. The chemical changes occurring in contraction are illustrated in **Figure 17.14**.

Cori Cycle (Lactic Acid Cycle)

The skeletal muscles are adapted in such a way that they can utilise the energy provided in the form of ATP by glycolysis for their contraction up to a certain stage. Therefore, in muscle contraction, a considerable amount of lactic acid is formed, which diffuses into the liver where it is oxidised back to pyruvic acid and converted to liver glycogen. To keep up the supply of energy for muscle contraction, liver glycogen splits to form glucose which enter the bloodstream and then the depleted muscles, where they get converted to muscle glycogen. This gets oxidised to lactic acid under anaerobic conditions. The cycle of events which repeats during muscle contraction is known as lactic acid cycle or Cori cycle (**Fig. 17.15**).

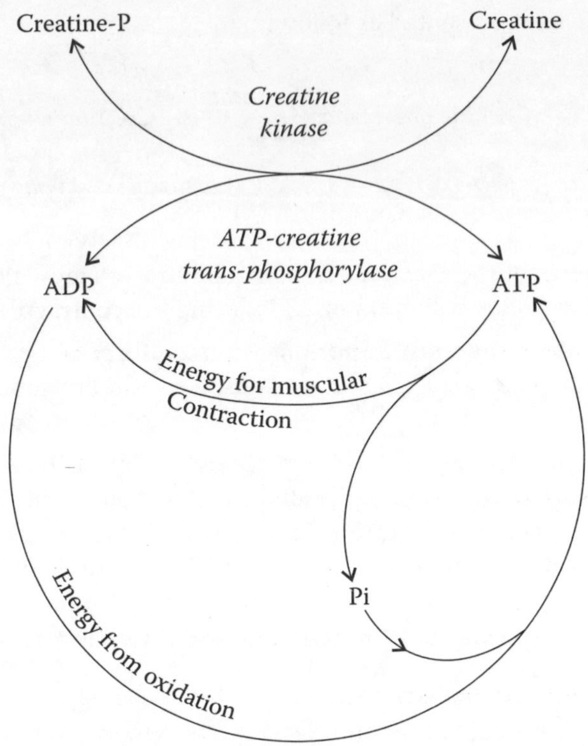

Figure 17.13 Relation between adenosine triphosphate and creatine phosphate.

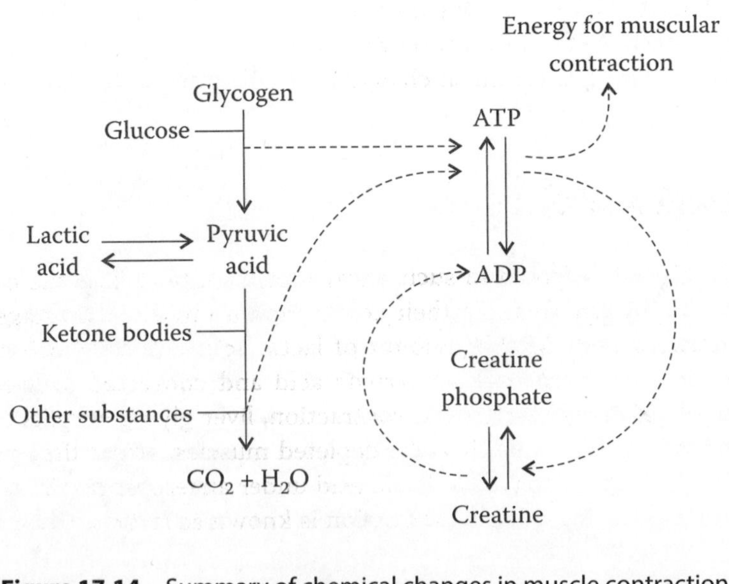

Figure 17.14 Summary of chemical changes in muscle contraction.

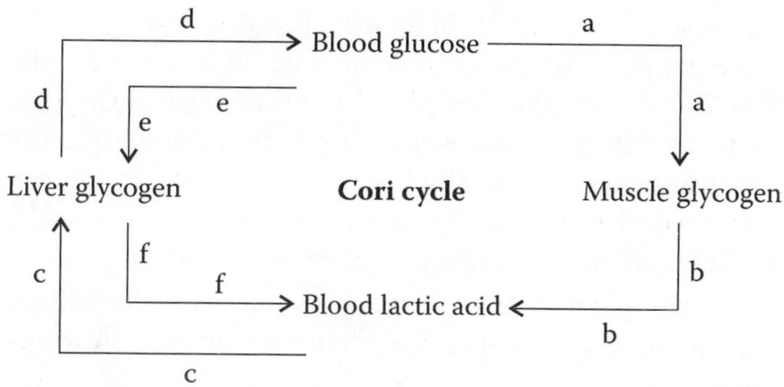

(a) Muscle glycogenesis
(b) Muscle glycolysis
(c) Gluconeogenesis
(d) Hepatic glycogenolysis
(e) Hepatic glycogenesis
(f) Hepatic glycolysis

Figure 17.15 Cori cycle.

Exercise: Skeletal muscles can function normally for some time in the absence of oxygen. When muscles work steadily as in *moderate exercise,* with a moderate supply of oxygen, the rate of oxidation produces sufficient ATP to supply energy for contraction. Very little lactic acid accumulates, because the pyruvic acid formed is completely oxidised via the tricarboxylic acid cycle. This supplies additional ATP for the contracting muscle.

However, in *sudden and severe exercise,* oxygen supply is inadequate due to sustained severe muscular contraction. But the muscles keep contracting to the maximum. For this, all the ATP produced are used much faster than the oxidative processes can form with the result that some more ATP must be provided now, by the rapid anaerobic glycolysis of muscle glycogen. The lactic acid formed accumulates and passes into the bloodstream and body fluids.

Fatigue: Muscular exhaustion sets in under the circumstances where the reserves of muscle ATP and creatine phosphate are used up and the muscles cannot obtain sufficient energy for further contraction. Consequently, the glycogen, ATP and creatine phosphate contents of such exhausted muscles are very low while the lactic acid and the inorganic phosphate content are very high.

Oxygen debt: A characteristic feature observed in severe exercise is that the breathing remains much above the resting level after the exertion is over. The excess oxygen consumed after the exercise, or in other words the resting oxygen consumption after completion of exercise, is called **oxygen debt.**

REGULATION OF BLOOD SUGAR

Blood sugar refers to the glucose present in blood. It is the only sugar present at all times in blood, biological fluids and tissues in physiologically significant amounts, though other monosaccharides are also absorbed in the same manner as glucose. The concentration of glucose in blood is remarkably constant in a normal healthy individual, ranging from 80 to 120 mg% (normoglycaemia). This value may be slightly low during the post-absorptive state, ranging from 75 to 90 mg%. The blood glucose level during the post-absorptive period is referred to as fasting blood sugar. Similarly, during the period of maximum absorption after a carbohydrate meal, the blood glucose may increase slightly, from 130 to 180 mg% but not beyond 180 mg%. This shows that in a normal healthy individual, the blood glucose level is maintained at a fairly constant level.

In the body, there are mechanisms operating to maintain the concentration of blood glucose at a fairly constant level; they are considered under the followings headings:

1. Alimentary mechanism
2. Role of liver
3. Role of hormones
4. Role of muscles and tissues
5. Role of kidneys
6. Role of blood glucose
7. Formation of fat

Alimentary mechanism: Following administration of glucose up to 200 grams orally, no glucose is detected in the urine and this is due to complete reabsorption of glucose by renal tubules. Increasing the amount of glucose up to 300–500 grams will cause distension of the stomach and consequently slow emptying and slow absorption from the intestines. In this way, rapid absorption causing a high rise of blood glucose is prevented. Though the glucose level may increase to some extent, it does not go beyond the renal threshold value. The maximum limit of absorption of glucose is 1.84 g per kg body weight per hour. Thyroxine and adrenocortical hormones increase absorption of glucose, whereas deficiency of vitamin B delays absorption. Other monosaccharides, such as galactose and fructose, absorbed along with glucose from the diet are rapidly converted to glucose.

Role of liver: Liver plays an important role in the regulation of blood glucose level as follows:

When the blood glucose tends to rise, the liver helps in restoring the normal value by

- Accelerating glycogenesis
- Increasing utilisation of glucose

The excess glucose is converted to glycogen and stored in the liver or if there is a need for energy, glucose is oxidised and utilised.

Insulin favours both glycogenesis and utilisation of glucose.

When the blood glucose tends to fall, as in fasting or during intake of low carbohydrate diet, liver helps in restoring the normal value by

- Accelerating glycogenolysis
- Accelerating gluconeogenesis
- Depressing utilisation of glucose

Glycogenolysis is the conversion of liver glycogen to blood glucose (**Fig. 17.16**). This causes a rise in blood glucose. Adrenaline, glucagon and thyroxine favour hepatic glycogenolysis.

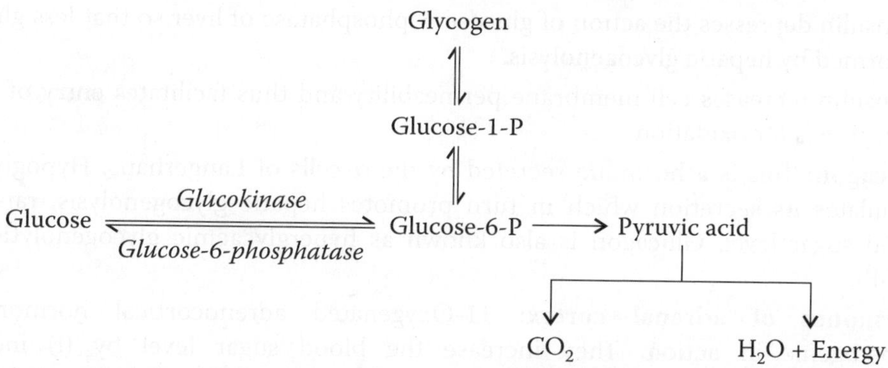

Figure 17.16 An illustration of glycogenesis, glycogenosis and glucose oxidation.

Gluconeogenesis is the conversion of non-carbohydrate substances to glycogen and glucose. The non-carbohydrate sources include glucogenic amino acids and certain intermediaries of carbohydrate metabolism, namely lactic acid, pyruvic acid and glycerol of fat. They enter the pathway of carbohydrate metabolism at various stages and get converted to glucose. 11-Oxy-corticosteroids increase, while insulin inhibits gluconeogenesis, which comes into the picture in states of starvation and in diabetes mellitus.

Role of hormones: Hormones play a very important part in regulating the level of blood glucose to normal limits. The blood glucose of an individual is the result of the opposing action of two sets of hormones, namely insulin acting on one hand and hormones of pituitary, adrenal cortex, medulla and thyroid acting on the other hand. Variation in the blood glucose value occurs, leading to abnormal carbohydrate metabolism, if there is disturbance in the secretion of these hormones. A brief account of the action of each of these hormones is given below.

1. **Insulin:** This hormone secreted by the β-cells of Langerhans is the strongest blood sugar lowering factor. It lowers the blood sugar level by
   - Accelerating glycogenesis in the liver
   - Increasing the rate of oxidation of glucose by tissue cells for the purpose of energy production
   - Depressing gluconeogenesis, thus reducing the rate of addition of glucose to the blood from other non-carbohydrate substances

   Diabetes mellitus which is characterised by abnormally high blood glucose levels (hyperglycaemia) is a chronic disorder caused by decreased secretion of insulin, due to degeneration of β-cells of Langerhans.

   Mechanism of insulin action:

   - Insulin promotes hexokinase reaction which is the initial reaction of glucose oxidation, whereby glucose is converted to glucose-6-phosphate. Adrenocortical hormones and hormones of pituitary inhibit this reaction while insulin antagonises this inhibition by promoting both oxidation and glycogenesis.
   - Insulin promotes the oxidation of sugars in the Krebs citric acid cycle, influencing at the site of acetyl-CoA.

- Insulin depresses the action of glucose-6-phosphatase of liver so that less glucose is formed by hepatic glycogenolysis.
- Insulin increases cell membrane permeability and thus facilitates entry of glucose into cells for oxidation.

2. **Glucagon:** This is a hormone secreted by the α-cells of Langerhans. Hypoglycaemia stimulates its secretion which in turn promotes hepatic glycogenolysis, raising the blood sugar level. Glucagon is also known as hyperglycaemic glycogenolytic factor (HGF).
3. **Hormones of adrenal cortex:** 11-Oxygenated adrenocortical hormones are diabetogenic in action. They increase the blood sugar level by (i) increasing gluconeogenesis from tissue proteins and (ii) diminishing the utilisation of glucose by enhancing the inhibitory influence of growth hormone on the hexokinase reaction. These reactions are antagonistic to those of insulin but similar to those of anterior pituitary hormones.
4. **Hormones of adrenal medulla:** Adrenaline (epinephrine) is diabetogenic in action. It increases the blood sugar level by increasing glycogenosis and glycolysis. Thus, it accelerates breakdown of both hepatic and muscle glycogen.
5. **Hormones of the pituitary:** These are (i) growth hormone, (ii) adrenocorticotropic hormones (ACTH) and (iii) thyroid-stimulating hormone (TSH).

   Growth hormone is the strongest blood sugar raising factor and therefore diabetogenic in action. Its action is direct, not mediated by gland, and opposite to that of insulin. It acts as follows:

   - It raises the blood sugar level.
   - It decreases utilisation of glucose by tissues. This is due to inhibition of the hexokinase reaction.
   - It increases gluconeogenesis.
   - It depresses hepatic and muscle glycogenesis.

   Adrenocorticotropic hormone (ACTH) and thyroid-stimulating hormone (TSH) stimulate the respective organs, namely adrenal cortex and thyroid, to secrete adrenal cortical hormone and thyroxine which produce diabetogenic effects. They decrease utilisation of glucose and cause hyperglycaemia.
6. **Hormone of thyroid:** Thyroxine is also diabetogenic. It increases blood sugar by (i) increasing the intestinal absorption of glucose, (ii) increasing hepatic glycogenolysis and (iii) increasing utilisation of glucose.

Role of muscles: Glucose is drawn from blood for muscular contraction When blood glucose is high, muscles withdraw the glucose and store it as glycogen or convert it into depot fat, thus reducing the blood glucose. When the blood glucose is low, as it occurs after severe muscular exercise, lactic acid which is formed is withdrawn from the tissues and muscles by the liver and is converted to liver glycogen. The latter is converted to glucose by hepatic glycogenosis and is discharged into the blood, thus raising the blood glucose level. The cycle by which lactic acid enters the liver and forms blood glucose, and again lactic acid, is called **Cori cycle** (*see* **Fig. 17.15**).

Role of kidneys: Kidneys function as the last outpost in the blood glucose regulating mechanism. Normally, the amount of glucose in the urine is negligible, because the filtered glucose is completely reabsorbed by the renal tubules by a phosphorylation mechanism, which is catalysed by an enzyme system. This mechanism continues normally, as long as the glucose in blood is well below the capacity of the tubular system to reabsorb it. But when the blood glucose value increases beyond the capacity of the tubular mechanism to reabsorb it, the excess glucose escapes in the urine, causing glycosuria. The blood glucose level above which glucose escapes in the urine to produce glycosuria is called the **renal threshold value of glucose**.

Role of blood glucose: Blood glucose regulates its own level. Hyperglycaemia stimulates secretion of insulin which brings down the blood glucose to the normal level. Hyperglycaemia stimulates insulin secretion by directly acting on the islet cells and insulin increases the rate of oxidation of glucose. Similarly, hypoglycaemia depresses insulin secretion and the blood glucose level is elevated to normal levels. Hypoglycaemia acts by directly acting on the islet cells to depress insulin secretion and stimulating the secretion of adrenaline and other diabetogenic hormones.

Formation of fat: Excess glucose is disposed off by formation of fat. Synthesis of fat from carbohydrates takes place readily in adipose tissue and mammary gland, and for this insulin is required.

Glycosuria

Normal urine contains a negligible amount of glucose, which is too insignificant to be detected by Benedict's reduction test. But when sugar is present in urine in sufficient concentration so as to give a positive result with Benedict's reagent, the condition is known as glycosuria or glucosuria. Under normal conditions, glucose is completely reabsorbed by the renal tubules, by a phosphorylation mechanism which is catalysed by an enzyme system. This mechanism functions normally as long as the glucose in blood is well below the capacity of the tubular enzyme system to reabsorb it. But when the glucose level in blood increases beyond the capacity of the tubular mechanism to deal with it, the excess glucose escapes in the urine, causing glycosuria. The renal threshold value for glucose, beyond which glucose appears in urine to cause glycosuria, varies from person to person, but on an average, it ranges from 160 to 180 mg%. It is generally higher in older people and in people with diseased kidneys. We say that the renal threshold value is high, when the blood glucose is abnormally high, with very little or no excretion of glucose in the urine.

Glycosuria can occur in two conditions:

1. In hyperglycaemia
2. In normoglycaemia

In **hyperglycaemia**, glycosuria may be due to either decreased secretion of insulin, as in diabetes mellitus, or due to hyperactivity of the hormones of the anterior pituitary, adrenal medulla, adrenal cortex and thyroid.

In **normoglycaemia**, glycosuria may occur due to physiological or hereditary causes.

- **Physiological glycosuria** includes alimentary glycosuria, emotional glycosuria, glycosuria in pregnancy and lactating glycosuria.
  - *Alimentary glycosuria:* Certain individuals with normal blood glucose may excrete glucose in urine after taking large amounts of glucose or carbohydrates. This may be due to a rapid rate of absorption of glucose into the blood as it often happens after surgical removal of a considerable part of the stomach. During such conditions, the liver and muscle cannot keep pace with the conversion of the rapidly absorbed glucose to glycogen. This results in glycosuria. It is temporary and is harmless.
  - *Emotional glycosuria:* Transient hyperglycaemia causing glycosuria may follow emotional factors such as fear, anger and anxiety. This is temporary and subsides after the emotional factor is removed. Glycosuria is the result of release of adrenaline which causes hyperglycaemia by promoting glycogenolysis.
  - *Pregnancy and lactating glycosuria:* Glycosuria may occur in late pregnancy due to an increased rate of glomerular filtration and lactation. The latter is due to the excretion of lactose in the urine.

  The blood glucose is normal. Glycosuria disappears after cessation of pregnancy lactation.

- **Hereditary glycosuria** refers to **renal glycosuria** (renal diabetes). This is a condition where glucose is excreted in the urine of individuals who do not show high blood glucose values or any abnormality in carbohydrate metabolism. They are otherwise healthy. Administration of a standard dose of glucose does not indicate blood glucose values higher those than in normal subjects, and their glucose tolerance curves are normal. Most of these cases are detected accidentally. The defect lies in the renal tubular enzyme mechanism which is responsible for reabsorption of glucose. Deficiency of the enzyme causes an impairment in the capacity to reabsorb glucose from the filtered urine and hence the glycosuria. It is a hereditary defect, affecting several members of the same family.

Glucose Tolerance

Administration of an additional amount of glucose to a normal person is followed by a rise in blood glucose, which promptly stimulates the secretion of insulin. This in turn increases the rate of oxidation of glucose in the cells and thereby quickly disposes the additional amount of glucose. In other words, the subject has well tolerated the glucose administered. On the other hand, administration of the same amount of glucose to a diabetic will result in a higher rise in blood sugar, which would take a longer time to settle to a normal level. This indicates a much slower rate of disposal of the administered glucose, and this is due to decreased insulin secretion as in diabetes. The diabetic shows a poor tolerance for the glucose administered, and the capacity to dispose the additional amount of glucose is poor.

Glucose Tolerance in Diabetes Mellitus

The characteristic feature in diabetes mellitus is hyperglycaemia. In maturity onset diabetes, i.e. non–insulin-dependent diabetes mellitus (NIDDM), there is hyperglycaemia and the plasma insulin is present at normal to elevated levels. Hyperglycaemia varies depending on the plasma insulin level. The diabetes is mild to moderate. The glucose tolerance is nearly normal. In juvenile diabetes, i.e. insulin-dependent diabetes mellitus (IDDM), there is hyperglycaemia and decreased secretion of insulin. The diabetes is severe. There is decreased tolerance of glucose.

These findings are presented in glucose tolerance test (GTT) curves of mild, moderate and severe diabetes.

The glucose tolerance, i.e. the capacity of the body to deal with an additional amount of glucose, is best studied by conducting a glucose tolerance test (GTT). This test is a standard procedure widely used to determine the capacity of the body to dispose a standard dose of glucose administered orally. It is a measure of insulin activity and therefore the diabetic state of the individual.

Oral Glucose Tolerance Test

The test is conducted in the morning, on a subject who is kept fasting for at least 12 hours after the last meal. The test is started with collection of a sample of venous blood and urine. These are samples of fasting blood and fasting urine. Immediately following this, a solution containing 50 grams of glucose dissolved in about 200 ml of water is given orally. Thereafter, samples of blood and urine are collected at 30 minutes' interval, for 2 hours in all. The usual procedure is to start the test at 10 a.m. and complete it by 12 noon. Each of the five specimens of blood is estimated for glucose and the urine qualitatively tested for glucose by Benedict's test. The results are plotted in a graph with the blood glucose values in the *Y*-axis and time intervals on the *X*-axis. The curve obtained is called the glucose tolerance test curve (GTT curve).

Normal GTT Curve The main features of a normal GTT curve (**Fig. 17.17**) are as follows:

1. Fasting blood sugar is between 80 and 100 mg%.
2. *Ascending limb:* The fasting blood sugar rises sharply to reach the peak value within 1 hour of ingestion of glucose, forming the ascending limb of the curve. It represents direct absorption of glucose into the bloodstream from the intestines.
3. The peak value which represents the stage of maximum absorption is well below the renal threshold value, usually below 180 mg%.
4. *Descending limb:* The blood sugar declines and reaches the fasting blood sugar level in about 2 hours, forming the descending limb of the curve. It represents glycogenesis and utilisation of glucose by tissues. At this stage, glucose leaves the blood faster than it entered by absorption. This stage represents the activity of insulin.
5. None of the urine samples show reduction. This indicates that glucose is not present in urine.

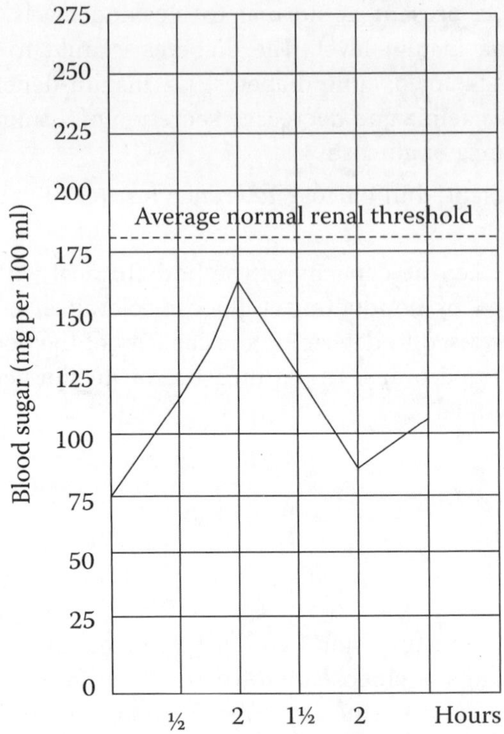

Figure 17.17 Normal glucose tolerance test curve.

Glucose Tolerance Test Curves in Diabetes Mellitus

The GTT curves of diabetic patients differ from the normal curve in the following aspects (**Fig. 17.18**):

1. The fasting blood sugar level is above 100 mg%. After ingestion of glucose, the level increases according to the severity of diabetes.
2. The peak level of absorption is much higher than the renal threshold value and this may be reached after 1–1½ hours. In very severe cases, the peak may not form even after 2 hours.
3. The blood sugar takes a longer time to return to the fasting level or it may not return as in severe cases. This shows improper utilisation of glucose due to lack of insulin.

The GTT curves in mild, moderate and severe types of diabetes are shown in **Figure 17.18**. The important features in each type are indicated below:

Mild diabetes:

- The fasting blood sugar value is within normal limits.
- The peak value is little above the renal threshold value.
- The descending limb is slightly prolonged to the right and takes more than 2 hours to reach the fasting level.
- Glycosuria is present.

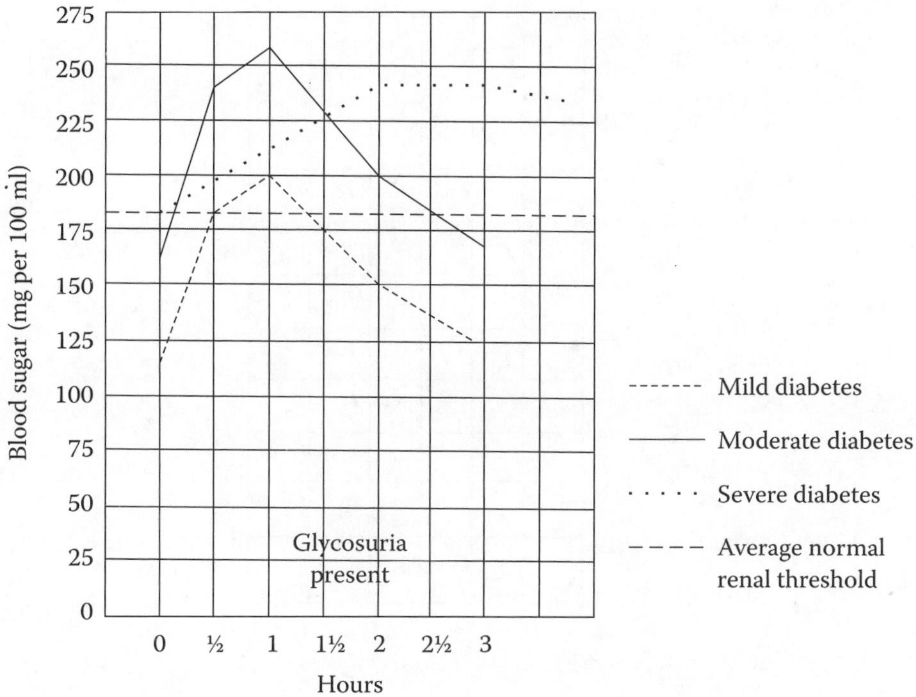

Figure 17.18 Glucose tolerance test curves in diabetes.

Moderate diabetes:

- The fasting blood sugar level is well above the normal limits.
- The peak value is well above the renal threshold value.
- The descending limb is well prolonged to the right and takes a much longer period to reach the fasting level.
- Glycosuria is more severe.

Severe diabetes:

- The fasting blood sugar level is raised above the renal threshold value.
- The peak value is high.
- The curve is markedly shifted to the right and does not return to the fasting level.
- Glycosuria is as a rule more severe than moderate diabetes. Sometimes, especially in elderly people, glycosuria may be mild due to a high renal threshold value.

'Lag' glycosuria type of curve: Lag glycosuria is a harmless condition. The important features of a lag curve are as follows (**Fig. 17.19**):

- The fasting blood sugar level is normal.
- The blood sugar rises rapidly after ingestion of glucose and reaches a peak, well above that of the normal curve.
- The descending limb is steep and the original level is regained rapidly.
- Glycosuria is present.

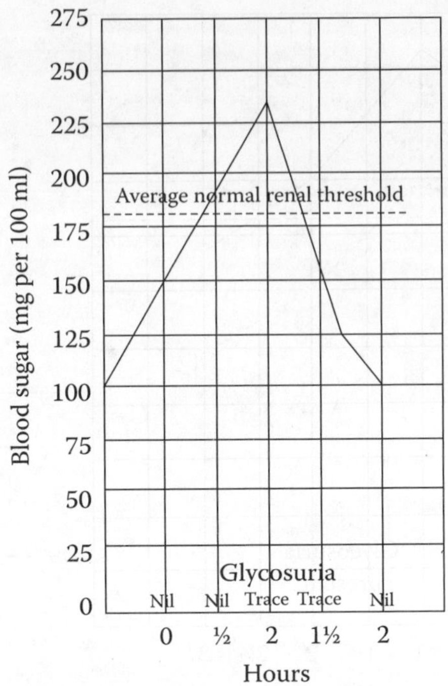

Figure 17.19 Lag glucose tolerance test curve.

Lag curve is obtained in two conditions:

(i) In subjects who had gastroenterostomy or partial gastrectomy, which favours rapid intestinal absorption

(ii) In potential diabetes

Diabetes mellitus: Diabetes mellitus is a chronic disease of carbohydrate metabolism mainly, but lipid and protein metabolism are also affected. Diabetes means chronic excretion of an excessive volume of the urine and mellitus means honey. So the word 'diabetes mellitus' refers to chronic excretion of a large volume of urine containing glucose.

The characteristic features of the disease are (i) glycosuria, (ii) hyperglycaemia and (iii) decreased glucose tolerance.

Normally, glucose is not detectable in urine by Benedict's test but in diabetes mellitus it is readily detectable. The blood glucose increases above the normal value of 120 mg%. Untreated diabetes exhibits the following symptoms:

- *Polyuria:* This means excretion of an increased quantity of urine. This is to excrete the additional quantity of glucose.
- *Polydipsia:* This means excessive thirst which leads to increased consumption of water. This is to replace the volume of water excreted due to polyuria.
- *Polyphagia:* Excessive appetite leads to polyphagia and increased intake of food. This is to replace the lost nourishment. The diabetic has voracious appetite, but in spite of overeating, he loses weight and becomes lean and emaciated.

Other symptoms include general weakness, vague pains in the body and neuritis. The biochemical disturbance in diabetes mellitus is due to deficiency of insulin which may be either relative or absolute. Relative deficiency may result from overproduction of diabetogenic factors such as glucagon, hormones of the pituitary, adrenaline and thyroxine, even though a normal amount of insulin is present. Absolute deficiency may result from inadequate secretion of insulin or destruction of insulin by increased activity of insulinases and insulin antagonists. Accordingly, two types of diabetes were identified:

(i) A milder type of diabetes which is resistant to insulin treatment.

(ii) A severe type of diabetes responding to treatment with insulin. This is due to absolute deficiency of insulin.

Clinically, two types of diabetes mellitus are recognised:

1. **Type I:** This is insulin-dependent diabetes mellitus and is referred to as **IDDM**. It is also known as juvenile diabetes. It requires insulin to control the hyperglycaemia.
2. **Type II:** This is non–insulin-dependent diabetes mellitus and is referred to as **NIDDM**. It is known as maturity onset diabetes mellitus.

   Type I-IDDM appears usually in childhood or in a younger age group. About 10% of persons affected with diabetes mellitus have **IDDM**. Insulin is either absent or nearly absent because of defective or absent β-cells in the pancreas. If the diabetes is not treated, hyperglycaemia, hyperlipoproteinaemia and episodes of ketoacidosis appear.

   Type II-NIDDM occurs usually in middle age and obese persons. About 90% of persons affected with diabetes mellitus have **NIDDM**. They have hyperglycaemia, but the symptoms are milder. They do not require insulin to control the hyperglycaemia and it can be controlled by diet. They do not develop ketoacidosis. Insulin is present at a normal or an elevated level. But, because of the continued elevated blood glucose levels, the **NIDDM** person may ultimately secrete more insulin for a given glucose load than a normal individual. The defect in **NIDDM** is attributed to a decreased number of **insulin receptors**. These are cells responding to insulin and to which insulin binds specifically, located on the plasma membrane.

When there is lack of insulin, the hexokinase reaction by which glucose is converted to glucose-6-phosphate and which is the initial reaction for oxidation of glucose is retarded, leading to defective utilisation of glucose by the body. As a result, the concentration of glucose increases in blood, contributing to hyperglycaemia. As glycolysis and tricarboxylic acid cycle are subsequently retarded, the body derives its energy requirements by increasing the oxidation of fats which in turn produces an excess amount of acetyl-CoA. Condensation of acetyl-CoA molecules produces an excess amount of ketone bodies. They are excreted in urine causing **ketonuria**. Accumulation of the ketone bodies, which are acid substances in the blood, causes acidosis and this condition is called **ketosis**. Ketonuria and ketosis develop in untreated cases of severe diabetes, and this may lead to diabetic coma. At this stage, the blood glucose is very high, above 600 mg%, and the urine shows a positive reaction for glucose and ketone bodies. If insulin is not administered promptly, the consequences become irreversible, resulting in death.

Increased formation of acetyl-CoA due to increased oxidation of fats also causes increased synthesis of cholesterol, leading to hypercholesterolaemia, which may result in earlier onset of atherosclerosis.

Along with the abnormal metabolism of carbohydrate and fat, catabolism of proteins also increases and this is mainly due to overactivity of corticosteroids owing to deficiency of insulin. The amino acids are deaminated and the keto acids are converted into carbohydrates, leading to increased gluconeogenesis. This results in increased excretion of urinary nitrogen. On account of excessive breakdown of protein, the patient loses weight and becomes emaciated.

The symptoms described so far are characteristic of severe diabetes as in **Type I**. However, there are less severe and milder types, manifesting a lesser degree of glycosuria and hyperglycaemia. Most of the mild cases respond to dietary restriction of carbohydrates as in **Type II**. But all severe cases require daily administration of insulin to reverse hyperglycaemia to normal levels.

Galactose Tolerance

Galactose like fructose is metabolised mainly by the liver. The metabolism of galactose differs from that of glucose in the following aspects:

1. It is absorbed from the intestines more rapidly than glucose.
2. The rate of increase in concentration in the blood after ingestion of galactose is lesser than that of glucose.
3. The renal threshold value for excretion of galactose is very low.

Galactose Tolerance Test

After ingestion of 40 grams of galactose in a fasting subject, the blood galactose level normally reaches a maximum of 15–30 mg/100 ml in 30–60 minutes, falling to zero at the end of 2 hours. Normal subjects excrete up to 3 grams of galactose in the urine during the 5 hours following ingestion of 40 grams of this sugar. Urine is collected for the succeeding 5 hours' period and estimated for galactose content. If it contains more than 5 grams, it indicates impairment of liver function. Increased excretion is a common finding in acute degeneration of liver. As the oral test is influenced by irregularities of intestinal absorption and renal efficiency, the intravenous galactose tolerance test is considered more reliable. For this, 0.5 gram of galactose/kg, body weight, is injected intravenously and the blood galactose level estimated at 30 minutes' intervals thereafter. In normal subjects, galactose disappears from the peripheral blood in 2 hours. When there is damage to the liver, it takes a longer time for clearance.

METABOLISM OF OTHER HEXOSES

Hexoses such as fructose, galactose and mannose undergo interconversion by way of the glycolytic pathway. They form phosphate esters by phosphorylation with ATP, in the presence of hexokinase enzymes, and enter the glycolytic pathway, at various stages (**Figs 17.20** and **17.21**).

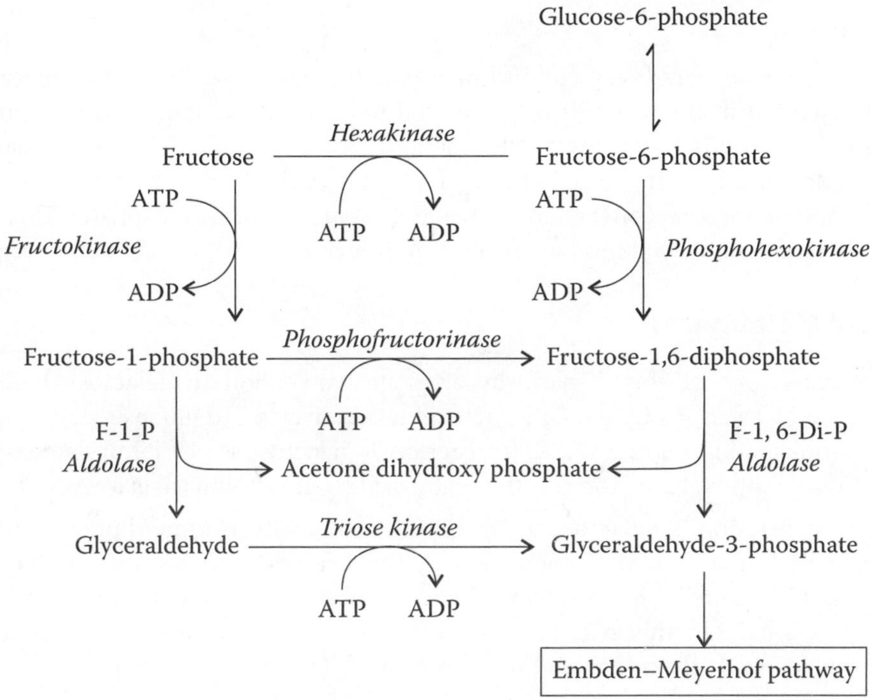

Figure 17.20 Fructose metabolism.

Fructose Metabolism

Fructose follows several metabolic pathways. Three of them considered important are explained here:

1. Some authors consider that fructose is mainly converted to fructose-1-phosphate by phosphorylation with ATP. The reaction, catalysed by fructokinase, is not influenced by insulin. This is the reason for fructose metabolism not being disturbed in diabetes mellitus. Fructose-1-phosphate is further split by aldolase to form the trioses, free glyceraldehyde and dihydroxyacetone phosphate. Free glyceraldehyde is phosphorylated to form glyceraldehyde-3-phosphate by triosekinase. Both trioses may be degraded via the glycolytic pathway or may again condense to form fructose-1-6-diphosphate which may be converted to form glucose. This pathway occurs mainly in liver.
2. Another possible pathway is that fructose-1-phosphate may get directly phosphorylated to form fructose-1-6-diphosphate, which can enter the glycolytic pathway and get metabolised like glucose.
3. A minor metabolic pathway is described for fructose, where it may directly get phosphorylated to fructose-6-phosphate which can enter the glycolytic pathway and get either converted to glucose or metabolised to form lactic acid. Whatever may be the pathway fructose takes, its end products are either glucose and glycogen or lactic acid due to glycolysis.

Fructosuria

Fructosuria is a rare hereditary condition in which about 10–20% of the fructose taken in food is excreted in the urine. It is postulated that in normal individuals, about 80% of the ingested fructose is converted to glucose and glycogen while the rest is broken down to form lactic acid. It is suggested that in fructosuria, there is lack of fructokinase, the enzyme required for the conversion of fructose to fructose-1-phosphate. This leads to accumulation of fructose in blood and excretion in urine.

Galactose Metabolism

Galactose enters the glycolytic pathway after its conversion to galactose-1-phosphate. The sequence of reactions by which galactose gets converted to glucose via the glycolytic pathway is indicated in **Figure 17.22**. In reaction 1, galactose is phosphorylated by ATP to form galactose-1-phosphate. The reaction catalysed by galactokinase is irreversible.

In the next reaction 2, galactose-1-phosphate reacts with uridine diphosphate-glucose (UDP-G), which also acts as a coenzyme in the presence of the enzyme galactose-1-phosphate-uridyltransferase, to form glucose-1-phosphate and uridine diphosphate-galactose (UDP-gal). In this reaction, an exchange of the hexose moieties between the substrate, galactose-1-phosphate and the coenzyme UDP-glucose takes place.

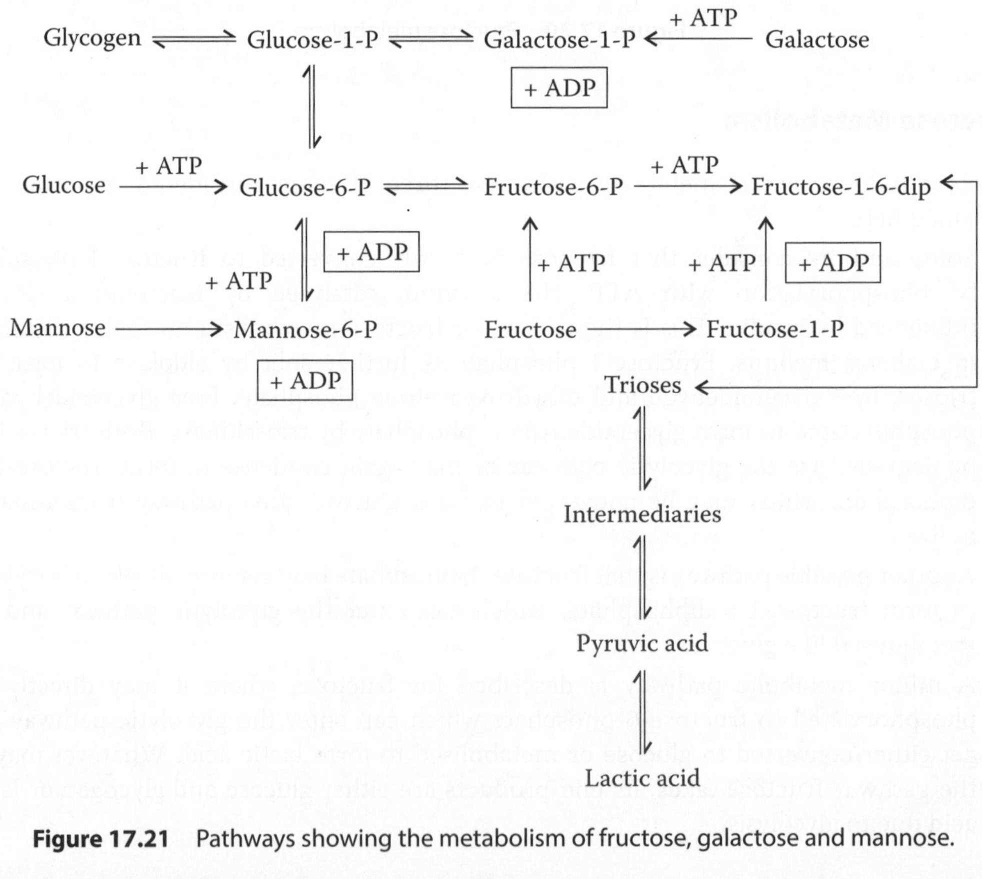

Figure 17.21 Pathways showing the metabolism of fructose, galactose and mannose.

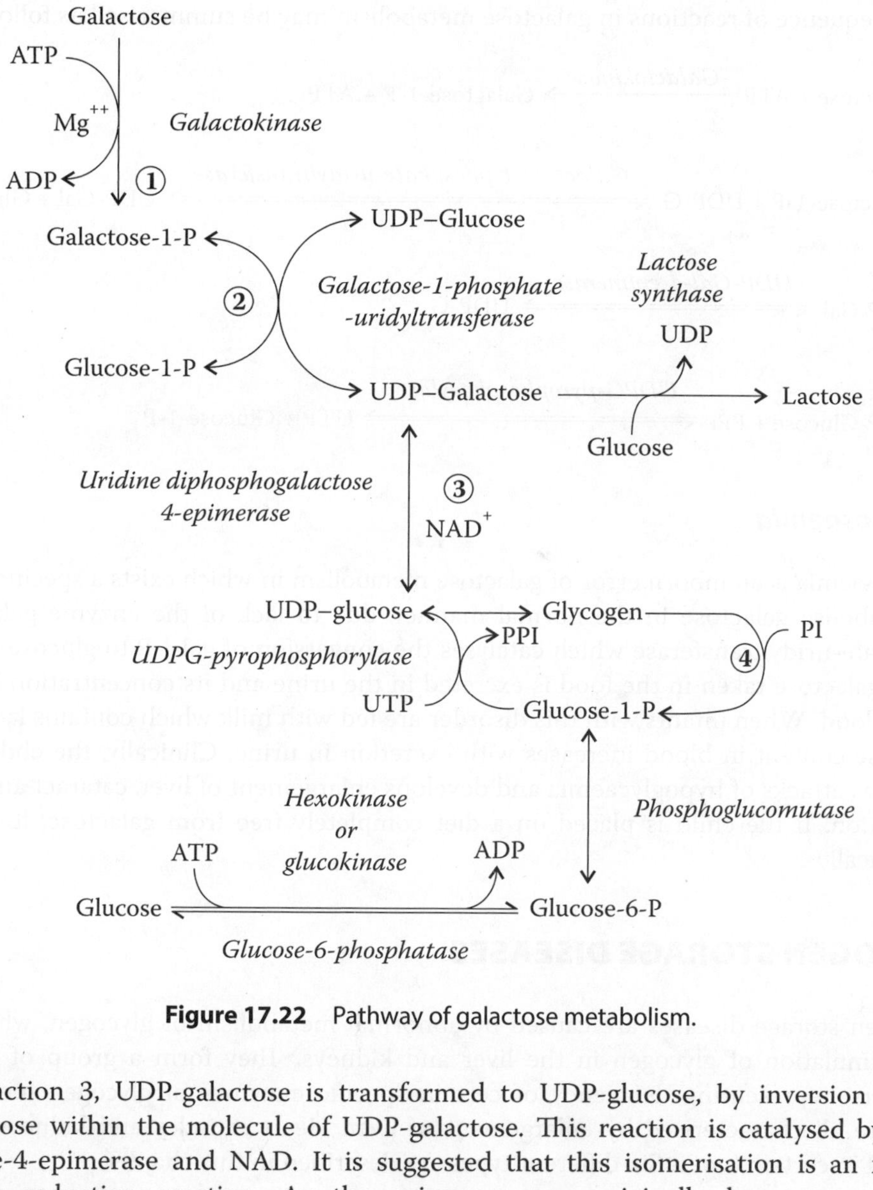

Figure 17.22 Pathway of galactose metabolism.

In reaction 3, UDP-galactose is transformed to UDP-glucose, by inversion of C-4 of galactose within the molecule of UDP-galactose. This reaction is catalysed by UDP-galactose-4-epimerase and NAD. It is suggested that this isomerisation is an internal oxidation–reduction reaction. As the epimerase was originally known as galacto-waldenase, this reaction is referred to as Walden inversion.

In reaction 4, glucose is liberated from UDP-glucose as glucose-1-phosphate, after incorporation into glycogen, followed by the action of phosphorylase. Glucose-1-phosphate is converted to glucose-6-phosphate which in turn forms glucose by the action of glucose-6-phosphatase. It may be noted that reaction 1 is irreversible, but other reactions are reversible. Thus, glucose-1-phosphate may be formed from galactose and galactose-1-phosphate may be formed from glucose. Compounds containing galactose, such as the galactosides of brain, may be synthesised in the body from glucose even in the absence of galactose in the diet.

The sequence of reactions in galactose metabolism may be summarised as follows:

1. $\text{Galactose} + \text{ATP} \xrightarrow{\textit{Galactokinase}} \text{Galactose-1-P} + \text{ATP}$

2. $\text{Galactose-1-P} + \text{UDP-G} \xrightleftharpoons{\textit{Galactose-1-phosphate-uridyltransferase}} \text{UDP-Gal} + \text{Glucose-1-P}$

3. $\text{UDP-Gal} \xrightleftharpoons{\textit{UDP-Gal-4-epimerase}} \text{UDP-G}$

4. $\text{UDP-Glucose} + \text{PPi} \xrightleftharpoons{\textit{UDPG-pyrophosphorylase}} \text{UTP} + \text{Glucose-1-P}$

Galactosaemia

Galactosaemia is an inborn error of galactose metabolism in which exists a specific inability to metabolise galactose in the normal manner, due to lack of the enzyme galactose-1-phosphate-uridyltransferase which catalyses the conversion of gal-l-P to glucose-1-P. As a result, galactose taken in the food is excreted in the urine and its concentration increases in the blood. When infants with this disorder are fed with milk which contains lactose, the galactose content in blood increases with excretion in urine. Clinically, the child fails to grow, has attacks of hypoglycaemia and develops enlargement of liver, cataract and mental retardation. If the child is placed on a diet completely free from galactose, it improves dramatically.

GLYCOGEN STORAGE DISEASES

Glycogen storage diseases are caused by abnormal metabolism of glycogen, which leads to accumulation of glycogen in the liver and kidneys. They form a group of inherited disorders, representing deficiency of certain specific enzymes of glycogen metabolism. They are all characterised by enlargement of liver. Heart muscles and kidneys are also affected in certain types. Six different types are described in this chapter.

1. **Von Gierke's disease (Type I):** Originally described by Von Gierke, the disease is characterised by an abnormal accumulation of glycogen in liver cells and cells of renal convoluted tubules. The glycogen is normal in structure. The characteristic features of the disease are enlargement of liver in infancy and severe hypoglycaemia. The underlying cause is failure of liver glycogen to break down and form blood glucose (glycogenolysis), due to deficiency or absence of the enzyme glucose-6-phosphatase. This leads to accumulation of glycogen in liver and kidneys where glucose-6-phosphatase is normally present. Clinical manifestations include hypoglycaemia, hyperuricaemia, hyperlipidaemia and ketosis.

2. **Pompe's disease (Type II):** This is a rare and most devastating type of glycogen storage disease, caused by the absence of α-1, 4-glycosidase (acid maltase), an enzyme normally found in lysosomes. The enzyme hydrolyses maltose and the outer branches of glycogen to yield free glucose. In its absence, glycogen is not degraded and accumulation of a large amount of glycogen of normal structure occurs in the lysosomes of all cells and tissues. Excessive accumulation of glycogen in cardiac muscle results in massive enlargement of the heart. An excessive amount of glycogen is also found in other muscles, especially tongue which is enlarged. Death from heart failure occurs at an early age.
3. **Coris disease (Type III):** This is caused by deficiency of the glycogen debrancher enzyme which is required for degradation of liver glycogen to blood glucose. Glycogen of abnormal structure containing very short outer chains accumulates in liver and muscles. Hypoglycaemia is present but is not as severe as in Von Gierke's disease.
4. **Andersen's disease (Type IV):** This condition is characterised by accumulation of glycogen in liver and cirrhosis. The structure of glycogen is abnormal. It has long, unbranched chains resulting from the absence of the branching enzyme which brings about branching between 1, 4 and 1, 6 transglucosidic linkages. Cirrhosis of liver, which is a unique feature of this disease, is probably the result of tissue reaction due to the abnormal glycogen. The victims rarely survive beyond the age of 4 years because of liver dysfunction.
5. **McArdle's disease (Type V):** This is a rare disease caused by the absence of muscle phosphorylase which is required for the breakdown of muscle glycogen (glycolysis) during muscular activity. In its absence, the muscle is unable to utilise its glycogen stores and derive energy by glycolysis. The normal release of lactate in blood following exercise is absent. The affected person suffers from painful muscular cramps and is unable to perform exercise.
6. **Her's disease (Type VI):** This is caused due to deficiency of liver phosphorylase which is required to convert liver glycogen to blood glucose. As a result, the glycogen content in liver becomes high and glucose formation from liver glycogen is decreased. On account of this, there is tendency towards hypoglycaemia.

Hypoglycaemia

A continuous supply of glucose is necessary for the normal functioning of brain and for the brain to derive energy. In a normal person, hypoglycaemia is prevented mainly by the combined action of two hormones **insulin** and **glucagon**.

1. Insulin lowers blood glucose.
2. Glucagon raises blood glucose by stimulating hepatic glycogenolysis and gluconeogenesis.

Epinephrine promotes glycogenolysis and inhibits secretion of insulin. The combined effect of glucagon and epinephrine along with diminished release of insulin is important in combating hypoglycaemia.

Hypoglycaemia is traditionally classified as follows:

1. Post-prandial hypoglycaemia
2. Fasting hypoglycaemia

Post-prandial hypoglycaemia is the hypoglycaemia following a meal. It is also called reactive hypoglycaemia. The most common cause is alimentary hyperinsulinism caused by exaggerated insulin release following a meal. This can occur in patients who have undergone gastrectomy, gastrojejunostomy or vagotomy. In all these conditions, the hypoglycaemia is due to rapid gastric emptying with quick absorption of glucose. This is followed by increased secretion of insulin leading to hypoglycaemia. However, the blood glucose level returns to normal even if the patient is not fed.

Fasting hypoglycaemia: This occurs during fasting. The main causes are as follows:

- Inadequate intake of food
- Underproduction of glucose, as occurring in states of hormone deficiency such as
  - Hypopituitarism
  - Adrenal deficiency
  - Glucagon deficiency

Hypoglycaemia due to other causes are as follows:

- Pancreatic islet cells diseases, for example tumours of pancreas
- Glycogen storage diseases due to the enzyme defect
- Galactosaemia due to the enzyme defect
- Transient postnatal hypoglycaemia in infants of a diabetic mother

Alcohol intoxication: Alcohol ingestion can induce hypoglycaemia in a person, after a period of fasting sufficient enough to deplete liver glycogen, as in the following conditions.

- After administration of anti-diabetic drugs such as sulphonylureas and insulin
- After strenuous exercise

The reactions leading to hypoglycaemia in alcohol intoxication are explained as follows:

Alcohol acts by (i) inhibiting hepatic gluconeogenesis and (ii) depleting liver glycogen stores.

Oxidation of ethanol produces excess of NADH (reducing equivalents). The quantity of NADH produced is so high that it exceeds the capacity of the liver to handle and the excess NADH block the conversion of lactate to glucose, resulting in hypoglycaemia and accumulation of lactate in blood. This leads to lactic acidosis. The hypoglycaemia may lead to irreversible damage to the central nervous system.

Symptoms of Hypoglycaemia

Symptoms of hypoglycaemia arise with a rapid decline in the blood glucose level to less than 50 mg%.

The symptoms in hypoglycaemia are due in part to release of epinephrine and to lack of supply of glucose to brain which leads to impaired functioning of the brain.

1. Symptoms due to release of epinephrine are sweating, trembling, hunger, nausea and vomiting.
2. Symptoms due to lack of supply of glucose to brain and decreased utilisation of oxygen by the brain are headache, restlessness, visual disturbances and difficulty with speech. Symptoms in more pronounced hypoglycaemia are convulsions, prolonged sleep, loss of consciousness and coma. Transient hypoglycaemia causes cerebral dysfunction. Severe and prolonged hypoglycaemia causes brain cell damage.

Hypoglycaemia During Pregnancy and Newborn

Hypoglycaemia may occur during pregnancy because the glucose consumption by the foetus increases and is drawn from the mother's nutrition.

The risk of developing hypoglycaemia, both maternal and foetal, is more during nights and when the interval between meals is prolonged.

Newborns, especially premature ones, have a greater susceptibility to hypoglycaemia because they have a larger brain/body weight ratio and the brain utilises a greater amount of glucose than the rest of the body.

Neonates have a limited capacity for ketogenesis and formation of free fatty acids. Ketone bodies and free fatty acids are important fuels for formation of glucose by the brain. Impairment of this function in neonates leads to hypoglycaemia.

18 CHAPTER

Glycoproteins and Proteoglycans

Chapter Outline

- Glycoproteins
- Proteoglycans

GLYCOPROTEINS

Glycoproteins are conjugated proteins composed of carbohydrates and proteins. They have high molecular weight ranging from 15,000 to over 1 million. They are of considerable biological significance and are widely distributed. They are present in plants, animals, humans, bacteria, fungi and viruses, and egg white. Most glycoproteins occur extracellularly and are secreted from cells. In humans, these include glycoproteins present in blood such as fibrinogen, immunoglobulins, ceruloplasmin, plasma proteins except albumin, blood group proteins, hormones such as chorionic gonadotropin, follicle stimulating hormone (FSH), thyroid stimulating hormone (TSH), various digestive enzymes secreted into the intestines, mucus secretion, collagen of connective tissue and cell membrane.

The carbohydrates are present as oligosaccharide groups. The constituent sugars are mannose, galactose, *N*-acetylglucosamine, *N*-acetlygalactosamine, arabinose, xylose, L-fucose and *N*-acetylneuraminic acid. They are attached covalently to a protein core (polypeptide chain), through the amide group of an asparagine, and to the hydroxyl group of L-serine, L-threonine and hydroxylysine residues. The proportion of carbohydrate in glycoprotein varies. Collagen and immunoglobulins contain less than 1% carbohydrates and glycophorin (a glycoprotein present in the red cell membrane) contains 60% carbohydrate. Blood group substances contain more than 80% carbohydrate.

Sialic acids are a family of sugars present in glycoproteins. They are derivatives of neuraminic acid.

Glycophorin is a major glycoprotein present in the human erythrocyte membrane. It is an integral membrane protein of the erythrocytes. It has 131 amino acid residues and is heavily glycosylated. It spans across the membrane lipid bilayer, having the free polypeptide portions outside the external and internal (cytoplasmic) surfaces. Its amino *N*-terminal segment extrudes out in the external environment carrying all the carbohydrate groups.

The carboxyl terminal segment extends into the cytoplasm of the erythrocyte and contains hydrophilic amino acids.

Functions: Glycoproteins participate in several functions of the body, as most membrane proteins and secretions from cells are glycoproteins.

1. Glycoproteins constitute the major active component of cellular membrane.
2. They form a considerable part of the mucus secreted by epithelial cells. They play an important role in lubrication and protection of tissues lining the ducts in the body.
3. A number of blood group substances are glycoproteins.
4. Most of the plasma proteins (except albumin), blood clotting proteins and immunoglobulins are glycoproteins.
5. Immunoglobulin antigenic sites situated in cellular membranes are glycoproteins.
6. Some hormones such as chorionic gonadotropin hormone, follicle stimulating hormone (FSH) and thyroid stimulating hormone (TSH) are glycoproteins.
7. Glycoproteins serve as transport molecules for transferrin, vitamins, lipids, minerals and trace elements. Ceruloplasmin, a glycoprotein, accounts for 95% of the total copper present in plasma.
8. The carbohydrate groups of glycoproteins in membranes provide a surface code for cellular identification by other cells and for contact inhibition, in the regulation of cell growth.

PROTEOGLYCANS

Mucopolysaccharides (MPS), an older name for proteoglycans, is still in use. They represent a class of compounds that contain complex macromolecules made of about 95% of carbohydrates and 5% of proteins. They are high-molecular-weight polyionic substances largely present in the extracellular matrix and the ground substance of the connective tissue. Proteoglycans are composed of long polysaccharide chains known as glycosaminoglycans (GAGs) linked covalently to a protein core. The polysaccharide chains consist of repeating units of a uronic acid and a hexosamine (amino sugar) residue. The hexosamine is either D-glucosamine or D-galactosamine. The uronic acid is either L-glucuronic acid or L-iduronic acid. Keratan sulphate is an exception as it does not contain any uronic acid. The hexosamines are generally acetylated. They are all acids because of the presence of sulphate esters on the hexosamine units. Hyaluronic acid is an exception as it is not sulphated. The carboxyl and sulphate groups contribute to the highly charged polyionic nature of the GAGs. Both the electric charge and the macromolecular structure of the proteoglycans help in their biological role as lubricants and support elements in connective tissues. GAGs are linked to their protein core through glycosidic bonds to serine or threonine or asparagine residues.

Six distinct classes of glycosaminoglycans are known and they are as follows:

1. Hyaluronic acid
2. Chondroitin sulphate (CS)

3. Dermatan sulphate (DS)
4. Keratan sulphate (KS)
5. Heparin
6. Heparan sulphate (HS)

Hyaluronic acid: Hyaluronic acid described as a jelly-like substance is present in connective tissue, cartilage, vitreous humour, umbilical cord, synovial fluid and capsules of certain strains of cocci. It acts as a lubricant in the joints and forms a jelly-like cementing substance in tissues. The polysaccharide chain is composed of repeating disaccharide units of D-glucuronic acid (GlcUA) and *N*-acetylglucosamine (GlcNAc) linked by a (1–3) bond and is attached to the next glucuronic acid (GlcUA) by 1–4 linkage. Hyaluronic acid is different from other GAGs in that it is not sulphated and is not linked with protein.

$$\text{D-Glucuronic acid} \xrightarrow{\beta\,1,3} N\text{-Acetylglucosamine} \xrightarrow{\beta\,1,4} \text{GlcUA}$$

(Repeating units of hyaluronic acid)

Hyaluronidase is an endoglycosidase enzyme present in testicular tissue, seminal fluid and spleen. It is also present in certain bacteria. Hyaluronidase catalyses cleaving of hexoseaminidic linkages on 1, 4 bonds of hyaluronic acids. It also acts on chondroitin sulphate. When the tissue hyaluronic acid is destroyed, the viscosity is reduced and this permits easy spreading of the materials in the tissue spaces. For this reason, hyaluronidase is referred to as 'spreading factor'. It has been observed that the invasive power of bacteria is due to the action of hyaluronidase present in them. Another observation is that hyaluronidase present in testicular secretion dissolves the viscous substance surrounding the ova, to permit penetration by spermatozoa.

Chondroitin sulphate: This is present mainly in the ground substance of cartilage, tendon and ligaments and is the most abundant MPS present in the body. The polysaccharide chain consists of repeating disaccharide units of D-glucuronic acid and *N*-acetylgalactosamine linked by (1–3) linkage. Each polysaccharide chain is attached to a specific serine residue in a protein core. Two types of chondroitin sulphate are known. These are chondroitin-4-sulphate and chondroitin-6-sulphate. In chondroitin-4-sulphate, the sulphate is esterified in the 4-hydroxyl position. In chondroitin-6-sulphate, the sulphate is esterified in the 6-hydroxyl position. Both are isomers.

$$\text{D-Glucuronic acid} \xrightarrow{\beta\,1,3} \underset{\substack{|\\ \text{4- or 6-Sulphate}}}{N\text{-Acetylgalactosamine}}$$

(Repeating units of chondroitin sulphate)

Dermatan sulphate: This is present in skin, connective tissues of blood vessels and heart valves. The polysaccharide chain consists of repeating disaccharide units of L-iduronic acid and *N*-acetylgalactosamine-4-sulphate in α-1,3 linkage. It has antithrombic action like heparin. It plays an important role in the development of the atheromatous plaques in arterial walls.

$$\begin{array}{ccc} \text{L-Iduronic acid} & \xrightarrow{\alpha\ 1,3} & N\text{-Acetylgalactosamine} \\ | & & | \\ \text{4-Sulphate} & & \text{4-Sulphate} \end{array}$$

(Repeating units of dermatin sulphate)

Keratan sulphate: This is present primarily in cornea and skin. The disaccharide chain consists of repeating units of β D-galactose and *N*-acetylglucosamine with sulphate attached to the sixth position of GlcNAc. There is no uronic acid in the molecule. Sulphate is present mostly on glucosamine and sometimes on galactose also. Two types of keratan sulphate have been distinguished. They differ in their carbohydrate content and tissue distribution.

$$\begin{array}{ccc} \text{Galactose} & \xrightarrow{\beta\ 1,4} & N\text{-Acetylglucosamine} \\ & & | \\ & & \text{6-Sulphate} \end{array}$$

(Repeating units of keratan sulphate)

Keratan sulphate I is isolated from cornea.

Keratan sulphate II is isolated from cartilage.

Heparin: This is present in the intracellular granules of the mast cells that line arterial walls in liver, lungs and skin. The repeating disaccharide unit is composed of *N*-glucosamine and either iduronic acid (mostly) or glucuronic acid linked by a 1–4 glucosidic linkage. Sulphate is present as sulphate ester in linkage with C-6 of glucosamine and also in amide linkage with the amino group of glucosamine. Heparin has few acetyl groups.

$$\begin{array}{ccc} \text{6-Sulphate} & & \\ | & & \\ N\text{-Glucosamine} & \longrightarrow & \text{D-Glucuronic acid} \\ | & & \text{or} \\ \text{3-Sulphate} & & \text{L-Iduronic acid} \\ \text{(Amide linkage)} & & \end{array}$$

(Repeating units of heparin)

Heparin has an anticoagulant property and is an extremely potent anticoagulant. It acts by reducing the formation of thrombin and fibrin.

Heparan sulphate: This is present on all cell surfaces and occurs as an extracellular substance in blood vessel walls. The repeating disaccharide unit is composed of *N*-glucosamine and either glucuronic acid mostly or iduronic acid, similar to heparin. It contains more glucuronic acid and less of iduronic acid than heparin. Heparan sulphate has fewer sulphates and more acetyl groups than heparin.

$$
\begin{array}{ccc}
N\text{-Glucosamine} & \xrightarrow{\alpha\ 1,4} & \text{D-Glucuronic acid} \\
| & & \text{or} \\
\text{4-Sulphate} & & \text{L-Iduronic acid} \\
 & & | \\
 & & \text{4-Sulphate}
\end{array}
$$

(Repeating units of heparan sulphate)

Mucopolysaccharidoses: They represent a group of inherited diseases that result from the deficiency of one or more enzymes responsible for the degradation of proteoglycans, particularly heparan sulphate, dermatan sulphate and keratan sulphate. These enzymes located in the lysosomes act on the polysaccharide chains of GAGs and remove the glycosyl groups, sulphate moieties and the glucuronic acid and iduronic acid residues. Deficiency of any of these enzymes results in accumulation and deposit of the proteoglycans and products of degradation in the lysosomes of various tissues and increased excretion of the degraded metabolites in urine. Accumulation of the degraded products in tissues can result in enlargement of the organs and deformity of the structure of bones and skin.

In general, the disease is characterised by coarse facies, corneal clouding, stiffness of joints, skeletal deformities, hepatosplenomegaly and mental retardation. There are seven types of mucopolysaccharidoses described. Each type is caused by deficiency of a specific lysosomal enzyme. These are named **Hurler's syndrome** caused due to deficiency of α-L-iduronidase, **Hunter's syndrome** caused by deficiency of iduronate sulphatase and **Sanfilippo** (A and B) caused by deficiency of heparan sulphate-*N*-sulphatase and *N*-acetylglucosaminidase. **Morquio** (A and B) is caused by deficiency of galactose-6-sulphatase and β-galactosidase. **Scheie** is caused by deficiency of α-L-iduronidase. In each case, an increased amount of specific metabolites is excreted in urine (**Table 18.1**). These are dermatan sulphate (DS) and heparan sulphate (HS) in Hurler, Hunter and Scheie; heparan sulphate (HS) in Sanfilippo; and keratan sulphate (KS) in Morquio. All the diseases are progressive and are fatal during either childhood or adolescence.

Table 18.1 Enzyme Defects and Excretion of Urinary Metabolites in Different Mucopolysaccharidoses

Mucopolysaccharidoses	Enzyme Defect	Metabolites in Urine
Hurler and Scheie	α-L-Iduronidase	DS, HS
Hunter	Iduronate sulphatase	DS, HS
Sanfilippo (A and B)	Heparan sulphate	
	N-Sulphatase	HS
	N-Acetylglucosaminidase	HS
Morquio (A and B)	Galactose-6-sulphatase	KS
	β-Galactosidase	

DS, Dermatan sulphate; HS, heparan sulphate; KS, keratan sulphate.

Functions of proteoglycans: Proteoglycans are complex molecules, having very high molecular weight, and are present in every tissue, mainly in the extracellular matrix. They perform varied functions in the body.

1. Proteoglycans bind to collagen and elastin in the extracellular matrix and play an important role in determining the structural organisation of the matrix.
2. The GAGs being polyionic bind cations such as Na and K and attract water by osmotic pressure into the extracellular matrix. This contributes to the characteristic turgor of tissues.
3. Proteoglycans act as sieves in the extracellular matrix because of the long extended structure of the polysaccharide chains and their ability to form gel at low concentration. This prevents passage of macromolecules passing from the extracellular matrix but allows free diffusion of smaller molecules.
4. The presence of hyaluronic acid in embryonic tissue permits cell migration during morphogenesis and wound repair.
5. Hyaluronic acid and chondroitin sulphate present in cartilage in high concentration contribute to the compressibility of cartilage in weight bearing.
6. Keratan sulphate and dermatan sulphate play an important role in corneal transparency.
7. Heparin has an anticoagulant property. It is an extremely potent anticoagulant.
8. Heparin binds with lipoprotein lipase present on the capillary surface and causes release of the enzyme into blood circulation. In plasma, lipoprotein lipase hydrolyses triglycerides present in chylomicrons and VLDL (very low density lipoprotein), releasing fatty acids.

19

CHAPTER

Lipid Metabolism

Chapter Outline

- Digestion of Lipids
- Absorption of Lipids
- Oxidation of Fatty Acids
- Synthesis of Fatty Acids
- Metabolism of Cholesterol
- Prostaglandins

Fat is the major source of energy for the body. It contains a large store of fatty acids sufficient to supply energy for several days. Body fat is derived from (i) the dietary fats, (ii) conversion of carbohydrates and proteins and (iii) fat depots such as subcutaneous tissues, omentum, peritoneum and suprarenal glands. The excess fat stored in subcutaneous and adipose tissues, retroperitoneal spaces and omentum is known as depot fat. It serves as the reserve food available for the purpose of energy. These are mainly glycerides of higher fatty acids such as palmitic, stearic and oleic acids. Fats act as insulators which serve to protect the body from extreme cold and heat. Certain constituents of fats in the diet such as essential fatty acids and fat-soluble vitamins are dietary essentials and are required for the maintenance of optimal functions of the body. They have to be provided in the diet, since they are not synthesised by the body.

Lipid metabolism differs from those of carbohydrates and proteins in that the proteins and carbohydrates after absorption pass through the portal vein first to enter liver and finally reach the systemic circulation, whereas fats after absorption first enter the lymphatics and systemic circulation and finally reach the liver.

Lipid metabolism comprises study of the following:

1. Absorption of lipids
2. Metabolism of fats and fatty acids which includes
   - Oxidation of fatty acids
   - Synthesis of fatty acids and fats
3. Energetics of fatty acid oxidation
4. Metabolism of cholesterol

DIGESTION OF LIPIDS

The major site of lipid digestion is small intestines. The main requisites for lipid digestion are pancreatic lipase and bile salts. Pancreatic lipase is a powerful lipolytic enzyme secreted by pancreatic juice. Bile salts derived from bile are effective emulsifying agents. The pancreatic duct and common bile duct open into the duodenum at a point close to the pylorus, and the pancreatic juice mixes with the bile shortly before entering the duodenum.

Bile salts have the unique ability to lower surface tension, emulsify fats and dissolve fatty acids and water-insoluble soaps. The alkaline content of pancreatic biliary secretions neutralises the acid of the chyme that enters the duodenum and shifts the pH of the food material to the alkaline side. This shift of pH is necessary for the activity of the enzymes contained in pancreatic juice and intestinal secretion.

No digestion of lipids occurs in the mouth or stomach because (i) the amount of lipase present in saliva and gastric juice is insignificant, (ii) there is no mechanism for emulsifying fatty materials in these regions and (iii) the acid pH of gastric juice is not conducive for lipid digestion.

Digestion of fats and other lipids poses a special problem, because they are insoluble in water and the lipolytic enzymes like other enzymes are soluble in an aqueous medium. This problem is overcome by emulsification of lipids by bile salts. By this process, large fats and oil globules are broken into fine particles. This increases the surface area of the lipids whereby a large surface of the lipids is exposed for interaction with lipase. The rate of digestion is also increased proportionately.

Pancreatic lipase acts at the oil–water interface of the finely emulsified lipid droplets formed by mechanical agitation in the gut in the presence of bile salts, phospholipids, phospholipase A_2 and colipase (a protein present in pancreatic secretion). Steapsin specifically cleaves the primary ester linkages at the 1 and 3 positions of the triglyceride (**Fig. 19.1**) and leaves behind monoglyceride with fatty acid esterified at carbon-2 of the glycerol. The hydrolysis of this linkage is difficult and is a slow process because the fatty acid is linked by a secondary ester bond to carbon-2. The enzyme that hydrolyses this linkage is esterase. As a result, the 2-monoglycerides appear to be the major end products of triglyceride digestion and less than one-fourth of the dietary triglyceride is completely broken down to glycerol and fatty acids. At the end of hydrolysis, the hydrolysed mixture consists of glycerol, fatty acid, monoglycerides, diglycerides and some unhydrolysed triglycerides. The monoglycerides along with the bile salts play an important role in stabilising and further emulsifying the fats in the small intestines. The finely emulsified fat droplets are reduced in size to *micelles*, 0.1–0.5 μm in diameter.

Several other enzymes secreted in the pancreatic juice take part in the hydrolysis of certain lipids, for example

1. Cholesterol esterase hydrolyses cholesterol ester to cholesterol and fatty acids.
2. Phospholipase A_2 hydrolyses the ester bond at carbon-2 of lecithin to form lysophospholipids.

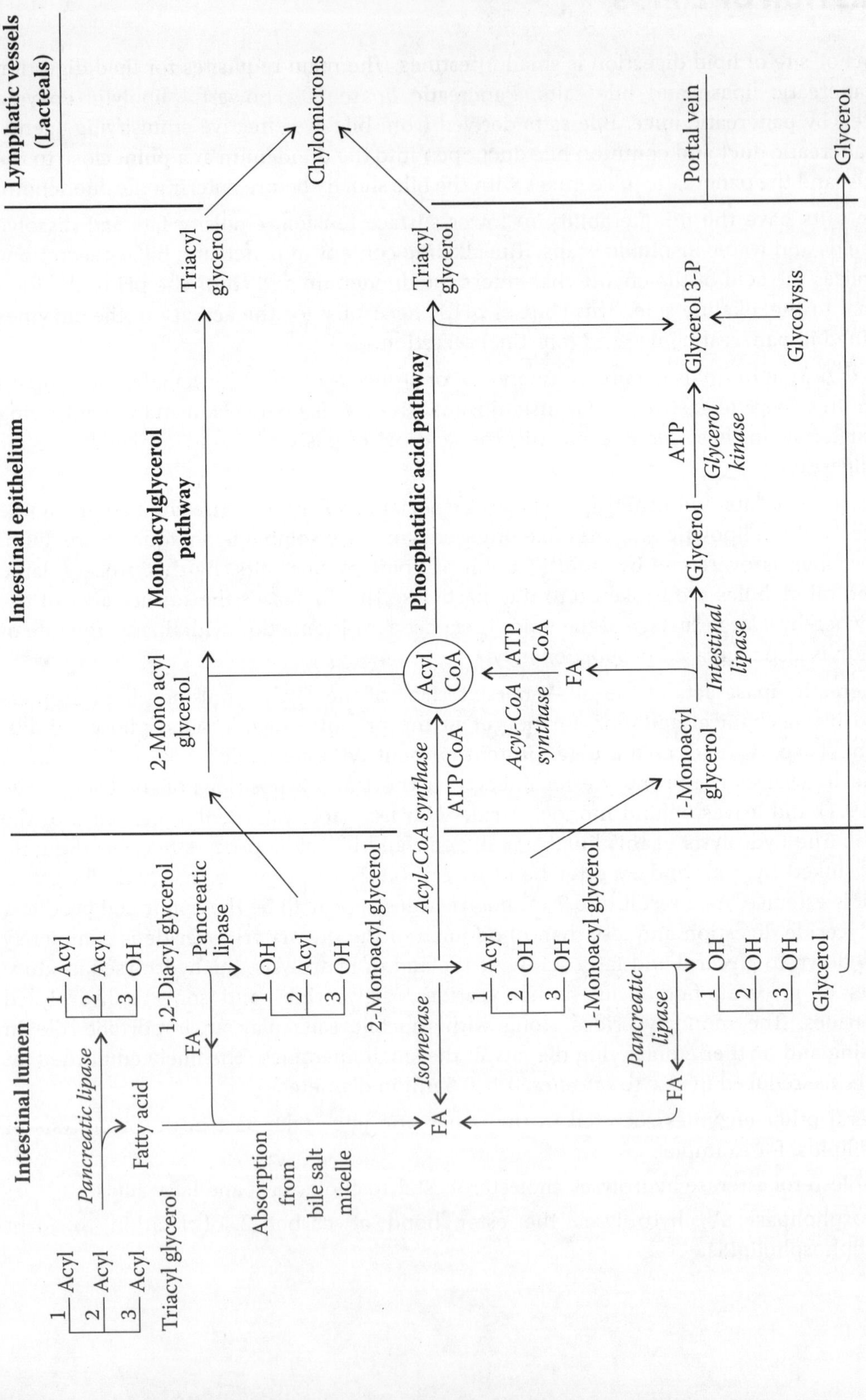

Figure 19.1 Digestion and absorption of triglycerides.

ABSORPTION OF LIPIDS

The products of digestion comprising monoglycerides, diglycerides, fatty acids and small amounts of unhydrolysed triglycerides and phospholipids leave the oil phase of the lipid emulsion and diffuse into the mixed micelles consisting of bile salts, lecithin and cholesterol furnished by the bile. The products of digestion are transported through the aqueous media of the intestinal lumen to the brush border of mucosal cells from where they are absorbed into the intestinal epithelium. The bile salts pass into the ileum where most of them are reabsorbed and returned to the liver for resecretion into the bile. This is enterohepatic circulation of the bile salts.

Within the intestinal epithelium, the products of digestion undergo further changes as indicated below:

1. 1-Monoglycerides may get hydrolysed further to form free glycerol and fatty acid by a lipase.
2. Fatty acids may combine with 2-monoglycerides and diglycerides to form triglycerides. This reaction requires activation of fatty acid by ATP and CoA and is catalysed by fatty acyl-CoA synthase.
3. Aggregates of triglycerides (80%) along with small amounts of extraneous phospholipids (7%) and cholesterol (9%) then get coated with a thin layer of protein to form ***chylomicron*** particles. The particles, about 1 μm in diameter, are secreted from the mucosal cells into the intracellular fluid and then discharged into the lacteals and lymphatics and finally they get into the systemic circulation for metabolic use. Triglycerides that follow this route have long-chain fatty acids of more than 10 carbons. Rapid absorption is assured by the maintenance of a sharp gradient of concentration across the cell membrane by the rapid removal of fatty acids and monoglycerides for the synthesis of triglycerides.
4. The glycerol released within the intestinal cells may be reutilised for triglyceride synthesis by activation with ATP to glycerol-3-phosphate. But the glycerol released in the intestinal lumen is not reutilised but passes directly to the portal vein.
5. The absorbed free cholesterol is re-esterified with fatty acid in the intestinal epithelium to form cholesterol ester.
6. The absorbed lysophospholipids, which is the hydrolysed product of phospholipid, together with some cholesterol, may be reacylated with acyl-CoA to regenerate phospholipids and cholesterol esters.

Majority of absorbed fatty acids with more than 10 carbon atoms in length are found as esterified fatty acids in the lymph of the thoracic duct. Fatty acids with a carbon chain shorter than 10–12 carbons are transported into portal venous blood as unesterified free fatty acids.

Differences exist in the rate of digestion and absorption of individual fatty acids. Unsaturated fatty acids with short chains are absorbed faster than those with long chains. Human milk fat is absorbed better than cow's milk fat because human milk contains a higher percent of unsaturated fatty acids. Also, fats and oils with low melting points (below 50°C) are more rapidly and completely digested and absorbed than those with higher melting points.

OXIDATION OF FATTY ACIDS

A large proportion of the absorbed fat is temporarily stored in the liver which is also the main site for the oxidation and synthesis of fatty acids.

The triglycerides which form an important source of energy are first hydrolysed by lipases to glycerol and fatty acids. Glycerol enters the glycolytic pathway of carbohydrate metabolism. The fatty acids are broken down by a system of degradation known as β-oxidation. The mechanism of the oxidation of fatty acids was primarily explained by Knoop in 1904 and the theory supporting Knoop's views is known as **Knoop's theory of 'β-oxidation'**.

In β-oxidation, oxidation of fatty acids takes place at the carbon atom in the β-position to the carboxyl group, resulting in the splitting of the two terminal carbon atoms, leaving a fatty acid chain shorter than the original acid by two carbon atoms.

Oxidation of phenyl-substituted fatty acids with an odd number of carbon atoms in the chain gives rise to benzoic acid and even-numbered acids give rise to phenylacetic acid. Such fatty acids after coupling with glycine are eliminated as hippuric acid and phenylaceturic acids, respectively.

While the major pathway for catabolism of fatty acids is β-oxidation, which occurs in mitochondria, there are minor pathways as well. The minor pathways are as follows:

1. **α-oxidation:** It predominantly takes place in the brain and liver. In this, one carbon is lost in the form of CO_2 per cycle.
2. **Omega oxidation:** Verkade proposed a theory that though the general pathways of the catabolism of fatty acids involve β-oxidation, certain fatty acids undergo oxidation at the carbon atom situated farthest from the carboxyl group, i.e. the omega carbon atom, producing a dicarboxyl acid, which then undergoes β-oxidation and cleavage to form successively, smaller dicarboxylic acids.
3. **Peroxisomal oxidation:** It is mainly for the trimming of very long-chain fatty acids.

β-Oxidation Cycle of Fatty Acid

Oxidation of fatty acids occurs in the mitochondrial matrix. The two carbon units removed from the fatty acid chain during its oxidative degradation are activated to form active acetate units known as acetyl-CoA. Acetyl-CoA is also the product of oxidative decarboxylation of pyruvic acid and it enters the citric acid cycle. Thus, acetyl-CoA forms a central meeting point for the oxidation of carbohydrates and fatty acids.

The detailed reactions involved in β-oxidation of fatty acids to form acetyl-CoA were worked out by Lynen, Mahler and Green. They found that coenzyme-A present in cells is necessary for the oxidation of fatty acids and that it participates in the first step of β-oxidation of fatty acids. CoA functions as a carrier for the whole fatty acid molecule during degradation as well as for the two carbon units which are split off. The CoA derivatives of fatty acids formed thus are known as fatty acyl derivatives. The fatty acids undergo a series of reactions, leading to the splitting off of acetyl-CoA and formation of an acyl-CoA derivative containing two carbon atoms less than the initial acyl-CoA compound. Repetition of the process shortens the fatty acid chain until it is split to acetyl-CoA units. The entire process takes place in five stages, catalysed by enzymes and coenzymes. The cycle which comprises the five stages of oxidation of fatty acids is known as **β-oxidation cycle of fatty acid**. The reactions are summarised as follows:

1. Condensation by thiokinase
2. Dehydrogenation by acyl dehydrogenase and FAD
3. Hydration by enoyl hydratase
4. Dehydrogenation by β-hydroxyacyl dehydrogenase and NAD
5. Thiolysis to form acetyl-CoA

Oxidation of a fatty acid $RCH_2CH_2CH_2COOH$ is illustrated in **Figure 19.2**.

Reaction 1 The initial step involves activation of the fatty acid with ATP and CoA to form an acyl thioester of CoA. Adenylic acid and inorganic pyrophosphate are liberated. The reaction catalysed by a thiokinase enzyme may be written as

$$RCH_2CH_2CH_2COOH + CoA + ATP \longrightarrow RCH_2CH_2CH_2CO \sim S\text{-}CoA + AMP + PPi.$$

In this reaction, energy is released by the splitting of ATP and this is used to link the fatty acid and CoA.

Reaction 2 The acyl thioester is next dehydrogenated in the α-, β-position by an acyl-CoA dehydrogenase bearing FAD prosthetic group and a metal cofactor iron or copper, resulting in the formation of α-, β-unsaturated acyl thioester of CoA.

$$RCH_2\underset{\beta}{CH_2}\underset{\alpha}{CH_2}CO \sim S\text{-}CoA + FAD \longrightarrow RCH_2CH = CHCO \sim S\text{-}CoA + FADH_9$$

Reaction 3 A molecule of water is added to the unsaturated linkage of the thioester of CoA, to form a β-hydroxyacyl-CoA. This reaction is catalysed by an enoyl-CoA hydratase.

$$RCH_2CH = CHCO \sim S\text{-}CoA + H_2O \longrightarrow RCH_2\overset{\beta}{CHOH}\overset{\alpha}{CH_2}CO \sim S\text{-}CoA$$

Reaction 4 The second dehydrogenation occurs in this reaction, when two hydrogen atoms are removed from the β-carbon atom of the β-hydroxy compound. The reaction is catalysed by a β-hydroxyacyl-CoA dehydrogenase and NAD. A β-keto compound is formed. This step evolves energy, and the β-keto linkage formed is energetically equivalent to a high-energy phosphate bond.

$$RCH_2CHOHCH_2CO \sim S\text{-}CoA + NAD \rightleftharpoons$$

$$RCH_2\overset{\overset{\displaystyle O}{\|}}{C} \sim S\text{-}CH_2CO \sim S\text{-}CoA + NADH + H^+$$

Reaction 5 A reaction similar to hydrolysis but involving CoA instead of water occurs, which splits the β-keto compound into a molecule of acetyl-CoA and a molecule of acyl-CoA which contains two carbon atoms less than the original one. This reaction described as thiolysis is catalysed by a β-keto acyl-CoA thiolase.

$$RCH_2\underset{\beta}{\overset{\overset{\displaystyle O}{\|}}{C}} \sim \underset{\alpha}{CH_2}CO \sim CoA + CoA \rightleftharpoons \underset{\text{Acyl-CoA}}{RCH_2\,CO \sim CoA} + \underset{\text{Acetyl-CoA}}{CH_3CO \sim CoA}$$

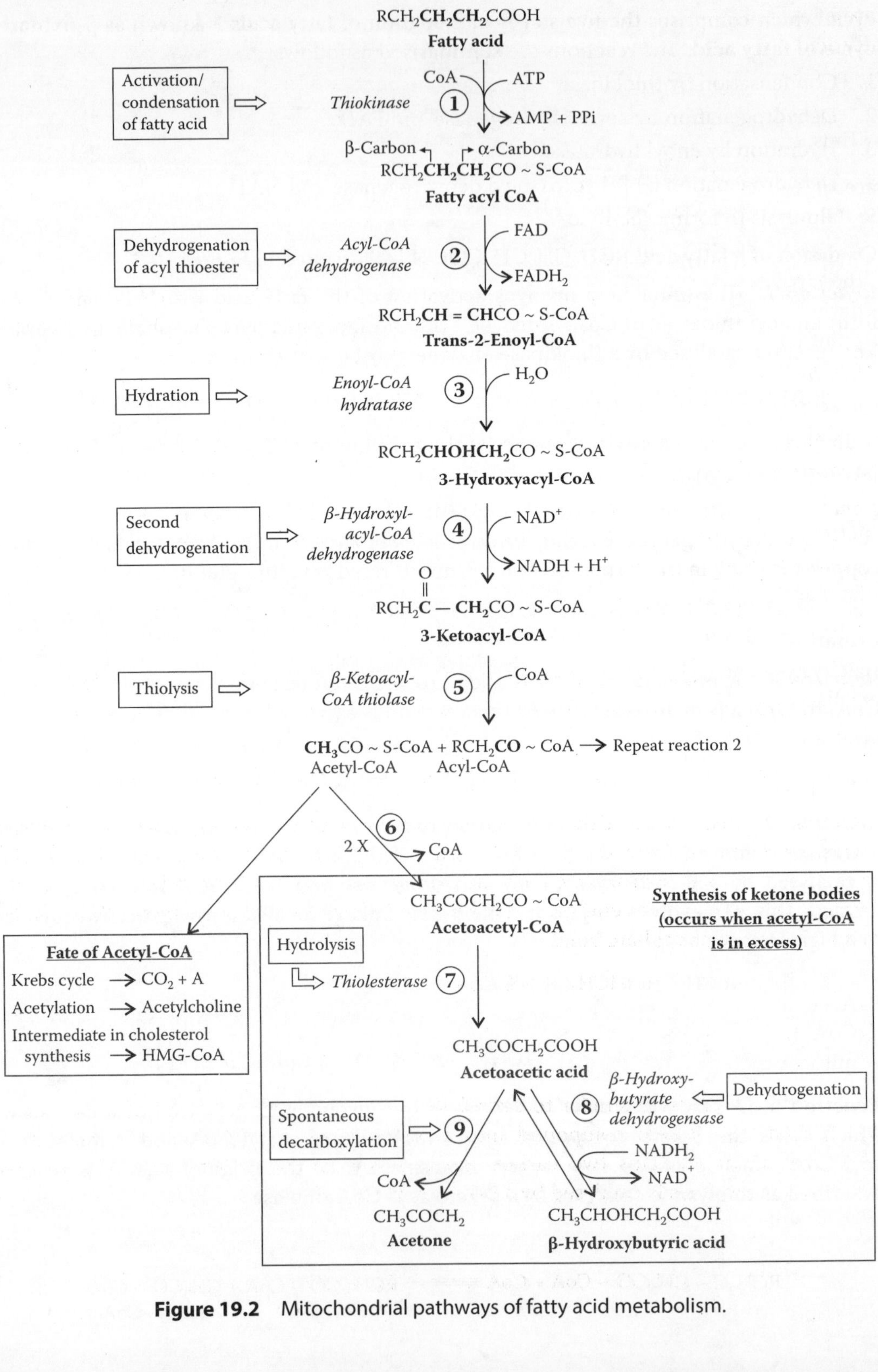

Figure 19.2 Mitochondrial pathways of fatty acid metabolism.

Fate of acyl-CoA: The acyl-CoA can repeat the sequence of reactions described under the fatty acid oxidation cycle, starting from reaction 2.

$$RCH_2CO \sim CoA \longrightarrow \text{Repeat from reaction 2}$$

Thus, fatty acids are enzymatically oxidised step by step, to form acetyl-CoA.

Fate of acetyl-CoA: Acetyl-CoA produced by the oxidation of fatty acids may undergo the following reactions:

- *Oxidation in citric acid cycle:* The major proportion of acetyl-CoA may be directed into the citric acid cycle for oxidation and production of energy. Acetyl-CoA which is also derived from the oxidative decarboxylation of pyruvic acid forms the central meeting point for the oxidation of carbohydrates and fats through the citric acid cycle.
- *Synthesis of acetylcholine:* Acetyl-CoA may be utilised for acetylation reactions. Choline is acetylated in the presence of acetyl-CoA to form acetylcholine and this takes place mainly in brain tissues.
- *Synthesis of cholesterol:* Acetyl-CoA is the starting material for the biosynthesis of cholesterol. It condenses with acetoacetyl-CoA to form β-hydroxymethylglutaryl–CoA (HMG CoA) which is an important intermediate in the synthesis of cholesterol.
- *Synthesis of fatty acids:* Acetyl-CoA units are the building blocks for the synthesis of fatty acids.

Formation of ketone bodies: When the rate of acetyl-CoA formation exceeds the capacity of the citric acid cycle to deal with ketone bodies, the following side reactions take place (*see* **Fig. 19.2**).

Reaction 6 Two molecules of acetyl-CoA condense with the loss of one molecule of CoA to form a molecule of acetoacetyl-CoA

$$2\ CH_3CO \sim CoA \rightleftharpoons CH_3COCH_2CO \sim CoA + CoA$$

Acetoacetyl-CoA follows two pathways:

(i) ***Reaction 7*** Acetoacetyl-CoA may be hydrolysed by a thiolesterase to form acetoacetic acid when CoA is liberated.

$$CH_3COCH_2CO \sim CoA + H_2O \longrightarrow CH_3COCH_2COOH + CoA$$

(ii) Acetoacetyl-CoA can condense with acetyl-CoA to form β-hydroxy-β-methylglutaryl-CoA (HMG-CoA). This reaction is catalysed by HMG-CoA synthase which is a mitochondrial enzyme. HMG-CoA is an intermediary in the synthesis of cholesterol.

$$CH_3COCH_2CO \sim CoA + CH_3CO \sim CoA + H_2O \rightleftharpoons$$

$$HOOC - CH_2 - \underset{\displaystyle CH_3}{\overset{\displaystyle OH}{\underset{|}{\overset{|}{C}}}} - CH_2CO \sim CoA + CoA$$

β-Hydroxy-β-methylglutaryl-CoA

HMG-CoA cleaves to form acetoacetic acid and acetyl-CoA in the liver by the action of the HMG-CoA lyase enzyme.

$$\text{HMG-CoA} \longrightarrow \text{Acetoacetic acid} + \text{Acetyl-CoA}$$

Reaction 8 A major fraction of the acetoacetic acid thus formed is reduced in the liver to β-hydroxybutyric acid by β-hydroxybutyrate dehydrogenase and NADH.

$$CH_3COCH_2COOH + NADH + H^+ \rightleftharpoons CH_3CHOHCH_2COOH + NAD^+$$

Reaction 9 A minor fraction of acetoacetic acid undergoes spontaneous decarboxylation to form acetone.

$$CH_3CO\text{-}CH_2COOH \longrightarrow CH_3COCH_3 + CO_2$$

Acetone may undergo two metabolic changes:

1. It may be further cleaved to yield acetic acid and formic acid.

$$CH_3COCH_3 \longrightarrow CH_3COOH + HCOOH$$

2. It can be transformed to propanediol which in turn gets oxidised to pyruvic acid.

$$CH_3COCH_3 \longrightarrow \underset{\text{Propanediol}}{CH_3CHOHCH_2OH} \longrightarrow CH_3COCOOH$$

Ketogenesis

Acetoacetate, β-hydroxybutyrate and acetone are collectively called **ketone bodies** or **acetone bodies**, and the process of their formation is known as **ketogenesis**. The main site of ketogenesis is the liver. These substances pass into the bloodstream in very small amounts under normal circumstances. The total concentration of ketone bodies in plasma is about 1 mg per 100 ml and the average excretion in urine in 24 hours is less than 125 mg. Normally, the ketone bodies are carried in the bloodstream, mainly to the kidneys and muscles, where acetoacetate is oxidised after conversion to acetoacetyl-CoA. The latter is then cleaved by thiolase when two molecules of acetyl-CoA are formed. They then enter the citric acid cycle. This process of oxidation of ketone bodies is called **ketolysis**.

Ketosis

When the rate of ketogenesis in the liver exceeds the rate of ketolysis in the periphery, the concentration of ketone bodies in the blood increases resulting in **ketonaemia**. At this stage, ketone bodies are excreted in a detectable quantity in the urine. This is **ketonuria**. When ketonuria and ketonaemia are marked, acetone which has a significant vapour pressure escapes in the exhaled air giving rise to acetone odour in the breath. The triad of ketonaemia, ketonuria and the acetone odour of the breath is referred to as **ketosis**. If ketosis is severe, acidosis will set in and this is accompanied by excretion of a large amount of water which is necessary to carry the ketone bodies. At this stage, the patient becomes profoundly acidotic and dehydrated and passes into the comatose stage. This occurs in diabetic coma which follows neglected and uncontrolled diabetes mellitus. The breath of patients suffering from diabetic coma smells of acetone. If prompt treatment is not given, death follows.

Causes of Ketosis Two main causes of ketosis are as follows:

1. Starvation
2. Diabetes mellitus

In starvation, there is deprivation of carbohydrates and in diabetes, carbohydrates are not efficiently utilised. The person survives on his own stores of glycogen in the liver for energy. When this is depleted, energy is derived by the breakdown of fats in the body. The accelerated fat metabolism leads to the formation of a large amount of acetyl-CoA and ketone bodies, giving rise to ketosis and ketonuria. A large amount of ketone bodies may be excreted in urine due to high fatty diet.

Energy Derived from Oxidation of Fatty Acids

The body derives energy from fats, mainly by the oxidation of acetyl-CoA. It may be assumed that the number of high-energy phosphate bonds generated during the oxidation of each unit of acetyl-CoA derived from a fatty acid is the same as that produced in pyruvate oxidation, minus the energy produced by oxidative decarboxylation of pyruvate. On this basis, 12 high-energy bonds (HEB) are produced in the citric acid cycle, per molecule of acetyl-CoA, as shown below:

	HEB
Total energy produced by the citric acid cycle for 2 molecules of acetyl-CoA	30
Oxidative decarboxylation of 2 molecules of pyruvic acid produces	6
Energy derived from the citric acid cycle minus oxidative decarboxylation of 2 molecules of pyruvic acid	24
Therefore, energy derived from 1 molecule of acetyl-CoA, through the citric acid cycle	12

Oxidation of NADH produced in reaction 4 of **Figure 19.2** accounts for 3 HEB whereas reaction 2, being on the flavoprotein level, yields 2 HEB. The energy derived from complete oxidation of 1 molecule of palmitic acid may be represented as follows: Palmitic acid $CH_3(CH_2)_{14}COOH$ produces eight acetyl fragments. The oxidation of these fragments yields $(8 \times 12) + (5 \times 7) = 131$ HEB.

Subtraction of energy expended in the initial step yields $(131 - 2) = 129$ HEB. Taking 9 kcal as the average energy value of one HEB, the approximate quantity of the free energy recoverable as HEB from the combustion of one molecule of palmitic acid is $129 \times 9 = 1161$ kcal.

SYNTHESIS OF FATTY ACIDS

The animal tissues contain fatty acids which have an even number of carbon atoms, from C_4 to C_{24}, increasing in length by the addition of two carbon atoms. Liver is the main site of synthesis and oxidation of fatty acids. Synthesis takes place in extrahepatic tissues also. In tissues, oxidation and synthesis of fatty acids are constantly renewed and tend to be in a state of equilibrium. When the amount of fatty acids synthesised and derived from the diet exceeds the amount degraded, the excess is stored in the tissues. Generally, unsaturated fatty acids are deposited in depot fat and long-chain fatty acids are deposited in adipose tissues. Short-chain fatty acids are oxidised. The main sources for the synthesis of fatty acids are as follows:

1. **Carbohydrates:** Pyruvic acid forms 'active acetate' or acetyl-CoA by oxidative decarboxylation. Acetyl-CoA forms fatty acids and the reaction is reversible.

$$\text{Acetyl-CoA} \rightleftharpoons \text{Fatty acids.}$$

2. **Proteins:** Amino acids, both glucogenic and ketogenic, are important sources for the synthesis of fatty acids. Glucogenic amino acids can form pyruvic acid which on oxidative decarboxylation forms acetyl-CoA. Ketogenic amino acids form acetate or acetoacetate which are direct sources for fatty acid synthesis. It may be noted that whatever be the major source, acetyl-CoA is the immediate precursor for the synthesis of fatty acids. In addition to acetyl-CoA, synthesis of fatty acids requires a source of reducing system, especially NADPH. The main source of supply of NADPH for this purpose is the hexose monophosphate shunt pathway of carbohydrate metabolism. Another important factor which influences lipogenesis is insulin, which has a direct influence on glucose metabolism. The synthesis of fatty acids is an endergonic reaction, i.e. energy requiring reaction.

Biosynthesis of Fatty Acids

It is believed that there are two pathways for the synthesis of fatty acids in tissues. These are (i) the mitochondrial system of fatty acid synthesis located inside the mitochondria and (ii) the non-mitochondrial system or the cytoplasmic system of fatty acid synthesis occurring outside the mitochondria.

Mitochondrial System of Fatty Acid Synthesis

This system involves a series of reactions which are essentially the reverse of those by which fatty acids are oxidised (*see* **Fig. 19.2**). It may be noted that all the steps of the oxidation of fatty acids are reversible except Reaction 3, i.e. conversion of the α-, β-unsaturated acyl-CoA to the corresponding β-hydroxy compound. The reactions occur anaerobically in mitochondria, starting with repeated condensation of acetate units to form acetyl-CoA followed by formation of the β-keto compound, β-hydroxyacyl-CoA and the active fatty acid derivatives. The reactions are catalysed by their respective enzymes. Up to this stage, all the reactions are reversible. However for the conversion of the α-, β-unsaturated fatty acid derivative to the saturated compound, an additional enzyme, enoyl-CoA reductase, is used. This requires reduced NADH as its coenzyme, which donates hydrogen atoms for the formation of the saturated fatty acid compound. This system of biosynthesis is particularly concerned with the synthesis of long-chain fatty acids, mainly stearic acid, and also with the process of elongation of the existing fatty acids of moderate chain lengths.

Extramitochondrial System of Fatty Acid Synthesis

A different and highly active system exists for the synthesis of palmitic acid from acetyl-CoA. This system, known as the extramitochondrial system, is localised in the cytosol fraction of the cell and is concerned almost entirely with the synthesis of palmitic acid which is the main fatty acid of the tissues. Synthesis occurs in liver, kidneys, brain, lungs and adipose tissue. Acetyl-CoA formed from pyruvate or fatty acids is the substrate from which synthesis starts and is the major building block for long-chain fatty acid synthesis. The end product is palmitic acid. Cofactors NADPH, ATP, Mn^{++} and HCO_3 (source of CO_2) are required for this enzyme system.

Formation of acetyl-CoA takes place in mitochondria and it cannot reach cytoplasm as such because the cell membrane is impermeable to acetyl-CoA. But the fatty acid synthesis occurs in cytoplasm and the enzymes responsible for the synthesis are extramitochondrial. Thus, the problem of the cell in transporting acetyl-CoA into the cytosol has to be overcome. This is overcome by allowing acetyl-CoA to form citrate in the mitochondria by condensing with oxaloacetate (citric acid cycle), and citrate which is permeable comes out of the mitochondria into the cytosol.

The process is reversed and acetyl-CoA is made available in the cytosol by a reaction catalysed by the enzyme ATP citrate lyase as shown below.

$$\text{Citrate} + \text{ATP} + \text{CoA} \longrightarrow \text{Acetyl-CoA} + \text{Oxaloacetate} + \text{ADP} + \text{P.}$$

The initial reaction for the biosynthesis of the fatty acid starts with carboxylation of acetyl-CoA to form malonyl-CoA. The reaction is catalysed by acetyl-CoA carboxylase, a biotin containing enzyme, and requires ATP. HCO_3^- is the source of CO_2 for carboxylation.

$$\text{Acetyl-CoA} + CO_2 + \text{ATP} \longrightarrow \text{Malonyl-CoA} + \text{ADP} + \text{P.}$$

The stepwise synthesis of the fatty acid from malonyl-CoA to palmitic acid is catalysed by a **multienzyme complex** known as **fatty acid synthase**. This is present in the soluble fraction of the cell.

To follow the complex reactions taking place in the process of synthesis, it is necessary to understand the structure and composition of the multienzyme complex and also the location of the binding and reactive sites of the enzyme. The fatty acid synthase is a dimer consisting of two identical monomers. Each monomer has a molecular weight of about 250,000 and consists of one polypeptide chain containing all the seven enzymes of fatty acid synthase and a terminal acyl carrier protein (ACP). The ACP plays a specific role of binding the acyl intermediates during the formation of the long-chain fatty acids. ACP is a heat-stable protein consisting of 77 amino acid residues. It has a prosthetic group 4′-phosphopantetheine attached to the serine moiety in the 36th position. The structure of 4′-phosphopantetheine is similar to that of coenzyme A and the SH group of 4′-phosphopantetheine is free to bind the acyl derivatives. It is believed that the growing fatty acyl group is transported from enzyme to enzyme in the manner of an assembly line while being attached to ACP (**Fig. 19.3**).

In close proximity to the SH group of the 4′-phosphopantetheine is another SH thiol of a cysteine residue attached to the ketoacyl synthase (condensing enzyme) of the other monomer (**Fig. 19.3**). The seven enzyme components of monomer 1 and monomer 2 are arranged in a specific sequence referred to as head-to-tail arrangement.

Monomer 1	Monomer 2
Acyl carrier protein	Ketoacyl synthase
Thioesterase	Ketoacyl reductase
Acetyl transacylase	Hydratase
Malonyl transacylase	Enoyl reductase
Enoyl reductase	Malonyl transacylase
Hydratase	Acetyl transacylase
Ketoacyl reductase	Thioesterase
Ketoacyl synthase	Acyl carrier protein

Step 1: The sequence of reactions from malonyl-CoA (page 359) obtained from the initial reaction (step 1: formation of malonyl-CoA) (page 357) continues.

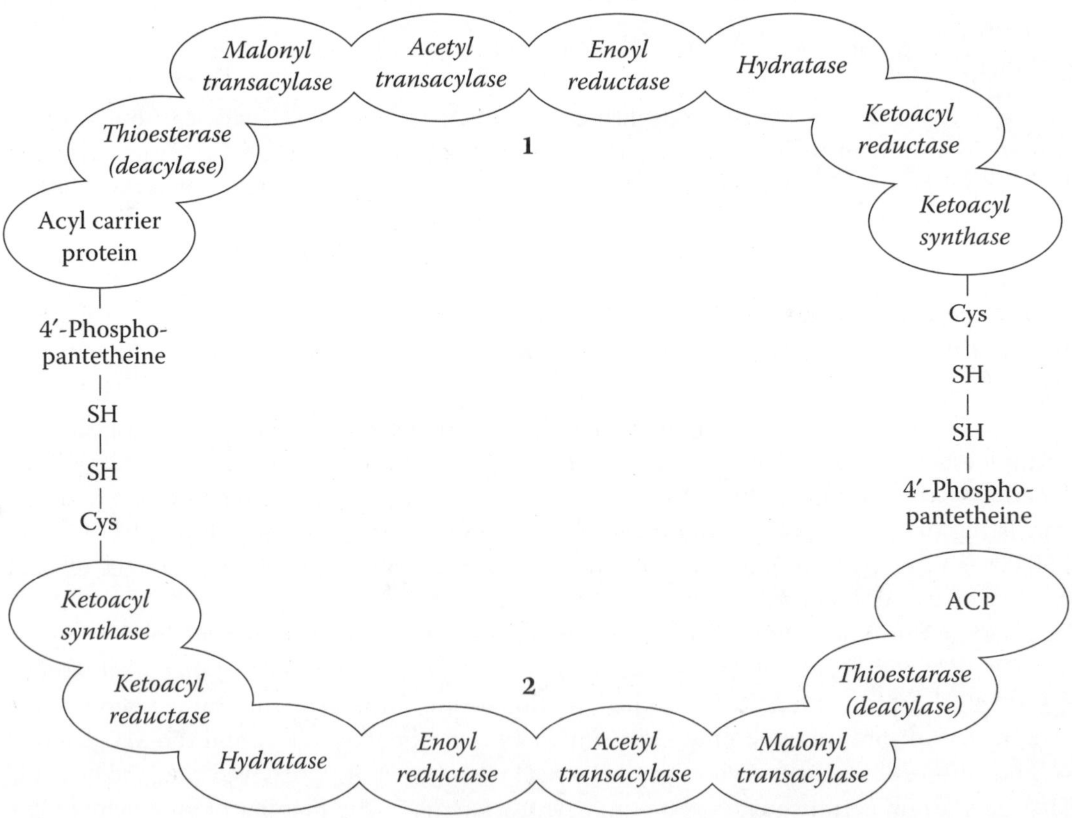

Figure 19.3 Components and sequence of enzymes of a fatty acid synthase multienzyme complex.

Step 2: The second step is formation of acetyl-S-ACP and malonyl-S-ACP. These reactions take place as follows (**Fig. 19.3**):

- Acetyl-S-ACP is formed by the transfer of the acetyl group of acetyl-S-CoA to the SH group of ACP of one of the monomers, say 1. This reaction is catalysed by acetyl transacylase.
- Malonyl-S-ACP is formed by the transfer of the malonyl group of malonyl-S-CoA to the SH group of ACP on monomer 2. This reaction is catalysed by malonyl transacylase.

Step 3: The third step is condensation of the acetyl-S-ACP from monomer 1 with malonyl-S-ACP on monomer 2 to form acetoacetyl-S-ACP. CO_2 is released. The reaction is catalysed by ketoacyl synthase, also called 'condensing enzyme.'

Step 4: The fourth step is reduction of acetoacetyl-CoA to form β-hydroxybutyryl ACP. This reaction requires NADPH for reduction and is catalysed by enoyl reductase.

Step 5: The fifth step is formation of enoyl-S-ACP (α–β unsaturated compound) by removal of a molecule of H_2O from β-hydroxybutyryl-S-ACP. The reaction is catalysed by hydratase.

Step 6: The final step is reduction of enoyl-S-ACP to butyryl-S-ACP which is a saturated compound. The reaction requires NADPH for reduction and is catalysed by enoyl reductase.

In this way, the steps may be repeated with butyryl-ACP by addition with another malonyl-ACP to form caproyl ACP (six carbons) and then eight carbons ACP and so on until a chain length of 16 carbons (palmityl ACP) is reached. This is then cleaved by thioesterase to form palmitic acid and ACP is released. Palmitic acid is released into cytosol. The reactions with ACP intact prior to its release are explained on page 357.

1. $CH_3CO\text{-}S \sim CoA + CO_2 \longrightarrow COOH\text{—}CH_2\text{—}CO{\sim}S\text{-}CoA$

   Aceyl-CoA → Malonyl-CoA

2. (a) ACP-SH + Acetyl-CoA ⟶ Acetyl-S-ACP

   (b) ACP-SH + Malonyl-CoA ⟶ Malonyl-S-ACP

3. $COOH\text{—}CH_2\text{—}CO{\sim}S\text{-}CoA + CH_3CO{\sim}S\text{-}CoA \xrightarrow{\textit{Ketoacyl synthase}} CH_3COCH_2CO{\sim}S\text{-}CoA$

   Malonyl-CoA + Acetyl-CoA → Acetoacetyl CoA

4. $CH_3COCH_2CO{\sim}S\text{-}CoA \xrightarrow{\textit{Ketoacyl reductase}} CH_3CHOH\ CH_2\ CO{\sim}S\text{-}CoA$

   Acetoacetyl-CoA → β-Hydroxybutyryl CoA

5. $CH_3CHOHCH_2CO{\sim}S\text{-}CoA \xrightarrow{\textit{Hydratase}} CH_3CH = CH\,CO{\sim}S\text{-}CoA$
   β-Hydroxybutyryl CoA — Enoyl-ACP

6. $CH_3CH = CHCO{\sim}S\text{-}CoA \xrightarrow{\textit{Enoyl reductase}} CH_3CH_2CH_2CO{\sim}S\text{-}CoA$
   Enoyl-ACP — Butyryl CoA

Repeat of reactions from step 2 wherein the butyryl-ACP condenses with a molecule of malonyl-ACP. The steps are repeated until a 16-C fatty acid (palmitic acid) is synthesised.

The overall reactions may be summarised as follows:

$$1\ \text{Acetyl-CoA} + 7\ \text{Malonyl-CoA} + 14\ \text{NADPH} + 14H^+ \longrightarrow 1\ \text{Palmitic acid} + 7\ CO_2 + 6\ H_2O + 8\ \text{CoA SH} + 14\ NADP^+.$$

Source of NADPH The main source of NADPH, the reducing coenzyme required for the reactions of the cytoplasmic synthesis of fatty acids, is obtained from the oxidative reactions of the hexose monophosphate shunt pathway. Other sources include the extramitochondrial isocitrate dehydrogenase reaction and the NADP-malate dehydrogenase reaction that converts malate to pyruvate. This enzyme, often known as the 'malic enzyme', is not the same as malate dehydrogenase of the citric acid cycle.

Regulatory Mechanisms of Lipogenesis

1. **Short-term mechanism:** Allosteric and covalent modifications of certain enzymes, the most important being acetyl-CoA carboxylase which is activated by citrate. The enzyme is inactivated by phosphorylation as well as by end product.
2. **Long-term mechanism:** Modifying the rates of gene expression which in turn controls the availability of the enzymes in the pathway.

Microsomal System for Chain Elongation

The main site for lengthening of the existing long-chain fatty acids is the microsomal fatty acid elongase system of enzymes. The acetyl donor is malonyl-CoA and the reducing coenzyme is NADPH.

Summary of Fatty Acid Synthesis

Step 1: Formation of malonyl-CoA by carboxylation of acetyl-CoA

Step 2: Formation of acetyl-ACP and malonyl-ACP by acetyl transacylase and malonyl transacylase, respectively

Step 3: Condensation of acetyl-ACP and malonyl-ACP to form acetoacetyl-ACP catalysed by ketoacyl synthase, also called condensing enzyme

Step 4: Reduction of acetoacetyl-ACP by the ketoacyl reductase enzyme to form β-hydroxyl-butyryl ACP

Step 5: Dehydration of β-hydroxyl-butyryl-ACP to form enoyl-ACP catalysed by the dehydratase enzyme.

Step 6: Reduction of enoyl-ACP by the enzyme enoyl reductase to form butyryl-ACP (4C).

Step 7: Repeat reactions from step 2 wherein the butyryl-ACP condenses with a molecule of malonyl-ACP. The steps are repeated until a 16-C fatty acid is synthesised.

Step 8: Release of fatty acid by the thioesterase enzyme

Role of Carnitine in Fatty Acid Metabolism

Carnitine (β-hydroxy-γ-trimethylammonium butyrate) is a betaine and has the formula of $(CH_3)_3N^+CH_2{-}CH(OH){-}CH_2{-}COO^-$. It is widely distributed in tissues, especially muscles. It acts as a carrier of acyl radicals between the mitochondria and the extramitochondrial components of the cell, as otherwise acyl radicals cannot penetrate the mitochondrial membrane readily. Acyl radicals are transferred to carnitine by two enzymes present in both compartments. These are (i) acetyl transferase which reacts with short-chain acyl-CoA molecules and (ii) acyl transferase which reacts with long-chain acyl-CoA molecules.

$$\text{Acetyl-CoA} + \text{Carnitine} \xrightleftharpoons{\textit{Acetyl transferase}} \text{Acetyl carnitine} + \text{CoA}$$

$$\text{Acyl-CoA} + \text{Carnitine} \xrightleftharpoons{\textit{Acyl transferase}} \text{Acyl carnitine} + \text{CoA}$$

Synthesis of Triglycerides or Neutral Fat

The mode of synthesis of triglycerides is illustrated in **Figure 19.4**. Glycerol and fatty acid, which are the starting materials for the synthesis of triglyceride, are first activated by ATP.

In liver, kidneys, heart and intestinal mucosa, glycerol is activated and phosphorylated to α-glycerophosphate by ATP, in the presence of the enzyme glycerokinase (**Fig. 19.4**).

In muscles and adipose tissues where glycerokinase is absent, α-glycerophosphate is formed from dihydroxyacetone phosphate by reduction with NADH in the presence of α-glycerophosphate dehydrogenase.

Fatty acids are activated to form acyl-CoA by ATP and CoA, in the presence of the enzyme thiokinase.

Two molecules of acyl-CoA combine with α-glycerophosphate to form α-β-diglyceride phosphate (phosphatidic acid) in the presence of glycerophosphate acyl transferase. The phosphatidic acid is next dephosphorylated by a phosphatase to form α-β-diglyceride. Another molecule of acyl-CoA is esterified with the diglyceride, to form a triglyceride (**Fig. 19.4**).

It may be noted that this pathway also represents the mode of synthesis of triglyceride from carbohydrates, the carbohydrate sources being glycerol and dihydroxyacetone phosphate.

Synthesis of Phospholipids—Lecithins, Cephalins and Lipositol

Lecithins and cephalins are derived from α-,β-diglyceride. For this, choline and ethanolamine are activated by ATP in the presence of a phosphokinase to form phosphoryl choline (choline-P) and phosphoryl ethanolamine (ethanolamine-P), respectively. ATP acts as the phosphate donor. These in turn react with cytidine triphosphate (CTP) to form cytidine diphosphocholine (CDP choline) and cytidine diphosphoethanolamine (CDP ethanolamine) (**Fig. 19.5**).

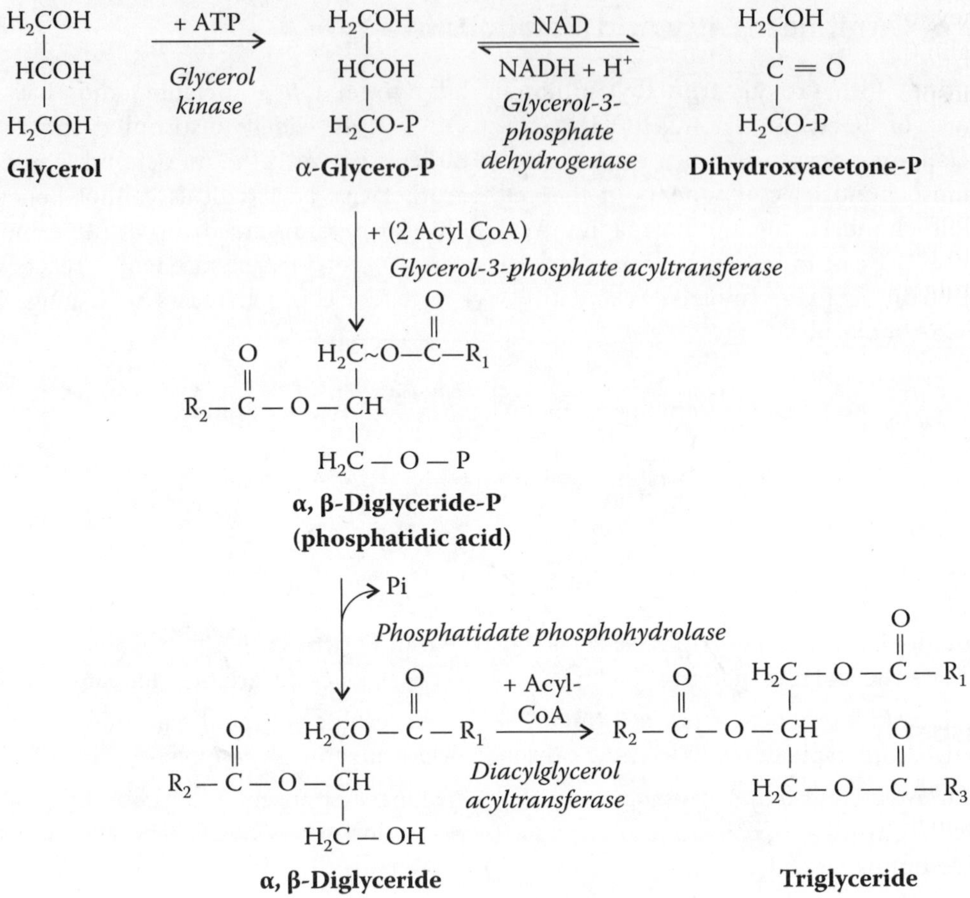

Figure 19.4 Biosynthesis of triglycerides.

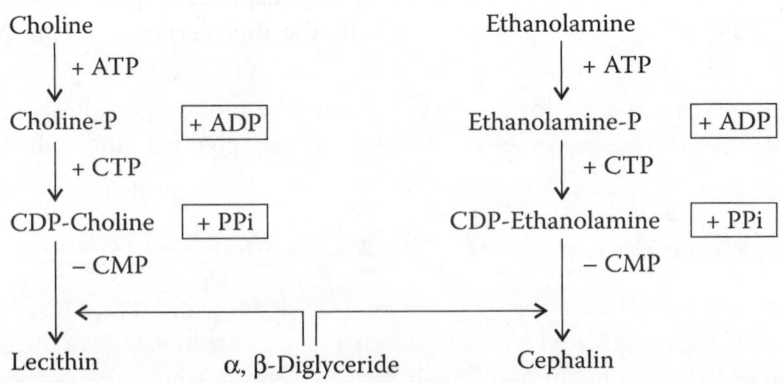

Figure 19.5 Synthesis of phospholipids.

They react with α-,β-diglyceride to form either lecithin (phosphatidylcholine) or cephalin (phosphatidylethanolamine).

Phosphatidylserine is formed by a direct reaction of phophatidylethanolamine with serine.

$$\text{Phosphatidylethanolamine} + \text{L-Serine} \rightleftharpoons \text{Phosphatidylserine} + \text{Ethanolamine}$$

Lipositol is derived from phosphatidic acid. For this, CTP first reacts with phosphatidic acid to form cytidine diphosphate diglyceride (CDP diglyceride) which in turn reacts with inositol to form phosphatidylinositol (lipositol).

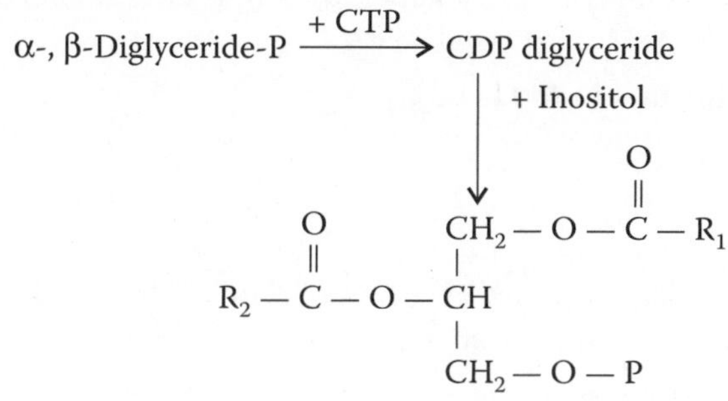

Lipositol

Transport of Lipids

Lipids after synthesis may be transferred from one site to another in response to physiological demands. When plenty of fats are supplied in the diet, the excess fats are sent to fat depots for storage. When the supply of fats is inadequate in the diet, the stored fats are mobilised from the depot and transported to liver for oxidation.

Interconversion between saturated fatty acids of different chain lengths by addition or removal of two carbon units is possible, for example

$$\text{Myristic acid} \underset{-\,C_2}{\overset{+\,C_2}{\rightleftharpoons}} \text{Palmitic acid} \underset{-\,C_2}{\overset{+\,C_2}{\rightleftharpoons}} \text{Stearic acid}$$

Formation of monounsaturated fatty acids from the corresponding saturated fatty acids is also possible, for example

$$\text{Palmitic} \xrightarrow{-2H} \text{Palmitoleic}$$

$$\text{Stearate} \xrightarrow{-2H} \text{Oleate}$$

Role of Liver in Fat Metabolism

Fat is not primarily stored in liver. Normal liver contains only about 4% of the body lipids. But liver plays a central role in the metabolism of lipids, as it forms the central meeting place for the different pathways of fat metabolism.

1. Liver facilitates digestion and absorption of fats by manufacturing bile acids and bile salts which are essential requisites for this purpose.

2. It is the main site of synthesis of fatty acids which are synthesised from acetate units and carbohydrates.
3. Liver is also the main organ where phospholipids, lipoproteins and cholesterol are synthesised. It also serves to remove them from blood.
4. In the liver, the lipids mobilised from the diet and depot are oxidised and metabolised to provide energy to the body.
5. It is in the liver that the blood lipids undergo the necessary changes for transportation in the plasma.
6. Liver brings about changes to fatty acids, by lengthening, shortening, saturating and desaturating them as and when necessary.
7. Ketone bodies are formed in the liver.

Fatty Livers

Normal healthy liver does not store fat beyond 4–5% of the total lipids. The liver fat consists mainly of neutral fat (triglycerides), phospholipids and small amounts of cholesterol. But in certain pathological conditions, liver may accumulate fat to the extent of about 30–40%, consisting mainly of triglycerides and cholesterol.

In severe cases, the accumulation of fat may be extensive, usually associated with destruction of liver cells. When this process becomes chronic, fibrotic changes occur in the liver cells, resulting in cirrhosis of liver and impaired liver functions.

The main causes leading to the formation of fatty livers may be considered under four headings:

1. Carbohydrate deprivation
2. Hepatotoxic agents
3. Deficiency of lipotropic factors
4. Cholesterol feeding

Carbohydrate deprivation: When carbohydrates are not completely oxidised as in the case of diabetes mellitus and starvation, fats are mobilised from depots, via the bloodstream to the liver in large quantities, for oxidation to yield energy. This causes accumulation of fats, i.e. triglycerides, in liver. The sources of mobilisation are as follows:

Fat depots in adipose tissues: Free fatty acids which are liberated in increasing amounts in the blood are taken to the liver and esterified.

Lipoproteins in extrahepatic tissues: Lipoproteins are hydrolysed by lipoprotein lipase, resulting in the liberation of increased amounts of free fatty acid in the plasma.

Hepatotoxic agents: Fat can accumulate in the liver and cause fatty liver, after prolonged administration of certain hepatotoxic agents such as chloroform, carbon tetrachloride, phosphorus and arsenic, bacteria and virus.

Deficiency of lipotropic factors: Substances such as choline, betaine, methionine and phospholipids are called **lipotropic factors** because they prevent and cure the accumulation of an abnormally large amount of fats in the liver. It may be noted that, for normal metabolism of fat, an effective synthesis of phospholipids is necessary. Impaired synthesis of phospholipids in the liver will cause accumulation of fat in the liver.

Deficiency of choline and betaine may arise when factors necessary for their synthesis are defective. Since choline and betaine are synthesised by methylation of ethanolamine, an inadequate supply of methionine which serves as the donor of methyl groups for methylation reactions will impair the synthesis of choline and betaine. Inadequate supply of methionine may arise if the appetite and metabolism of the animal are increased by feeding with excess of B vitamins, when the available methionine will be utilised in the increased metabolism, rather than for the transmethylation reactions. Thus, deficiency of lipotropic factors results in accumulation of fat in the liver. Similarly, deficiency of unsaturated fatty acids which are necessary for the synthesis of phospholipids causes fatty livers.

Cholesterol feeding: Another factor which leads to the formation of fatty liver is feeding the animal with an excessive amount of cholesterol which forms cholesterol ester by combining with the available fatty acids, thus creating a deficiency of fatty acids which are again important constituents for the synthesis of phospholipids.

Lipotropic Factors

Substances which prevent and cure the accumulation of an abnormally large amount of fats in the liver are called lipotropic substances. It has been found that rats fed on low protein diet develop fatty liver. Diets deficient in choline and lecithin also produce fatty liver. On further study, it was observed that methionine could replace choline in the diet and in the absence of choline, methionine could prevent infiltration of fat. This shows that phospholipids, choline and methionine are lipotropic factors. The lipotropic action of methionine is based on its ability to provide methyl groups for transmethylation reactions and synthesis of choline and betaine. In other words, any substance capable of donating methyl groups for synthesis of choline has the property of being lipotropic. On the other hand, substances such as guanidoacetate and nicotinamide which get irreversibly methylated in the body are said to deflect methyl groups from the synthesis of choline. These substances are called **antilipotropic substances**.

METABOLISM OF CHOLESTEROL

Cholesterol is the principal steroid of the diet and is found only in fats of animal origin. Egg yolk, brain, liver and meat are rich sources of cholesterol in diet. Cholesterol is present in tissues and blood either as free cholesterol or as cholesteryl ester. Plasma lipoproteins, particularly low density lipoproteins (LDL), are rich in cholesterol. Approximately 80% of the cholesterol in plasma is present in LDL.

Cholesterol is the precursor of all steroid hormones in the body, bile acids and vitamin D. It is synthesised mainly in liver and is eliminated from the body in bile as cholesterol or bile acids.

The body derives a greater part of cholesterol, about 0.7 g/day, by synthesis, whereas about 0.3 g/day is provided by diet.

Absorption of Cholesterol

It may be noted that the amount of cholesterol provided by diet per day is only about 0.3 gram whereas about 0.7 gram of cholesterol is synthesised by the body. Cholesterol is absorbed readily from the intestine along with other lipids, mostly as cholesterol esters. Ester formation with fatty acids is brought about by cholesterol esterase of pancreatic juice. After absorption, virtually all the absorbed cholesterol get incorporated into the chylomicrons and are transported in the blood by way of lymphatic circulation, just like the triglycerides. It has been found that the peak of absorption into the lymph occurs in about 6–8 hours after ingestion. The concentration of cholesterol in lymph in a fasting state is about one-third the concentration in the plasma and of this, 70% is in the ester form.

Factors Influencing Absorption of Cholesterol

Absorption of cholesterol is accelerated by bile acids and bile salts.

The plant sterols such as β-sitosterol interfere and reduce the absorption of cholesterol from the intestine.

Absorption is interfered by the presence of dihydrocholesterol in the intestines.

Presence of saturated fatty acids in food favours absorption of cholesterol whereas unsaturated fatty acids lower the absorption. In this connection, it has been observed that intake of fats of animal origin, such as butter containing a high amount of saturated fatty acids, causes a rise in serum cholesterol whereas addition of vegetable fats, such as gingelly oil, cottonseed oil, corn oil and safflower oil which contain a fairly high amount of unsaturated fatty acids, lowers the level of serum cholesterol. But coconut oil, although a vegetable fat, is an exception in that it increases the absorption of cholesterol, thus elevating the serum cholesterol level. But it may be said that, as a general rule, a fairly good correlation exists between the iodine number (measure of degree of unsaturation) of a fat and its ability to lower the serum lipids. Fats which have the highest iodine number are useful in producing the greatest effect on lowering of the serum lipids. Besides absorption from diet, the cholesterol of blood is derived partly from reabsorption of endogenous cholesterol derived from the intestinal lumen and liver.

Plasma Cholesterol Concentration

The total concentration of cholesterol in plasma ranges from 150 to 220 mg per 100 ml for a normal adult. Out of this, about 60 mg is in the free state and about 150 mg is in the ester form. It is important to maintain the plasma cholesterol level at the normal range without undue rise because it has been observed that hypercholesterolaemia is a contributing factor in the causation of a disease process called **atherosclerosis**. The main feature of this disease is deposition of cholesterol and other lipids in the connective tissue of the walls of the arteries. Atherosclerosis is more common in adults past middle age, whose diets are rich in animal fat. Certain diseases such as severe diabetes, nephrosis and hypothyroidism are accompanied by elevated plasma cholesterol and extensive atherosclerotic changes. Cholesterol is present in plasma in combination with lipoproteins.

Biosynthesis of Cholesterol

Cholesterol is synthesised from acetyl-CoA. All the reactions of synthesis occur in the cytoplasm of the cell, but some of the enzymes are microsomal and are bound to the membranes of the endoplasmic reticulum. All the carbon atoms are derived from acetyl-CoA.

The sequence of events starting from acetyl-CoA is summarised as follows:

1. **Synthesis of mevalonate from acetyl-CoA (Reactions 1 to 3; Fig. 19.6)**

   Reaction 1 The biosynthesis starts with condensation of two molecules of acetyl-CoA to form one molecule of acetoacetyl-CoA. The reaction is catalysed by acetoacetyl-CoA thiolase, a cytosolic enzyme.

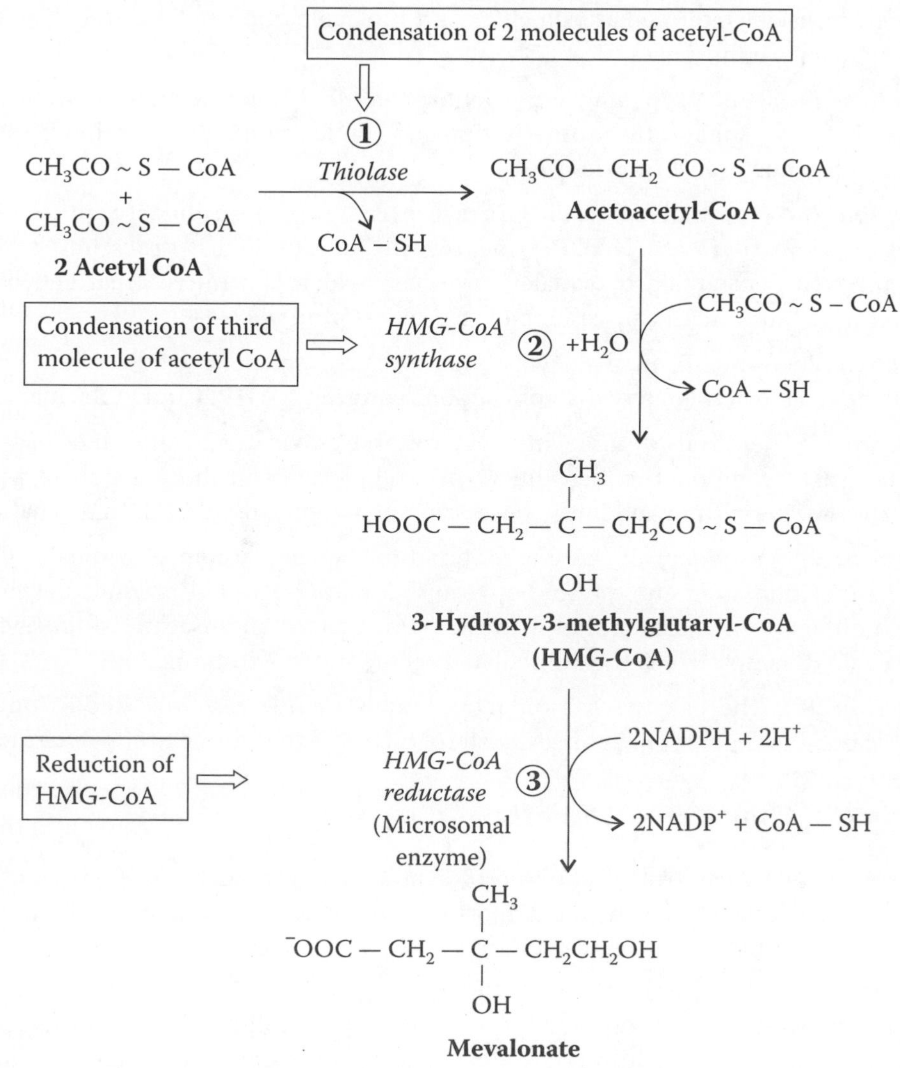

Figure 19.6 Biosynthesis of mevalonate.

Reaction 2 Acetoacetyl-CoA condenses with a third molecule of acetyl-CoA to form 3-hydroxy-3-methylglutaryl CoA which is known as HMG-CoA. The reaction is catalysed by HMG-CoA synthase, which is a microsomal enzyme. Remember that there is an HMG-CoA synthase enzyme which participates in the synthesis of ketone bodies. It is a mitochondrial enzyme and is different.

Reaction 3 HMG-CoA is reduced by HMG-CoA reductase and two NADPH in two stages to form **mevalonate**. HMG-CoA reductase is an important microsomal enzyme and catalyses the rate-limiting reaction in the pathway of cholesterol synthesis. It is the site of action of the most effective class of cholesterol-lowering drugs.

2. **Synthesis of cholesterol from mevalonate (Reactions 4 to 10; Fig. 19.7):**

   Reaction 4 (a to d) Mevalonate which is the key intermediate is phosphorylated three times in succession by ATP, forming first mevalonate-5-phosphate (Reactions 4a–c), a transient intermediate which loses a molecule of phosphate and CO_2 to form isopentenyl pyrophosphate (Reaction 4d).

   Reaction 5 Three isopentenyl pyrophosphate molecules form one molecule of farnesyl pyrophosphate after isomerisation and condensation. The reaction is catalysed by a cytoplasmic prenyl transferase.

   Reaction 6 Two molecules of farnesyl pyrophosphate condense in a reaction involving reduction with **NADPH** to form the unsaturated hydrocarbon **squalene**. The reaction is catalysed by squalene synthase which is a microsomal enzyme. The structure of squalene closely resembles that of a steroid nucleus.

   Reaction 7 A microsomal enzyme system called squalene oxidocyclase converts squalene to lanosterol in a two-step reaction requiring **NADPH** and molecular oxygen.

   Reaction 8 Removal of three methyl groups by oxidation from lanosterol forms zymosterol, a compound which differs from cholesterol in the position of a double bond in the ring system and in the possession of a double bond in the side chain.

   Reaction 9 Movement of the double bond in the ring system of zymosterol to the normal position as in cholesterol between C-5 and C-6 would produce desmosterol, which differs from cholesterol only in the possession of an unsaturated linkage in the side chain. Desmosterol is the immediate precursor of cholesterol.

   Reaction 10 The enzyme Δ^{24} reductase catalyses this reaction. Reduction of the double bond in the side chain of desmosterol gives rise to the final product, **cholesterol**.

Regulation of Cholesterol Synthesis

The primary site for control of cholesterol synthesis is the HMG-CoA reductase step. Synthesis of cholesterol is controlled mostly by regulating the activity of HMG-CoA reductase which catalyses the conversion of HMG-CoA to mevalonate.

A high dietary cholesterol suppresses hepatic synthesis of cholesterol by a feedback mechanism whereby HMG-CoA reductase in liver is inhibited by mevalonate, the immediate product in the pathway, whereas a diet containing low cholesterol increases cholesterol synthesis in the liver and intestines.

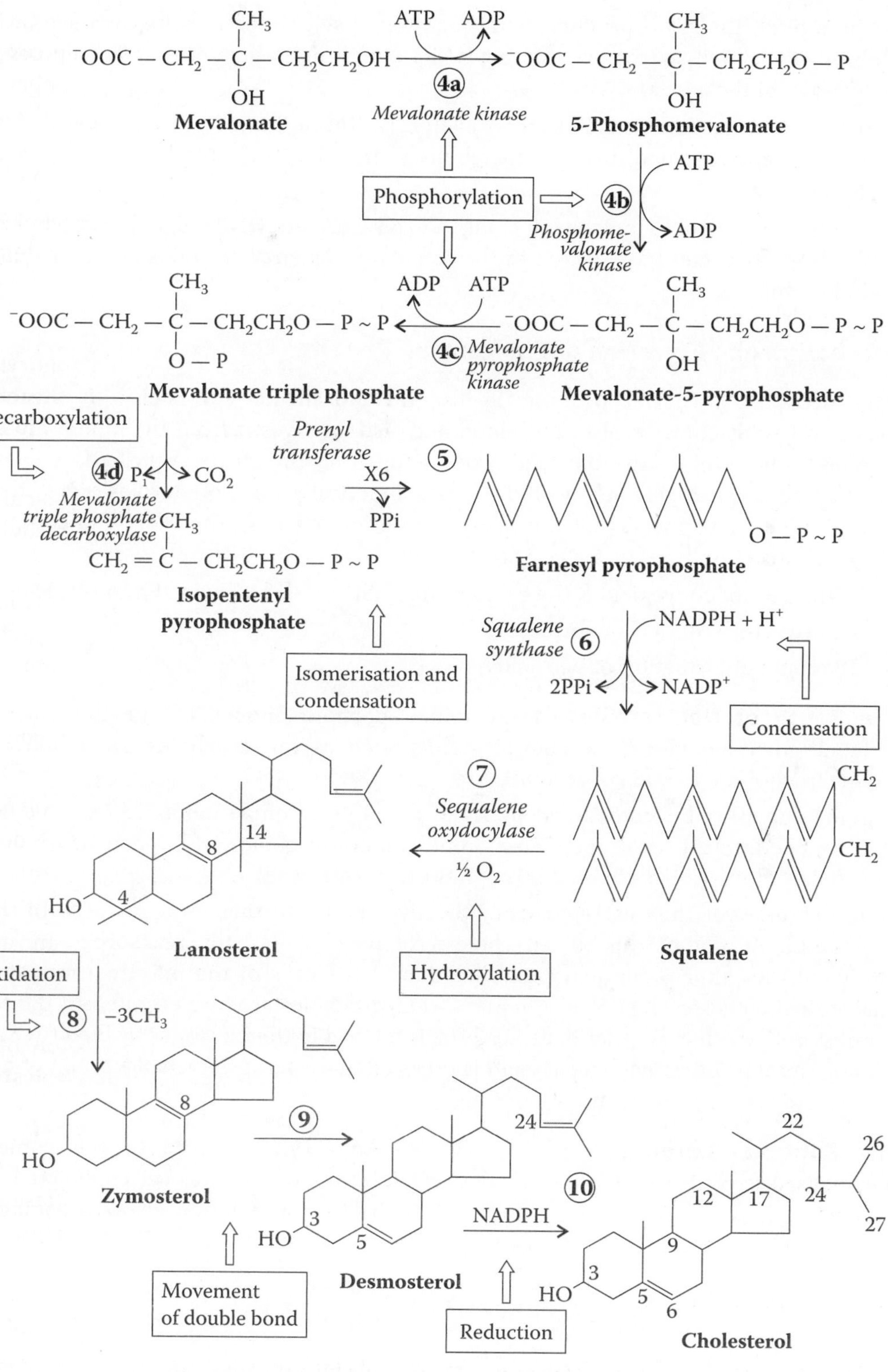

Figure 19.7 Biosynthesis of cholesterol. *X6, six times.*

Cholesterol, the main product of the pathway, itself suppresses its own synthesis by inhibiting the activity of the pre-existing HMG-CoA reductase in liver and promotes rapid inactivation of the enzyme.

LDL cholesterol inhibits cholesterol synthesis. The influx of cell cholesterol released by LDL receptors when LDL is metabolised inhibits cholesterol synthesis (refer to pages 378–379).

Insulin and thyroid hormone increase HMG-CoA activity and enhance cholesterol synthesis whereas glucagon decreases the activity of the enzyme and suppresses synthesis of cholesterol.

Catabolism and Excretion of Cholesterol

Liver occupies a central position in the metabolism of cholesterol. It synthesises cholesterol, adds cholesterol to the blood and also removes it from the blood. Liver also excretes cholesterol in the bile after converting it to bile acids. Very little cholesterol metabolised is excreted as sterols in the faeces. Practically, no cholesterol is excreted in the urine. Therefore, it appears that cholesterol is utilised for the synthesis of other compounds which are structurally related; these are steroids.

For the sake of convenience, the catabolism of cholesterol is divided into two routes:

1. The excretory route via neutral sterols
2. The route of formation of bile acids

The Route of Neutral Sterols A minor portion, about 20% of the cholesterol metabolised, is converted to neutral sterols such as dihydrocholesterol (cholestanol), 7-dehydrocholesterol and coprosterol.

Some cholesterol accompanied by small amounts of cholestanol are excreted by the liver via bile into the small intestines. Some amount of cholesterol, 7-dehydrocholesterol and cholestanol are also excreted through the intestinal wall.

The cholesterol thus excreted from the liver and intestinal wall mixes with dietary cholesterol. A part of this mixed cholesterol may be partially reabsorbed by way of the lymphatics after preliminary esterification in the cells of the intestinal mucosa. The unabsorbed cholesterol, cholestanol and 7-dehydrocholesterol are excreted in the faeces. Coprosterol, which is another neutral sterol, is formed in the intestines by direct reduction of cholesterol by intestinal bacteria and is excreted in the faeces. A small amount of neutral sterol is excreted in the sebum of the skin.

The Route of Formation of Bile Acids Approximately 80% of the cholesterol metabolised is converted by liver tissues to bile acids, which later get conjugated in the liver with glycine and taurine by enzymes of the liver as follows. Prior to conjugation, the bile acids are activated to acyl-CoA

$$\text{Cholic acid} \xrightarrow[\text{ATP, Mg}^{++}]{\text{CoA}} \text{Cholyl-CoA} \xrightarrow[\text{Glycine}]{\text{Taurine}} \begin{cases} \longrightarrow \text{Taurocholic acid} \\ \longrightarrow \text{Glycocholic acid} \end{cases}$$

The conjugated bile acids are excreted via the bile into the intestines from where a major portion is reabsorbed via the intestinal mucosa to enter the portal blood and then return to the liver. This minor circuit of bile acid is the enterohepatic circulation. A small amount from the intestines passes into the systemic circulation.

The unabsorbed bile acids are acted upon by the intestinal bacteria and the products are excreted in the faeces. Thus, it may be seen that bile represents the main route for the excretion of cholesterol which is held in solution by the emulsifying action of bile salts. This can lead to the formation of cholesterol stones (calculi) in the biliary passages such as gall bladder and common bile duct and cause obstruction to the circulation of bile pigments resulting in obstructive jaundice, under abnormal conditions.

Bile acids: Bile acids are important end products of the metabolism of cholesterol in liver. The four bile acids, isolated from human bile, are cholic acid, deoxycholic acid, chenodeoxycholic acid and lithocholic acid. They are explained in page 41.

- **Cholic acid** is present in the largest amount in the bile itself, forming a maximum of 60% of the total. It is a saturated sterol having three OH groups on the nucleus in positions 3, 7 and 12 (*see* **Fig. 2.14**).
- **Deoxycholic acid** lacks the OH group in position 7 and constitutes 25% of the total (*see* **Fig. 2.14**).
- **Chenodeoxycholic acid** lacks the OH group in position 12 and constitutes about 15–20% of the total.
- **Lithocholic acid** has only one OH group in position 3.

PROSTAGLANDINS

Prostaglandins (PG) comprise a group of biologically active lipids, widely distributed in mammalian tissues and body fluids. They were originally discovered in seminal fluid but now they are known to be present in almost all tissues. They have many and varied roles in both physiological and pharmacological processes. They are also considered to be local hormones because their action appears to be confined to the cells of origin or neighbouring cells.

All prostaglandins are derived from a parent compound known as prostanoic acid. This is a 20-carbon carboxylic acid consisting of a cyclopentane ring and two aliphatic side chains (**Fig. 19.8**).

In vivo, prostaglandins are synthesised from arachidonic acid by cyclization of the centre of the 20-carbon chain at C-10, to form a cyclopentane ring, and this is catalysed by an enzyme complex known as prostaglandin endoperoxide synthase. The 5-carbon cyclopentane ring comprising C-8 to C-12 is formed by the joining of the 8th and 12th carbons. Two arms of the prostaglandin, C-8 to C-l and C-12 to C-20, extend from C-8 and C-12 respectively (**Fig. 19.8**).

There are several series of prostaglandins present in various tissues, each exerting different effects and actions. Of these, two groups classified as PGE and PGF series are considered to be the primary compounds. The PGE series has a ketone group at C-9 and hydroxyl at C-11 of the ring. The PGF series has two hydroxyl groups on the ring, one at C-9 and the other at C-11. Both series have a double bond between C-13 and C-14 and a hydroxyl at C-15.

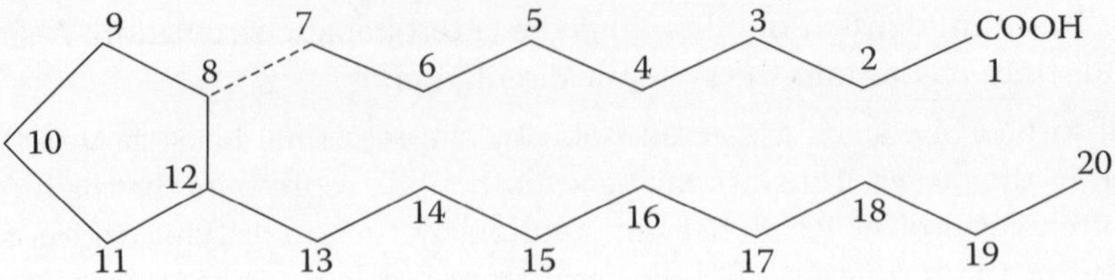

Prostanoic acid

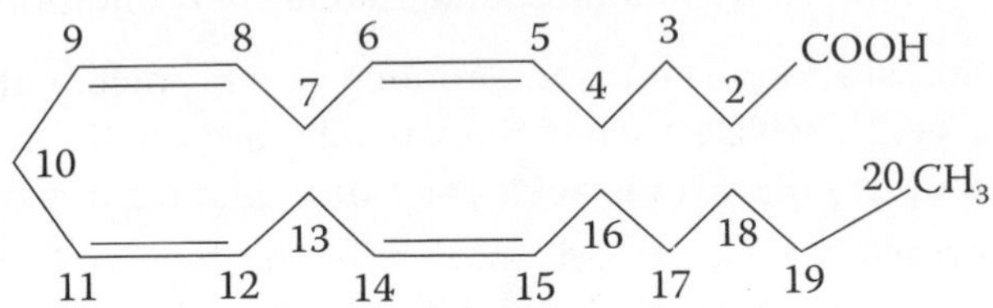

Figure 19.8 Arachidonic acid.

The PGE series are classified further as PGE_1, PGE_2 and PGE_3. The numericals following PGE represent the number of double bonds in the acyl side chains. The PGF series are further represented as $PGF_1\alpha X$, $PGF_2\alpha$ and PGF3α. The α and β in the nomenclature refer to the configuration of the hydroxyl group on C-9. Only those PGF compounds with the C-9 hydroxyl in the α position occur naturally. The most prevalent series of PG are those possessing two double bonds, namely PGE_2 and $PGF_2\alpha$. The PGE_3 and $PGF_3\alpha$ are found rarely. The structures of PGE_1 and $PGF_1\alpha$ are shown in **Figure 19.9**.

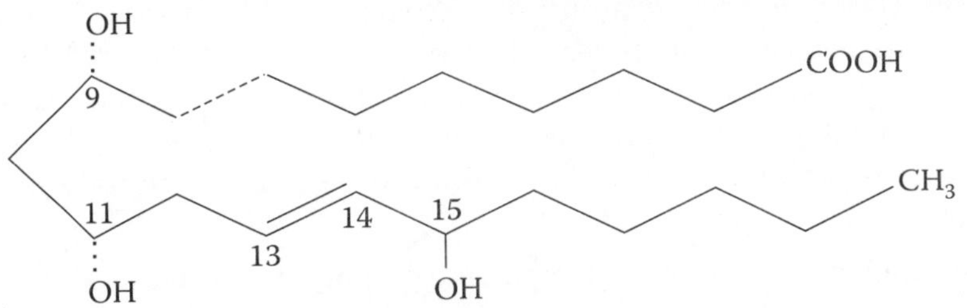

$PGF_1\alpha$

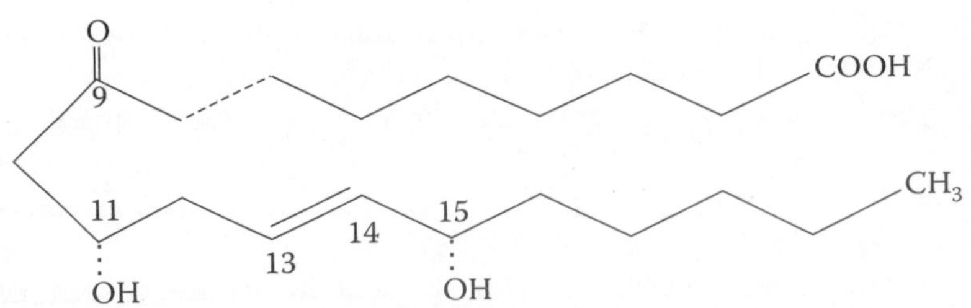

PGE_1

Figure 19.9 $PGF_1\alpha$ and PGE_1.

In addition to the prostaglandins, there are two other related series of compounds, namely prostacyclins (PGI) and thromboxanes (TX). Prostacyclins are like prostaglandins and are derivatives of prostanoic acid, whereas thromboxanes, though a comparable substance with prostaglandins, is not a derivative of prostanoic acid. Both play an important role in aggregation of blood platelets and therefore are important in clotting of blood. Prostacyclin PGI_2 and thromboxane TXA_2 possess two double bonds and are most prevalent. PGI_2 is an intermediate in the biosynthesis of prostaglandins and it also serves as a precursor in the synthesis of TXA_2. PGI_2 are produced in the walls of the blood vessels and are potent inhibitors of platelet aggregation. TX are formed in platelets and when released cause vasoconstriction and aggregation of platelets. Thus, prostacyclins and thromboxanes exert opposing actions.

Metabolism: The major site for the metabolism of prostaglandins is the lungs. On entering the circulation, prostaglandins are rapidly converted into inactive metabolites and excreted in the urine. The inactivation is brought about by way of oxidation and reduction processes.

Function: Prostaglandins exert their effects by modulating the production of cyclic AMP (cAMP). Thus, they can act as stimulators of adenyl cyclase in some endocrine glands, such as thyroid, and adenohypophysis, in corpus luteum and platelets. They also act as inhibitors of adenyl cyclase in the case of adipose tissue. The most potent stimulator of adenyl cyclase is PGI_2 whereas TXA_2 is an inhibitor. Sometimes, prostaglandins oppose one another in their action. Thus, PGE_2 causes dilatation of blood vessels and bronchi whereas $PGF_2\alpha$ constricts them.

Biological effects: Prostaglandins are potent biologically active substances. As little as 1 mg/ml cause contraction of smooth muscles in animals. They are used therapeutically for various purposes on the basis of their biological effects. These include the following:

- Prevention of conception
- Induction of labour at term
- Termination of pregnancy
- Lowering of blood pressure
- Control of inflammation
- Relief of asthma and nasal congestion
- Prevention or alleviation of peptic ulcer. Here, they act by inhibiting acid secretion.
- Inhibit platelet aggregation

20 CHAPTER

Lipid Transport

Chapter Outline

- Plasma Lipoproteins
- Metabolism of Lipoproteins
- Atherosclerosis
- Disorders of Lipoprotein Metabolism

The major lipids in plasma, namely triglycerides, phospholipids and cholesterol, are combined with specific apoproteins to form complexes called **lipoproteins** and circulate in blood. These apoproteins are synthesised in the intestines and liver. Their main function is transport of lipids from the intestines and liver to extrahepatic tissue where they can be stored or oxidised for energy. Free fatty acids mobilised from adipose tissue circulate in plasma, bound with plasma albumin.

Triglycerides (TGL) form the major fraction of lipids in the plasma lipoprotein complex. They are esters of glycerol with fatty acids. The chemistry of TGL is explained in page 28. Plasma TGL may be of exogenous or endogenous origin. Exogenous TGL is derived from dietary lipids and is carried in the chylomicron fraction of the lipoprotein. Endogenous TGL is synthesised in the liver, mostly from carbohydrates, and is carried in the VLDL (very low density lipoprotein) fraction of lipoprotein.

Phospholipids present in plasma are lecithin, cephalin and sphingomyelin. Lecithin forms the major fraction. The phospholipids exist in plasma, mostly in association with α- and β-globulins, and are carried with the α- and β-lipoprotein fractions. The plasma phospholipids are synthesised and metabolised in the liver.

Cholesterol exists in plasma in two forms, namely the free and the esterified forms. Both are carried along with β-globulins and form a considerable portion of the LDL lipoprotein fraction.

Free fatty acids (FFA) are referred to as unsaturated fatty acids (UFA) or non-esterified fatty acids (NEFA). They circulate in the blood in very small quantities, bound with plasma albumin. The usual concentration varies between 8 and 25 mg per 100 ml of blood. The FFAs of blood include palmitic, stearic, oleic and linoleic acids. These are derived by lipolysis of TGL of adipose tissues. The plasma FFA level is usually high in a fasting condition and in an uncontrolled state of diabetes mellitus.

PLASMA LIPOPROTEINS

There are five main classes of plasma lipoproteins, namely chylomicrons (CM), very low density lipoproteins (VLDL), intermediate density lipoprotein (IDL), low density lipoproteins (LDL) and high density lipoproteins (HDL). Each class differs in the relative amounts of cholesterol, triglycerides and phospholipid and in the chemical composition of the protein carriers. The plasma lipoproteins are classified on the basis of their densities depending on the proportion of lipids and proteins in the lipoprotein molecules. The various lipoproteins are separated by ultracentrifugation and the rate of flotation is expressed in Svedberg (Sf) units. The composition of the lipoprotein fractions and their density obtained by ultracentrifugation are given in **Table 20.1**. Plasma lipoproteins may also be separated according to their electrophoretic mobility into α-lipoproteins, β-lipoprotein, pre-β-lipoprotein and chylomicron (**Fig. 20.1**).

Table 20.1 Average Composition of Plasma Lipoproteins

Lipoprotein Fractions	Chylomicron	VLDL	IDL	LDL	HDL_2	HDL_3
Diameter (mm)	90–1000	30–90	25–30	20–25	10–20	7.5–10
Density (g/ml)	<0.95	0.95–1.006	1.006–1.019	1.019–1.063	1.063–1.125	1.126–1.210
Sf	>400	20–400	12–20	2–12	–	–
Protein (%)	1–2	7–10	11	21	33	57
Total lipid (%)	98–99	90–93	89	79	67	43
Triglycerol (% of total lipid)	88	56	29	13	16	13
Phospholipid (% of total lipid)	8	20	26	28	43	46
Cholesteryl ester (% of total lipid)	3	15	34	48	31	29
Cholesterol (free) (% of total lipid)	1	8	9	10	10	6

HDL, high density lipoprotein; IDL, intermediate density lipoprotein; LDL, low density lipoprotein; Sf, Svedberg unit; VLDL, very low density lipoprotein.

Four bands can be visualised on electrophoresis. The chylomicrons remain in the origin as a broad band. The second band called β-lipoprotein migrates with β-globulins of plasma proteins and occupies the β-globulin zone. It contains LDL. The third band called pre-β-lipoprotein migrates in front of the LDL band. This fraction contains VLDL. The fourth band called the α-lipoprotein migrates with the α-globulin of plasma protein and occupies the α-globulin region. This fraction contains HDL. IDL migrates with β-lipoprotein.

Plasma lipoprotein analysis is done routinely in clinical laboratories by electrophoresis on cellulose acetate or agarose gel media, and the lipoprotein fractions are visualised after staining.

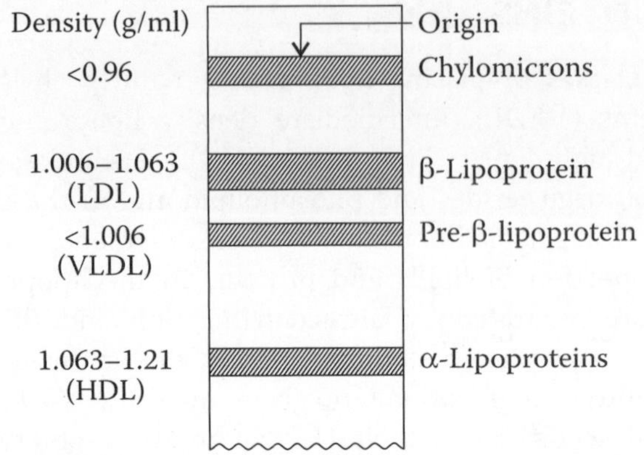

Figure 20.1 Separation of plasma lipoprotein fractions by electrophoresis.

Apolipoproteins: The protein components of the lipoproteins are called apolipoproteins. They were initially classified as A, B and C. But now there are eight different proteins with further sub-classifications. They are named as apolipoproteins or apoproteins A-I, A-II, B (B-100, B-48), C-I, C-II, C-III, D and E. One or more apoproteins are present in each lipoprotein. The major apoproteins that are present in different lipoprotein fractions are as given in **Table 20.2.**

Table 20.2 Major Apoproteins Present in Lipoproteins

Apolipoproteins	Lipoproteins
A-I	HDL, chylomicrons
A-II	HDL, chylomicrons
B-100	LDL, VLDL, IDL
B-48	Chylomicron, chylomicron remnants
C-I	VLDL, HDL, chylomicrons
C-II	VLDL, HDL, chylomicrons
C-III	VLDL, HDL, chylomicrons
D	Subfraction of HDL
E	VLDL, HDL, chylomicrons Chylomicron remnants

Apoproteins A-I and A-II are present in HDL and CM.

Apoprotein B-100 is present in LDL, VLDL and IDL.

Apoprotein B-48 is present in CM and CM remnants.

Apoproteins C-I, C-II and C-III are present in VLDL, HDL and CM.

Apoprotein D is present in HDL.

Apoprotein E is present in VLDL, HDL, CM and CM remnants.

The apoproteins help in solubilising the lipids, and each lipoprotein fraction moves in combination with one or more specific apoprotein. Thus, they act as lipid transfer proteins. They also act as enzyme cofactors; for example, C-II is a cofactor for lipoprotein lipase.

METABOLISM OF LIPOPROTEINS

Chylomicrons

Chylomicrons are rich in triglycerides and are derived from intestinal absorption of lipids. They are secreted from the intestinal mucosal cells into the intracellular fluid. From here, they enter the lacteals and the lymphatics and finally into the systemic circulation. Chylomicrons are responsible for the transport of all dietary lipids into the circulation. Chylomicron particles have a diameter of about 0.2–1.0 μ and contain about 88% of triglycerides, small amounts of phospholipid, cholesterol and protein. The principal apoprotein component of chylomicron is apo-B-48 which is incorporated into the chylomicron in the intestine itself (**Fig. 20.2**). This is the **nascent chylomicron**. In the circulation, apoproteins C and E are added. Apo-A is also present in chylomicron. The milky appearance (lactescence) of plasma seen after an average fatty meal is due to the presence of chylomicrons which have the property of scattering light. The lactescence clears after 12–14 hours as the plasma passes through various organs, and this is due to the clearing action of the enzyme lipoprotein lipase, located on the surface of endothelial cells of capillaries and also distributed in adipose tissue.

Chylomicrons are metabolised in extrahepatic tissues by hydrolysis with lipoprotein lipase. The triglycerol is hydrolysed, progressively to diacylglycerol and then to monoacylglycerol which is finally hydrolysed to free fatty acid and glycerol. Some of the free fatty acids return to the circulation and are attached to albumin, but the bulk are transported to the extrahepatic tissue. Approximately 90% of the triglycerol of chylomicron is lost by hydrolysis with lipoprotein lipase. Apo-C and Apo-A return to the circulating HDL. The chylomicron remnant that remains after delipidation is about half the diameter of the original chylomicron and is rich in cholesterol and cholesteryl esters. It contains phospholipids. Similar changes occur to VLDL resulting in the formation of IDL which is a VLDL remnant. Chylomicron remnants are taken up by the liver where most of the cholesterol and the remaining triglycerides are hydrolysed and metabolised. The uptake of a chylomicron remnant by liver is mediated through a receptor, specific for Apo-E (**Fig. 20.2**). The fatty acids are used for phospholipid synthesis.

The **primary function** of chylomicron is transport of dietary fats, mainly triglycerides to liver and adipose tissues, and transport of smaller amounts of cholesterol and phospholipids from intestines to liver.

VLDLs are composed primarily of TGLs and they contain apoproteins B (B-100) and C. Apo-C and E are added in the circulation to the nascent VLDL. Their particle size is smaller than chylomicron. The main bulk of VLDL is synthesised in the liver and a small amount in the intestinal cells. VLDLs transport TGL from liver to extrahepatic tissues where the lipids can be stored or oxidised for energy. The transport and fate of VLDL are similar to those of CM. VLDLs are hydrolysed by lipoprotein lipase and the TGL is delivered to the tissues. The remnants of the VLDL after delipidation are known as IDL and are returned to the liver (**Fig. 20.3**).

The remains of VLDL, after they deliver their triglycerides and apo-C, are rich in cholesterol esters and are called **IDL**. They contain a small amount of triglycerol. IDLs have two fates. Half of them are taken up directly by the liver and the other half are converted

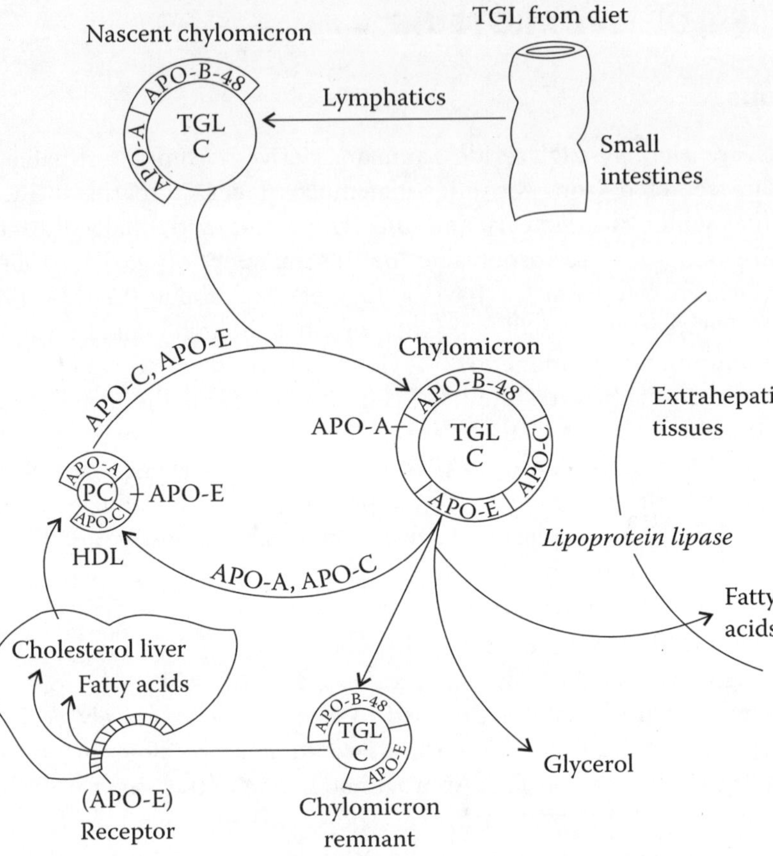

Figure 20.2 Chylomicron metabolism. *C, cholesterol; HDL, high density lipoprotein; P, phospholipid; TGL, triglycerol.*

to **LDL**. IDLs usually do not accumulate in plasma like LDL even after an overnight fast (**Fig. 20.3**).

Low Density Lipoproteins

Low density lipoproteins are particularly rich in cholesterol. Approximately 80% of the plasma cholesterol is present in the LDL fraction and about 75% of the cholesterol in LDL is in the form of cholesteryl esters. The main apoprotein in LDL is apo-B-100. The source of LDL in plasma is IDL which is a breakdown product of VLDL (**Fig. 20.3**). About 70% of the circulating LDL is degraded by the liver and 30% is degraded in extrahepatic tissues. The **primary function** of LDL is transport of excess cholesterol and its esters from liver to extrahepatic tissues. This process has been implicated as a potential factor in atherosclerosis.

LDL is **metabolised** through LDL receptors. Since LDL is the major source of cholesterol in plasma, the plasma cholesterol level depends on the formation and removal of LDL from circulation. Liver plays an important role in removing 70% of LDL in plasma, as hepatocytes have specific receptors, known as the LDL apo-B-100-E receptors, on their

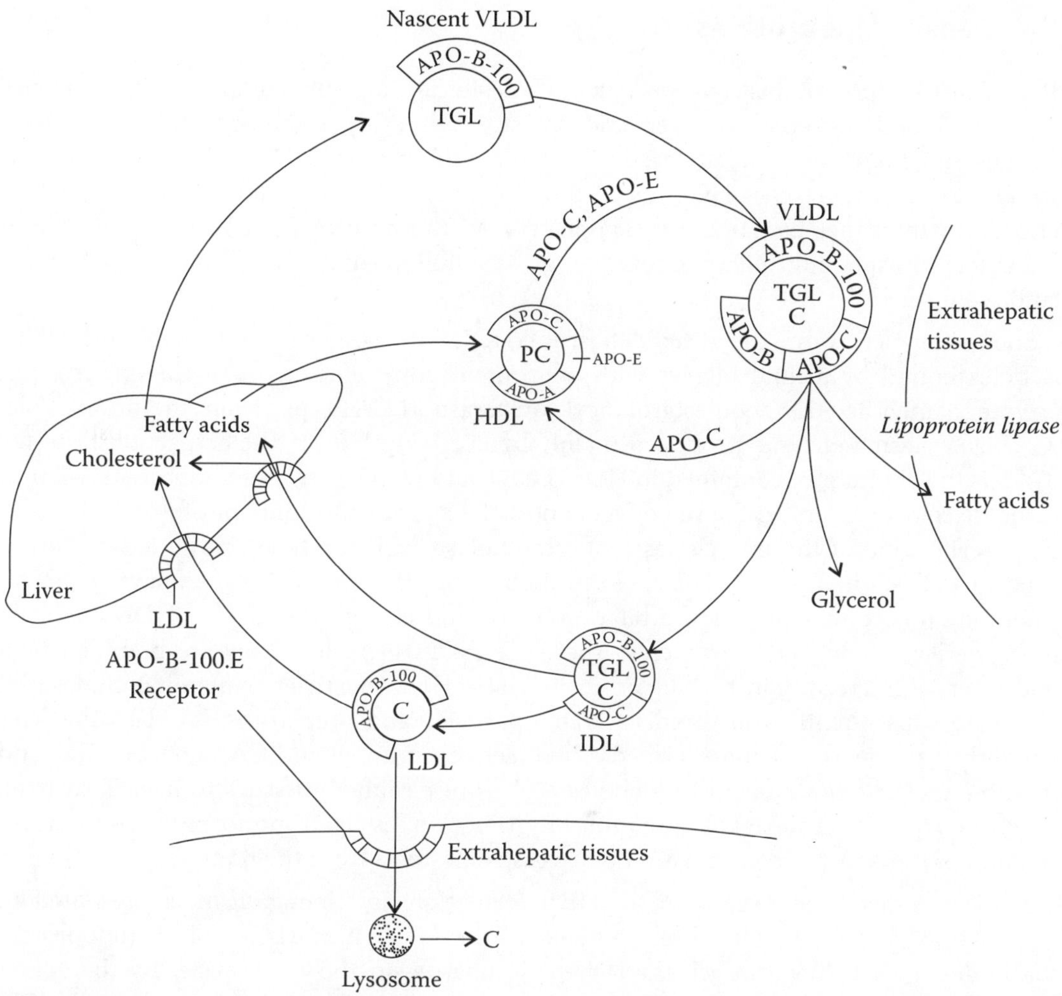

Figure 20.3 LDL formation and metabolism of VLDL and LDL. C, *cholesterol; IDL, intermediate density lipoprotein; LDL, low density lipoprotein; P, phospholipid; TGL, triglycerides; VLDL, very low density lipoproteins.*

surface to take in LDL. The LDLs from plasma are taken up into the liver by binding to these specific receptors that are in the form of pits coated with a protein called ***clathrin*** located on the surface of cell membrane. Once LDL binds to the LDL receptor, the LDL particle rich in cholesterol is taken up intact by **endocytosis** within the hepatocytes and it becomes an endosome. In the next step, the endosomes fuse with lysosomes where they are degraded by lysosomal enzymes. Eventually, the LDL receptors separate from LDL and return to the cell surface. Inside the lysosomes, the cholesteryl ester of LDL is hydrolysed by the lysosomal cholesterol esterase to produce free cholesterol and free fatty acid. Free cholesterol then diffuses into cytoplasm. This influx of cholesterol inhibits the activity of HMG-CoA reductase and cholesterol synthesis. By this mechanism which regulates cholesterol synthesis, most of the LDLs deliver cholesterol to the extrahepatic tissue (**Fig. 20.3**).

High Density Lipoproteins

High density lipoproteins are protein-, cholesterol- and phospholipid-rich particles synthesised and secreted by liver and intestines. Freshly secreted **HDL** are known as '**nascent HDL**' and are released by liver and intestines into blood circulation (*see* **Fig. 20.2**). The nascent HDL released by liver contains apoproteins C and E but that released by intestines contains only apoprotein A. The nascent HDL released into blood consists of phospholipid bilayers containing free cholesterol and apoproteins and have a flat discoid shape.

Soon after secretion, the discoid nascent HDLs are converted into spherical HDL_3 particles bound by a lipid bilayer with apoprotein embedded in it. In this process, an enzyme named lecithin cholesterol acyltransferase (LCAT) plays an important role. LCAT is a plasma enzyme produced mainly by liver (**Fig. 20.4**). The actual substrate for LCAT is the cholesterol contained in HDL. LCAT and LCAT activator apoprotein A-l bind to the discoid HDL and catalyse conversion of the surface phospholipid into lysolecithin and esterification of the free cholesterol into cholesteryl ester. Lysolecithin is transferred to plasma albumin. The cholesteryl esters diffuse into the interior of the bilayer of HDL, generating a core that pushes the bilayers apart, and change the discoid HDL gradually into spherical-shaped HDL particles. These are HDL_3 particles. They are bounded by a lipid layer with apoprotein embedded in it. These HDL_3 particles containing cholesteryl esters are subsequently converted to HDL_2 particles and then transported to the liver where they are degraded and excreted. The mechanism in which LCAT acts on HDL and provides a vehicle for transporting cholesterol from peripheral tissues to liver is referred to as the '**reverse cholesterol transport**'. By this process, HDL performs the important function of transport and elimination of excess cholesterol from the body.

A diagrammatic representation of HDL formation and metabolism is presented in **Figure 20.4**. The figure illustrates the role of three enzymes—LCAT, LPL (lipoprotein lipase) and HRHL (heparin releasable hepatic lipase)—in the HDL cycle. By the action of LPL, 90% of the triglycerides of CM is lost and this results in the formation of a CM remnant. The figure explains the conversion of nascent HDL derived from liver and intestines to HDL_3 and subsequently to HDL_2. The process actually involves a transfer of lipids between the HDL_3 and VLDL and CM that undergo catabolism in the plasma. Cholesteryl esters formed in the LCAT reaction are transferred to the VLDL. At the same time, triglycerides and cholesterol released from CM and VLDL during the extrahepatic lipoprotein lipase reaction are accepted by the circulating HDL. The resulting HDL is enriched in triglycerides and cholesteryl ester. This is HDL_2 and is the HDL which is present in plasma. In liver, HRHL hydrolyses surface phospholipids on the HDL_2 particles entering liver and releases cholesterol for uptake into the liver. This also allows the formation of smaller and more dense HDL. It may be noted that androgens increase HRHL activity, thereby increasing plasma HDL_2 concentration in men. Oestrogens decrease HRHL activity, thereby lowering the plasma HDL_2 concentration in women.

Two pathways are open to HDL_2: (i) partial hydrolysis by hepatic lipase resulting in the conversion of HDL_2 back to HDL_3 and (ii) enter liver and get excreted in the bile either as cholesterol or as cholic acid in the bile salts (**Fig. 20.4**).

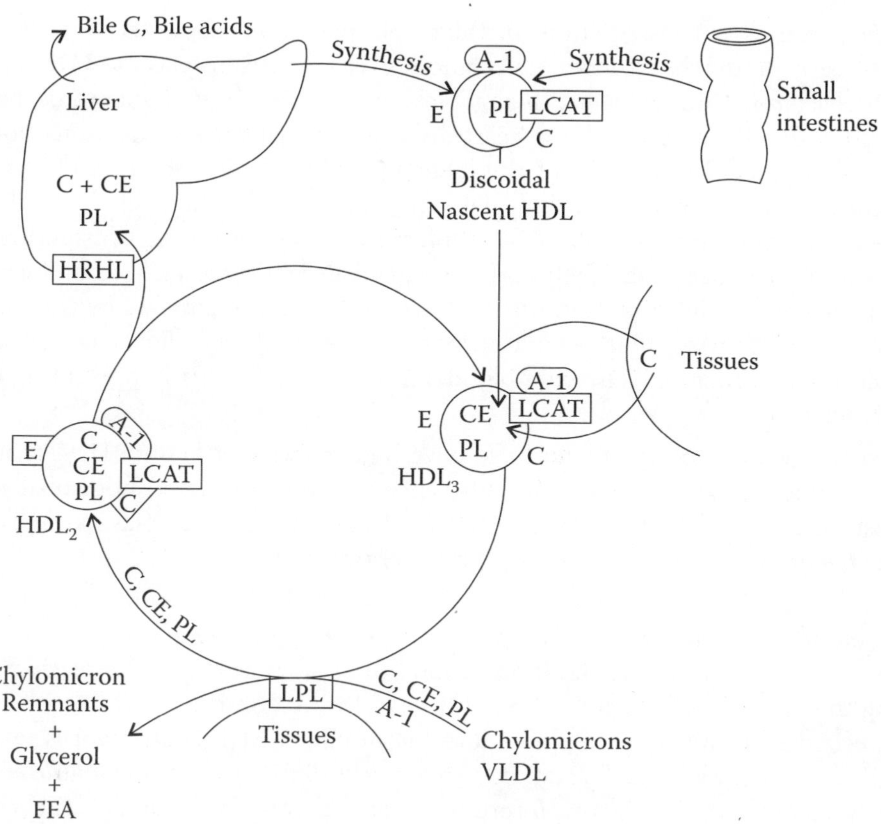

Figure 20.4 HDL formation and HDL metabolism. *C, cholesterol; CE, cholesteryl ester; HRHL, heparin-releasable hepatic lipase; LPL, lipoprotein lipase; PL, phospholipid; TGL, triglycerol.*

HDL_2 and HDL_3: HDLs are separated into two fractions by ultracentrifugation. HDL_2 is composed of 33% protein and 67% lipids and its density range is 1.063–1.125. HDL_3 is the spherical HDL and contains 57% protein and 43% lipids. Its density range is 1.126–1.210. Apoproteins A-I and A-II are present in these two classes. HDL_2 represents plasma HDL.

ATHEROSCLEROSIS

The most serious consequence of elevation of plasma lipoproteins is atherosclerosis which is a disease of the arteries that causes coronary heart disease and stroke. Atherosclerosis is characterised by accumulation of cholesteryl esters that form **atherosclerotic plaques** on the inner surface of the arterial walls, resulting in narrowing of the arterial lumen and reduction in blood flow. Consequently, the cells and tissues that are supplied with oxygen by the arterial blood become anoxic and ultimately die. Atherosclerosis can occur in many different arteries in the body, but the most frequent location is the coronary arteries. Reduced blood flow along these arteries results in myocardial infarction, which is commonly known as '**heart attack**'. The affected persons have high plasma LDL cholesterol. This disease however is correlated with a low concentration of plasma HDL.

While there is an association of high plasma total cholesterol with coronary artery disease, a much stronger correlation exists between plasma LDL cholesterol and atherosclerosis. In contrast, high levels of plasma HDL cholesterol have been associated with a decreased risk for heart disease and that HDL gives protection against coronary heart disease. Because of this beneficial effect, HDL cholesterol is called the **good cholesterol** as distinct from LDL cholesterol and VLDL cholesterol that are considered harmful and are called **bad cholesterol**. The reason for considering HDL as good cholesterol is that HDL functions by removing excess cholesterol from the blood and extrahepatic tissues and transport it to the liver where it is degraded, by the mechanism referred to as 'reverse cholesterol transport' (page 380). It reflects the efficiency of cholesterol scavenging by HDL from blood and tissues and helps in preventing the onset of atherosclerosis.

In general, women before menopause have higher levels of plasma HDL than men of the corresponding age. However, the difference which is mediated hormonally explains that oestrogens tend to raise plasma HDL and androgens lower plasma HDL and this protects the premenopausal women against atherosclerosis.

When there is a deficiency or absence of LDL receptors as in familial hypercholesterolaemia, LDL uptake by the receptor is defective and LDL accumulates in plasma. There is a significant elevation in total plasma cholesterol. The plasma LDLs, on entering the arterial wall, deposit their cholesteryl esters on the arterial intima. Some of the deposited LDL undergo oxidation, and the modified LDL cholesterol is taken up by macrophages resulting in the formation of 'foam cells'. Subsequently, the foam cells develop into fatty streaks which are the forerunners of atheromatous plaque. The correlation between elevated total plasma cholesterol and heart attacks and stroke has led to the view that LDL cholesterol is harmful.

Normal concentration of plasma lipids:

Total lipids	400–800 mg%
Cholesterol	150–220 mg%
Triglycerides	35–160 mg%
Phospholipids	145–200 mg%
HDL cholesterol	>40 mg%
LDL cholesterol	<180 mg%
VLDL cholesterol	<40 mg%
Free fatty acids	8–25 mg%

DISORDERS OF LIPOPROTEIN METABOLISM

Some individuals have inherited defects in lipoprotein metabolism. These include hyperlipoproteinaemias and hypolipoproteinaemias.

Hyperlipoproteinaemias

Hyperlipoproteinaemias represent the presence of excess amounts of plasma lipoproteins. They are classified as Type I, II, III, IV and V hyperlipoproteinaemias, based on plasma TGL and cholesterol levels and on the pattern observed in plasma lipoprotein electrophoresis.

- *Type I:* In this disorder, there is an abnormal increase in the chylomicron fraction, due to a genetic deficiency of lipoprotein lipase. The plasma TGL is exceedingly high and a correspondingly prominent chylomicron band is seen in the electrophoretic pattern. The affected person suffers from eruptive xanthomas.
- *Type II:* This is characterised by hypercholesterolaemia and elevated plasma LDL. Electrophoresis shows a prominent β-lipoprotein band. This type is referred to as Type IIa. In Type IIb, the VLDL and LDL fractions are increased and plasma electrophoresis shows increased concentration of pre-β-lipoprotein and β-lipoprotein bands. The patients have an increased risk of developing atherosclerosis and myocardial infarction at an early age.
- *Type III:* This is also known as 'broad β disease' since it is characterised by the appearance of a broad band between the normal β-lipoprotein and pre-β-lipoprotein bands in plasma electrophoresis. This abnormal lipoprotein is known as 'floating β-lipoprotein'. Plasma TGL and cholesterol are elevated. The hyperlipidaemia is due to abnormality of apo E which interferes with the clearance of chylomicrons and VLDL remnants by liver. The patients have an increased risk of developing atherosclerosis, especially in coronary arteries and peripheral vessels.
- *Type IV:* The characteristic features are overproduction of VLDL and elevated plasma TGL. A prominent pre-β-lipoprotein band appears in plasma electrophoresis. It is associated with coronary heart disease and diabetes mellitus.
- *Type V:* This is a rare disorder in which there is overproduction of chylomicrons and VLDL and elevated plasma TGL. On plasma electrophoresis, chylomicron and pre-β bands appear prominent. The cause of the defect is not known.

Hypolipoproteinaemias

Hypolipoproteinaemia represents deficiency or absence of plasma lipoproteins. This includes two rare inherited diseases:

1. **Abetalipoproteinaemia:** This condition is characterised by the absence of β-lipoprotein (LDL) in plasma. Chylomicrons and VLDL are absent. This is due to the inability to synthesise apolipoprotein B-100.
2. **α-lipoproteinaemia (Tangier disease):** The plasma HDL is low or nearly absent. The plasma cholesterol and phospholipid are low. The disorder is probably due to a defect in HDL biogenesis. The affected patients have enlarged tonsils with orange discolouration and accumulation of cholesteryl esters in tissues. There is overproduction of triglycerides due to the absence of apo C-II which normally activates lipoprotein lipase. As a result, the patients develop hypertriacylglycerolaemia.

21

CHAPTER

Protein Metabolism

Chapter Outline

- General Pathway of Protein Metabolism
- Nitrogen Metabolism
- Anabolism of Protein
- Catabolism of Proteins
- Urea Synthesis—Krebs-Hensleit Cycle
- Metabolism of Individual Amino Acids
- Common Pathway of Carbohydrate, Fat and Protein Metabolism
- Metabolism in Starvation
- Role of Vitamins and Hormones on Metabolism

Absorption: The end products of protein digestion in the intestines are the amino acids. Being readily soluble in water, they are promptly absorbed from the intestines to reach the liver via portal circulation. In the liver, they are utilised for various synthetic purposes. A small amount enters the systemic circulation via the lacteals and thoracic duct.

The rate of absorption of amino acids from the intestines depends upon the nature of the amino acid isomer. Natural L-isomers are absorbed by the process of active transportation across the intestine, from the mucosa to the serosa, in the presence of adequate supply of pyridoxal phosphate whereas D-isomers are absorbed from the mucosa by free diffusion.

Blood in systemic circulation contains at all times a small amount of amino acids which include a small proportion of amino acids synthesised and added by the liver. The amino nitrogen content of blood during basal conditions varies from 3 to 6 mg%. It rises to a maximum of 10 mg%, about 3 hours after the intake of a protein meal.

Metabolic pool: The amino acids from the blood diffuse in the body fluids and reach all the tissue cells, where they are taken up by tissues by the active transportation process. At the same time, most of the tissue proteins undergo disintegration constantly and release their amino acid content which enter the circulation. This is an endogenous source of amino acids. They constantly keep mixing with the exogenous amino acids derived from the food, and this mixture of amino acids which is drawn upon from both anabolic and catabolic reactions constitutes a hypothetical reservoir of amino acids called the metabolic pool of amino acids. The metabolic pool of amino acids can be compared to the currency of protein metabolism from where the amino acids can be withdrawn for synthetic purposes. At the same time, the amino acids formed by breakdown of body proteins are discharged into the pool. Both synthesis of amino acids and breakdown of body proteins are influenced by hormones. Synthesis of amino acids is enhanced by anabolic hormones such as growth hormone, insulin and testosterone. Catabolism of proteins is accelerated by the adrenocorticotropic hormone (ACTH) and thyroxine.

Storage: In tissues, amino acids are not stored as such but either are metabolised for incorporation into proteins or split further by deamination and transamination and are taken up for synthesis of compounds of physiological interest. But reserves of protein accumulate mostly in the liver, where they are drawn upon, in conditions of inadequate protein intake.

GENERAL PATHWAY OF PROTEIN METABOLISM

A general scheme of the usual metabolic pathway of proteins and amino acids is outlined in **Figure 21.1**.

The amino acid pool is derived from the food and from the breakdown of body proteins.

The amino acids from the 'pool' are utilised for two purposes: (i) synthetic purpose and (ii) catabolic purpose.

Whatever may be the purpose for which they are utilised, they first undergo splitting by deamination into two moieties, namely

1. Nitrogenous moiety (NH_3)
2. Non-nitrogenous moiety (α-keto acids)

1. The nitrogenous moiety (NH_3), i.e. ammonia, may be utilised as follows:
   - For synthesis of purines
   - Excreted as ammonia
   - For synthesis of pyrimidines
   - Diverted to enter the urea cycle (ornithine cycle) for synthesis of urea
2. The non-nitrogenous moiety (α-keto acids) enters the carbohydrate pathway to get metabolised via the Krebs cycle and through the carbohydrate pathway, it enters the pathways of fatty acids metabolism.

A few amino acids take special metabolic routes to form unusual end products such as nicotinic acid, creatinine and sulphate.

Excretion: Proteins are excreted mostly as non-protein nitrogen after utilisation. The average excretion per day via the usual routes is given below:

1. *Faeces:* 1–2 grams of nitrogen per day
2. Urine is the major route of excretion. About 13 grams of nitrogen per day are excreted. All these are in the form of non-protein nitrogenous constituents. They are as follows:
   - Urea 85%
   - Ammonia 3%
   - Creatinine 5%
   - Uric acid 1%

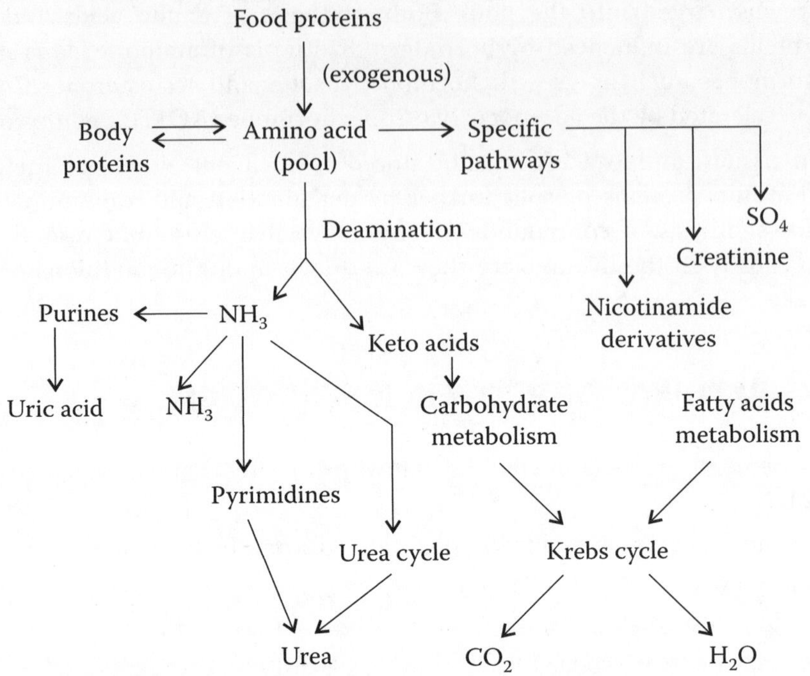

Figure 21.1 General scheme of the pathway of proteins and amino acid metabolism.

NITROGEN METABOLISM

Since nitrogen is an essential constituent of all proteins and is uniquely characteristic of proteins, the overall metabolism of protein can be assessed in terms of the nitrogen contained in the proteins. For this reason, it is customary to represent the overall protein metabolism in the form of nitrogen metabolism, which can be conveniently studied under the following headings:

1. Significance of nitrogen
2. Intake of nitrogen in food
3. Nitrogen content of the body
4. Excretion of nitrogen
5. Nitrogen balance

1. **Significance of nitrogen:** The efficiency of metabolism can be expressed in terms of nitrogen because the carbon and hydrogen of the proteins finally form CO_2 and H_2O indistinguishable from the end products of the metabolism of carbohydrates and fats. Certain proteins contain phosphoric acid which is also a constituent of nucleic acid, phospholipids and certain intermediaries of carbohydrate metabolism. Certain amino acids contain sulphur. But in contrast to these elements, nitrogen is uniquely characteristic of proteins. Apart from it being a highly concentrated constituent of proteins, nitrogen forms specialised excretory products such as urea and ammonia.

2. **Intake of nitrogen in food:** The nitrogen content of food is derived exclusively from food proteins. Nitrogen in food includes (i) traces of inorganic nitrogen ingested in the form of nitrites and nitrates and (ii) non-protein nitrogen (NPN) derived from nucleic acids and amino acids.
3. **Nitrogen content of the body:** Nitrogenous compounds are widely distributed in the tissues and body fluids. It is estimated that about 20% of the net weight of the tissues is formed by proteins.

   Distribution in blood: In blood, nitrogen is present in two forms:

   - *Protein nitrogen:* This is the form of nitrogen present in plasma proteins and conjugated proteins.
   - *Non-protein nitrogen (NPN):* These are nitrogen-containing compounds that do not get precipitated by protein-precipitating agents such as tungstic acid and picric acid. They are either the end products or the intermediaries formed during the metabolism of proteins, amino acids and nucleoproteins.

   The non-protein nitrogen constituents present in blood in detectable amounts are urea, free amino acids, uric acid, creatine and creatinine. Urea forms 50% and free amino acids form 25% of the total NPN. The remaining 25% includes creatine, creatinine and uric acid; very small amounts of bilirubin, choline, epinephrine, thyroxine, glutathione and ATP are also included in this group.

   Urea constitutes 50% of the total NPN and forms the major waste product of protein metabolism. It is formed in the liver from where it passes into the bloodstream to reach the kidneys for excretion. The average normal concentration of blood urea ranges from 20 to 40 mg%. Free amino acids which constitute about 25% of the total NPN are in transit from one organ to another for purposes of synthesis or breakdown. The average normal content of amino nitrogen is 4–10 mg%.

   Uric acid which forms about 1% of the total NPN is the end product of purine metabolism. Its level in blood fluctuates with the level of dietary purines. The average normal concentration of blood uric acid is 2–5 mg%.

   Creatine is present only in trace and is formed by the breakdown of creatine phosphate in the muscle.

   Creatinine is also the waste product formed from the breakdown of creatine phosphate. Its concentration in blood is slightly more than creatine and ranges from 1 to 3 mg%.

   Ammonia and other NPN constituents are present in traces.
4. **Excretion of nitrogen:** Nitrogen is excreted in urine and faeces. Urine is the major route of excretion for nitrogen. The daily excretion of total nitrogen in an average normal adult is 13 grams, and all this is in the form of NPN constituents. These are urea, ammonia, creatine, creatinine and uric acid.

   In urine, urea comprises about 85% of the total NPN. It is the chief end product of amino acid catabolism. It serves as the most significant index of the extent of protein breakdown.

   Ammonia, which forms about 3% of the total NPN constituents in urine, is present in blood only in traces. It is present in urine in a fairly significant amount because it is actually formed in the cells of renal tubules. From there, it passes largely into the tubular urine, where it acts as a base and combines with H^+ ions to form NH_4, thus serving to lower the H^+ ion concentration of blood. This mechanism is an important factor in the renal regulation of acid–base balance. The output of ammonia increases with increasing levels of dietary protein and after ingestion of acid-forming substances such as NH_4C1. Ammonia is high in acidosis and is less after ingestion of alkalies.

Under normal conditions, proteins are not found in urine.

Creatine is not present in a significant amount in urine, because it is completely reabsorbed by the renal tubules. It is present in the urine of pre-pubertal children and pregnant women. It is increased in conditions associated with muscle wasting and muscle dystrophy.

Creatinine is creatine anhydride and is formed from creatine. It forms 5% of the total NPN constituents of urine.

Uric acid: 1% of the total nitrogen of NPN constituents is formed by uric acid. The output fluctuates with the level of dietary purines as it is the end product of purine metabolism. About 90% of the urates filtered through glomeruli are reabsorbed by the tubules. In urine, uric acid is present as soluble sodium and potassium urates, at the average pH of urine (pH6), whereas they are precipitated in highly acid urine.

Excretion of nitrogen in faeces varies with the protein content of the food ingested. On an average, it amounts to 1–2 grams per day. Very small amounts of nitrogen are excreted in milk, sweat and menstrual fluid.

Nitrogen balance: Since nitrogen is taken to represent proteins, the nitrogen of the food and the nitrogenous products excreted represent broadly the intake and excretion of proteins and therefore the state of protein metabolism.

Nitrogen balance may be defined as the difference that exists between the intake and output of nitrogen, both being expressed in terms of grams N per day.

Intake represents the nitrogen ingested and output represents excretion of nitrogen via urine and faeces.

A man is said to have a positive nitrogen balance when the intake of nitrogen in food exceeds the nitrogen output. Such a condition prevails when new tissues are being formed as occurring during the growth of young, during pregnancy and during convalescence.

A negative nitrogen balance exists when the output of nitrogen exceeds intake. Such a condition would prevail when there is more protein destruction and less intake of protein. A negative nitrogen balance exists in the following circumstances:

1. During fasting and gastrointestinal disorders, when the intake of protein is inadequate
2. During fevers, infections and wasting diseases where the protein catabolism is accelerated
3. When loss of protein occurs from the body as in lactation and albuminuria
4. When there is inadequate supply of essential amino acids in the food

It is evident that nitrogen balance, which means intake should be equal to output, could be achieved only in healthy adults, who do not suffer from the abnormal conditions mentioned in the preceding text. Such a balance can be achieved when the diet supplied is adequate, containing all the fulfilment of vitamins, minerals and proteins of a high biological value. The diet should supply sufficient calories and contain a proper amount of carbohydrate and fat.

ANABOLISM OF PROTEIN

Anabolism of protein includes the following:

1. Protein turnover
2. Synthesis of protein

Protein turnover: Proteins in the body are constantly broken down and resynthesised. Replacement of proteins lost by constant wear and tear is necessary at all stages to promote growth, to facilitate recovery from chronic illness and to maintain nitrogen balance in both young and old.

Liver plays an important role in the synthesis of proteins. The proteins after synthesis from amino acids in the liver are deposited in the cytoplasm of the cells in a labile form, where they are rapidly used up to replace loss of proteins as occurring during haemorrhage and during starvation. The loss of protein from the liver is accompanied by loss of enzymes from liver.

Since liver is also the site of synthesis of plasma proteins, the concentration of plasma proteins tends to fall in liver diseases. Liver is depleted of its valuable products and becomes susceptible to infections and injury by agents such as phosphorus, arsenic and alcohol. Liver is considerably affected when there is a disturbance in protein metabolism, and treatment of liver diseases should be supported by a diet containing a high proportion of protein.

Amino acids from the metabolic pool, formed by the amino acids absorbed from the food and the amino acids broken down from body proteins, reach the extracellular fluid, from where they are taken up by various tissues for synthesis of proteins. The uptake of amino acids from the extracellular fluid by the tissues is accomplished by the process of active transport. The rate of uptake of amino acids and turnover of proteins by cells of tissues varies in different tissues, the rate being high in plasma protein, intestinal mucosa and liver.

CATABOLISM OF PROTEINS

Catabolism of proteins is essentially catabolism of amino acids.

Amino acids in the body are highly reactive and undergo rapid changes. They may be utilised as such to form new protein or they may replace amino acids that are lost. They contribute to the formation of blood proteins, tissue proteins, hormones, enzymes and certain other physiologically important compounds.

In general, amino acids catabolise with the separation of the amino group, leaving behind the carbon skeleton, which becomes an α-keto acid. The ammonia enters the ammonia pool where it is utilised in various anabolic and catabolic reactions. The majority of the α-keto acids enter the carbohydrate pool. A few participate in the formation of ketone bodies and fatty acids.

The catabolic pathway of amino acids involves the following reactions:

I. Removal of amino groups
II. Fate of the amino group
III. Fate of carbon skeleton

Removal of Amino Group from Amino Acid

This reaction is accomplished by (i) oxidative deamination, (ii) transamination and (iii) transdeamination.

Oxidative deamination: A large amount of amino acids after absorption from the intestines reach the liver where they lose their amino groups.

This process described as oxidative deamination is accompanied by oxidation and is catalysed by specific amino acid oxidases or more appropriately dehydrogenases present in liver and kidneys. The D-amino acid oxidase and L-amino acid oxidase act on D-amino acids and L-amino acids, respectively. L-Glutamic acid dehydrogenase acts on glutamic acid. The first two are flavoproteins containing FAD and FMN as coenzymes. They are less active and are present in tissues in very small amounts.

The process of oxidative deamination takes place in the following two stages.

The first stage is oxidation or in other words dehydrogenation. This is followed by the second stage, hydrolysis, when ammonia and keto acid are liberated. The net reaction may be described as transformation of an amino acid $RCHNH_2COOH$ to the corresponding keto acid RCO COOH with the liberation of NH_3.

The reaction which is catalysed by the specific amino acid oxidase with FAD as a coenzyme may be represented as

$$\underset{\text{Amino acid}}{RCHNH_2COOH} + FAD \longrightarrow \underset{\text{Imino acid}}{RC = NHCOOH} + FADH_2$$

The imino acid, which is formed as an intermediate, is unstable and spontaneously undergoes hydrolysis to form the keto acid, liberating ammonia.

$$RC{=}(NH)\,COOH + H_2O \longrightarrow R\overset{\overset{\displaystyle O}{\|}}{C}\,COOH + NH_3$$

The reduced FAD ($FADH_2$) is reoxidised spontaneously by oxygen. H_2O_2 is formed.

$$FADH_2 + O_2 \longrightarrow H_2O_2 + FAD$$

H_2O_2 is decomposed by the catalase present in cells.

The overall reaction of oxidative deamination by amino acid oxidase may be written as

$$\underset{\textbf{Amino acid}}{\begin{array}{c} \mathrm{H} \\ | \\ \mathrm{R-C-NH_2} \\ | \\ \mathrm{COOH} \end{array}} \xrightarrow{-2H} \underset{\textbf{Imino acid}}{\begin{array}{c} \mathrm{R-C=NH} \\ | \\ \mathrm{COOH} \end{array}} \xrightarrow{+H_2O} \underset{\textbf{Keto acid}}{\begin{array}{c} \mathrm{R-C=O+NH_3} \\ | \\ \mathrm{COOH} \end{array}}$$

$$\underset{\textbf{Alanine}}{CH_3CHNH_2COOH} \xrightarrow{-2H} CH_3C=NHCOOH \xrightarrow{+H_2O} \underset{\textbf{Pyruvic acid}}{CH_3\overset{O}{\overset{\|}{C}}COOH + NH_3}$$

$$\underset{\textbf{Aspartic acid}}{COOHCHNH_2CH_2COOH} \longrightarrow COOHC=NHCH_2COOH \longrightarrow \underset{\textbf{Oxaloacetic acid}}{COOH\overset{O}{\overset{\|}{C}}CH_2COOH + NH_3}$$

$$\underset{\textbf{Glutamic acid}}{COOH-CHNH_2CH_2CH_2COOH} \xrightarrow{-2H} COOHC=NHCH_2CH_2COOH \xrightarrow{+H_2O} \underset{\boldsymbol{\alpha}\textbf{-Ketoglutaric acid}}{COOH\overset{O}{\overset{\|}{C}}CH_2CH_2COOH + NH_3}$$

Oxidative deamination of glutamic acid is catalysed by glutamate dehydrogenase which has NAD as a coenzyme. The reduced NAD is oxidised via the oxidative chain by the nicotinamide-linked dehydrogenase.

By oxidative deamination, amino acids are split to form α-keto acids and ammonia. Keto acids are metabolites of carbohydrate metabolism and are oxidised in the Krebs cycle to yield energy. Ammonia which is highly toxic may be converted to urea or detoxified to glutamine.

Transamination: The process of transfer of an amino group from an amino acid to α-keto acid, resulting in the formation of a new amino acid and keto acid, is known as transamination. In other words, it is deamination of an amino acid, coupled with amination of a keto acid. It is an important method by which many amino acids undergo interconversion in metabolic reactions.

Transamination is catalysed by transaminases, with pyridoxal phosphate functioning as a coenzyme. There are two active transaminases in tissues, catalysing interconversions. These are (i) glutamate oxaloacetate transaminase (GOT) and (ii) glutamate pyruvate transaminase (GPT).

The mechanism of their action is illustrated in **Figures 21.2(a)** and **(b)** respectively.

1. **Glutamate-oxaloacetate transaminase (GOT; Fig. 21.2a)** catalyses the transfer of NH_2 from glutamate to oxaloacetate resulting in the formation of α-ketoglutarate and aspartate.

$$\text{L-Glutamate} + \text{Oxaloacetate} \rightleftharpoons \alpha\text{-Ketoglutarate} + \text{L-Aspartate}$$

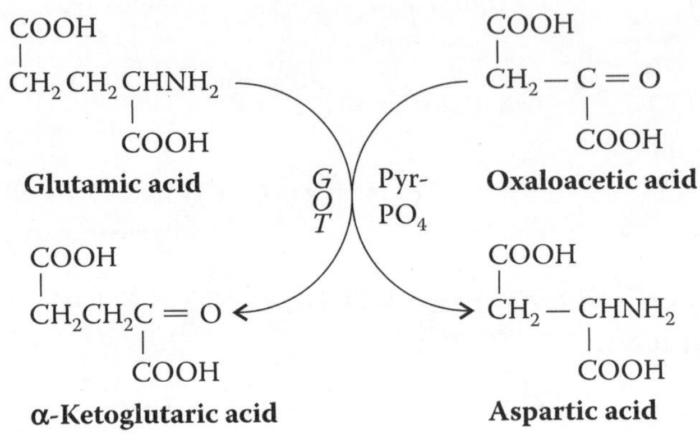

Figure 21.2(a) Illustration of transaminase (GOT) action.

2. **Glutamate-pyruvate transaminase (GPT; Fig. 21.2b)** catalyses the transfer of NH_2 from glutamate to pyruvate, resulting in the formation of α-ketoglutarate and alanine.

$$\text{L-Glutamate} + \text{Pyruvate} \rightleftharpoons \alpha\text{-Ketoglutarate} + \text{L-Alanine}$$

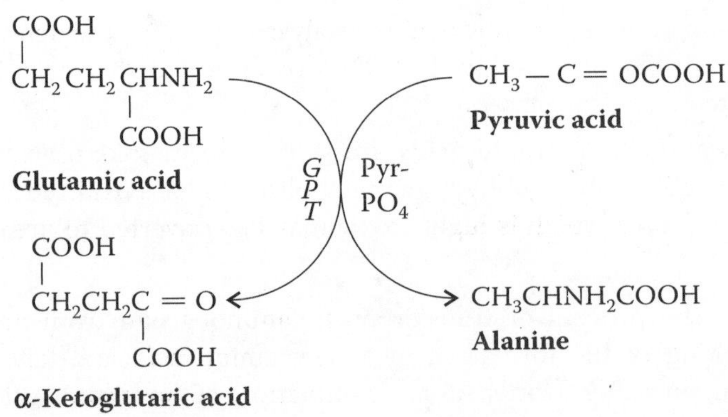

Figure 21.2(b) Illustration of transaminase (GPT) action.

The reactions indicated in **Figure 21.2** are of great clinical importance. The concentrations of these transaminases in serum, referred to as serum glutamic oxaloacetate transaminase (SGOT) and serum glutamic pyruvate transaminase (SGPT), are increased in certain pathological conditions (page 94).

Transdeamination: This is a combination of transamination and deamination. Transdeamination has been suggested as a possible method by which some amino acids lose their amino groups. As an example, transdeamination of glutamic acid is explained here.

The amino group is first removed from glutamic acid, by transamination with pyruvic acid to form alanine, which gets deaminated next by a specific amino acid oxidase as in oxidative deamination.

$$\text{L-Glutamic acid} + \text{Pyruvic acid} \longrightarrow \text{Alanine} + \alpha\text{-Ketoglutarate}$$

$$\text{Alanine} \longrightarrow NH_3 + \text{Pyruvic acid}$$

It is transamination of glutamic acid followed by deamination of alanine in this case.

Fate of the Amino Group

Ammonia released by deamination of amino acids enters the general ammonia pool where it may be utilised for either anabolic or catabolic purposes. These include the following:

1. Synthetic pathway
2. Formation of urea
3. Glutamine pathway
4. Direct excretion

Synthetic pathway: The amino groups are utilised for the synthetic purpose:

- α-keto acids derived from carbohydrates may be reductively aminated to form new amino acids by the reversal of transdeamination reaction.
- Ammonia may be utilised for the synthesis of purines and pyrimidines.

Glutamine pathway: When a large amount of ammonia is formed, it is necessary to prevent their accumulation in the cells, as they are toxic substances. This is accomplished by detoxication, when ammonia couples with glutamic acid to form glutamine. Synthesis of glutamine occurs in extrarenal tissues. The reaction requires energy and involves participation of ATP.

$$\text{Glutamic acid} + NH_2 + \text{ATP} \longrightarrow \text{Glutamine} + \text{ADP} + H_3PO_4$$

Glutamine formed thus passes from the tissues via blood to the kidneys, where it is hydrolysed to glutamic acid by glutaminase.

$$\text{Glutamine} \xrightarrow{+H_2O} \text{Glutamine acid} + NH_3$$

The ammonia is excreted in urine. 60% of the ammonia present in urine is formed by this source.

Formation of urea: Liver is the site of formation of urea. If deamination of amino acids occurs in the liver, the ammonia is utilised in the formation of urea, when it would enter the 'ornithine' cycle. (Refer to pages 396–398 for details.)

Direct excretion of ammonia: Deamination takes place in kidneys also. When ammonia is not required for immediate synthetic purpose, it may get excreted directly in the urine. 40% of the total ammonia present in urine is derived from this source. It should be noted that ammonia, irrespective of the site of formation, is transported to the kidneys from where it is excreted. This accounts for the absence of ammonia in normal systemic blood.

Fate of Carbon Skeleton

The carbon skeletons left behind after deamination are identified as α-keto acids. They may take any one of the following pathways:

1. **Synthesis of amino acids:** They may get reductively aminated by reversal of transdeamination or undergo transamination to form once again the original amino acids.
2. **Glucogenic pathway:** Keto acids may get converted to carbohydrates. Some keto acids are intermediaries in carbohydrate metabolism; for example, pyruvic acid, oxaloacetic acid and α-ketoglutaric acid are derived from amino acids which are known as glucogenic amino acids. The keto acids can be converted to amino acids and vice versa. The keto acids themselves are interconvertible via the citric acid cycle.

   The pathways of three important glucogenic amino acids are shown below. Though the routes vary with each amino acid, they all converge at pyruvic acid.

   $$
   \begin{array}{lcl}
   \text{Glucose} & & \\
   \updownarrow & & \\
   \text{Pyruvic acid} & \rightleftharpoons & \text{Alanine} \\
   \updownarrow & & \\
   \text{Oxaloacetic acid} & \rightleftharpoons & \text{Aspartic acid} \\
   \updownarrow & & \\
   \alpha\text{-Ketoglutaric acid} & \rightleftharpoons & \text{Glutamic acid}
   \end{array}
   $$

   Glucogenic amino acids constitute more than 50% of the amino acids, derived from animal protein. The process of conversion of the keto acids of glucogenic amino acids to carbohydrate metabolites is known as **gluconeogenesis**.
3. **Ketogenic pathway:** A few amino acids may get converted to fat and these are classified as ketogenic amino acids. On deamination, they form α-keto acids which are more closely related to fats rather than carbohydrates. They metabolise to produce acetoacetic acid and ketone bodies instead of glucose.

   They enter the tricarboxylic acid cycle at the stage of acetate. Ketogenic amino acids constitute only a minority and follow specialised and complex pathways. Examples are leucine, isoleucine, phenylalanine and tyrosine. Among these, leucine is solely ketogenic whereas the other three are both ketogenic and glucogenic.

Branched chain amino acids: Three amino acids, two ketogenic (leucine and isoleucine) and one glucogenic (valine), follow different pathways. The resulting α-keto acids after deamination undergo oxidative decarboxylation and then follow a series of reactions similar to those undergone by fatty acids. They give rise to propionate and ketone bodies ultimately.

Transpeptidation: Amino acids link with one another to form peptides. When peptides are hydrolysed, amino acids are formed. Transpeptidation is a process by which peptides or amino acids are transferred from a peptide chain or protein to amines, amino acids or peptides, to form a new peptide or protein. Transpeptidation plays an important role in protein synthesis.

During the process of transfer, the peptide bond is broken with liberation of energy which is utilised for the synthesis of the new peptide bond. The enzymes which catalyse such reactions are called **transpeptidases**. Examples are cathepsin, trypsin and chymotrypsin. The transfer of the glutamyl radicle from glutamine or glutathione to certain amino acids is an example of transpeptidation. The reaction is catalysed by glutamyl transpeptidase present in kidney, liver and brain. It transfers the glutamyl radicle to various amino acid acceptors. For example,

$$\text{Glutathione } (\gamma\text{-glutamyl cysteinyl glycine}) + \text{L-Leucine} \longrightarrow \gamma\text{-Glutamyl L-leucine} + \text{Cysteinyl glycine}$$

The γ-glutamyl dipeptide may get lengthened by further addition of peptides or amino acids. For each COOH group forming a peptide, a molecule of ATP is formed.

Transamidation: Transfer of the amide group as a source of amino group to a keto group is transamidation. Synthesis of glucosamine (in the form of glucosamine-6-phosphate) is an example of this reaction.

$$\text{Glutamine} + \text{Fructose-6-P} \longrightarrow \text{Glucosamine-6-P}$$

Glutamine contributes its amide group to form glucosamine-6-phosphate. This reaction is catalysed by a transamidase and the energy is derived from the cleavage of the amide bond of glutamine.

Transamidination: Transfer of an amidine group from one amino acid to another is transamidination. Synthesis of creatine is an example. The amidine group from arginine is transferred to glycine to form guanidoacetate which gets methylated to form creatine.

Energy Derived from Oxidation of Amino Acid

It is difficult to arrive at a generalised formula for derivation of energy due to oxidation of amino acids. For the purpose of convenience, amino acid oxidation can be dealt in two portions.

1. The amino group forms urea and gets excreted.
2. The carbon and hydrogen skeletons are oxidised to CO_2 and H_2O through the Krebs cycle. The CO_2 may be represented as HCO_3 at physiological pH. Thus if we take oxidation of glutamate as an example, one molecule of glutamate will form half a molecule of urea, one molecule of HCO_3^- and one molecule of H_2O, at physiological pH. It has been estimated that about 490 kcals of free energy is formed by this process. The conversion of this energy to ATP is derived as follows.

On deamination, glutamic acid forms α-ketoglutaric acid, ammonia and reduced NAD.

Oxidation of reduced NAD via the cytochrome chain yields three molecules of high-energy phosphate bonds per molecule of glutamate. Oxidation of α-ketoglutarate via the tricarboxylic acid cycle step by step to oxaloacetate yields 18 molecules of high-energy phosphate bonds (HEPB) as shown below.

α-Ketoglutarate to succinate	6 ATP
Succinate thiokinase	2 ATP
Succinate to fumarate	4 ATP
Malate to oxaloacetate	6 ATP
	18 ATP

Ammonia is converted to urea. This is an endergonic process and requires expenditure of three molecules of HEPB for each molecule of urea formed.

UREA SYNTHESIS—KREBS–HENSLEIT CYCLE

Urea is the chief end product of amino acid metabolism and it is synthesised in liver. An increase in dietary protein is followed by an increase in urine urea. A normal healthy man excretes 25–30 grams of urea per day. The normal blood urea level is 15–35 mg per 100 ml.

Krebs and Hensleit, who studied about synthesis of urea, showed that urea is formed when liver slices are incubated with ammonium salts. They demonstrated that when liver is damaged as in acute hepatic necrosis, blood amino acids increase while blood urea and urine urea decrease. They also found that addition of amino acids, namely arginine, ornithine and citrulline, considerably increased the rate of formation of urea and attributed a catalytic effect to these three amino acids towards the formation of urea. They observed that liver contains a fairly high concentration of the enzyme arginase which is necessary for synthesis of urea. With these observations, Krebs and Henseleit proposed a cyclic mechanism for the synthesis of urea, which involves participation of ornithine, citrulline and arginine with carbon dioxide and ammonia entering the cycle at different stages. This cycle is known as the Krebs–Hensleit urea cycle. This cycle starts from ornithine which goes through the formation of citrulline and arginine. Arginine undergoes hydrolysis to form urea and ornithine, and the cycle is repeated with ornithine. The ornithine, citrulline, arginine cycle is shown in **Figure 21.3**.

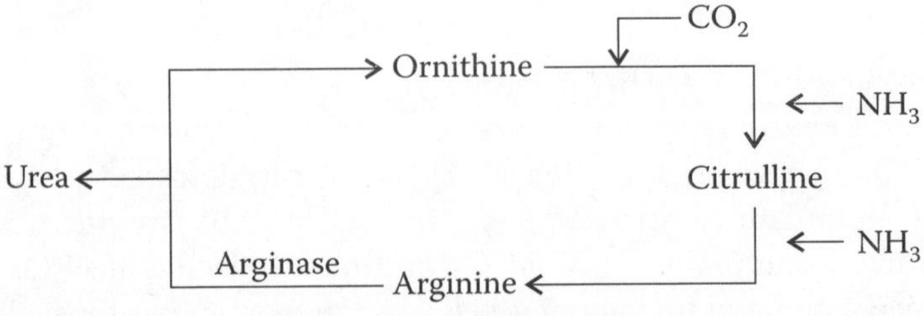

Figure 21.3 Reactions of synthesis of urea.

The reactions of synthesis of urea and the intermediates formed are represented in **Figure 21.4**. The overall reactions of the cycle may be expressed as follows. Two molecules of ammonia and one molecule of carbon dioxide are converted to one molecule of urea for each turn of the cycle, regenerating ornithine to start another fresh cycle. The actual

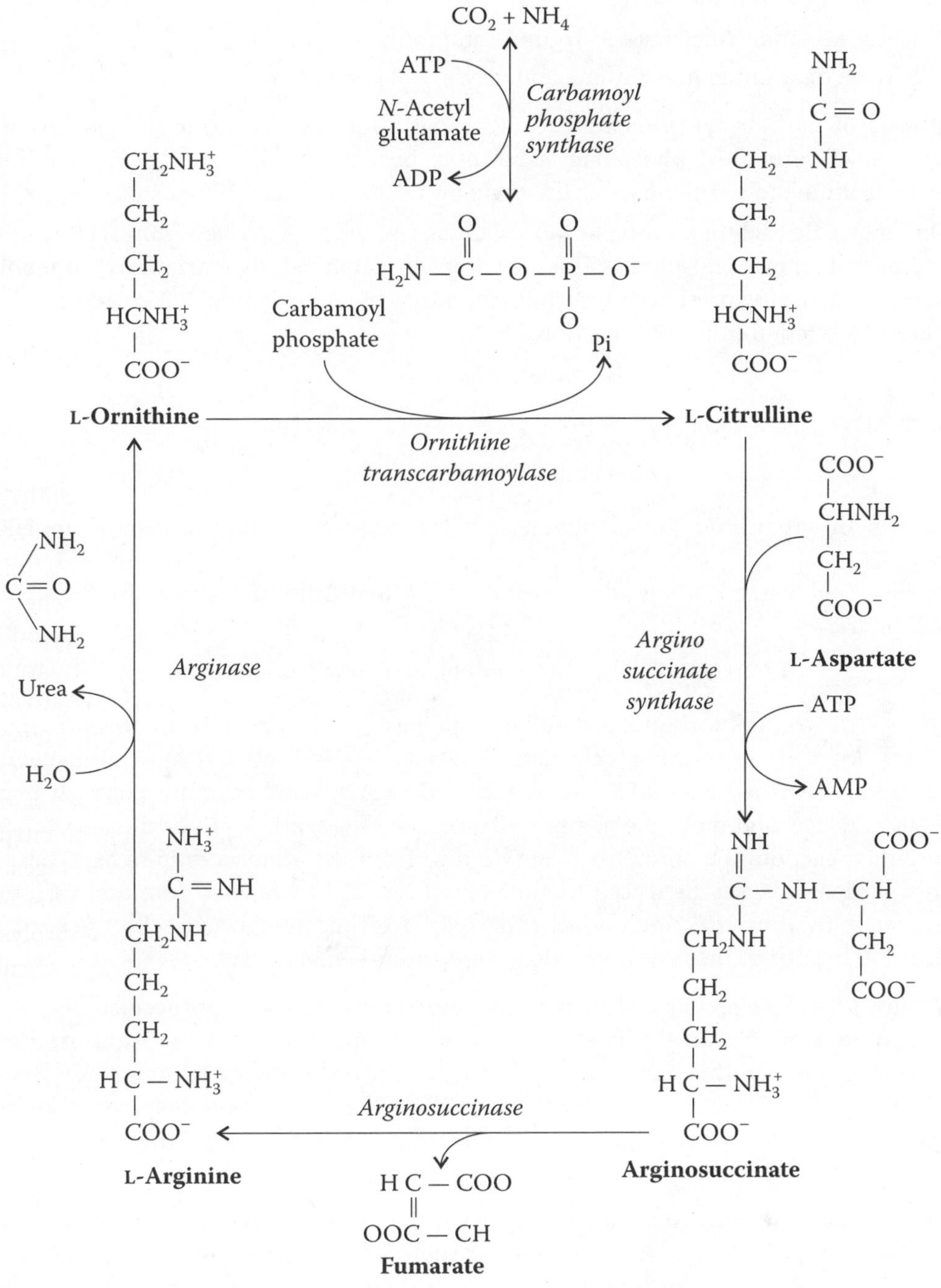

Figure 21.4 Urea cycle reactions of urea biosynthesis.

process involves complex reactions, with derivation of energy. The sequence of reactions may be described in five steps as follows:

1. Synthesis of carbamoyl phosphate
2. Synthesis of citrulline
3. Synthesis of arginosuccinate
4. Cleavage of arginosuccinate to arginine and fumarate
5. Cleavage of arginine to ornithine and urea

Synthesis of carbamoyl phosphate: Carbamoyl phosphate is formed in the first step. Formation of carbamoyl phosphate is essential because the CO_2 and NH_3 required to convert ornithine to citrulline enter the cycle in this form.

One molecule each of ammonium ion, CO_2 and phosphate derived from ATP condense to form carbamoyl phosphate. This reaction is catalysed by **carbamoyl phosphate synthase**, an enzyme present in liver mitochondria. In addition, Mg^{++}, *N*-acetyl glutamine and biotin are required for the reaction.

$$CO_2 + NH_4^+ + 2ATP \xrightarrow[\text{N-AGA, Biotin, } Mg^{++}]{\textit{Carbamoyl phosphate synthase}} \text{Carbamoyl phosphate} + 2ADP + Pi$$

Synthesis of citrulline: This reaction involves transfer of the carbamoyl moiety of carbamoyl phosphate to ornithine to form citrulline which is carbamoyl ornithine. Inorganic phosphate is liberated. The reaction is catalysed by **ornithine transcarbamoylase** of liver mitochondria.

$$\text{Carbamoyl phosphate} + \text{Ornithine} \rightleftharpoons \text{Citrulline} + Pi$$

Synthesis of arginosuccinate: Citrulline condenses with aspartate in the presence of ATP and Mg^{++} to form arginosuccinate. The reaction is catalysed by **arginosuccinate synthase** and is reversible. ATP is cleaved to form AMP and pyrophosphate. It may be noted that the second molecule of ammonia required for synthesis of urea enters the cycle during this reaction, the ammonia being derived from the amino group of aspartate. The source of aspartate may be traced to glutamate (**Fig. 21.5**) which by transamination with oxaloacetate can form α-ketoglutarate and aspartate. Thus, integration with the citric acid cycle is established at the levels of oxaloacetate and α-ketoglutarate.

Cleavage of arginosuccinate to arginine and fumarate: Arginosuccinate is cleaved reversibly to arginine and fumarate and the reaction is catalysed by **arginosuccinase**. Fumarate may enter the citric acid cycle to get converted to malate and oxaloacetate. Oxaloacetate may then get transaminated to form aspartate, thus helping to keep the supply of aspartate to regenerate arginine. Note the integration of the urea cycle with the citric acid cycle at this point.

Cleavage of arginine to ornithine and urea: Arginase in liver hydrolyses arginine to ornithine and urea. Arginase catalyses the hydrolytic cleavage of the guanido group of arginine. Arginase is activated by Mn^{++}. Ornithine and lysine are potent competitive inhibitors with arginine. This reaction completes the urea cycle and regenerates ornithine,

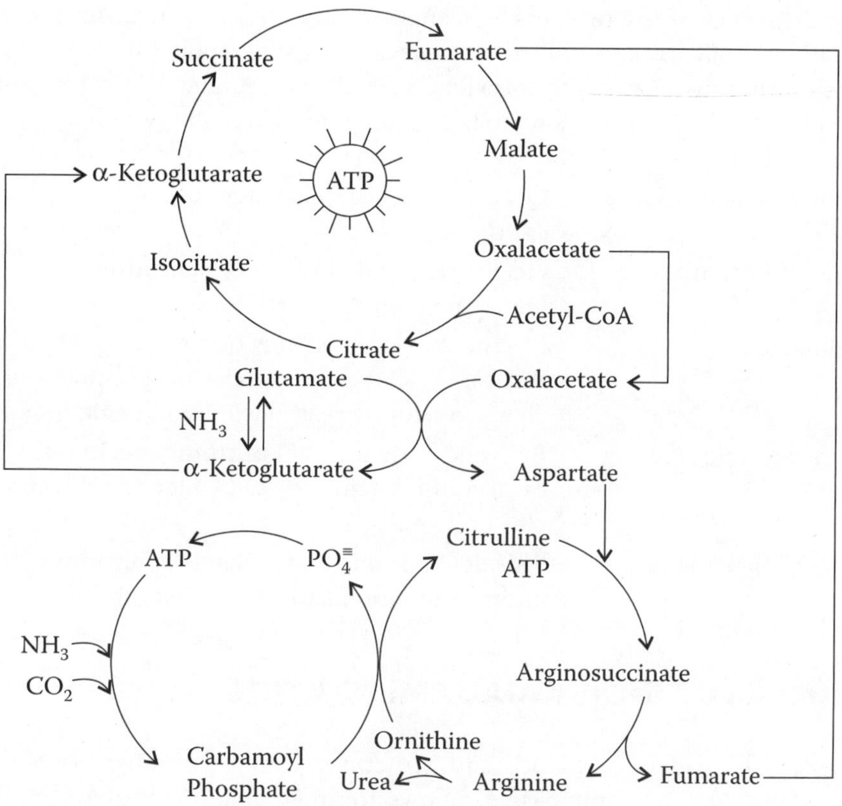

Figure 21.5 Synthesis of urea—integration with the citric acid cycle.

the substrate for reaction 2. Ornithine passes into the mitochondria by way of the enzyme ornithine translocase and reacts with another molecule of carbamoyl phosphate, and the cycle is repeated.

Overall reactions of the urea cycle: The overall process of urea synthesis requires three molecules of ATP and participation of five amino acids and five enzymes. Out of the three ATP molecules, two are converted to ADP + Pi in reaction (1) and one is converted to AMP + PPi in reaction (3). The five amino acids are *N*-acetylglutamate, aspartate, arginine, ornithine and citrulline.

Urea synthesis is not an independent process but is connected with vital metabolic reactions in the body. Synthesis of urea gains importance because of its integration with the citric acid cycle, which serves as a source of supply of aspartate (**Fig. 21.5**). In addition to this, fumarate derived from arginosuccinate integrates with the citric acid cycle. Urea by itself has no physiological effect in the body though its increase in blood is a consequence of renal damage. However, it has some diuretic action. A common observation is that a high protein diet is followed by increased excretion of urine, and to replace the water lost, one feels thirsty and drinks more water.

Uraemia: This is a pathological clinical state when blood urea increases above 50 mg%. Acute uraemia is associated with anuria (suppression of excretion of urine).

Metabolic disorders of the urea cycle: Deficiency of each of the five enzymes concerned in urea synthesis may occur resulting in the respective metabolic disorder. All disorders of urea synthesis cause ammonia intoxication and have similar clinical symptoms. The symptoms include vomiting, aversion to high protein food, irritability, lethargy, intermittent ataxia and mental retardation. Only a few cases have been reported for each disorder.

1. Hyperammonaemia-Type I	Occurs due to deficiency of **carbamoyl phosphate synthase**
2. Hyperammonaemia-Type II	Occurs due to deficiency of **ornithine transcarbamoylase**
3. Citrullinaemia	Occurs due to deficiency or absence of **arginosuccinate synthase**. Citrulline levels in plasma and CSF are elevated with increased excretion of citrulline in urine.
4. Argininosuccinic aciduria	Reflects absence of **argininosuccinase**. The levels of argininosuccinic acid in blood, CSF and urine are elevated.
5. Hyperargininaemia	This defect is due to deficiency of **arginase**. The levels of arginine in blood and CSF are elevated.

METABOLISM OF INDIVIDUAL AMINO ACIDS

Amino acids vary widely in nature and structure. Some are indispensable and some are dispensable. No single amino acid follows the metabolic pathway of another amino acid, and it is necessary to deal with the metabolism of individual amino acids that are physiologically important. The metabolic reactions and the metabolic products of amino acids are not only interrelated but integrate with the metabolic pathways of carbohydrates and lipids. Some amino acids have specific functions to perform in metabolism.

For the purpose of understanding the significance of the metabolism of individual amino acids, they may be classified under two groups, namely essential and non-essential amino acids.

Essential amino acids are indispensable and are required for nutrition, promotion of normal growth and maintenance of nitrogen balance. They are not synthesised in the body and are required to be supplied in an adequate amount in diet. Ten amino acids are classified under essential amino acids. They are lysine, arginine, threonine, valine, leucine, isoleucine, histidine, methionine, tryptophan and phenylalanine. The amino acids *arginine* and *histidine* are considered semi-essential because they are synthesised in the body in smaller amounts. It is necessary to include all the eight essential amino acids in the diet, to maintain nitrogen balance. Even if a single amino acid is excluded, the value of nutrition is impaired and this would lead to syndromes of malnutrition, fatty liver and states of vitamin deficiency and anaemia.

Other amino acids are non-essential and do not present unusual features. But a few of them are physiologically important and take part in the general metabolic reactions. Non-essential amino acids are glycine, alanine, serine, glutamic acid, proline, aspartic acid, cysteine and tyrosine.

This section will deal with the metabolism of individual amino acids. An overview of the amino acids discussed in this section is presented in **Tables 21.1** and **21.2**.

Table 21.1 Essential Amino Acids

Amino Acid	Metabolic Fate of Carbon Skeleton (Ketogenic/Glucogenic*)	Catabolic Pathway	Related Disease/ Disorder
Lysine	Ketogenic	The reactions of lysine are 1. Oxidative deamination to α-amino-adipic acid 2. This is followed by deamination to α-ketoadipic acid 3. α-Ketoadipic acid is decarboxylated to glutaric acid	Hyperlysinaemia due to a deficiency of enzymes in the metabolic pathway Mental retardation is a feature
Threonine	Glucogenic and ketogenic	1. Deamination to form α-ketobutyrate 2. Splitting into two halves—acetaldehyde and glycine	
Valine	Glucogenic	Undergo a similar sequence of reactions as that of leucine and isoleucine Transamination, oxidative deamination and FAD-dependent dehyrogenation Subsequent individual reactions generate succinyl-CoA	Maple Syrup Urine disease in infants
Leucine and Isoleucine	Leucine: Ketogenic Isoleucine: Ketogenic and glucogenic	Undergo a similar sequence of reactions as that of valine and isoleucine. Transamination, oxidative deamination and FAD-dependent dehyrogenation. Subsequent individual reactions generate acetoacetate + acetyl-CoA in case of leucine Acetyl-CoA + Propionyl-CoA in case of isoleucine	Maple Syrup Urine disease in infants
Histidine	Glucogenic	Metabolic routes: 1. Histamine pathway 2. Urocanic acid pathway	Imidazole aminoaciduria Histidinuria
Methionine	Glucogenic	1. Transfer of the methyl group 2. Utilisation of homocysteine 3. Utilisation of methyl group in transmethylation reactions	Homocystinuria
Tryptophan	Ketogenic and glucogenic	Major pathways: 1. Nicotinamide pathway with minor pathways 2. Serotonin pathway	Hartnup syndrome
Phenylalanine	Ketogenic and glucogenic	Conversion to tyrosine catalysed by phenylalanine hydroxyse	Phenylketonuria
Arginine (and Ornithine)	Glucogenic	1. Involved in urea formation. 2. Required for synthesis of nitric oxide and creatine	Hyperargininaemia due to absence of the arginase enzyme in liver

Ketogenic/Glucogenic*—**Ketogenic** amino acids are amino acids which are converted to acetoacetate or acetyl-CoA and ultimately into ketone bodies while **glucogenic** amino acids are those that can be converted into pyruvate, oxaloacetate, fumarate, α-ketoglutarate and succinyl-CoA and ultimately to glucose.

Table 21.2 Non-Essential Amino Acids

Amino Acid	Metabolic Fate of Carbon Skeleton (Ketogenic/ Glucogenic*)	Synthesised from	Catabolic Pathway	Related Disease/ Disorder
Glycine	Glucogenic	Serine Threonine	Required for biosynthesis of creatine, haem, purines, glutathione Conjugating agent Neurotransmitter Completely degraded by the glycine cleavage system	Non-ketotic hyperglycinaemia, hyperoxaluria
Alanine	Glucogenic	Transamination or reanimation of pyruvic acid Catabolism of pyrimidines such as cytosine and uracil	Interorgan transport of nitrogen Glucose-alanine cycle	No reported disorder probably due to its vital role in intermediary metabolism
Serine	Glucogenic	3-Phosphoglyceric acid (by the addition of formaldehyde to glycine)	Conversion to pyruvate by deamination Involved in one-carbon metabolism, formation of cysteine, alanine and selenocysteine	No disorder reported
Proline and Hydroxyproline	Glucogenic	Citric acid cycle intermediates	Does not undergo transamination Converted to dehydroproline and then to glutamate	Hyperprolinaemia Types I and II due to deficiency of proline oxidase (POX) and pyroline-5-carboxylate reductase (P5C) enzyme respectively
Aspartic acid	Glucogenic	Citric acid cycle intermediates	Contributes its α-amino nitrogen to urea, involved in purine and pyrimidine synthesis	No known disorder reported
Cysteine and Cystine	Glucogenic	From serine (and sulphur from methionine)		Cystinuria Cystinosis
Tyrosine	Ketogenic and glucogenic	Phenylalanine (on its hydroxylation)		Alcaptonuria Ochronosis *Pheochromocytomas*: Albinism Aminoaciduria

Ketogenic/Glucogenic*—**Ketogenic** amino acids are amino acids which are converted to acetoacetate or acetyl-CoA and ultimately into ketone bodies while **glucogenic** amino acids are those that can be converted into pyruvate, oxaloacetate, fumarate, α-ketoglutarate and succinyl-CoA and ultimately to glucose.

Glycine (CH_2NH_2COOH)

Amino acid glycine is the simplest of the amino acids. It is non-essential because it is readily synthesised. It is a glucogenic amino acid. It participates in a variety of metabolic reactions.

Synthesis:

Glycine is synthesised from two sources, namely (i) serine and (ii) threonine.

1. **Synthetic pathway from serine:** This involves three routes, via glyoxylic acid, choline and serine.
   - *Glyoxylic acid route*
     - Serine on decarboxylation forms ethanolamine.
     - Ethanolamine is oxidatively deaminated to form glycolaldehyde.
     - On oxidation, glycolaldehyde forms glycolic acid and glyoxylic acid. The latter may be aminated to form glycine (**Fig. 21.6**).

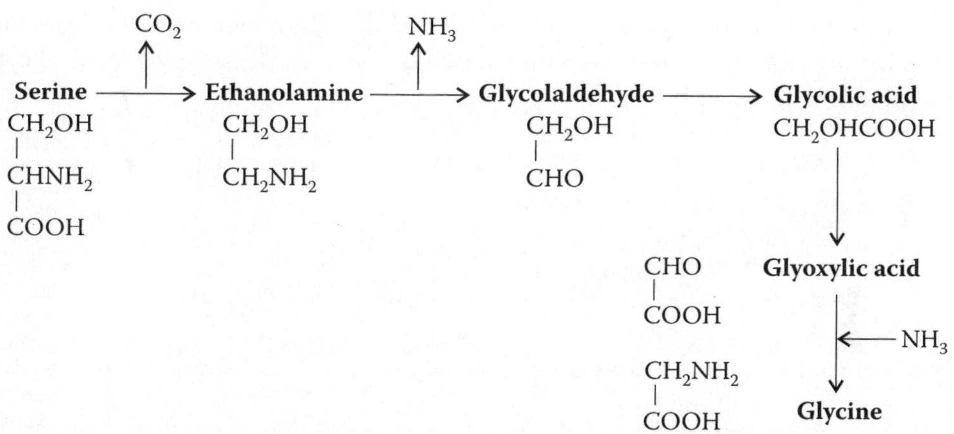

Figure 21.6 Synthetic pathway for glycine from serine via glyoxylic acid.

   - *Choline route*:
     - Serine on decarboxylation forms ethanolamine.
     - Successive methylation of ethanolamine thrice leads to the formation of choline.
     - Choline on oxidation forms betaine.
     - Successive demethylation of betaine results in the formation of glycine (**Fig. 21.7**).

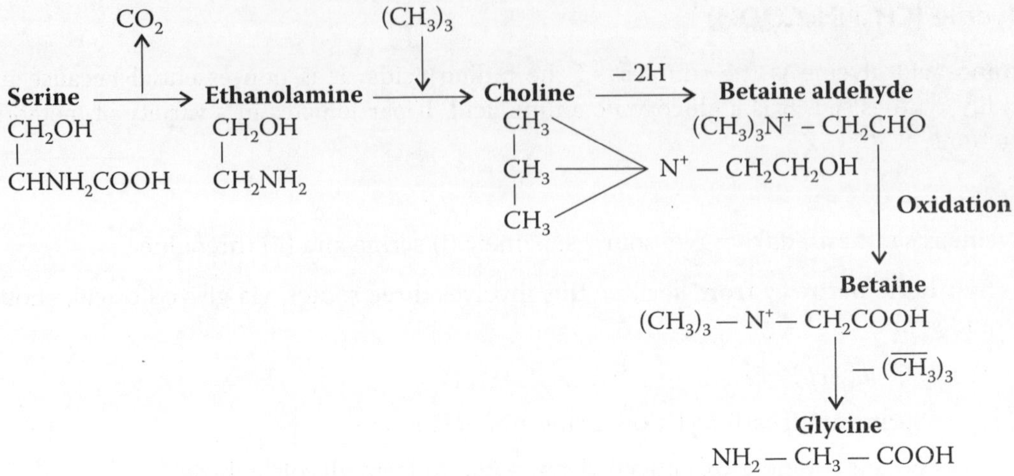

Figure 21.7 Synthesis of glycine via the choline route.

- *Serine route*: Glycine and serine are interconvertible.

  Serine may split reversibly between the α and β carbon atoms to yield glycine and formaldehyde. The interconversion requires the presence of pyridoxal phosphate and folic acid.

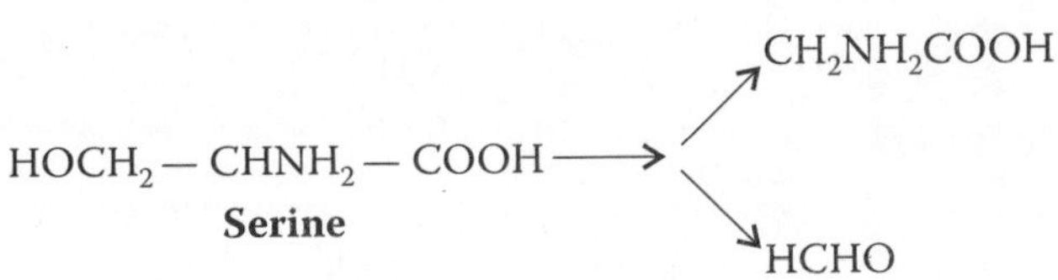

2. **Synthetic pathway from threonine:** Glycine can arise from threonine.

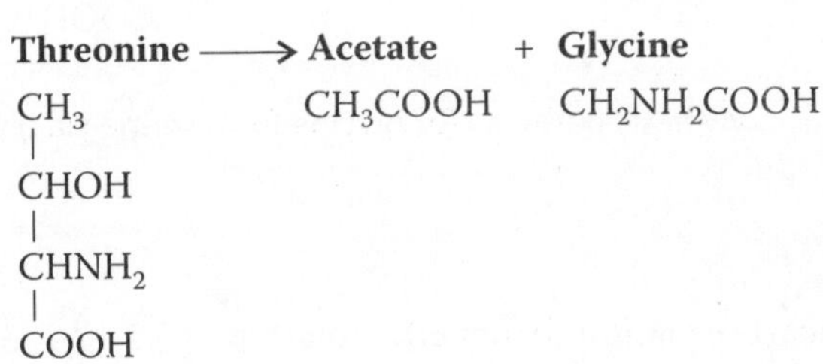

See **Figure 21.8** for reactions of glycine.

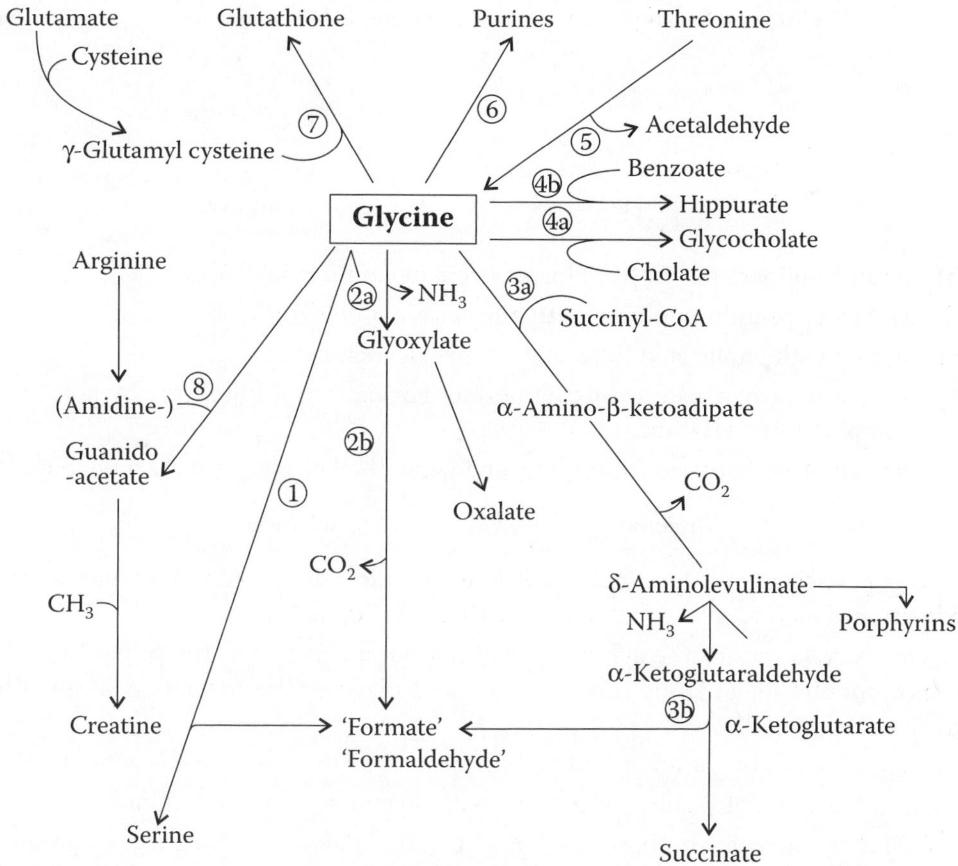

Figure 21.8 Glycine metabolism.

1. Glycine combines with formaldehyde to form serine which splits to form glycine and formaldehyde.

$$\text{Glycine} + \text{Formaldehyde} \rightleftharpoons \text{Serine}$$

2. (a) Glycine on oxidative deamination by glycine oxidase present in the liver and kidney forms glyoxylic acid. NH_3 is liberated.

$$\text{Glycine} \xrightarrow{-NH_3} \text{Glyoxylic acid}$$

   (b) Glyoxylic acid may be decarboxylated further to produce CO_2 and formate.
3. Glycine participates in the synthesis of porphyrins. This takes place along the glycine-succinate cycle, which is finally degraded into succinate and formaldehyde. The actual synthesis of porphyrin involves the following reactions:
   (a) Succinyl-CoA condenses with glycine to form α-amino-β-ketoadipic acid. Decarboxylation of the latter results in the formation of δ-aminolevulinic acid, which may condense with another molecule to form porphyrin.

Glycine + Succinyl-CoA ⟶ α-Amino-β-ketoadipic acid

↓ $-CO_2$

δ-Aminolevulinic acid

↓ × 2

Porphyrin

(b) Aminolevulinate may split to form succinate and formaldehyde.

4. Glycine forms 'pseudo-peptides' with bile acids and benzoic acid in liver.
   (a) Glycine with cholic acid (bile acid) forms glycocholate.
   (b) Glycine with benzoate forms hippurate. Formation of hippurate by glycine is an example of detoxication.
5. Glycine can be synthesised from threonine when the latter gives out acetaldehyde.

Threonine ⟶ Glycine + Acetaldehyde

6. Glycine participates in the synthesis of a purine ring. Glycine combines with ammonia, formate and CO_2 to give rise to a purine ring (*see* **Fig. 6.19**).
7. Glycine is required for the synthesis of glutathione which is a tripeptide. Glutathione is a compound of glutamic acid, cysteine and glycine. The formation of glutathione involves two steps:
   (a) Combination of glutamic acid and cysteine to form γ-glutamylcysteine
   (b) Condensation of γ-glutamylcysteine with glycine to form glutathione

   ATP is required for both (a) and (b) steps. The major metabolic role of glutathione is that it functions as a coenzyme for glyceraldehyde-3-phosphate dehydrogenase. Glutathione protects haemoglobin from being oxidised by H_2O_2 (**Fig. 21.9**).

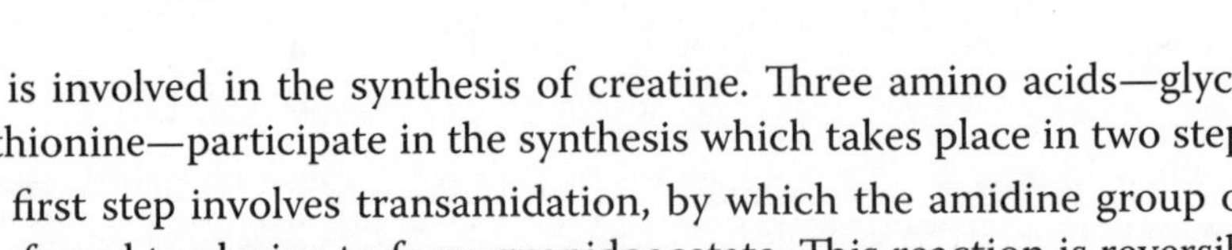

Figure 21.9 Glutathione (reduced form)—a tripeptide.

8. Glycine is involved in the synthesis of creatine. Three amino acids—glycine, arginine and methionine—participate in the synthesis which takes place in two steps:
   (a) The first step involves transamidation, by which the amidine group of arginine is transferred to glycine to form guanidoacetate. This reaction is reversible and takes place in the kidneys. Arginine after losing the amidine group forms ornithine.
   (b) The second step involves transmethylation, when the methyl group from activated methionine is transferred to guanidoacetate to form creatine. This reaction takes place in the liver.

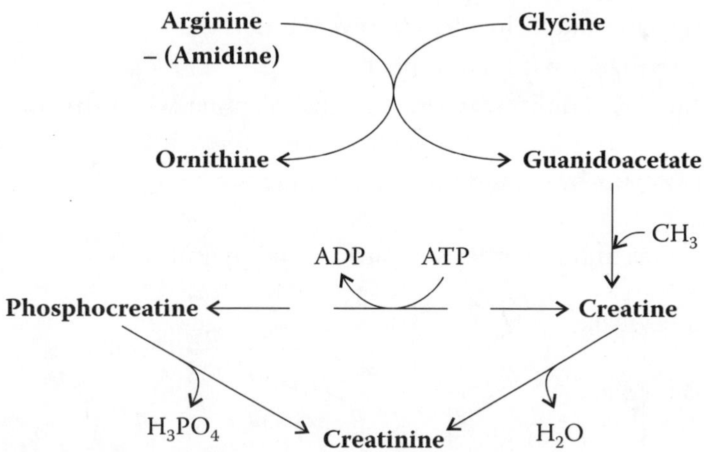

Figure 21.10 Synthesis of creatine and phosphocreatine—formation of creatinine.

Creatine is stored in muscle as phosphocreatine which is an important storage form of high-energy phosphate compound. Under physiological pH and temperature, phosphocreatine spontaneously loses phosphoric acid, leaving behind creatine. Creatine may lose water to form creatinine, which is excreted in urine (**Fig. 21.10**).

Alanine (CH_3CHNH_2COOH)

Alanine is the simplest of optically active amino acids. It is non-essential and is readily synthesised in the body. It is both glucogenic and ketogenic.

On deamination, alanine forms pyruvic acid which gets oxidised to CO_2 and H_2O in the citric acid cycle to yield energy.

Pyruvic acid may also undergo transamination to form alanine.

β-alanine is a constituent of pantothenic acid.

Alanine is also an end product of the catabolism of pyrimidines such as cytosine and uracil.

Serine ($CH_2OHCHNH_2COOH$)

Serine is a non-essential and glucogenic amino acid.

Besides being present in proteins, it is a constituent of phospholipids. Serine is the precursor of glycine and is formed in the body by the addition of formaldehyde to glycine. Formaldehyde which forms the β-carbon of serine is carried by an intermediate compound, 5-hydroxymethyl tetrahydrofolic acid.

Serine undergoes a variety of metabolic reactions. These are illustrated in **Figure 21.11**.

1. Serine on deamination forms pyruvate. The reaction is catalysed by serine dehydrogenase and pyridoxal phosphate.
2. Serine with phosphate forms phosphoserine which forms phosphoproteins with proteins.

3. Serine forms glycine and formaldehyde reversibly.
4. It participates in the formation of cephalins.
5. Decarboxylation of serine gives rise to ethanolamine which on methylation forms choline.
6. Serine forms cysteine by condensing with homocysteine, which in turn is converted to homoserine.
7. Serine participates in the synthesis of purines and pyrimidines.

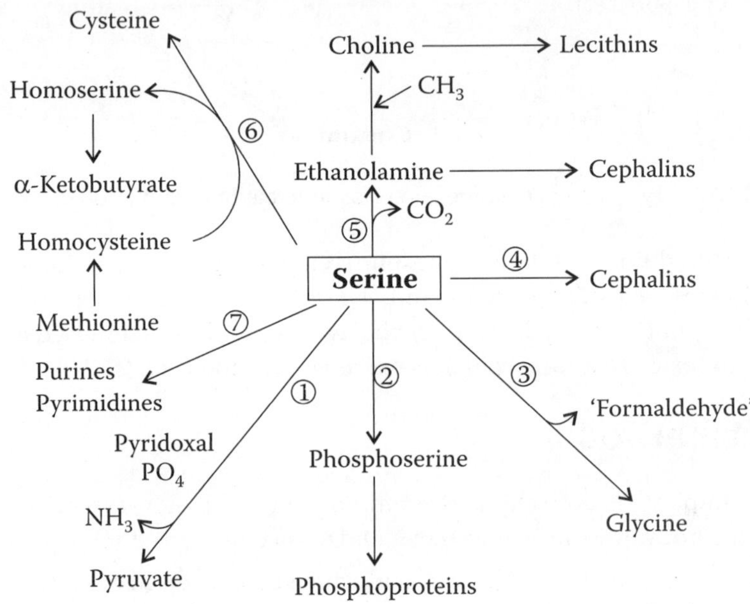

Figure 21.11 Metabolism of serine.

Lysine ($NH_2CH_2CH_2CH_2CH_2CHNH_2COOH$)

Lysine is an essential amino acid. It is the only amino acid which on deamination keeps away from participating in transamination reactions. The reactions of lysine are as follows (**Fig. 21.12**):

1. Oxidative deamination to α-aminoadipic acid
2. This is followed by deamination to α-ketoadipic acid
3. α-ketoadipic acid is decarboxylated to glutaric acid

Fate of glutaric acid:

- A minor pathway involves oxidation of glutaric acid to α-ketoglutaric acid which may enter the citric acid cycle.
- A major pathway involves decarboxylation of glutaric acid to butyric acid which may be oxidised to acetoacetic acid and acetic acid.
- Lysine undergoes bacterial decomposition in the large intestines to form cadaverine which is toxic. It is detoxified later.

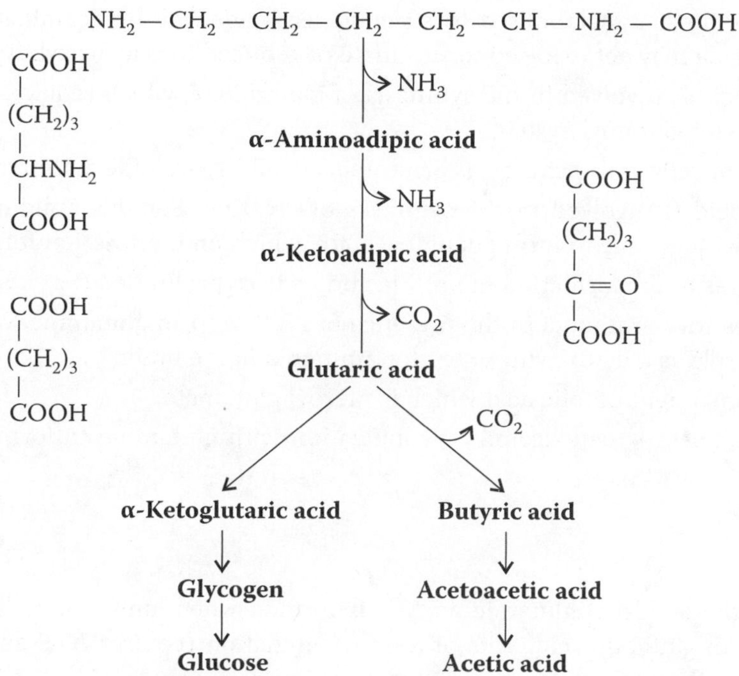

Figure 21.12 Lysine metabolism.

Glutamic Acid [$COOH(CH_2)_2CHNH_2COOH$]

Glutamic acid is an important glucogenic amino acid, present in high concentration in brain tissues. It plays a special role in the brain metabolism. Important metabolic reactions are as follows:

1. Glutamic acid is synthesised from α-ketoglutaric acid, which on transamination forms glutamic acid. Deamination of glutamic acid by glutamic dehydrogenase forms α-ketoglutarate.

   Glutamic acid may get transaminated with pyruvic acid to form α-ketoglutaric acid and alanine. This reaction is catalysed by a transaminase. Both reactions are reversible.

   (a) Glutamic acid $\xrightleftharpoons{-NH_3}$ α-Ketoglutaric acid

   (b) Glutamic acid + Pyruvic acid $\rightleftharpoons$ α-Ketoglutaric acid

2. Glutamic acid is formed from the metabolic breakdown of histidine.
3. Glutamic acid on decarboxylation forms γ-aminobutyric acid (GABA). The reaction is catalysed by a decarboxylase in the presence of pyridoxal phosphate which acts as a coenzyme.

   GABA is a regulator of neuronal activity and is a naturally occurring tranquilliser. It is presumed that a transaminase present in brain may destroy GABA leading to epileptiform convulsions and administration of an inhibitor. Amino oxyacetate was found to bring about general sedation and relaxation of muscles.

GABA is further metabolised to succinic semi-aldehyde by deamination. Succinic semi-aldehyde may get oxidised to succinate or reduced to γ-hydroxybutyrate.

4. Glutamic acid is involved in the synthesis of glutathione, which requires combination of glycine with glutamyl cysteine.
5. On reduction, glutamic acid forms ornithine, citrulline, arginine and urea (urea cycle).
6. Glutamic acid is involved in the synthesis of creatine. For this amidine of arginine combines with glycine to form guanidoacetate, which on methylation forms creatine.
7. It contributes to the formation of proline and hydroxyproline.
8. It combines with ammonia in the presence of ATP to form glutamine, which plays an important role as a detoxifying agent for ammonia in the brain.

   It is a constituent of folic acid which is pteroyl glutamate.
9. Phenylacetic acid is detoxicated by conjugation with glutamine to form phenylacetyl glutamine.

Glutamine

Glutamine is the amide of glutamic acid. It is formed when ammonia is detoxicated by conjugation with glutamic acid. This process of amidation requires ATP and is catalysed by glutamine synthetase.

$$\mathrm{COOH(CH_2)_2\underset{\substack{|\\ NH_2}}{C}HCOOH + NH_3 \longrightarrow CONH_2(CH_2)_2\underset{\substack{|\\ NH_2}}{C}HCOOH}$$

Glutamine is deaminated by a special enzyme, glutaminase, which is present in the kidneys liberating free NH_3. This mechanism of storing or releasing NH_3 by glutamine helps in the regulation of acid–base balance of the body.

Glutamine itself acts as a conjugating agent in detoxication of phenylacetic acid, resulting in the formation of phenylacetyl glutamine (**Fig. 21.13**).

It participates in the synthesis of purines, pyrimidines and NAD.

Proline and Hydroxyproline

Proline and hydroxyproline are non-essential and glucogenic amino acids. They are present in collagen.

They are pyrrolidines having a cyclic structure (page 57).

They do not possess a free NH_2 group but have an NH group. Strictly speaking, they are imino acids rather than amino acids.

The hydroxylation of proline to hydroxyproline is not reversible and requires ascorbic acid. Proline is further metabolised to form glutamate by the opening of the ring in the presence of proline oxidase present in kidney. Proline, glutamic acid and ornithine are reversibly converted to one another.

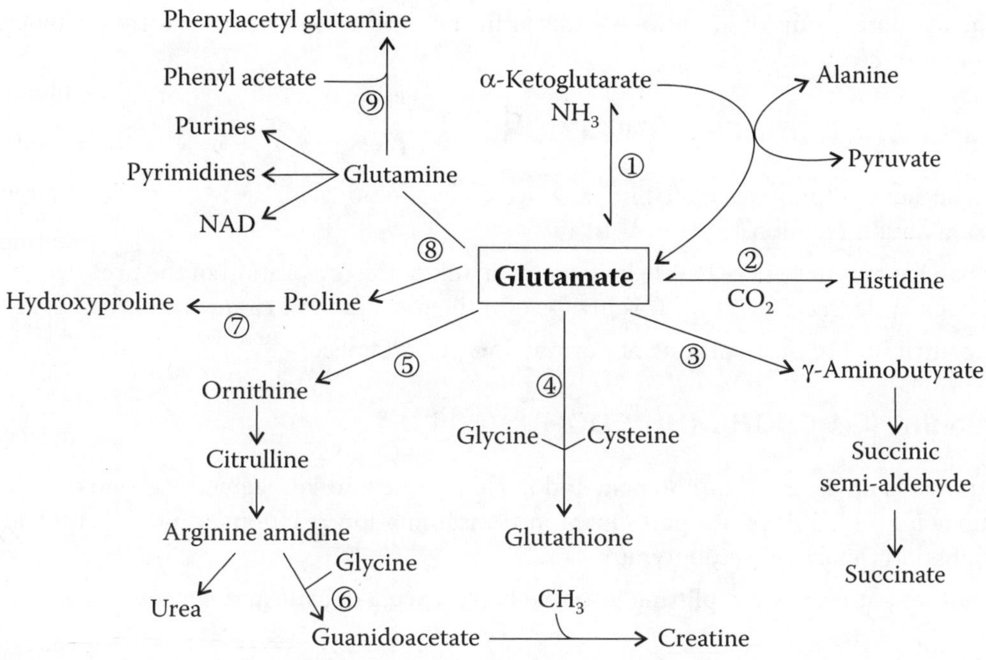

Figure 21.13 Metabolism of glutamic acid.

Arginine and Ornithine

$$\underset{\underset{NH_2}{|}}{\underset{C=NH}{|}}\!\!HNCH_2CH_2CH_2CHNH_2COOH \quad \text{(Arginine)}$$

$$NH_2CH_2CH_2CH_2CHNH_2COOH \quad \text{(Ornithine)}$$

Arginine is a glucogenic amino acid and an important metabolite in the formation of urea. It is an important metabolite of the urea cycle and participates in the formation of urea. Arginine is broken down to form urea and ornithine by the action of arginase in liver. The relationship and interconversion between arginine, ornithine, proline and glutamic acid as occurring in the urea cycle is shown below.

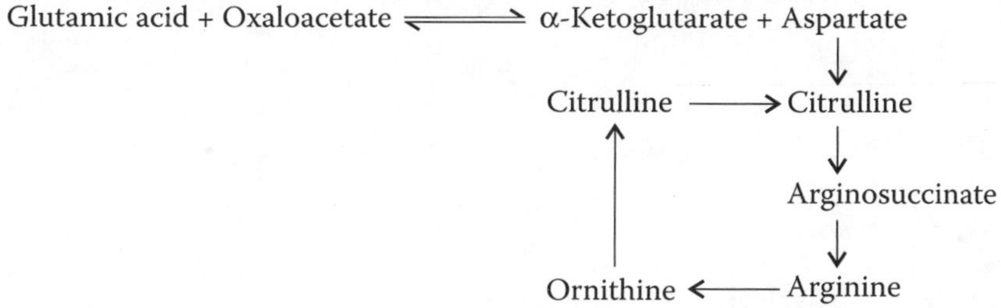

The amidine group of arginine is utilised in the synthesis of guanidoacetate which is a precursor of creatine.

Aspartic Acid ($COOHCH_2CHNH_2COOH$)

Aspartic acid is non-essential and a glucogenic amino acid. It is involved mainly in transamination reactions.

It participates in the urea cycle by forming a link in the integration of the urea cycle with the Krebs cycle (*see* **Fig. 21.5**). It is involved in the formation of camosine and anserine.

It contributes to the synthesis of purines and pyrimidines.

Threonine ($CH_2CHOHCHNH_2COOH$)

Threonine is an essential amino acid and is glucogenic and ketogenic. It is one of the few amino acids which does not participate in transamination reactions, though it undergoes deamination to form α-ketobutyrate.

Another pathway is its splitting into two halves, acetaldehyde and glycine.

$$\underset{\textbf{Threonine}}{CH_3CHOHCHNH_2COOH} \xrightarrow{-NH_2} \underset{\textbf{α-Ketobutyric acid}}{CH_3CH_2COCOOH}$$

$$\underset{\textbf{Threonine}}{CH_3CHOHCHNH_2COOH} \longrightarrow \underset{\textbf{Acetaldehyde}}{CH_3CHO} + \underset{\textbf{Glycine}}{CH_2NH_2COOH}$$

Valine, Leucine and Isoleucine

Valine, leucine and isoleucine are **branched chain amino acids**. All three are essential and contain branched chain aliphatic groups. Valine is glucogenic, leucine is ketogenic while isoleucine is both glucogenic and ketogenic. All the three amino acids undergo similar reactions during their metabolic breakdown. They are initially deaminated to their corresponding α-keto acids which further undergo decarboxylation, followed by a sequence of reactions similar to those undergone by fatty acids.

Valine and isoleucine form propionate while leucine and some amount of isoleucine form ketone bodies as their end products.

Valine

$$CH_3-\underset{\underset{CH_3}{|}}{CH}-\underset{\underset{NH_2}{|}}{CH}-COOH$$

Valine is α-amino-isovaleric acid. It is glucogenic.

Valine on deamination forms α-keto-isovaleric acid, which gets further metabolised to form isobutyric acid. The latter forms propionic acid which gets degraded to its CoA derivatives and finally to succinyl-CoA which is a metabolite of the Krebs cycle.

Valine ⟶ α-Ketoisovaleric acid ⟶ Isobutyric acid
↓
Propionic acid
↓
Krebs cycle ⟵ Succinyl-CoA ⟵ CoA derivatives

Leucine

Leucine is α-amino-isocaproic acid.

$$\begin{array}{ccccccccc} CH_3 & - & CH & - & CH_2 & - & CH & - & COOH \\ & & | & & & & | & & \\ & & CH_3 & & & & NH_2 & & \end{array}$$

Leucine is a ketogenic amino acid. On deamination, it forms α-keto-isocaproic acid which gets further metabolised to successively form isovaleryl-CoA, β-methylcrotonyl-CoA, β-hydroxy-β-methylglutaryl-CoA, (HMG-CoA) and finally to acetyl-CoA.

Leucine ⟶ α-Keto-isocaproic acid ⟶ Isovaleryl-CoA
↓
β-Methylcrotonyl-CoA
↓
Acetyl-CoA ⟶ β-Hydroxy-β-methylglutaryl-CoA

HMG-CoA is an intermediate in the synthesis of cholesterol.

Isoleucine

Isoleucine is α-amino-β-methylvaleric acid.

$$\begin{array}{ccccccccc} & & & & & & NH_2 & & \\ & & & & & & | & & \\ CH_3 & - & CH_2 & - & CH & - & CH & - & COOH \\ & & & & | & & & & \\ & & & & CH_3 & & & & \end{array}$$

Isoleucine is ketogenic and glucogenic. On deamination, it forms α-keto-β-methylvaleric acid which further metabolises via α-methylbutyryl-CoA to ultimately form propionyl-CoA and acetyl-CoA. Propionyl-CoA leads to the formation of glucose while acetyl-CoA forms acetoacetic acid.

Isoleucine ⟶ α-Keto-β-methylvaleric acid ⟶ α-Methylbutyryl-CoA ⟶ Propionyl-CoA + Acetyl-CoA

Propionyl-CoA ↓ Glucose; Acetyl-CoA ↓ Acetoacetic acid

It may be noted that these three amino acids are examples of proteins integrating with fat and carbohydrate metabolism.

Maple Syrup Urine Disease

A metabolic block in the metabolism of the three branched chain amino acids—valine, leucine and isoleucine—gives rise to an inborn error of metabolism called Maple Syrup Urine disease in infants. The characteristic feature of this disorder is the unusual odour of the urine, similar to that of maple syrup, due to excessive excretion of these amino acids and the corresponding α-keto acids. The concentration of these amino acids in blood is also high. The affected infants are mentally retarded.

Histidine

Histidine contains an imidazole ring. It is nutritionally semi-essential as it can be synthesised in an adequate amount by adult humans, but is essential for the growth of young animals. It is a glucogenic amino acid, because it gives rise to glutamic acid during its metabolism.

Histidine, besides being an integral part of tissue protein, is found in the muscles as carnosine and anserine which are conjugated compounds of histidine. Carnosine is alanylhistidine and anserine is alanyl-methylhistidine.

The metabolic fate of histidine is complex.

It follows two major pathways, which are as follows:

1. Histamine pathway
2. Urocanic acid pathway

Histidine also undergoes a minor metabolic pathway, leading to the formation of conjugation products, namely carnosine, anserine and ergothioneine.

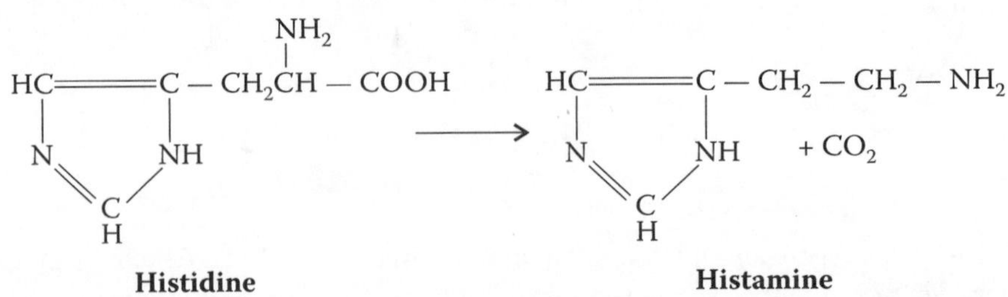

Histidine → **Histamine**

Histamine pathway: Histidine is decarboxylated to histamine by a specific histidine decarboxylase present in the liver, kidneys and intestines. The same reaction is catalysed in many tissues by a non-specific aromatic amino acid decarboxylase which is also known to catalyse the decarboxylation of 3,4-dihydroxyphenylalanine (dopa) and 5-hydroxytryptophan.

Histamine is a powerful stimulant of gastric HCl secretion. It is also a powerful vasodilator and causes lowering of blood pressure. A larger dose may cause vascular collapse. Histamine is implicated in urticarial and anaphylactic reactions and is released following burns. Because of its pharmacological potency, it is necessary that its concentration in blood is regulated. In man, the histamine level is maintained low by

- Excreting it in urine as such or by the action of histaminase which disposes histamine by its acetyl derivative after methylation
- Oxidising it to imidazoleacetic acid, which may get excreted in the urine as such or as a ribotide or as a methyl derivative.

Urocanic acid pathway: This is the major pathway of histidine degradation. It takes place in the liver by the action of the enzyme histidase.

- When histidine gets deaminated to form urocanic acid, which in turn is converted by urocanase to an intermediate, formiminoglutamic acid (figlu).
- Figlu is ultimately metabolised to form ammonia, glutamic acid and formic acid. But prior to the ultimate degradation, figlu is split to form the formimino group (**Fig. 21.14**).
- The formimino group is transferred to tetrahydrofolic acid (FH_4) to form formiminotetrahydrofolic acid.
- Then ammonia is split off to form a formyl folic acid derivative, which serves as the source of one-carbon moiety.

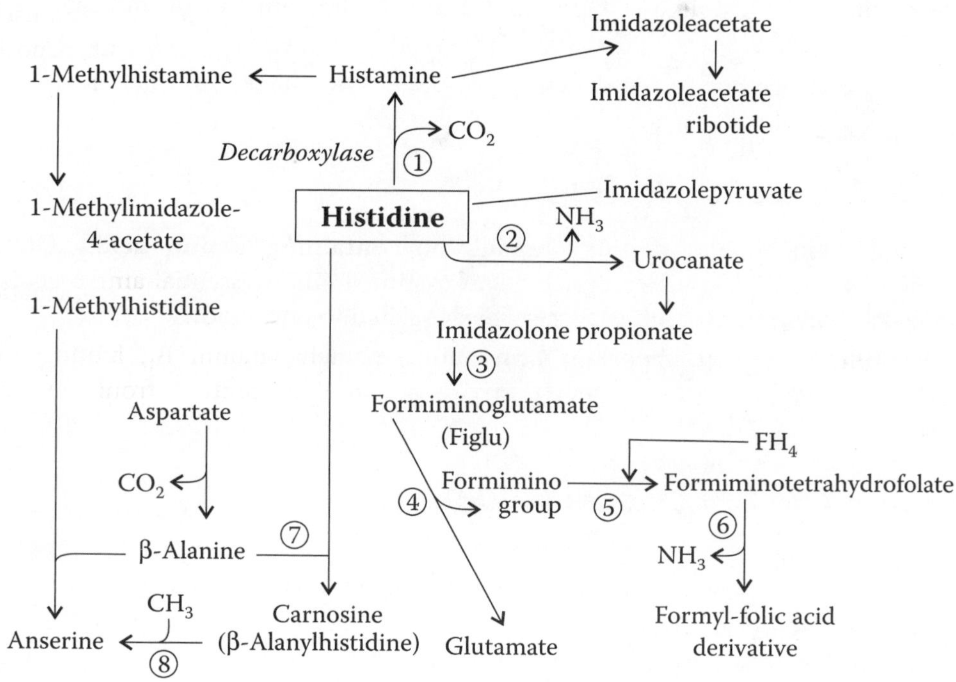

Figure 21.14 Histidine metabolism.

Because of these metabolic reactions, figlu is excreted in urine, in folic acid deficiency, thereby indicating impairment of further metabolism of figlu.

Minor pathway:

- Histidine combines with alanine to form the pseudo-peptide carnosine.
- Carnosine may be methylated to form anserine which may also be formed when 1-methylhistidine combines with β-alanine. These two compounds are found in muscles. Ergothioneine and the betaine of thiol histidine are other histidine compounds found in red blood cells and liver.

Histidine compounds have a reducing property and interfere with certain methods used in the determination of glucose and uric acid. Large amounts of histidine are excreted in urine during pregnancy from the fifth week up to childbirth. It is said that during this period, histidase which splits histidine in liver is absent and this helps in conserving histidine which is indispensable for the growth of the foetus.

Inherited Disorders of Histidine Metabolism

Two types of disorders have been noted:

1. **Imidazole aminoaciduria:** This is a rare condition, characterised by excretion of histidine, methylhistidine, carnosine and anserine in abnormally large quantities. It is also associated with cerebromacular degeneration, which involves cerebral degeneration and blindness.
2. **Histidinuria:** This is also a rare disorder, characterised by the presence of increased concentration of histidine in blood and urine. A large amount of imidazole pyruvic acid is excreted.

Both disorders are due to the deficiency of the enzyme histidase which is required to convert histidine to urocanic acid.

Methionine, Cysteine and Cystine

Methionine, cysteine and cystine are **sulphur-containing amino acids**. Of these, methionine is essential, whereas cysteine and cystine are non-essential amino acids. The metabolism of these three amino acids is closely related to one another.

Certain physiologically important compounds, namely vitamin B_1, biotin, anterior pituitary hormone and glutathione, derive their sulphur content from these three amino acids.

Methionine (CH_3-S-$CH_2CH_2CHNH_2COOH$)

Methionine contains sulphur and has a methyl group. It is essential for growth and maintains nitrogen balance. Methionine follows three important metabolic routes:

1. Transfer of methyl group
2. Utilisation of homocysteine
3. Utilisation of methyl group in transmethylation reactions

Transfer of methyl group: Methionine is the most important methyl donor in the body. It readily gives up its methyl group for synthesis of various compounds. The demethylated derivative is homocysteine.

Utilisation of homocysteine: Homocysteine, which contains sulphur, condenses with serine to form cystathionine. This involves transfer of sulphur to the carbon chain of serine (**Fig. 21.15**).

Cystathionine is further split to yield cysteine and homoserine (**Fig. 21.15**). Homoserine undergoes deamination to form α-ketobutyrate.

The condensation of homocysteine with serine to form cystathionine and the splitting of cystathionine are catalysed by cystathionine synthetase and coenzyme pyridoxal phosphate.

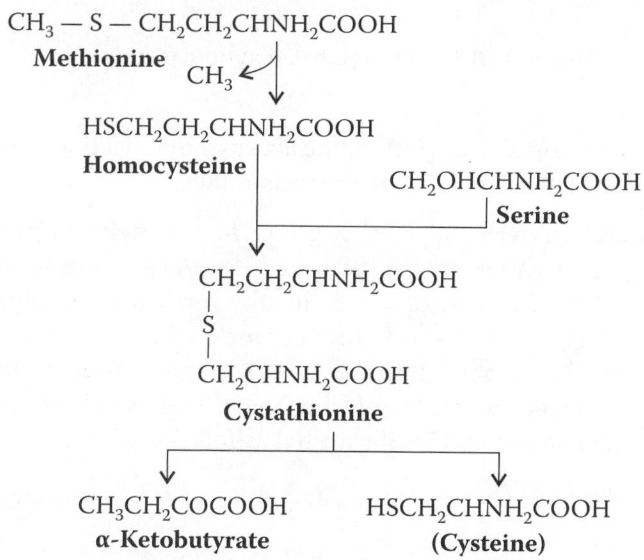

Figure 21.15 Utilisation of homocysteine.

Utilisation of methyl groups in transmethylation reactions: Transmethylation is a process by which the methyl group of methionine and certain other compounds containing methyl groups are transferred to other compounds. By this process, various physiologically active compounds such as choline, creatine and epinephrine are synthesised in the body.

Transmethylation also plays an important role in detoxication reactions. For example, toxic pyridine derivatives such as nicotinic acid are detoxified by transmethylation.

Besides methionine, the other methyl donors are choline and betaine. There is a close interrelation between the methylation reactions of methionine, choline and betaine. These reactions which are reversible are illustrated in **Figure 21.16**. The mechanism of the transmethylation reactions of methionine, choline and betaine is discussed in the following section.

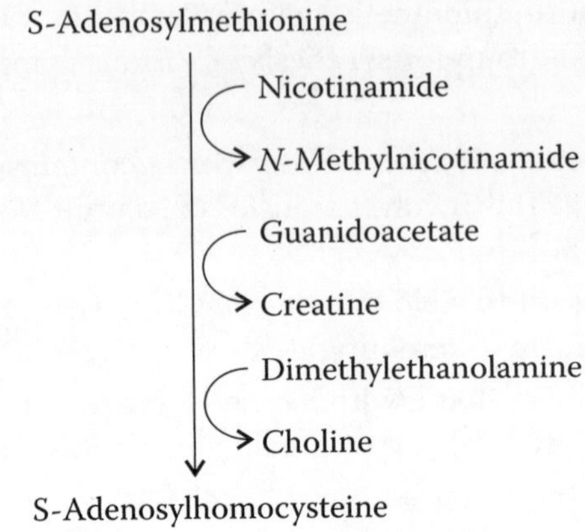

Figure 21.16 Transmethylation from methionine.

Transmethylation of methionine: Methionine acts as a methylating agent in the formation of (i) choline, (ii) creatine and (ii) *N*-methylnicotinamide.

Methionine donates its terminal methyl group for methylation of these compounds. For this, methionine requires to be activated by ATP. Activation is catalysed by a methionine-activating enzyme of liver, in the presence of cofactors Mg^{++} ions and glutathione (GSH). The 'active methionine' which is formed is known as S-adenosylmethionine. In the activation reaction, ATP gives away its adenosine moiety to methionine and loses three molecules of phosphate, one as orthophosphate and two as pyrophosphate. The activation may be illustrated as follows:

$$\text{Methionine} + \text{ATP} \longrightarrow \text{S-Adenosylmethionine} + \text{Pyrophosphate} + \text{Orthophosphate.}$$

Active methionine which contains adenine, attached to methionine through sulphur, acts as the methyl donor in transmethylation reactions. The S-methyl linkage in active methionine is a high-energy bond. This increases the free energy, chemical reactivity and lability of the methyl group.

$$\text{Adenine-ribose} - \overset{\overset{\large CH_3}{\wr}}{\underset{+}{S}} - CH_2CH_2CHNH_2COOH$$

S-Adenosylmethionine

Synthesis of choline: Choline is a component of phospholipids and is a lipotropic factor. It contains three methyl groups. Choline is formed by methylation of dimethylethanolamine which in turn is derived from ethanolamine by successive methylation by active methionine. Ethanolamine is derived from serine by decarboxylation (**Fig. 21.17**).

Formation of creatine: Creatine is formed by methylation of guanidoacetate. Synthesis of creatine may be described to occur in two steps:

(i) Formation of guanidoacetate, which takes place in the kidney, is accomplished by the transfer of the amidine group of arginine to glycine

(ii) Methylation of guanidoacetate by active methionine, to form creatine, takes place in the liver and the reaction is catalysed by the enzyme guanidoacetate methyl transferase.

Formation of N-methylnicotinamide: Nicotinamide is excreted in urine as its methyl derivative *N*-methylnicotinamide, after conjugation with the methyl group as a detoxication mechanism. This is necessary because of the toxicity of nicotinic acid. Methylation of nicotinamide is accomplished by 'active' methionine.

The three important methylation reactions of methionine have been diagrammatically illustrated in **Figure 21.16.**

Transmethylation of choline and betaine: Choline which contains three methyl groups can methylate homocysteine to convert it to methionine. For this, choline must be first oxidised to betaine which then serves as the methylating agent (**Fig. 21.17**).

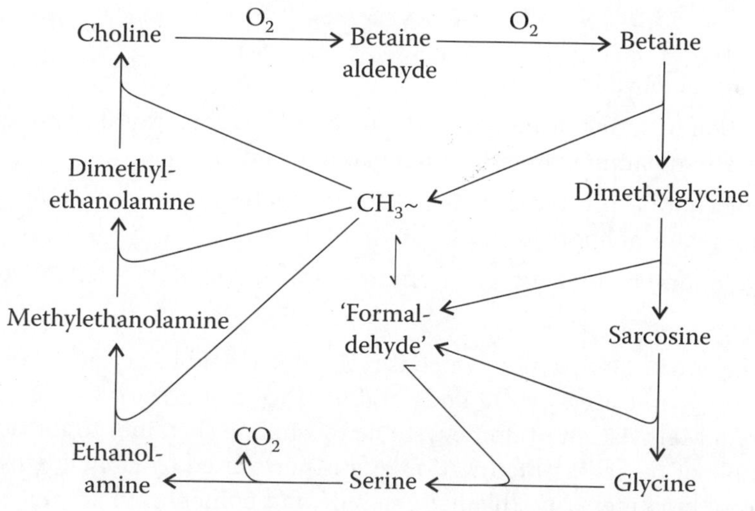

Figure 21.17 Interrelations of choline and glycine derivatives in transmethylation.

Betaine containing three methyl groups is acted upon by a specific transmethylase which catalyses the transfer of one methyl group from betaine, leaving behind dimethylglycine. The methyl group is utilised for the conversion of homocysteine to methionine. Folic acid and vitamin B_{12} are required for the conversion. One of the methyl groups of dimethylglycine is transferred and oxidised to a formaldehyde fragment, leaving sarcosine which is monomethylglycine. The only methyl group of sarcosine is also removed and oxidised to a formaldehyde fragment leaving behind glycine, which in turn can be interconverted to serine by the addition of a 'formaldehyde' fragment. Decarboxylation of serine produces ethanolamine. This is methylated in three successive steps to methylethanolamine, dimethylethanolamine and choline. Oxidation of choline produces betaine. These reactions are important in connection with the phenomenon of lipotropism.

The methyl donors, methyl acceptors and the respective methyl derivatives are enlisted in **Table 21.3.**

Table 21.3 Donors and Acceptors of Methyl Groups

Methyl Donors	Methyl Acceptors	Methylated Derivatives
	Ethanolamine	Methylethanolamine
	Methylethanolamine	Dimethylethanolamine
S-Adenosyl-methionine, betaine } ⟶ CH_3 ~ →	Dimethylethanolamine	Choline
↓	Guanidoacetate	Creatine
Formaldehyde	Nicotinamide	*N*-methylnicotinamide
↓ Formate	Norepinephrine	Epinephrine
↓	Homocysteine	Methionine
CO_2	Carnosine	Anserine

Glycine + Formaldehyde ⟶ Serine.

Decarboxylation of serine produces ethanolamine. This is methylated in three successive steps to methylethanolamine, dimethylethanolamine and choline.

Oxidation of choline produces betaine. These reactions are important in connection with the phenomenon of lipotropism.

The methyl donors, methyl acceptors and the respective methyl derivatives are enlisted in **Table 21.3.**

Labile methyl groups: Methylation which is reversible is said to be caused by labile methyl groups. They are synthesised by the body and for this, a source of folic acid and vitamin B_{12} are required. Methylation of homocysteine by choline (betaine) to form methionine is the only example of reversible methylation and is performed by labile methyl groups. The methyl groups of creatine, *N*-methylnicotinamide and epinephrine are not labile, because their initial methylations are irreversible.

Fate of methyl groups:

1. Methyl groups are utilised in the intact form for various transmethylation reactions (*see* **Fig. 21.17**). The labile methyl groups of betaine or choline can be used to replace methionine in the diet.
2. Ultimately, the methyl groups are oxidised to CO_2. Formaldehyde and formate are intermediaries formed in the oxidation.
3. The methyl carbon can participate in the formation of one-carbon units, namely formaldehyde and formate fragments. These can conjugate with glycine to synthesise serine.

Metabolism of one-carbon units: One-carbon units are (i) methyl groups (CH_3), (ii) formaldehyde or hydroxymethyl (HCHO) and (iii) formate or formyl (HCOOH).

The sources of methyl groups have been already discovered. These are S-adenosylmethionine and betaine. Free formaldehyde is derived from the oxidation of methyl groups of sarcosine and dimethylglycine. Hydroxymethyl fragments are derived from the β-carbon of serine. Formyl groups are derived from free formate, released from formylkynurenine, δ-carbon of glycine and δ-aminolevulinate.

The formimino fragment is derived from formiminoglutamate, a metabolite of histidine.

Both formate and formaldehyde units are interconvertible by means of a redox reaction. The transport of these units is accomplished by coenzymes tetrahydrofolic acid (FH_4) and vitamin B_{12}. The latter facilitates reduction of formate to formaldehyde.

Vitamin B_{12} also aids in the preservation of compounds in the reduced condition, for example the SH state of homocysteine. This is necessary for the acceptance of formaldehyde units prior to conversion to methyl groups. In any case, vitamin B_{12} and FH_4 are required for the synthesis of methyl groups.

Inborn Error of Methionine Metabolism

Homocystinuria is a rare inborn error of methionine metabolism, characterised by excretion of a large quantity of homocystine in urine and a high concentration of homocystine and methionine in plasma.

The clinical manifestations are mental retardation, skeletal deformities involving spine, bilateral posterior dislocation of the lenses and enlarged liver. The nature of the defect is due to a genetic deficiency or absence of the hepatic cystathionine synthetase, which under normal conditions is responsible for the condensation of homocysteine with serine to form cystathionine. Deficiency of the enzyme results in the accumulation of plasma homocystine and methionine and causes homocystinuria.

Cysteine and Cystine

Cysteine and cystine are sulphur-containing amino acids.

They are non-essential and glucogenic. Cysteine and homocysteine are reversibly convertible to cystine and homocystine, respectively, by oxidation and reduction reactions (**Fig. 21.18**).

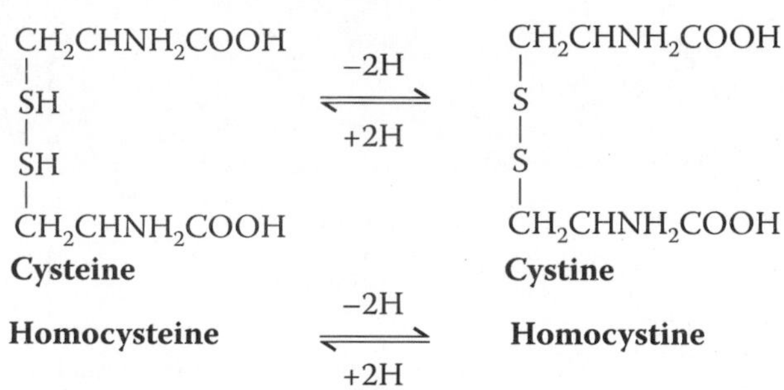

Figure 21.18 Reversible conversion of cysteine and homocysteine.

Cysteine differs from cystine in that it has two hydrogen atoms more. Similar is the case with homocysteine and homocystine. The oxidation of cysteine is catalysed by cytochrome C and cytochrome oxidase. The reduction of cystine to cysteine is effected by reducing agents in the tissues such as sulphydryl groups of glutathione, certain enzymes and H_2S. This cysteine and cystine form an important pair of the oxidation–reduction system in reactions of biological oxidation. Insulin, melanin, coenzyme A, hair and nails derive their sulphur content from cysteine. Glutathione which is an important reactivator of enzymes is a tripeptide composed of cysteine, glutamic acid and glycine.

Synthesis: The carbon skeleton and the amino group of cysteine are provided by serine whereas the sulphur is derived from methionine, which after activation with ATP gives up its methyl group to some appropriate acceptor, leaving homocysteine.

Homocysteine condenses with serine to form the thioether cystathionine, which is split specifically to cysteine and homoserine (**Fig. 21.19**). Homoserine undergoes deamination to form α-ketobutyrate, which is excreted in the urine. These reactions are catalysed by cystathionine synthetase and the coenzyme pyridoxal phosphate. The synthesis of cysteine from methionine is irreversible.

Metabolic reactions: The metabolic reactions of cysteine and cystine are as follows (**Fig. 21.19**):

1. Cysteine is reversibly oxidised to cystine.

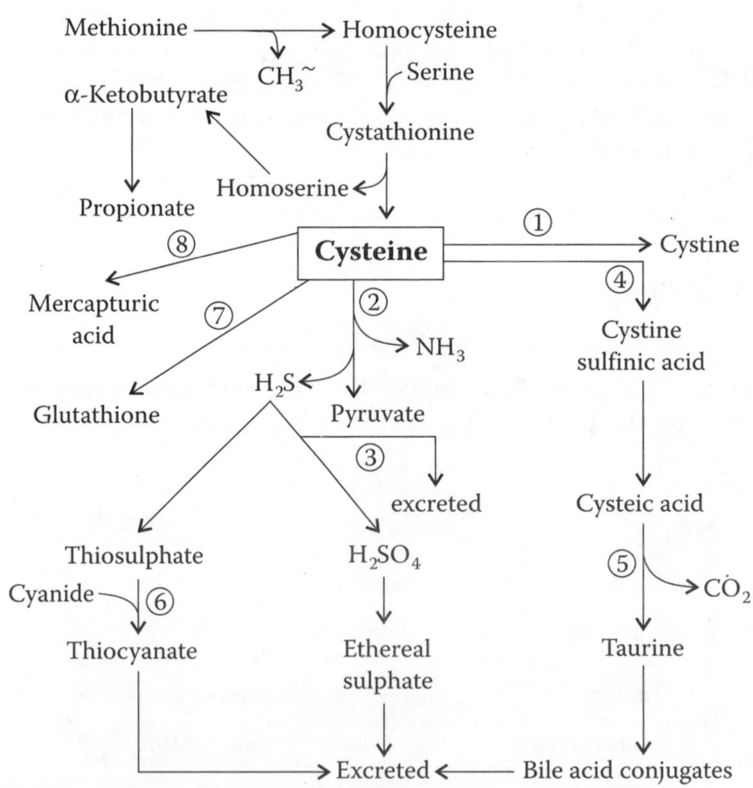

Figure 21.19 Metabolism of cysteine and cystine.

2. Cysteine is converted by deamination and desulphydration to pyruvic acid. NH_3 and H_2S are liberated. The presence of pyridoxal phosphate is required for the conversion. Formation of pyruvic acid shows that cysteine is a glucogenic amino acid.
3. The H_2S evolved is oxidised to inorganic sulphate which is excreted in urine and faeces. This forms the major route. A minor fraction of the total sulphate in the urine is excreted in the form of ethereal sulphate. The major sources of urinary sulphur are cystine, cysteine and methionine derived from dietary proteins.
4. Some amount of cysteine is metabolised via pathways of cysteine-sulphinic acid to cysteic acid.
5. Cysteic acid is decarboxylated to form taurine which participates in conjugation of bile acids.
6. Thiosulphate, another product of sulphur oxidation, is used in the detoxication of cyanide to form thiocyanate. The detoxication is catalysed by the enzyme rhodenase.
7. Cysteine is utilised in the synthesis of glutathione. Glutamic acid combines with cysteine to form glutamylcysteine, which condenses with glycine to form glutathione.
8. Cysteine takes part in detoxication. Acetylated cysteine couples with certain aromatic compounds to form mercapturic acid.

Inborn Errors in the Metabolism of Cystine

Two distinct types of inborn errors in the metabolism of cystine are described. These are cystinuria and cystinosis:

1. **Cystinuria:** The characteristic feature of this disorder is excretion of a large amount of cystine (20–30 times normal) in the urine. It is also associated with the excretion of a fairly high quantity of basic amino acids (diamino acids) such as lysine, arginine and ornithine. The condition is complicated by recurrent formation of calculi in the renal tract. The lesion in cystinuria is traced to a defect in an enzyme system of the kidney which is responsible for the tubular reabsorption of compounds having diamine structures such as cystine. This leads to defective reabsorption of cystine and consequently in its excessive excretion. In normal conditions, cystine is utilised rapidly and does not appear in the urine. The mechanism of calculi formation in cystinurics is explained as follows. Cystine is one of the least soluble amino acids and in urine with a pH range from 5 to 7, it can be kept in solution only to the extent of 300–400 mg per litre. But in patients excreting 1/2–1 grams of cystine per day, the concentration of the substance reaches a saturation level, particularly at night time, when urine is passed in the most concentrated form. Cystine crystals separate out of the solution and form calculi. The plasma level of cystine in these patients is not elevated.
2. **Cystinosis:** This disorder presents a complex syndrome. It is described under different names, namely cystine storage disease, De Toni–Fanconi syndrome, cystine rickets and cystinosis. The characteristic features are marked aminoaciduria, renal glycosuria and low plasma inorganic phosphate. The condition is associated with vitamin D-resistant rickets in childhood and osteomalacia in adult life. Other common features are chronic acidosis, proteinuria, polyuria and electrolyte disturbance which may lead to potassium depletion. The cause is not known. An important biochemical finding

is the widespread deposition of cystine crystals in bone marrow and lymph glands. Prognosis is poor and death ensues before puberty.

Tryptophan

Tryptophan is an essential amino acid. Deficiency causes tissue wasting and negative nitrogen balance. Tryptophan is the only amino acid containing the indole nucleus. It has an alanine side chain. It is glucogenic and ketogenic in its metabolic pathways (**Fig. 21.20**).

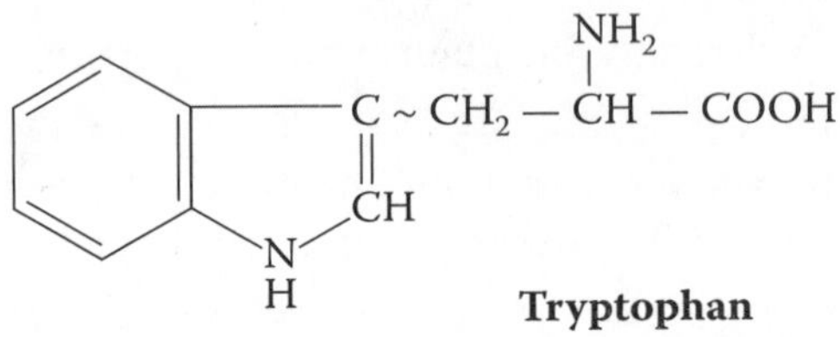

Tryptophan

Tryptophan is the precursor of an important physiological compound called serotonin, which is a vasoconstrictor present in serum, gastrointestinal tract and central nervous system.

The chief end product of tryptophan metabolism is nicotinamide, a B vitamin. This establishes an important interrelationship between tryptophan, which is an essential amino acid, and nicotinic acid, which is a vitamin. It means that tryptophan which is a protein can replace nicotinic acid in the diet. It is known that increased intake of tryptophan leads to excretion of nicotinic acid in urine.

Tryptophan undergoes several metabolic pathways. The major pathways are as follows:

1. Nicotinamide pathway with minor pathways
2. Serotonin pathway

Nicotinamide pathway: This is the main pathway and proceeds as follows:

- Tryptophan is oxidised by molecular oxygen, in the presence of a peroxidase enzyme system called tryptophan pyrrolase, present in the liver, to form formylkynurenine.
- Formylkynurenine is then hydrolysed to kynurenine and formic acid by kynurenine formylase.
- Kynurenine is oxidised to 3-hydroxykynurenine by the enzyme kynurenine hydroxylase and coenzyme riboflavin (FMN or FAD).

  In the absence or deficiency of riboflavin, kynurenine follows a minor pathway, to get decomposed to anthranilate and alanine by kynureninase (present in kidneys and liver) and coenzyme pyridoxal phosphate. In the absence or deficiency of pyridoxal phosphate, this reaction does not take place but kynurenine conjugates and kynureninate are excreted in the urine.
- 3-Hydroxykynurenine is split into alanine and 3-hydroxyanthranilate by the enzyme kynureninase and the coenzyme pyridoxal phosphate.

  When there is a deficiency of pyridoxal phosphate, 3-hydroxykynurenine takes a minor pathway leading to the excretion of xanthurenate.

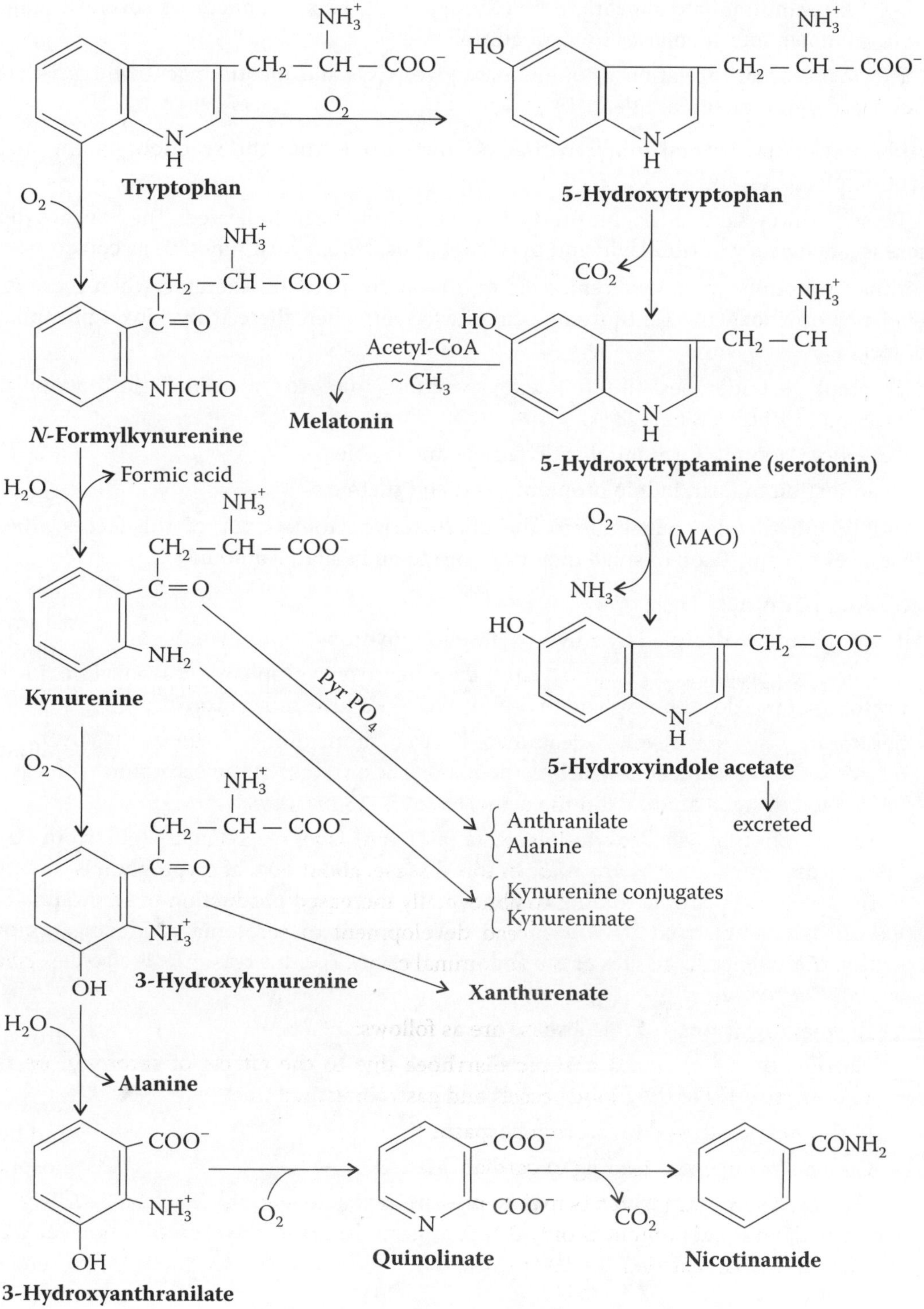

Figure 21.20 Metabolism of tryptophan.

- 3-Hydroxyanthranilate appears to be oxidised, cyclised and undergoes several changes via unknown intermediaries to form quinolinate.
- Enzymatic decarboxylation of quinolinate gives CO_2 and nicotinic acid, which is later converted into nicotinamide.

Minor pathways: Several minor pathways emerge out from the reactions of the main nicotinamide pathway.

These pathways and their end products have already been indicated. They occur when there is a deficiency of riboflavin and pyridoxal phosphate, which function as cofactors.

Thus, anthranilic acid, kynurenic acid and its derivatives are excreted when there is a deficiency of riboflavin. Xanthurenic acid is excreted when there is pyridoxal phosphate deficiency.

Tryptophan undergoes the following reactions due to microbiological action in putrefaction (pages 233 and 234):

- Decarboxylation to form indole ethylamine and indole
- Deamination to form indole propionic acid and skatole

Indole and skatole contribute to the characteristic foul odour of the faeces. These substances are non-toxic in small quantities but toxic in a large amount.

Serotonin pathway:

- Tryptophan is hydrolysed by a hydroxylase to 5-hydroxytryptophan.
- 5-hydroxytryptophan is decarboxylated by 5-hydroxytryptophan decarboxylase, in the presence of pyridoxal phosphate to 5-hydroxytryptamine or **serotonin**.
- Serotonin is oxidatively deaminated by monoamine oxidase (MAO) to 5-hydroxyindoleacetic acid which is the major end product of the serotonin pathway. It is excreted in small amounts in the urine, about 5–18 mg/day.

  The excretion of 5-hydroxyindolacetate (5-HIAA) is increased many fold, from 70 to 500 mg/day in malignant *carcinoid*. In this disease, about 60% of tryptophan is directed to the serotonin pathway leading to abnormally increased production of serotonin. The disease is characterised by widespread development of serotonin-producing tumour cells in the argentaffin tissues of the abdominal cavity. For this reason, it is also described as ***argentaffinoma***.

  The main symptoms of this disease are as follows:

  - Flushing of the skin and chronic diarrhoea due to the effects of serotonin on the smooth muscles of the blood vessels and gastrointestinal tract
  - Respiratory distress due to bronchospasm
  - Cardiac involvement leading to cardiac distress

  The blood serotonin which is mainly present in platelets is high, about 0.5–2.7 μg/ml, whereas the normal content is only 0.1–0.3 μg/ml. In urine, the excretion of 5-HIAA is greatly increased, reaching 70–500 mg per day.

Serotonin (Enteramin or Thrombocytin)

Serotonin is a vasconstrictor stored in platelets in the gastrointestinal tract and central nervous system. When platelets disintegrate, serotonin is liberated which produces vasoconstriction. It also stimulates smooth muscle contraction.

Serotonin, when given in small doses, increases the frequency and amplitude of the heart beat and respiration and stimulates the activity of the intestines. Serotonin has a stimulating effect on the metabolism of the brain. Excess of serotonin brings about stimulation of cerebral activity and deficiency produces a depressant effect.

Melatonin

Acetyl methoxy serotonin is melatonin. It is a hormone isolated from the pineal body and peripheral nerves. It is derived from serotonin, which on acetylation with acetyl-CoA is further methylated at the hydroxyl group by methionine to form melatonin in the pineal tissue. Melatonin reverses the darkening effect of the melanocyte-stimulating hormone by causing aggregation of the melanin granules in the melanocytes.

Inborn Error of Metabolism

Hartnup syndrome: Hartnup disease is an inborn error in the metabolism of tryptophan. It manifests the following features:

1. A general aminoaciduria with increased excretion of tryptophan derivatives such as indoleacetic acid and tryptophan itself
2. Pellagra-like skin rash, localised to exposed areas, apparently due to photosensitivity
3. Neurological episode, characterised by ataxia and mental deterioration

No abnormality is found in the plasma amino acid concentration. In general, this condition is said to be due to a highly specific disturbance in the renal tubular reabsorption of many amino acids.

Phenylalanine and Tyrosine

There is a close relationship between the essential amino acid phenylalanine and tyrosine which is non-essential, because both are **aromatic amino acids** and tyrosine is derived from phenylalanine.

Phenylalanine

The conversion of phenylalanine to tyrosine is irreversible. The important reactions of phenylalanine in the body are performed only after its conversion to tyrosine in the liver. The reactions are catalysed by the enzyme phenylalanine hydroxylase and cofactors NADPH, molecular oxygen, Fe^{++} and tetrahydrobiopterin, a pteridine cofactor (**Fig. 21.21**). The same enzyme phenylalanine hydroxylase hydroxylates tryptophan to 5-hydroxytryptophan.

Independent of its conversion to tyrosine, phenylalanine undergoes the following reactions as part of its metabolism (**Fig. 21.21**):

1. Phenylalanine gets deaminated to form phenylpyruvate.
2. Some amount of phenylpyruvate is reduced to phenyl-lactate.
3. Traces of phenylpyruvate may get decarboxylated to phenylacetate. Some of phenylacetate is excreted as phenylacetyl glutamine.

Both phenyl-lactate and phenylpyruvate may undergo reconversion to phenylalanine and metabolise via tyrosine (**Fig. 21.21**).

Phenylketonuria (PKU): This is an inborn error of metabolism of phenylalanine. Genetically, the familial distribution is typical of Mendelian recessive character. It is common among sisters and brothers of the patients but rare in their parents.

The metabolic error in phenylketonuria is incomplete conversion of phenylalanine to tyrosine due to deficiency or complete absence of the enzyme phenylalanine hydroxylase in the foetal liver. This leads to diversion of the usual metabolic pathway towards conversion to phenylpyruvate and its metabolites, resulting in the accumulation of phenylalanine and phenylpyruvate in the blood and their excretion in urine.

The main features of the disorder are as follows:

1. Excretion in the urine of an unusually large amount of phenylpyruvate and less (not less than normal) of phenylalanine, phenyl-lactate and phenyl acetylglutamine. Phenylacetate is mainly conjugated with glutamine to form phenylacetyl glutamine which gives 'mousy' odour to the urine of phenylketonuric infants. The excretion of 5-hydroxyindoleacetic acid is also less than normal, as the same enzyme phenylalanine hydroxylase hydroxylates tryptophan to 5-hydroxytryptophan.
2. Plasma shows an elevated level of phenylalanine, from 20 to 60 mg%, whereas the normal value is only 1 mg%.
3. One common feature associated with phenylketonuria is a mental defect, which may vary from feeble mindedness to imbecility. Epileptic attacks are also common.
4. Hair and skin pigmentation are found to be lighter than normal, and this may be due to inhibition of the normal pathways of tyrosine metabolism.

Tyrosine

Normally, phenylalanine after hydroxylation to tyrosine takes the following pathways:

1. Acetoacetate and fumarate pathway
2. Pathway to epinephrine
3. Pathway to melanin
4. Pathway to thyroxine
5. Minor pathways

Acetoacetate and fumarate pathway: This is the major pathway of tyrosine metabolism.

- Tyrosine is converted reversibly to p-hydroxyphenyl-pyruvate by transamination with α-ketoglutarate. The reaction is catalysed by a transaminase.

- The major pathway of p-hydroxyphenylpyruvate involves its oxidation and decarboxylation to 2, 5-dihyroxyphenyl-acetate which is known as homogentisate. This reaction is unusual because it involves the migration of the side chain on the aromatic ring. Ascorbic acid is necessary for this step.

  The conversion of p-hydroxyphenylpyruvate to homogentisate is the site of a rare metabolic error known as **tyrosinosis**. In this condition, inhibition of further oxidation of p-hydroxyphenylpyruvate to homogentisate occurs, leading to excretion of a large amount of p-hydroxyphenylpyruvate and tyrosine in the urine, after an ordinary diet.

  It has been found that ascorbic acid is necessary for the formation of homogentisic acid and when there is a deficiency of ascorbic acid, some p-hydroxyphenylpyruvate gets converted to p-hydroxyphenylacetate and p-hydroxyphenyl-lactate, to take a minor pathway (*see* **Fig. 21.21**).
- Otherwise, homogentisate is oxidised to form the open chain compound maleyl-acetoacetate. This reaction is catalysed by the enzyme homogentisate oxidase in the presence of Fe^{++}, in the liver.
- Next, maleyl-acetoacetate is isomerised (from cis to trans) to fumarylacetoacetate, under the influence of an enzyme requiring glutathione as cofactor. Fumarylacetoacetate is hydrolysed to fumarate and acetoacetate.

  Because of the nature of the end products, i.e. fumarate, which is a carbohydrate derivative, and acetoacetate, which is a derivative of fat metabolism, tyrosine is classified as both glucogenic and ketogenic amino acid.

Alcaptonuria: Further breakdown of homogentisate to maleyl-acetoacetate is blocked in an inborn error of metabolism of tyrosine, due to deficiency of the enzyme homogentisate oxidase resulting in the disorder called **alcaptonuria**. Consequently, homogentisate is excreted in the urine in high concentration. But the blood level of homogentisate in alcaptonuria is low because there is little or no reabsorption of homogentisate by the renal tubules. Clinically, the condition is characterised by excretion of urine which, upon standing and exposure to air, gradually becomes darker and finally becomes black. This is due to the oxidation of homogentisate (which by itself is colourless) to a black pigment. Alkalinity speeds up this reaction. It has been observed that no harmful effects result, although several grams of homogentisate might be excreted per day.

This condition is usually recognised in early infancy, when napkins moistened with the urine become darkly stained. On other occasions, the abnormality is detected for the first time in a routine medical check-up when the urine shows a reducing property.

Ochronosis: In later life, accumulation of dark pigments derived from homogentisate in the cartilages, tendons, joints, ligaments, bones and sclera of the eyes gives rise to a condition known as **ochronosis**. Arthritis is a troublesome feature when joints are affected. Genetically, the disease is inherited in the manner of a typical Mendelian recessive character occurring frequently among brothers and sisters of the affected person but rarely among their parents and children. It is relatively more common in males.

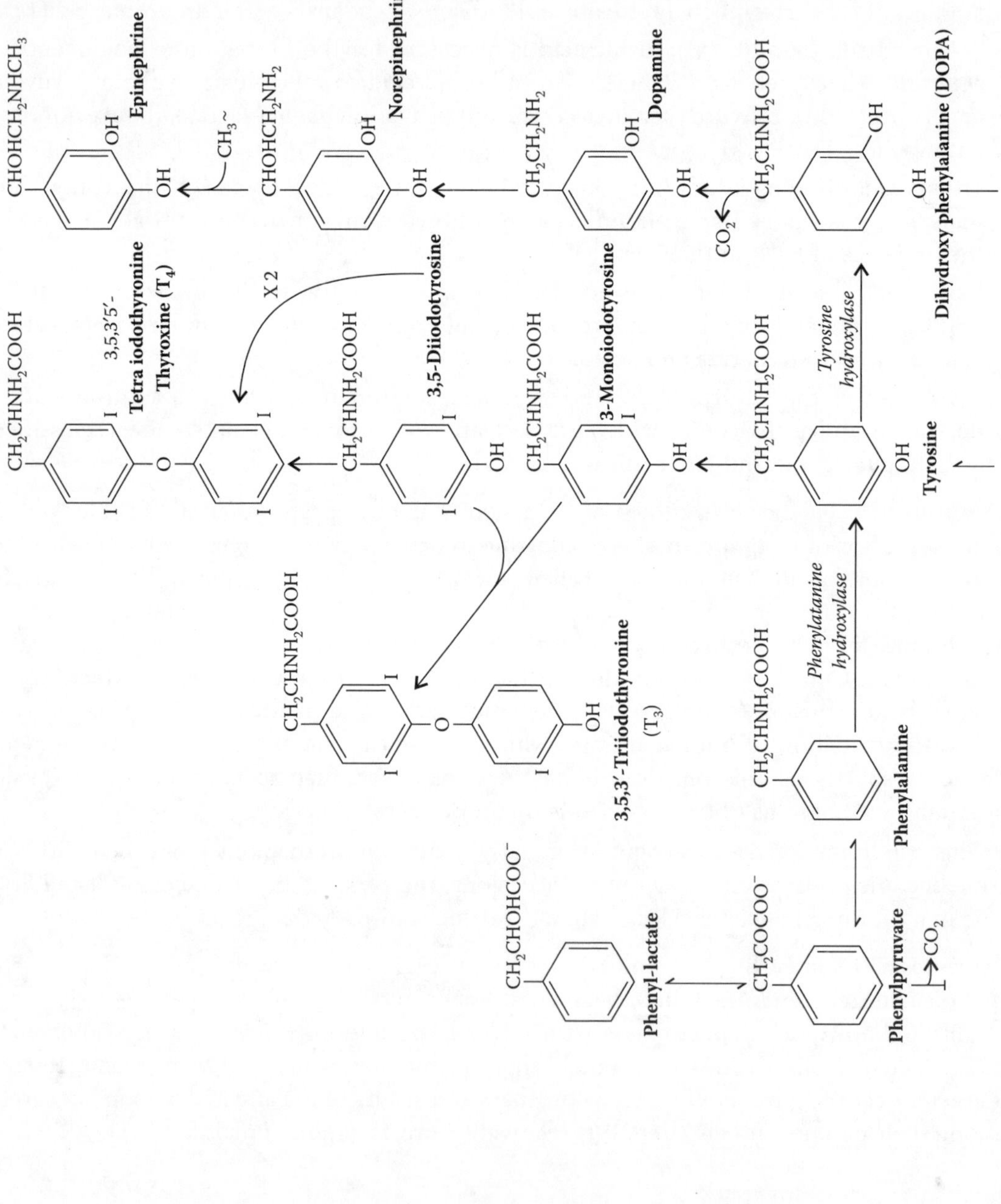

$CH_2CHOHCOO^-$
Phenyl-lactate
CH_2COCOO^-
Phenylpyruvate
CO_2
CH_2CHNH_2COOH
Phenylalanine
Phenylatanine hydroxylase
CH_2CHNH_2COOH
OH
Tyrosine
Tyrosine hydroxylase
CH_2CHNH_2COOH
OH
OH
Dihydroxy phenylalanine (DOPA)
CO_2
$CH_2CH_2NH_2$
OH
OH
Dopamine
$CHOHCH_2NH_2$
OH
OH
Norepinephrine
CH_3~
$CHOHCH_2NHCH_3$
OH
OH
Epinephrine
CH_2CHNH_2COOH
I
OH
3-Monoiodotyrosine
CH_2CHNH_2COOH
I
I
OH
3,5-Diiodotyrosine
X 2
CH_2CHNH_2COOH
I
I
O
I
I
3,5,3′5′-
Tetra iodothyronine
Thyroxine (T_4)
CH_2CHNH_2COOH
I
I
O
I
OH
3,5,3′-Triiodothyronine
(T_3)

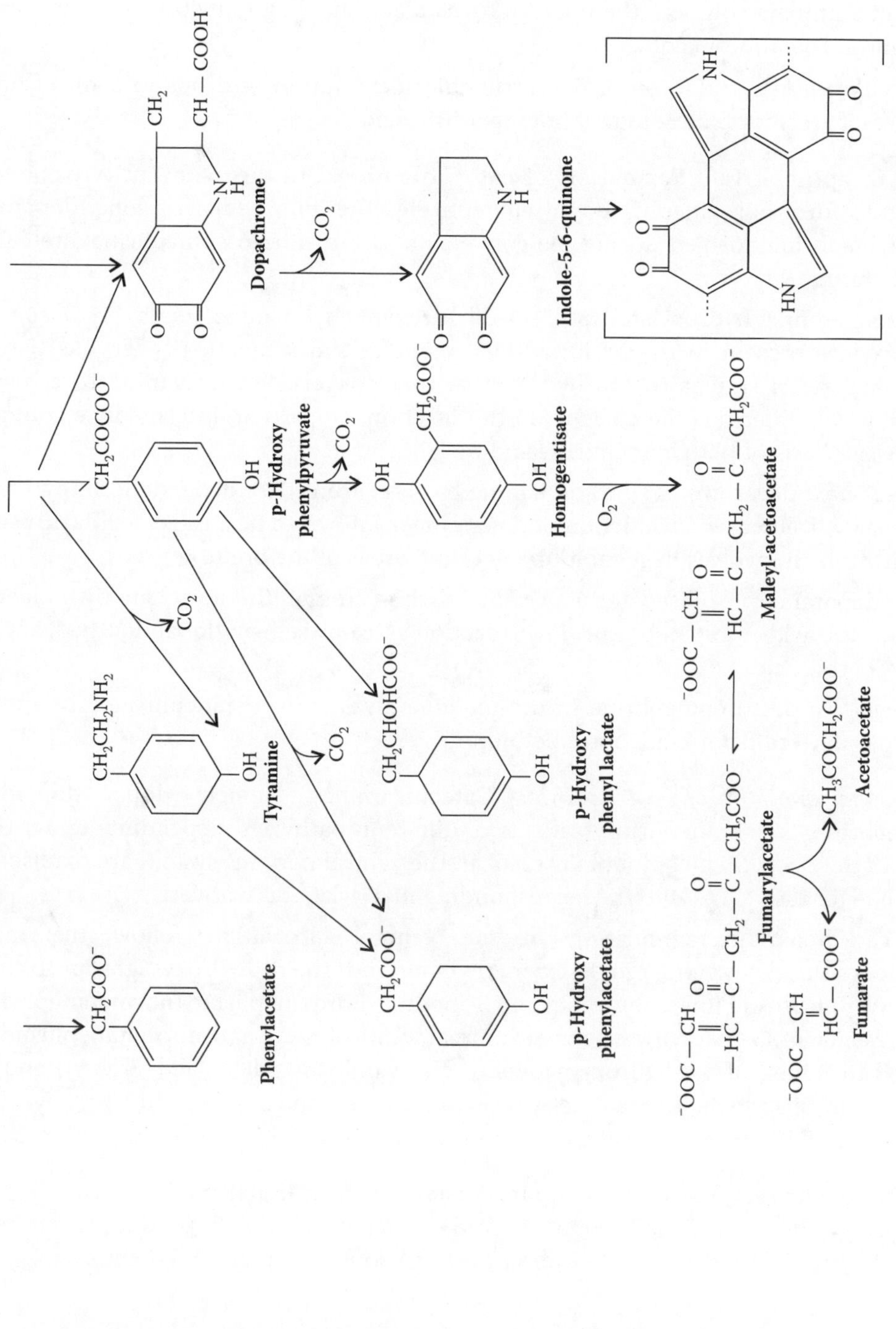

Figure 21.21 Metabolism of phenylalanime and tyrosine.

Tests for homogentisic acid:

- *Benedict's test*: When 1 ml of the urine is boiled with 5 ml of Benedict's qualitative reagent, the mixture first becomes greenish brown with a brown precipitate, which later turns yellow.
- *Silver nitrate test*: When 5 ml of 3% silver nitrate is mixed with 0.5 ml of urine and a few drops of ammonia solution, the mixture turns black showing reduction of ammoniacal silver nitrate solution in cold.
- *Ferric chloride test*: Addition of 5% ferric chloride solution in drops to 5 ml of urine produces a green or blue colour, if homogentisic acid is present.

Pathway of epinephrine: Formation of catecholamines: In this pathway, tyrosine gets converted to form norepinephrine and epinephrine. The intermediaries dopa, dopamine and norepinephrine, formed during the conversion of tyrosine to epinephrine, are called **catecholamines.**

1. Tyrosine is first hydroxylated to 3, 4-dihydroxyphenyl-alanine (dopa) by a specific hydroxylase present in the brain, adrenal medulla and sympathetic nervous tissues. This enzyme is similar to the hydroxylase that converts phenylalanine to tyrosine. Tetrahydrobiopterin is the cofactor in the reaction. Dopa is an intermediate common to the synthesis of both epinephrine and melanin.
2. Dopa is next decarboxylated to dopamine by a decarboxylase dependent on pyridoxal phosphate. Decreased production of dopamine is known to be a cause for **Parkinson's disease** which involves degeneration of certain areas of the brain.
3. Next, dopamine is oxidised at the proximal carbon atom in the side chain by molecular oxygen to yield norepinephrine. The reaction is catalysed by dopamine hydroxylase and ascorbic acid.
4. Methylation of norepinephrine in the medulla gives rise to epinephrine. The methyl group is derived from S-adenosylmethionine.

Further metabolism of adrenaline: Catecholamines, namely dopa, dopamine, norepinephrine and epinephrine, take two different pathways depending upon their location in the body. Small amounts present in the central nervous system are oxidised by monoamine oxidase (MAO) to the corresponding mandelate derivatives.

The catecholamines circulating in the general circulation follow the major metabolic route. They undergo S-oxymethylation on the 3-hydroxyl group to form 3-methoxyepinephrine (metanephrine) and 3-methoxynorepinephrine (normetanephrine), in the presence of O-methyltransferase. Some amount of meta and normetanephrine are converted to 3-methoxy, 4-hydroxymandelic acid (vanillylmandelic acid [VMA]) and are excreted in urine as such. The mandelate derivatives are also converted to VMA by MAO and are excreted in urine. The rest of the products are excreted in the conjugated form.

Pheochromocytomas: These are tumours arising in the adrenal medulla. They secrete an excessive amount of norepinephrine and epinephrine, which produce widespread metabolic dysfunction. Details of this disease are given in **Chapter 26, Hormones**.

Pathway to melanin: Dopa is oxidised, cyclised and further oxidised to dopachrome by tyrosinase, present in specialised cells called the melanocytes, which are located in skin and eyes. Dopachrome is spontaneously decarboxylated to 5, 6-dihydroxyindole, which is oxidised to indole 5, 6-quinone. Polymerisation of indole 5, 6-quinone produces melanin. Melanin exists in oxidised (black) as well as reduced (brown) forms. In nature, melanin is combined with proteins, forming melanoprotein.

Albinism: It is an inborn error or melanin metabolism. There is complete absence of pigmentation by melanin due to a hereditary deficiency of tyrosinase in the melanocytes. The skin and hair are whitish, the eyes are similarly depigmented and the iris is pinkish and translucent. The pupils are red and there is usually marked photophobia, nystagmus and defective vision.

Pathway to thyroxine: This pathway leads to the synthesis of thyroxine and occurs in thyroid gland. As the first step, inorganic iodide is oxidised to organic iodine.

$$2\,I \longrightarrow I_2$$

A series of reactions follow, involving iodination of tyrosine:

1. Tyrosine is iodinated in the third position to form 3-monoiodotyrosine (monoiodotyrosine).
2. Next, iodination occurs in the fifth position to form 3, 5-diiodotyrosine (diiodotyrosine).
3. Two molecules of diiodotyrosine couple to form one molecule of tetraiodotyrosine, which is thyroxine. Alanine is liberated.
4. A molecule of triiodothyronine may be formed by conjugation of one molecule of monoiodotyrosine and one molecule of diiodotyrosine. Triiodothyronine may also be formed by deiodination of thyroxine.

Pitt Rivers and Gross have established that triiodothyronine is five times more powerful and active than thyroxine. Synthesis of thyroxine is accelerated by TSH and inhibited by certain antithyroid agents.

Minor pathways: These involve decarboxylation and sulphatation of tyrosine. A very minor and insignificant pathway emerges when tyrosine gets decarboxylated to tyramine in the kidney.

Another reaction is the conjugation of the phenolic hydroxyl of tyrosine with sulphate to form tyrosine-o-sulphate. This unusual ester is found to be a constituent of the peptide liberated in the transformation of fibrinogen to fibrin.

Aminoaciduria: Normally, the amino acids are almost completely reabsorbed by the renal tubules and only small amounts are excreted in the urine.

Aminoaciduria refers to conditions where one or more free amino acids are excreted in urine in an abnormally large amount. A normal adult excretes daily in urine about 1 gram of free amino acids and about 2 grams of amino acids in a conjugated form.

During pregnancy, increased amounts of certain amino acids, mainly threonine and histidine, are excreted in urine. Excretion of threonine increases steadily throughout pregnancy, whereas histidine excretion reaches a maximum level in the fourth month and remains at the same level throughout pregnancy.

An abnormally high amount of amino acids is excreted in urine in a variety of inherited disorders, described as **aminoaciduria**. The main causes leading to aminoaciduria are as follows:

1. Increase in the concentration of one or more amino acids in plasma. This is referred to as *overflow aminoaciduria*. This may occur as a consequence of the following defects:
   - An inherited defect in certain enzymes of the metabolic pathway of amino acids as in phenylketonuria, maple syrup urine disease, histidinuria and homocystinuria
   - Severe liver damage which would lead to impaired deamination and increase in plasma amino acids
2. Defect in the process of renal tubular reabsorption. This is referred to as *renal aminoaciduria*. This may occur due to
   - Inherited defect of the enzyme system involved in the renal tubular reabsorption for one or more amino acids
   - Renal tubular damage leading to defective reabsorption and transport mechanism. In renal aminoaciduria, there is excretion of a large amount of amino acids in the urine but no increase in the plasma amino acids. An example of an inherited defect in the mechanism of renal tubular reabsorption of amino acids is cystinuria.

COMMON PATHWAY OF CARBOHYDRATE, FAT AND PROTEIN METABOLISM

Interconversion of carbohydrate and fat: The pathways of carbohydrate and fat metabolism meet at the common intermediate, acetyl-CoA. Fatty acids are reversibly oxidised to acetate units which form acetyl-CoA.

Pyruvic acid, a carbohydrate metabolite, reversibly undergoes decarboxylation to form acetyl-CoA which meets acetyl-CoA from fatty acids. Acetyl-CoA from both sources can condense with oxaloacetic acid, a product of carbohydrate metabolism, and enter the citric acid cycle.

Fats on hydrolysis liberate glycerol which is converted to glyceraldehyde-3-phosphate, a carbohydrate metabolite. As this reaction is also reversible, an integration between carbohydrate and fat metabolism is established at this point, when glycerol (fat) enters the carbohydrate pathway and vice versa.

Conversion of protein to carbohydrate: Many amino acids are glucogenic; examples are glutamic acid, histidine, serine, glycine, cystine and cysteine whereas leucine, tyrosine and phenylalanine are ketogenic.

Both types of amino acids get metabolised in the same citric acid cycle. Glutamic acid is converted to α-ketoglutaric acid and enter the citric acid cycle at this point. Histidine is metabolised to glutamic acid. Cysteine, cystine, glycine and serine are deaminated to form pyruvic acid.

The ketogenic amino acids—leucine, isoleucine and tyrosine—are metabolised to acetate and acetyl-CoA which enter the citric acid cycle.

Integration of urea formation with the citric acid cycle is an example of conversion of amino acids to carbohydrates. Amino acids—ornithine, citrulline and arginine—constitute the Krebs–Henseleit urea cycle for the formation of urea. Arginosuccinate, which is an intermediate formed in this cycle, splits to form succinate which in turn enters the Krebs citric acid cycle.

Again in the process of urea formation, citrulline condenses with aspartate which in turn is derived by transamination of oxaloacetate, an important component of the citric acid cycle. The details of the integration of the urea cycle with the citric acid cycle are discussed in **Figure 21.5**.

The relationship between the carbohydrate, fat and protein metabolism and their integration via the Krebs citric acid cycle which serves as the common metabolic pathway are shown in **Figure 21.22**.

METABOLISM IN STARVATION

Starvation is deprivation of food of any kind, in any form continuously, for more than 1 day. The following changes in metabolism take place when food is completely withdrawn as in starvation.

The three main reserves of the body—carbohydrates, fats and proteins—are oxidised one after another for derivation of energy. First the carbohydrate storage of the body, namely glycogen from liver and muscles, is oxidised to supply energy for the body. Next, the fat reserves are burnt and finally, when the carbohydrate and fat reserves are exhausted, the tissue proteins are broken down. During the first few days of starvation, the subcutaneous tissues and other fat depots get drained and the skin becomes dry and lies loosely attached to the subcutaneous tissues. There is loss of a large quantity of extracellular fluid and dehydration sets in.

Carbohydrate metabolism: The liver glycogen breaks down first to support blood glucose (glycogenolysis). This is associated with hypoglycaemia at the earlier stage of starvation. However, when the glycogen store is depleted, proteins are broken down to form glucose (gluconeogenesis).

Fat metabolism: After exhausting the glycogen store, the neutral fat from adipose tissues is mobilised and taken to the liver, where it is completely oxidised to form acetyl-CoA. Excess amounts of acetyl-CoA condense to form the ketone bodies, acetoacetic acid, β-hydroxybutyric acid and acetone. They are excreted in urine causing ketonuria.

The ketone bodies also circulate in the blood in abnormally high concentration causing ketosis. The resulting acidosis leads to increased excretion of urinary ammonia. The metabolic changes are similar to those produced in advanced diabetes mellitus. When starvation is prolonged, the subject passes into a state of coma simulating that of diabetic coma.

Protein metabolism: The tissue proteins are the last to get depleted. That is why the total nitrogen excretion in the urine is much less on the first 2 or 3 days of the fast, as the body then concentrates on the carbohydrate reserves. The length of this period

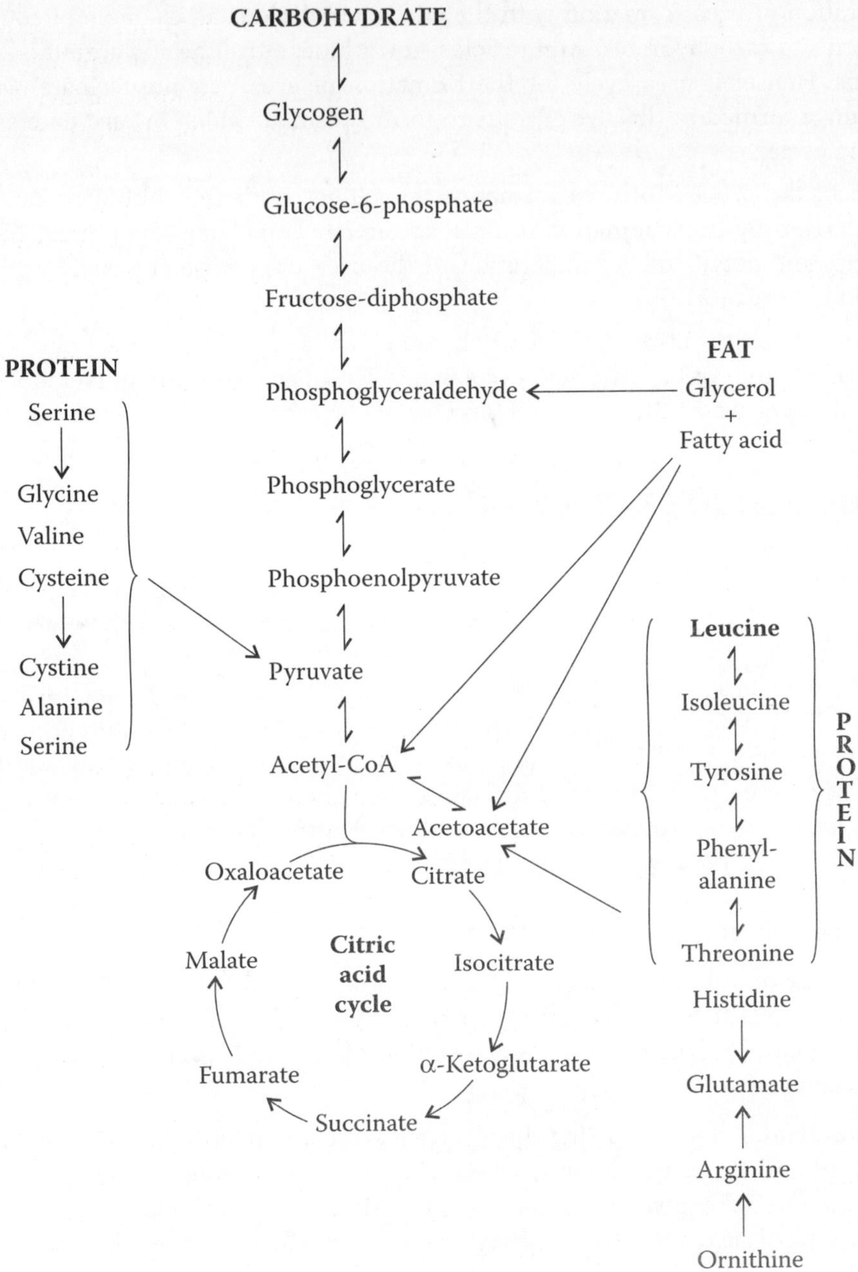

Figure 21.22 Diagrammatic illustration of the integration of the metabolic pathways of carbohydrates, proteins and fats.

varies with the amount of glycogen stores. Then there is a steady increase in the nitrogen excretion, corresponding to the tissue protein breakdown. This is followed by increased ammonia excretion which corresponds to the ketosis and production of acid proteins and phosphoric acid derived from protein breakdown.

Mineral metabolism: Excretion of phosphate and sulphate in urine increases, corresponding to the excretion of nitrogen due to breakdown of protein. Both features decline towards the later stage. The urinary excretion of sodium, potassium, chloride and magnesium are reduced throughout the fasting period, because of the restricted intake of these minerals. The plasma $NaHCO_3$ is reduced when ketosis supervenes.

ROLE OF VITAMINS AND HORMONES ON METABOLISM

Role of Vitamins on Metabolism

Most of the members of B vitamins and vitamin C function as coenzymes in important metabolic reactions involving carbohydrate, protein and fat.

Thiamine: Thiamine pyrophosphate (TPP) plays an important role in carbohydrate metabolism where it serves as cocarboxylase in reactions involving decarboxylation of α-keto acids. It also helps in the synthesis of fats from carbohydrates and proteins.

Riboflavin: The coenzymes of riboflavin FMN and FAD are involved in biological oxidation–reduction reactions. They participate in reactions of protein metabolism, by serving as coenzymes for amino acid oxidases.

Riboflavin is necessary for the conversion of kynurenine to 3-hydroxykynurenine, a step in tryptophan metabolism. Protein synthesis is impaired in riboflavin deficiency. Riboflavin is required for normal fat metabolism. It acts as a cofactor for acyl-CoA dehydrogenase which is necessary for oxidation of fatty acids.

Niacin: The coenzymes of nicotinic acid NAD and NADP play an important role in the metabolism of carbohydrate, protein and fat. They serve mainly as hydrogen-transferring agents, functioning as coenzymes to dehydrogenases. Nicotinamide has an important relationship with protein metabolism because it is derived from tryptophan which is an essential amino acid.

Pyridoxine: This is mainly concerned with the metabolism of amino acids. The coenzyme pyridoxal phosphate serves as cotransaminase in reactions concerned with the metabolism of tyrosine and glutamic acid. It is also necessary for the normal metabolism of tryptophan.

Pyridoxal phosphate acts as a codecarboxylase in decarboxylation reactions occurring in metabolic pathways. It also acts as a cofactor for the conversion of linoleic to arachidonic acid.

Biotin: This vitamin is necessary for the extramitochondrial biosynthetic pathway of fatty acids.

It helps in the deamination of amino acids such as threonine, serine and aspartic acid. It participates in the Krebs–Henseleit cycle of urea formation for the conversion of ornithine to citrulline ('transcarbamoylation' reaction). It is necessary for the biosynthesis of purines.

Pantothenic acid: Acetyl-CoA, derived from CoA which is the coenzyme of pantothenic acid, is an important enzyme in the major metabolic pathways like the tricarboxylic acid cycle. It is formed during the intermediary stages of carbohydrate and fat metabolism and occupies a position in the common pathway of carbohydrate, fat and protein metabolism.

It helps in the formation of acetylcholine. Acetyl-CoA is a precursor of cholesterol and thus helps in the synthesis of cholesterol and steroid hormones.

Coenzyme A is necessary for lipid metabolism. The first step in the oxidation of fatty acids is initiated by CoA. Acyl carrier protein (ACP) which contains protein-bound pantothenic acid is necessary for the biosynthesis of fatty acids. Some amino acids require CoA for their action.

Folic acid: This group of vitamins serves as coenzymes in reactions involving the transfer and utilisation of the single carbon moiety.

It is necessary for the synthesis of purines, pyrimidines and nucleic acids.

Folic acid is essential for the normal growth and maturation of red blood cells.

Histidine requires folic acid for its metabolic pathway.

Vitamin B_{12} is necessary for the synthesis of nucleic acids. It is involved in the biosynthesis of protein. It helps in the formation of labile methyl groups and functions as a cofactor in transmethylation reactions. Along with folic acid, vitamin B_{12} maintains normal haemopoiesis.

Vitamin C: Ascorbic acid helps in the formation and maintenance of the intercellular ground substance of the matrix of the tissues. It is involved in cellular oxidation–reduction reactions where it functions as a hydrogen transport agent.

Vitamin C is necessary for the normal metabolic pathway of tyrosine and tryptophan.

Vitamin C is required for the conversion of folic to folinic acid, and both are necessary for normal maturation of erythrocytes.

Vitamin D: It is associated with the metabolism of calcium and phosphorus. It helps the formation of bone and development of teeth.

Avitaminosis

Avitaminosis may be acute or chronic, due to lack of single or more vitamins. Acute deficiencies are due to inadequate intake of vitamins. They respond to treatment more quickly than chronic types because of the absence of pathological changes which are invariably present in chronic deficiencies.

Chronic avitaminosis occurs on account of inadequate intake of vitamins due to undernutrition over a longer period. It is more common in aged than in young. Beriberi, scurvy and xerophthalmia occur due to deficiency of a single vitamin. An example of multiple avitaminosis is pellagra. Pellagrins suffer from lack of most of the B vitamins though niacin is particularly deficient.

The common causes of avitaminosis are as follows:

1. Unbalanced diet containing an inadequate amount of vitamins
2. Excessive intake of alcohol
3. Severe and prolonged fever

4. Gastric achlorhydria. In this condition, absorption of all the water-soluble vitamins is impaired.
5. Biliary obstruction. Absorption of fat-soluble vitamins is interfered in biliary obstruction.

Hypervitaminosis

Sometimes, indiscriminately large doses of vitamins are recommended as part of treatment. Two vitamins that produce toxic manifestations in humans are vitamins **A** and **D**.

The toxic effects recognised by eskimos by eating the liver of polar bears and arctic foxes, which are particularly rich in vitamin A, have been described in page 102.

No toxicity is reported for riboflavin, pantothenic acid, PABA or ascorbic acid. Instances of toxic and even fatal manifestations following repeated parenteral administration of large doses of thiamine have been reported. In rats, excessive doses of dehydroascorbic acid have caused permanent diabetes, identical with that produced by alloxan.

Vitamin Inter-Relationship

An inter-relationship exists between excessive intake of vitamin A and manifestations of vitamin K deficiency. It is observed that continued intake of excess of vitamin A, especially in children, produces coarse skin, falling of hair, irritability, anorexia, loss of weight and haemorrhages associated with hypoprothrombinaemia. The haemorrhage can be prevented by simultaneous administration of vitamin K and vitamin E.

Another inter-relationship exists between administration of vitamin A and action of vitamin E. The antioxidant property of vitamin E prevents destruction of vitamin A in the intestines. In rats, deficiency of vitamin A is reported to be associated with manifestations resembling vitamin C deficiency, such as swollen and bleeding gums, swollen joints, bleeding from lacrimals and low blood vitamin C level. The symptoms disappear after administration of vitamin C.

The inter-relationship between ascorbic acid and folic acid is described on page 123. It may be noted that ascorbic acid is required for the conversion of folic acid to folinic acid. In this connection, reference has already been made that the megaloblastic anaemia of scorbutic infants and animals could be relieved by administration of folinic acid.

A relationship between ascorbic acid and adrenocortical hormone is noteworthy. Administration of ACTH causes a prompt fall in the concentration of ascorbic acid in the adrenal cortex of normal animals.

Vitamin B_{12} functions in conjunction with folic acid and vice versa, in metabolic reactions.

Role of Hormones on Metabolism

Androgens influence protein metabolism. They increase the rate of incorporation of amino acids into protein.

Epinephrine exerts influence on carbohydrate metabolism. It accelerates glycogenolysis in the liver, thus increasing the blood sugar. It accelerates glycolysis in muscles, thus increasing the formation of lactic acid.

Adrenocortical hormones exert characteristic metabolic effects:

1. They regulate the distribution of sodium and potassium between extracellular and intracellular fluids, and direct excretion by the kidney.
2. They have a specific influence on carbohydrate and protein metabolism. They also influence fat metabolism indirectly.

Thyroxine stimulates growth and development. It favours protein anabolism. It increases the rate of intestinal absorption of monosaccharides and causes a rise in the blood sugar level. Thyroxine enhances gluconeogenesis. It promotes ketogenesis and ketosis. It mobilises unesterified fatty acids from adipose tissues, thus increasing their concentration in the blood.

Insulin has a profound influence on carbohydrate metabolism.

It decreases blood sugar.

It increases oxidation of glucose.

It decreases gluconeogenesis.

Insulin affects fat metabolism by decreasing ketogenesis and increasing lipogenesis.

Parathyroid hormone influences mineral metabolism. It increases serum calcium and decreases serum inorganic phosphate.

Anterior pituitary hormone: Growth hormone induces protein anabolism. It brings about characteristic changes on carbohydrate metabolism also. Growth hormone produces hyperglycaemia by inhibiting insulin action. It stimulates mobilisation of fat depots and causes an increase in plasma lipids.

Posterior pituitary hormones: Vasopressin raises blood pressure and also exerts an antidiuretic effect. Oxytoxin influences contraction of uterus.

Relation Between Vitamin and Hormones

Some vitamins act in close co-ordination with hormones. The inter-relationships which are important are as follows:

1. **Vitamin A and adrenocortical hormones:** Gross deficiency of vitamin A is associated with diminished synthesis of adrenocortical hormones. Administration of vitamin A corrects the condition.
2. **Vitamin A and thyroxine:** Thyroxine is necessary for the conversion of carotene to vitamin A. Vitamin A deficiency produces hypertrophy of thyroid gland and a diminished rate of synthesis of thyroxine.
3. **Vitamin D and parathyroid hormone:** Vitamin D and parathyroid hormone are closely related to one another. Vitamin D helps absorption of calcium from intestines and parathyroid hormone mobilises calcium from bones, to maintain the blood calcium level.

4. **Vitamin E and sex hormones:** Deficiency of vitamin E in rats causes intrauterine death of foetus, sterility in female rats and degeneration of the germinal epithelium in male rats. Administration of vitamin E restores normal gestation and foetal development.
5. **Pyridoxine and pregnancy:** Deficiency of pyridoxine occurs in pregnancy, due to a greater demand of the vitamin by the foetus.
6. **Folic acid and pregnancy:** Folic acid is required for the maintenance of normal pregnancy and prevention of megaloblastic anaemia.

CHAPTER 22

Protein Synthesis

Chapter Outline

- Gene and Genetic Code
- Ribonucleic Acid
- Steps in Protein Synthesis

GENE AND GENETIC CODE

The basic instructions to build a protein with specific hereditary traits are written in the DNA of the gene. **Gene** is a segment of the DNA strand present in chromosomes. It decides the type of proteins to be synthesised by the cell and provides a coded message essential for the synthesis of the protein. The genetic message is in the form of specific sequences of nucleotides along the DNA strands.

A gene does not build protein directly. RNA acts as a bridge between genetic information and protein synthesis. The genetic message from the DNA in the nucleus is carried to the ribosomes, the site of protein synthesis located in the cytoplasm by the messenger RNA (mRNA) molecules. In response to this, the polypeptides are formed by incorporation of amino acids in a specific order.

Both nucleic acids and proteins have specific sequences of monomers that confer information. In nucleic acids, the monomers are the four types of nucleotides (adenine, guanine, thymine and cytosine) that differ in the nitrogenous bases. Genes are typically hundreds or thousands of nucleotides long, each gene having a specific sequence of bases. A protein also has monomers arranged in a particular linear order and that is the protein primary structure. Monomers are the 20 amino acids. Thus, nucleic acids and proteins contain information written in two different chemical languages, namely nucleotide sequences and amino acids. To get from one to the other requires two major steps called **transcription** and **translation**.

Protein synthesis comprises complex processes but they are carried out with speed and precision. All the different RNAs, namely mRNA, tRNA and rRNA, take part in the synthesis of protein. The meanings of certain terms, used in explaining synthesis of protein, are enlisted in the following section:

1. **Gene:** It is a segment of a DNA strand present in the chromosomes in nucleus. It decides the type of protein to be synthesised by the cell and provides a coded message essential for the synthesis of a polypeptide.
2. **Codon:** The genetic instructions for a polypeptide are written in the DNA as a series of three nucleotide words called **codons**. These are the smallest units that can code for a single amino acid. The coded messages are transcribed into complementary base sequences of mRNA.
3. **Genetic code:** A collection of codons is genetic code. It is described as a dictionary that gives the correspondence between a sequence of nucleotide bases and a sequence of amino acids. The codons exist in the DNA or they are transcribed into mRNA and then translated into a sequence of amino acids during protein synthesis.
4. **Triplet code:** Each codon consists of a sequence of three nucleotides. This is triplet code. Each codon codes for one particular amino acid. Taking into account that there are four different nitrogenous bases, adenine, guanine, thymine and cytosine in a DNA molecule, the maximum number of possible three-letter code words will be (4^3) or 64. This is more than sufficient to code all the 20 amino acids.
5. **Nonsense codon:** Out of 64 codons, three codons do not code for any specific amino acid. These are nonsense codons. But two of these nonsense codons are utilised as termination codons, i.e. as stop signals to terminate polymerisation of amino acids in the formation of a protein.
6. **Degeneracy of the code:** The remaining 61 codons have to code for 20 amino acids. That means more than one codon must decode the same amino acid except in the case of methionine and tryptophan which have a single codon. This means that there is degeneracy in the genetic code. Degeneracy literally means the existence of multiple codons for a single amino acid.

RIBONUCLEIC ACID

Ribonucleic acid (RNA) is a polymer of purine and pyrimidine ribonucleotides linked together by 3′-5′ phosphodiester bridges. They are found in the nucleoli, cytoplasm and ribosomes. RNA exists as a single strand and is capable of folding back on itself and acquire double-stranded characteristics.

RNA contains ribose as its pentose sugar. The purine bases are adenine and guanine. The pyrimidine components are cytosine and uracil. The genetic information within the single strand of RNA is contained in the sequence (primary structure) of purine and pyrimidine nucleotides and is complementary to the 'template' strand of the gene from which it was transcribed. An **RNA** molecule can bind specifically to its template DNA strand via the base pairing rules. The sequence of the RNA molecule is the same as that of the coding strand of the gene except that U (uracil) replaces T (thymine) in the DNA strand.

Types of Ribonucleic Acid

There are four types of cellular RNA—tRNA, mRNA, rRNA and hnRNA.

The **transfer RNA (tRNA)** molecules are the smallest of the RNAs. Approximately 18% of the RNAs are tRNA. Originally, tRNA was called soluble RNA (sRNA). tRNAs are generated by nuclear processing of a precursor molecule in the nucleus and are passed on to the cytoplasm. They have two functions: (i) tRNA molecules transport specific activated amino acids from the activated aminoacyl complex to the ribosomes where proteins are synthesised and (ii) tRNAs serve as adaptors that recognise specific codons in the mRNA template so that the correct amino acid is incorporated into the growing polypeptide chain.

There are about 20 species of tRNA in every cell, each corresponding to each of the 20 amino acids required for protein synthesis. As a class, tRNA molecules are described to have many features in common, although each specific tRNA differs from the others in its nucleotide sequence.

General Structure of Ribonucleic Acid

A tRNA molecule consists of a single RNA strand that has about 75–80 nucleotides, folded upon itself to form a three-dimensional structure. It is described to have the appearance of a cloverleaf, with two free ends and representing primary, secondary and tertiary structure (**Fig. 22.1**).

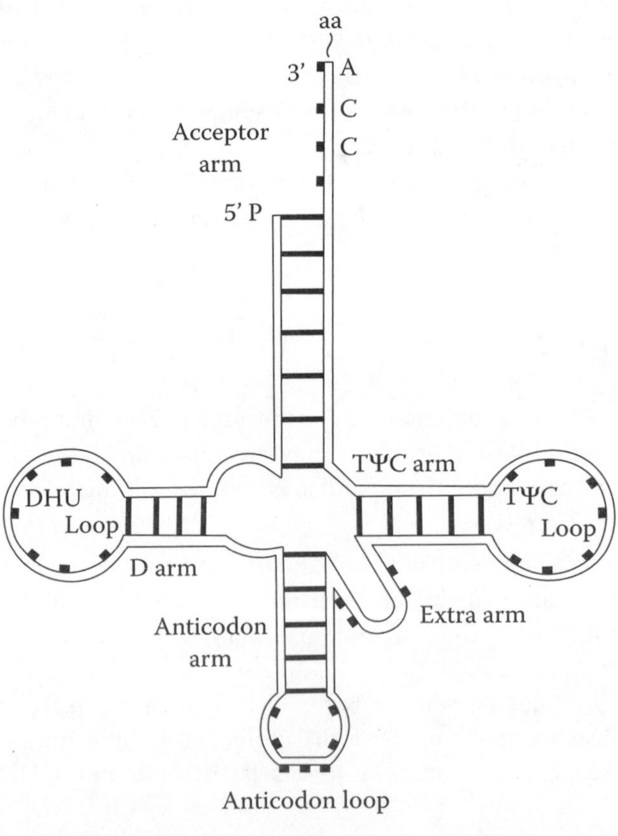

Figure 22.1 Structure of a tRNA molecule.

The primary structure, i.e. the nucleotide sequence, is stabilised by a large number of hydrogen bonds formed between complementary bases in different parts of the RNA strand. This allows formation of base-paired double-stranded stems, helical structures and loop formation at the end of stems.

All tRNA molecules have four arms and three loops. The four arms are the (i) acceptor arm, (ii) anticodon arm, (iii) D arm and (iv) TψC arm.

1. The acceptor arm is the long arm. It has a base-paired stem consisting of seven base pairs. At one of the free ends of this stem, at 3′-terminal, the nucleotide base sequence CCA which represents cytidine cytidine and adenine resides. The activated amino acid (aa) is attached to this end. The other free end of the stem at the 5′ terminal is phosphorylated (5′P).
2. The anticodon arm is at the other end of the stem. It has a nucleotide sequence complementary to the triplet codon on the mRNA template. The anticodon triplet recognises the mRNA codons and is unique. It has five base pairs.
3. The D arm has the base dihydrouridine. It has three or four base pairs.
4. The TψC arm (thymidine pseudo-uridine cytidine) is named so for the presence of thymidine, pseudo-uridine and cytidine. ψ stands for the base pseudo-uridine. It has five base pairs.

The extra arm is the most variable feature of tRNA. It provides a basis for classification.

The first loop is the dihydrouracil (DHU) loop. It is named so because of the presence of the base DHU. It is important for proper recognition of a tRNA species by its charging enzyme.

The second loop is the anticodon loop. This is at the end of the anticodon stem. The loop contains seven nucleotides of which the centre three form the anticodon triplet bases that pair with the triplet codon of mRNA.

The third loop is the thymidine pseudo-uridine cytidine (TψC) loop. It contains seven nucleotides. It is involved in the binding of aminoacyl-tRNA to the ribosomal surface at the site of protein synthesis.

mRNAs or messenger RNAs are single-stranded RNA molecules having high molecular weight. They are processed from nuclear RNA precursors known as hnRNA. mRNAs are the direct carriers of genetic information from the nucleus to the cytoplasmic ribosome and represent about 2% of the cellular RNA. They are transcribed by the DNA template in the nucleus and are complementary to the template strand of their respective structural gene.

Human mRNAs have unique structural features. The information within mRNA lies in a linear sequence. The 5′ end of mRNA is attached to a 7-methylguanosine by a 5′-5′ pyrophosphate linkage. This structure is referred to as a **cap**. The function of capping is to block the action of RNA exonucleases and phosphatases which could attack the 5′ terminus of the mRNA. Also, the cap functions in the recognition of mRNA by the translating machinery.

The translation of mRNA on the ribosomes begins at the 5′ end and proceeds towards the 3′ end. During translation, the mRNAs serve as templates on which specific amino acids are assembled to form the specific protein molecule (*see* **Fig. 22.8** later in the text). To the 3′ end of the mRNA is attached a string of adenylic acids AAA consisting of 20–200 nucleotides in length, and this is called the polyadenylic acid tail or **poly (A) 'tail'** (**Fig. 22.2**). Polyadenylation occurs after capping but before splicing. Polyadenylation increases the stability of mRNA. Some mRNAs do not have a poly (A) tail.

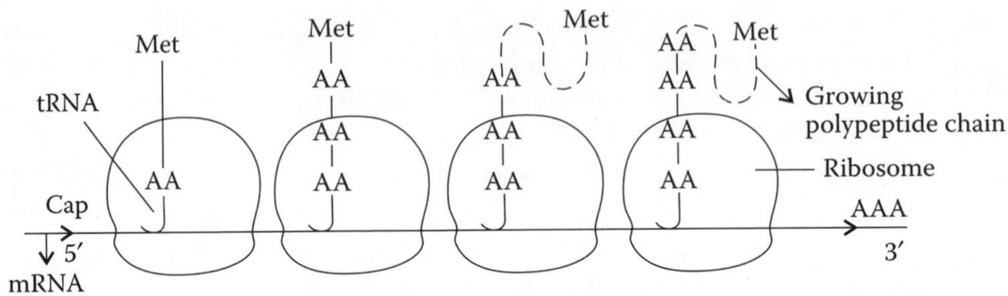

Figure 22.2 Polyribosome and protein synthesis. *AA, amino acid; AAA, poly (A) 'tail'; Met, methionine.*

rRNAs are **ribosomal RNAs** found in cytoplasm and are the most abundant type of RNAs present in cells. They are the components of the mammalian ribosomes and are classified into four types that differ in their size and sedimentation velocity S (Svedberg unit). They are 5 S, 5.8 S, 18 S and 28 S rRNAs. The rRNAs in the ribosomes are necessary (i) for ribosomal assembly and (ii) because they play an important role in the binding of mRNA to ribosomes and its translation.

Ribonucleic Acid Synthesis

hnRNA: The heterogeneous nuclear RNA constitutes the fourth class of RNA. They are much larger than the mature mRNA and are heterogeneous in size. They are formed from DNA and are the primary transcripts and precursors of mRNA. The hnRNA is processed within the nucleus. The **introns** that are the intervening sequences are removed and the **exons** that are the coding regions are spliced to form mature mRNA, which enters the cytoplasm to serve as a template for protein synthesis.

Ribosomes are cytoplasmic nucleoprotein structures that act as the machinery for the synthesis of proteins, where mRNA and tRNA molecules interact to translate information transcribed from the gene (DNA) by the mRNA into specific proteins. They occur as free ribosomes in the cytoplasm or as ribosomes bound to membranes of rough endoplasmic reticulum (RER). Ribosomes are rich in rRNA and consist of several components. They are classified according to their sedimentation velocity (S). The mammalian ribosome has a molecule weight of 4.2×10^6 and its sedimentation velocity is 80 S (Svedberg units). It contains two major subunits. The 60 S large subunit contains a 5 S, a 5.8 S and a 28 S rRNA and also more than 50 specific polypeptides. The 40 S small subunit contains a single 18 S rRNA and approximately 30 polypeptide chains.

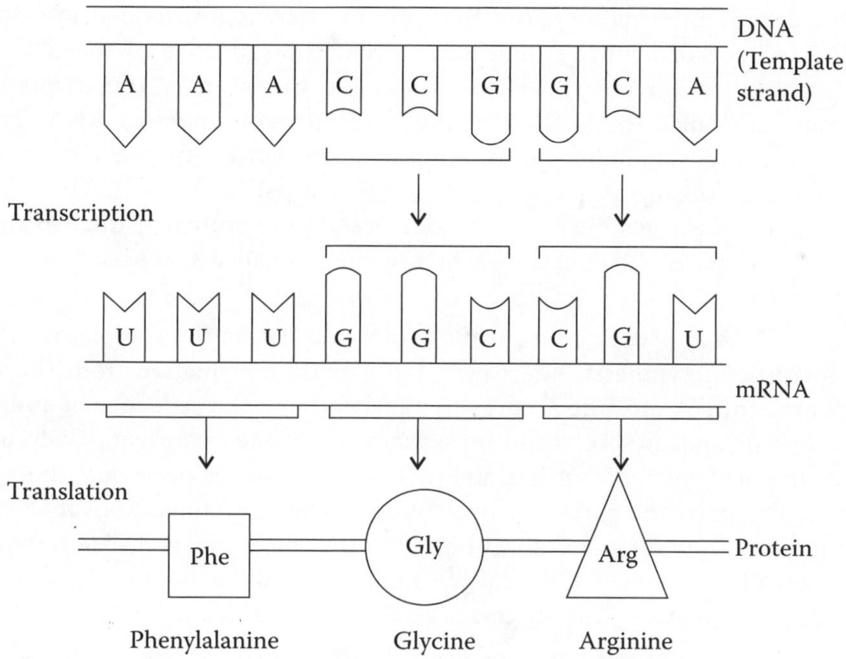

Figure 22.3 Triplet codes: Transcription and translation.

A ribosome as seen in an electron microscope is made of two subunits, one small and the other big (**Fig. 22.3**). Each ribosome has an mRNA-binding site and two tRNA-binding sites referred to as the **P site** and **A site**. These two sites (P and A) are present in the large subunit. The P site known as the peptidyl tRNA site holds the tRNA carrying the growing polypeptide chain. The A site referred to as the aminoacyl tRNA binding site holds the tRNA carrying the next amino acid to be added to the polypeptide chain (*see* **Fig. 22.9** later in the text). Only one polypeptide chain can grow from each ribosome.

Polyribosomes (polysomes): Several ribosomes combine to form polyribosomes. They attach to an mRNA strand and travel down the length of the strand from codon to codon, assembling amino acids as they are formed. Ribosomes play an important role in translating the mRNA message (*see* **Fig. 22.2**).

STEPS IN PROTEIN SYNTHESIS

An overview of protein synthesis: When a protein is to be synthesised, the genetic information flows in a sequence:

$$\text{DNA} \xrightarrow{\text{Transcription}} \text{RNA} \xrightarrow{\text{Translation}} \text{Protein}$$

The synthesis of an RNA molecule from DNA is a complex process.

First, the genetic information from the gene in DNA is transcribed into the specific nucleotide sequence of an RNA molecule so that the sequence of the RNA molecule is complementary to that in the DNA. These are the primary transcripts of mRNA molecules and are called the **hnRNA** or the **heterogeneous nuclear RNA**. The hnRNA molecule is then processed and the resulting RNA molecule which is a transcript of the genes protein building instructions is called **messenger RNA (mRNA)**. It is called so because it functions as a genetic message from DNA to the protein synthesising machinery of the cell. The process by which hnRNA is formed is called **transcription** and it takes place in the nucleus.

Once the mRNA is processed from the hnRNA, it enters the cytoplasm to serve as a template for protein synthesis. Thereafter, the genetic information from the nucleotide sequence of the mRNA must be accurately translated into the sequence of amino acids of the corresponding specific protein to be synthesised in the cytoplasm. Code words exist for each amino acid sequence of a protein. The cell possesses necessary and appropriate machinery to recognise the particular nucleotide sequence on the mRNA molecule on one hand and the corresponding amino acid on the other hand and translate the information from the nucleotide sequence of the mRNA molecule into the amino acid sequence of the corresponding polypeptide. This process is known as **translation**.

The sequence of events that take place in protein biosynthesis are as follows:

1. Transcription of genetic information from DNA to RNA
2. Recognition of amino acids by specific tRNA molecules
3. Translation of information contained in RNA by the tRNA at the ribosomes

Transcription

Transcription is synthesis of RNA molecules under the direction of DNA. The template for RNA synthesis is DNA. The transcription takes place by polymerisation of ribonucleotides in the $5' \rightarrow 3'$ direction.

A specific gene in one of the strands of DNA is activated in response to an external signal, either from intracellular or from extracellular components, to transcribe hnRNA which is the precursor and primary transcript of mRNA. The genetic information of the cell stored in the nucleotide sequence of DNA is converted to an analogous base sequence in the mRNA.

An mRNA molecule is complementary to its DNA template because the RNA bases are assembled on the DNA template according to the base pairing rules. To give an example, for a codon CCG (cytidine cytidine guanine) on the coding strand of a DNA, GGC (guanine guanine cytidine) will be the codon at the corresponding position along the mRNA molecule (**Fig. 22.4**).

This is the mRNA code word for glycine. In another example where U (uracil) of mRNA pairs with A (adenine) of DNA, the DNA codon GCA is transcribed as an mRNA codon CGU which is the code word for arginine (**Fig. 22.4**). After transcription, the newly formed mRNA separates from the DNA strand and passes into the cytoplasm.

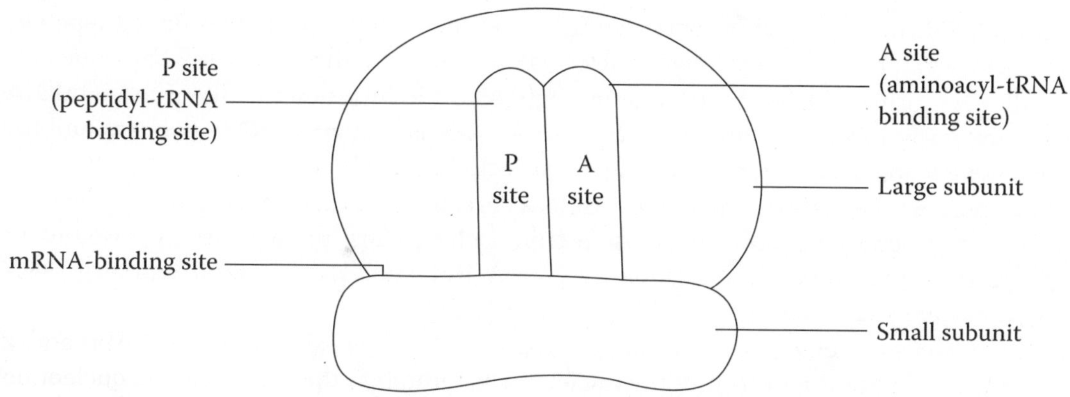

Figure 22.4 Structure of a ribosome.

Transcription is divided into the following three stages:

1. Initiation
2. Elongation
3. Termination

Initiation: This is the stage when RNA polymerase recognises an active gene starting point and moves along the DNA till the beginning of the bond formation. As an RNA polymerase molecule moves along a DNA gene from the initiation site at 5′ end, it separates the two strands of the DNA and hooks together the RNA nucleotides as they base pair along the DNA templates in a specific sequence. The reaction is catalysed by RNA polymerase. The enzyme translocates to the next position.

Elongation: This refers to the binding, bond formation and translocation cycle. As the RNA polymerase continues to move along the coding strand, the unwound DNA binds the initiating triphosphate and continues to base pair with the growing RNA chain. Successive ribonucleotides are added to the growing RNA molecule elongating it in the $5' \rightarrow 3'$ direction. Each ribonucleotide is linked to the other by a phosphodiester linkage. The enzyme translocates to the next position and continues synthesis.

Termination: This refers to the final stage of transcription and release of the newly formed RNA molecule. The DNA template strand has a transcription termination signal in the form of a specific nitrogenous base sequence in the coding strand. When RNA polymerase reaches the termination site, the signal is recognised by a termination protein factor called the rho (P) factor and addition of nucleotides to the RNA strand is stopped. The core enzyme separates from the DNA template and the primary transcript of the RNA molecule is released.

Post-Transcription Processing

The immediate product of transcription in mammalian cells is a precursor RNA molecule, the primary transcript. This has to be subsequently modified to a mature functional RNA molecule because primary transcripts may contain information that is discontinuous or in a repeated form or they may contain information for multiple molecules linked together. The primary transcripts have longer nucleotide sequences than the final mRNA.

All RNA primary transcripts undergo extensive modifications in the nucleus before they are ready to serve as mature active RNA. This is known as **RNA processing**. The processing involves several modifications that include the following:

1. **Capping:** The newly transcribed mRNA precursor molecule is promptly capped on the 5′ end by 7-methylguanosine triphosphate caps, in the nucleus, prior to its transport to cytoplasm. The capping serves as protection for the mRNA against 5′ → 3′ exonucleolytic attack.
2. **Addition of nucleotides:** A string of 20–200 adenylates called **poly (A) tail** is added at the 3′ end of the mRNA in the nucleus. This prohibits the action of 3′ exonucleases and enhances the stability of specific mRNAs. Absence of a 'poly(A) tail' in the mRNA molecule is associated with rapid degradation of mRNA.
3. **Specific nucleolytic processing:** Extra nucleotide sequences in both 5′ and 3′ ends of the primary transcripts of tRNA are subjected to nucleolytic processing and reduced to size by a specific class of ribonucleases.
4. **Processing of the hnRNA, the primary transcript to mRNA, by splicing:** The hnRNA contains long intervening sequences called **introns** that separate the **exons**, the coding regions. In the nucleus, the introns are removed and the exons are spliced to form mature mRNA.

   RNA splicing: In the formation of mRNA, the introns are cleaved out of the primary transcript and the exons are appropriately spliced, i.e. joined together. This takes place in the nucleus before the resulting mature mRNA enters the cytoplasm. The mRNA molecules are much smaller than their primary transcript hnRNA. The excision of the introns and formation of the final mRNA molecule by ligation of exons is called **RNA splicing**.

   An enzyme complex named spliceosome catalyses the accurate removal of introns and joining of the exons. The splicing process is remarkably precise. If an error of even a single base occurs, the correct reading frame would be destroyed and functional mRNA is not produced. **Thalassaemia** arises due to a defect in the splicing process and a defect in mRNA synthesis. The 5′ end of the primary transcript is retained and the cap structure is added. This prevents attack by 5′ exonucleases. To the 3′ end, several adenylate molecules are added to form a poly(A) tail. The presence of a poly(A) tail at the 3′ end is associated with the stability of the specific mRNAs. The correctly spliced mRNA transcript leaves the nucleus and enters the cytoplasm carrying only information from DNA that is necessary for translation of the specific protein.

   After transcription, the two strands of the DNA rewind simultaneously and the DNA regains its double helix structure. This is followed by unwinding of the next segment of the DNA strands for transcription. The correctly spliced mRNA transcript leaves the nucleus and enters the cytoplasm bound to a free ribosome for translation.

Translation

Translation means translating the genetic message in the mRNA and build a protein accordingly. It requires a close relationship between mRNA which is the carrier of information for the synthesis of protein, tRNA the amino acid adaptor molecule, rRNA and ribosomes, the site of protein synthesis. Translation can be divided into three stages, namely

1. Initiation
2. Elongation
3. Termination

The various stages in translation are represented in **Figures 22.5–22.12**.

To initiate translation, the mRNA must first form an initiation complex with a ribosome small unit (40 S) and met-tRNA. Methionine is attached as the first amino acid to a specific tRNA by activation. Activation of amino acids involves formation of aminoacyl-tRNAs, by binding of an amino acid to a specific tRNA. The reactions take place in two steps:

1. The first step is activation of the amino acid by ATP. Aminoacyl AMP is formed. The reaction is catalysed by aminoacyl-tRNA synthetase.
2. The second step is linking of the activated amino acid to tRNA. The same enzyme must accurately recognise the amino acid it activates and link it to the tRNA, specific for the amino acid. This process is known as **'charging'** of the tRNA. The activated amino acid binds to the 3′ end of the tRNA which has the trinucleotide sequence CCA.

$$1.\quad \text{Amino acid} + \text{ATP} \rightleftharpoons \text{Aminoacyl AMP} + \text{PP}_i$$

$$2.\quad \text{Aminoacyl AMP} + \text{tRNA} \rightleftharpoons \text{Aminoacyl-tRNA} + \text{AMP.}$$

The tRNAs carrying activated amino acids reach the mRNA in the ribosomal site, recognise their codons in the mRNA and assemble the amino acids in a correct sequence as dictated by the mRNA template.

Initiation: This starts when the ribosome small unit (40 S) binds to a start codon AUG which is a specific sequence of nucleotides, at the 5′ end on the mRNA strand situated next to the cap structure of mRNA (**Fig. 22.5**). Initiation follows in the 5′ → 3′ direction. At the same time, the initiator tRNA molecule which carries methionine as the first incoming amino acid and which has anticodon UAC reaches the mRNA and fits into the P site of the ribosome (**Fig. 22.5**). The anticodon of met-tRNA UAC base pairs with AUG of the start codon of the mRNA.

Now the large ribosome unit (60 S) joins the small unit (40 S) initiation complex to form a complete functional ribosome (**Fig. 22.6**). Proteins called initiation factors referred to as eLFs are required to bring the translation components together. GTP provides energy for the initiation process. Note that the initiator tRNA bearing the growing polypeptide is in the P site ready for the elongation cycle to start and the A site holds the tRNA bearing the next amino acid to be added to the polypeptide chain (**Fig. 22.7**).

Elongation: This is a step-wise formation of peptide bonds. As each ribosome moves over the successive codons of the mRNA strand, the appropriate tRNA that reads the codon attaches to the mRNA and deposits its amino acid at each step on the ribosome. Peptide bonds are formed between the activated carboxyl group of the growing polypeptide and the amino group of the aminoacyl tRNA (**Figs 22.8** and **22.9**). Elongation consists of three steps and the reactions are catalysed by proteins called elongation factors (eEF). They utilise the energy released by GTP hydrolysis for the movements.

1. **Codon recognition:** An incoming aminoacyl-tRNA binds to the mRNA codon in the A site. Selection of the correct aminoacyl-tRNA is enhanced by elongation factor (EF1) (**Fig. 22.8**). This step requires hydrolysis of GTP.

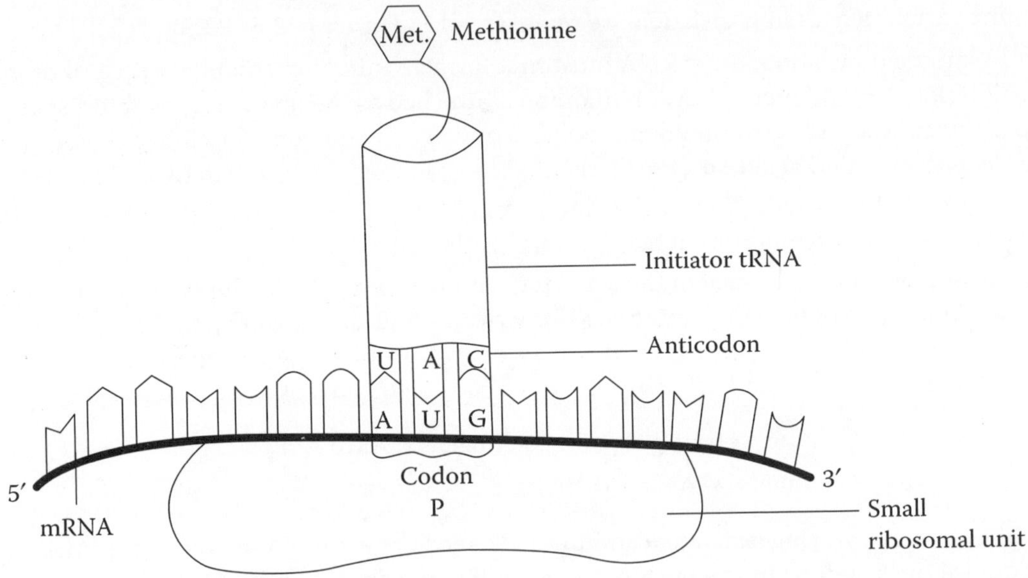

Figure 22.5 Initiation: A small ribosomal subunit binds to mRNA.

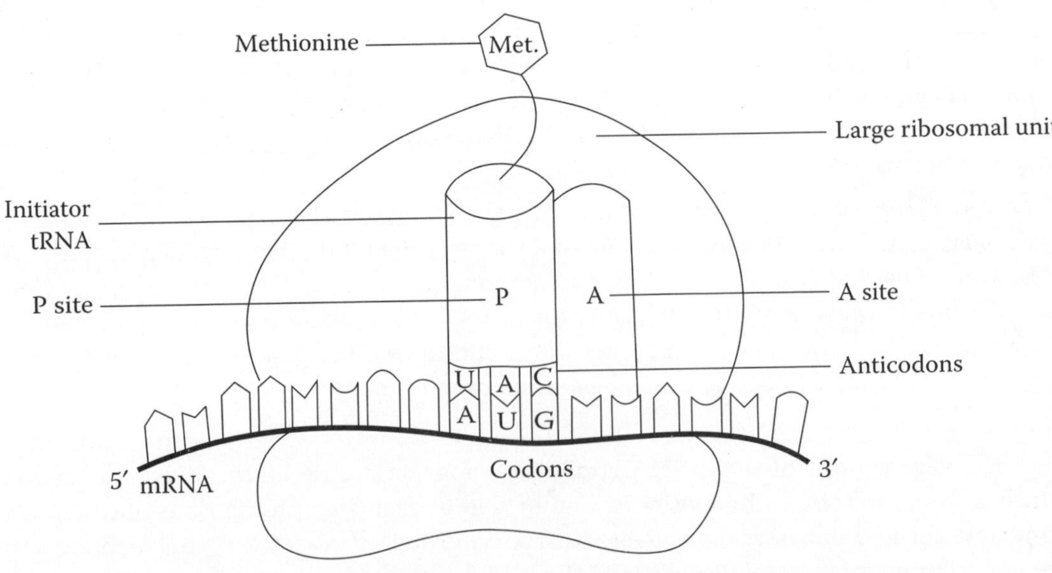

Figure 22.6 The large ribosomal subunit joins the small subunit.

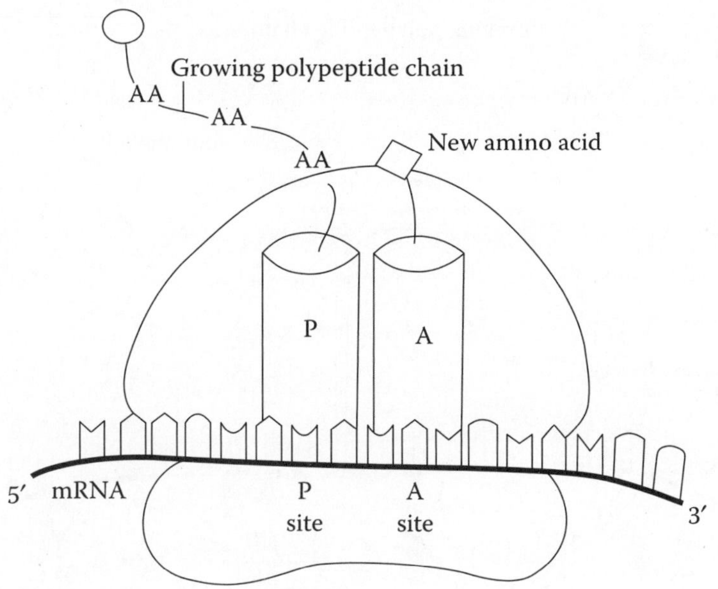

Figure 22.7 The initiator tRNA bearing the growing polypeptide is in the P site. A site holds the tRNA bearing the next amino acid.

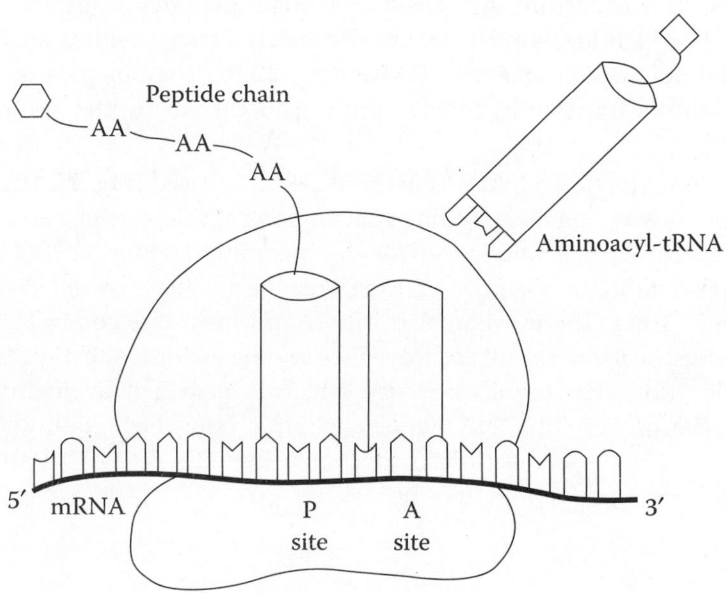

Figure 22.8 Elongation: Codon recognition. An incoming aminoacyl tRNA binds to the codon in A site.

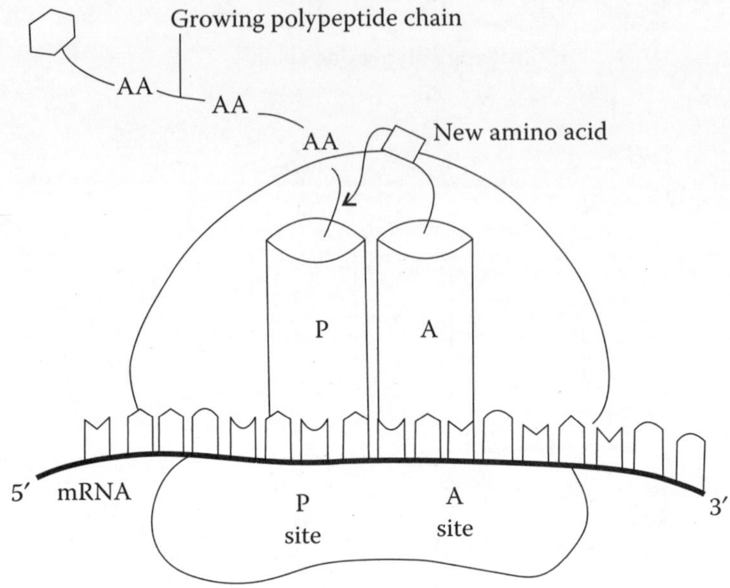

Figure 22.9 Peptide bond formation. A peptide bond is formed between the new amino acid and the growing polypeptide chain.

2. **Peptide bond formation:** An enzyme named peptidyl transferase catalyses the formation of a peptide bond between the newly arrived amino acid in **A site** and the growing polypeptide chain in **P site** (**Fig. 22.9**). The polypeptide separates from the tRNA and is transferred to the amino acid carried by the tRNA in the **A site** (**Fig. 22.10**).
3. **Translocation:** The tRNA that was in the **P site** is released (**Fig. 22.10**). The aminoacyl tRNA in the **A site** attached to the growing polypeptide is translocated to the **P site** (**Fig. 22.11**). Now the **A site** is free for the incoming aminoacyl-tRNA and is aligned with the next codon. In this process, the ribosome advances by one codon towards the 3′ end (**Fig. 22.11**). The movement of ribosomes from one codon to the next codon is called **translocation** and is accomplished by means of elongation factor 2 (eEF-2). The translocation step requires energy which is provided by hydrolysis of a GTP molecule. The process of tRNA binding, peptide bond formation and translocation, resulting in step-wise elongation of the polypeptide, is repeated until a termination codon is encountered.

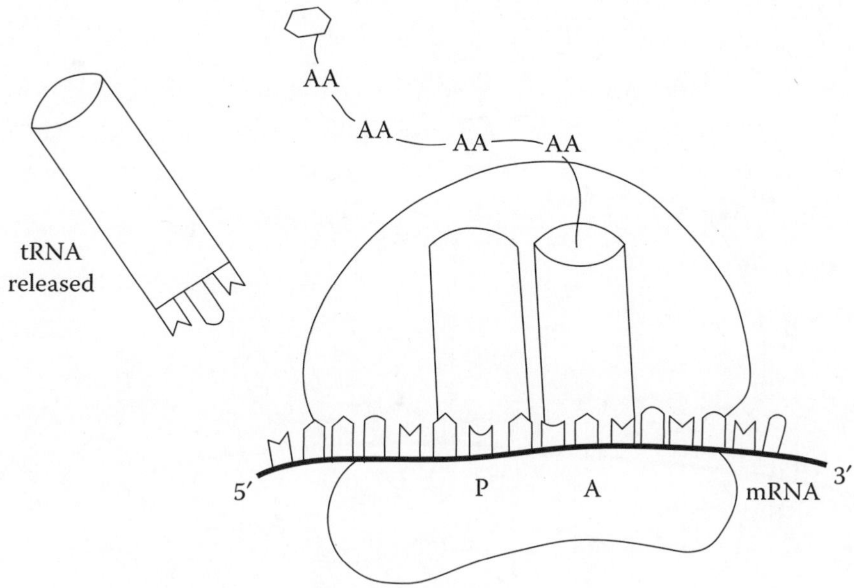

Figure 22.10 Translocation. The tRNA in the P site is released.

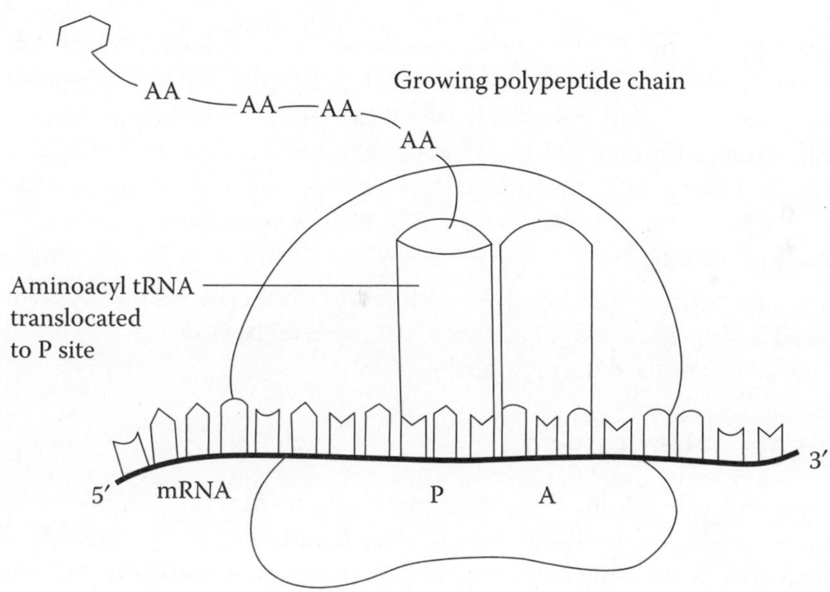

Figure 22.11 Translocation. The aminoacyl tRNA in the A site is translocated to the P site. The ribosome is advanced by one codon.

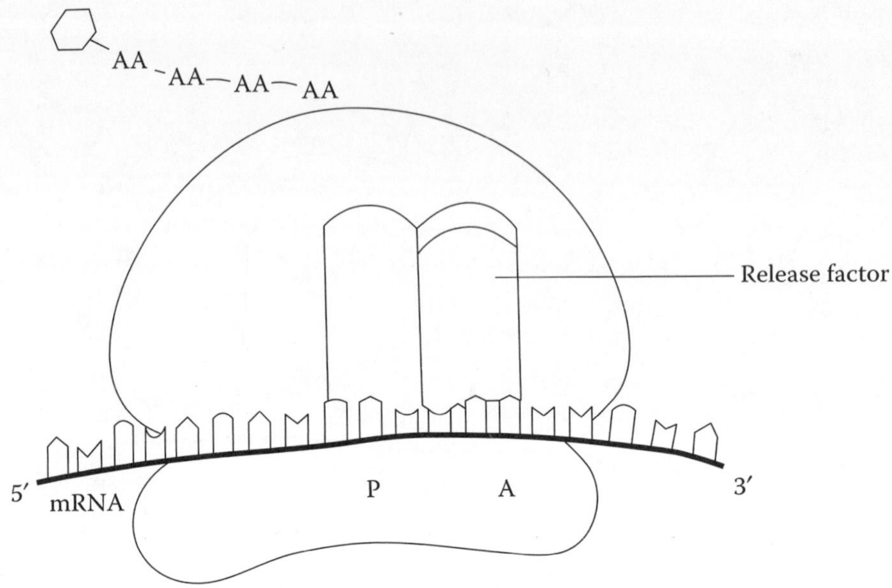

Figure 22.12 Termination. The peptide-tRNA linkage is hydrolysed release factor. The polypeptide and the tRNA separate from rib.

Termination: This is the final stage of translation. The codons UAG, UAA and UGA are termination codons of mRNA and act as stop signals. When a ribosome reaches a terminating codon, a protein, called **release factor** (eRF), binds to the termination codon and in conjunction with peptidyl transferase hydrolyses the peptide-tRNA ester linkage (**Fig. 22.12**). Following this, the polypeptide, tRNA and mRNA are released and the ribosome dissociates into its subunits (**Fig. 22.13**). The completed protein is thus released from tRNA and ribosome.

Four high-energy phosphate bonds are utilised to synthesise each peptide linkage. Two ATPs are used during activation of amino acid. One GTP provides energy for the initiation process. One GTP is utilised during translocation.

Post-Translational Processing

Most proteins emerging from ribosomes are ready to function immediately. But some proteins must undergo several alterations after translation of the mRNA, to form the active protein. The process of such alterations is called '**post-translational modifications of proteins**'. These modifications include the following:

1. **Removal of *N*-terminal amino acids** of the protein molecules, by specific aminopeptidases; for example, collagen is synthesised as procollagen. Specific enzymes carry out hydroxylations and oxidation of specific amino acid residues within the procollagen molecule to provide cross-links for greater stability. Amino-terminal peptides are cleaved off the molecule to form the final collagen molecule.

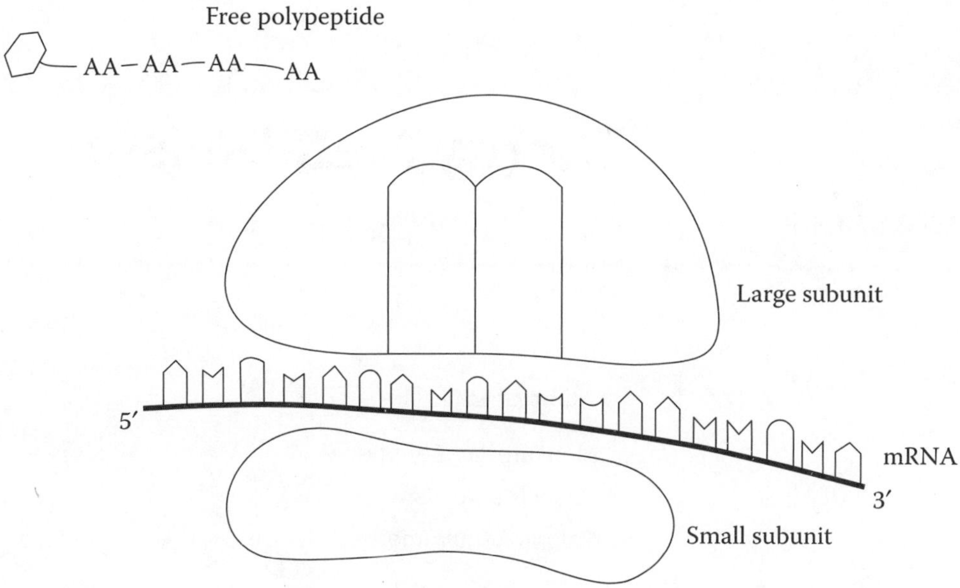

Figure 22.13 Completion of protein synthesis: Release of free polypeptide chain, separation of ribosomal subunits and mRNA.

2. **Trimming:** Insulin, a protein having two polypeptide chains with interchain and intrachain disulphide bridges, is synthesised initially, as a single long precursor polypeptide proinsulin molecule that is not active functionally. The polypeptide chain folds to allow the disulphide bridges to form. A specific protease clips out a segment at the head of the folding, resulting in the generation of the functional insulin molecule having two polypeptide chains.
3. **Covalent modification by hydroxylation, acetylation, phosphorylation** and **glycosylation** are common. The hydroxylated amino acids, for example hydroxyproline and hydroxylysine present in proteins, arise as a result of post-translational modification.
4. **Phosphorylation:** Glycogen synthase and glycogen phosphorylase are the regulatory enzymes of glycogen synthesis and degradation. Phosphorylation converts the enzymes from their inactive 'b' form to their active 'a' form.
5. **Glycosylation** of proteins alters the physical properties of protein and makes them more stable. Glycosylation may involve addition of a few carbohydrate residues or formation of large, branched oligosaccharide chains. It is carried out by a variety of glycosyltransferases.
6. **Methylation:** Methyl groups in certain amino acids, namely arginine, lysine and histidine, are donated by S-adenosylmethionine to the transcribed protein as a post-translational modification.

23 CHAPTER

Energy Metabolism

Chapter Outline

- Measurement of Energy
- Basal Metabolism
- Caloric Requirement

In living tissues, the bulk of energy is derived from the oxidation of the three main classes of foodstuffs, namely carbohydrates, fats and proteins. The energy derived is utilised as follows:

1. A considerable amount of energy is converted to heat and is utilised to maintain the body temperature.
2. Some portion of energy is utilised for the performance of work like muscular contraction, secretory function and nerve impulse conduction.
3. Some amount of energy is stored temporarily in the high-energy phosphate bonds or stored for a longer period in the form of fat and glycogen to provide energy whenever required.

MEASUREMENT OF ENERGY

Energy in the form of heat is measured in terms of calories (small calorie). It refers to the amount of heat required to raise the temperature of 1 gram of water by 1°C from 15°C to 16°C. For the purpose of nutrition, it is common to use the large calorie written as 'C', Cal or kilocalorie, which is 1000 times the small calorie mentioned above.

In nutrition studies, the caloric value of a given food is determined by igniting the weighed food in a bomb calorimeter which consists of a metal vessel, surrounded by a measured volume of water. The ignition is done in an atmosphere of oxygen by means of an electric spark. The increase in the temperature of the surrounding water, multiplied by the weight of the food, gives the number of calories liberated by the combustion of the food. The caloric values of carbohydrate, fat and protein as determined by burning in a bomb calorimeter are given below.

1 gram of carbohydrate yields ... 4.1 Cal

1 gram of fat yields ... 9.4 Cal

1 gram of protein yields ... 5.6 Cal

It has been found that when the same substances are utilised by the body, carbohydrates and fats give the same caloric values as in a bomb calorimeter, whereas proteins yield only 4.1 Cal. This is because proteins are incompletely oxidised in the body, and urea which is the end product of protein metabolism in the body retains some energy without availing it to the body. However, in the bomb calorimeter, urea is completely burnt.

As it is customary to round off the caloric values to the nearest figure, the rounded-up figures for the three main classes of foodstuffs are given below and these figures will be taken to represent their caloric values when energy calculation referring to them is made.

1 gram of carbohydrate yields ... 4 Cal

1 gram of fat yields ... 9 Cal

1 gram of protein yields ... 4 Cal

Respiratory Quotients of Foodstuffs

A simple method applied to calculate the caloric values of the foodstuffs in the body is to determine their 'respiratory quotient'.

The respiratory quotient (R.Q.) of any foodstuff is the ratio of the volume of carbon dioxide eliminated to the volume of oxygen utilised for its oxidation.

In the process of oxidation, carbohydrates, fats and protein react with definite amounts of oxygen to form definite amounts of carbon dioxide and water. The R.Q. for the three main foodstuffs are given below.

1. **Carbohydrates:** Complete oxidation of one molecule of glucose may be represented as follows:

$$C_6H_{12}O_6 + 6\ O_2 \longrightarrow 6\ CO_2 + 6\ H_2O.$$

The R.Q. for carbohydrate is $\frac{6\ CO_2}{6\ O_2} = 1.$

2. **Fats:** The R.Q. for fats is lower because the oxygen content of fat in relation to the carbon content is low. Consequently, they need more oxygen from outside for oxidation. Complete oxidation of a typical fat (triolein) may be represented as follows:

$$C_{57}H_{104}O_6 + 80\ O_2 \longrightarrow 57\ CO_2 + 52\ H_2O.$$

The R.Q. for triolein is $= \frac{57\ CO_2}{80\ O_2} = 0.71.$

The R.Q. of fats in general is about 0.7.

3. **Protein:** The R.Q. of protein is more difficult to determine, since it is not completely burned. Some amount of C, H and O are retained in the body without utilisation and therefore not excreted in the urine and faeces. However, the proteins catabolised during a given period can be calculated by obtaining the urine nitrogen excreted

during the period, because nitrogen represents the index of protein catabolism. Based on this, it has been calculated that 100 grams of proteins, when metabolised, give rise to 16 grams of nitrogen in urine. Thus by estimating the nitrogen content of urine, the amount of protein metabolised is calculated as follows.

16 grams of urinary nitrogen represent 100 grams of proteins. 1 gram of urinary nitrogen represents $= \frac{100}{16}$ 6.25 grams of protein.

The R.Q. of proteins obtained by applying this calculation is found to be about 0.8.

The R.Q. of a mixed diet containing the normally allowed quantities of carbohydrate, fats and protein has been calculated to be about 0.85 for a normal individual. The R.Q. increases and reaches the value of 1, when more carbohydrate is included in the diet. It reaches a lower value when more fat is included in the diet.

BASAL METABOLISM

Besides the energy derived from food, the body also derives energy from its own metabolism when it is under basal condition, i.e. at complete physical and mental rest. This energy is derived solely from stored sources. Most of it is dissipated in the form of heat and part of it is expended for the maintenance of respiration, circulation, muscle tone, gastrointestinal contraction and functional activities of organs such as kidneys, liver and endocrine glands.

This metabolism is called basal metabolism. The term 'basal metabolic rate' (BMR) may be defined as the heat produced per unit time under basal condition, i.e. at complete physical and mental rest, in the post-absorptive state, which means 14–18 hours after taking food.

Basal metabolism varies with the size of the body, age and sex of the individual and is expressed as Cal per square meter of the body surface per hour. The average normal BMR for an young adult of 20–25 years is about 40 Cal/m^2/hr and this would amount to about 1300–1600 Cal per day for a man weighing 70 kg, having a surface area of 1.75 m^2.

For clinical purpose, derivations of BMR from the average normal are expressed in terms of percentage increase or decrease. Values between 10% and 15% are considered to be within the normal limits. Values above +15% are high and below –15% are clinically low.

Factors Influencing BMR

1. **Surface area:** The basal metabolism is proportional to the surface area of the body and the BMR of different individuals when expressed in terms of the surface area is remarkably constant.

   The surface area can be calculated if the body weight and height of the individual are known, by applying the formula of DuBois which states that surface area in cm^2. = (Weight in kg)$^{0.425}$ × (height in cm)$^{0.725}$ × 71.84. Calculated tables are available for different weights and heights for ready reference.

2. **Age:** The BMR in the newborn is low. It rises to a maximum at the age of 5 years, above which the rate begins to decline with a relative rise just before puberty.
3. **Sex:** Generally, the BMR for women is 6–10% lower than that in males. In woman, the BMR rises just before and during menstruation.
4. **Climate:** The BMR is lower in warm climate.
5. **State of nutrition:** The BMR is lowered in states of undernutrition and starvation.
6. **Sleep:** The BMR falls by about 10% during sleep. During 8 hours of sleep, the total energy output would be about 520 Cal, at the rate of 65 Cal per hour.
7. **Hormones:** Two hormones, thyroxine and epinephrine, influence the BMR. Of these, thyroxine has more influence, as approximately 40% of the basal oxygen consumption is due to the action of thyroid hormone. BMR is increased from +30 to +60% in hyperthyroid conditions and falls from −30 to −50% in hypothyroid conditions (myxoedema). Therefore, determination of BMR is of great value in the diagnosis of diseases of thyroid.

   Epinephrine has a direct but rapid and brief effect on the BMR which is increased in pheochromocytoma (tumour of the adrenals) and decreased in adrenal insufficiency (Addison's disease).
8. **Other diseases:** BMR is raised in fevers and infectious diseases, the rise being proportional to the elevation of the temperature.
9. BMR is raised in all conditions where there is increased cellular activity, for example leukaemia and polycythaemia.
10. BMR will show a high false value when the test is conducted on a patient with a perforated eardrum.

Specific Dynamic Action

The specific dynamic action (SDA) of a foodstuff is the extra heat produced, over and above the caloric value of a given amount of food. This extra heat is produced when the food is used by the body and is drawn from the food stores.

Protein has the greatest SDA, about 50% above its caloric value. For example, when a certain amount of protein which contains say 100 Cal (25 grams) is metabolised, 130 Cal of heat is produced instead of 100 Cal. This extra 30 Cal is the product of the SDA of protein. Carbohydrate comes next. It produces an increase of about 5–6%, i.e. when carbohydrate containing 100 Cal is metabolised, it produces 105 Cal of heat. Fats produce an increase of about 10%. The origin of this extra heat is not clearly known, though it is suggested that the activity of the tissues metabolising these foodstuffs is responsible for this. However, on a mixed diet, the SDA of the whole diet is found to be less than the sum of the SDA of the individual foodstuff.

Knowledge about the SDA of each foodstuff is necessary because this extra energy must be provided for in the diet, in terms of food, besides the calculated quantity of food and it is customary to add 10% to the total required calories to provide energy for the SDA.

CALORIC REQUIREMENT

Energy Equilibrium

A normal individual is said to maintain energy equilibrium when his daily diet supplies as much energy as he expends. If the energy supplied through food is less than what he expends, he loses weight. If the caloric value of the diet is much higher than the energy he expends, the excess energy would be stored as fat. It is, therefore, necessary to calculate the exact caloric requirement for an individual, if he should maintain his energy equilibrium.

Calculation of Caloric Requirement

In order to calculate the caloric requirement for an individual, the amount of energy he expends due to various kinds of activities during different parts of the day must be known. Besides his activities, one should not forget about the energy expended to maintain him under basal conditions, which is constant for any individual. The average value of BMR for a normal adult weighing 70 kg ranges from 1300 to 1600 Cal per day. While calculating the energy requirement for any individual, it is necessary to add the energy expended for basal metabolism to the energy required by him to carry out various types of routine activities.

Approximate increments in caloric requirements per hour, above the basal level, for different muscular activities are given in **Table 23.1**.

Table 23.1 Approximate Increments in Hourly Caloric Requirements Based on the Physical Activity Level

Activity	Increased Requirement of Cal/per hour	Nature of Occupation
Sitting quietly	35	Watchman, peon
Standing quietly	40	Watchman, peon
Reading	40	Students
Typing	75	Typist
Housework	110	Housewife
Carpentry	150	Carpenter
Sawing wood	380	Woodcutter
Walking fast	550	Labourer-Athlete
Walking upstairs	1000	Labourer-Athlete

It may be seen from the table that the metabolism of a man increases as he engages in active work or exercise and accordingly the total amount of energy output also increases. An interesting observation made by Benedict is that mental work does not involve an appreciable increase in total metabolism. For instance, the effort involved in solving mathematical problems increases the metabolism only by 3–4%. Depending upon the type of work a person does daily, he may lead the following type of life:

1. **Sedentary life:** A person can be classified under sedentary life, if his daily work is of the type referred in 1, 2 or 3 of **Table 23.1**. He expends for this type of work an average of 40 Cal of energy per hour and in 16 hours will expend 640 Cal (40 × 16). Giving allowance for working lesser or more number of hours, values ranging from 500 to 700 Cal per day may be taken as the normal average figures for those who come under this group.
2. **Light work:** Typist, clerk, manager, director and businessmen can be classified under this group. He may expend a minimum of 75 Cal per hour and for 16 hours expend 1200 Cal (75 × 16). Giving allowance for working lesser number of hours, a range of 700–1200 Cal may be taken as the average value.
3. **Moderate work:** A housewife doing house work, a mechanic and a carpenter can be classified under this group. These persons expend on an average 100–150 Cal of energy per hour and will expend in 16 hours, 100 × 16 = 1600 to 150 × 16 = 2400 Cal. A range of 1600–2400 Cal may be taken as the average value.
4. **Severe work:** A labourer or an athlete comes under this group. He expends 380–500 Cal per hour by doing this type of work and will expend for 16 hours, 6080 (380 × 16) to 8000 (500 × 16) Cal of energy.

As a general rule, the energy requirement for an average normal woman is 15% less than that for men. Extra provision of 200–500 Cal should be made for pregnant and lactating women.

While calculating the caloric requirement, allowance must be made for the following activities:

1. 8 hours of sleep
2. Basal metabolism
3. Muscular activity
4. Specific dynamic action (SDA)

A normal adult man weighing 70 kg and having a body surface area of say 1.7 m^2, has a BMR of about 65 Cal per hour (at the rate of 40 Cal per m^2 per hour approximately). This rate increases with the severity of exercise.

It is usual to allow 6% of the total calories for SDA, and this works out to an average of 175 Cal for a total caloric requirement of 3000. If allowance for SDA is not made, the subject will lose weight, as this amount of energy will be drawn from his tissues.

The caloric requirement for a man doing light work is calculated as shown below. For the sake of convenience, 24 hours of the day is split usually into three periods, each of 8 hours' duration. Each period represents routine activities such as

1. 8 hours of sleep
2. 8 hours of light work

3. 8 hours of a lighter type of work, which may include, for instance, 6 hours of sitting quietly and 2 hours of light exercise. Accordingly, he expends energy as follows.

8 hours of sleep at 65 Cal per hour	= 520 Cal
8 hours of light work at 65 + 100 (165 Cal per hour)	= 1320 Cal
6 hours of sitting quietly at 65 + 35 (100 Cal per hour)	= 600 Cal
2 hours of light exercise at 65 + 110 (175 Cal per hour)	= 350 Cal
	Total = 2790 Cal
Specific dynamic action at 6%	= 168 Cal
Therefore, daily caloric requirement	= **2958 Cal**

(Basal metabolism for an average man is taken as 65 Cal and added to the caloric requirement in doing work at every stage.)

The daily caloric requirement for a man who does light work is approximately 3000 Cal. Similarly, the energy expended by persons doing more strenuous work or leading a sedentary life can be calculated. Care should be taken to provide extra calories during periods of growth, puberty, pregnancy and convalescence. **Table 23.2** indicates the daily requirements of calories at various ages for different levels of activity, as recommended by the Food and Nutrition Board of National Research Council.

Table 23.2 Energy Requirements

	Calories per day	
Levels of Activity and Age	**Males**	**Females**
Adults		
Sedentary work	2400	2000
Light work	3000	2400
Moderate work	3500	3000
Strenuous work	4500	3500
Pregnancy (later half)	–	2400
Lactating period	–	3000
Children		
16–24 years	3800	2400
13–15 years	3200	2600
10–12 years	2500	2500
7–9 years	2000	2000
4–6 years	1600	1600
1–3 years	1200	1200
Under 1 year	110/kg	110/kg

24 CHAPTER

Elements of Nutrition

Chapter Outline

- Well-Balanced Diet
- Essential Components of Diet and Their Importance
- Nutritive Values of Some Common Foods
- Nutrition During Pregnancy
- Nutrition for Lactating Women

WELL-BALANCED DIET

Having known the energy expended for various types of activities, it is possible to chart out the quality and quantity of food that would furnish the required energy. The foremost requirement in recommending diet is to prescribe one which permits and maintains growth and reproduction and provides all nutrients in a required amount. Such a diet is known as **well-balanced diet**. The proximate principles of food are carbohydrates, proteins and fats, supplemented by small amounts of vitamins, minerals and essential fatty acids. Of these, carbohydrates, proteins and fats contribute to the bulk of energy required for the body. Carbohydrates serve as the major source of energy and next comes fats. Proteins serve to provide amino acids for tissue growth and repairs primarily, but if the intake of carbohydrates and fats is inadequate, proteins are utilised for supply of energy. The components of a well-balanced diet will vary depending upon the age, sex, physiological needs such as pregnancy and lactation and the nature of physical activity.

While designing the quality and quantity of a balanced diet, the total calories are distributed among the three classes of food in the following proportion. As a general rule, 55–70% is derived from carbohydrates, 20–30% from fats and 10–15% from protein. The proportion of carbohydrates, fats and protein should be approximately 4:1:1. Thus, a diet containing 400 grams of carbohydrates, 100 grams of protein and 100 grams of fats can provide 3000 calories which is the requirement for a normal average adult. But these proportions vary under different physiological conditions and with climate. For example, more calories are required in cold climate to retain a constant body temperature. In such a situation, the extra calories can be met by increasing the fat content of the diet.

ESSENTIAL COMPONENTS OF DIET AND THEIR IMPORTANCE

Foods contain several chemical constituents known as nutrients. The essential constituents are carbohydrates, proteins, fats, vitamins and minerals. They have all been dealt in detail in the respective chapters. In this chapter, a brief description of their importance in nutrition and major deficiency manifestations is discussed.

Carbohydrates

On an average, 55–70% of the daily intake of calories is supplied by carbohydrates. The carbohydrate requirement under normal conditions is 6–7 grams per kg body weight. A normal adult weighing 70 kg will therefore require 420–500 grams of carbohydrate per day. Substituting the caloric value of 1 gram of carbohydrate as 4 Cal, the carbohydrates taken per day yield approximately (500 × 4) = 2000 Cal.

The main sources of carbohydrates are rice, cereals, potatoes and tubers. Food carbohydrates include sugars such as glucose, fructose and sucrose. **Dietary fibre carbohydrates** present in undigestible plant cell wall components such as cellulose, pectins and gums add bulk to the diet. The importance of the dietary fibre carbohydrates lies in the fact that they absorb water in the intestinal lumen and produce bulky and soft faeces that are easier to be eliminated. It is observed that dietary fibre consumption decreases bowel transit time, reduces enterohepatic circulation of bile salts and delays intestinal absorption of cholesterol and sugar. This helps in reducing serum cholesterol and prevention of high incidence of cardiovascular diseases, diabetes mellitus and cancer of colon. Whole cereals, pulses with husk and vegetables are rich sources of fibre.

Proteins

The accepted recommendation of protein intake for a normal adult is 1 gram per kg body weight. Therefore, an average man weighing about 70 kg requires 70 grams of proteins per day. Substituting the caloric value of 1 gram of protein to be 4 Cal, the proteins taken per day yield approximately (70 × 4) = 280 Cal per day. The requirement of protein is increased in growing children, pregnant and lactating women and in conditions of increased metabolism as in fever and convalescence.

Proteins differ in quality, and the nutritive value of a protein depends largely on the content of amino acids of the protein molecules. Proteins of a high biological value have a high content of essential amino acids and they must be supplied in diet to maintain nitrogen balance. Generally, proteins of animal origin are considered to have a high biological value as they contain most of the essential amino acids necessary for the maintenance of nitrogen balance and for promoting growth. Examples of proteins of a high biological value are proteins of egg, milk, dairy products, liver, meat and fish. Proteins of plant origin such as nuts and legumes have a poor biological value. Proteins such as gelatin, zein of corn and gliadin of wheat are considered incomplete protein, because they lack essential amino acids. Proteins, besides supplying essential amino acids, are important sources of sulphur and phosphorus.

Biological value of protein is defined as the percentage of the protein nitrogen that is retained in the body. A protein of a high biological value contains all essential amino acids in adequate quantities and when ingested are absorbed and utilised to the optimum for incorporation into peptides.

The biological values of proteins for some common foods are listed below:

Rice (milled)	70	Groundnut	54
Wheat	60	Soyabean	64
Maize	50	Milk (cow)	85
Ragi	60	Egg (hen)	98
Bengal gram	62	Meat	82
Black gram	54	Fish	80

Foods Containing High-Quality Protein

Egg and milk are high-quality proteins. They are used as a reference standard for comparing the quality of other proteins. Meat protein is also of high protein quality. Some vegetable proteins that are used as major food sources are relatively deficient in one or more essential amino acids. For example, tryptophan and lysine are deficient in maize (corn), lysine is deficient in wheat and methionine is deficient in some beans. So, in a mixed diet of vegetable proteins, deficiency of an amino acid in one vegetable source is compensated by its abundance in another vegetable source. These are described as **complementary proteins**.

Limiting Amino Acids

The essential amino acids most deficient in a protein is called its limiting amino acid. The deficient essential amino acids (limiting amino acids) of wheat, corns and pulses are lysine, tryptophan and methionine, respectively.

Protein Deficiency

Protein Energy Malnutrition When there is insufficient supply of dietary protein, cells lack amino acids for their synthetic activities and growth slows down or stops. The earliest feature of protein deficiency is indigestion and failure of absorption of food because of lack of synthesis of digestive enzymes. As a result, chronic diarrhoea sets in. Next, the liver cells fail to synthesise plasma albumin and this leads to water retention and oedema. Skeletal muscles and red blood cells fail to maintain their structure and functions, resulting in wasting of muscles and anaemia. These clinical symptoms comprise a spectrum of diseases in early childhood and are collectively known as **protein energy malnutrition**. Two diseases, namely **marasmus** and **kwashiorkor**, will be considered under this section.

Marasmus: This occurs in infants below 1 year of age, particularly after weaning of the mother's milk. The infant fed on diet low in both protein and calories becomes undernourished and loses weight considerably with chronic diarrhoea. If not corrected, the condition leads to extreme wasting of subcutaneous fat and muscles. There is no oedema in marasmus.

Kwashiorkor: This affects children above 1 year of age when they are fed with diet low in protein but relatively adequate calories. The child is undernourished and loses weight. There is wasting of subcutaneous fat and muscles. This condition differs from marasmus in that there is oedema of feet and this is due to hypoalbuminaemia.

Fat

Lipids are indispensable components of diet, because they provide the highest caloric value to the diet. One gram of fat yields 9.4 Cal. This is more than twice the caloric value of carbohydrate or protein. In addition, dietary fats provide essential fatty acids as they are not synthesised in the body. Linoleic, linolenic and arachidonic acids are major precursors for the biosynthesis of prostaglandins. A high ratio of unsaturated fatty acids to saturated fatty acids in the diet is considered to reduce serum cholesterol and thus prevent the premature onset of atherosclerosis. Fats of animal origin contain a higher proportion of saturated fatty acids than those of plant origin, and cholesterol is present only in foods of animal origin. Fats also serve as transport media for the transport of fat-soluble vitamins that are contained in fatty foods. Besides these functions, fats contribute to the palatability and flavour of the food.

The recommended supply of calories by way of dietary fats is 20–30% of the total caloric intake and this includes about 3% contribution by essential fatty acids. It is found that 60–80 grams of fat per day would supply the recommended calories. However, at higher caloric levels, more than 30% would be derived from fats. Accordingly, for calculating the dietary requirement, 1–2 grams of fat per kg body weight per day are recommended. This works out to 70–140 grams of fat for a man weighing 70 kg.

Substituting the caloric value of 1 gram of fat as 9 Cal approximately, the total caloric value of an average amount of 100 grams of fat would be 900 Cal.

Sources of fat: Liver, fish oils, egg yolk, butter, vegetable fats, oils, nuts and seeds are good sources of fat.

Vitamins

Among vitamins, B-Complex, vitamin C, vitamins A and D are important constituents of diet. Water-soluble vitamins such as thiamine and vitamin C are lost in cooking water. Polishing cereals result in loss of B vitamins. Inadequate intake of vitamins leads to vitamin deficiency. To ensure adequate intake of vitamins, it is always better to include fresh fruits and vegetables in the diet.

Minerals

Inclusion of certain minerals in diet is necessary for the maintenance of normal health. Calcium and phosphorus are important for the growth and maintenance of healthy bones and teeth. Iron and copper are necessary for the maturation of erythrocytes and prevention of anaemias. Milk and milk products are good sources of calcium and phosphorus while green vegetables and fruits form the chief sources of iron and copper.

NUTRITIVE VALUES OF SOME COMMON FOODS

Milk: It contains proteins of a high biological value. These are lactalbumin, lactoglobulin and casein. Casein is a phosphóprotein. The sugar present in milk is lactose. It is high in human milk. Fats in milk are in the form of fine emulsion. Butter is milk fat. It is rich in Vitamin A. Milk is a good source of calcium and phosphorus.

Egg: It is a good source of protein, fat and vitamins. The main protein in egg white is egg albumin. Ovalbumin and ovoglobulin are other proteins present in egg white. Ovovitellin is phosphoprotein present in egg yolk. The proteins have a high biological value. Egg is rich in cholesterol and is present in yolk. Avidin, a glycoprotein present in egg white, reacts with biotin and prevents absorption of biotin. The yolk is a rich source of vitamin A and riboflavin.

Meat: It is a good source of proteins that has a high biological value and it contains all essential amino acids. Meat contains B vitamins and iron.

Fish: It is a rich source of proteins of a high biological value. The fat content of fish is low, less than 1%, and is easily digestible.

Pulses (legumes): They are important sources of proteins for vegetarians. Grams, peas, lentils and beans belong to this group. Legumes are a good source of B vitamins, calcium, phosphorus and iron.

Soyabean: It is a rich source of protein. It contains all essential amino acids except methionine. The fat content is fairly high and contains a high amount of unsaturated fatty acids. It is a good source of B vitamins, calcium, phosphorus and iron. Processed soyabean flour is used as a milk substitute.

Cereals: They include wheat, rice, maize, barley and oats. They are rich sources of starch and contain less protein. Rice is a good source of thiamine. Raw milled rice is deficient in thiamine and niacin.

Vegetables: Green leafy vegetables are rich sources of vitamins, such as carotenes, ascorbic acid and folic acid and contain calcium.

Fruits: They contain sugars, organic acids, carotene, B vitamins and ascorbic acid. Citrus fruits contain ascorbic acid. Mangoes and papayas are rich sources of carotene. Dates contain a good amount of iron.

Taking into consideration the foods that commonly form part of Indian diets, balanced diets have been suggested by Nutrition Experts groups for various types of population. The quantity and composition of such diets are given in **Table 24.1**.

Table 24.1 Balanced Diet for an Adult Man (Vegetarian)

Food Items	Sedentary Work (g)	Moderate Work (g)	Heavy Work (g)
Cereals	400	475	650
Pulses	70	80	80
Green leafy vegetables	100	125	125
Other vegetables	75	75	100
Roots and tubers	75	100	100
Fruits	30	30	30
Milk	200	200	200
Fats and oils	35	40	50
Sugar and jaggery	30	40	55

NUTRITION DURING PREGNANCY

During pregnancy, a normal woman weighing about 58 kg requires a daily intake of food supplying 2000–2200 Cal and an additional allowance of 300 Cal. The ICMR has recommended 120 Cal in the first trimester and 300 Cal in the second and third trimesters of pregnancy. The additional calories are required to provide for the growth and development of the foetus and growth of the uterus, placenta and mammary glands.

Protein: The ICMR nutrition group has recommended an additional daily intake of 12 grams of protein during the second and third trimesters for increased blood formation and synthesis of plasma proteins. Proteins of a high biological value, namely milk, egg, meat and fish, should be included in the diet. Carbohydrates and fats containing essential fatty acids should be included in the food.

Vitamins and minerals: The ICMR has recommended an additional allowance of 500–600 mg calcium and 200 IU vitamin D per day. This is necessary as otherwise the calcium stores in the bones of the mother will be depleted by the growing foetus leading to osteomalacia in extreme cases. Diets should include an adequate amount of milk and milk products.

Folic acid: An additional daily allowance of 50 and 200 (μg of folic acid and 0.5 μg vitamin B_{12}) is recommended.

Iron: It is required for the formation of an additional amount of haemoglobin for the mother and formation of foetal blood. An extra daily allowance of 10–15 mg iron is recommended during pregnancy and foods rich in iron should be taken regularly.

The diet of pregnant women should include an adequate amount of milk, eggs, green leafy vegetables and citrus fruits.

NUTRITION FOR LACTATING WOMEN

Milk production varies in lactating mothers. The daily output of milk in lactating women is about 850 ml. The energy value of 850 ml of milk is estimated to be equivalent to 600 kcal. With 80% efficiency to convert food energy into milk energy, a mother needs an additional allowance of 750 kcal daily during the lactation period.

Protein and fat requirement: During lactation, an extra daily allowance of 20 grams of dietary protein of which 25% should be in the form of animal protein of a high biological value is recommended. The diet should contain an adequate quantity of essential fatty acids. This can be provided by including vegetable oils in the diet.

Calcium: An additional dietary calcium of 500–600 mg should be provided daily.

Vitamins: The recommended daily additional allowances during lactation are 400 μg vitamin A, 0.4 mg thiamine, 0.4 mg riboflavin, 5 mg nicotinic acid, 50 μg folic acid, 0.5 μg vitamin B_{12} and 30 mg ascorbic acid.

25

CHAPTER

Water and Mineral Metabolism

Chapter Outline

- Water Metabolism
- Mineral Metabolism (Sodium, Potassium and Chloride Metabolism)

WATER METABOLISM

Water forms 60–70% of the body weight and is distributed throughout the body, being closely associated with the distribution of electrolytes in the body. The total quantity of water is distributed throughout two main compartments:

1. Intracellular compartment, which comprises the fluid present inside the cells
2. Extracellular compartment, which comprises the fluid present outside the cells. This includes the fluid in plasma and interstitial fluid.

Functions: The body water is of utmost physiological importance and has specific functions to perform:

- It acts as a solvent for the secretory and excretory products.
- It acts as a carrier of nutritive elements to tissues and removes waste materials from tissues.
- It is a regulator of body temperature.
- Water is a solvent for electrolytes. It helps to regulate the electrolyte balance of the body and maintains a healthy equilibrium of osmotic pressure exerted by the solutes dissolved in water. A state of health is possible only as long as the osmotic pressure exerted by the solutes remains constant.

Water balance: A healthy body maintains water balance precisely, even on variable intake or output of fluids. The chief physiological regulatory mechanism which prevents excessive loss of body water by excretion is due to the action of antidiuretic hormone (ADH) or vasopressin, secreted by the posterior lobe of pituitary. It reduces the excretion of water by the kidneys, by increasing the rate of reabsorption of water with solutes, from the renal tubules. In diabetes insipidus, due to the failure of ADH secretion, there is excessive excretion of urine.

A body is said to maintain water balance, when the amount of water gained by the body is equal to the amount of water excreted or lost from the body. This is shown in **Table 25.1**.

Table 25.1 Water Balance

Water Intake in ml per day	Water Output in ml per day
Water intake as such = 1100	Water excreted in urine = 1000
Water intake in diet = 900	Water excreted in stools = 200
Water produced during metabolism = 200	Water lost through skin and lungs = 1000
Total intake 2200	Total output 2200

Water gain: Body gains water in the following ways:

1. Water consumed as drinking water and beverage
2. Water consumed in the foods
3. Water formed by the oxidation of foodstuffs in the body. This is the water gained in the metabolism. A normal diet giving rise to 2500–3000 calories is said to yield 200 ml of water by the metabolic process.

Water lost: Body loses water by the following routes:

1. Water is lost from the skin and lungs and this represents insensible perspiration. This amounts to about 850 ml per day. The quantity increases in fevers.
2. Water is lost in sweat. The amount of water lost depends upon the work and humidity of the environment. This varies from 0 to 1 litre per day.
3. Water is lost in the urine and this amounts to 1000–1500 ml. The water lost in stools amounts to about 200 ml.

Since the efficient functioning of the body fluid depends so much on its amount and its composition in different parts of the body, precise knowledge about the different fluid compartments, the amount and the chemical composition of fluid in each compartment and the significance of the distribution in health is essential. The volume and chemical composition of the fluids in such compartments are maintained fairly constant in spite of the wide variations to which they are exposed.

Mode of distribution of body fluid: The water which forms 60–70% of the body weight is distributed arbitrarily in two major compartments as

1. Intracellular fluid (ICF) comprising about 50% of the body weight
2. Extracellular fluid (ECF) comprising 20% of the body weight. This includes (i) plasma (5% of body weight) and (ii) interstitial fluid (15% of body weight).

Factors influencing distribution of body fluid: Under normal healthy conditions, the total amount of water retained in the body is maintained at a constant level though its distribution is subjected to changes continuously. The principal factors controlling the location and the amount of fluid in the various compartments are the osmotic forces which are maintained by the solutes, i.e. the substances dissolved in the body water. The solutes may be divided into three categories:

1. Organic compounds having a small molecular size, for example glucose and urea. They do not exert much effect on the distribution of water because they diffuse freely across the cell membranes.
2. Organic compounds having a large molecular size, for example proteins. They help in the exchange of fluid between the circulating blood and the interstitial fluid. The plasma proteins are responsible for about 25 mm of the total osmotic pressure of the plasma.
3. The inorganic electrolytes: These constitute the various cations and anions of the body fluids. The main cations are Na^+ and K^+ ions. Ca^{++} and Mg^{++} are present in smaller amounts. The main anions are Cl^- and HCO_3^-. $HPO_4^=$, $SO_4^=$, organic acids and proteins are present in lesser amounts. The inorganic electrolytes are important factors in directing the movement of the fluid in the various compartments and in determining their quantity. The electrolyte composition of ECF (plasma and interstitial fluid) is presented in **Table 25.2**. The concentration of electrolytes is expressed in terms of mEq/L (which is 1/1000 of Eq. wt.) because of their small amount. For conversion of mg/100 ml into mEq wt/L, the following formula is applied:

$$\text{mEq/L} = \frac{\text{mg/L (= mg/100 ml} \times 10) \times \text{Valence}}{\text{'Atomic weight'}}$$

Table 25.2 Electrolyte Composition of ECF Expressed in mEq/L

	Plasma	Interstitial Fluid
Cations		
Na^+	142	138
K^+	5	5
Ca^{++}	5	5
Mg^{++}	3	3
Total	**155**	**151**
Anions		
HCO_3^-	27	32
Cl^-	103	108
$HPO_4^=$	2	2
$SO_4^=$	1	1
Organic acids	6	6
Proteins	16	2
Total	**155**	**151**

It may be seen from the table that the patterns of the electrolyte composition of plasma and interstitial fluid are identical. The predominant cation of the ECF is Na^+. It makes up more than 90% of the total base and its concentration is 142 mEq/L. The high concentration of Na^+ in the plasma and the relative impermeability of Na^+ ions across the cell wall membrane are important factors in controlling the distribution of water throughout the body. It is this function of Na^+ which makes it important in maintaining fluid balance.

The concentration of Na^+ in the plasma is controlled by nerve receptors in the hypothalamus. A drop in the concentration of Na^+ in the serum will initiate a loss of fluid from the body so that normal concentration is restored. An increase in the serum Na^+ concentration will stimulate retention of water, thus diluting the serum back to its normal level. Thus, sodium ions in plasma control the retention or loss of water from the body.

MINERAL METABOLISM (SODIUM, POTASSIUM AND CHLORIDE METABOLISM)

Since the metabolism of sodium, potassium and chloride are closely related to one another, the three elements are studied together. Sodium is the main cation of the ECF and potassium the main cation of the ICF. Potassium is also an important constituent of the ECF though it is present in lesser concentration. Chloride forms the chief anion of the ECF and exists along with sodium mostly.

Functions

1. Sodium, potassium and chloride regulate the acid–base balance of the body fluids. Chloride is required for the chloride shift mechanism and the formation of HCl in gastric juice.
2. They regulate the water balance by maintaining the osmotic pressure of the body fluids.
3. They help to preserve the normal neuromuscular irritability, by maintaining a state of equilibrium on account of their relative proportion in the ECF and ICF.
4. Sodium, potassium and chloride help in the preservation of the permeability of the cells.
5. The plasma proteins are kept in solution as proteinates by sodium and potassium, because both albumin and globulin are soluble in dilute neutral solutions of salts (NaCl).

Source:

Sodium and chloride: The main source of sodium is the salt or sodium chloride which is used in cooking. Sodium chloride is present in the plants, animal tissues and food ingested. An average adequate diet contains 8–15 grams of NaCl. The recommended amount of sodium for adults is 5–15 grams per day.

Potassium: Vegetables are rich sources of potassium. The recommended amount of potassium for adults is about 4 g/day.

Distribution:

Sodium: It is present as the major cation throughout the ECF of the body. In blood, it is present mainly in the serum. The normal average serum concentration of sodium is about 320 mg/100 ml (142 mEq/L). Erythrocytes contain very little sodium.

Potassium: It is present as the major cation of the ICF and is present mainly inside the cells. But a lesser amount is also present in the serum. The normal average serum concentration of potassium is about 19 mg/100 ml (5 mEq/L). Potassium concentration in erythrocytes is about 440 mg/100 g (112 mEq/L).

Chloride: It is the chief anion of ECF. It is present in the plasma and is expressed as NaCl. The normal plasma concentration is 500–550 mg/100 ml. The chloride concentration in CSF is higher than in plasma, 600–620 mg/100 ml.

The strict localisation of large amounts of sodium and chloride in the ECF and potassium in ICF is mainly due to the high degree of selective impermeability of the cell membrane to these ions, under normal conditions. This pattern may deviate from the normal, under certain functional and pathological states. In such cases, potassium will move from the ICF to ECF while sodium from ECF moves into the cells. These changes are always accompanied by alteration in the concentration of chloride and bicarbonate in the ECF.

The distribution of Cl^- and HCO_3^-, between plasma and RBC, is identical and takes place in accordance with Donnan's Law of Equilibrium, which governs the distribution of diffusible monovalent ions. The chloride and bicarbonate shift mechanism are important factors in the maintenance of acid–base balance.

It must be clearly understood that Na^+ ions predominate in the plasma and K^+ ions predominate in the cells. Na^+ and K^+ ions usually have a reciprocal influence on each other so that when the concentration of one increases, the other is diminished. For example, when the amount of K^+ ion in the diet is suddenly increased, a fall in the sodium content of plasma occurs to compensate for the increased intake of potassium, by increased excretion of sodium and chloride.

The concentration of sodium, chloride and potassium in blood may vary slightly, but within physiological limits, under the following physiological conditions:

1. A slight fall in the plasma sodium and chloride may occur during periods of active digestion, when gastric juice containing HCl is secreted in large amounts. But it will resume its normal level in the post-digestive period and this is due to reabsorption of the chloride from the intestines.
2. A slight fall in the plasma potassium level may occur during periods of increased carbohydrate utilisation, when potassium from ECF passes into the cells.

Absorption: Sodium, potassium and chloride are readily absorbed from the gastrointestinal tract. After absorption, sodium is distributed throughout ECF. Very little sodium enters ICF. Potassium passes through the cell membrane to reach the cells. Sodium, potassium and chloride get excreted almost entirely in the urine in a short period.

Excretion:

Sodium and chloride: Much NaCl is not lost through the skin under normal conditions. However, during prolonged strenuous exercise, excessive sweat is accompanied by considerable loss of NaCl with onset of symptoms such as muscle cramps, headache and mental confusion. It is important to remember that administration of water alone without addition of salt will bring down the level of sodium and chloride still further and thus aggravate the symptoms.

Under normal conditions, the digestive fluids are completely reabsorbed in the intestines. But in severe diarrhoea and vomiting, large amounts of water and electrolytes are lost from the body. The dehydration has to be treated by administration of water and electrolytes.

Potassium: It is excreted mainly through the kidneys. Some potassium is also secreted by the distal tubules and this adds to the quantity of potassium in urine. Under normal conditions, excretion of potassium takes place as follows. When potassium is excreted in the urine, K^+ ions from within the cells pass out to the ECF and get excreted along with chloride. Simultaneously, Na^+ ions and H^+ ions from ECF move in the opposite direction to ICF in exchange for K^+ ions which have moved out. This results in increased H^+ ion concentration inside the cells and reduced H^+ ion concentration in ECF, with a corresponding increase in HCO_3^- in ECF. This causes a tendency for a metabolic type of alkalosis and this is a normal process. But when there is impairment in renal functions, the exchange between Na^+ ions and H^+ ions with K^+ ions in the cells does not take place efficiently. Potassium excretion is reduced, resulting in a rise in the serum potassium level. Care should be taken not to administer potassium intravenously, in renal diseases.

While dealing with the metabolism of electrolytes, the metabolism of sodium and chloride will be discussed as one unit and potassium separately.

Metabolism:

Sodium and chloride: The metabolism of sodium and chloride are so much interrelated that abnormality in the metabolism of one is always accompanied by abnormality in the other. Thus loss of sodium in gastrointestinal fluids, sweat and urine is accompanied by loss of chloride also, though there is always more loss of chloride than sodium. This produces a low level of plasma chloride and a compensatory increase in bicarbonate with consequent alkalosis.

The metabolism of sodium is markedly influenced by adrenocortical hormones. This is seen clearly in adrenocortical insufficiency, which is associated with increased excretion of sodium in the urine and reduced serum sodium concentration.

Under normal conditions, 99% or more of NaCl is reabsorbed by the renal tubules. The reabsorption is enhanced by aldosterone. But in chronic renal diseases accompanied by acidosis, the tubular reabsorption of sodium is impaired, resulting in its excretion in the urine. Loss of sodium in acidosis is also due to buffering of the acids.

Hyponatraemia means low serum sodium. Two types of hyponatraemia have to be differentiated.

1. Hyponatraemia with true loss of sodium
2. Hyponatraemia due to overhydration

In the first type, i.e. hyponatraemia with true loss of sodium, there is loss of total body sodium and this is always indicated by loss of body weight. Clinical conditions exhibiting this type of hyponatraemia are as follows:

- Excessive vomiting and diarrhoea resulting in excessive loss of fluid from the gastrointestinal tract

- Chronic renal disease with acidosis. Here, the loss of sodium in the urine is due to two factors:
  - (i) Poor renal reabsorption of sodium
  - (ii) Loss of sodium due to buffering of the acids. As referred earlier, the serum potassium level is high in these cases.
- Addison's disease due to adrenocortical insufficiency.

The second type is hyponatraemia due to overhydration. Hyponatraemia is due to either administration of large quantities of salt-free water or accumulation of fluid due to oedema. Hyponatraemia due to oedema occurs in (i) congestive heart failure and (ii) cirrhosis of liver.

Hypernatraemia means an increased serum sodium level. This is not common. It may occur in the following conditions:

1. Hyperactivity of adrenal cortex as in Cushing's disease
2. Prolonged administration of cortisone, ACTH and sex hormones

Potassium: Potassium is the main cation of the intracellular fluid and is also an important constituent of the ECF. It is this fraction that influences muscle activity. Potassium is essential for growth and for building up of cells. This is indicated by a fairly high retention of potassium during infancy, childhood and pregnancy. Potassium ions are essential for contraction of cardiac and skeletal muscles. During muscular contraction, potassium from the muscle cells is lost into the ECF and after muscle contraction it is returned to the muscle cells. Potassium is essential for the activity of nerves and is present in nerve fibres. It is related to carbohydrate metabolism.

The activity of the striated muscles is dependent on the concentration of the potassium in ECF. Any variation in the concentration of this fraction will cause abnormalities in the conduction and activity of cardiac muscle. Low serum potassium is associated with extreme weakness of muscles and sometimes paralysis.

Hyperkalaemia means increased serum potassium. This occurs in the following conditions:

1. Renal failure
2. Advanced dehydration
3. Addison's disease. Adrenal insufficiency causes hyperkalaemia along with high intracellular potassium. The hyperkalaemia in adrenal insufficiency is due to diminished capacity of the kidney to excrete potassium. Hyperkalaemia along with high intracellular K is a characteristic feature in Addison's disease.
4. Intravenous administration of an excess amount of potassium. Hyperkalaemia produces characteristic effects on (i) cardiovascular system, (ii) central nervous system and (iii) muscles, as follows:

   Cardiovascular system: (a) Bradycardia followed by peripheral vascular collapse and finally cardiac arrest and (b) characteristic ECG changes with elevated T wave and widening of the QRS complex.

   Central nervous system: Depression and mental confusion.

Muscles: Extreme weakness of muscles, flaccid paralysis of the limbs and weakness of respiratory muscles

Hypokalaemia means decreased serum potassium concentration. Low serum potassium may develop in any illness leading to malnutrition, wasting and negative nitrogen balance. Long-standing potassium deficiency may cause injury to myocardium and severe renal damage leading to chronic renal disease such as chronic pyelonephritis.

Causes leading to hypokalaemia are as follows:

1. Intravenous administration of potassium-free fluids for a longer time, as a measure of replacement of gastric fluid, lost by continuous suction.
2. Prolonged diarrhoea and vomiting, resulting in considerable loss of gastrointestinal fluid. Potassium from ICF is transferred to ECF to compensate the loss of potassium in ECF. But this is also quickly excreted in the urine.
3. Overactivity of adrenal cortex (Cushing's syndrome) may induce potassium deficit. This is due to the action of ACTH which increases excretion of potassium.
4. Prolonged administration of diuretics may induce hypokalaemia, because of excretion of potassium in the urine.
5. Hypokalaemia may develop during heart failure. It is important to keep watch over the serum potassium level while treating heart failure with digitalis because one of the complications in heart failure is depletion of the potassium content of myocardium which in turn increases the sensitivity of myocardium to digitalis, resulting in digitalis toxicity. Administration of potassium at this stage will relieve manifestations of digitalis toxicity. But the depletion of potassium and digitalis toxicity would be aggravated, when diuretics are administered to fully digitalised patients.
6. Hypokalaemia may develop during treatment of diabetic coma with insulin, which acts by increasing the utilisation of glucose, by promoting glycogenesis. Since potassium is necessary for glycogenesis, it is withdrawn from the ECF, leading to hypokalaemia, which may prove fatal sometimes. This factor has to be remembered when treating diabetic coma.
7. Hypokalaemia is the characteristic feature of a rare disease called 'familial periodic paralysis.' In this condition, potassium from ECF is withdrawn and transferred to the cells.

Sulphur

Sulphur, a nutritionally essential element, is present in all the cells of the body, occurring mainly in protein, in the form of sulphur-containing amino acids. It is present in certain enzymes, hormones (insulin, anterior pituitary) and substances such as glutathione, thiamine, biotin, coenzyme A, lipoic acid, taurocholic acid, chondroitin sulphate of cartilages and tendons, and keratin of hair.

Source:

Organic: Sulphur-containing amino acids (cystine, cysteine and methionine)

Inorganic: Sodium, potassium and magnesium sulphates

Sulphur in blood: The total sulphur in blood (plasma) averages to about 3.4 mg%. This is present in three distinct forms:

1. Inorganic sulphate (1 mg%)
2. Neutral sulphate (1.9 mg%)
3. Ethereal sulphate (0.5 mg%)

Absorption: Sulphur in food is ingested in two forms: (i) as inorganic sulphate of sodium, potassium and magnesium and (ii) as organic sulphate, from sulphur, containing amino acids, sulpholipids, glycoproteins and chondroitin sulphuric acid. They are absorbed from the intestines into portal blood and reach the liver.

Metabolism: In the liver, sulphur undergoes the following changes. Most of the organic sulphur is oxidised to inorganic sulphates (SO_4). But a small portion escapes oxidation. The unoxidised sulphur is utilised for the formation of sulphur-containing substances such as insulin, anterior pituitary hormone, taurocholic acid and glutathione and the rest is excreted in the urine as neutral sulphur (**Fig. 25.1**).

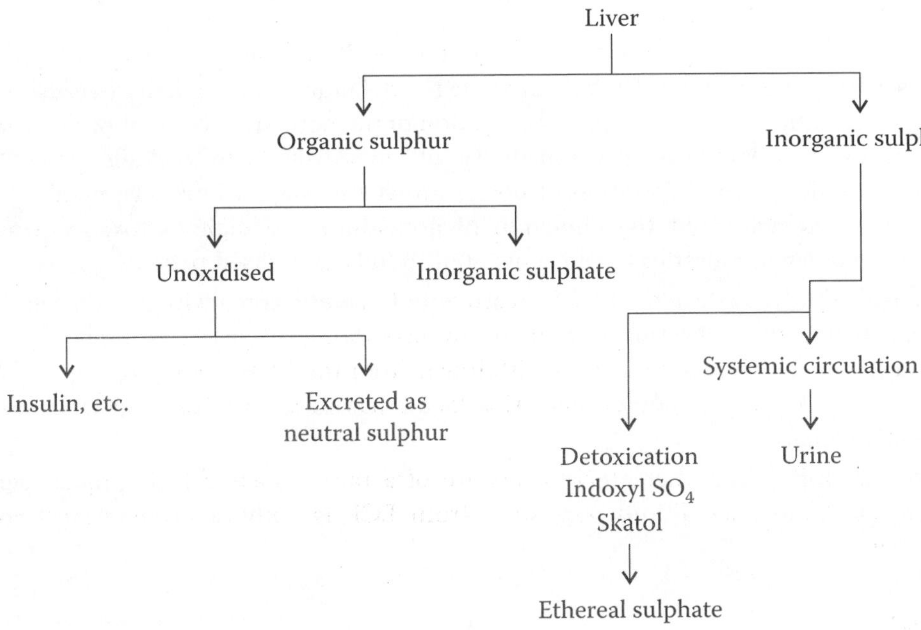

Figure 25.1 Metabolism of sulphur.

Some inorganic sulphate obtained by oxidation of the major portion of the organic sulphur, along with some inorganic sulphate absorbed as such, enter the systemic circulation and get excreted in the urine. A part of the inorganic sulphate combines in the liver with various phenolic substances produced by putrefaction, to form ethereal sulphate which is excreted in urine. This is a mechanism of detoxication. Cysteine also acts as a conjugating agent in the detoxication of bromobenzene.

Excretion: Sulphur is excreted in the urine in the three forms in which it occurs in the plasma. The total amount of sulphur excreted in urine is about 1 gram per day under normal conditions.

The excretion of sulphur varies with the intake of sulphur-containing protein and the rate of tissue catabolism.

Three forms of sulphur excreted in urine are as follows:

1. Inorganic sulphate—85% of the total excretion. This includes sulphates of sodium, potassium, calcium, magnesium and ammonium.
2. Ethereal sulphate—10% of the total excretion. This includes sulphates of phenol, cresols, indoxyl and skatol.
3. Neutral sulphate—5% of the total excretion. This is unoxidised sulphur and includes cysteine, taurine, cyanides and thiocyanates.

Calcium

This mineral element is present in great abundance in the body, being almost entirely distributed in the bones and teeth. A very small amount is present in the body fluids. An adult weighing 70 kg has about 1200 grams of calcium in his body.

Blood calcium: In the blood, calcium is present exclusively in the plasma, to the extent of 9–11 mg%.

The calcium content of plasma during infancy and early childhood is slightly more than the average adult values. In the plasma, calcium exists in two physiologically distinct fractions.

1. Diffusible or ionised fraction
2. Non-diffusible or unionised fraction

A small fraction of about 0.5 mg% is present, bound as an unionised complex anion with citrate.

The diffusible or ionised form constitutes 60% of the total calcium. It is capable of passing through an artificial, semi-permeable membrane. Parathormone exerts its influence almost entirely on the diffusible calcium ions. Thus when there is parathyroid deficiency, the blood ionic calcium falls below the normal value. This affects the central nervous system, which produces increased irritability of the peripheral nerves. At a later stage, muscle spasm sets in leading to generalised convulsions and this is **tetany**. It can be cured by administration of parathormone. Conversely, when there is hyperactivity of the parathyroids, the ionic calcium content in the blood increases. The calcium is deposited on various organs such as heart, lungs and arteries, the excess being mobilised from the bones, which in turn become soft and weak.

The non-diffusible form constitutes 40% of the total serum calcium. The fraction cannot pass through the semi-permeable membrane, because it is bound with the plasma albumin. It is reduced in hypoproteinaemia.

Source: Milk, milk products and vegetables (beetroot).

Requirement: 1–1.5 grams daily. Growing children and pregnant women require more.

Metabolism: Maintenance of the plasma calcium level within the normal range is of vital importance because certain fundamental processes, such as membrane permeability, neuromuscular excitability and coagulation, are dependent on the plasma calcium level.

Factors maintaining the plasma calcium concentration:

1. Parathyroid hormone is the most important factor in the regulation of the concentration of calcium ions in the body fluids. It has dual action and acts as follows:
   - Parathormone mobilises calcium from the bones in a fasting condition, to maintain the plasma calcium. The action of parathormone on bones is called 'calcium mobilising action.'
   - At the same time, it lowers the serum phosphate concentration. This is brought about by decreasing the reabsorption of phosphate and causing 'phosphaturic action.'
2. Vitamin D maintains the plasma calcium concentration by enhancing the absorption of calcium from the intestines. Intestinal absorption of calcium is low in rickets. The plasma phosphate usually falls before the plasma calcium, due to the stimulation of parathyroid activity, which while trying to maintain the plasma calcium concentration simultaneously lowers the plasma phosphate (dual action of parathormone).
3. **Plasma proteins:** About 40% of the plasma calcium, which constitutes the non-diffusible form, is bound to plasma proteins, mainly albumin. So an increase or a decrease in the albumin fraction may be accompanied by an increase or a decrease in the serum calcium concentration. A reduced calcium level on account of this fraction will not lead to tetany, as this hypocalcaemia is due to hypoproteinaemia.
4. **Plasma phosphate:** To a certain extent, a reciprocal relationship exists between the concentration of calcium and phosphate but usually in one direction, i.e. an increase in serum phosphate concentration may cause a fall in serum calcium concentration. The mechanism involved is not known. But clinically, this is seen in advanced renal failure, when the serum phosphate concentration is fairly high. Tetany may occur under such conditions due to low serum calcium.

The calcium phosphate ratio is important in ossification. In the serum of children, the product of Ca × P (in mg per 100 ml) is about 50, and in rickets it may be less than 30. Normally, in adults the product of Ca × P is about 26–40 mg%. Products above 40 are seen when bone growth or healing takes place.

Regulation of blood and bone calcium and phosphorus: The bone calcium exists in two forms:

1. The more soluble intercrystalline form (labile part)
2. The less soluble crystalline hydroxyapatite form

The more soluble fraction is said to be in equilibrium with the calcium salts of the blood plasma and tends to keep up 70% of the normal serum calcium content. This is independent of the parathormone activity. The remaining 30% is supplied in just the amount needed and kept by a 'feedback mechanism' which is controlled by parathormone. Thus, when the level of serum calcium falls below normal, the parathormone secretion is stimulated and the increased secretion promotes the solution of the bone salt calcium, which is mobilised to the blood. As the blood calcium rises, the secretion of parathormone is reduced automatically, preventing further mobilisation of calcium from the bones. Thus, the bone undergoes metabolic turnover of decalcification and recalcification continuously. This process is controlled besides parathormone, by factors such as vitamin D, vitamin C, vitamin A and anterior pituitary hormone. In rickets, the amount of calcium and phosphate in bones is very low, due to inadequacy of vitamin D which in turn impairs absorption and utilisation of calcium and phosphate. Consequently, the bones become less rigid and bend, resulting in bowlegs and other deformities. In scurvy, the epiphyseal junction of growing bones is affected leading to bone deformities.

Factors controlling the absorption of calcium:

1. *Site:* Calcium is absorbed more readily from the upper part of the small intestines.
2. *Intestinal pH:* As the calcium salts are soluble in acid solution, absorption is increased when the intestinal pH is acidic. The maximum absorption takes place from the duodenum before the gastric acidity is neutralised. Subsequent absorption is favoured by the presence of organic acids such as lactic and citric acids, amino acids and fatty acids.
3. *Magnesium in the food:* An excess of magnesium diminishes absorption of calcium, especially if calcium is not present in adequate amounts.
4. Phytic acid (inositol hexaphosphate), which occurs in cereal grains, forms insoluble phytin salts with calcium, magnesium and iron, thus interfering with their absorption. This phenomenon is the basis of the rachitogenic effect of cereals such as oatmeal.
5. Oxalates in food, as present in leafy vegetables such as spinach, interfere with absorption, by forming calcium oxalate.
6. *Calcium–phosphorus ratio:* If there is an excess of both calcium and phosphorus in the diet, the faecal excretion of both increases creating calcium deficiency, due to the formation of insoluble $Ca_3(PO_4)_2$. The optimum ratio of absorption of calcium to phosphorus is about 1:1.5–1.2.
7. *Abnormal fat metabolism:* Impaired fat metabolism leads to impaired absorption of calcium because of excessive formation of free fatty acids which form insoluble fatty acids of calcium (calcium soaps). Thus, calcium absorption is impaired in diseases such as sprue and steatorrhoea where fat is poorly absorbed.
8. *Protein in the diet:* Calcium absorption is favoured during increased protein consumption because calcium salts are more soluble in aqueous solutions of amino acids.
9. *Vitamin D:* Intestinal absorption of calcium is enhanced by vitamin D.

Diseases associated with calcium metabolism:

1. **Hyperparathyroidism:** This occurs due to increased secretion of parathyroid hormone by hyperactive and hyperplastic tumours of parathyroids. The following changes are noted:
    - Hypercalcaemia (12–24 mg/100 ml)
    - Diminished serum phosphate

- Increased urinary excretion of calcium and phosphorus
- Bones become soft and fragile due to constant mobilisation

2. **Hypoparathyroidism:** This denotes hypoactivity of parathormone and occurs generally after surgical removal of the parathyroids. The serum calcium level may drop below 7 mg/100 ml, leading to tetany. This is accompanied by increased serum phosphate concentration. The urinary phosphate and calcium are low.
3. **Rickets:** Deficiency of vitamin D in children causes impairment of intestinal absorption of calcium and phosphorus and produces rickets which is characterised by defective calcification. The serum calcium and phosphate remain normal or may be slightly lowered. But the faecal excretion of both is increased because of their poor absorption. The alkaline phosphatase activity is raised because of increased osteoblastic activity. Another type of rickets known as renal rickets is caused by an inherited defect in the renal tubules by which the reabsorption of phosphates is impaired. This disease is not relieved by vitamin D therapy.

Excretion: Calcium is excreted in the faeces, urine and sweat. About one-fourth of the total excretion occurs in the urine, and this represents the unionised calcium. The rest of the calcium is excreted in the faeces and this is mainly the unabsorbed dietary calcium. Normally, 0.4–0.8 gram of calcium is excreted in the faeces per day. The renal threshold level for calcium is 6.5–8 mg/100 ml. Approximately 200 mg of calcium is excreted in the urine in 24 hours. The urinary calcium excretion is decreased in

1. Vitamin D deficiency
2. Hypoparathyroidism
3. Inadequate intake of calcium
4. Lactation

Functions:

1. Calcium is essential for growth, as it plays an important role in the formation of bones and development of teeth.
2. It is necessary for coagulation of blood. It is also necessary for the clotting and digestion of milk. Its presence is required for the formation of calcium paracaseinate.
3. Calcium ions are necessary for muscle contraction. Muscle contraction is impaired when there is a deficiency of calcium ions. Excess of calcium increases the contractility of heart muscles and the heart stops during systole.
4. Calcium ions are necessary for the normal transmission of nerve impulses. A low calcium level is associated with increased neuromuscular irritability.
5. Calcium ions are necessary for the maintenance and regulation of acid–base balance and water balance in the body.
6. Calcium and phosphate ions activate certain enzymes in the intermediary metabolism of carbohydrate, fat and protein.
7. Calcium ions are required for the maintenance of the permeability of intercellular cement substances. The capillary permeability increases or decreases with the amount of calcium.

Phosphorus

Phosphorus is present in every cell, in both inorganic and organic combinations. As inorganic combination, it is present with calcium in the skeleton and teeth up to 80%. As organic phosphorus, it is present along with proteins as phosphoproteins and nucleoproteins. It is present along with carbohydrates as hexose and triose phosphates and along with lipids as phospholipids. These are distributed in various tissues of the body.

Distribution: The total amount of phosphorus in the body is about 700 grams. In blood, phosphorus is present in the erythrocytes and plasma in two forms as (i) inorganic phosphorus and (ii) organic phosphorus.

Metabolism: The concentration of plasma inorganic phosphorus is 3–4.5 mg% in adults. In children, it is slightly high (4.5–6.5 mg%). The organic phosphorus includes glycerophosphates, hexose phosphates, nucleotides and lipid phosphorus. The blood phosphorus decreases during periods of increased carbohydrate metabolism, due to increased utilisation for phosphorylation of carbohydrate metabolites.

Source: The chief sources of calcium in the diet are milk, cheese, egg, meat, fish, cereals and vegetables.

Requirement: 1–1. 5 grams per day

Absorption: In the intestines, phosphate is derived from nucleoproteins, phosphoproteins and inorganic phosphorus of food. Phosphorus is readily absorbed from the intestines. The absorption and metabolism of phosphorus are similar to those of calcium in many respects.

Factors influencing absorption:

1. *Site:* Like calcium, phosphorus is absorbed from the upper part of the small intestines.
2. *Intestinal pH:* Similar to calcium, phosphates are soluble in acid medium and factors increasing intestinal acidity favour absorption while factors increasing intestinal alkalinity impair absorption by being precipitated as calcium phosphate. Maximum absorption takes place from the duodenum before the gastric acidity is neutralised.
3. *Other substances:* Phytic acid, iron, beryllium, aluminium and strontium form insoluble phosphates and thus interfere with the absorption of phosphorus. The presence of these substances can even induce rickets.
4. Factors such as Ca:P ratio, vitamin C and abnormal fat metabolism have effects similar to those of calcium. As in the case of calcium, parathormone and vitamin D maintain the concentration of plasma phosphorous in a similar manner and with the same effects.

Excretion: About two-third of the ingested phosphorus is excreted in the urine and the remainder in the faeces. The urinary phosphorus increases as the calcium intake decreases. Parathormone increases phosphate excretion, due to inhibition of the reabsorption of phosphorus from the glomerular filtrate by the renal tubular epithelium. Phosphate excretion is impaired and this causes retention of plasma phosphate in renal diseases. Retention of phosphorus is a prominent cause of acidosis in severe renal diseases and the serum calcium is bound to be low.

Functions: The functions of phosphorus are closely related to those of calcium. A few, not mentioned under calcium, are given below:

1. Phosphorus is required for the formation of certain physiologically important phosphorus-containing compounds such as phospholipids, coenzymes and enzymes of intermediary metabolism.
2. Phosphorus contributes to the formation of high-energy-bond compounds such as ATP, ADP and creatine phosphate. These are required for phosphorylation of sugars in carbohydrate metabolism.
3. Phosphorus is an important constituent of phosphate buffers in the blood and urine.

Magnesium

Magnesium (Mg) is one of the principal cations of soft tissues. The body contains about 21 grams of Mg, out of which 70% is present in the bones in combination with Ca and P. The remaining 30% is distributed in the soft tissues and body fluids.

In blood, Mg is present in the cells as well as in the plasma. More than 50% is present inside the blood cells and in this respect, it is similar to potassium. The Mg content of the red blood cells is 5–7 mg% and that of plasma is 1.7–2.3 mg/100 ml. The magnesium in the serum exists in two forms. About 80% is in the diffusible form and the remainder is in the non-diffusible form, being bound to plasma proteins. Little is known regarding the factors involved in the regulation of the Mg content of blood.

Source: Magnesium is a component of chlorophyll. It is abundantly present in green vegetables and marine foods. Other sources are nuts, soybean, peas and derivatives of cocoa.

Requirement: The recommended daily allowance of magnesium is 300–350 mg.

Metabolism: The metabolism of Mg is similar to that of Ca and P, and an inter-relationship exists among them in some aspects.

Absorption: Like Ca, absorption of Mg takes place readily from the small intestines. Certain dietary constituents such as calcium, protein, fat, phosphate, phytic acid and alkalies impair the absorption of Mg because magnesium salts are less soluble in their presence. Vitamin D does not seem to play a dominant role on the absorption of Mg.

Excretion: Two-thirds of the dietary Mg is excreted in the faeces and the rest in urine.

There is a reciprocal relationship between the plasma Mg and Ca in certain respects. For example, in hypermagnesaemia induced by intravenous injection of Mg, there is a fall in the serum Ca level, whereas in oxalate poisoning which induces a decrease in serum Ca, there is an increase in plasma Mg. A relationship also exists between plasma Mg and P rather than with serum Ca in certain conditions; for example, when parathormone is administered, there is a decrease in serum phosphate, whereas plasma magnesium is increased.

It has been found that Mg^{++} and Ca^{++} ions exert antagonistic effects on cell permeability. Hypermagnesaemia up to 20 mg% induced by injection of Mg results in immediate and profound anaesthesia, along with paralysis of voluntary muscles. These effects could be reversed instantaneously by intravenous injection of a corresponding amount of Ca. Serum magnesium tends to rise in renal failure.

Mg^{++} ions are activators of various enzymes involved in intermediary metabolism such as phosphorylase, phosphoglucomutase and enolase.

Deficiency symptoms: High levels of plasma Mg induce depression of the nervous system and anaesthesia while a low level produces tetany. Deficiency of magnesium in rats produces vasodilatation, hyperirritability and finally convulsions which are fatal. These convulsions are found similar to those of tetany produced by hypocalcaemia. Hypomagnesaemia in man is rare. However, a clinical syndrome has been described, characterised by muscle tremors, twitching and occasional convulsions, associated with magnesium deficiency. Hypomagnesaemia has been observed in clinical hyperparathyroidism, prolonged vomiting and diarrhoea and in diuretic therapy.

Iron

Iron is an essential constituent of haemoglobin, cytochromes and other components of respiratory enzyme systems such as cytochrome oxidase, catalase and peroxidase. The main functions of iron are as follows:

1. Transport of oxygen to the tissues
2. Participation in the cellular oxidation mechanism

Requirement: The requirement of iron varies with age and circumstances. More iron is required during growth, pregnancy and lactation, because of an increased demand for synthesis of haemoglobin.

Adults: Men require about 10 mg per day.

Women require 15–20 mg per day during their reproductive age.

Source: Meat, liver, kidney, spleen, egg yolk, fish, wheat, nuts, green leafy vegetables and oat meal.

Absorption: A peculiar feature of iron metabolism is that only a small part of the dietary iron is absorbed under normal conditions because the body has limited capacity to excrete iron. Absorption of iron from intestines is controlled in such a way that accumulation in tissues in toxic amounts is prevented. Ordinarily, less than 10% of the ingested amount is absorbed by a normal person. The iron that is not absorbed is excreted in faeces. The rate of iron absorption is increased in children and in conditions of iron deficiency. Prior administration of iron hinders subsequent absorption for 12–24 hours.

Factors controlling iron absorption:

1. Iron absorption is facilitated by acid medium. The HCl and other organic acids of gastric juice and reducing substances containing SH groups (cysteine and ascorbic acid) play an important role in iron absorption. The acids first liberate ferric iron from ferric compounds and they are further reduced to ferrous iron by the reducing substances. In this form, iron is more soluble and therefore more readily absorbed.

2. Absorption of iron occurs mainly in the stomach and duodenum. Absorption is therefore impaired in patients with surgical removal of stomach and proximal portion of the small intestines. Absorption is also impaired in various malabsorption syndromes such as steatorrhoea.
3. A diet high in phosphate, phytic acid and oxalate impairs absorption because they form insoluble compounds with iron.
4. Alkalinity impairs absorption of iron by forming insoluble basic iron compounds.
5. Presence of bile acids also impairs iron absorption because they form insoluble salts with iron.

Absorption of iron occurs mainly from stomach and duodenum and is controlled by a regulatory mechanism which exists within the intestinal mucosal cells. Iron in food exists in a ferric state. Ferric iron is reduced to ferrous iron by reducing substances such as cysteine and ascorbic acid that are present in food and is absorbed into the mucosal cells. Two steps are involved in the absorption of iron: (i) ferrous iron is taken up by the mucosal cells from the intestinal lumen and (ii) intestinal mucosa transfers iron to plasma. Most of the iron entering the mucosal cells is not transferred to plasma but remains trapped within the mucosal cells and is excreted into the lumen when the cells are shed. The ferrous iron absorbed into the mucosal cells is promptly oxidised to ferric iron and is bound to an intracellular protein molecule known as 'apoferritin' present within the cells in small amounts. The ferric protein complex that is formed is known as 'ferritin'. In normal conditions, the intestines have a low content of apoferritin and this helps in restricting the amount of iron that can be absorbed. Apoprotein content increases in states of iron deficiency and this facilitates more absorption of iron. Thus, acceptance or rejection of iron by absorption is regulated by the amount of ferritin present in the intestinal mucosal cells. Entrance of iron is stopped when the capacity of the cells for storing ferritin is exhausted.

Ferritin: The ferric protein complex contains 23% of iron in the ferric form. The iron is present as micelles composed of ferric hydroxide ferric phosphate complex and is bound firmly to apoprotein. Apoprotein which is present in small amounts is unstable and breaks down quickly unless ferric iron is present to convert it to ferritin. Ferritin is the chief storage form of iron and is present in gastrointestinal mucosa, bone marrow, liver and spleen. The mechanism of absorption and transport of iron are illustrated in **Figure 25.2.**

Transport of iron in the plasma: The iron released from ferritin is again reduced to ferrous iron, leaves the intestines and enters the plasma. Diminished oxygen tension in the blood may increase more transfer of iron from the intestinal mucosal cells into the plasma. Here the ferrous iron undergoes reoxidation to ferric form and then combines with a specific metal-binding β-globulin known as *siderophilin* or *transferrin* to form a red ferric protein complex. Transferrin is a glycoprotein. The concentration of iron in plasma transferrin is 50–180 μg per 100 ml. Under normal circumstances, almost all the iron bound to transferrin is taken up rapidly by the bone marrow to synthesise haemoglobin. Transferrin is the main form in which iron is transported in the blood and iron in transferrin is in the ferric form. The iron content of the whole blood is 40–60 mg per 100 ml and most of it is present in haemoglobin. In haemoglobin, the iron is present in the ferrous form.

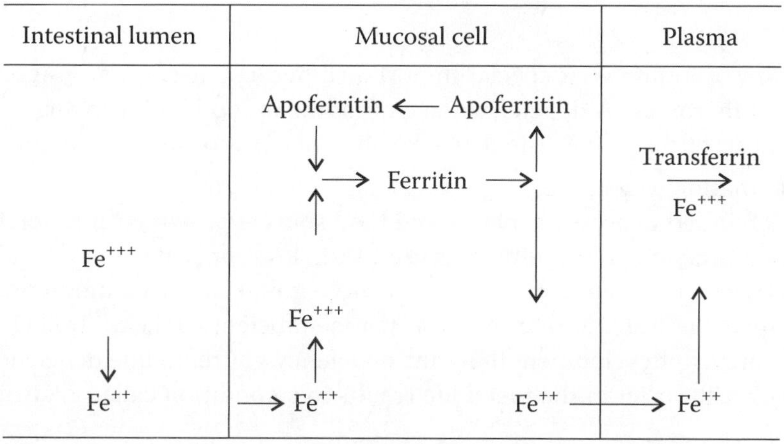

Figure 25.2 Illustration of the mechanism of absorption and transport of iron.

The iron in the plasma is released when the tissues need it. It passes out of the capillaries into the cells where it is stored or utilised. The storage mechanism in the liver is identical with that described in the gastrointestinal mucosal cells. Iron is also stored in spleen, bone marrow and all reticuloendothelial cells. If the iron present in the blood exceeds the capacity of the body to store it as ferritin, it accumulates in the liver as minute microscopic particles called **haemosiderin** which is similar to ferritin and in which iron is present in the form of colloidal iron oxide in association with protein. When iron is deposited all over the body, the condition is called **haemosiderosis**. This may occur in cases of

1. Excessive parenteral iron therapy
2. Repeated blood transfusions
3. Excessive haemolysis

Haemochromatosis: When iron accumulates in the tissues for many years, the skin acquires a bronzed pigmentation and this condition is known as haemochromatosis. The cause of this is not known. This may be associated with hepatic cirrhosis, pancreatic fibrosis and diabetes. This condition is sometimes referred to as **bronze-diabetes.**

States of iron deficiency:

1. Iron deficiency may occur as a result of malabsorption from the gastrointestinal tract, especially after surgical removal of portions of stomach and small intestines.
2. In women, iron deficiency anaemia is common during pregnancy.

Excretion: The efficiency of excretion of endogenous iron is such that only small quantities are lost. Normally in men, about 0.5–1.15 mg of iron is excreted per day and in women, double the amount may be lost due to menstrual bleeding. Some amount is lost in faeces, urine and sweat.

Iodine

The metabolism of iodine is of special importance because it plays an important role in the synthesis of thyroxine. A deficient intake of iodine in food and drinking water leads to deficient synthesis of thyroxine. The thyroid gland enlarges to compensate the deficiency.

Sea foods, marine vegetation, vegetables and fruits grown near the sea coast are particularly rich in iodine whereas plants and food sources grown far interior, especially at high altitudes, are deficient in iodine because of the low concentration of iodine in water and soils. Such regions are endemic areas for **simple goitre**. It is a common practice to add iodide to the drinking water and to the table salt in sufficient concentration (1 in 5000 to 1 in 200,000) to prevent development of iodine deficiency goitre. Iodine deficiency occurring in childhood or still earlier in the foetal life results in a condition called **cretinism**.

Requirement: An average adult requires 100–200 μg of iodine per day. Children require about 50 μg per day.

Distribution: A normal adult body contains about 20–50 mg of iodine. Out of this, about 20% is present in thyroid gland. The rest is distributed in the muscles, skin, bones, liver and blood.

Blood iodine: Almost the entire amount of iodine in the plasma is bound to plasma protein and this is known as **protein-bound iodine (PBI)**. The normal value of PBI is 4–10 μg per 100 ml of plasma. It is precipitated along with protein of plasma, when treated with protein-precipitating reagents. The level of plasma PBI is a measure of the concentration of circulating thyroid hormone. The value of PBI is high in hyperthyroidism (8–30 μg%) and low in hypothyroidism (0–3 μg%). Thus, estimation of plasma PBI is useful in the diagnosis of thyroid diseases. A small amount of iodine also circulates in the form of inorganic iodide which is largely trapped and utilised by the thyroid gland to synthesise thyroxine. It may be noted that when there is diminished intake of iodine in a normal person, the concentration of iodine in thyroid gland is not diminished whereas all the other tissues show reduced concentration. This is because the thyroid has remarkable capacity for trapping and storing iodine even under adverse conditions. In thyroid, iodine is stored in follicular colloid as iodothyroglobulin, which is a composite protein molecule containing thyroxine, diiodotyrosine and smaller amounts of triiodothyronine. When there is a demand, these substances are drawn from thyroglobulin and passed into the systemic circulation.

Absorption and circulation: Iodine and iodides are readily absorbed from the intestines. Absorption can also occur from other mucous membranes, lungs and skin. In blood, iodine is found as PBI and inorganic iodine. Inorganic iodine is rapidly withdrawn from the circulation by thyroid, where it is oxidised to free iodine. It is then incorporated in tyrosine to form diiodotyrosine, triiodothyronine and thyroxine, which are all stored in thyroglobulin. Thyroxine is released from thyroglobulin to enter circulation when it is necessary. In blood, it is loosely bound with plasma protein to form PBI.

Excretion: Iodine is excreted as inorganic iodide. The major route of excretion is through kidneys. 40–80% is excreted in the urine. Some amount is also excreted by liver, skin, lungs, milk and saliva. A lesser amount is excreted in faeces.

Goitrogenic substances: Certain food sources such as cabbage, cauliflower and peanuts inhibit the synthesis of thyroxine and are said to be goitrogenic. For diseases associated with iodine metabolism, refer to thyroxine in **Chapter 26, Hormones**.

Copper

Copper, though present in small quantities, is widely distributed in all the tissues. The adult human body contains 100–150 mg of copper. Liver contains a fairly high concentration of copper and it is its main storage site. The copper in liver is called **hepatocuprein**. The concentration of copper in foetal liver is 5–10 times more than that of the adult. Copper is present in kidneys, heart, bone marrow and hair.

In blood, copper is present in both the erythrocytes and the plasma, in almost an equal amount. It is increased in pregnancy. The average concentration of copper present in normal plasma is about 100 μg/100 ml in adults.

In the erythrocytes, copper is present as a copper-containing protein called **erythrocuprein** which is colourless. The concentration of erythrocuprein per 100 ml of packed cells is 30–36 mg in a normal adult.

In the plasma, copper is present in two forms. About 96% of plasma copper is present firmly bound to α_2-globulin as **ceruloplasmin** which is blue in colour. The normal concentration of plasma ceruloplasmin is about 30 mg per 100 ml. Ceruloplasmin is the main transport form of copper in plasma.

A smaller amount, about 4%, is present loosely bound to albumin. Another copper-containing protein has been isolated from human brain and this is called **cerebrocuprein**.

Absorption: Copper is absorbed in small amounts, mainly from the upper part of the small intestines. Very little amount is retained in the body, depending on the amount of copper present in the tissues. 85–95% of the ingested copper is excreted in the faeces. Copper is not excreted in the urine, as it is largely bound with the proteins of plasma. Copper favours absorption of iron from the intestines.

Functions:

1. Copper is an essential constituent of enzymes such as cytochrome, cytochrome oxidase, catalase, tyrosinase, monoamine oxidase, ascorbic acid oxidase and uricase.
2. Its chief function is in haemopoiesis. Along with iron, it helps in the synthesis of haemoglobin and maturation of red blood cells. Deficiency of copper causes a microcytic anaemia, similar to that resulting from iron deficiency. But the anaemia cannot be corrected by administration of iron.
3. There appears to be a relationship between copper and iron metabolism. When there is a deficiency of copper, there is a decrease in the movement of iron from the tissues to the plasma, causing a fall in the iron content of blood. A well-established disease

caused by abnormal metabolism of copper is **Wilson's disease** which is also described as hepatolenticular degeneration. It is a hereditary condition involving increased absorption of copper from the intestines, leading to accumulation of copper in the tissues, its excessive excretion in urine and failure to synthesise ceruloplasmin. The disease is characterised by the following findings:

1. Excessive accumulation of copper in the liver and lenticular nucleus in the brain
2. Excessive excretion of copper in the urine
3. Low levels of copper and ceruloplasmin in the plasma
4. A generalised aminoaciduria arises on account of impairment of renal tubular reabsorption due to damage caused by local deposit of excessive copper

Zinc

Zinc is widely distributed in plants and animal tissues and is essential for growth. The average concentration of zinc in blood is 900 μg per 100 ml. Of this, about 75% is present in the red blood cells in carbonic anhydrase, 3% is in white blood cells and 22% is in the plasma, bound mostly to albumin. In leukaemia, the zinc content of white blood cells is reduced. When there is an amelioration of the disease process due to treatment, the normal level is restored. Zinc is a constituent of crystalline insulin. In this connection, it is of interest to note that the zinc content of diabetic pancreas is less than normal. Zinc is present in enzymes such as carbonic anhydrase, liver alcohol dehydrogenase, uricase and kidney phosphatase.

Requirement: A daily intake of 0.3 mg/kg is recommended and this amount is easily obtained from the diet.

Absorption: Zinc is poorly absorbed from the intestines and almost all the zinc taken in the food is excreted in the faeces. A small amount is excreted in the urine and this is derived from the metabolic processes in the kidney. Zinc in serum is lowered in liver diseases. In rats, poor growth of the body and fur coat has been reported.

Molybdenum

The importance of molybdenum is due to the fact that it is an essential component of metalloflavoproteins such as xanthine oxidase, aldehyde oxidase and hydrogenase.

Molybdenum is absorbed from the intestines and is excreted mainly in the urine. In man, no deficiency symptoms are known and the human requirement is also not known. In cattle, ingestion of excessive amounts of molybdenum results in a disease known as 'teart', which is characterised by persistent scouring. This toxicity is overcome, if copper is given.

Molybdenum is essential for plant growth. It is added as manure to the soil for satisfactory growth of clover.

Cobalt

Cobalt has gained importance in nutrition because it is an essential component of vitamin B_{12} and it influences haemopoiesis. As cobalt mainly originates from the intestinal micro-organisms, its requirement by way of diet is much less. Even in pernicious anaemia, as little as 1–2 μg of vitamin B_{12} which contains 0.045–0.09 μg of cobalt per day is found sufficient to maintain normal bone marrow function.

Cobalt is readily absorbed from intestines. About 65% of the amount ingested is excreted in the urine and the remainder in the faeces. Cobalt inhibits certain respiratory enzymes such as cytochrome oxidase and succinate dehydrogenase.

Manganese

Manganese occurs in the tissues in very small amounts. Blood contains 12–18 μg/100 ml. It is poorly absorbed and retained. It is mostly excreted in the faeces. The daily requirement of manganese is 6–8 mg.

Functions: Manganese is involved in activating several enzymes, namely phosphatases, arginase, carboxylase, cholinesterase and mitochondrial respiratory enzyme systems.

No deficiency manifestations are noticed in man.

In rats, manganese specifically appears to function in haemoglobin formation. Deficiency of manganese in rats impairs their growth due to poor bone formation.

Fluorine

Fluorine is found particularly in bones and teeth. It is present in sea water. Bones of fish and marine animals contain more fluorine than those of land animals.

Fluorine is readily absorbed from the intestines. About 75% is excreted in the urine. Unabsorbed fluorine is excreted in faeces. Fluorine after absorption is mostly distributed in the bones and teeth. Though not nutritionally essential, the importance of fluorine has been recognised in dentistry, because of its peculiar effect on the enamel. Ingestion of water containing abnormally large amounts of fluorine for long periods during the stage of development and formation of permanent teeth in children result in **dental fluorosis**. This is characterised by mottling or pitting of the surface of the enamel which becomes bleached showing chalky white patches. In later stages, the enamel becomes abnormally fragile and chips off. It has also been found that intake of drinking water containing a minimum amount of fluorine, i.e. 1 part per million, renders the teeth more resistant to caries. This has led to widespread fluoridation of water supplies, with encouraging results in the prevention of dental caries. On this basis, topical application of fluoride in mild dose has been recommended for the prevention of caries. It is believed that the fluorine is absorbed by the hydroxyapatite crystals on the surface of the enamel to form a protective layer of acid-resistant fluorapatite. Another possibility is that the fluoride ions act by inhibiting the activity of the enzymes of the oral bacteria, which are otherwise responsible for the local production of acids from carbohydrates mainly. These acids are believed to be important factors in the causation of dental caries. A more serious condition known as

fluorosis results when workers in the industry of aluminium and fertilisers are exposed to the fumes of fluorine. Osteosclerosis is the predominant feature of fluorosis. The bones show increased density with calcification of ligaments and tendons. When the vertebrae are involved, they suffer from severe back pain.

Fluorine is known to inhibit enzymes requiring Ca, Mg, Mn, Cu and Zn, for example enolase, esterases and bone alkaline phosphatases.

Selenium

Selenium is irregularly distributed in soils and is considered as an element with toxic properties, particularly to cattle grazing plants grown in soils rich in selenium. Selenium toxicity is known to occur in persons exposed occupationally to industries of paints, glass and electronics. Selenium deficiency occurs in people living in certain rural areas where the soil in which foodstuffs are grown is deficient in selenium. Deficiency causes dilatation of heart resulting in congestive heart failure. Selenium forms an integral part of an enzyme called glutathione peroxidase which protects vital cellular components, such as cell membranes, against oxidative damage by hydroperoxides. This action of selenium is similar to the antioxidant property of vitamin E. Vitamin E has a specific effect on selenium metabolism and the vitamin E sparing effects of selenium are discussed in **Chapter 5, Vitamins**.

26

CHAPTER

Hormones

Chapter Outline

- Thyroxine
- Parathyroid Hormone
- Insulin
- Glucagon
- Adrenal Hormones
- Sex Hormones
- Pituitary Hormones
- Melatonin
- Relaxin
- Gastrointestinal Hormones
- Other Gut Hormones

Hormones are secretions of endocrine glands. They discharge their secretions into the blood from where they are carried to specific organs and tissues called **target organs**. Such hormones function by exercising specific and biological action on these target organs. Certain hormones exert influence directly on various biological and metabolic functions and act as integrators of metabolic processes.

The mode of action of hormones is similar to that of enzymes, as hormones exert specific control on metabolic reactions in very low concentration. Most of the hormones are proteins or polypeptides, for example anterior pituitary hormones, parathormone and insulin. Some are derivatives of amino acids, for example thyroxine, norepinephrine and epinephrine, and a few are steroid in nature, for example sex hormones and adrenocortical hormones. Evidences suggest that the metabolic effects of most of the hormones are preceded by increased production of mRNA in the tissues of target glands.

Hormones present in the blood are bound to plasma protein fractions and are transported along with them. For example, thyroxine and corticosteroids are bound to globulin and oestrogens and androgens are bound to albumin. Binding with proteins is important because hormones are prevented from being diffused across the capillaries or excreted in the urine across the glomerular membrane, thereby helping to maintain the concentration of circulating hormones. Liver plays an important role in the regulation of hormone metabolism. In liver, steroid hormones are structurally altered to form inactive compounds. Some steroid hormones are conjugated with sulphate and glucuronic acid to form soluble compounds for excretion in urine. This chapter will briefly deal with the chemistry and metabolic effects of the hormones in the body.

THYROXINE

This hormone secreted by thyroid gland has a molecular weight of about 680,000. It is stored in the colloid of the thyroid follicles, in the form of a glycoprotein called thyroglobulin.

Hydrolysis of thyroglobulin yields monoiodotyrosine, diiodotyrosine, triiodothyronine and thyroxine. Of these, triiodothyronine is considered to be 4–10 times more active than thyroxine. Naturally occurring thyroxine is laevorotatory, whereas synthetic thyroxine does not show any optical rotation.

Biosynthesis and metabolism: Thyroxine is synthesised in thyroid gland from tyrosine (page 433). The first inorganic iodide is oxidised to organic iodine ($2I \longrightarrow I_2$). Tyrosine is iodinated in the third position to form 3-monoiodotyrosine. The next iodination occurs in the fifth position to form 3, 5-diiodotyrosine (**Fig. 26.1**).

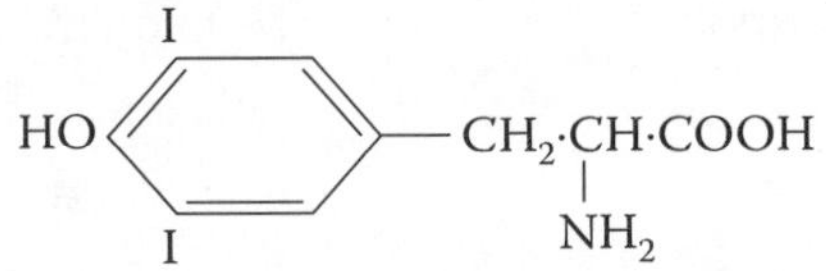

Figure 26.1 3,5-Diiodotyrosine.

Two molecules of diiodotyrosine couple to form a molecule of tetraiodotyrosine which is thyroxine (**Fig. 26.2**). Alanine is liberated.

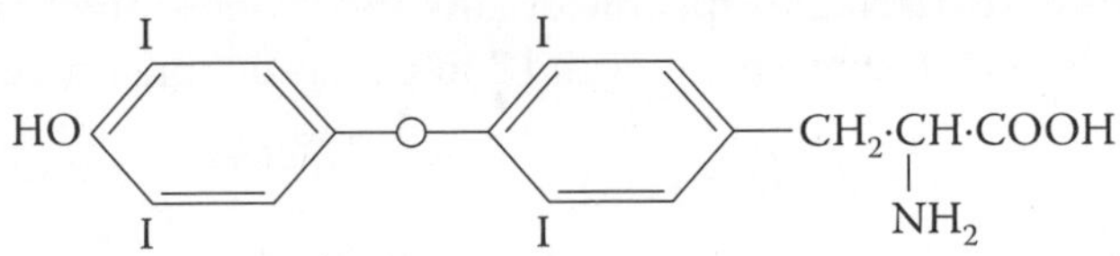

Figure 26.2 Thyroxine.

Triiodothyronine may be formed either by conjugation of one molecule of monoiodotyrosine and one molecule of diiodotyrosine or by deiodination of thyroxine.

Synthesis of thyroxine is accelerated by thyroid stimulating hormone (TSH) and inhibited by antithyroid agents such as thiocarbamides and aminobenzenes. Thyroid has the capacity of trapping inorganic iodine from circulation and storing it for utilisation in the synthesis of thyroxine and its precursors. Depending upon the need for thyroxine and its iodinated derivatives, a proteolytic enzyme hydrolyses thyroglobulin, under the stimulating influence of TSH.

Circulating thyroid hormone: Circulating blood contains 6–12 μg% thyroxine, a small amount of triiodothyronine and traces of inorganic iodide. Thyroxine and triiodothyronine are sometimes called circulating thyroid hormone. These two hormones are loosely bound to plasma proteins. Thyroxine is bound to a specific α-globulin known as thyroxine binding globin (TBG) which moves between α_1 and α_2 globulin, electrophoretically. The iodine present in the hormones is referred to as protein bound iodine (PBI) and its concentration in blood is 4–10 μg per 100 ml. The small amount of inorganic iodide present in blood (2 μg per 100 ml) is used up rapidly by thyroid for synthesis of thyroxine.

Thyroxine and triiodothyronine may also get conjugated with glucuronic acid and sulphates and get excreted in bile. A part of the hormone may be reabsorbed into portal circulation to constitute enterohepatic circulation.

Metabolic effects of thyroxine: Thyroxine produces a widespread enhancement of metabolism in almost all the tissues of the body. These may be discussed under the following headings:

1. *Calorigenic effect:* Thyroxine has the unique property of increasing the rate of energy exchange and oxygen consumption of all tissues except the thyroid gland itself. The high level of metabolism can be shown by an increase in the basal metabolic rate (BMR). The calorigenic effect of thyroxine is greater at a low level of metabolism, as in hypothyroidism. In myoxedematous conditions, 1 mg of thyroxine produces about a 2.8% increase in BMR. BMR is increased in hyperthyroidism and decreased in hypothyroid states where tissue oxidation and oxygen consumption are less.
2. *Protein metabolism:* In small physiological doses, thyroxine promotes protein anabolism, resulting in retention of nitrogen and positive nitrogen balance. Cessation of growth occurs in hypothyroid children and thyroidectomised animals. Normal growth is resumed following administration of thyroxine.

   In larger doses, thyroxine stimulates catabolism of proteins, resulting in negative nitrogen balance and increased urinary excretion of creatine, the latter being due to increased catabolism of muscle protein.
3. *Carbohydrate metabolism:*
   - Thyroxine increases the rate of absorption of monosaccharides by the intestines.
   - Thyroxine enhances hepatic glycogenolysis, thus increasing the blood sugar concentration.
   - Thyroxine also favours gluconeogenesis. All these factors contribute to the hyperglycaemic state of hyperthyroidism.
4. *Lipid metabolism:* Thyroxine increases the rate of oxidation of fats, ultimately leading to ketosis. It promotes liberation of free fatty acids from adipose tissues and raises the concentration of free fatty acids in blood.

   Serum cholesterol is considered to be decreased in hyperthyroidism and increased in hypothyroidism, even though thyroxine increases the rate of biosynthesis of cholesterol. This is because thyroxine increases the rate of breakdown of cholesterol to a greater extent than the rate of biosynthesis.
5. *Electrolytes and water metabolism:* Thyroxine initiates an increased urinary excretion of water, potassium, sodium and chlorides by mobilising them from intracellular fluid and increasing the plasma volume. This is the picture given by hyperthyroid cases. In hypothyroidism, there is an increase in the interstitial fluid and a decrease in blood volume.
6. *Calcium metabolism:* Small doses of thyroxine bring about retention of calcium and this is probably due to stimulation of protein metabolism which increases the bone

matrix formation. Large doses of thyroxine lead to increased excretion of calcium in urine, by mobilisation of calcium from the bones.

7. *Vitamins:* Deficiency of thyroxine causes deficiency of vitamin A and increase in serum carotene, probably due to an interference in the synthesis of vitamin A from carotene.

   Thyroxine also increases the requirements of B complex group of vitamins and vitamin C.

8. *Induction of metabolism:* Thyroxine accelerates metamorphosis of amphibians. It is a well-known fact that very small tadpoles can be metamorphosised into minute frogs by administration of small doses of thyroxine.

Agents interfering with the synthesis of thyroid hormone: There are chemical agents that have the property of interfering with the synthesis of thyroid hormone at different stages, for example (i) thyroxine, (ii) iodine, (iii) thiocyanate and (iv) antithyroid agents.

1. *Thyroxine:* Administration of thyroxine produces regressive changes in the thyroid gland, leading to reduced formation of thyroxine. It probably acts by inhibiting the action of TSH on thyroid gland.
2. *Iodine:* Synthesis of thyroxine is impaired when the iodine intake is inadequate. This leads to compensatory hyperplasia of the thyroid gland resulting in iodine deficiency goitre. On the other hand, administration of iodine to individuals with hyperthyroidism leads to regressive changes in thyroid gland and diminished output of thyroxine.
3. *Thiocyanate:* This substance inhibits the uptake, concentration and storage of iodine by the thyroid, causing decreased synthesis of thyroxine and goitre formation. The thyroid gland will have no difficulty in synthesising the hormone, if sufficient iodine enters the gland either by passive diffusion or following administration of iodine parenterally, because thiocyanate does not interfere with the synthesising mechanism.
4. *Antithyroid agents:* These are chemical agents which inhibit the synthesis of thyroid hormone. They act most probably by blocking the oxidation of inorganic iodide to free iodine which is a preliminary step for iodination of tyrosine and thereafter synthesis of thyroxine. For this reason, these substances are used in the treatment of hyperthyroidism. They are grouped under two categories:
   - *Compounds containing thiocarbamide grouping:* Examples are thiourea, thiouracil and related compounds.
   - *Compounds containing aminobenzene grouping:* Examples are sulphonamides and aniline derivatives.

Diseases associated with abnormal metabolism of thyroxine:

1. *Hyperthyroidism:* Excessive secretion of thyroxine produces hyperthyroidism or thyrotoxicosis and this is usually associated with the enlargement of thyroid gland, as in exophthalmic goitre or Graves' disease. The disease manifests symptoms such as tachycardia, tremors of fingers and protrusion of eyeballs (exophthalmos). The person loses weight, becomes irritable and puts on an anxious and nervous appearance.

   In thyrotoxicosis, the BMR is greatly increased, ranging from +20 to +60%. Treatment consists of administration of iodine or antithyroid drugs in mild cases and removal of thyroid gland in severe cases.

2. *Hypothyroidism:* Deficiency of thyroxine causes a hypothyroid state. Hypothyroidism may arise due to a deficient intake of iodine or may follow surgical removal of thyroid.

   Hypothyroidism in infants is known as **cretinism**. The child is underdeveloped both physically and mentally. Hypothyroidism in an adult is known as myxoedema. The typical features of myxoedema are puffiness of the face, thickening of the skin due to infiltration of a semifluid material in the subcutaneous tissue, hoarseness of voice, sluggishness in speech and mental retardation. The temperature of the body and the pulse rate are reduced. The BMR in hypothyroidism is greatly reduced, reaching levels from –20 to –60%. Treatment consists of administration of iodine and thyroxine in appropriate doses.

PARATHYROID HORMONE

Parathyroid hormone is secreted by a pair of parathyroid glands which lie embedded in the lower end of the thyroid gland, one on either side. It is a protein and has a molecular weight of about 8000. In its purified form, the hormone consists of a long, straight polypeptide chain and is soluble in water. As it is inactivated by proteolytic enzymes and hydrolysed by acids, it is ineffective when administered orally. It is stable to reducing agents and unstable to oxidising agents.

Metabolic actions: Parathyroid hormone (parathormone) exerts a profound effect on the metabolism of calcium and phosphorus. The two important metabolic functions are mobilisation of calcium from the bones and phosphaturic action. The parathyroid hormone regulates the blood calcium level by a negative feedback mechanism whereby low blood calcium brings about stimulation of parathyroid hormone secretion while an increase in blood calcium suppresses the secretion of the parathyroid hormone. This mechanism is strengthened by the action of a hypocalcaemic agent known as **calcitonin**, secreted by thyroid when there is an increased concentration of serum calcium. Calcitonin secreted by the C cells of thyroid gland lowers the serum calcium.

The metabolic actions of parathyroid hormone can be studied best by observing (i) the effects of removal of parathyroid glands and (ii) the effects of parathyroid hormone injection.

1. *Effects of removal of parathyroid glands are as follows:*
   - Reduction in the serum calcium concentration
   - Reduction in the urinary excretion of calcium
   - Increase in the serum inorganic phosphorus
   - Reduction in the urinary excretion of inorganic phosphorus

   The most important effect of parathyroidectomy is reduction in the serum calcium concentration, leading to a condition called **tetany**. It is a manifestation of neuromuscular hyperexcitability, characterised by fibrillary muscle twitchings in the beginning stage, leading eventually to a generalised type of painful, clonic and tonic spasm. The convulsions may become violent with the onset of laryngeal spasm, resulting in asphyxia and death.

2. *Effects of parathyroid hormone injection are as follows:*
   - Increase in serum calcium concentration
   - Increased urinary excretion of calcium
   - Increased urinary excretion of inorganic phosphorus
   - Decrease in serum inorganic phosphorus

Other findings are an increase in serum alkaline phosphatase and an increase in the concentration of citrate in the blood.

Parathyroid hormone accelerates mobilisation of calcium and phosphate from the bones with a consequent increase in the concentration of calcium in the blood and increased excretion of urinary calcium and phosphate. It diminishes the renal tubular reabsorption of inorganic phosphate from the glomerular filtrate, leading to excessive loss of phosphate in the urine and a consequent fall of the serum phosphate level.

The increased level of serum alkaline phosphatase in hyperparathyroidism is due to the osteoblastic activity in areas of healing in the bones.

The high concentration of blood citrate and increased excretion of citrate in urine are again due to the mobilisation of citrate along with bone calcium with which it forms a soluble and loose complex. The excess citrate is excreted in the urine. Besides these actions, parathyroid hormone increases the absorption of calcium from the intestines, in the presence of a sufficient amount of vitamin D.

Repeated injections of parathyroid hormone lead to loss of calcium and phosphorus from bones to an extent of presenting the characteristic picture of diffuse osteitis fibrosa cystica, which shows resorption of trabecular and cortical bone. This leads to fractures and deformities. The increased concentration of calcium in the blood is followed by deposit of calcium phosphate in various tissues, including myocardium, kidneys, stomach and arteries. Calculi may develop in the kidneys and urinary tract due to high concentration of calcium and phosphate in the urine.

Effect of Vitamin D: The action of vitamin D on calcium metabolism is similar to that of the parathyroid hormone. Vitamin D enhances absorption of calcium from intestines and increases the serum calcium concentration. It can also mobilise calcium from bones and produce hypercalcaemia and hypercalciuria like the parathyroid hormone.

Abnormalities of parathyroid hormone secretion:

1. *Hypoparathyroidism* arises due to diminished parathyroid hormone secretion. Accidental removal of the parathyroids during thyroid surgery is the common cause of hypoparathyroidism. The findings in hypoparathyroidism are the same as those under the effects of parathyroidectomy in varying degrees.
2. *Hyperparathyroidism* arises due to increased secretion of the parathyroid hormone. It is usually caused by tumours of parathyroids. It is a primary bone disease and presents a picture of general decalcification. When there is excessive destruction of bones, bone pains and spontaneous fractures set in. Formation of urinary calculi is another common feature.

INSULIN

Insulin is secreted by the β-cells of the islets of Langerhans of the pancreas. Insulin has been isolated and prepared in a crystalline form. It is a protein composed of two long polypeptide chains and has a molecular weight of 5734. Crystalline insulin contains zinc.

Structure: The structure of insulin is complex and has been established by Sanger in 1958. It is composed of two polypeptide chains, the glycyl or A chain and the phenylalanine or B chain.

The **glycyl chain** is acidic and consists of 21 amino acids. It contains glycine as the N terminal residue. The amino acid residue situated at the terminal end of the chain is important because it contains a free amino group and is open to chemical reactions.

The **phenylalanine chain** is basic and contains 30 amino acids. It has phenylalanine as the N terminal residue. The structure of insulin is graphically represented in **Figure 26.3**. The two chains are linked by two cystine residues.

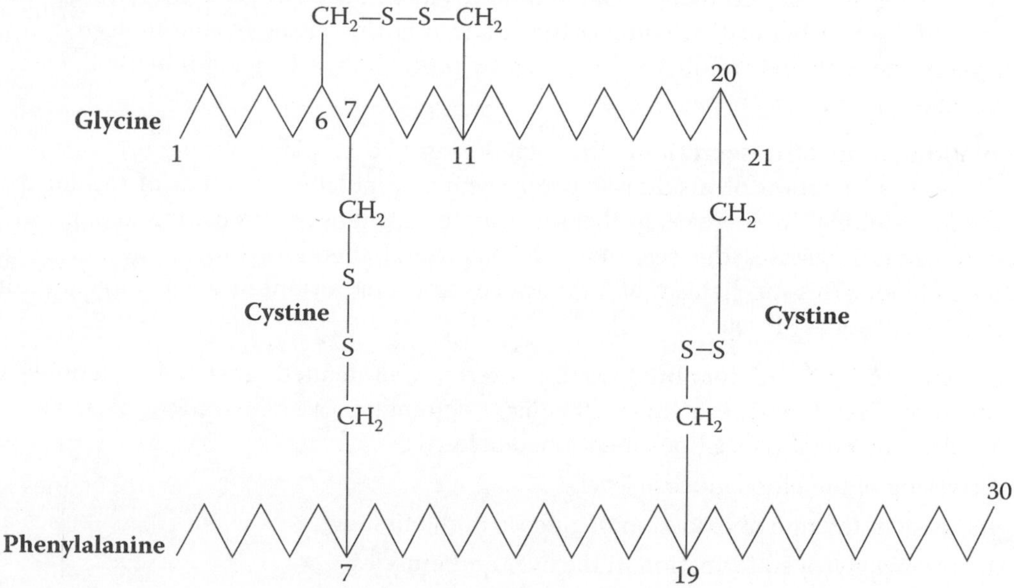

Figure 26.3 Structure of insulin.

Insulin has six molecules of ammonia, present as amide groups (NH_2). Out of these, four are present in the glycyl chain. Two are associated with glutamic acid residues in positions 5 and 15 and two with aspartic acid residues in positions 18 and 21. The other two are present in the phenylalanine chain, associated with asparagine and glutamine in positions 3 and 4. Both the chains are joined at two points, i.e. between the 7th amino acid of each chain at one end and between the 20th and 19th amino acids of each chain at the other end by disulphide (cystine) bridges. There are three disulphide (cystine) bridges in one molecule of insulin. The third cystine is an intrachain link between the cystine residues in positions 6 and 11 of the glycyl chain. The biological activity of insulin is lost when the disulphide linkages are reduced.

Biosynthesis of insulin: Insulin is produced in the β-cells of Langerhans in the pancreas. It is synthesised first as proinsulin in the ribosomes of the rough endoplasmic reticulum.

Proinsulin, which consists of a single polypeptide chain, is made up of A and B chains linked together by another polypeptide chain. Proinsulin is biologically inactive.

The proinsulin molecule is transported to the Golgi apparatus where it is packaged into secretory granules containing the prohormone. The granules mature as they traverse towards the plasma membrane. Within the secretory granules, the proinsulin molecule undergoes proteolytic cleavage and is converted to form the active insulin which is secreted into the circulation on demand.

Metabolism: Insulin circulates in blood mostly along with β- and γ-globulin fractions of plasma protein. The normal concentration of plasma insulin is 4–25 μU/ml. Insulin is degraded by insulinase which is present in the liver. Insulin is rapidly metabolised by an enzyme in the liver, named glutathione insulin transhydrogenase. It brings about cleavage of the S–S bonds that connect the A and B chains of the insulin molecule. After this, the A and B chains are further degraded by proteolysis. Glucagon inhibits the action of insulinase.

Regulation of insulin secretion: The blood sugar level plays an important role in regulating the secretion of insulin. Hyperglycaemia stimulates secretion of insulin from pancreas, resulting in increasing the quantity of insulin in circulating blood, while hypoglycaemia depresses the secretion of insulin and therefore lowers the amount of insulin in blood. This mechanism of feedback control is important in the maintenance of a normal blood glucose level.

Metabolic actions of insulin: Insulin exerts well-defined metabolic actions on carbohydrate, lipid and protein metabolism. Parenteral administration of insulin is followed by the metabolic actions mentioned below:

1. Lowering of the blood glucose level
2. Increase in the rate of oxidation of glucose in the tissues
3. Increasing glycogen formation in the liver and muscles
4. Depressing gluconeogenesis
5. Accelerating the rate of conversion of glucose to lipid (lipogenesis)
6. Decreasing ketogenesis
7. Increasing protein synthesis

The first four actions of insulin refer directly to carbohydrate metabolism. Insulin is administered parenterally to reduce hyperglycaemia in diabetes mellitus. It brings down the blood glucose level by increasing the oxidation of glucose and promoting glycogenesis in liver and muscles. Insulin acts by promoting the passage of glucose across the cell membrane from extracellular fluid into the cells. Normally, the cell wall forms a barrier for the entry of glucose and related sugars.

Insulin has an equally important effect on lipid metabolism. Injection of insulin promotes lipogenesis and decreases ketogenesis. Lack of adequate secretion of insulin as in diabetes mellitus produces increased breakdown of lipids with the formation of acetyl-CoA and ketone bodies.

Insulin promotes synthesis of protein. It acts by accelerating the entry of amino acids into the cells for incorporation into proteins. It is also observed that insulin increases the synthesis of messenger RNA and ribosomal RNA which are necessary adjuncts for synthesis of proteins.

Another action of insulin associated with utilisation of glucose is lowering of the levels of potassium and inorganic phosphorus in the blood. This is apparently due to the utilisation of these elements in the mechanism of phosphorylation and glycogen formation.

Insulin antagonists: These are substances present in the body and they counteract the metabolic actions of insulin.

1. They are hormones, which have diabetogenic action. They act by depressing the utilisation of glucose and accelerating the mechanism of glycogenolysis in liver. Examples are epinephrine, growth hormone, glucocorticoids and glucagon.
2. Certain factors present in blood, and closely associated with plasma protein fractions, have antagonistic action. These are as follows:
   - *Synalbumin factor:* This is associated with plasma albumin. Normally, it is present in a very small amount in the blood. The amount of this fraction increases in a severe type of uncontrolled diabetes, especially juvenile diabetes.
   - Insulin antibodies appear in the blood of those who have had a prolonged treatment with insulin. Sometimes, they are present in high concentration and act by resisting the action of insulin in bringing down hyperglycaemia.

Commercial insulin: Insulin, being quickly absorbable and rapid in action, is marketed in three types of combination which are absorbed more slowly. They vary in the duration of their action.

1. *Protamine zinc insulin:* This is a combination of insulin with protamine. It is absorbed more slowly than plain insulin. One injection of protamine zinc insulin can lower the blood sugar for more than 24 hours, whereas the same effect will be produced by two or three injections of plain crystalline insulin.
2. *Globin insulin:* This is a combination of insulin with globin. It is not long acting like protamine zinc insulin. Its duration of action is 12–15 hours.
3. *Ultralente insulin:* This is a slow-acting insulin, prepared in the presence of high concentrations of zinc and acetate, in order to produce large crystals which are slowly absorbed.
4. *Lente insulin:* This is a mixture of ultralente and plain insulin in the proportion of 7:3. Its duration of action is between that of ultralente and plain insulin.

GLUCAGON

Glucagon, which is also known as the hyperglycaemic glycogenolytic factor (HGF), is a hormone formed by the α-cells of the islets of Langerhans in pancreas. It is a protein consisting of a straight polypeptide chain, which contains 29 amino acid residues. It has a molecular weight of 3485. Glucagon is very active when administered intravenously and has an effect opposite to that of insulin. The blood sugar rises immediately, reaches a peak in about 30 minutes and returns to the original level in an hour.

Mode of action: Glucagon raises the blood glucose level by promoting glycogenolysis of liver glycogen. This process is accomplished by glucagon by its specific action on the liver where it activates the phosphorylase enzyme system, which undergoes continual enzymatic inactivation during glycogenesis and activation during glycogenolysis. Active phosphorylase contains phosphate which is removed when it becomes inactive. The removal of phosphate is catalysed by an inactivating enzyme, phosphorylase phosphatase. Reactivation of phosphorylase which involves addition of phosphate to the latter by another enzyme, dephosphorylase kinase, is accelerated by glucagon in the presence of cyclic 3′,5′-AMP. It may be noted that the glycogenolytic action of glucagon is different from that of epinephrine in that epinephrine breaks both liver glycogen and muscle glycogen, the latter forming lactic acid, whereas glucagon acts only on liver glycogen.

Glucagon affects lipid metabolism by increasing the mobilisation of fat from adipose tissues into blood, thus causing hyperlipaemia. It also promotes ketogenesis.

Glucagon stimulates catabolism of proteins. This is reflected by an increased excretion of urea and creatinine in urine.

ADRENAL HORMONES

There are two parts in the adrenals—the medulla and the cortex.

The medulla is related to the sympathetic nervous system and secretes two hormones, epinephrine and norepinephrine. The medulla consists of chromaffin tissues which means tissues answering chromaffin reaction. The reaction refers to the property of oxidation of epinephrine and certain related compounds by bichromate or iodate resulting in the formation of coloured compounds.

The cortex is an epithelial structure. It secretes hormones which are essential for maintaining life. Their actions are metabolic in nature.

Hormones of Adrenal Medulla

Adrenal medullary hormones are **epinephrine** (**adrenaline**) and **norepinephrine** (**noradrenaline**). For structure, refer to **Figure 21.21**.

The naturally occurring forms are laevorotatory whereas the synthetic forms are racemic. Both are derivatives of tyrosine. Epinephrine is formed from norepinephrine by methylation.

Biosynthesis and metabolism: Tyrosine is the precursor of norepinephrine and epinephrine. The pathway of synthesis of the hormones is outlined below. For details, refer to **Figure 21.21**.

1. Tyrosine is oxidised to 3,4-dihydroxyphenylalanine (dopa).
2. Dopa undergoes decarboxylation to dopamine.
3. Oxidation of dopamine in the side chain yields norepinephrine.
4. Methylation of norepinephrine gives rise to epinephrine.

Norepinephrine, epinephrine and dopamine are called **catecholamines** and they are present in adrenal medulla.

Both epinephrine and norepinephrine are present in blood in very small amounts, bound to plasma proteins. In urine, small amounts of the hormones are excreted normally in the concentration of about 10–15 μg of epinephrine and 30–50 μg of norepinephrine daily. Epinephrine and norepinephrine are excreted in free and conjugated forms as sulphate and glucuronide, respectively.

The bulk of the catecholamines is metabolised by processes involving methylation and oxidative deamination in the presence of monoamine oxidase. The major metabolite of these reactions, 3-methoxy-4-hydroxymandelic acid (vanillyl mandelic acid [VMA]) is excreted in the urine normally in amounts up to 3 mg daily.

Pheochromocytoma: Abnormally large amounts of epinephrine and norepinephrine are produced by certain tumours of chromaffin tissue arising in the medulla. These tumours are called pheochromocytomas. They are manifested by the excretion of an increased amount of catecholamines and VMA in the urine. The content of norepinephrine predominates over epinephrine in pheochromocytoma. The characteristic manifestation of this disease is a persistent type of hypertension.

Epinephrine is secreted in response to stimulation of the nerve fibres of the splanchnics following stress, fear, anger, pain, hypoglycaemia, haemorrhage, muscular activity, anaesthesia and some drugs.

Metabolic actions of epinephrine: Injection of epinephrine causes the following metabolic changes:

1. Increased blood sugar concentration due to acceleration of glycogenolysis in liver
2. Increased lactic acid concentration due to an accelerated rate of glycolysis in muscles. The hyperglycaemic effect of norepinephrine is considered much less than epinephrine, about 1/20th the capacity of epinephrine.
3. Epinephrine depresses the hexokinase activity and probably contributes to the low uptake of glucose by the muscle cells and diminished utilisation of glucose. This action of epinephrine is antagonistic to that of insulin.
4. Both epinephrine and norepinephrine cause an increase in the free fatty acid content of the blood. This is due to the stimulation of hydrolysis of triglycerides by these hormones.
5. Both hormones increase oxygen consumption and thus increase the BMR. This is attributed to the accelerated rate of formation of lipids and oxidation of fatty acids.
6. Both hormones cause an increase in the blood pressure.

Hormones of Adrenal Cortex

The adrenal cortex secretes several hormones which have important metabolic functions in the body. All of them are structurally similar and belong to the group of steroids.

The hormones of adrenal cortex may be classified into four main groups, on the basis of their biological activity and number of carbon atoms contained in their structure. These are as follows:

1. Oestrogens—18 carbon atoms
2. Androgens—19 carbon atoms
3. Progesterone—21 carbon atoms
4. Corticoids—21 carbon atoms.

Hormones 1, 2 and 3 are discussed under Sex Hormones in page 513. We shall consider corticoids in this section.

Corticoids

The common name applied to corticoids is corticosterone. They are all derivatives of pregnane, containing 21 carbon atoms.

Corticoids have three essential features in their structure (**Fig. 26.4**):

1. A double bond between C-4 and C-5
2. A ketone group at C-3
3. A ketone group at C-20
4. Additional features: The following additional features exercise a well-marked effect upon the biological activity of these compounds:
    - A hydroxyl (OH) group at C-21 enhances sodium retention. It is also necessary for the activity of carbohydrate metabolism.
    - The presence of O or OH group at C-11 is essential for the activity of carbohydrate metabolism. It decreases sodium retention.
    - An OH group at C-17 increases the activity of carbohydrate metabolism.

Classification: On the basis of the relationship between structure and biological functions, the adrenal cortical hormones may be classified into three groups:

I. **Hormones possessing an O or OH group at C-11:** These determine the activity of carbohydrate and protein metabolism. They are referred to as 11-oxygenated corticosteroids or 11-oxysteroids. They are also known as glucocorticoids. The following hormones are included in this group (**Fig. 26.4**):
    - Corticosterone (compound B)
    - 11-Dehydrocorticosterone (compound A)
    - 11-Dehydro-17-hydroxycorticosterone (compound E; cortisone)
    - 17-Hydroxycorticosterone (compound F; hydrocortisone; cortisol)

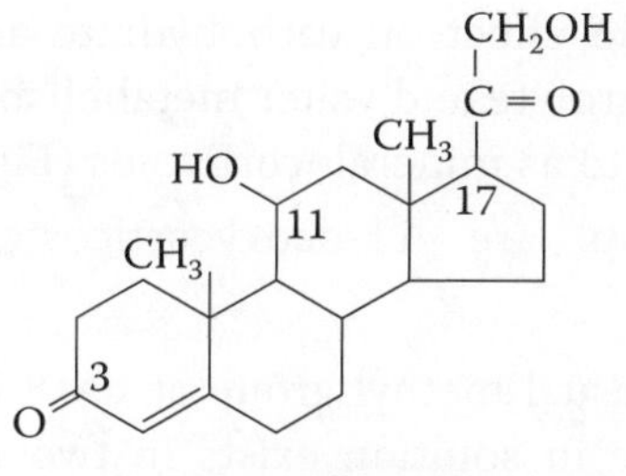

Corticosterone

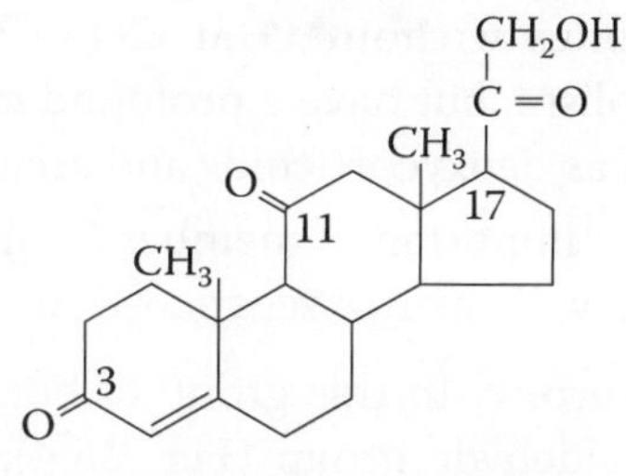

11-Dehydrocorticosterone

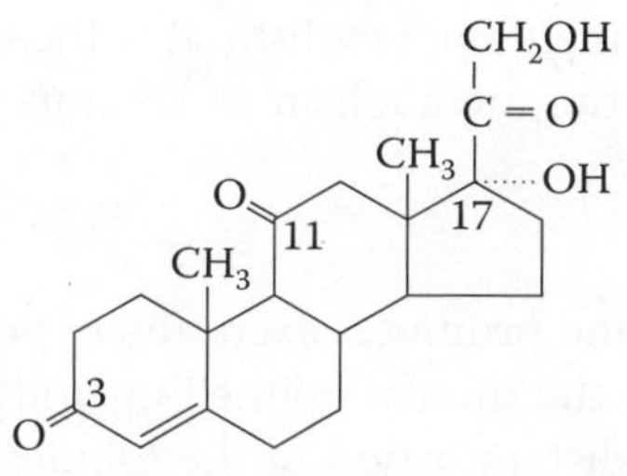

11-Dehydro-17-hydroxycorticosterone

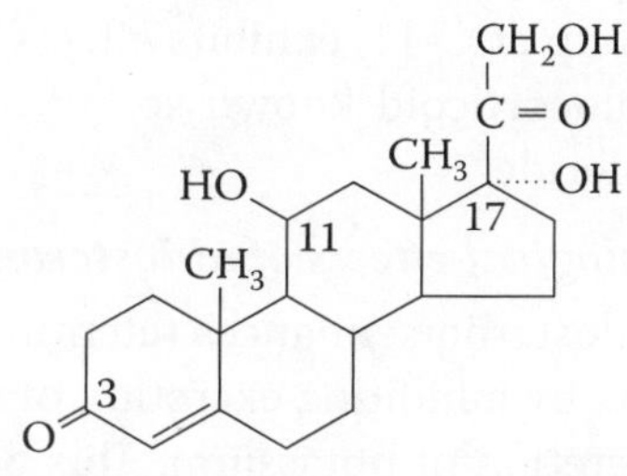

17-Hydroxycorticosterone

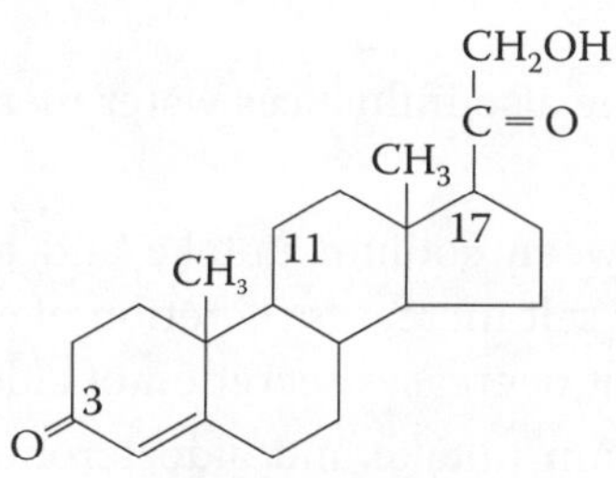

11-Deoxycorticosterone

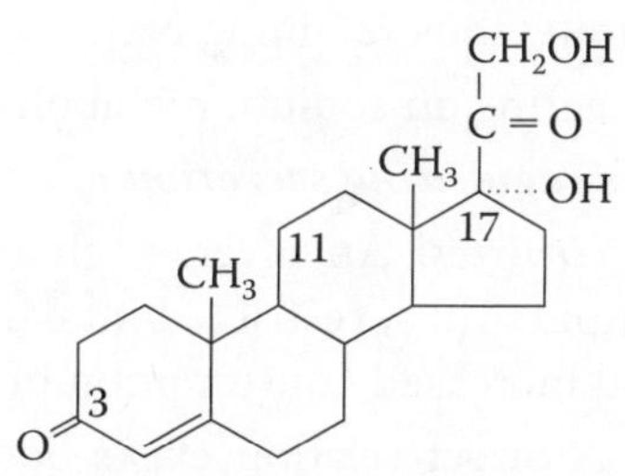

11-Deoxy-17-hydroxycorticosterone

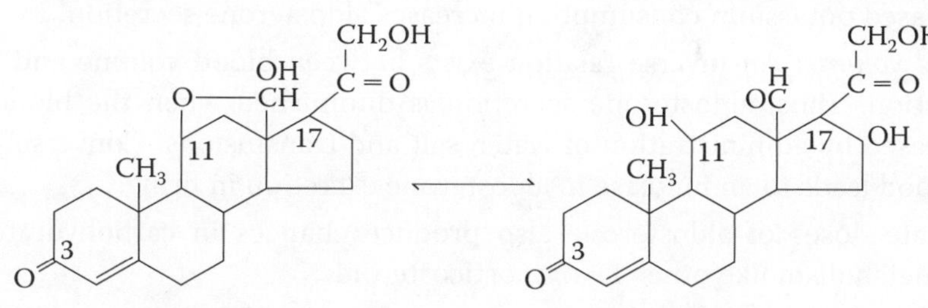

(Hemiacetal) **(Aldehyde)**

Aldosterone

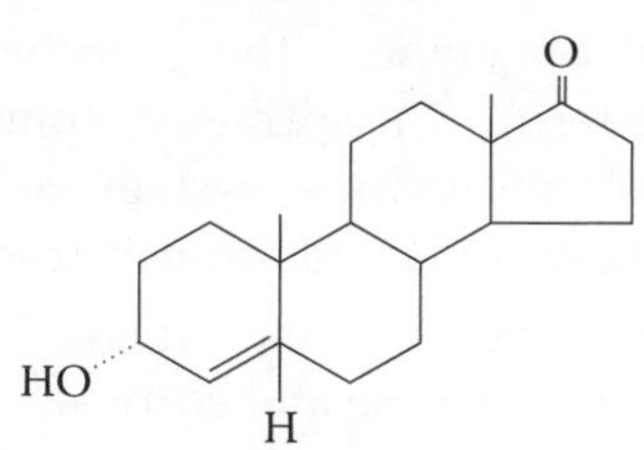

Etiocholanolone

Figure 26.4 Hormones of the adrenal cortex and etiocholanolone.

II. **Hormones without O at C-11:** These have no effect on carbohydrate and protein metabolism, but have a profound effect on electrolyte and water metabolism. They are known as deoxycorticoids and are also referred to as mineralocorticoids (**Fig. 26.4**).

The important members of this group are 11-deoxycorticosterone and 11-deoxy-17-hydroxycorticosterone.

III. **Aldosterone:** In this group of hormones, the usual methyl group at C-18 is replaced by an aldehyde group (**Fig. 26.4**). Aldosterone in solution exists in two tautomeric forms, with hemiacetal and aldehyde structures. Aldosterone, though possessing an OH group at C-11, exhibits effects mostly on mineral metabolism. It is the most active mineralocorticoid known so far and regulates the metabolism of sodium, potassium and chloride.

Physiological effects of aldosterone:

1. Aldosterone enhances retention of sodium and promotes excretion of potassium. It acts by inhibiting excretion of sodium from the tubular epithelium and promoting excretion of potassium. This occurs at the distal portion of the tubules, where K^+ and H^+ ions from the tubular cells are exchanged for Na^+ ions from the glomerular filtrate, thus retaining Na^+.
2. By acting on sodium metabolism, aldosterone also influences water metabolism.

Factors regulating secretion of aldosterone:

1. *Electrolytes:* An inverse relation exists between sodium uptake and aldosterone output. Thus, restricted intake of sodium or salt increases secretion of aldosterone and increased consumption of sodium or salt decreases secretion of aldosterone.

   A direct relation exists between potassium uptake and aldosterone secretion. Thus, restriction of potassium intake decreases aldosterone secretion and increased potassium consumption increases aldosterone secretion.
2. *Blood volume:* An inverse relation exists between blood volume and aldosterone secretion. Thus, aldosterone secretion is diminished when the blood volume is increased by administration of water, salt and transfusions. Conversely, acute loss of blood leads to an increase in aldosterone excretion in urine.

Adequate doses of aldosterone also produce changes in carbohydrate, lipid and protein metabolism like other 11-oxycorticosteroids.

Sex hormones, namely oestrone, progesterone and androsterone, have been isolated from the adrenal cortex.

Biosynthesis of adrenocortical hormones: The probable precursor of adrenocortical hormones is acetate or cholesterol. The primary compound formed from acetate or cholesterol is pregnenolone. An enzyme system oxidises pregnenolone to form progesterone, which takes two pathways for subsequent transformation (**Fig. 26.5**):

1. Progesterone may first undergo 17 and then 21-hydroxylation followed by 11-hydroxylation to form cortiscosterone and cortisol.
2. Progesterone may undergo 21-hydroxylation to form first 11-deoxycorticosterone and then 11-hydroxylation to form corticosterone. Finally by the conversion of C-18 methyl to an aldehyde, aldosterone is formed.

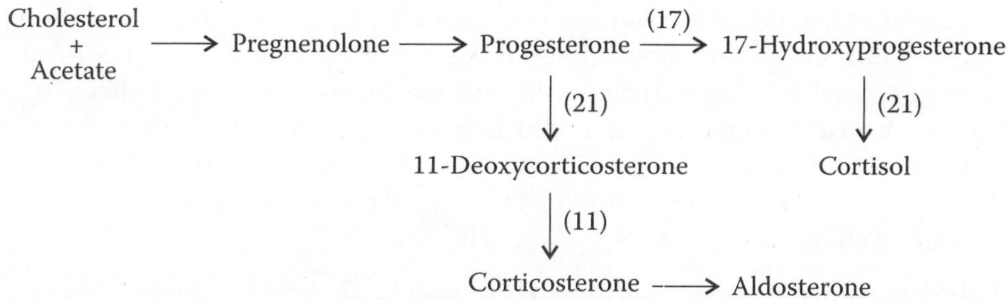

Figure 26.5 Illustration of biosynthesis of adrenocortical hormones. (11), (17) and (21) in the figure indicate the hydroxylation points.

The three layers of adrenal cortex named from the outermost to interior produce corticosteriods as indicated below:

1. Zona glomerulosa secretes aldosterone.
2. Zona fasciculata secretes corticosterone and cortisol.
3. Zona reticularis secretes androgens.

Metabolism and excretion of corticoids: The average concentration of corticoids in blood is as follows:

- 17-hydrocorticosterone; cortisol, (F) = 12 μg/100 ml
- Corticosterone (B) = 1 μg/100 ml
- Aldosterone = 0.05 μg/100 ml

Under normal conditions, 10% of blood cortisol is present in the free state and 90% is bound to plasma protein. Out of the latter, 30% is bound to albumin and 60% to a specific α_2-globulin, known as **transcortin**. The normal plasma cortisol concentration is found to exhibit a diurnal rhythm with maximum values in the morning at about 8 a.m. and low values in the evening from 4 p.m. to midnight. Plasma cortisol concentration increases in the third trimester of pregnancy.

Corticosterones are rapidly inactivated in liver with loss of their biological activities, accompanied by the following changes:

1. Loss of a 4-5 unsaturated bond and a 3-ketone group in ring A
2. Reduction at C-3, C-4, C-5 and C-20, giving rise to dihydro and tetrahydro derivatives
3. Oxidation and removal of the 17-hydroxy group to form 17-ketosteroids. The corticoids and their metabolites may be excreted in urine in the following forms:
   - As biologically active corticoids in their original form but conjugated to a large extent
   - As biologically inactive reduction and conjugated products
   - As 17-ketosteroids, mostly conjugated

Regulation of corticoid secretion: ACTH stimulates the secretion of adrenocortical hormones. Circulating corticosteroids have a reciprocal action too; that is, they control the secretion of ACTH by a negative feedback mechanism. For example, when the level of circulating corticosteroids is increased, secretion of ACTH is depressed and vice versa. Secretion of aldosterone is not regulated by ACTH but by Na/K balance (page 508). Aldosterone enhances retention of sodium by increasing reabsorption of sodium by the renal tubular epithelium. More recent evidences suggest that a substance called angiotensin II, formed by renin which in turn is secreted by what are known as juxtaglomerular cells of the kidney and located in the walls of the renal afferent arterioles, acts directly on the aldosterone producing cells of the zona glomerulosa, stimulating them to secrete aldosterone.

Metabolic functions of corticosteroids: These may be classified under two headings:

1. Effects on electrolyte and water metabolism, influenced by the 11-deoxy type of hormones
2. Effects on carbohydrate, protein and fat metabolism, influenced by 11-oxygenated cortical hormones

The metabolic effects and functions of the corticoids can be studied best by observing the effects of (i) adrenalectomy and (ii) injection of ACTH and corticoid hormones.

Effects of adrenalectomy: Adrenalectomy stimulates the characteristic findings presented by Addison's disease which represents typical metabolic manifestations due to absence or reduced secretion of corticoids, particularly aldosterone. The effects on various metabolism are briefly discussed in this section. Adrenalectomy produces

- Increased excretion of urine
- Increased excretion of sodium and chloride
- Decreased concentration of plasma sodium and chloride
- Dehydration
- Fall in blood pressure and circulatory collapse
- Retention of potassium in blood

The primary organ involved in the excretion of sodium and retention of potassium is the kidneys. In the absence of aldosterone, the renal tubular cells are unable to reabsorb sodium, chloride and water from the glomerular filtrate, even though the plasma sodium concentration is low. They are also unable to excrete potassium adequately in spite of the increased plasma potassium concentration.

This is followed by a disturbance in the water metabolism. The equilibrium between the ECF and the ICF components is changed because there is an increase in the intracellular potassium and a decrease in the extracellular sodium and chloride. The plasma bicarbonate level decreases resulting in metabolic acidosis.

11-Deoxycorticosterone available as a synthetic acetate (DOCA) is next best to aldosterone in the regulation of electrolyte and water metabolism. DOCA which is more easily available than aldosterone is absorbed from the mucous membrane and is administered sublingually.

Effects of 11-deoxycorticosterone on metabolism:

1. *Carbohydrate metabolism*
   - Low blood sugar level
   - Decrease in liver glycogen

- Decrease in intestinal absorption of glucose
- Increased sensitivity to insulin

These effects are due to the absence of the 11-oxygenated adrenocortical hormones. Hypoglycaemia occurs due to an increased rate of utilisation of glucose which is otherwise antagonised by adrenocortical hormones. The highest activity on carbohydrate metabolism is exhibited by cortisol followed by cortisone.

2. *Protein metabolism:* Administration of small amounts of glucocorticoids is followed by a protein anabolic effect resulting in positive nitrogen balance. Large amounts of glucocorticoids produce a catabolic effect on proteins, resulting in increased excretion of nitrogen in urine and negative nitrogen balance. This is followed by an increase in the total body carbohydrate because the extra proteins catabolised are converted to glucose. The glucose/nitrogen (G/N) ratio increases.
3. *Lipid metabolism:* The effects of glucocorticoids on lipid metabolism are secondary to their effects on carbohydrate metabolism:
   - They depress the synthesis of lipids from carbohydrates.
   - They increase mobilisation of depot fat to the liver.
   - They increase ketogenesis in the liver.
   - Cortisone causes an increase in plasma lipoprotein, phospholipids and cholesterol.

Anti-inflammatory action: Some corticoids inhibit inflammatory reaction caused by physical, chemical or bacterial agents. Cortisol is most powerful in producing this effect whereas corticosterone is inactive as an anti-inflammatory agent.

Effect of corticosteroids on immune reactions: Certain corticoids such as cortisol and cortisone possess a powerful antiallergic property. They can prevent the production of antibodies following the introduction of an antigen and also alleviate serious manifestations of hypersensitivity such as anaphylactic shock.

Other miscellaneous effects of corticosteroids: Administration of glucocorticoids produces lymphopenia and eosinopenia. The mechanism of this effect is not known. The converse is also true; that is, a high percentage of circulating lymphocytes and eosinophils is observed in adrenocortical insufficiency.

Diseases associated with adrenocortical functions: The diseases may be classified under two broad headings, namely

1. *Hypoadrenocorticism-Addison's disease:* This condition refers to the hypofunction of the adrenal cortex, as a result of destruction of its tissues, most commonly by tuberculosis. The effects produced depend upon the amount of tissue destroyed. The findings are characteristic, similar to those produced after adrenalectomy and these are mainly due to lack of aldosterone.

   Addison's disease presents characteristic clinical findings such as muscular weakness, gastrointestinal disturbance, low body temperature, low blood pressure and pigmentation of skin. The latter is probably due to the activity of the melanocyte stimulating hormone which is inherent in the structure of ACTH. In Addison's disease, ACTH is increased in amount, because of the deficiency of corticosteroids. Addisonian patients can be maintained in a satisfactory condition by administration of DOCA along with a daily intake of 10–15 grams of NaCl.

2. *Hyperadrenocorticism:* This condition refers to hyperfunctioning of the adrenal cortex, caused due to tumours of the adrenal cortex or hyperplasia of cortical tissue initiated by increased secretion of ACTH.

   Prolonged and continuous administration of steroid hormones or ACTH may also lead to hyperadrenocorticism.

   The characteristic findings are as follows:

   - Hyperglycaemia and glycosuria
   - Retention of sodium and water, resulting in oedema and increased blood volume
   - Negative nitrogen balance due to increased gluconeogenesis
   - Hypokalaemia and alkalosis
   - Hirsutism

Cushing's syndrome: This disease, first recognised by Cushing in 1932 and attributed to basophilic tumours of pituitary, is now claimed to be due to hyperfunctioning of adrenocortex. Administration of cortisol and ACTH for long periods can produce this syndrome but the same can be reversed after discontinuation of the agents. The characteristic findings of this syndrome are as follows:

- Excessive adiposity of the face, neck and trunk
- Tendency to purpura
- Sexual dystrophy

Other findings are hyperglycaemia and hypokalaemia.

Primary aldosteronism: Certain tumours of the adrenal cortex may lead to the production of an excessive amount of aldosterone, which may produce widespread disturbances in the body. The secretion of other corticosteroids may remain normal. This syndrome is termed **primary aldosteronism** or **Conn's syndrome**.

The metabolic changes observed in this condition are significant of the action of aldosterone. These are hypokalaemia, hypernatraemia, alkalosis (due to retention of Na), hyperaldosteronuria, polyuria not responding to ADH, polydipsia, hypertension, muscular weakness due to loss of K and intermittent tetany. Polyuria and polydipsia are the result of lack of reabsorption of water due to degeneration of the tubules.

Laboratory tests for adrenocortical functions: Various laboratory tests are employed to help in the diagnosis of diseases of adrenal cortex. Important among them are as follows:

1. *Estimation of 17-hydroxycorticoids in blood and urine:* The normal value of blood hydroxycortisone is 5–15 μg/100 ml. After injection of 25 units of ACTH, the level rises normally up to 45 μg/100 ml. In adrenal insufficiency, there is no increase in the value.

   The average normal values of 17-hydroxycorticoids in a 24-hour specimen of urine are about 10 mg in a male and about 7 mg in a female and most of the hormone is excreted in the conjugated form. An intravenous injection of 20 units of corticotrophin in a normal person increases the level of urine 17-hydroxycorticoid from 10 to 30 mg whereas in cases of adrenal insufficiency, the level is as low as 3 mg in 24 hours' urine and there is no rise in the level after intravenous administration of corticotrophin. The level of 17-hydroxycorticoids in hyperadrenocorticism is above 12 mg in 24 hours' urine and this may rise to 40 mg or more after injection of ACTH.

2. *Eosinophil count in blood:* The normal response of ACTH to circulating eosinophils is to effect a rapid decline. The eosinophil counts are made before and after the injection of 25 units of corticotrophin. If the reduction in the eosinophil count is more than 50%, the functioning of adrenals is considered normal. If the reduction is less than 50%, adrenal insufficiency is suspected.
3. *Estimation of 17-ketosteroids in urine:* Determination of 17-ketosteroids gives valuable information about the functioning of adrenal cortex because 17-ketosteroids are derived mainly from adrenal cortex in females and from adrenal cortex and testes in males.

SEX HORMONES

The sex hormones are produced by the testes and ovaries. They are concerned with the functions of reproduction, development of the accessory reproductive organs and control of secondary sex characteristics. Structurally, the sex hormones belong to the group of steroids. The male sex hormones are referred to as **androgens** and the female sex hormones as **oestrogens**.

Male Sex Hormones (Androgens; Fig. 26.6)

Androgens produce masculinising effects and help in maintaining primary and secondary male characteristics. They are produced by the interstitial cells of Leydig of testes. They have also been isolated from adrenal cortex and ovaries. There are four naturally occurring androgens in man. These are testosterone, androsterone, isoandrosterone and dehydroisoandrosterone.

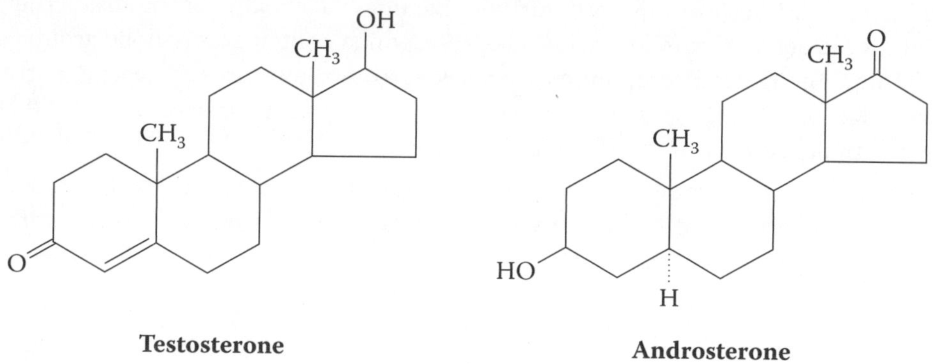

Figure 26.6 Male sex hormones.

Androgens contain 19 carbon atoms and possess the following features:

1. They have two methyl groups, one at C-10 and another at C-13.
2. Most of them have a ketone group at C-3 and a double bond at C4-C5.

These two features are characteristic of all active steroid hormones except oestrogens. This arrangement in the structure from C-3 to C-5 is referred to as an α, β-unsaturated ketone group. Any change occurring in this group will result in the reduction of the specific activity of the hormone.

Biosynthesis and metabolism: The probable precursor of androgens is either acetate or cholesterol. Androgens give rise to the intermediate pregnenolone, which is also the precursor of the adrenocortical hormones. It is converted to progesterone which leads to the formation of testosterone.

Synthesis of the androgens occurring mainly in the testes is accelerated by gonadotropic hormones.

About 4–12 mg of testosterone are secreted daily in a normal man. The normal average concentration of plasma testosterone in a male is about 0.6 μg per 100 ml.

Testosterone is metabolised in the liver where it undergoes conversion to inactive compounds, when the α, β-unsaturated system in ring A is destroyed. In the liver, testosterones are conjugated with sulphate or glucuronate to form water-soluble products and are excreted in the urine. The metabolic products excreted in urine are known as 17-ketosteroids. They include androsterone, etiocholanolone, dehydroepiandrosterone and epiandrosterone. Normally, testosterone is not excreted in urine.

Urinary 17-ketosteroids: Urine contains a small amount of 17-ketosteroids which represent metabolic products derived mainly from testosterone. In a male, they are derived from adrenal cortex and testes in the proportion of 2/3 and 1/3, respectively. In a female, they are derived mainly from the adrenal cortex. These compounds have a ketone group at position 17 and this enables the ketosteroids to form characteristic colour reactions, namely *Zimmermann reaction* with *m*-dinitrobenzene and *Pincus reaction* with antimony trichloride. This is the basis of the quantitative determination of the ketosteroids in biological fluids.

The urinary 17-ketosteroids are further classified as acidic or neutral. The acidic compounds are derived from bile acids. Oestrone which contains a phenolic group belongs to this group. The neutral compounds are derived from the testes and adrenal cortex. The determination of neutral urinary 17-ketosteroids is important clinically because it reflects on the functional activity of these organs.

As the urinary ketosteroids are present as esters, they have to be first liberated free, by hydrolysis before quantitative estimation. The values of urinary 17-ketosteroids in a 24-hour urine sample of

1. An adult man during the reproductive period = 7–20 mg
2. An adult woman during the reproductive period = 5–15 mg
3. Normal children from 6 to 12 years = 1.5–5.0 mg

High values are obtained in conditions of hyperfunctioning of testicular and adrenocortical hormones as in tumours of testes and adrenal cortex. Low values are obtained in hypofunctioning of adrenal cortical and testicular hormones as in hypogonadism.

Metabolic actions of androgens:

1. Testosterone promotes anabolism of protein by stimulating protein biosynthesis and transport of amino acids into cells.

   The protein anabolic effect results in

   - Decreased urinary excretion of nitrogen
   - Increase in body weight which is mainly due to an increase in skeletal muscle mass and bones

   In clinical practice, small doses of testosterone are administered to promote protein anabolism and in higher doses it produces undesirable androgenic action.

2. Testosterone produces specific stimulation of the growth and functional activity of prostate, seminal vesicles, epididymis and vas deferens. It is used clinically as a replacement therapy in eunuchoidism.

Female Sex Hormones

Two types of female sex hormones are secreted by the ovary:

1. The oestrogenic hormones produced by the cells of the developing graafian follicles (oestrogens)
2. The progestational hormones produced by corpus luteum derived from the ruptured follicles (progesterone)

Oestrogens

In humans, the three naturally occurring oestrogens are oestrone, β-oestradiol and oestriol (**Fig. 26.7**). They are steroids and have the following common features in their structure:

1. 18 C atoms
2. 3 double bonds in ring A
3. Absence of a methyl group at C-10
4. Presence of an OH group at C-3

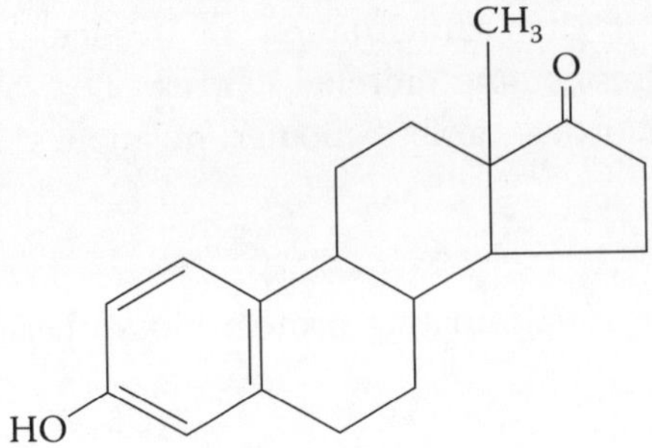

Oestrone

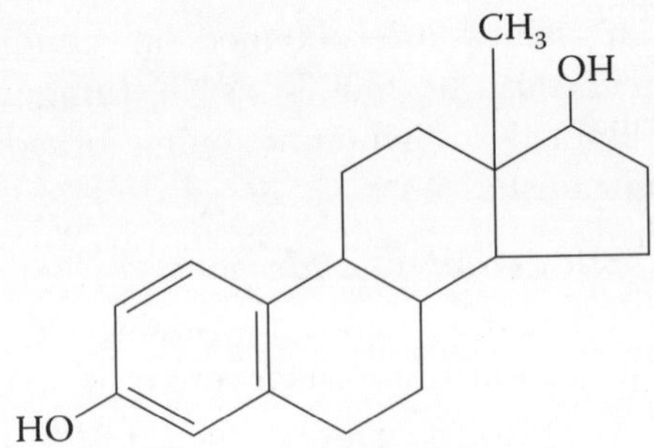

Oestradiol

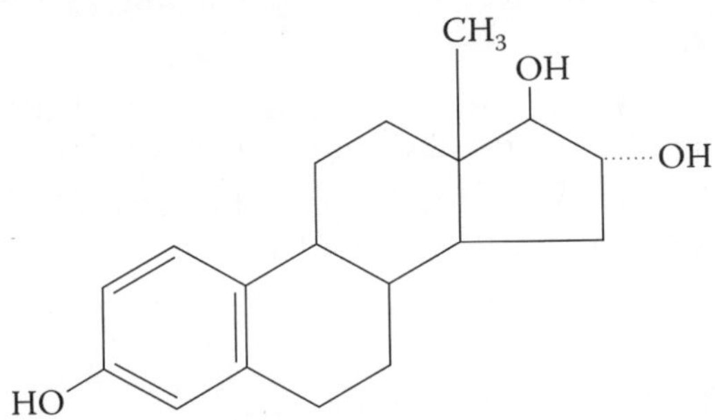

Oestriol

Figure 26.7 Oestrogens.

Oestrone has three double bonds in ring A, an OH group at C-3 and a ketone group at C-17. It is found in non-pregnant urine, placenta, adrenal cortex and urine of adult males.

Oestradiol has two OH groups, one at C-3 and one at C-17. It is the chief hormone produced by the ovarian follicles and is also present in placenta and pregnant urine. It occurs in α and β forms; the α form is more powerful than the β form.

Oestriol has three OH groups, one at C-3, one at C-16 and one at C-17. It is present in pregnant urine and placenta. The main sites of formation of oestrogens are the maturing follicles of ovary and corpus luteum. They are also formed in the adrenal cortex and placenta. The three gonadotropic hormones, namely FSH, LH and LTH (p. 521), stimulate secretion of oestrogens. Oestrogens are soluble in oil, ether, alcohol, acetone and alkalies.

Metabolism: Oestradiol is the primary oestrogen produced by the ovary. Oestradiol, oestrone and oestriol are interconvertible and exist in the ovary in a state of equilibrium.

The probable precursor of oestrogens is cholesterol. In blood, oestrogen and metabolites are present in both the free and the conjugated forms. The conjugated form is bound to the γ-globulin of the plasma proteins.

Liver plays an important role in the metabolism of oestrogens, mainly by inactivating them. The liver cells contain an enzyme system called estrinase, which converts oestradiol to the less active oestrone and oestriol. After conjugation with glucuronide and sulphate, they are returned to systemic circulation from where they get excreted in the urine as oestrone sulphate and oestriol glucuronides. A small amount of oestrogens enter the biliary circulation and get excreted in bile.

Urinary oestrogens represent the activity of oestrogens.

The normal values of urinary oestrogens for an adult man = 21.6–26.2 μg/24 hours (derived from adrenal cortex and testosterone), an adult woman = 10–50 μg/24 hours and during pregnancy = 365–1500 μg/24 hours.

The urinary oestrogen of a normal newborn during the first week is high and is derived entirely from the maternal circulation.

The urinary excretion of oestrogen in girls at the age of 8–10 years is generally more than that in boys. It increases progressively with a marked rise before the menarche. During the reproductive period, oestrogen production follows a cyclic pattern. It is rather low during the earlier follicular phase, but rises gradually to reach an initial peak value at the time of ovulation. It drops to a lower level subsequently and rises again to reach a second peak value on about 21–24 days of the cycle, when the corpus luteum becomes well established. The level again falls to a low value just before the menstrual bleeding. At menopause, the oestrogen level is low.

Physiological functions: Oestrogens exert specific effects on the growth and development of the female reproductive organs, namely fallopian tubes, uterus, endometrium, cervix, vaginal mucous membrane and female secondary characteristics.

Synthetic oestrogens: Two synthetic oestrogens, namely ethylestradiol and diethylstilbestrol, are widely used. They act even when given by mouth.

Progesterone

Progesterone is mainly secreted by the corpus luteum of the ovary. It is also formed in the placenta, adrenal cortex and testes (**Fig. 26.8**).

Progesterone makes its appearance suddenly on the day of ovulation or 1 or 2 days earlier. It exerts its action in the later half of the menstrual cycle and is concerned mainly with the preparation of the endometrium for implantation of the fertilised ovum for conception.

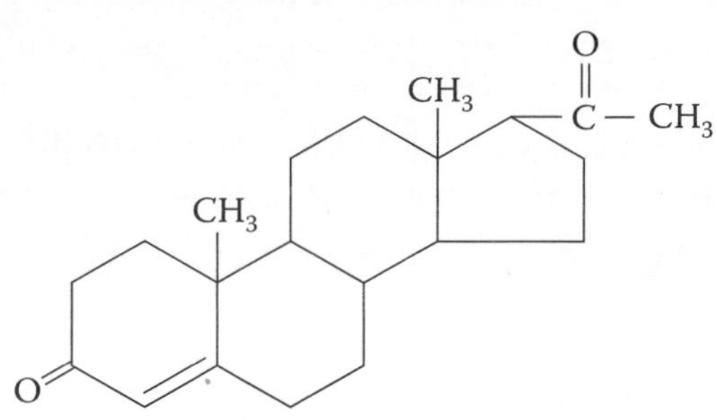

Figure 26.8 Progesterone.

During pregnancy, progesterone is produced by the corpus luteum in the earlier period and by the syncytial cells of the placenta in the later period. The chief excretion product of progesterone in urine is pregnanediol.

Progesterone is a steroid and contains 21 carbon atoms. It has methyl groups at C-10 and C-13.

Progesterone is soluble in all organic solvents except petroleum, ether, acetone and pyridine. It is soluble in water.

Biosynthesis and metabolism: The probable precursor of progesterone is acetate or cholesterol. Progesterone serves as an intermediate in the biosynthesis of adrenal corticoids, androgens and oestrogens (page 517).

As in the case of oestrogens, liver forms the important site for the metabolism of progesterone. Liver removes the hormone from circulation and inactivates about 10% of it by degradation and reduction. The chief metabolite formed is pregnanediol which is conjugated with glucuronic acid and then passed on to systemic circulation, from where it is excreted in urine. A part of the conjugated pregnanediol is also excreted in the bile which enters the intestines, to be excreted in faeces.

During the reproductive period, pregnanediol in urine appears almost suddenly about 12–14 days before the onset of menstrual bleeding, i.e. within 1 or 2 days after ovulation. The amount excreted daily may vary from 3 to 10 mg reaching a peak on about the 21st day of the menstrual cycle and then dropping almost abruptly to zero, 2 or 3 days before the onset of the bleeding. If pregnancy occurs, pregnanediol excretion continues to increase and may reach values of 50–100 mg, nearing full term. Thus, the presence of a significant amount of pregnanediol in urine is considered a satisfactory test for pregnancy.

Physiological action:

1. Progesterone produces characteristic progestational changes in the endometrium during the reproductive period. It prepares the endometrium for the reception and implantation of fertilised ovum.
2. It stimulates the development and growth of mammary glands and sensitises them for the action of lactogenic hormone.
3. The suppression of ovulation and menstruation during pregnancy is due to the action of progesterone which along with oestrogens helps in the maintenance of the quiescent state of uterus. If pregnancy does not occur, the concentration of progesterone decreases at the end of the menstrual cycle and menstrual bleeding starts which is associated with shredding of the mucosa of the endometrium.
4. It is responsible for increasing the BMR during the luteal phase of a normal menstrual cycle, i.e. from 14 to 28 days. There is a slight rise in basal temperature during this period.

PITUITARY HORMONES

Hypophysis has three parts—the anterior pituitary, the posterior pituitary and the pars intermedia.

Hormones of Anterior Pituitary

Anterior pituitary is most important because

1. It controls the functional activity and structural integrity of other important endocrine glands, namely thyroid, adrenal and gonads, through the so-called tropic hormones.
2. It produces **growth hormone** which exerts a direct action on certain fundamental aspects of protein, carbohydrate and fat metabolism.

Tropic Hormones

The tropic hormones secreted by the anterior pituitary are given in the following text. These hormones exert their effects solely by stimulating their respective target glands, so much so that hypophysectomy leads to atrophy of thyroid, adrenal cortex and gonads.

1. **Thyrotropic hormone (thyroid stimulating hormone [TSH]):** It is a glycoprotein and has a high cystine content.

   Actions:
   - TSH plays an important role in the regulation of secretion of thyroxine.
   - Secretion of TSH by the anterior pituitary, on the other hand, is controlled by the level of circulating thyroxine. An increase in the concentration of circulating thyroxine depresses and a decrease in the quantity of circulating thyroxine increases the TSH production.

   Effects of injection of TSH:
   - Increases the iodine content of the gland
   - Increases the rate of synthesis of thyroxine
   - Liberates thyroxine from thyroglobulin
   - Increases the concentration of plasma PBI
2. **Adrenocorticotropic hormone (ACTH):** It is a protein containing a straight-chain polypeptide consisting of 39 amino acid residues. Two forms, α-corticotrophin and β-corticotrophin, have been isolated.

   Actions: ACTH is the main regulator of the activities of adrenal cortex.

   Effects of administration of ACTH:
   - Increased secretion of adrenal corticosteroids
   - Increased rate of synthesis of proteins
   - Increased secretion of mineralocorticoids and glucocorticoids
3. **Gonadotropic hormones:** The three gonadotropic hormones exercising important effects on the gonads are as follows:
   - Follicle-stimulating hormone (FSH)
   - Interstitial cell-stimulating hormone (ICSH) or luteinising hormone (LH)
   - Lactogenic hormone (prolactin); luteotropic hormone (LTH)

   In a female, gonadotropic hormones promote growth, maturation and expulsion of the ova and stimulate production of internal secretions of the ovary.

   In a male, they stimulate spermatogenesis and stimulate production of androgen.

4. **Follicle-stimulating hormone (FSH):** It is a water-soluble glycoprotein, containing about 3–11% carbohydrate.

   Actions: In a female, FSH stimulates the growth and maturation of the Graafian follicles and prepares them for ovulation.

   In the male, FSH stimulates spermatogenesis.

5. **Interstitial-cell-stimulating hormone (ICSH) (luteinising hormone [LH]):** It is a carbohydrate, containing protein.

   Actions: In the female, ICSH (LH) acts in conjunction with FSH to promote maturation of the Graafian follicles, ovulation of mature follicles and development of corpus luteum. It stimulates secretion of oestrogen and progesterone.

   In the male, ICSH stimulates the production of testosterone by the testes.

6. **Lactogenic hormone (prolactin):** Prolactin is responsible for stimulating lactation in the postpartum woman. As a luteotropic hormone, it stimulates corpus luteum for continued production of progesterone.

   Chorionic gonadotrophin: The placenta produces a gonadotropic hormone which has action similar to that of ICSH. Its concentration in blood and urine increases steadily during pregnancy. It promotes functioning of the corpus luteum during pregnancy.

Growth Hormone (Somatotropin)

Growth hormone has a single polypeptide chain composed of 190 amino acids.

Actions: Administration of growth hormone results in *gigantism* in young and *acromegaly* in adults. It exerts direct action on the metabolism of protein, carbohydrates and lipids.

1. *Protein metabolism:* It stimulates anabolism of protein in general. It promotes synthesis of protein and induces a positive nitrogen balance. It retards amino acid catabolism.
2. *Carbohydrate metabolism:* It produces hyperglycaemia (diabetogenic effect).

   It inhibits insulin action resulting in decreased utilisation of glucose.

   It inhibits the hexokinase reaction. This is opposite to the action of insulin which enhances hexokinase reaction.
3. *Lipid metabolism:* It stimulates mobilisation of fats from fat depots to blood. It increases ketogenesis.
4. *Mineral metabolism:* Growth hormone enhances absorption of calcium from the intestines. It helps in retaining phosphate, sodium and potassium and stimulates the growth of the long bones at the epiphysis.

Posterior Lobe Hormones

Posterior pituitary hormones consist of two principal fractions:

1. Vasopressin (pitressin, antidiuretic hormone, ADH), which raises the blood pressure and decreases the secretion of urine
2. Oxytocin (pitocin) which causes contraction of uterine muscles

Chemistry and structure: Vasopressin and oxytocin have similar chemical structures (**Figs 26.9** and **26.10**).

Both are octapeptides and contain eight amino acids, out of which six are common to both. These are glycine (amide), proline, aspartic acid (amide), glutamic acid (amide), tyrosine and cystine. These are represented in a cyclic form with two cysteinyl residues forming disulphide bridges. Three of these eight amino acids are present in the form of amides.

Oxytocin contains in addition leucine and isoleucine, while vasopressin contains in those places arginine or lysine and phenylalanine.

S——S (H.Cys. to Cys.)							
H.Cys.	Tyr.	Ile.	Glut. (NH_2)	Asp. (NH_2)	Cys.	Pro.	Leu.	Gly. (NH_2)

Figure 26.9 Oxytocin.

S——S (H.Cys. to Cys.)								
H.Cys.	Tyr.	Phe.	Glut. (NH_2)	Asp. (NH_2)	Cys.	Pro.	Arg. or Lys.	Gly. (NH_2)

Figure 26.10 Vasopressin.

Site of formation: Vasopressin and oxytocin are formed in the neurones of the hypothalamic nuclei. They migrate along their axons and are stored in the nerve cell endings in the neurohypophysis. The discharges of ADH, particularly from this structure, are controlled by the hypothalamic neurones and are influenced by the degree of concentration of the plasma. Thus when there is a tendency towards reduction in plasma water content, antidiuresis is stimulated which results in renal tubular reabsorption of an increased amount of water.

In the absence of ADH, the urine cannot be concentrated and large volumes of low specific gravity urine are excreted. This condition is **diabetes insipidus**.

Functions:

1. Vasopressin stimulates the peripheral blood vessels and causes a rise in the blood pressure. It is used to counteract the low blood pressure of shock following surgery, postpartum haemorrhage and uterine inertia. The rise in blood pressure is more gradual than that of epinephrine.
2. Being an antidiuretic, vasopressin helps in regulating water balance. It acts by reabsorption of water from the epithelial cells of renal tubules (distal portion). Deficiency or lack of ADH causes diabetes insipidus.

3. Oxytocin produces contraction of the uterus. It causes ejection of milk from the lactating breast.
4. It stimulates contraction of gall bladder, intestines and urinary bladder.

Hormones of the Middle Lobe of the Pituitary (Pars Intermedia)

The middle lobe of the pituitary secretes a hormone, originally known as intermedin. It is now called melanocyte stimulating hormone (MSH) because it increases the deposition of the pigment melanin by the melanocytes of the human skin.

Secretion of MSH is inhibited by epinephrine, norepinephrine, hydrocortisone and cortisone. In adrenocortical deficiency, as in Addison's disease, where the production of corticosteroids is diminished, MSH secretion is increased resulting in increased synthesis of melanins. Brown pigmentation of the skin is a characteristic finding in Addison's disease. The pigmentation increases as the disease progresses.

Excess pigmentation of skin can be suppressed by oral administration of 30–50 mg of cortisone daily.

Chemistry: Two types of MSH (α-MSH and β-MSH) have been isolated. They are straight-chain peptides and contain 13 and 18 amino acid residues, respectively. The amino acid sequence for seven amino acids in both MSH are found to be identical with the sequence of seven amino acids (4–10) in ACTH. The similarity in structure between MSH and ACTH explains the mild but definite melanophore-expanding activity of ACTH.

MELATONIN

Melatonin is *N*-acetyl-5-methoxyserotonin. It is a hormone secreted by the pineal gland (page 427). It lightens the colour of the skin of certain animals such as frogs and fish. It blocks the action of MSH and ACTH.

RELAXIN

Relaxin is a hormone produced during pregnancy and parturition by the tissues of the reproductive system, namely ovaries, placenta and uterus. It is concerned with the phenomenon of pelvic relaxation which consists in the separation of symphysis pubis, leading to expansion of the size of pelvic cavity to facilitate parturition.

Relaxin acts by increasing the vascularisation of the connective tissue of the symphysis pubis. Its production is probably stimulated by progesterone.

GASTROINTESTINAL HORMONES

There are three major gastrointestinal hormones: (i) gastrin, (ii) secretin and (iii) cholecystokinin. They are all polypeptides produced by the mucosal endocrine cells of the stomach and small intestines. They regulate the motor and secretory functions of the stomach, small intestines, pancreas, liver and biliary tract.

Gastrin

Gastrin is produced by the mucosal cells of the pyloric region of the stomach and is the most effective activator of gastric acid secretion. From the pyloric region, it is carried to the parietal cells of the fundus of the stomach where it stimulates the gastric glands to secrete gastric juice rich in HCl. Gastrin has 17 amino acids in its polypeptide chain. The activity resides in the C-terminal tetrapeptide sequence (peptides 14–17) of the polypetide chain. Certain factors are known to increase the release of gastrin. They are vagal stimulation, acetylcholine, intake of food rich in proteins and amino acids, particularly glycine. The gastrin level increases with age and in conditions where gastric acid secretion is low as in pernicious anaemia. Gastrin release and gastric secretion are elevated in a condition known as **Zollinger–Ellison syndrome**, characterised by gastrointestinal ulcers. The increased secretions are caused by gastrin-producing pancreatic tumours.

Two active forms of gastrin, namely gastrin I and gastrin II, have been identified. The polypeptide of gastrin I has 17 amino acids and that of gastrin II has 14 amino acids.

Secretin

Secretin is formed and liberated from the duodenal mucosal cells. The secretion is stimulated by HCl in the acid chyme in the stomach. From the duodenum, it is carried by the bloodstream to the pancreas where it stimulates to produce a flow of pancreatic juice rich in bicarbonate but low in enzyme. Secretin also stimulates the flow of intestinal juice and is one of the factors that increases the secretion of bile by the liver. Secretin has some of the actions of glucagon, for example increasing cardiac output and lypolysis. It consists of a polypeptide chain with 27 amino acids of which 14 are identical to those found in glucagon.

Cholecystokinin

Pancreozymin (cholecystokinin) stimulates pancreas to produce pancreatic juice rich in enzymes and bicarbonate. The enzymes include trypsinogen, chymotrypsinogen, lipase, nucleases and procarboxypeptidase. Pancreozymin stimulates the release of both insulin and glucagon from the pancreatic islets like secretin. This may explain why an oral glucose load is more effective in stimulating insulin release than intravenous administration of glucose. Pancreozymin has 33 amino acid residues, and most of the biological activity of the hormones resides in the C-terminal 8 amino acids.

OTHER GUT HORMONES

Several substances are secreted by gastrointestinal mucosa with a polypeptide structure and having hormonal actions. Some of them are mentioned below:

Enterogastrone is produced by the duodenal mucosa. It inhibits gastric motility and gastric secretion of HCl. Its formation is stimulated by the presence of fat as it reaches the duodenum.

Parotin is secreted by the salivary gland. It stimulates calcification of teeth.

Moulin stimulates gastric motility.

Enterocrinin stimulates secretion of fluid and enzymes by the intestinal mucosa.

Gastric inhibitory polypeptide inhibits gastric acid secretion and gastric motility. It stimulates release of insulin from pancreas.

Vasoactive intestinal peptide inhibits gastric acid secretion. It stimulates pancreatic and intestinal secretion.

Enteroglucagon stimulates the release of insulin.

Chymodenin stimulates the secretion of chymotrypsin by the pancreas.

Bulbogastrone inhibits gastric HCl secretion.

27
CHAPTER

Renal Function Tests

Chapter Outline

- Urine
- Renal Function Tests

URINE

General Characteristics of Urine

Colour: Normal urine is clear and straw coloured. The colour is lighter when a large amount of water is consumed and darker in fevers and after excessive perspiration. This is mainly due to the presence of the pigment urochrome. In jaundice, the urine is highly coloured due to excretion of bile pigments. In alcaptonuria and methaemoglobinaemia, urine may be coloured dark brown.

Odour: Freshly voided urine has a mild aromatic odour. It develops an ammoniacal odour on standing, due to the formation of ammonia by bacterial decomposition of urea. Urine in ketosis emits the smell of acetone.

Volume: The daily normal output of urine varies from 1 to 2 litres, the average volume being 1.5 litres. The volume depends upon the amount of water consumed, the temperature of the environment, the nature of the diet and the mental and physical state of the body. The volume of urine output increases in cold climate and after drinking an excess amount of water. It decreases in hot climate and after heavy perspiration. It is also reduced after loss of fluid from the body as in vomiting and diarrhoea. The volume of urine passed during daytime is nearly twice the volume of urine passed during night.

Specific gravity: Normal urine has a specific gravity of 1.010–1.030, and this depends upon the concentration of the solutes in urine. Under normal conditions, about 50 grams of solids are excreted in urine daily. In renal diseases, when kidneys are damaged, the concentrating capacity of the kidneys is impaired. When the damage is extensive, specific gravity and osmolar concentration of urine may be nearly the same as those of glomerular filtrate. Thus, determination of the specific gravity of urine is an important factor to assess the concentrating capacity of urine.

Reaction: Normal urine is slightly acidic with an average pH of 6. Under physiological conditions, urine is acidic after a high protein diet, due to the excretion of phosphates and sulphates released from the breakdown of proteins. Fever may also produce acid urine. Urine on standing turns alkaline, and this is due to the formation of ammonia from urea by bacterial decomposition. After a heavy meal, urine may be alkaline. In acidosis, acid urine is excreted and the acidity is due to the high ratio of acid phosphate (NaH_2PO_4) to basic phosphate (Na_2HPO_4).

Constituents of Urine

Normal Constituents of Urine

These may be divided into two categories: (i) organic and (ii) inorganic.

1. **Organic constituents:** They may be subdivided into two groups—nitrogenous and non-nitrogenous:
   - ***Nitrogenous constituents:*** These are urea, ammonia, creatine, creatinine, uric acid, amino acids, allantoin and hippuric acid. They are also known as non-protein nitrogenous (NPN) constituents.
     - *Urea:* About 25–35 grams of urea are excreted daily in urine. As it is the end product of protein metabolism, the amount of excretion is an index of the intake of protein in diet. Urea excretion in urine is increased in states of exaggerated protein catabolism as in fevers and increased adrenocortical activity. It is decreased in the last stages of severe hepatic diseases and in acidosis.
     - *Ammonia:* Normally, less than 1 gram of ammonia is excreted in 24 hours. In acidosis, when kidneys are normal, a large amount is excreted. In acidosis, ammonia is formed in the renal tubules as a measure to neutralise excess H^+ ions (p. 257). When acidosis is associated with renal damage, the mechanism of ammonia formation fails.
     - *Creatine and creatinine:* Creatinine is the anhydride of creatine. The daily excretion of creatinine in normal urine is 1–2 grams. Increased excretion of creatinine is found in chronic uraemia.

       Creatine is not present in a significant amount in urine, because it is completely reabsorbed by the tubules. It is present in an appreciable quantity in the urine of prepubertal children and pregnant women. It is increased in muscle dystrophies, hyperthyroidism and starvation.
     - *Uric acid:* This is the end product of metabolism of purines derived from dietary nucleoproteins and from the breakdown of cellular nucleoproteins. Very little uric acid, about 0.7 gram, is excreted in 24 hours. Uric acid is present as soluble sodium and potassium urates at the normal pH of urine whereas they are precipitated in highly acid urine. Increased excretion of uric acid in urine is found in gout, leukaemia and severe liver disease.

       Uric acid has a mild reducing property, and this may give a positive result for reduction with Fehling's solution, if present in an increased amount.

- *Amino acids:* All amino acids are excreted in urine in varying concentrations. Some are in free form and some in combined form. The average daily urinary excretion in normal subjects is about 150–200 mg of free amino acids and 2 grams of conjugated amino acids. During pregnancy, about 200 mg of histidine is excreted daily. The excretion of essential amino acids is much less, about 4 mg, while for other amino acids it is about 50 mg per day. Newborn infants at birth excrete about 3 mg of amino acid nitrogen per pound body weight per day. The excretion declines gradually up to 1 mg per pound body weight per day. Premature infants excrete 10 times more amino acid N than full-term infants.

  Aminoaciduria refers to abnormal excretion of high amount of amino acids in urine, due to inherited disorders (pages 433 and 434).
- *Allantoin:* A very small amount (5–25 mg per day) of allantoin, a partial oxidation product of uric acid, is present in human urine.
- *Hippuric acid:* Benzoate derived from vegetables, fruits and preservatives of foods is conjugated by glycine to form hippuric acid, which is excreted in urine in small amounts. Endogenously, benzoate may be derived from the intestinal bacterial action of aromatic amino acids. The daily urinary excretion of hippuric acid is about 0.5 gram.

• ***Non-nitrogenous constituents:*** These are oxalic, glucuronic and citric acids and traces of fatty acids. Small amounts of certain aromatic hydroxy acids derived from aromatic amino acids are also present.
  - *Oxalic acid:* Small amounts, say 10–25 mg, of oxalic acid are excreted daily as calcium oxalate. Oxalic acid is probably derived from fruits and vegetables. Larger amounts are excreted in a metabolic disorder called primary oxaluria.
  - *Glucuronic acid:* A variety of substances, after conjugation with glucuronic acid in liver, are excreted as glucuronates in urine. Under normal conditions, the daily excretion is 0.3–1.0 gram.

    Glucuronic acid is increased, after ingestion of drugs such as aspirin and sulphonamide. As it has a mild reducing property, excretion of a larger amount will show reduction with Benedict's reagent.
  - *Citrate:* About 0.2–1.2 gram of citrate are excreted daily. This is derived from diet and citric acid cycle.
  - *Organic acids:* About 50–200 mg of lactic acid are excreted daily in urine under normal conditions.

Traces of acetoacetic acid, β-hydroxybutyric acid and acetone derived from fatty acid metabolism are excreted in urine. Larger amounts are excreted in cases of starvation and diabetes mellitus, passing on to the stage of ketosis.

2. **Inorganic constituents:** These are chlorides, phosphates and sulphates of Na, K, Ca and Mg.
   • ***Chlorides:*** About 10 grams of chlorides are excreted as NaCl in 24 hours. The amount excreted varies with the dietary intake. It is reduced when a considerable amount of fluid is lost from the body, as after excessive perspiration, diarrhoea and vomiting.

- ***Phosphate:*** Two types of phosphates, namely alkaline phosphates and earthy phosphates, are excreted in urine. Alkaline phosphates are phosphates of Na and K and constitute two-third of the total phosphate. Earthy phosphates are phosphates of Ca and Mg. They are precipitated in alkaline urine. The urinary phosphorus are derived mainly from proteins in the diet. Some phosphates are derived from the breakdown of cellular nucleoproteins.

  Increased excretion of phosphate occurs in rickets, osteomalacia and hyperparathyroidism.

  Decreased excretion of phosphate occurs in renal diseases and hypoparathyroidism.

- ***Sulphate:*** Sulphur in urine is present in three forms: (i) inorganic sulphate, (ii) organic or ethereal sulphate and (iii) neutral sulphate. The total sulphate excretion ranges from 0.7 to 1.5 grams per day. Out of this, 0.6–1.0 gram is inorganic, 0.06–0.12 gram is ethereal sulphate and 0.04–0.15 gram is neutral sulphate.

  The *inorganic sulphate* is mainly derived from protein of food. It is combined with Na, K, Ca and Mg.

  The *ethereal sulphate* or *organic sulphate* is combined with phenol, cresol, indole and skatole to form ethereal sulphate. Some ethereal sulphate compounds are derived from protein metabolism. Indole, a product of intestinal putrefaction, is oxidised to indoxyl in liver and is conjugated with sulphate to form indoxyl sulphate. Potassium salt of indoxyl sulphate is indican. The presence of indican in urine is an index of intestinal putrefaction.

  Neutral sulphate is contributed by the sulphur-containing amino acids (cysteine, cystine, methionine and mercaptans), thiosulphate, vitamin B_1 and taurine.

- ***Sodium and potassium:*** These are the chief cations present in the urine. Normal healthy adults excrete 3–5 grams of sodium and 1–3 grams of potassium per day.

  Under normal conditions, the adrenocortical hormone stimulates the reabsorption of sodium and depresses the absorption of potassium by renal tubules. In Addison's disease, the urinary excretion of sodium is increased and that of potassium is diminished.

- ***Calcium and magnesium:*** The normal daily output of calcium in urine is about 0.1–0.3 gram and that of magnesium is 0.1–0.2 gram. The amount excreted depends upon the capacity of absorption of these elements from intestines. Under normal conditions, the presence of vitamin D promotes absorption of calcium while excess of phosphate in the intestines prevents absorption of calcium.

  The parathyroid hormone promotes urinary excretion of calcium by mobilising it from bones and therefore urinary calcium is increased in hyperparathyroidism and certain decalcifying bone diseases.

Abnormal Constituents of Urine

These are proteins, glucose, reducing substances other than glucose, ketone bodies, bilirubin, blood and porphyrin.

1. **Protein:** The glomeruli of a normal healthy kidney do not permit the passage of substances such as proteins which have a molecular weight of more than 70,000. When the glomeruli are diseased as in kidney diseases such as glomerulonephritis, nephrosis and nephrosclerosis, the membrane becomes permeable to such substances, resulting in their excretion in urine. Since the albumin fraction of plasma protein passes through the diseased glomerular membrane more readily than globulin because of its comparatively smaller size, urinary excredon of protein is referred to as **albuminuria.** The latter may arise due to prerenal factors when the pathology lies before the kidneys are reached, due to renal factors when the lesion is located in the kidneys or due to postrenal factors when inflammation is located in the lower urinary tract.
2. **Bence Jones protein:** These are low-molecular-weight L-chains of immunoglobulins, overproduced by proliferating plasma cells. They are formed in a significant amount in multiple myeloma (page 212) and are excreted in the urine. Bence Jones protein has the peculiar property of being precipitated, when the urine containing this protein is heated to 50–60°C and redissolve as the temperature is elevated to 100°C.
3. **Glucose:** The average normal blood glucose level is 100 mg% and the glomerular filtration rate is 125 ml per minute. The entire amount of glucose is reabsorbed into the blood by the proximal tubules and no glucose appears in the urine. Even when the blood glucose level is raised, the entire amount is reabsorbed up to a limit of 350 mg of glucose presented to the tubules for absorption. If more than this is presented, reabsorption fails, and glucose is excreted in urine. Glycosuria, which may result due to various causes, both physiological and pathological, is discussed on page 325. The most common pathological condition manifesting glycosuria is diabetes mellitus.
4. **Reducing substances other than glucose:** Certain other reducing substances may be excreted in urine. These are lactose, fructose, galactose, pentose, glucuronates and homogentisic acid.
   - *Lactose:* Excretion of lactose in urine is common during pregnancy and lactation. (Refer to page 326.)
   - *Fructose:* Fructosuria is a rare disorder of fructose metabolism. (Refer to page 334.)
   - *Galactose:* This sugar is excreted in the urine of infants affected by galactosaemia, which is an inborn error of galactose metabolism. (Refer to page 336.)
   - *Pentose:* Excretion of pentose in urine may be due to physiological or inherited causes. Excretion due to physiological causes is common after ingestion of large quantities of fruits containing pentose, for example plums, cherries, grapes and prunes. Essential pentosuria is a rare hereditary disease characterised by excretion of a large amount of pentose in urine, due to the inability to metabolise L-xylulose. (Refer to page 313.)
   - *Glucuronate:* Glucuronic acid derived from glucose is a conjugating agent and may appear in urine in a significant amount as a result of detoxication of toxic substances. When present in an appreciable amount, it reduces Benedict's solution and may be mistaken for the presence of glucose.
   - *Homogentisic acid:* Excretion of homogentisic acid is a rare phenomenon and occurs in alcaptonuria (page 429), which is an inborn error of tyrosine metabolism. Urine

containing homogentisic acid darkens in colour when exposed to air. For special tests to detect homogentisic acid, refer to page 429.

All reducing sugars and reducing substances mentioned in the preceding text reduce Benedict's solution. The presence of glucose, lactose and fructose may be identified by doing the osazone test. Fructose may be differentiated from glucose by doing Seliwanoff's test.* Pentose and galactose may be identified by Bial's test and Tollen's phloroglucinol test.†

5. ***Ketone bodies:*** Acetoacetic acid, β-hydroxybutyric acid and acetone are ketone bodies and are excreted in a significant amount in ketosis which results from accelerated lipid metabolism, as is common in severe diabetes mellitus and starvation (pages 353 and 354).
6. ***Bilirubin:*** A considerable amount of bilirubin is excreted in jaundice. The details of bilirubin excretion in urine are given in **Chapter 9, Catabolism of Haem**.
7. ***Blood:*** Excretion of blood in urine is termed haematuria. This may arise as result of a lesion in either the kidney or the urinary tract. The presence of haemoglobin in urine is haemoglobinuria. This condition may arise also as a result of rapid haemolysis, for example incompatible blood transfusion.
8. **Porphyrins:** Both uroporphyrins and coproporphyrins are excreted in varying amounts in porphyrias which are inborn errors of metabolism of porphyrins. For details, refer to page 181.

Formation of Urine

The main functions of kidney are as follows:

1. Regulation of water balance, electrolyte balance and osmotic pressure of body fluids
2. Regulation of acid–base balance
3. Removal of metabolic waste products and toxic substances from the body

In order to maintain a fluid of constant composition in the body, kidneys eliminate urine, which may vary in composition and rate of production from time to time. Many of the substances present in urine are higher in concentration than those in blood, for example urea. Some are in a negligible quantity in urine, for example glucose.

Urine serves as a channel for excretion of waste products formed in the body. Excess water, either consumed or formed during metabolism, is also eliminated.

Urine formation involves two processes:

1. **Glomerular filtration:** A filtration process through Bowman's capsule
2. **Tubular reabsorption:** The glomerular filtrate is absorbed and concentrated to form urine.

---

* *Seliwanoff's test*: When ketoses are heated with HCl and resorcinol, a bright red colour is formed. This is a more specific test for ketoses.

† *Tollen's phloroglucinol test*: This is a test for galactose. When galactose is treated with phloroglucinol and HCl, a red colour is formed.

Glomerular filtration: The first step in the formation of urine is filtration of the non-protein substances across the glomeruli. The glomeruli filter out a protein-free filtrate of the excretory products collected from the systemic circulation. The composition of the glomerular filtrate is nearly the same as that of plasma without its proteins. For effective filtration, the blood pressure in the glomerular capillaries should be greater than the sum of the osmotic pressure of the plasma protein and the pressure in Bowman's capsule. This pressure is known as 'filtration pressure'.

The normal volume of a glomerular filtrate formed is about 125 ml per minute and for a day about 170 litres are formed. The filtration rate is affected by factors which alter renal blood flow. The rate is reduced in clinical conditions of lowered blood pressure, dehydration, haemoconcentration, cardiac failure and renal ischaemia. A reduced filtration rate leads to retention of nitrogen, particularly urea and creatinine.

Tubular reabsorption: The second step in the formation of urine is processing of the glomerular filtrate by tubular reabsorption. The glomerular filtrate passes through minute and lengthy tubules in the kidneys, where most of the water and dissolved substances such as glucose, urea, phosphate, uric acid, sodium, potassium and chloride are reabsorbed and returned to the blood. The rest of the filtrate pass through the collecting tubules and enter the ureters to get emptied in the bladder as urine.

Reabsorption of water: Under normal conditions, the rate of formation of glomerular filtrate has been estimated to be about 125 ml per minute and for a day about 170 litres are formed. But the rate at which urine passes into the bladder under the same condition is approximately 1–2 ml per minute. From this, it is obvious that during its passage through the uriniferous tubules, about 99% of the glomerular filtrate is reabsorbed. 70–80% is reabsorbed in the proximal portion of the tubules by the passive mechanism of **obligatory reabsorption**. About 13–20% is reabsorbed in the lower portion of the tubules, where concentration of urine also takes place. This is known as **facultative reabsorption**, and the process is controlled by antidiuretic hormone (ADH) of the posterior pituitary. As the absorption takes place against the osmotic pressure of urine, it utilises energy, which is provided by the metabolic activity of the renal tubular cells. The specific gravity of urine is 1.010–1.030.

Tubular reabsorption is described as 'selective reabsorption', because it involves absorption of selected substances such as glucose, urea, electrolytes and uric acid besides a large amount of water. Out of the 170 litres of glomerular filtrate formed daily, 168.5 litres of water, 100 grams of NaCl, 360 grams of $NaHCO_3$, 170 grams of glucose and smaller amounts of phosphate, sulphate, amino acids, urea and urates are reabsorbed in order to excrete 1500 ml of urine containing 60 grams of NaCl, urea and other waste products. The absorption of the various constituents is described in the following section.

1. **Glucose:** Normal arterial blood contains about 80–120 mg% of glucose. This amount is filtered in the glomerular filtrate. Under normal conditions, the entire amount of glucose from the glomerular filtrate is reabsorbed in the proximal tubules by the phosphorylation mechanism and returned to the blood. The absorption is complete even when blood glucose is raised. The maximum rate at which glucose can be reabsorbed is about 350 mg per minute. If more glucose than this is presented in the

filtrate, the excess is excreted in urine and for this, it will carry an additional amount of water. This represents the polyuria in glycosuria. The maximum limit of absorption for glucose by tubules is known as tubular maximum for glucose (TMG). This is 375 ± 80 mg of glucose per minute for normal men and 305 ± 75 mg for women.

2. **Sodium, potassium and chloride:** Under normal conditions, more than 99% of NaCl leaving plasma is reabsorbed in tubules and this is significantly influenced by aldosterone. About 85–90% of the filtered Na is reabsorbed with chloride in the proximal segment; the remaining Na is involved in the exchange with H^+ ions for the maintenance of acid–base balance. Absorption of this portion takes place in the distal tubules and is influenced by the pH of blood and the capacity of the tubular cells of the kidney to acidify the urine.

   Potassium also undergoes extensive reabsorption, about 90%, by the tubules. The mechanism of excretion of K is different from that of Na, because, simultaneously with reabsorption, some K is actively excreted into the tubular lumen by distal tubular cells.
3. **Urea:** About 40% of urea from the glomerular filtrate is reabsorbed under normal conditions. The amount of urea absorbed depends upon the volume of water reabsorbed. During a low output of urine, which corresponds with more water reabsorption, more urea is reabsorbed and less is excreted. Maximum reabsorption, about 70%, occurs when the urine volume is less than 0.35 ml per minute. When the urine volume is 1 ml per minute, about 60% is reabsorbed and at 2 ml or more per minute, 40% is reabsorbed.
4. **Phosphate:** Reabsorption of phosphate takes place in the proximal segment and is influenced by the parathyroid hormone which specifically increases phosphate excretion by decreasing its reabsorption. It has been suggested that vitamin D may influence this mechanism.
5. **Bicarbonate:** Normal urine does not contain HCO_3^- ions because the bicarbonate of the glomerular fluid is almost completely (90%) reabsorbed in the proximal segment or is converted to CO_2 which may later be absorbed as a result of increasing acidity of the fluid in this portion of the tubule. If the plasma bicarbonate concentration is excessively high as in alkalosis, some may escape reabsorption and get excreted in the urine.
6. **Uric acid:** 90–95% of the filtered uric acid is reabsorbed in the tubules. Uricosuric agents such as benemid block uric acid reabsorption. Benemid is valuable in the treatment of acute gout because it lowers the plasma uric acid concentration by its uricosuric action.
7. **Amino acids:** Only small amounts of amino acids are excreted in the urine under normal conditions. The major fraction that enters the glomerular filtrate is reabsorbed. Aminoaciduria is the result of an inherited defect in the enzyme systems concerned with the mechanism of reabsorption.

Tubular excretion: In addition to the flow of substances from the plasma along the glomeruli, certain substances such as glucose and urea also pass across the tubular cells back into the plasma. Some substances (creatinine) flow, both from the plasma and directly across the proximal tubular cells to enter into the tubular lumen whereas substance such as inulin flows in one direction only, i.e. across the glomeruli (**Fig. 27.1**).

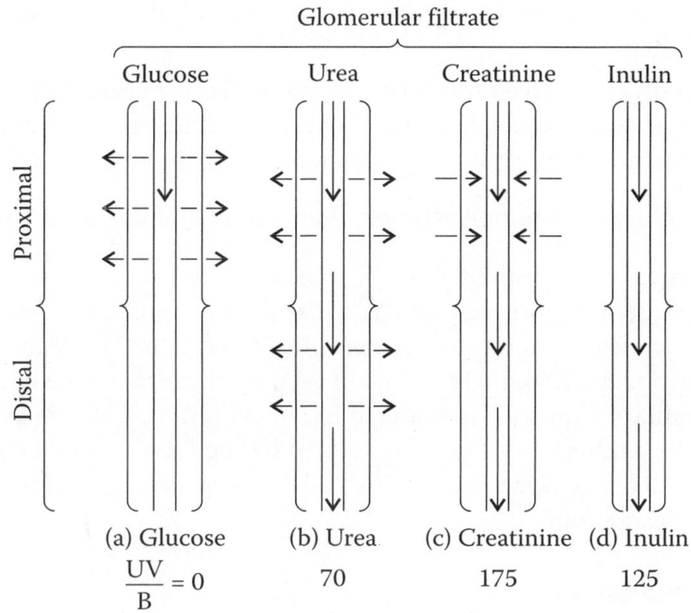

Figure 27.1 Mode of tubular reabsorption and results of clearance studies for glucose, urea, creatine and inulin.

Figure 27.1(a) shows complete reabsorption of glucose along the proximal length of the tubules.

Figure 27.1(b) shows reabsorption of urea in both proximal and distal tubules.

Figure 27.1(c) shows excretion of creatinine both from glomeruli and from directly across the proximal tubules.

Note that inulin is completely filtered (**Fig. 27.1d**) by glomeruli without reabsorption of any kind. Because of this property of inulin, excretion of inulin is taken as an index of glomerular filtration.

Regulation of acid–base balance: Kidneys play an important role in the regulation of acid–base balance. For details, refer to **Chapter 14, Acid–Base Balance**.

RENAL FUNCTION TESTS

Determination of renal function is necessary to locate the site of impairment of renal function and to assess the severity of the impairment. Determination of renal function depends mostly on the excretory functions of the kidneys of certain substances which are either present normally in the blood and urine, such as urea, or foreign substances injected intravenously. These substances are analysed in both blood and urine during a specified time, under controlled conditions. Such tests are called **clearance tests**. The result of the test, wherein the kidneys are said to clear these substances from blood as waste products, is expressed as the volume of plasma that would be required at the existing plasma concentration to furnish the amount of that substance appearing in the urine in 1 minute.

Suppose 'U' denotes the concentration of the substance, for example urea in urine in mg per 100 ml, and 'V' indicates the volume in ml of urine excreted per minute, then U × V will be the quantity of the substance excreted per minute. If 'B' represents the concentration of the substance in blood in mg per 100 ml, then $\frac{UV}{B}$ will be the actual volume of blood cleared of the substance per minute, i.e. clearance. If the substance used for the test is completely filtered at the glomeruli and is subsequently completely reabsorbed by the tubules, its clearance will be zero, for example glucose (**Fig. 27.1a**). If the substance used for the test is completely filtered without reabsorption, the clearance will be equivalent to the rate of glomerular filtration, for example inulin (**Fig. 27.1d**). If the substance used is filtered through the glomeruli and is also excreted by the tubular epithelium, for example creatinine (**Fig. 27.1c**), its clearance will exceed the rate of glomerular filtration by the amount of tubular excretion.

Inulin Clearance Test

Rate of glomerular filtration: Inulin is a polysaccharide which is excreted quantitatively by the kidneys within a short time following its injection intravenously. It passes through glomerular filtration entirely and does not undergo any reabsorption in the tubules. For this reason, inulin excretion serves as an index of glomerular filtration. It is obvious that inulin exists in plasma and glomerular filtrate in identical concentration. Since the quantity of inulin excreted per minute in the bladder urine is equal to the amount entering the glomerular filtrate per minute, it follows that the inulin clearance UV/B will represent the volume of glomerular filtrate formed per minute. By applying this procedure, the average rate of glomerular filtration has been estimated as about 125 ml per minute, in healthy normal adults.

The value may be lowered by 25–45% in elderly but apparently normal subjects. Determination of the rate of glomerular filtration by employing the inulin clearance test is useful in finding out the efficiency of renal function in health and disease. Some applications are as follows:

1. If the rate of glomerular function (GFR) and the rate of urine flow (RUF) are known, the quantity of water reabsorbed in the tubules per minute may be calculated as GFR – RUF.
2. If the inulin clearance (IC) and the clearance of another substance (CX) are known, the proportion of the substance X reabsorbed in the tubule may be calculated as

$$\frac{IC - CX}{IC}$$

For example, inulin clearance (125) minus urea clearance (75) divided by inulin clearance (125) is equal to 0.4. This indicates that 40% (0.4 × 100) of the urea of the glomerular filtrate is reabsorbed during its passage through the tubules.

3. When a substance is found to have a clearance value higher than that of inulin, it means that the substance is not only filtered but an extra amount is also added through excretion by the tubules.

Inulin clearance is reduced in the following conditions:

1. States of reduced renal blood flow
2. Conditions of partial obliteration or reduction in the number of functioning glomeruli, as occurring in glomerulonephritis, glomerulosclerosis and destructive lesions of the renal parenchyma
3. State of reduced glomerular filtration pressure

The test is of limited value in actual practice because of the tedious and cumbersome procedures involved in carrying out the test.

For clinical purpose, the urea clearance test is preferred because of the easy performance of the test.

Urea Clearance Test

The most commonly employed clearance test for clinical purposes is urea clearance test. Urea clearance is defined as the volume of blood which would contain the amount of urea removed in the urine in 1 minute by renal action. The concept of 'clearance' is extended to several substances other than urea for the purpose of determining the efficiency of renal function in health and diseases.

The urea clearance test is performed as follows:

The test is done in the morning. No coffee or tea is allowed. The subject is given about two glasses (250 cc) of water to drink and the time is noted. Water is given to enable him to have an adequate flow of urine. Immediately after drinking the water, the patient is asked to void urine which is discarded. Exactly 1 hour later, the patient is asked to void urine which should be collected in a urine glass and the volume measured (V_1). Blood from vein is collected now. One hour later, the subject is asked to void urine which is collected in a glass. The volume of this urine is also measured (V_2). The blood urea (B) and urine urea (U) are determined. The volume of urine passed per minute (V) is equal to

$$\frac{V_1 + V_2}{120} = V$$

It has been shown that when the volume of urine excreted is relatively high, the amount of urea excreted per minute is directly proportional to the blood urea content. But when urinary volume is small, this relation does not hold good. The critical urinary volume below which there is no proportionate increase in the rate of urea excretion is called the *augmentation limit.* In adults, the augmentation limit is 2 ml per minute.

The calculation for clearance above and below 2 ml per minute is different. When urinary volume is 2 ml or more per minute, the clearance is termed *maximum clearance.* When it is below 2 ml, it is termed *standard clearance.* It has been found that below the augmentation limit, the rate of urea excretion varies with the square root of the urine volume. When the rate of urine flow is less than 2 ml, the clearance does not represent full capacity of the kidneys.

Accordingly, the calculation for standard clearance (CS) is derived as

$$CS = \frac{U \times \sqrt{V}}{B} \text{ ml of blood per minute.}$$

The average value for standard clearance is 54 ml per minute for clinical purposes. It is expressed as the percentage of normal standard clearance:

$$\text{Percentage average for CS} = \frac{U \times \sqrt{V}}{B} \times \frac{100}{54}$$

Maximum clearance (Cm) is calculated as follows. As the amount of urea excreted per minute is directly proportionate to the blood urea content,

$$Cm = \frac{U \times V}{B} \text{ ml of blood per minute}$$

The average value for maximum clearance is 75 ml.

The percentage of average normal for maximum clearance (Cm) is

$$= \frac{U \times \sqrt{V}}{B} \times \frac{100}{54}$$

The results obtained from the urea clearance test are interpreted as follows:

Over 70%	Normal renal function	
70–40%	Mild deficit	
40–20%	Moderate deficit	
Below 20%	Severe deficit	Renal damage
Below 5%	Uraemic coma	

The value of urea clearance in a given healthy individual is not constant, as it may vary with flow of blood through the kidneys. In severe renal diseases, it is lowered significantly. Clearances have no significance in patients with enlarged prostate and in patients who cannot co-operate by micturating completely at the specified time.

Endogenous Creatinine Clearance

Determination of endogenous creatinine clearance without exogenous administration of creatinine is frequently done as a renal function test for the following reasons:

1. At a normal level of blood creatinine, it is totally filtered by healthy glomeruli.
2. The values for endogenous creatinine clearance are nearly the same as those for inulin clearance, in normal healthy subjects, and are sometimes taken as a measure of GFR. The normal values for creatinine clearance are 95–105 ml per minute. But, when the concentration of creatinine in plasma is raised by intravenous injection of creatinine and in renal diseases, the creatinine clearance value exceeds that of inulin clearance, indicating tubular excretion of this substance. However, the test is not free from

criticism, because even in health, a small amount of creatinine is secreted into urine by the tubules.

Concentration Tests

An early sign of renal disease is impairment of the capacity of the tubules to perform osmotic work and concentrate glomerular filtrate. This can be detected by determining the specific gravity of urine, after a period of deprivation of water. If the specific gravity is 1.010, which is the same as that of glomerular filtrate, it indicates that the kidneys have lost the capacity to perform osmotic work.

Addis test: The subject is deprived of fluids for 24 hours (from 8 a.m. of the first day to 8 a.m. on the next day). The urine excreted up to 8 p.m. on the first day is discarded. The urine excreted from 8 p.m. of the first day to 8 a.m. on the next day is collected and its specific gravity determined. If the concentrating power of the kidneys is normal, the urine will have a specific gravity of more than 1.025–1.034. If the specific gravity is less than 1.025, renal damage is indicated.

Mosenthal test: The test is less taxing than Addis test because there is no restriction of fluid intake. On the day of the test, the test is started at 8 a.m., when the patient empties the bladder and discards the urine. From 8 a.m. to 8 p.m. on the same day, urine collections are made at 2-hourly intervals. The specific gravity of each specimen is determined and thereafter all the specimens are returned to the same vessel. All the urine excreted during the 12-hour period from 8 p.m. to 8 a.m. of the next day is collected as one specimen. The specific gravity and volume of this specimen are also noted. In normal cases, the specific gravity of one or more of the 2-hourly specimen should be 1.018 or more. The difference between the highest and lowest readings should not be less than 0.009. The volume of the 12-hour night specimen of urine should be less than 725 ml and its specific gravity 1.018 or more.

Urea concentration test: Following a period of restricted fluid intake, urea is given and the urine urea determined. The ability of the kidneys to excrete urine with a high concentration of urea indicates normal functioning of the kidneys.

Technique: The test is started in the morning. The patient is asked to empty the bladder at 7 a.m., and 15 grams of urea dissolved in about 200 ml of water are given to drink. He is asked to void urine at hourly intervals for the next 3 hours, i.e. at 8 a.m., 9 a.m. and 10 a.m. The volume and the urea content of each specimen of urine are determined. In normal conditions, the concentration of urine urea is 2.5% or more. Values of 2% and lesser concentration indicate some degree of renal failure. The test is not specific and is given up in preference to the urea clearance test.

Dye tests: Kidneys have the capacity to remove from blood a number of foreign substances when introduced into the body. Dyes are widely used for this purpose. Examples are phenol-sulfonephthalein (PSP), phenol red and indigo carmine. They are excreted in urine within a short period. The rate of excretion of the dye serves as a measure to assess the efficiency of renal functions in health and diseases. A measured amount of the dye (PSP or phenol red or indigo carmine) is injected intravenously to the subject.

Urine specimens are collected at 15, 30, 60 and 120 minutes, after injection of the dye. Note (i) the time elapsing between the injection and the first appearance of the dye in urine, (ii) the time of appearance of maximum colour of the dye and (iii) the time required for complete excretion of the dye. The results are interpreted as follows:

	Normal	**Abnormal**
Appearance of colour	5–20 minutes	Beyond 20 minutes
Appearance of maximum colour	About 45 minutes	After 1 hour
Complete excretion	14 hours	Beyond 14 hours

28

CHAPTER

Liver Function Tests

Chapter Outline

- Functions of Liver
- Classification of Liver Function Tests
- The Tests

FUNCTIONS OF LIVER

Liver is the largest and the most significant metabolic organ of the body. It is the centre of diverse metabolic reactions that occur in the body. The functions performed by liver may be classified under five categories:

1. **Circulatory function:** Liver transfers blood from portal to systemic circulation. It acts as a storage organ for blood and regulates blood volume.
2. **Excretory function:** Liver forms bile and excretes it into the intestines.
3. **Metabolic function:** Liver controls the metabolism of carbohydrate, protein and lipid. It is also concerned with the metabolism of minerals and vitamins. It regulates heat production and stores nutrients.
4. **Protective function—detoxication:** Foreign bodies from blood are removed by the Kupffer cells. Detoxication takes place in liver, which also helps in removing ammonia from blood.
5. **Haematological function:** Blood formation in embryo takes place in the liver. Liver is the site of production of fibrinogen, prothrombin and heparin which are necessary for coagulation of blood. Destruction of erythrocytes takes place in liver. Liver cells receive blood supply from portal vein (70%) and hepatic artery (30%). Blood leaves the liver lobules by the hepatic veins.

In view of the versatility of liver as the centre of metabolic functions, it is essential that the liver should maintain efficiency in its functions.

For clinical purpose, the efficiency of liver is assessed by liver function tests (LFT). These tests are widely employed to locate the nature of the dysfunction and diagnose liver disease. However, these tests have limitations. Since the liver has enormous reserve, it is often difficult to get correct information of the extent of damage inflicted on the liver with the results of LFT. Normal results are obtained even when one-fifth of the liver is functioning.

CLASSIFICATION OF LIVER FUNCTION TESTS

For the sake of convenience, the various liver function tests may be grouped under four headings:

I. Tests based on excretory functions
II. Tests based on metabolic functions
III. Tests based on the capacity for detoxication
IV. Tests based on enzymes of liver

THE TESTS

Tests Based on Excretory Functions

The main excretory product of liver is bile. It is formed and stored in the liver. It is concentrated in gall bladder for excretion into the intestines. In normal health, very little bile pigment is present in blood and the amount excreted in urine is negligible. When the formation of bile and its circulation within and outside the liver encounter any obstacle, bile pigments escape into the blood and urine in an abnormally large amount, resulting in jaundice. The causation of jaundice, the types and biochemistry of jaundice are described in **Chapter 9, Catabolism of Haem**. The laboratory tests described in the following section constitute the liver function tests based on the excretory functions of liver. They are employed to detect the different types of jaundice.

1. Tests for bile pigments in blood
    - Van den Bergh reaction
    - Serum bilirubin estimation
    - Icterus index
2. Serum alkaline phosphatase estimation
3. Tests for bile salts and bile pigments in urine
    - Gmelin's test for bilirubin
    - Fouchet's test for bilirubin
    - Hay's test for bile salts
    - Schlesinger's test for urobilinogen
    - Wallace-Diamond test for urobilinogen
4. Dye excretion tests
    - Bromsulphalein test
    - Rose Bengal test

The salient features of each of these tests are given in the following section.

Tests for bile pigments in blood:

Van den Bergh reaction and serum bilirubin estimation: The significance of Van den Bergh reaction and the technique employed to estimate the bilirubin content of blood by this test are described on page 190.

Icterus index (Meulengracht test): The intensity of the yellow colour of the jaundiced serum serves as a measure of the severity of jaundice. The yellow colour of the serum is diluted with sodium citrate solution and compared with the known standards of potassium dichromate solutions corresponding to 10 units. The ratio of the unknown to the standard, multiplied by 10, gives the number of units of icterus index of the serum. Normal values for the icterus index are 4 to 6 units. Values above 10 units indicate jaundice. This test is not frequently used because a direct estimation of the bilirubin can be obtained by Van den Bergh reaction.

Serum alkaline phosphatase estimation: Alkaline phosphatase is excreted by liver into bile. In obstructive jaundice, it is reabsorbed into circulation and therefore the serum alkaline phosphatase value is high. The normal value for alkaline phosphatase is 53–128 U/L per 100 ml of serum.

For details, refer to page 94.

Tests for bile salts and bile pigments in urine: Bilirubin in urine will be present when there is accumulation of bilirubin in blood. This is a common finding in obstructive jaundice. Excretion of bilirubin in urine occurs earlier than its accumulation in the tissues.

The tests used to find out the presence of bile pigments in the urine are as follows:

1. **Gmelin's test:** About 3 ml of urine taken in a test tube are layered carefully with about 5 ml of concentrated nitric acid. If bilirubin is present in the urine, rings of colours of green, blue, red and yellow appear at the junction of the two liquids.
2. **Fouchet's test:** 10 ml of acidified urine taken in a test tube are treated with about 5 ml of 10% barium chloride, the contents mixed and filtered. To the precipitate on the filter paper are added 1 or 2 drops of Fouchet's reagent (trichloroacetic acid with ferric chloride). A green or blue colour indicates the presence of bilirubin in the urine.
3. **Hay's test (test for bile salts):** Bile salts are excreted in urine along with bile pigments in obstructive jaundice in the early stages. To about 5 ml of urine taken in a test tube, a small pinch of flowers of sulphur are sprinkled. If bile salts are present in the urine, the sulphur flowers sink to the bottom of the test tube, due to lowering of the surface tension by bile salts. Otherwise the sulphur flowers remain on the surface of the urine.
4. **Schlesinger's test (test for urobilinogen):** The widely used test for detecting urobilinogen in urine is Schlesinger's test. On addition of an alcoholic solution of zinc acetate to the urine and mixing the solution, a green fluorescence is produced, if urobilinogen is present in the urine. Urobilinogen is excreted in urine in haemolytic jaundice. Normal urine contains mere traces of urobilinogen which is not detectable by Schlesinger's test.
5. **Wallace-Diamond test:** 1 ml of Ehrlich's reagent (a solution of *p*-dimethylamino-benzaldehyde, acidified with hydrochloride) is added to about 10 ml of urine and

allowed to stand for 3 minutes. If the colour changes to red, urobilinogen is present in the urine. If the colour remains light pink, the urine is normal.

Dye excretion tests: The capacity of the liver to remove a dye from the blood is determined by dye excretion tests. This is a measure of the efficiency of the liver cells to excrete normally certain substances from the blood into the bile.

1. **Bromsulphalein test (BSP):** Normally, liver has the capacity to excrete nearly completely test doses of dyes such as bromsulphalein and Rose Bengal in the bile within a short period. When bromsulphalein is injected intravenously (5 mg per kg body weight in normal cases), 95% of the dye disappears in 30 minutes and the entire amount in 45 minutes from the blood. Removal of BSP is delayed and impaired in hepatic insufficiency due to liver cell damage.
2. **Rose Bengal test:** This is another dye excretion test. 10 ml of a 1% solution of the dye is injected intravenously. In normal cases, 50% of the dye disappears in 8 minutes.

Tests Based on Metabolic Functions of Liver

Liver plays an important role in the metabolism of carbohydrates, proteins and lipids. It is also involved in the metabolism of minerals and vitamins.

1. **Carbohydrate metabolism:** Liver regulates carbohydrate metabolism by promoting glycogenesis, glycogenolysis and gluconeogenesis. For details on these aspects, refer to pages 307–309.

   The tests based on carbohydrate metabolism are as follows:
   - Glucose tolerance test
   - Galactose tolerance test
   - Epinephrine tolerance test

   Glucose tolerance test: This is explained in detail in pages 326–332.

   Galactose tolerance test: Normal liver metabolises galactose, converting it to glucose. As this function is impaired in acute liver damage, the galactose tolerance test is considered specific, to detect intrinsic hepatic dysfunction. For more details about the test, refer to page 332.

   Though the test is a good index to detect severe hepatocellular damage, it fails to reveal lesser degrees of liver damage. As the test is time consuming and involves several analytical procedures, it is not worthwhile to follow it as a routine investigation.

   Epinephrine tolerance test (glycogen storage test): This is a test to measure hepatic glycogenolysis and is used for the diagnosis of glycogen storage diseases (Von Gierke's disease). Epinephrine given to normal subjects raises the blood glucose level by hepatic glycogenolysis, and this is directly influenced by hepatic glycogen storage. Patients with parenchymal liver disease fail to show a normal rise.

   The subject is allowed a high carbohydrate diet for 3 days. After an overnight fast, the blood sugar level is estimated and 0.01 ml of 1:1000 solution of epinephrine/kg body weight is injected. Following this, his blood sugar is estimated at intervals of 15 minutes up to 1 hour. In normal cases, an increase of more than 40 mg over the fasting level is observed in the course of 1 hour. In hepatic diseases, the rise is not significant.

2. **Protein metabolism:** Liver plays an important role in the metabolism of proteins absorbed from diet. Besides providing the bulk of plasma proteins, it is responsible for the formation of proteins concerned with blood coagulation, namely prothrombin and fibrinogen. It synthesises several enzymes of varied metabolic importance. Liver is also the site of deamination of amino acids and urea formation.

   Liver disease is associated with the failure to maintain the serum albumin level whereas serum globulin, particularly γ-globulin, which is formed in the reticuloendothelial system is increased. In such cases, the total protein level may be decreased or increased. A decrease in serum total protein is usually due to a fall in the albumin fraction (hypoalbuminaemia). An increase in serum total protein may be due to an increase in the globulin fraction. For more details, refer to pages 204–207.

   Hypoalbuminaemia: The role of liver in the metabolism of plasma protein and other blood proteins is described in **Chapter 10, Blood and Cerebrospinal fluid**. Hypoalbuminaemia is an indication of acute or chronic liver disease, such as cirrhosis. The severity of hypoalbuminaemia is taken as an indication of the extent of liver damage. Persistence of hypoalbuminaemia in spite of treatment indicates a poor prognosis. An increase in the serum total protein is seen in parenchymal liver damage and this is usually due to an increase in the globulin, mainly γ-globulin which contains an increased amount of antibodies. Based on the significance of serum protein levels in health and diseases and the role of liver on various aspects of protein metabolism, certain tests have been devised to determine the capacity of liver in the regulation of protein metabolism. They are as follows:

   - Estimation of plasma proteins
   - Determination of the serum albumin–globulin ratio
   - Fractionation of serum proteins by electrophoresis
   - Determination of prothrombin time
   - Determination of plasma fibrinogen
   - Tests of altered protein fraction production
     - Cephalin-cholesterol flocculation test
     - Thymol turbidity test

   Estimation of plasma protein, determination of the albumin–globulin ratio, electrophoretic separation and quantitative estimation of fractions of serum proteins, the concentration and significance of each of these constituents in health and diseases are discussed in **Chapter 3, Proteins**.

   Plasma prothrombin time: Prothrombin is synthesised in liver and vitamin K is necessary for its production. Prothrombin time is reduced in liver diseases. If prothrombin time is persistently low even after administration of vitamin K, severe liver damage is indicated.

   Determination of plasma fibrinogen: Fibrinogen is also manufactured in liver. The normal value is 0.2–0.4 g%. It is reduced in liver disease.

Tests of altered protein fraction production: Altered protein fractions are produced in liver diseases and these can be detected in the blood by employing flocculation and turbidity tests. Two tests commonly used are as follows:

1. Cephalin-cholesterol flocculation test
2. Thymol turbidity test

Cephalin-cholesterol flocculation test: The test depends upon the formation of flocculation when the serum containing globulins is added to cephalin-cholesterol emulsion. A positive result is obtained if the γ-globulin content of the serum is high and if the albumin content of the serum is decreased below the concentration which would inhibit the reaction.

The test is performed by adding 0.2 ml of serum to a mixture of 4 ml of saline with 1 ml of the cephalin-cholesterol emulsion. The mixture is allowed to stand for 24 hours and the tubes are observed for the formation of flocculation. No flocculation occurs with normal serum. Varying degrees of both precipitation and flocculation are seen with sera of active liver disease. The test is of value only in acute hepatitis and not in chronic cases.

Thymol turbidity test: This test is considered to be more sensitive than the cephalin-cholesterol flocculation test. Positive results are obtained with sera containing high concentration of lipoproteins. 0.1 ml of serum is added to 6 ml of a thymol solution and the solution is left aside for 30 minutes. The turbidity obtained is measured. The normal thymol turbidity value is 0–4 units. The value is increased in acute inflammatory liver diseases. It remains elevated for some time after apparent clinical recovery. This is due to the persistent portal zone infiltration for some time after the liver cells are restored to normalcy. Thymol turbidity is high in prolonged obstructive jaundice with high serum lipoprotein values.

3. **Lipid metabolism:** Liver plays an important role in lipid metabolism, for two main reasons:
   - The bile salts which are necessary for emulsification and absorption of fats are excreted by liver.
   - Liver is concerned with cholesterol metabolism.

   Serum phospholipids and serum cholesterol which constitute major fractions of the total blood lipids are derived from liver. The normal value for total serum cholesterol ranges from 150 to 250 mg per 100 ml. 60–70% of the total cholesterol is present as ester cholesterol. In obstructive jaundice, the total as well as ester cholesterol values are increased. In parenchymatous liver diseases, there is a reduction in the value of total and ester cholesterol. A fall in the level of ester cholesterol is considered an indication of hepatocellular damage.

Tests Based on the Capacity for Detoxication

Liver deals with toxic substances by conjugating them with glycine and glucuronic acid to produce less toxic substances. The well-known detoxication occurring in liver is the conjugation of benzoic acid with glycine to form hippuric acid, which is excreted in urine. Excretion of hippuric acid is a measure of hepatic function connected with detoxication.

Hippuric acid test: The test may be carried out by either oral or intravenous methods. The oral test consists in the administration of a standard dose of sodium benzoate (6 grams) orally followed by a 4-hour collection of urine. The amount of hippuric acid excreted is estimated. In normal subjects, 2.5 grams or more of hippuric acid are excreted in 1 hour. The output of hippuric acid is low in intrahepatic rather than extrahepatic diseases.

Tests Based on Enzymes of Liver

Enzymes such as alkaline phosphatase, transaminases, lactic dehydrogenase, cholinesterase, aldolase, phosphohexose isomerase and isocitric dehydrogenase are derived from liver and are elevated in liver disease.

Enzymes such as alkaline phosphatase (ALP), transaminases, 5′-nucleotidase and gamma-glutamyl transferase (GGT) are derived from liver and consequently their levels in blood are altered in liver disease. Measurement of these enzymes is useful in the diagnosis and treatment of various liver disorders.

1. Aspartate aminotransferase (AST), formerly called SGOT, is also found in muscles and many other tissues besides the liver while alanine aminotransferase (ALT), formerly called SGPT, is almost exclusively found in the liver.
2. If ALT and AST are found together in elevated amounts in the blood, liver damage is most likely present.

Alkaline phosphatase, 5′-nucleotidase and gamma-glutamyl transpeptidase are secreted by the biliary canalicular cells and are elevated when there is obstruction to flow of bile. Increased ALP in the absence of an elevation of either 5′-nucleotidase or GGT eliminates liver disease and is suggestive of bone disorder since ALP is also found in bone.

For normal blood levels, see page 553.

29 CHAPTER Elements of Biochemical Genetics

Chapter Outline

- Mendelian Inheritance
- Chromosomes and Genes
- Inborn Errors of Metabolism

All living organisms are made up of cells built on the same general plan. Most of them are like their parents in general plan but differ from them in certain details. Offsprings always arise from pre-existing cells which are contributed by the parents. In this manner, a general continuity is established from a generation to the next and this is known as heredity. The study of heredity is called **genetics** (genesis means origin).

MENDELIAN INHERITANCE

John Gregor Mendel was the first man to give interpretation on transmission of characters in 1865. In 1900, the year which marks the beginning of genetics as a science, De Vries and Tschermark von Seysenegg arrived at conclusions similar to those of Mendel and recognised the importance of his work. The generalisations formulated by Mendel have become the foundation of the science of genetics and are expressed as the law of genetic segregation and the law of independent assortment.

Law of Genetic Segregation: This explains that there are factors which control development and retain their individuality from generation to generation. Every individual normally possesses a pair of each of these factors, which divide to form the gametes containing only one member of each pair. This is known as the **law of segregation**.

Mendel's own experiment on garden peas is traditionally used to illustrate this law (**Fig. 29.1**). Tall pea plants were crossed with short plants and the offsprings in the first filal (F_1) generation were all tall. When these hybrids were allowed to self-fertilise, they gave a second filal (F_2) generation consisting of tall plants and short plants in the ratio of 3:1. The short peas of this generation when self-fertilised bred true, giving nothing but short peas. A third of the remaining tall plants also bred true, giving tall plants, whereas the other two-thirds of the tall plants gave rise to tall and short plants in the ratio of 3:1.

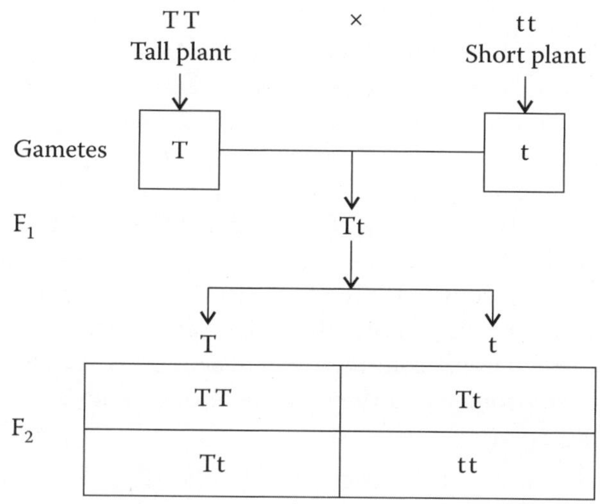

Figure 29.1 Diagram illustrating law of genetic segregation.

Mendel concluded that tallness (T) and shortness (t) were dependent on a pair of alternative factors. Each pea plant contained two of these factors in all its cells except in the gametes, where only one of the pair was represented. The gametes are denoted T and t. Zygote contains two of these factors. The hybrid which is tall is represented as Tt in which tallness dominates. So the factor tallness (T) is said to be 'dominant' to the factor shortness or t which is 'recessive'. Mendel's experiment on pea plants can be represented as follows.

Many other characteristics are also inherited in the same way. In some cases, the two factors are not completely dominant or recessive to one another but interact to give an intermediate condition.

Law of Independent Assortment: This states that when more than one pair of factors are considered, each pair segregates independently from all other pairs. When round yellow peas were crossed with wrinkled green peas, the seeds of the first (F_1) generation were all round and yellow, since these two are the dominant factors. When the F_1 generation was self-fertilised, the resulting F_2 generation had all the four possible combinations of factors, round, yellow, wrinkled and green showing an independent assortment of characters.

CHROMOSOMES AND GENES

Every person begins life as a single cell known as the zygote which is formed by the fusion of the sperm with the ovum (gametes). The hereditary traits of the new individual or zygote are derived from the characteristics of the gametes, and these are determined by a series of thread-like structures present in their nuclei and known as **chromosomes**. Each chromosome is subdivided into a large number of genes and they represent the specific units determining hereditary traits. The genes in turn are largely composed of DNA. Each zygote is estimated to contain 10,000–50,000 genes. The genes are so characteristically arranged in the same order along the length of the chromosome that each gene can be said to have its own specific position in any one particular chromosome. This is called its **locus**.

There are 23 chromosomes in the nucleus of each human gamete. Each of the chromosomes is different from the others in its genetical properties. The nucleus of the ovum and the sperm fuse during fertilisation and the resulting zygote will have 46 chromosomes in its nucleus, made up of 23 pairs. Generally, each member of such a pair of homologous chromosomes has similar genetical properties to those of its fellow. The number of genes present and the arrangement of their loci are the same in each member of the pair. But one pair of chromosomes called the ***sex chromosomes*** is different, in these aspects. The pair of sex chromosomes in males is made up of one long chromosome (the X chromosome) derived from the mother and one short chromosome (the Y chromosome) derived from the father. The pair is represented as XY. The genes represented in each are different from the other. The pair of sex chromosome in females is made up of XX chromosomes and they resemble one another in the same way as the members of the other 22 pairs.

Growth in living organisms is nothing but multiplication of cells which occurs by cell divisions (**mitosis**). Prior to each cell division, the chromosomes are duplicated in such a way that each of the daughter cells receives a set of chromosomes exactly like the other and like those of the parent cells. They also possess the same complement of genes. The exception to this rule occurs in the formation of the gametes. Here, a special type of cell division called **meiosis** occurs, by which only one member of each pair of chromosomes appears in the gamete. Thus, there are 23 chromosomes in each gamete.

When conception takes place, a gene derived from the male pairs with its counterpart derived from the female. The genes that pair are called **alleles** and they carry the same instruction. If the two alleles are identical, a person is said to be ***homozygous*** for that gene. When the alleles carry different instructions, he is said to be ***heterozygous***. It has been established that each gene has a specific role in the biochemical functioning of the cells and hence of the body as a whole. When a gene undergoes mutation, i.e. a sudden change in the structure of genetic material, this is reflected in its functional behaviour.

Normal and Abnormal Human Chromosomes Complement

Human cells are diploid in nature, having 22 pairs of homologous chromosomes in each cell. Tjio and Levan found that the chromosomal constitution (**karyotype**) of females is 22 + XX and that of males is 22 + XY, where X and Y represent the sex chromosomes. The remaining 22 pairs are known as **autosomes**. It is possible to divide chromosomes into seven distinct groups depending on the chromosome length and the position of centromere (central point). **Figure 29.2** shows the arrangement of chromosomes into standard karyotype. This is obtained by growing white cells for several days in an artificial medium which is then treated with the alkaloid colchicine. The latter arrests the cell division at a stage called metaphase stage and makes the cells suitable for examination because chromosomes are readily observable microscopically in this stage. After treatment with colchicine, the cells are immersed in hypotonic salt solution and then spread on a slide and squashed with a cover slip to spread the chromosomes. Photographs are taken after fixing and staining. According to the length, size and shape of the chromosomes, the photographs are cut out and arranged in an order as shown in **Figure 29.2**.

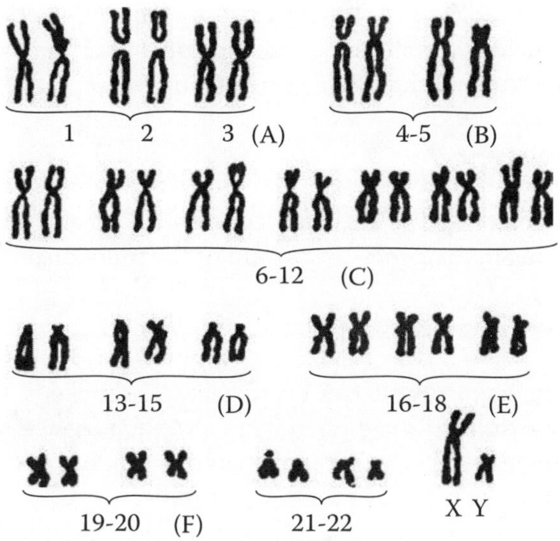

Figure 29.2 Chromosomes arranged into standard karyotype. 21-22 and XY chromosomes represent group G.

The first three lengthy pairs of chromosomes constitute group A. These are easily distinguished from one another because of the difference in length and centromere position. Group B is composed of pairs 4 and 5 which cannot be distinguished from each other. Group C is formed by chromosome pairs 6 through 12 plus X chromosome. Group D consists of three chromosome pairs 13, 14 and 15 which cannot be distinguished from one another. They are of the same length. Group E is formed of pairs 16, 17 and 18 and group F consists of pairs 19 and 20. Group G includes chromosome pairs 21 and 22 and Y chromosome. With this grouping, moderate changes and any abnormal chromosome can be detected by an experienced observer.

During cell division, each daughter cell receives an exact complement of chromosomes. Accidentally, in cell division, one daughter cell may receive an extra chromosome and the other daughter cell may be deficient in a chromosome. If there is deficiency in the chromosome, the condition is known as *monosomic* and when there is an extra chromosome, it is known as *trisomic.*

Trisomy 21 syndrome: The condition known as trisomy 21 syndrome or Mongolian idiocy, first discovered by Lejeune, in 1959 is a rare disorder. It is associated with mental retardation, short broad fingers and toes, a round flattened face with a long protruding tongue, characteristic eyelid folds and unusual palm and finger prints. These are persons affected with **Mongolism**. They were found to have 47 chromosomes. The extra chromosome was found in group G (21 or 22), most probably associated with 21, and hence the condition is known as trisomy 21 syndrome.

Group D trisomy: Very rarely we come across abnormalities in newborn infants such as anophthalmia, cleft palate, hare-lip, polydactyly, haemangiomata and congenital heart defects. These abnormalities accompany a trisomic condition involving group D (13, 14 or 15).

Group E trisomy: This condition is characterised by ear deformities, spasticity due to a central nervous system defect, umbilical hernia and congenital heart defects. Chromosome 18 is trisomic in this disease and the infants do not survive for more than a few months.

Phenotype and Genotype

The term 'phenotype' refers to the external appearance of an individual and the term 'genotype' is used to indicate the genetic make-up of the individual.

Abnormalities of Sex Chromosomes

The sex chromosome status in a male is **XY** and that in a female is **XX**. The presence of Y chromosome in a male results in male phenotype and the absence of Y chromosome in a female results in female phenotype. There are two outstanding sex abnormalities. One is *Klinefelter's syndrome* and the other is *Turner's syndrome.*

Victims of *Klinefelter's syndrome* are phenotypic males. They are somewhat enuchoid with underdeveloped genitalia, sparse body hair and retarded intelligence. Jacob and Strong (1959) found that these persons have 47 chromosomes, including a normal Y chromosome. The extra chromosome was found to be similar to the usual X chromosome. So, the karyotype pattern of these persons would be 22 + XXY instead of 22 + XY.

Turner's syndrome persons are phenotypic females, having underdeveloped ovaries. They are characteristically short, with webbing of the neck and impaired intelligence. On examination, these persons were found to contain only 45 chromosomes (monosomic) with the absence of the Y chromosome. The karyotype pattern may be represented as 22 + XO, O indicating the absence of one of the X chromosomes.

Apart from the abnormalities arising in the number of chromosomes, abnormality may also occur in the structure of the chromosome. These variant chromosomes are designated 'aberrant'. The aberration takes place during crossing over in meiosis or it may result from an environmental factor like radiation. The aberrations are either deletion or translocation. Due to structural changes, 'isochromosomes' or 'ring chromosomes' may also result. Isochromosomes are those in which both arms are identical instead of being unequal. Ring chromosomes are formed when a chromosome after breaking on both the sides of the centromere occasionally forms a ring by joining of the two proximal ends.

Gene Action

As explained in **Chapter 6, Nucleoproteins and Nucleic Acids**, the chemical entities of chromosomes are the basic protein histone and deoxyribonucleic acid (DNA). These two constitute 90% of the chromosomes. The remaining 10% is constituted by non-histone proteins and ribonucleic acid (RNA). It has been shown that genetic information is stored in DNA. Genes play an important role in the synthesis of enzyme and other cellular proteins. The sequence of purine and pyrimidine bases in the DNA molecule determines the sequence of amino acids and the structure of the protein. Gene represents a section of a DNA molecule which determines the sequence of amino acids for a particular peptide chain. Until recently, it was thought that one gene is responsible for one enzyme. But now it has been proposed that one gene is responsible for one polypeptide chain. Generally, two or more polypeptide chains are needed to form a functional enzyme.

Mutation

Occasionally, a gene may undergo a sudden change in the structure of genetic material. This is called **mutation**. It leads to disturbance of the normal functioning of the genetic material. The new form of the gene so produced is doubled at each cell division in the same way as other genes so that a mutant form persists.

On the molecular level, mutation consists in the loss or gain of one or more base or in the conversion of one base to another in the nucleotide chain of the DNA molecule. By impairment of a particular gene, the production of one of the polypeptide chains of the functional enzyme involved in the metabolic process is affected. So, the protein formed will have diminished activity and the net result will be a metabolic block. For example, let us consider the conversion of substrate S to product P, catalysed by enzyme E. If the gene controlling E mutates, then the conversion of S to P is blocked and if S is supplied continuously from other metabolic steps, it will accumulate or get excreted.

INBORN ERRORS OF METABOLISM

Inborn errors of metabolism may be considered as genetically determined biochemical disorders. They are highly specific and represent a wide range of metabolic processes. In each disorder, the body fails to perform a specific biochemical step pertaining to the normal metabolic pathway. This is due to a congenital deficiency or absence of the enzyme specifically concerned in catalysing the particular biochemical step, resulting in a block at this point in the metabolic pathway. This leads to unusual accumulation of metabolites in the body fluids and their excretion in urine. They are always associated with characteristic clinical signs and symptoms. The absence of the enzyme and the accumulation of the metabolite may be illustrated as follows.

Let us consider a series of reactions catalysed by enzymes α, β, γ and δ respectively written as:

$$R_1 \xrightarrow{\alpha} R_2 \xrightarrow{\beta} R_3 \xrightarrow{\gamma} R_4 \xrightarrow{\delta} R_5$$

Congenital absence of enzyme γ will result in the failure to form metabolite R_4 from R_3 and lead to the accumulation of R_3 in the body fluids and excretion in urine in excessive amount.

The important inborn errors pertaining to different metabolites have been already explained in the chapters concerned and the student may refer to the following pages in those chapters:

	Pages
Gout (nucleic acid metabolism)	153–154
Lesch–Nyhan syndrome	154
Porphyrias (porphyrin metabolism)	181–183
Abnormal haemoglobins (haemoglobinopathies)	165–172
Carbohydrate metabolism:	
Essential pentosuria	313–314
Fructosuria	334
Galactosemia	336
Glucose-6 phosphate-dehydrogenase deficiency	95
Glycogen storage diseases:	336–337
Von Gierke's disease	336
Andersen's disease	337
Pompe's disease	337
McArdle's disease	337
Her's disease	337
Amino acid metabolism:	
Maple syrup urine disease	414
Histidinuria	416
Homocystinuria	421
Cystinuria	423
Cystinosis	423–424
Hartnup syndrome	427
Phenylketonuria	428
Alcaptonuria	429
Albinism	433
Cretinism	490, 499
Diabetes insipidus	521
Wilson's disease	491–492

Normal Clinical Laboratory Values

Blood = (B), Plasma = (P), Serum = (S)

Albumin (S) : 3.5–5.2 g/dl

ALT/SGPT (S) : Males <45 U/L
Females <34 U/L

AST/SGOT (S) : Males <35 U/L
Females < 31 U/L

Ammonia nitrogen (P) : 15–45 μgN/dl

Amylase (S) : 28–100 U/L

Bicarbonate (S) : 22–26 mEq/L

Bilirubin (S) : Total 0.0–1.2 mg/dl;
direct (conjugated): 0.0–0.2 mg/dL

Calcium (S/P-hep) : 8.6–10.2 mg/dl

Ceruloplasmin (S) : 20–60 mg/dl

Chloride (S/P) : 96–106 mEq/L

Cholesterol (S) : 150–220 mg/dl; desirable <200 mg/dl

Creatinine (S) : 0.8–1.2 mg/dl

Creatine kinase total (S) : Males 46–171 U/L
Females 34–145 U/L

CK-MB (S) : <5 μg/L

Fibrinogen (P) : 0.2–0.6 g/dl

Glucose (P/S) : 70–110 mg/dL

Haemoglobin (S) : Male: 14–18 gm/dl
Female: 12.0–16.0 gm/dl

Lipoprotein fractions (S):

- HDL cholesterol : >40 mg/dl
- LDL cholesterol : <180 mg/dl, recommended <150 mg/dl
- VLDL cholesterol : <40 mg/dl
- Triglycerides (S) : 40–165 mg/dl, recommended <150 mg/dl

pH (B) arterial : 7.35–7.45

Phosphorus inorganic (S/P-hep) : 2.5–4.5 mg/dl

Protein (S) total	: 6–8 g/dl
Acid phosphatase	: 1.5–4.5 U/L
Alk phosphatase	: 53–128 U/L
Potassium (S)	: 3.5–5.1 mEq/L
Sodium (S)	: 136–145 meq/L
TSH (S)	: 0.4–4.2 μIU/ml
Thyroxine (T4) (S)	: 4.6–11.0 μg/dl
Urea nitrogen (S)	: 6–20 mg/dl
Uric acid (S)	: Males: 3.5–8.0 mg/dl Females: 2.6–7.3 mg/dl

Cerebrospinal Fluid

Proteins	: 15–40 mg/dl
Chloride	: 700–760 mg NaCl per 100 ml
Glucose	: 40–70 mg/dl

REFERENCES

1. Harper's Biochemistry, 24th Edition. 1996.
2. Varley H. Practical Clinical Biochemistry, 1969.
3. King EJ and Wooton IDP. Microanalysis in Medical Biochemistry, 1964.
4. Burtis CA, Ashwood ER and Bruns DE. Tietz Textbook of Clinical Chemistry and Molecular Diagnostics.

Bibliography

Anderson's Pathology. Edited by John M. Kissane, 9th Edition; 1990.

Carl A. Burtis, Edward R. Ashwood and David E. Bruns, *Tietz Textbook of Clinical Chemistry and Molecular Diagnostics.* 5th Edition; 2012.

Donald Voet and Judith G. Voet. *Biochemistry*; 1990.

Dorothy E. Schumm. *Essentials of Biochemistry*, 2nd Edition; 1995.

F.P. Antia. *Clinical Dietetics and Nutrition*, 3rd Edition; 1986.

Harper's Biochemistry, 24th Edition; 1996.

Harper's Illustrated Biochemistry, 29th Edition; 2012.

Harper's Review of Biochemistry, 19th Edition; 1983.

Ian D.K. Halkerston. *Biochemistry*, 2nd Edition; 1988.

Ivan M. Roitt. *Essential Immunology*, 6th Edition; 1988.

Lippincott's Illustrated Reviews. *Biochemistry*, 2nd Edition; 1994.

Lubert Stryer. *Biochemistry*, 3rd Edition; 1988.

M. Swaminathan. *Handbook of Food and Nutrition,* 1986.

N.V. Bhagavan. *Medical Biochemistry*; 1992.

Neil A. Campbell. *Biology*, 3rd Edition; 1993.

Peter N. Campbell and Anthony D. Smith. *Biochemistry Illustrated*, 2nd Edition; 1998.

Rex Montgomery, Thomas W. Conway and Arthur A. Spector. *Biochemistry, A Case-Oriented Approach*, 5th Edition; 1990.

Rypins. *Basic Sciences Review*, 16th Edition; 1993.

Sheila Sherlock. *Diseases of the Liver and Biliary System*, 4th Edition; 1968.

Thomas M. Devlin. *Textbook of Biochemistry with Clinical Correlations*, 3rd Edition; 1993.

Todd–Sanford. *Clinical Diagnosis by Laboratory Methods*, 15th Edition; 1977.

Index

D

E

I

M

P

Q

R

S

V

W

X

Z